A TREASURY OF GREAT SCIENCE FICTION

A
Treasury
of GREAT
SCIENCE FICTION

VOLUME ONE

Edited by Anthony Boucher

DOUBLEDAY & COMPANY, INC.

Garden City, New York

This book is for
PHYLLIS
as what is not?

All of the characters in this book are fictitious, and any resemblance to actual persons, living or dead, is purely coincidental.

Before the Curtain . . .

FIRST OF ALL, let's reach a clear understanding of what this treasury is not.

It is not a definitive anthology of the very best of all science fiction: such a collection would, inevitably, contain too many stories which are over-familiar and readily accessible elsewhere.

It is not a scholarly survey of the history and development of science fiction: too many stories of the utmost importance to the scholar are tough going for the lay reader.

It is not, indeed, any kind of shaped or patterned anthology, but simply a very large collection of stories which are (I think) of high quality and (I hope) unfamiliar to many readers.

Most of the stories here, including three of the book-length novels, are new to hard covers in America; nine of them have never appeared in book form at all. Only one story has been hitherto published in a science fiction anthology; and that one has been out of print for ten years.

My primary concern was simply to get together a great deal of good reading in modern (1938–58) s.f. which had been overlooked by earlier anthologists; and I was astonished to find that, after the anthological Gold Rush of the 1950's, there was so much high grade ore still unmined— enough to make the biggest s.f. anthology ever . . . and to trace, after all, an unintended pattern: the pattern of almost kaleidoscopic variety.

When man entered the Space Age two years ago, the writers and editors of science fiction, who had so long been living in this new age, hoped for a fresh surge of reader interest, an expression of gratitude for accurate prophecy in the past and of interest in the possible accuracy of other, as yet unfulfilled prophecies.

It seemed a logical enough expectation, but it was a fallacious one. The new readers did not arrive—to some extent, at least, because they were put off by the cry of the press (never happier than when it can claim a miracle and coin a cliché): "Science has caught up with science fiction!"

Factually we have dipped a toe into the ocean of space. Science has caught up with the space flight concepts of s.f. to about the same extent that a child taking its first step has caught up with Herb Elliott.

But facts are impotent against loud and frequent assertion. Readers believe that science has "caught up"; and somehow the very fact of s.f.'s accurate prophecies turns into a weapon against it, as if a literature of prophecy should become outmoded the instant one of its predictions was fulfilled.

This is all fairly foolish, but even if it made some sense it still should not deter readers from the joys of that speculative entertainment known as science fiction. Scientific prophecy, technological prediction—this is only one of s.f.'s functions. And even if science "caught up" with every single scientific datum in these stories*, they would still remain enjoyable in their own various manners as fiction.

There is good solid straight science-cum-fiction here, especially by Robert A. Heinlein, than whom no one writes better science fiction in its strictest straitest sense.

But there are also (and all falling within the general editors'-publishers'-readers' definition of s.f.):

—a dazzlingly inventive adventure novel by Alfred Bester which is deliberately (and successfully) modeled on Alexandre Dumas;

—a serious and bitter story by Judith Merril, of such literary quality that Martha Foley chose it for *The Best American Short Stories*;

—a happy study in sheer mechanical gadgetry by the master of technological tales, George O. Smith;

—a charming, sexy, and malicious caprice by Mildred Clingerman;

—a warm and plausible picture of Abraham Lincoln by Oscar Lewis;

—a spirited pastiche of Sherlock Holmes by Poul Anderson;

—a vivid and intricate melodrama of transgalactic politics by A. E. van Vogt, which resembles Ruritania in five dimensions (and which has, quite possibly, the best curtain line in all imaginative fiction);

—a powerful poetic prophecy by Ray Bradbury;

—as good a sports-story-not-by-Bill-Gault as I've ever read, by Malcolm Jameson, who invents a new future sport for our excitement;

—a quiet, convincing, Wells-like document by John Wyndham;

—a Sturgeon novella which (like most Sturgeon stories) will not fit into the most offbeat of categorical descriptions;

. . . Well, you take my meaning. Prophecy (though it is here, along with that other basic s.f. ingredient, satire) is not all. Science fiction is fiction, and the best of it is damned good fiction; I hope you'll find that these samples prove my point.

For suggestions, stimuli, and other aids to anthologizing, I wish particularly to thank Poul and Karen Anderson, John W. Campbell, Jr., Mildred Clingerman (chiefly just for existing), Kendell Foster Crossen, H. L. Gold, the late Henry Kuttner, J. Francis McComas, Judith Merril, Robert P. Mills, and most especially Walter I. Bradbury.

ANTHONY BOUCHER

Berkeley, California

---

* As indeed it occasionally has. Notice especially the manipulative miniature "hands" in Heinlein's *Waldo* (1942). These now exist (for the handling of radioactive matter) and are known, properly and gratefully, as *waldoes*.

6

CONTENTS

Volume One

BEFORE THE CURTAIN . . .   5
by Anthony Boucher

RE-BIRTH   9
by John Wyndham

THE SHAPE OF THINGS THAT CAME   136
by Richard Deming

PILLAR OF FIRE   141
by Ray Bradbury

WALDO   170
by Robert A. Heinlein

THE FATHER-THING   245
by Philip K. Dick

THE CHILDREN'S HOUR   255
by Henry Kuttner and C. L. Moore

GOMEZ   288
by C. M. Kornbluth

THE [WIDGET], THE [WADGET], AND BOFF   308
by Theodore Sturgeon

SANDRA   370
by George P. Elliott

BEYOND SPACE AND TIME   380
by Joel Townsley Rogers

THE MARTIAN CROWN JEWELS   400
by Poul Anderson

THE WEAPON SHOPS OF ISHER   413
by A. E. van Vogt

RE-BIRTH
by John Wyndham

CHAPTER ONE

WHEN I WAS QUITE SMALL I would sometimes dream of a city—which was strange because it began before I even knew what a city was. But this city, clustered on the curve of a big blue bay, would come into my mind. I could see the streets, and the buildings that lined them, the waterfront, even boats in the harbor; yet, waking, I had never seen the sea, or a boat. . . .

And the buildings were quite unlike any I knew. The traffic in the streets was strange, carts running with no horses to pull them; and sometimes there were things in the sky, shiny fish-shaped things that certainly were not birds.

Most often I would see this wonderful place by daylight, but occasionally it was by night when the lights lay like strings of glowworms along the shore, and a few of them seemed to be sparks drifting on the water, or in the air.

It was a beautiful, fascinating place, and once, when I was still young enough to know no better, I asked my eldest sister, Mary, where this lovely city could be.

She shook her head, and told me that there was no such place—not now. But, perhaps, she suggested, I could somehow be dreaming about times long ago. Dreams were funny things, and there was no accounting for them; so it might be that what I was seeing was a bit of the world as it had been once upon a time—the wonderful world that the Old People had lived in; as it had been before God sent Tribulation.

But after that she went on to warn me very seriously not to mention it to anyone else; other people, as far as she knew, did not have such pictures in their heads, either sleeping or waking, so it would be unwise to mention them.

That was good advice, and luckily I had the sense to take it. People in our district had a very sharp eye for the odd, or the unusual, so that even my lefthandedness caused slight disapproval. So, at that time, and for some years afterward, I did not mention it to anyone—indeed, I almost forgot about it, for as I grew older the dream came less frequently, and then very rarely.

But the advice stuck. Without it I might have mentioned the curious understanding I had with my cousin Rosalind, and that would certainly have led us both into very grave trouble—if anyone had happened to believe me. Neither I nor she, I think, paid much attention to it at that time; we simply had the habit of caution. I certainly did not feel unusual. I was a normal little boy, growing up in a normal way, taking the ways of the world about me for granted. And I kept on like that until the day I met Sophie. Even then, the difference was not immediate. It is hindsight that enables me to fix that as *the* day when the first small doubts started to germinate in my hitherto plain field of acceptance.

That day I had gone off by myself, as I often did. I was, I suppose, nearly ten years old. My next sister, Sarah, was five years older, and the gap meant that I played a great deal alone. I had made my way down the cart track to the south, along the borders of several fields until I came to the high bank, and then along the top of the bank for quite a way.

The bank was no puzzle to me then; in common with the rest of the landscape, it simply existed, it just *was*. It had no significance; it was far too big for me to think of as a thing that men could have built. It had never occurred to me to connect it with the wondrous doings of the Old People whom I sometimes heard about. It was simply the bank, coming round in a wide curve, and then running straight as an arrow toward the distant hills— just a part of the world, and no more to be wondered at than the river, the sky, or the hills themselves.

I had often gone along the top of it, but seldom explored on the farther side. For some reason I regarded the country there as foreign—not so much inimical, as outside my territory. But there was a place I had discovered where the rain, in running down the far side of the bank, had worn a sandy gully. If one sat in the start of that and gave a good push off, one could go swishing down at a fine speed, and finally fly a few feet through the air to land in a pile of soft sand at the bottom.

I must have been there half a dozen times before, and there had never been anyone about, but on this occasion, when I was picking myself up after my third descent, a voice said, "Hullo!"

I looked around. At first I could not tell where it came from, then a shaking of the top twigs in a bunch of bushes caught my eye. While I was gazing at it the branches parted, and a face looked out at me. It was a small face, sunburned, and clustered about with dark curls. The expression was somewhat serious, but the eyes sparkled. We regarded one another for a moment, then:

"Hallo," I responded.

She hesitated, then pushed the bushes further apart. I saw a girl a little shorter than I was, and perhaps a little younger. She wore reddish-brown dungarees with a yellow shirt. The cross stitched to the front of the dungarees was of a darker brown material. Her hair was tied on each side of her head with yellow ribbons. She stood still for a few seconds as though uncertain about leaving the security of the bushes, then curiosity got the better of her caution, and she stepped out.

I stared at her because she was completely a stranger. From time to time there were gatherings or parties which brought together all the children for miles around, so that it was astonishing to encounter one that I had never seen before.

"What's your name?" I asked her.

"Sophie," she told me. "What's yours?"

"David," I said. "Where's your home?"

"Over there," she said, waving her hand vaguely toward the foreign country beyond the bank.

Her eyes left mine and went to the sandy runnel down which I had been sliding.

"Is that fun?" she inquired, with a wistful look.

I hesitated a moment before inviting her. "Yes," I told her. "Come and try."

She hung back, studying me with a serious expression for a second or two, then made up her mind quite suddenly. She scrambled to the top of the bank ahead of me.

She sped down the runnel with curls and ribbons flying. When I landed she had lost her serious look, and her eyes were dancing with excitement.

"Again," she said, and panted back up the bank.

It was on her third descent that the misadventure occurred. She sat down and shoved off as before. I watched her swish down and come to a stop in a flurry of sand. Somehow she had contrived to land a couple of feet to the left of the usual place. I made ready to follow, and waited for her to get clear. She did not.

"Go on," I told her, impatiently.

She tried to move, and then called up, "I can't. It hurts."

I risked pushing off anyway, and landed close beside her.

"What's the matter?" I asked.

Her face was screwed up. Tears stood in her eyes. "My foot's stuck," she said.

Her left foot was buried. I scrabbled the soft sand clear with my hands. Her shoe was jammed in a narrow space between two up-pointed stones. I tried to move it, but it would not budge.

"Can't you sort of twist it out?" I suggested.

She tried, lips valiantly compressed.

"It won't come."

"I'll help pull," I offered.

"No, no! It hurts," she protested.

I did not know what to do next, but I was favorably impressed by her stoicism. All the other small girls I knew—and some of the boys, too—would have been yelling their heads off in the circumstances. Very clearly her predicament was painful. I considered the problem.

"We'd better cut the laces so you can pull your foot out of the shoe. I can't reach the knot," I decided.

"No!" she said, alarmedly. "No, I mustn't."

She was so emphatic that I was baffled. If she would pull her foot out of the shoe, we might knock the shoe itself free with a stone, but if she would not, I did not see what was to be done. She lay back on the sand, the knee of the trapped leg sticking up in the air.

"Oh, it is hurting so," she said. She could not hold back the tears any longer. They ran down her face. But even then she didn't howl. She made small puppyish noises.

"You'll *have* to take it off," I told her.

"No!" she protested again. "No. I mustn't. Not ever. I mustn't."

Whatever the reason for it, there was no mistaking her intensity. I sat down beside her, at a loss. Both her hands held on to one of mine, gripping it tightly while she cried. It was obvious that the pain of her foot was increasing. For almost the first time in my life I found myself in charge of a situation which demanded a decision. I made it.

"It's no good. You've *got* to get it off," I told her. "If you don't, you'll probably stay here and die."

She did not give in at once, but her argument weakened until at last she consented. She watched apprehensively while I cut the lace. Then she said: "Go away! You mustn't look."

I hesitated, but childhood is a time thickly beset with incomprehensible, though important, conventions; I withdrew a few yards and turned my back. I heard her breathing hard. Then she was crying again. I turned around to help her.

"I can't do it," she said, looking at me fearfully through her tears. I knelt down to see what I could do about it.

"You mustn't ever tell," she said. "Never, *never*. Promise?"

I promised.

She was very brave about it. Nothing more than the puppy noises.

When I did succeed in getting the foot free, it looked queer; I mean, it was all twisted and puffy—I didn't even notice then that it had more than the usual number of toes. . . .

I managed to hammer the shoe out of the cleft, and handed it to her. But she found she could not put it on her swollen foot. Nor could she put the foot to the ground. I thought I might carry her on my back, but she was heavier than I expected, and it was clear that we should not get far that way.

"I'll have to go and fetch somebody to help," I told her.

"No, I'll crawl," she said.

I walked beside her, carrying the shoe, and feeling useless. She kept going gamely for a surprisingly long way, but she had to give it up. Her trousers were worn through at the knees, and the knees themselves were sore and bleeding. I had never known anyone, boy or girl, who would have kept on till that pitch; it awed me slightly. I helped her to stand up on her sound foot, and steadied her while she pointed out where her home was, and the trickle of smoke that marked it. I set off half-running, with a high sense of responsibility. When I looked back she was on all fours again, disappearing into the bushes.

I found the house without much difficulty, and knocked, a little nervously.

A tall woman answered. She had a fine, handsome face with large bright eyes. Her dress was russet and a little shorter than those most of the women at home wore, but it carried the conventional cross, from neck to hem and breast to breast, in a green that matched the scarf on her head.

"Are you Sophie's mother?" I asked.

She looked at me sharply and frowned. She said, with anxious abruptness: "What is it?"

I told her.

"Oh," she said. "Her foot!"

She looked hard at me again for a moment, then she stood the broom she was holding against the wall, and asked briskly:

"Where is she?"

I led her by the way I had come. At the sound of her voice Sophie crawled out of the bushes.

Her mother looked at the swollen, misshapen foot and the bleeding knees.

"Oh, my poor darling!" she said, holding her and kissing her. Then she added: "He's seen it?"

"Yes," Sophie told her. "I'm sorry, Mummy. I tried hard, but I couldn't do it myself, and it did hurt so."

Her mother nodded slowly. She sighed.

"Oh, well. It can't be helped now. Up you get."

Sophie climbed on to her mother's back, and we all went back to the house together.

The commandments and precepts one learns as a child are just a set of bits; parts of no pattern, few of them even touching one another. Some lodge and are remembered by rote, but they mean little until there is example— and, even then, the example needs to be recognized.

Thus, I was able to sit patiently and watch the hurt foot being washed, cold-poulticed, and bound up, and perceive no connection between it and the affirmation which I had heard almost every Sunday of my life. I could repeat the words of the affirmation, just as I could repeat many other sets of words, but it had simply never occurred to me that they had any connection with real life or real people. They were just something that got said on Sunday:

"And God created man in his own image. And God decreed that man should have one body, one head, two arms and two legs; that each arm should be jointed in two places and end in one hand; that each hand should have four fingers and one thumb; that each finger should bear a flat finger-nail . . ."

And so on until:

"Then God created woman, also, and in the same image, but with these differences, according to her nature: her voice should be of higher pitch than man's; she should grow no beard; she should have two breasts . . ."

And so on again.

I knew it all, word for word—and yet the sight of Sophie's six toes stirred nothing in my memory. They looked no less proper to her foot than my five did to my own. I saw the foot resting in her mother's lap. Watched her mother pause to look down at it for a still moment, lift it, bend to kiss it gently, and then look up with tears in her eyes. I felt sorry for her distress, and for Sophie, and for the hurt foot—but nothing more.

While the bandaging was being finished I looked around the room curiously. The house was a great deal smaller than my home, a cottage, in fact, but I liked it better. It felt friendly. And although Sophie's mother was anxious and worried she spoke to me now and then as if I was as real a person as herself. She did not give me the feeling that I was the one regrettable and unreliable factor in an otherwise orderly life, the way most people did at home. And the room itself seemed to me the better, too, for not having groups of words hanging on the wall that people could point to in disapproval. At home they had been doing that since long before I had been able to read the words. Instead, this room had several drawings of horses, which I thought very fine.

Presently, Sophie, tidied up now, and with the tearstains washed away, hopped to a chair at the table. Quite restored but for the foot, she inquired with grave hospitality whether I liked eggs.

I said I did.

Afterward, her mother told me to wait where I was while she carried Sophie upstairs. She returned in a few minutes, and sat down beside me. She took my hand in hers and looked at me seriously for some moments. I could feel her anxiety strongly; though quite why she should be so worried was not, at first, clear to me. I was surprised by her, for there had been no sign before that she could think in that way. I thought back to her, trying to reassure her and show her that she need not be anxious about me, but it didn't reach her. She went on looking at me with her eyes shining, much as Sophie's had when she was trying not to cry. Her thoughts were all worry and shapeless as she kept on looking at me, I tried again but still couldn't reach them. Then she nodded slowly, and said in words:

"You're a good boy, David. You were very kind to Sophie. I want to thank you for that."

I felt awkward, and looked at my shoes. I couldn't remember anyone saying before that I was a good boy. I knew no form of response designed to meet such an event.

"You like Sophie, don't you?" she went on, still looking at me.

"Yes," I told her. And I added: "I think she's awfully brave, too. It must have hurt a lot."

"Will you keep a secret—an important secret—for her sake?" she asked.

"Yes, of course," I agreed, but a little uncertain in my tone for not realizing what the secret was.

"You—you saw her foot?" she said, looking steadily into my face. "Her —toes?"

I nodded. "Yes," I said again.

"Well, that is the secret, David. Nobody else must know about that. You are the only person who does, except her father and me. Nobody else must know. Nobody at all—not ever."

"No," I agreed, and nodded seriously again.

There was a pause—at least, her voice paused, but her thoughts went on, as if "nobody" and "not ever" were making desolate, unhappy echoes there. Then that changed and she became tense and fierce and afraid inside. It was no good thinking back to her. I tried clumsily to emphasize in words that I had meant what I said.

"Never—not anybody at all," I assured her earnestly.

"It's very, very important," she insisted. "How can I explain to you?" But she didn't really need to explain. Her urgent, tight-strung feeling of the importance was very plain. Her words were far less potent. She said:

"If anyone were to find out, they'd—they'd be terribly unkind to her. We've got to see that that never happens."

It was as if the anxious feeling had turned into something hard, like an iron rod.

"Because she has six toes?" I asked.

"Yes. That's what nobody but us must ever know. It must be a secret between us," she repeated, driving it home. "You'll promise, David."

"I'll promise. I can swear, if you like," I offered.

"The promise is enough," she told me.

It was so heavy a promise that I was quite resolved to keep it completely —even from my cousin Rosalind. Though, underneath, I was puzzled by its evident importance. It seemed a very small toe to cause such a degree of anxiety. But there was a great deal of grown-up fuss that seemed disproportionate to causes. If I had not learned long ago that a grown-up could scarcely ever give a satisfactory answer to a simple question I would have asked her just *why* it was so important, and *why* anybody should be unkind to Sophie on account of it. But as one was liable sometimes to get punished simply for putting a question at all, I had got into the habit of not asking things much. So I held on to the main point—the need for secrecy. That would not be difficult. I could just tuck it in among my rather large range of private secrets, though it would be unusual to have one I could not share even with Rosalind.

Sophie's mother kept on looking at me with a sad, but unseeing expression until I became uncomfortable. She noticed as I fidgeted, and smiled. It was a kind smile.

"All right, then," she said. "We'll keep it secret, and never talk about it again?"

"Yes," I agreed.

On the way down the path from the door, I turned around.

"May I come and see Sophie again soon?" I asked.

She hesitated, giving the question some thought, then she said:

"Very well—if you are sure you can come without anyone knowing."

Not until I had reached the bank and was making my homeward way along the top of it did the monotonous Sunday precepts join up with reality. Then, suddenly, the Definition of Man recited itself in my head: "—and each leg shall be jointed twice and have one foot, and each foot five toes, and each toe shall end with a flat nail . . ." And so on, until finally: "And any creature that shall seem to be human, but is not formed thus is not human. It is neither man nor woman. It is a Blasphemy against the true Image of God, and hateful in the sight of God."

I was abruptly perturbed—and considerably puzzled, too. A Blasphemy was, as had been impressed upon me often enough, a frightful thing. Yet there was nothing frightful about Sophie. She was simply an ordinary little girl—if a great deal more sensible and braver than most. Yet, according to the Definition . . .

Clearly there must be a mistake somewhere. Surely having one very small toe extra—well, two very small toes, because I supposed there would be one to match on the other foot—surely that couldn't be enough to make one "hateful in the sight of God?"

The ways of the world were very puzzling. In the course of my ten years I had accumulated quite a lot of lore of one kind and another, bits from church, bits from my parents, bits from lessons, bits from other children, bits from adventuring on my own, but they were still disjointed and not to be relied upon for guidance. When I did something amiss, I still had little but the scale of the punishment to indicate whether I had committed an enormity, or a peccadillo. The things I knew did not connect to make a clear course of conduct. The best I could do was to cling to the simpler things that I did understand—things like a promise being a promise. That, at least, was clear and straightforward.

CHAPTER TWO

I REACHED HOME by my usual method. At a point where the woods had lapped up the side of the bank and grown across it I scrambled down on to a narrow, little-used track. From there on I was watchful, and kept my hand on my knife. I was supposed to keep out of the woods, for it did occasionally—though very rarely—happen that large creatures penetrated as far into civilized parts as Waknuk, and there was just a chance that one might encounter some kind of wild dog or cat. However, and as usual, the only creatures I heard were small ones, hurriedly making off.

After a mile or so I reached cultivated land, with the house in sight across three or four fields. I worked along the fringe of the woods, observing carefully from cover, then crossed all but the last field in the shadows of the hedges, and paused to prospect again. There was no one in sight but old Jacob slowly shoveling muck in the yard. When his back was safely turned I cut swiftly across the bit of open ground, climbed in through a window, and made my way cautiously to my own room. One of the troubles about home was that if one walked in by a door there would almost certainly be some person who, after a what-have-you-been-up-to-now? question, would find one a useful, but uncongenial job.

Our house is not easy to describe. My grandfather, Elias Strorm, built the first part of it over fifty years before; since then it had grown new rooms and extensions at various times. By now, it rambled off on one side into stock-sheds, stores, stables, and barns, and on the other into washhouses, dairies, cheese-rooms, farmhands' rooms, and so on until it three-quarters enclosed a large, beaten-earth yard which lay to leeward of the main house and had a midden for its central feature.

Like all the houses of the district to which it had given its name, it was constructed on a frame of solid, roughly dressed timbers, but, since it was the oldest house there, most of the spaces in the outer walls had been filled in with bricks and stones from the ruins of some of the Old People's buildings, and plastered wattle was used only for the internal walls.

My grandfather, in the aspect he wore when presented to me by my father as an example, appeared to have been a man of somewhat tediously unrelieved virtue. It was only later that I pieced together a portrait that was more credible, if less creditable.

Elias Strorm came from the east, somewhere near the sea. Why he came is not quite clear. He himself maintained that it was the ungodly ways of the East which drove him to search for a less sophisticated, stauncher-minded region; though I have heard it suggested that there came a point when his native parts refused to tolerate him any longer. Whatever the cause, it persuaded him to Waknuk—then undeveloped, almost frontier country—with all his worldly goods in a train of six wagons, at the age of forty-five. He was a husky man, a dominating man, and a man fierce for rectitude. He had eyes that could flash with evangelical fire beneath bushy brows. Respect for God was frequently on his lips, and fear of the devil constantly in his heart, and it seems to have been hard to say which inspired him the more.

Soon after he had started the house he went off on a journey and brought back a bride. She was shy, pretty in the pink and golden way, and twenty-five years younger than himself. She moved, I have been told, like a lovely colt when she thought herself unwatched; as timorously as a rabbit when she felt her husband's eye upon her.

All her answers, poor thing, were dusty. She did not find that a marriage service generated love; she did not enable her husband to recapture his youth through hers; nor could she compensate for that by running his home in the manner of an experienced housekeeper.

Elias was not a man to let shortcomings pass unremarked. In a few seasons he straightened the coltishness with admonitions, faded the pink and gold with preaching, and produced a sad, gray wraith of wifehood who died, unprotesting, a year after her second son was born.

Grandfather Elias had never a moment's doubt of the proper pattern for his heir. My father's faith was bred into his bones, his principles were his sinews, and both responded to a mind richly stored with instances from the Bible, and from Nicholson's *Repentances*. In faith father and son were at one; the difference between them was only in approach; the evangelical flash did not appear in my father's eyes; his virtue was more legalistic.

Joseph Strorm, my father, did not marry until Elias was dead, and when he did, he was not a man to repeat his father's mistakes. My mother's views harmonized with his own. She had a strong sense of duty, and never doubted where it lay.

Our district, and, consequently, our house as the first there, took the name Waknuk because of a tradition that there had been a place of that name there, or thereabouts, long, long ago, in the time of the Old People. The tradition was, as usual, vague, but certainly there had been some buildings there, for remnants and foundations had remained until they were taken for new buildings. There was also the long bank, running away until it reached the hills and the huge scar there that must have been made by the Old People when, in their superhuman fashion, they had cut away half a mountain in order to find something or other that interested them. It may have been called Waknuk then; anyway, Waknuk it had become, an orderly, law-abiding, God-respecting community of some hundred scattered holdings, large and small.

My father was a man of local consequence. When, at the age of sixteen, he had made his first public appearance by giving a Sunday address in the church his father had built, there had still been fewer than sixty families in the district. But as more land was cleared for farming and more people came to settle, he was not submerged by them. He was still the largest landowner, he still continued to preach frequently on Sundays and explain with practical clarity the laws and views held in heaven upon a variety of matters and practices, and he continued upon the appointed days to administer the laws temporal, as a magistrate. For the rest of the time he saw to it that he, and all within his control, continued to set a high example to the district.

Within the house, life centered, as was the local custom, upon the large living room which was also the kitchen. As the house was the largest and best in Waknuk, so was the room. The great fireplace there was an object of pride—not vain pride, of course; more a matter of being conscious of having given worthy treatment to the excellent materials that the Lord had provided: a kind of testament, really. The hearth was solid stone blocks. The whole chimney was built of bricks and had never been known to catch fire. The area about its point of emergence was covered with the only tiles in the district, so that the thatch which covered the rest of the roof had never caught fire, either.

My mother saw to it that the big room was kept very clean and tidy. The floor was composed of pieces of brick and stone and artificial stone cleverly fitted together. The furniture was whitely scrubbed tables and stools, with a few chairs. The walls were whitewashed. Several burnished pans, too big to go in the cupboards, hung against them. The nearest approach to decoration was a number of wooden panels with sayings, mostly from *Repentances*, artistically burnt into them. The one on the left of the fireplace read: ONLY THE IMAGE OF GOD IS MAN. The one on the right: KEEP PURE THE STOCK OF THE LORD. On the opposite wall two more said: BLESSED IS THE NORM, and IN PURITY OUR SALVATION. The largest was the one on the back wall, hung to face the door which led to the yard. It reminded everyone who came in: WATCH THOU FOR THE MUTANT!

Frequent references to these texts had made me familiar with the words long before I was able to read; in fact I am not sure that they did not give me my first reading lessons. I knew them by heart, just as I knew others elsewhere in the house which said things like: THE NORM IS THE WILL OF GOD, and, REPRODUCTION IS THE ONLY HOLY PRODUCTION, and, THE DEVIL IS THE FATHER OF DEVIATION, and a number of others about Offenses and Blasphemies.

Many of them were still obscure to me; others I had learnt something about. Offenses, for instance. That was because the occurrence of an Offense was sometimes quite an impressive occasion. Usually the first sign that one had happened was that my father came into the house in a bad temper. Then, in the evening, he would call us all together, including everyone who worked on the farm. We would all kneel while he proclaimed our repentance and led prayers for forgiveness. The next morning we would all be up before daylight, and gather in the yard. As the sun rose we would sing a hymn while my father ceremonially slaughtered the two-headed calf, four-legged chicken, or whatever other kind of Offense it happened to be. Sometimes it would be a much queerer thing than those. The most exciting time I remember was when a goose proudly led her brood into the yard one day. She must somehow have reared them in the woods, for they were already the size of hens. Not only were they web-winged instead of feathered, but they also had exceedingly sharp beaks and vicious tempers. There was a very active scene in the yard before a much-pecked and scratched company assembled to ask a blessing on their liquidation.

But Offenses were not limited to the livestock. Sometimes it would be some stalks of corn, or some vegetables, that my father produced and cast on the kitchen table in anger and shame. If it was merely a matter of a few rows of vegetables, they just came out and were destroyed. But if a whole field had gone wrong we would wait for good weather, and then set fire to it, singing hymns while it burnt. I used to find that a very fine sight.

It was because my father was a careful and pious man with a keen eye for an Offense that we used to have more slaughterings and burnings than anyone else. Any suggestion that we were more afflicted with Offenses than other people hurt and angered him. He had no wish at all to throw good money away, he pointed out. If our neighbors were as conscientious as ourselves, he had no doubt that their liquidations would far outnumber ours; unfortunately there were certain persons with elastic principles.

So I learned quite early to know what Offenses were. They were things which did not look *right*—that is to say, did not look like their parents, or parent-plants. Usually there was only some small thing wrong—though sometimes a thing might have gone altogether wrong, and be very queer indeed. But however much or little was wrong it was an Offense, and if it happened among people it was a Blasphemy—at least, that was the technical term though commonly both kinds were called Deviations.

Nevertheless, the question of Offenses was not always as simple as one might think. When there was disagreement the district's Inspector would be sent for. He would examine the dubious creature or plant carefully, and more often than not he would decide it was an Offense—but sometimes he would proclaim it simply a Cross. In that case it was usually allowed to survive although nobody thought much of Crosses. My father, however, seldom called in the Inspector, he preferred to be on the safe side and liquidate anything doubtful. There were people who disapproved of his meticulousness, saying that the local Deviation-rate, which had shown a steady over-all improvement and now stood at half what it had been in my grandfather's time, would have been better still but for my father. Nevertheless, the Waknuk district had a great name for Purity.

Ours was no longer a frontier region. Hard work and sacrifice had produced a stability of stock and crops which could be envied even by some communities to the east of us. You could now go some thirty miles to the south or southwest before you came to Wild Country—that is to say parts where the chance of breeding true was less than fifty per cent. After that, everything grew more erratic across a belt which was ten miles wide in some places and up to twenty in others, until you came to the mysterious Fringes where nothing was dependable, and where, to quote my father, "the Devil struts his wide estates, and the laws of God are mocked." Fringes country, too, was said to be variable in depth, and beyond it lay the Badlands about which nobody knew anything. Usually anybody who went into the Badlands died there, and the one or two men who had come out of them did not last long.

It was not the Badlands, but the Fringes that gave us trouble from time to time. The people of the Fringes—at least, one calls them people, because although they were really Deviations they often looked quite like ordinary human people, if nothing had gone too much wrong with them—these people, then, had very little where they lived in their border country, so they came out into civilized parts to steal grain and livestock and clothes and tools and weapons, too, if they could; and sometimes they carried off children.

Occasional small raids used to happen two or three times a year, and nobody took much notice of them as a rule—except the people who got raided, of course. Usually they had time to get away and lost only their stock. Then everybody would contribute a little in kind, or in money, to help them set up again. But as time went on and the frontier was pushed back there were more Fringes people trying to live on less country. Some years they got very hungry, and after a time it was no longer just a matter of a dozen or so making a quick raid and then running back into Fringes country; they came instead in large, organized bands and did a lot of damage.

In my father's childhood mothers used to quieten and awe troublesome infants by threatening, "Be good now. Or I'll fetch Old Maggie from the Fringes to you. She's got four eyes to watch you with, and four ears to hear you with, and four arms to smack you with. So you be careful." Or Hairy Jack was another ominous figure who might be called in. ". . . and he'll take you off to his cave in the Fringes where all his family lives. They're all hairy, too, with long tails; and they eat a little boy each for breakfast every morning, and a little girl each for supper every evening." Nowadays, however, it was not only small children who lived in nervous awareness of the Fringes people not so far away. Their existence had become a dangerous nuisance and their depredations the cause of many representations to the government in Rigo.

For all the good the petitions did, they might never have been sent. Indeed, with no one able to tell, over a stretch of five or six hundred miles, where the next attack would come, it is difficult to see what practical help could have been given. What the government did do, from its comfortable situation far, far to the east, was to express sympathy in encouraging phrases, and suggest the formation of a local militia—a suggestion which, as all able-bodied males had as a matter of course been members of a kind of unofficial militia since frontier days, was felt to amount to disregard of the situation.

As far as the Waknuk district was concerned the threat from the Fringes was more of a nuisance than a menace. The deepest raid had come no nearer than ten miles, but every now and then there were emergencies, and seemingly more every year, which called the men away, and brought all the farm work to a stop. The interruptions were expensive and wasteful; moreover, they always brought anxiety if the trouble was near our sector: nobody could be sure that they might not come further one time. . . .

Mostly, however, we led a comfortable, settled, industrious existence. Our household was extensive. There were my father and mother, my two sisters, and my Uncle Axel to make the family, but also there were the kitchen girls and dairymaids, some of whom were married to the farm men, and their children, and, of course, the men themselves, so when we were all gathered for the meal at the end of the day's work there were over twenty of us; and when we assembled for prayers there were still more because the men from the adjoining cottages came in with their wives and children.

Uncle Axel was not a real relative. He had married one of my mother's sisters, Elizabeth. He was a sailor then, and she had gone east with him and died in Rigo while he was on the voyage that had left him a cripple. He was a useful all-around man, though slow in getting about because of his leg, so my father let him live with us. He was also my best friend.

My mother came of a family of five girls and two boys. Four of the girls were full sisters; the youngest girl and the two boys were half-sister and half-brothers to the rest. Hannah, the eldest, had been sent away by her husband, and nobody had heard of her since. Emily, my mother, was next in age. Then came Harriet, who was married to a man with a big farm at Kentak, almost fifteen miles away. Then Elizabeth, who had married Uncle Axel. Where my half-aunt Lilian and my half-uncle Thomas were I did not know, but my half-uncle Angus Morton owned the farm next to us, and a mile or more of our boundaries ran together, which annoyed my father, who could scarcely agree with half-uncle Angus about anything. His daughter, Rosalind, was, of course, my cousin.

Although Waknuk itself was the biggest farm in the district, most of them were organized along the same lines, and all of them growing larger, for with the improving stability-rate there was the incentive to extend; every year felling of trees and clearing went on to make new fields. The woods and spurs of forest were being nibbled away until the countryside was beginning to look like the old, long-cultivated land in the east.

It was said that nowadays even people in Rigo knew where Waknuk was without looking it up on the map.

I lived, in fact, on the most prosperous farm in a prospering district. At the age of ten, however, I had little appreciation of that. My impression was of an uncomfortably industrious place where there always seemed to be more jobs than people, unless one was careful, so on this particular evening I contrived to lie low until routine sounds told me that it was near enough to the mealtime for me to show myself safely.

As I wandered into the yard I encountered Janet, bringing in a big jug of milk from the dairy. She looked at me suspiciously.

"And where've you been?" she inquired. "Your father was wanting you to give the pony some exercise."

I was ready for that. "Fishing," I told her, unblushingly. "Down below the mill."

I hung about, watching the horses being unharnessed and turned out. Presently the bell on the gable-end tolled a couple of times. Doors opened, and people came into the yard, making for the kitchen. I went along with them. The warning: WATCH THOU FOR THE MUTANT! faced me as I went in, but it was much too familiar to stir a thought. What interested me exclusively at the moment was the smell of food.

CHAPTER THREE

I USUALLY WENT OVER to see Sophie once or twice a week after that. What schooling we had—which was a matter of half a dozen children being taught to read and write and do some sums by one or another of several old women—took place in the mornings. It was not difficult at the midday meal to slip away from the table early and disappear until everyone would think someone else had found a job for me, but I felt it would be unwise to do that too often, and made a point of letting someone find work for me two or three afternoons a week.

Very often I did not need to go all the way to Sophie's home to find her. Sometimes I'd hear her call, but see no sign of her until she came pushing out of the bushes, or popping up from behind a tuft of grass.

When her ankle was quite recovered she was able to show me the favorite corners of her territory. Most often we went to the stream. She liked to watch the fish in the pools there. In order not to disturb them we'd crawl to the bank and push our heads over very slowly and carefully. There were some queer things to be seen sometimes.

One day we were watching a fish with a dark line on its back that broke into speckles on its sides. It hung suspended, facing upstream, opening its mouth in a leisurely way now and then to gulp morsels that were washed toward it. Sophie nudged me. I followed her line of sight, and saw a larger fish, lurking beneath an overhanging bush like a long shadow. It was watching the midstream fish attentively, and for all its present lack of motion it looked tense and ready to pounce, but beneath and behind it was something else again. A creature on long, stilty legs with sharp-looking claws wide, and reaching forward. Its tail was curled under it and fanning very gently as it crept closer and closer to the intent larger fish.

We watched, fascinated. The drama was painfully prolonged. Still the larger fish awaited the perfect moment, while the other creature inched delicately nearer to it.

Suddenly Sophie shouted "No!" and threw a stone. When the ripples cleared the tableau had vanished.

"What did you do that for?" I said. I had wanted to see how it would work out.

"The horrible thing was going to get him. They nearly always do."

"Are there a lot of them in there?" I asked, looking down into the water.

"Oh, yes. My father catches them sometimes. They're nice to eat, although they're horrible."

"It looked like an Offense," I said. "You ought to burn Offenses, not eat them."

"Why?"

I was not sure about that, but I knew it was the proper thing to do. I told her that we always did it at home.

"But that's silly if they're good to eat," she decided.

It was, I explained, a matter of principle. I did not know quite what that meant, either, but I was sure it was what my father would have said in the circumstances.

"Oh," said Sophie, vaguely, but she looked a little impressed, all the same.

One day I took her over our side of the big bank to see the steam-engine. There wasn't another steam-engine within a hundred miles, and we were very proud of it. Corky, who looked after it, was not about, but the doors at the end of its shed were open, letting out the sound of a rhythmic groaning, creaking, and puffing. We ventured onto the threshold and peered into the gloom inside. It was fascinating to watch the big timbers moving up and down with wheezing noises while up in the shadows of the roof a huge crossbeam rocked slowly backward and forward, with a pause at the end of each tilt as though it were summoning up energy for the next effort. Fascinating—but, after a time, monotonous.

Ten minutes of it were enough, and we withdrew to climb to the top of the woodpile beside the shed. We sat there with the whole heap quivering beneath us as the engine chugged ponderously on.

"My Uncle Axel says the Old People must have had much better engines than this," I told her.

"My father says that if one-quarter of the things they say about the Old People are true, they must have been magicians, not real people, at all," Sophie countered.

"But they *were* wonderful," I insisted.

"Too wonderful to be true, he says," she told me.

"Doesn't he think they were able to fly, like people say?" I asked.

"No. That's silly. If they could've, we'd be able to."

"But there are lots of things they could do that we are learning to do again," I protested.

"Not flying," she shook her head. "Things can either fly, or they can't; and we can't," she said.

I thought of telling her about my dream of the city and the things flying over it, but after all, a dream isn't much evidence of anything, so I let it pass. Presently we climbed down, leaving the engine to its panting and creaking and made our way over to her home.

John Wender, her father, was back from one of his trips. A sound of hammering came from the outside shed where he was stretching skins on frames, and the whole place smelled of his operations. Sophie rushed to him and flung her arms round his neck. He straightened up, holding her against him with one arm.

"Hullo, Chicky," he said.

He greeted me more gravely. We had an unspoken understanding that we were on a man-to-man basis. It had not always been like that. When he first saw me he had looked at me in a way that had scared me and made me afraid to speak in his presence. Gradually, however, that had changed. We became friends. He showed me and told me a lot of interesting things—all the same I would look up sometimes to find him watching me uneasily.

And no wonder. Only some years later could I appreciate how badly troubled he must have been when he came home to find Sophie had sprained her ankle, and that it had been David Strorm, the son of Joseph Strorm, of all people, who had seen her foot. He must, I think, have been greatly tempted by the thought that a dead boy could break no promise. It would have been understandable. Perhaps Mrs. Wender saved me.

But I think he would have been reassured had he known of an incident at my home about a month after I met Sophie.

I had run a splinter into my hand and when I pulled it out it bled a lot. I went to the kitchen with it only to find everybody too busy getting supper to be bothered with me, so I rummaged a strip out of the rag-drawer for myself. I tried clumsily for a minute or two to tie it, then my mother noticed. She made tchk-tchk noises of disapproval and insisted on it being washed. Then she wound the strip on neatly, grumbling that of course I must go and do it just when she was busy. I said I was sorry, and added:

"I could have managed it all right by myself if I'd had another hand."

My voice must have carried, for silence fell on the whole room like a clap.

My mother froze. I looked around the room at the sudden quiet. Mary, standing with a pie in her hands, two of the four men waiting for their meal, my father about to take his seat at the head of the table, and the others; they were all staring at me. I caught my father's expression just as it was turning from amazement to anger. Alarmed, but uncomprehending, I watched his mouth tighten, his jaw come forward, his brows press together over his still-incredulous eyes. He demanded:

"What was that you said, boy?"

I knew the tone. I tried to think in a desperate hurry how I had offended this time. I stumbled and stuttered.

"I—I s-said I couldn't manage to tie this for myself," I told him.

His eyes had become less incredulous, more accusing.

"And you wished you had a third hand!"

"No, father. I only said *if* I had another hand——"

"——you would be able to tie it. If that was not a wish, what was it?"

"I only meant *if*," I protested. I was alarmed, and too confused to explain that I had only happened to use one way of expressing a difficulty which might have been put in several ways. I was aware that the rest had stopped gaping at me, and were now looking apprehensively at my father. His expression was grim.

"You—my own son—were calling upon the Devil to give you another hand!" he accused me.

"But I wasn't. I only——"

"Be quiet, boy. Everyone in this room heard you. You'll certainly make it no better by lying."

"But——"

"Were you, or were you not, expressing dissatisfaction with the form of the body God gave you—the form in his own image?"

"I just said *if* I——"

"You blasphemed, boy. You found fault with the Norm. Everybody here heard you. What have you to say to that? You know what the Norm is?"

I gave up protesting. I knew well enough that my father in his present mood would not try to understand. I muttered, parrot-like:

" 'The Norm is the Image of God.' "

"You *do* know. And yet, knowing this, you deliberately wished yourself a Mutant. That is a terrible thing, an outrageous thing. You, my son, committing blasphemy before his parents!" In his sternest pulpit voice, he added: "What is a Mutant?"

" 'A thing accursed in the sight of God and man,' " I mumbled.

"And *that* is what you wished to be! What have you to say?"

With a heart-sunk certainty that it would be useless to say anything I kept my lips shut and my eyes lowered.

"Down on your knees!" he commanded. "Kneel and pray!"

The others all knelt, too. My father's voice rose:

"Lord, we have sinned in omission. We beg thy forgiveness that we have not better instructed this child in thy laws. . . ." The prayer seemed to go booming on for a long time. After the "Amen" there was a pause, until my father said:

"Now go to your room and pray. Pray, you wretched boy, for a forgiveness you do not deserve, but which God, in his mercy, may yet grant you. I will come to you later."

I went to my room, but I did not pray. I sat miserably on the side of my bed while a feeling of bewildered shame gave way slowly to a feeling of injustice that glowed in my chest like a hot coal.

In the night, when the anguish which had followed my father's visit was somewhat abated, I lay awake, puzzling. I had had no idea of wishing for a third hand, but even if I had . . . ? If it was such a terrible thing just to think of having three hands, what would happen if one really had them —or anything else wrong; such as, for instance, an extra toe . . . ?

And when at last I fell asleep I had a dream.

We were all gathered in the yard, just as we had been at the last Purification. Then it had been a little hairless calf that stood waiting, blinking stupidly at the knife in my father's hand; this time it was a little girl, Sophie, standing barefooted and trying uselessly to hide the whole long row of toes that everyone could see on each foot. We all stood looking at her, and waiting. Presently she started to run from one person to another, imploring them to help her, but none of them moved, and none of their faces had any expression. My father started to walk toward her, the knife shining in his hand. Sophie grew frantic; she flitted from one unmoving person to another, tears running down her face. My father, stern, implacable, kept on coming nearer; still no one would move to help her. My father came closer still, with long arms outspread to prevent her bolting as he cornered her.

He caught her, and dragged her back to the middle of the yard. The sun's edge began to show above the horizon, and everyone started to sing a hymn. My father held Sophie with one arm just as he had held the struggling calf. He raised his other hand high, and as he swept it down the knife flashed in the light of the rising sun, just as it had flashed when he cut the calf's throat. . . .

If John and Mary Wender had been there when I woke up struggling and crying, and then lay in the dark trying to convince myself that the terrible picture which still hung in my mind was nothing more than a dream, they would, I think, have felt quite a lot easier in their minds.

CHAPTER FOUR

THIS WAS A TIME when I passed out of a placid period into one where things kept on happening. There wasn't much reason about it; that is to say, only a few of the things were connected with one another. It was more as if an active cycle had set in, just as a spell of different weather might come along.

My meeting with Sophie was, I suppose, the first incident; the next was that Uncle Axel found out about me and my half-cousin, Rosalind Morton. He—and it was lucky it was he, and no one else—happened to come upon me when I was talking to her, and I was doing it out loud because, although that way was slower, I could still be a lot clearer when I did it like that.

It must have been a self-preservative instinct which had made us keep the thing to ourselves, for we'd no active feeling of danger—I had so little, in fact, that when Uncle Axel found me sitting behind a rick chatting apparently to myself, I made very little effort to dissemble. He may have been there a minute or more before I became aware of somebody just around the corner of my eye, and turned to see who it was.

My Uncle Axel was a tall man, neither thin nor fat, but sturdy, and with a seasoned look to him. I used to think when I watched him at work that his weathered hands and forearms had some sort of kinship with the polished wood of the helves they used. He was standing in his customary way, with much of his weight upon the thick stick he used because his leg had been wrongly set when it was broken at sea. His bushy eyebrows, a little touched with gray, were drawn closer by a half-frown, but the lines on his tanned face were half-amused as he regarded me.

"Well, Davie boy, and who would you be chattering away so hard to? Is it fairies, or gnomes, or only the rabbits?" he asked.

I just shook my head. He limped closer, and sat down beside me, chewing on a stalk of grass from the rick.

"Feeling lonely?" he inquired.

"No," I told him.

He frowned a bit again. "Wouldn't it be more fun to do your chatting with some of the other kids?" he suggested. "More interesting than just sitting and talking to yourself?"

I hesitated, and then because he was Uncle Axel and my best friend among the grown-ups I said:

"But I was."

"Was what?" he asked, puzzled.

"Talking to one of them," I told him.

He frowned, and went on looking puzzled.

"Who?"

"Rosalind," I told him.

He paused a bit, looking at me harder.

"H'mm—I didn't see her around," he remarked.

"Oh, she isn't here. She's at home—at least, she's near home, in a little secret tree-house her brothers built in the woods," I explained. "It's a favorite place of hers."

He was not able to understand what I meant at first. He kept on talking as though it were a make-believe game; but after I had tried for some time to explain he sat quiet, watching my face as I talked, and presently his expression became very serious. After I'd stopped he said nothing, for a minute or two, then he asked:

"This isn't play-stuff, it's the real truth you're telling me, Davie boy?" And he looked at me hard and steadily as he spoke.

"Yes, Uncle Axel, of course," I assured him.

"And you've never told anyone else—nobody at all?"

"No. It's a secret," I told him, and he looked relieved.

He threw away the remains of his grass-stalk, and pulled another out of the rick. After he had thoughtfully bitten a few pieces off that and spat them out he looked directly at me again.

"Davie," he said, "I want you to make me a promise."

"Yes, Uncle Axel?"

"It's this," he said, speaking very seriously. "I want you to *keep* it secret. I want you to promise that you will never, never tell anyone else what you have just told me—*never*. It's very important; later on you'll understand better how important it is. You mustn't do anything that would even let anyone guess about it. Will you promise me that?"

His gravity impressed me greatly. I had never known him to speak with so much intensity. It made me aware, when I gave my promise, that I was vowing something more important than I could understand. He kept his eyes on mine as I spoke, and then nodded, satisfied that I meant it. We shook hands on the agreement. Then he said:

"It would be best if you could forget it altogether."

I thought it over, and then shook my head.

"I don't think I could do that, Uncle Axel. Not really. I mean, it just *is*. It'd be like trying to forget——" I broke off, unable to express what I wanted to.

"Like trying to forget how to talk, or how to hear, perhaps?" he suggested.

"Rather like that—only different," I admitted.

He nodded, and thought again.

"You hear the words inside your head?" he asked.

"Well not exactly 'hear,' and not exactly 'see,' " I told him. "There are—well, sort of shapes—and if you use words you make them clearer so that they're easier to understand."

"But you don't *have* to use words—not say them out loud as you were doing just now?"

"Oh no, it just helps to make it clearer sometimes."

"It also helps to make things a lot more dangerous, for both of you. I want you to make another promise: that you'll never do it out loud any more."

"All right, Uncle Axel," I agreed again.

"You'll understand when you're older how important it is," he told me, and then he went on to insist that I should get Rosalind to make the same promises. I did not tell him anything about the others because he seemed so worried already, but I decided I'd get them to promise, too. At the end he put out his hand again, and once more we swore secrecy very solemnly.

I put the matter to Rosalind and the others the same evening. It crystallized a feeling that was in all of us. I don't suppose that there was a single one of us who had not at some time made a slip or two and brought upon himself, or herself, an odd, suspicious look. A few of these looks had been warnings enough to each; it was such looks, not comprehended, but clear enough as signs of disapproval just below the verge of suspicion, that had kept us out of trouble. There had been no acknowledged, cooperative policy among us. It was simply as individuals that we had all taken the same self-protective, secretive course. But now, out of Uncle Axel's anxious insistence on my promise, the feeling of a threat was strengthened. It was still shapeless to us, but it was more real. Furthermore, in trying to convey Uncle Axel's seriousness to them I must have stirred up an uneasiness that was in all their minds, for there was no dissent. They made the promise willingly, eagerly, in fact, as though it was a burden they were relieved to share. It was our first act as a group; it *made* us a group by its formal admission of our responsibilities toward one another. It changed our lives by marking our first step in corporate self-preservation, though we understood little of that at the time. What seemed most important just then was the feeling of sharing.

Then, almost on top of that personal event came another which was of general concern; an invasion in force from the Fringes.

As usual, there was no detailed plan to deal with it. As near as anyone came to organization was the appointment of headquarters in the different sectors. Upon an alarm it was the duty of all able-bodied men in the district to rally at their local headquarters, when a course of action would be decided according to the location and extent of the trouble. As a method of dealing with small raids it had proved good enough, but that was all it was intended for. As a result, when the Fringes people found leaders who could promote an organized invasion there had been no adequately organized system of defense to delay them. They were able to push forward on a broad front, mopping up little bands of our militia here and there, looting as they liked and meeting nothing to delay them seriously until they were twenty-five miles or more into civilized parts.

By that time we had our forces in somewhat better order, and neighboring districts had pulled themselves together to head off a further widening, and harry the flanks. Our men were better-armed, too. Quite a lot of them had guns, whereas the Fringes people had only a few that they had stolen, and depended chiefly on bows, knives, and spears. Nevertheless, the width of their advance made them difficult to deal with. They were better woodsmen and cleverer at hiding themselves than proper human beings, so that they were able to press on another fifteen miles before we could contain them and bring them to battle.

It was exciting for a boy. With the Fringes people little more than seven miles away, our yard at Waknuk had become one of the rallying points. My father who had had an arrow through his arm early in the campaign, was helping to organize the new volunteers into squads. For several days there was a great bustling and coming and going as men were registered and sorted, and finally rode off with a fine air of determination and all the women of the household waving handkerchiefs at them.

When they had all departed, and our workers, too, the place seemed uncannily quiet for a day. Then there came a single rider, dashing back. He paused long enough to tell us that there had been a big battle and the Fringes people, with some of their leaders taken prisoner, were running away as fast as they could, then he galloped on with his good news.

That same afternoon a small troup of horsemen came riding into the yard, with two of the captured Fringes leaders in the middle of them.

I dropped what I was doing, and ran across to see. It was a bit disappointing at first sight. The tales about the Fringes had led me to expect creatures with two heads, or fur all over, or half a dozen arms and legs. Instead, they seemed at first glance to be just two ordinary men with beards—though unusually dirty, and with very ragged clothes. One of them was a short man with fair hair which was tufted as though he had trimmed it with a knife. But when I looked at the other I had a shock which brought me up dumbfounded, and staring at him. I was so jolted I just went on staring at him, for, put him in decent clothes, tidy up his beard, and he'd be the image of my father.

As he sat his horse, looking round, he noticed me; casually at first, in passing, then his gaze switched back and he stared hard at me. A strange look that I did not understand at all came into his eyes.

He opened his mouth as if to speak, but at that moment people came out of the house—my father, with his arm still in a sling, among them—to see what was going on.

I saw my father pause on the step and survey the group of horsemen, then he, too, noticed the man in the middle of them. For a moment he stood staring, just as I had done; then all his color drained away, and his face went blotchy gray.

I looked quickly at the other man. He was sitting absolutely rigid on his horse. The expression on his face made something clutch suddenly in my chest. I had never seen hatred naked before, the lines cut deep, the eyes glittering, the teeth suddenly looking like a savage animal's. It struck me with a slap, a horrid revelation of something hitherto unknown, and hideous; it stamped itself on my mind so that I never forgot it.

Then my father, still looking as though he was ill, put out his good hand to steady himself against the doorpost, and turned back into the house.

One of the escort cut the rope which held the prisoner's arms. He dismounted, and I was able to see then what was wrong with him. He stood some eighteen inches taller than anyone else, but not because he was a big man. If his legs had been right, he would have stood no taller than my father's five-foot-ten, but they were not; they were monstrously long and thin, and his arms were long and thin, too. It made him look half-man, half-spider.

The escort gave him food and a pot of beer. He sat down on a bench, and his bony knees stuck up to seem almost level with his shoulders. He looked around the yard, noticing everything as he munched his bread and cheese. In the course of his inspection he perceived me again. He beckoned. I hung back, pretending not to see. He beckoned again. I became ashamed of being afraid of him. I went closer, and then a little closer still, but keeping warily out of range, I judged, of those spidery arms.

"What's your name, boy?" he asked.

"David," I told him. "David Strorm."

He nodded, as though that was satisfactory.

"The man at the door, with his arm in a sling, that would be your father, Joseph Strorm?"

"Yes," I told him.

Again he nodded. He looked around the house and the outbuildings. "This place, then, would be Waknuk?" he asked.

"Yes," I said again.

I don't know whether he would have asked more, for at that point somebody told me to clear off. A little later they all remounted, and soon they moved away, the spidery man with his arms tied together once more. I watched them ride off in the Kentak direction, glad to see them go. My first encounter with someone from the Fringes had not, after all, been exciting; it had been unpleasantly disturbing.

I heard later that both the captured Fringes men managed to escape that same night. I can't remember who told me, but I am perfectly certain it was not my father. I never once heard him refer to that day, and I never had the courage to question him about it.

Then scarcely, it seemed, had we settled down after the invasion and got the men back to catching up with the farm work, than my father was in the middle of a new row with my half-uncle, Angus Morton.

Differences of temperament and outlook had kept them intermittently at war with each other for years. My father had been heard to sum up his opinion by declaring that if Angus had any principles they were of such infinite width as to be a menace to the rectitude of the neighborhood; to which Angus was reputed to have replied that Joseph Strorm was a flinty-souled pedant, and bigoted well beyond the brink of stupidity. It was not, therefore, difficult for a row to blow up, and the latest one occurred over Angus's acquisition of a pair of greathorses.

Rumors of greathorses had reached our district though none had been seen there. My father was already uneasy in his mind at what he had heard of them, nor was the fact that it was Angus who had imported them a recommendation; consequently, it may have been with some prejudice that he went to inspect them.

His doubts were confirmed at once. The moment he set eyes on the huge creatures standing twenty-six hands at the shoulder, he knew they were *wrong*. He turned his back on them with disgust, and went straight to the Inspector's house with a demand that they should be destroyed as Offenses.

"You're out of order this time," the Inspector told him cheerfully, glad for once that his position was incontestable. "They're government-approved, so they are beyond my jurisdiction anyway."

"I don't believe it," my father told him. "God never made horses the size of these. The government *can't* have approved them."

"But they have," said the Inspector. "What's more," he added, with satisfaction, "Angus tells me that knowing the neighborhood so well he has got attested pedigrees for them."

"Any government that could pass creatures like that is corrupt and immoral," my father announced.

"Possibly," admitted the Inspector, "but it's still the government."

My father glared at him. "It's easy to see *why* some people would approve them," he said. "One of those brutes could do the work of two, maybe three, ordinary horses—and for less than double the feed of one. There's a good profit there, a good incentive to get them passed. But that doesn't mean that they're *right*. I say a horse like that is not one of God's creatures—and if it isn't his, then it's an Offense, and should be destroyed as such."

"The official approval states that the breed was produced simply by mating for size, in the normal way. And I'd defy you to find any characteristic that's identifiably wrong with them, anyway," the Inspector told him.

"It does not follow that they are *right*," my father persisted. "A horse that size is *not* right—you know that unofficially as well as I do, and there's no getting away from it. Once we allow things that we know are not right, there's no telling where it will end. A God-fearing community doesn't have to deny its faith just because there's been pressure brought to bear in a government licensing office. There are plenty of us here who know how God intended his creatures to be, even if the government doesn't."

The Inspector smiled. "As with the Dakerses' cat?" he suggested.

My father glared at him. The affair of the Dakerses' cat rankled.

About a year previously it had somehow come to his knowledge that Ben Dakers's wife housed a tailless cat. He investigated, and when he had collected evidence that it had not simply lost its tail in some way, but had never possessed one, he condemned it, and in his capacity as a magistrate ordered the Inspector to make out a warrant for its destruction as an Offense. The Inspector had done so, with reluctance, whereupon Dakers promptly entered an appeal. Such shilly-shallying in an obvious case outraged my father's principles, and he personally attended to the demise of the Dakerses' cat while the matter was still *sub judice*. His position, when a notification subsequently arrived stating that there was a recognized breed of tailless cats with a well-authenticated history, was awkward, and somewhat expensive. It had been with very bad grace that he had chosen to make a public apology rather than resign his magistracy.

"This," he told the Inspector sharply, "is an altogether more important affair."

"Listen," said the Inspector patiently. "The type is approved. This particular pair has confirmatory sanction. If that's not good enough for you, go ahead and shoot them yourself—and see what happens to you."

"It is your moral duty to issue an order against these so-called horses," my father insisted.

The Inspector was suddenly tired of it.

"It's part of my official duty to protect them from harm by fools or bigots," he snapped.

My father did not actually hit the Inspector, but it must have been a near thing. He went on boiling with rage for several days and the next Sunday we were treated to a searing address on the toleration of Mutants which sullied the Purity of our community. He called for a general boycott of the owner of the Offenses, speculated upon immorality in high places, hinted that some there might be expected to have a fellow feeling for

Mutants, and wound up with a peroration in which a certain official was scathed as an unprincipled hireling of unprincipled masters and the local representative of the Forces of Evil.

Though the Inspector had no such convenient pulpit for reply, certain trenchant remarks of his on persecution, contempt of authority, bigotry, religious mania, the law of slander, and the probable effects of direct action in opposition to government sanction achieved a wide circulation.

It was very likely the last point that kept my father from doing more than talk. He had had plenty of trouble over the Dakerses' cat which was of no value at all: but the greathorses were costly creatures; besides, Angus would not be one to waive any possible penalty.

So there was a degree of frustration about that made home a good place to get away from as much as possible.

Now that the countryside had settled down again and was not full of unexpected people, Sophie's parents would let her go out on rambles once more, and I slipped away over there when I could get away unnoticed.

Sophie couldn't go to school, of course. She would have been found out very quickly, even with a false certificate, and her parents though they taught her to read and write did not have any books for her to read, so that it wasn't much good to her. That was why we talked—at least I talked—a lot on our expeditions, trying to tell her what I was learning from my reading books.

The world, I was able to tell her, was generally thought to be a pretty big place, and probably round. The civilized part of it, of which Waknuk was only a small district, was called Labrador. This was thought to be the Old People's name for it, though that was not very certain. Round most of Labrador there was a great deal of water called the sea, which was important on account of fish. Nobody that I knew, except Uncle Axel, had actually seen this sea because it was a long way off, but if you were to go three hundred miles or so east, north, or northwest you would come to it sooner or later. But southwest or south, you wouldn't; you'd get to the Fringes and then the Badlands, which would kill you.

It was said, too, though nobody was sure, that in the time of the Old People Labrador had been a cold land, so cold that no one could live there for long, so they had used it then only for growing trees and for their mysterious mining. But that had been a long, long time ago. A thousand years? Two thousand years? Even more, perhaps? People guessed, but nobody really knew. There was no telling how many generations of people had passed their lives like savages between the coming of Tribulation and the start of recorded history. Only Nicholson's *Repentances* had come out of the wilderness of barbarism, and that only because it had lain for, perhaps, several centuries sealed in a stone coffer before it was discovered. And only the Bible had survived from the time of the Old People themselves.

Except for what these two books told, the past, further back than three recorded centuries, was a long oblivion. Out of that blankness stretched a few strands of legend, badly frayed in their passage through successive minds. It was this long line of tongues that had given us the name Labrador, for it was unmentioned in either the Bible or *Repentances*, and they may have been right about the cold, although there were only two cold months in the year now; Tribulation could account for that, it could account for almost anything.

For a long time it had been disputed whether any parts of the world other than Labrador and the big island of Newf were populated at all. They were thought to be all Badlands which had suffered the full weight of Tribulation, but it had been found that there were some stretches of Fringes country in places. They were grossly deviational and quite godless, of course, and incapable of being civilized at present, but if the Badland borders were withdrawing there as ours were, it might one day be possible to colonize them.

Altogether, not much seemed to be known about the world, but at least it was a more interesting subject than Ethics, which an old man taught to a class of us on Sunday afternoons. Ethics was why you should, and shouldn't do things. Most of the don'ts were the same as my father's, but some of the reasons were different, so it was confusing.

According to Ethics, mankind—that was us, in civilized parts—was in the process of climbing back into grace; we were following a faint and difficult trail which led up to the peaks from which we had fallen. From the true trail branched many false trails that sometimes looked easier and more attractive; all these really led to the edges of precipices, beneath which lay the abyss of eternity. There was only one true trail, and by following it we should, with God's help and in his own good time, regain all that had been lost. But so faint was the trail, so set with traps and deceits, that every step must be taken with caution, and it was too dangerous for a man to rely on his own judgment. Only the authorities, ecclesiastical and lay, were in a position to judge whether the next step was a re-discovery, and so, safe to take; or whether it deviated from the true re-ascent, and so was sinful.

The penance of Tribulation that had been put upon the world must be worked out, the long climb faithfully retraced, and, at last, if the temptations by the way were resisted, there would be the reward of forgiveness—the restoration of the Golden Age. Such penances had been sent before: the expulsion from Eden, the Flood, pestilences, the destruction of the Cities of the Plain, the Captivity. Tribulation had been another such punishment, but the greatest of all. It must, when it struck have been not unlike a combination of all these disasters with something else, too, which caused a desolation far more frightful than flood and fire. Why it had been sent was as yet unrevealed, but, judging by precedent, there had very likely been a phase of irreligious arrogance prevailing at the time.

Most of the numerous precepts, arguments, and examples in Ethics were condensed for us into this: the duty and purpose of man in this world is to fight unceasingly against the evils that Tribulation loosed upon it. Above all, he must see that the human form is kept true to the divine pattern in order that one day it may be permitted to regain the high place in which, as the image of God, it was set.

However, I did not talk much about this part of Ethics to Sophie. Not, I think, because I ever actually classified her in my mind as a Deviation; but it had to be admitted that she did not quite qualify as a true image, so it seemed more tactful to avoid that aspect. And there were plenty of other things to talk about.

CHAPTER FIVE

NOBODY AT WAKNUK seemed to trouble about me if I was out of sight. It was only when I hung about that they thought of jobs that needed doing.

The season was a good one, sunny, yet well watered so that even farmers had little to complain of other than the pressure to catch up with the work that the invasion had interrupted. Except among the sheep the average of Offenses in the spring births had been quite unusually low. The impending crops were so orthodox that the Inspector had posted only a single field, belonging to Angus Morton, for burning. Even among the vegetables there was little deviation; the *solonaceae* as usual provided most of what there was. All in all, the season would likely set up a Purity record, and condemnations were so few that even my father was pleased enough to announce guardedly in one of his addresses that Waknuk appeared to be giving the forces of Evil quite a setback this year.

With everyone so busy I was able to get away early, and during those long summer days Sophie and I roamed more widely than before, though we did our adventuring with caution, and kept it to little-used ways in order to avoid encounters. Sophie's upbringing had given her a timidity toward strangers that was almost an instinct. Almost before one was visible she vanished noiselessly. The only adult she had made friends with was Corky who looked after the steam-engine. Everyone else was dangerous.

We discovered a place up the stream where there were banks of shingle. I liked to take off my shoes, roll up my trousers, and paddle there, examining the pools and crannies. Sophie used to sit on one of the large, flat stones that shelved into the water, and watch me wistfully. Later we went there armed with two small nets that Mrs. Wender had made, and a jar for the catch. I waded about fishing for the little shrimp-like creatures that lived there while Sophie did her best to scoop them up by reaching from the bank. She did not do very well at it. After a time she gave up, and sat watching me enviously. Then, greatly daring, she pulled off a shoe, and looked at her naked foot reflectively. After a minute she pulled off the other. She rolled her cotton trousers above her knees, and stepped into the stream. She stood there for a thoughtful moment, looking down through the water at her feet on the washed pebbles. I called to her:

"Come over this way. There're lots of them here."

She waded toward me, laughing and excited.

When we had enough of it we sat on the flat rock, letting our feet dry in the sun.

"They're not really horrible, are they?" she said, regarding hers judicially.

"They're not horrible at all. They make mine look all knobbly," I told her, honestly. She was pleased about that.

A few days later we went there again. We stood the jar on the flat stone beside our shoes while we fished, and industriously scampered back to it now and then with our catch, oblivious of all else until a voice said:

"Hullo, there. David!"

I looked up, aware of Sophie standing rigid behind me.

The boy who had called stood on the bank, just above the rock where our things lay. I knew him. Alan, the son of John Ervin, the blacksmith, about two years older than I was. I kept my head.

"Oh, hullo Alan," I said, unencouragingly.

I waded to the rock and picked up Sophie's shoes.

"Catch!" I called, as I threw them to her.

One she caught, the other fell in the water, but she retrieved it.

"What are you doing?" Alan asked.

I told him we were catching the shrimp-things. As I said it I stepped casually out of the water onto the rock. I had never cared much for what I knew of Alan at the best of times, and he was by no means welcome now.

"They're no good. Fish are what you want to go after," he said, contemptuously.

He turned his attention to Sophie, who was wading to the bank, shoes in hand, some yards further up.

"Who's *she*?" he inquired.

I delayed answering while I put on my shoes. Sophie had disappeared into the bushes now.

"Who is she?" he repeated. "She's not one of the——" He broke off suddenly. I looked up and saw that he was staring down at something beside me. I turned quickly. On the flat rock was a footprint, still undried. Sophie had rested one foot there as she bent over to tip her catch into the jar. The mark was still damp enough to show the print of all six toes quite clearly. I kicked over the jar. A cascade of water and struggling shrimps poured down the rock, obliterating the footprint, but I knew, with a sickly feeling, that the harm had been done.

"Ho!" said Alan, and there was a gleam in his eye that I did not like. "Who is she?" he demanded again.

"She's a friend of mine," I told him.

"What's her name?"

I did not answer that.

"Huh, I'll soon find out, anyway," he said, with a grin.

"It's no business of yours," I told him.

He took no notice of that; he had turned and was standing looking along the bank toward the point where Sophie had disappeared into the bushes.

I ran up the stone and flung myself on him. He was bigger than I was, but it took him by surprise, and we went down together in a whirl of arms and legs. All I knew of fighting was what I had learned from a few sharp scuffles. I simply hit out, and did my furious best. My intention was to gain a few minutes for Sophie to put her shoes on and hide; if she had a little start, he would never be able to find her, as I knew from experience. Then he recovered from his first surprise and got in a couple of blows on my face which made me forget about Sophie and sent me at it, tooth and nail, on my own account.

We rolled back and forth on a patch of turf. I kept on hitting and struggling furiously, but his weight started to tell. He began to feel more sure of himself, and I more futile. However, I had gained something: I'd stopped him going after Sophie straight away. Gradually he got the upper hand, presently he was sitting astride of me, pummeling me as I squirmed. I kicked out and struggled, but there wasn't much I could do but raise my arms to protect my head. Then, suddenly, there was a yelp of anguish, and the blows ceased. He flopped down on top of me. I heaved him off, and sat up to see Sophie standing there with a large, rough stone in her hand.

"I hit him," she said proudly, and with a touch of wonderment. "Do you think he's dead?"

Alan lay white-faced and still, with the blood trickling down his cheek, but he was breathing all right, so he certainly wasn't dead.

"Oh, dear," said Sophie in sudden reaction, and dropped the stone.

We looked at Alan, and then at one another. Both of us, I think, had the impulse to do something for him, but we were afraid.

"No one must ever know. *No one*," Mrs. Wender had said, so intensely. And now this boy did know. It frightened us.

I got up. I reached for Sophie's hand and pulled her away.

"Come along," I told her urgently.

John Wender listened carefully and patiently while we told him about it.

"You're quite sure he saw? It wasn't simply that he was curious because Sophie was a stranger?" he asked at the end.

"No," I said. "He saw the footmark; that's why he wanted to catch her." He nodded slowly.

"I see," he said, and I was surprised how calmly he said it.

He looked steadily at our faces. Sophie's eyes were big with a mixture of alarm and excitement. Mine must have been pink-rimmed, with dirty smears trailing from them. He turned his head and met his wife's gaze steadily.

"I'm afraid it's come, my dear. That is it," he said.

He got up and went round the table to her. He put his arms round her, bent down and kissed her. Tears stood in her eyes.

"Oh, Johnny, dear. Why are you so sweet to me, when all I've brought you is——?" He stopped that with another kiss.

They looked steadily into each other's eyes for a moment, then, without a word, they both turned to look at Sophie.

Mrs. Wender became her usual self again. She went briskly to a cupboard, took out some food, and put it on the table.

"Wash first, you dirty things," she told us. "Then eat this up. Every bit of it."

While I washed I put the question I had wanted to ask often before.

"Mrs. Wender, if it's just Sophie's toes, couldn't you have cut them off when she was a little baby? I don't expect it would have hurt her much then, and nobody need have known."

"There'd have been marks, David, and when people saw them they'd know why. Now hurry up and eat that supper," she told me, and went busily off into the other room.

"We're going away," Sophie confided to me presently, through a mouthful of pie.

"Going away?" I repeated blankly.

She nodded. "Mummy said we'd have to go if anybody ever found out. We nearly did when you saw them."

"But—you mean, right away? Never come back?" I asked, in dismay.

"Yes, I think so."

I had been hungry, but I suddenly lost my appetite. I sat fiddling with the food on my plate. The sounds of bustling and bumping elsewhere in the house took on an ominous quality. I looked across the table at Sophie. In my throat there was a lump that wouldn't be swallowed.

"Where?" I asked, unhappily.

"I don't know—a long way, though," she told me.

We sat on. Sophie prattled between mouthfuls; I found it hard to swallow because of the lump. Everything was abruptly bleak to the horizon, and beyond. Nothing, I knew, was going to be quite the same ever again. The desolation of the prospect engulfed me. I had to struggle hard to keep back tears.

Mrs. Wender brought in a series of satchels and packs. I watched glumly as she dumped them close to the door, and went away again. Mr. Wender came in from outside and collected some of them. Mrs. Wender reappeared and took Sophie away into the other room. The next time Mr. Wender came for some more of the packs I followed him out.

The two horses, Spot and Sandy, were standing there patiently with some bundles already strapped onto them. I was surprised not to see the cart, and said so.

John Wender shook his head.

"A cart keeps you to the tracks; with packhorses you go where you like," he told me.

I watched him strapping more bundles on while I gathered courage.

"Mr. Wender," I said, "Please can't I come too?"

He stopped what he was doing, and turned to look at me. We faced one another for some moments, then slowly, regretfully, he shook his head. He must have seen that tears were close behind my eyes, for he put his hand on my shoulder, and let it rest there.

"Come along inside, Davie," he said, leading the way back to the house.

Mrs. Wender was back in the living room, standing in the middle of the floor, and looking round as if for things forgotten.

"He wants to come with us, Martie," said Mr. Wender.

She sat down on a stool, and held her arms out to me. I went to her, unable to speak. Looking over my head she said:

"Oh, Johnny. That awful father! I'm afraid for him."

Close to her like that I could catch her thoughts. They came faster, but easier to understand than words. I know how she felt, how she genuinely wished I could go with them, how she leaped on, without examining the reasons, to knowing that I could not and must not go with them. I had the complete answer before John Wender had put the first sentence of his reply into ordinary words.

"I know, Martie. But it's Sophie I'm afraid for—and you. If we were to be caught we'd be charged with kidnaping as well as concealment."

"If they take Sophie nothing could make things worse for me, Johnny."

"But it's not just that, dear. Once they are satisfied that we are out of the district we'll be someone else's responsibility, and they'll not bother much more about us. But if Strorm were to lose his boy there'd be hue and cry for miles around, and I doubt whether we'd have a chance of getting clear. They'd have posses out everywhere looking for us. We can't afford to increase the risk to Sophie, can we?"

Mrs. Wender was silent for some moments. I could feel her fitting the reasons into what she had known already. Presently her arm tightened round me.

"You *do* understand that, don't you, David? Your father would be so angry if you came with us that we'd have much less chance of getting Sophie away safely. I want you to come, but for Sophie's sake we daren't do it. Please be brave about it, David. You're her only friend, and you can help her by being brave. You will, won't you?"

The words were like a clumsy repetition. Her thoughts had been much clearer, and I had already had to accept the inevitable decision. I could not trust myself to speak. I nodded dumbly, and let her hold me to her in a way my own mother never did.

The packing was finished a little before dusk. When everything was ready Mr. Wender took me aside.

"Davie," he said, man to man, "I know how fond you are of Sophie. You've looked after her like a hero, but now there's one more thing you can do to help her. Will you?"

"Yes," I told him. "What is it, Mr. Wender?"

"It's this. When we've gone don't go home at once. Will you stay here till tomorrow morning? That'll give us more time to get her safely away. Will you do that?"

"Yes," I said, reliably.

We shook hands on it. It made me feel stronger and more responsible— rather like I had on that first day when she twisted her ankle.

Sophie held out her hand with something concealed in it as we came back.

"This is for you, David," she said, putting it into my hand.

I looked at it. A curling lock of brown hair tied with a piece of yellow ribbon. I was still staring at it when she flung her arms around my neck and kissed me, with more determination than judgment. Her father picked her up and swung her high on top of the leading horse's load.

Mrs. Wender bent to kiss me, too.

"Good-by, David, dear." She touched my bruised cheek with a gentle forefinger. "We'll never forget," she said, and her eyes were shiny.

They set off. John Wender led the horses, with his gun slung across his back, and his left arm linked in his wife's. At the edge of the woods they paused and turned to wave. I waved back. They went on. The last I saw of them was Sophie's arm waving as the dusk beneath the trees swallowed them up.

The sun was getting high and the men were long ago out in the fields when I reached home. There was no one in the yard, but the Inspector's pony stood at the hitching post near the door, so I guessed my father would be in the house.

I hoped that I had stayed away long enough. It had been a bad night. I started it with a determinedly stout heart, but in spite of my resolutions it weakened somewhat when darkness fell. I had never before spent a night anywhere but in my own room at home. There, everything was familiar, but the Wenders' empty house seemed full of queer sounds. I managed to find some candles and light them, and when I had blown up the fire and put some more wood on, that, too, helped to make the place less lonely—but only a little less. Odd little noises kept occurring inside and outside the house.

The night stretched out before me in a prospect of terrors, yet nothing actually happened. The sounds like creeping footsteps never brought anything into view, the tapping was no prelude to anything at all, nor were the occasional dragging noises. They were beyond explanation, but also, luckily, apparently beyond manifestation, too, and at length, in spite of them all I found my eyes blinking as I swayed on my stool. I summoned up courage and dared to move, very cautiously, across to the bed. I scrambled across it, and very thankfully got my back to a wall again. For a time I lay watching the candles and the uneasy shadows they cast in the corners of the room, and wondering what I should do when they were gone, when, all of a sudden, they *were* gone—and the sun was shining in.

I had found some bread for my breakfast in the Wenders' house, but I was hungry again by the time I reached home. That, however, could wait. My first intention was to get to my room unseen, with the very thin hope that my absence might not have been noticed, so that I would be able to pretend that I had merely overslept, but my luck was not running; Mary caught sight of me through the kitchen window as I was slipping across the yard. She called out:

"You come here at once. Everybody's been looking all over for you. Where've you been?" And then, without waiting for an answer, she added: "Father's on the rampage. Better go to him before he gets worse."

My father and the Inspector were in the seldom used, rather formal room at the front. I seemed to have arrived at a crucial time. The Inspector looked much as usual, but my father was thunderous.

"Come here!" he snapped, as soon as I appeared in the doorway.

I went nearer, reluctantly.

"Where've you been?" he demanded. "You've been out all night. Where?"

I did not answer.

He fired half a dozen questions at me, looking fiercer every second when I did not answer them.

"Come on now. Sullenness isn't going to help you. Who was this child—this Blasphemy—you were with yesterday?" he shouted.

I still did not reply. He glared at me. I had never seen him angrier. I felt sick with fright.

The Inspector intervened then. In a quiet, ordinary voice he said to me:

"You know, David, concealment of a Blasphemy—not reporting a human deviation—is a very, very serious thing. People go to prison for it. It is everybody's duty to report any kind of Offense to me, even if they aren't sure, so that I can decide. It's always important, and very important indeed if it is a Blasphemy. And in this case there doesn't seem to be any doubt about it, unless young Ervin was mistaken. Now he says this child you were with has six toes. Is that true?"

"No," I told him.

"He's lying," said my father.

"I see," said the Inspector calmly. "Well, then if it isn't true, it can't matter if we know who she is, can it?" he went on in a reasonable tone.

I made no reply to that. It seemed the safest way. We looked at one another.

"Surely, you see that's so? If it is *not* true——" he was going on persuasively, but my father cut him short.

"I'll deal with this. The boy's lying." To me he added: "Go to your room."

I hesitated. I knew well enough what that meant, but I knew, too, that with my father in his present mood it would happen whether I told or not. I set my jaw, and turned to go. My father followed, picking up a whip from the table as he came.

"That," said the Inspector curtly, "is my whip."

My father seemed not to hear him. The Inspector stood up.

"I said, that is *my* whip," he repeated, with a hard, ominous note in his voice.

My father checked his step. With an ill-tempered gesture he threw the whip back on the table. He glared at the Inspector, and then turned to follow me.

I don't know where my mother was, perhaps she was afraid of my father. It was Mary who came, and made little comforting noises as she dressed my back. She wept a little as she helped me into bed, and then fed me some broth with a spoon. I did my best to put up a brave show in front of her, but when she had gone my tears soaked into my pillow. By now it was not so much the bodily hurts that brought them—it was bitterness, self-contempt, and abasement. In wretchedness and misery I clutched the yellow ribbon and the brown curl tight in my hand.

"I couldn't help it, Sophie," I sobbed. "I couldn't help it."

CHAPTER SIX

In the evening, when I grew calmer, I found that Rosalind was trying to talk to me. Some of the others were anxiously asking what was the matter, too. I told them about Sophie. It wasn't a secret any more now. I could feel that they were shocked. I tried to explain that a person with a deviation—a small deviation, at any rate—wasn't the monstrosity we had been told. It did not really make any difference—not to Sophie, at any rate.

They received that very doubtfully indeed. The things we had all been taught were against their acceptance, though they knew well enough that what I was telling them must be true to me. You can't lie when you talk with your thoughts. They wrestled with the novel idea that a Deviation might not be disgusting and evil—not very successfully. In the circumstances they could not give me much consolation, and I was not sorry when one by one they dropped out and I knew that they had fallen asleep.

I was tired out myself, but sleep was a long time coming. I lay there, picturing Sophie and her parents plodding their way southward toward the dubious safety of the Fringes, and hoping desperately that they would be far enough off now for my betrayal not to hurt them.

And then when sleep did come it was full of dreams. Faces and people moved restlessly through it; scenes, too. Once more there was the one where we all stood round in the yard while my father disposed of an Offense which was Sophie, and I woke up hearing my own voice shouting to him to stop. I was afraid to go to sleep again, but I did, and that time it was quite different. I dreamt again of the great city by the sea, with its houses and streets, and the things that flew in the sky. It was years since I had dreamt that one, but it still looked just the same, and in some quite obscure way it soothed me.

My mother looked in in the morning, but she was detached and disapproving. Mary was the one who took charge, and she decreed that there was to be no getting up that day. I was to lie on my front, and not wriggle about, so that my back would heal more quickly. I took the instruction meekly for it was certainly more comfortable to do as she said. So I lay there and considered what preparation I should have to make for running away, once I was about again and the stiffness had worn off. It would, I decided, be much better to have a horse, and I spent most of the morning concocting a plan for stealing one and riding away to the Fringes.

The Inspector looked in in the afternoon, bringing with him a bag of buttery sweets. For a moment I thought of trying to get something out of him—casually, of course—about the real nature of the Fringes. After all, as an expert on Deviation he might be expected to know more about them than anyone else. On second thought, however, I decided it might be impolitic.

He was sympathetic and kindly enough, but he was on a mission. He put his questions in a friendly way. Munching one of the sweets himself, he asked me:

"How long have you known that the Wender child—what is her name, by the way?"

I told him, there was no harm in that now.

"How long have you known that Sophie deviates?"

I didn't see that telling the truth could make things much worse.

"Quite a long time," I admitted.

"And how long would that be?"

"About six months, I think," I admitted.

He raised his eyebrows, and then looked serious.

"That's bad, you know," he said. "It's what we call abetting a concealment. You must have known that was wrong, didn't you?"

I dropped my gaze. I wriggled uncomfortably under his straight look, and then stopped because it made my back twinge.

"It sort of didn't seem like the things they say in church," I tried to explain. "Besides, they were awfully little toes."

The Inspector took another sweet and pushed the bag back to me.

" '——And each foot shall have five toes,' " he quoted. "You remember that?"

"Yes," I admitted, unhappily.

"Well, every part of the definition is as important as any other; and if a child doesn't come within it, then it isn't human, and that means it doesn't have a soul. It is not in the image of God, it is an imitation, and in the imitations there is always some mistake. Only God produces perfection. Although Deviations may look like us in many ways, they cannot be really human. They are something quite different."

I thought that over.

"But Sophie *isn't* really different—not in any other way," I told him.

"You'll find it easier to understand when you are older, but you do know the definition, and you must have realized Sophie deviated. Why didn't you tell your father or me about her?"

I explained about my dream of my father treating Sophie as he did one of the farm Offenses. The Inspector looked at me thoughtfully for some seconds, then he nodded:

. "I see," he said. "But Blasphemies are not treated the same way as Offenses."

"What happens to them?" I asked.

But he evaded that. He went on:

"You know, it's really my duty to include your name in my report. However, as your father has already taken action, I may be able to leave it out. All the same, it is a very serious matter. The Devil sends Deviations among us to weaken us and tempt us away from Purity. Sometimes he is clever enough to make a nearly perfect imitation, so we have always to be on the lookout for the mistake he has made, however small, and when we see one it must be reported at once. You'll remember that in future, won't you?"

I avoided his eye. The Inspector was the Inspector, and an important person; all the same I could not believe that the Devil had sent Sophie. I found it hard to see how the very small toe on each foot could make that much difference.

"Sophie's my friend," I said. "My best friend."

The Inspector kept on looking at me, then he shook his head, and sighed.

"Loyalty is a great virtue, but there is such a thing as misplaced loyalty. One day you will understand the importance of a greater loyalty. The Purity of the Race——" He broke off as the door opened. My father came in.

"They got them, all three of them," he said to the Inspector, and gave a look of disgust at me.

The Inspector got up promptly, and they went out together. I stared at the closed door. The misery of self-reproach struck me so that I shook all over. I could hear myself whimpering as the tears rolled down my cheeks. I tried to stop it, but I couldn't. My hurt back was forgotten. The anguish my father's news had caused me was far more painful than that. My chest was so tight with it that it was choking me.

Presently the door opened again. I kept my face to the wall. Steps crossed the room. A hand rested on my shoulder. The Inspector's voice said:

"It wasn't that, old man. You had nothing to do with it. A patrol picked them up, quite by chance, twenty miles away."

A couple of days later I said to Uncle Axel, "I'm going to run away."

He paused in his work, and gazed thoughtfully at his saw.

"I'd not do that," he advised. "It doesn't usually work very well. Besides," he added after a pause, "where would you run to?"

"That's what I wanted to ask you," I explained.

He shook his head. "Whatever district you're in they want to see your normalcy certificate," he told me. "Then they know who you are and where you're from."

"Not in the Fringes," I suggested.

He stared at me. "Man alive, you'd not want to go to the Fringes. Why they've got nothing there, not even enough food. Most of them are half-starving, that's why they make the raids. No, you'd spend all the time there just trying to keep alive, and lucky if you did."

"But there must be some other places," I said.

"Only if you can find a ship that'll take you, and even then . . ." He shook his head again. "In my experience," he told me, "if you run away from a thing just because you don't like it, you don't like what you find either. Now, running to a thing, that's a different matter, but what would you want to run to? Take it from me, it's a lot better here than it is most places. No, I'm against it, Davie. In a few years' time when you're a man and can look after yourself it may be different. I reckon it'd be better to stick it out till then, anyway; much better than have them just catch you and bring you back."

There was something in that. I was beginning to learn the meaning of the word "humiliation," and did not want any more of it at present. But from what he said the question of where to go would not be easily solved even then. It looked as if it would be advisable to learn what one could of the world outside Labrador, in preparation. I asked him what it was like.

"Godless," he told me. "Very godless indeed."

It was the sort of uninformative answer my father would have given. I was disappointed to have it from Uncle Axel, and told him so. He grinned.

"All right, Davie, boy, that's fair enough. So long as you'll not chatter, I'll tell you something about it."

"You mean it's secret?" I asked, puzzled.

"Not quite that," he said. "But when people are used to believing a thing is such-and-such a way, *and* the preachers want them to believe that that's the way it is, you get no thanks for upsetting their ideas. Sailors soon found that out in Rigo, so mostly they only talk about it now to other sailors. If the rest of the people want to think it's nearly all Badlands outside, they let them; it doesn't alter the way it really is, but it does make for peace and quiet."

"My book says it's all Badlands, or bad Fringes country," I told him.

"There are other books that don't but you'll not see them about much, not even in Rigo, let alone in the backwoods here," he said. "And, mind you it doesn't do to believe everything every sailor says, either. Often you're not sure whether any couple of them are talking about the same place or not, even when they think they are. But when you've seen some of it, you begin to understand that the world's a much queerer place than it looks from Waknuk. So you'll keep it to yourself?"

I assured him I would.

"All right. Well, it's this way . . ." he began.

To reach the rest of the world (my Uncle Axel explained) you start by sailing downriver from Rigo until you get to the sea. They say that it's no good sailing on straight ahead, to the east, that is, because either the sea goes on for ever, or else it comes to an end suddenly, and you sail over the edge. Nobody knows for sure.

If you make to the northeast they say there is a great land where the plants aren't very deviational, and animals and people don't *look* deviational, but the women are very tall and strong. They rule the country entirely, and do all the work. They keep their men in cages until they are about twenty-four years old, and then eat them. They also eat shipwrecked sailors. But as no one ever seems to have met anyone who has actually been there and escaped, it's difficult to see how all that can be known. Still there it is—no one has ever come back denying it, either.

The only way I know is south—I've been south three times. To get there you keep the coast to starboard as you leave the river. After a couple of hundred miles or so you come to the Straits of Newf. As the Straits widen out you keep the coast of Newf to port and call in at Lark for fresh water—and provisions, too, if the Newf people will let you have any. After that you bear southeast a while and then south, and pick up the mainland coast again to starboard. When you reach it you find it is Badlands—or at least very bad Fringes. There's plenty growing there, but sailing close inshore you can see that nearly all of it is deviational. There are animals, too, and most of them look as if it'd be difficult to classify them as Offenses against any known kinds.

A day or two's sail further on there's plenty of Badlands coastline, with no doubt about it. Soon you're following round a big bay, and you get to where there are no gaps, it's all Badlands.

When sailors first saw those parts they were pretty scared. They felt they were leaving all Purity behind, and sailing further and further away from God, where he'd not be able to help them. Everybody knows that if you walk on Badlands you die, and they'd none of them expected ever to see them so closely with their own eyes.

And a shocking sight it must have been at first, to see how the things which are against God's laws of nature flourish there just as if they had a right to. You can see giant, distorted heads of corn growing higher than small trees; big saprophytes growing on rocks, with their roots trailing out on the wind like bunches of hair, fathoms long; in some places there are fungus colonies that you'd take at first sight for big white boulders; you can see succulents like barrels, but as big as small houses, and with spines ten feet long. There are plants which grow on the cliff tops and send thick, green cables down a hundred feet and more into the sea; and you wonder whether it's a land plant that's got to the salt water, or a sea plant that's somehow climbed ashore. There are hundreds of kinds of queer things, and scarcely a normal one among them—it's a kind of jungle of Deviations, going on for miles and miles. There don't seem to be many animals, but occasionally you catch sight of one, though you'd never be able to name it. There are a fair number of birds, though, seabirds mostly; and once or twice people have seen big things flying in the distance, too far away to make out anything except that the motion didn't look right for birds. It's a weird, evil land, and many a man who sees it suddenly understands what might happen here if it weren't for the Purity Laws and the Inspectors.

It's bad, but it isn't the worst.

Further south still you begin to find patches where only coarse plants grow, and poorly at that, and soon you begin to come to stretches of coast, and land behind it, twenty, thirty, forty miles long, maybe, where nothing grows, nothing at all.

The whole seaboard is empty—black and harsh and empty. The land behind looks like a huge desert of charcoal. Where there are cliffs they are sharp-edged, with nothing to soften them. There are no fish in the sea there, no weed either, not even slime, and when a ship has sailed there the barnacles and the fouling on her bottom drop off and leave her hull clean. You don't see any birds. Nothing moves at all, except the waves breaking on the black beaches.

It is a frightful place. Masters order their ships well out for fear of it, and very relieved the sailors are to keep clear of it.

And yet it can't always have been like that because there was one ship whose captain was foolhardy enough to sail close inshore. Her crew were able to make out great stone ruins. They all agreed that they were far too regular to be natural, and they thought they might be the remains of one of the Old People's cities. But nobody knows any more about them. Most of the men in that ship wasted away and died, and the rest were never the same afterward. No other ship has risked going close in.

For hundreds of miles the coast goes on being Badlands with stretches of the dead, black land, so far, in fact, that the first navigators gave up and turned back saying that they thought it must go on like that to the ends of the earth.

The preachers and the church people were pleased to hear it, for it was very much what they had been teaching, and for a time it made people lose interest in exploring.

But later on curiosity revived, and better-found ships sailed south again. A ship called the *Venture*, which had long been given up for lost, came sailing home to Rigo. She was battered and under-manned, her canvas was patched, her mizzen jury-rigged, and her condition foul, but she triumphantly claimed the honor of being the first to reach the lands beyond the Black Coasts. She brought back a number of objects including gold and silver and copper ornaments, and a cargo of spices to prove it. Strict churchgoers refused to touch the spices for fear they might be tainted, but other people preferred to believe that they were the kinds of spices referred to in the Bible. Whatever they were, they are profitable enough now for ships to sail south in search of them.

The lands down there aren't civilized. Mostly they don't have any sense of sin there so they don't stop Deviations; and where they do have a sense of sin, they've got it mixed up. A lot of them aren't ashamed of Mutants; it doesn't seem to worry them when children turn out wrong, provided they're right enough to live and to learn to look after themselves.

You'll find islands where the people are all thickset, and others where they're thin; there are even said to be some islands where both the men and women would be passed as true images if it weren't that some strange deviation has turned them all completely black—though even that's easier to believe than the one about a race of Deviations that has dwindled to two feet high, grown fur and a tail, and taken to living in trees.

All the same, it's queerer there than you'd ever credit. Pretty nearly anything seems possible once you've seen it.

That seems blasphemous at first, but after a bit you start asking yourself, well, what real evidence have *we* got about the true image? You find that the Bible doesn't say anything to contradict the Old People being like us, but, on the other hand it doesn't give any definition of Man, either. No, the definition comes from Nicholson's *Repentances* and he admits that he was writing some generations after Tribulation came. You find yourself wondering whether he *knew* he was in the true image, or whether he only thought he was. . . .

Uncle Axel had a lot more to say about southern parts than I can remember, and it was all very interesting in its way, but it didn't tell me what I wanted to know. At last I asked him point-blank.

"Uncle Axel, are there any cities there?"

"Cities?" he repeated. "Well, here and there you'll find a town, of a kind. As big as Kentak, maybe, but built differently."

"No," I told him. "I mean big places." I described the city in my dream, but without telling him it was a dream.

He looked at me oddly. "No, I never heard of any place like that," he told me.

"Further on, perhaps. Further than you went?" I suggested.

He shook his head. "You can't go further on. The sea gets full of weed. Masses of weed with stems like cables. A ship can't make her way through it, and it's trouble enough to get clear of it once you get in it at all."

"Oh," I said. "You're quite sure there's no city?"

"Sure," he said. "We'd have heard of it by this time if there was."

I was disappointed. It sounded as if running away to the South, even if I could find a ship to take me, would be little better than running away to the Fringes. For a time I had hoped, but now I had to go back to the idea that the city I dreamt of must be one of the Old People's cities after all.

Uncle Axel went on talking about the doubts of the true image that his voyages had given him. He labored it rather a lot, and after a while he broke off to ask me directly:

"You understand, don't you, Davie, why I've been telling you all this?"

I was not sure that I did. Moreover, I was reluctant to admit the flaw in the tidy, familiar orthodoxy I had been taught. I recalled a phrase which I had heard a number of times.

"You lost your faith?" I inquired.

Uncle Axel snorted, and pulled a face.

"Preacher-words!" he said, and thought for a moment. "I'm telling you," he went on, "that a lot of people saying that a thing is so doesn't *prove* it is so. I'm telling you that nobody, *nobody* really *knows* what is the true image. They all *think* they know—just as we think we know, but, for all we can prove, the Old People themselves may not have been the true image." He turned, and looked long and steadily at me again.

"So," he said, "how am I, and how is anyone to be sure that this 'difference' that you and Rosalind have does not make you something nearer to the true image than other people are? Perhaps the Old People were the image; very well then, one of the things they say about them is that they could talk to one another over long distances. Now *we* can't do that, but you and Rosalind can. Just think that over, Davie. You two *may* be nearer to the image than we are."

I hesitated for perhaps a minute, and then took a decision.

"It isn't just Rosalind and me, Uncle Axel," I told him. "There are others, too."

He was startled. He stared at me.

"Others?" he repeated. "Who are they? How many?"

I shook my head.

"I don't know who they are—not names, I mean. Names don't have any thinking-shapes, so we've never bothered. You just know who's thinking, like you know who's talking. I only found out who Rosalind was by accident."

He went on looking at me seriously, uneasily.

"How many of you?" he repeated.

"Eight," I told him. "There were nine, but one of them stopped about a month ago. That's what I wanted to ask you, Uncle Axel, do you think somebody found out? He just stopped suddenly. We've been wondering if anybody knows. . . . You see, if they found out about him . . ." I let him draw the inference himself.

Presently he shook his head.

"I don't think so. We should be pretty sure to have heard of it. It looks to me more as if it'd be an accident of some kind, being quite sudden like that. You'd like me to try to find out?"

"Yes, please. It's made some of us afraid."

I told him what I could, which was very little. It was a relief to know that he would try to find out what had happened. Now that a month had gone by without a similar thing happening to any of the rest of us we were less anxious than we had been, but still far from easy.

Before we parted he returned to his earlier advice to remember that no one could be certain of the true image.

Later, I understood why he gave it. I realized, too, that he did not greatly care what was the true image. Whether he was wise or not in trying to forestall both the alarm and the sense of inferiority that he saw lying in wait for us when we should become better aware of ourselves and our difference, I cannot say. At any rate, I decided, for the moment, not to run away from home. The practical difficulties were clearly greater than they had seemed.

CHAPTER SEVEN

THE ARRIVAL OF MY SISTER, Petra, came as a genuine surprise to me, and a conventional surprise to everyone else.

There had been a slight, not quite attributable, sense of expectation about the house for the previous week or two, but it remained unmentioned and unacknowledged. For me, the feeling that I was being kept unaware of something afoot was unresolved until there came a night when a baby howled. It was penetrating, unmistakable, and certainly within the house, where there had been no baby the day before. But in the morning nobody referred to the sound in the night. No one, indeed, would dream of mentioning the matter openly until the Inspector should have called to issue his certificate that it was a human baby in the true image. Should it unhappily turn out to violate the image and thus be ineligible for a certificate, no mention would ever be made of it, and the whole regrettable incident would be deemed not to have occurred.

As soon as it was light my father sent a stablehand off on a horse to summon the Inspector, and, pending his arrival, the whole household tried to dissemble its anxiety by pretending we were just starting another ordinary day.

The pretense grew thinner as time went on, for the stablehand, instead of bringing back the Inspector forthwith, as was to be expected when a man of my father's position and influence was concerned, returned with a polite message that the Inspector would certainly do his best to find time to pay a call in the course of the day.

It is very unwise for even a righteous man to quarrel with his local Inspector and call him names in public. The Inspector has too many ways of hitting back.

My father became very angry, the more so since the conventions did not allow him to admit what he was angry about. Furthermore, he was well aware that the Inspector intended him to be angry. He spent the morning hanging around the house and yard, exploding with bad temper now and then over trivial matters, so that everyone crept about on tiptoe and worked very hard indeed, in order not to attract his attention.

My sister Mary disappeared now and then toward my mother's room, and for the rest of the time tried to hide her anxiety by loudly bossing the household girls. I felt compelled to hang about in order not to miss the announcement when it should come. My father kept on prowling.

The suspense was aggravated by everyone's knowledge that on the last two similar occasions there had been no certificate forthcoming. My father must have been well aware—and no doubt the Inspector was aware of it, too—that there was plenty of silent speculation whether my father would, as the law allowed, send my mother away if this occasion should turn out to be similarly unfortunate. Meanwhile, since it would have been both impolitic and undignified to go running after the Inspector, there was nothing to be done but bear the suspense as best we could.

It was not until mid-afternoon that the Inspector ambled up on his pony. My father pulled himself together, and went out to receive him. The effort to be even formally polite nearly strangled him. Even then, the Inspector was not brisk. He dismounted in a leisurely fashion, and strolled into the house, chatting about the weather. Father, red in the face, handed him over to Mary who took him along to Mother's room. Then followed the worst wait of all.

Mary said afterward that he hemmed and hawed for an unconscionable time while he examined the baby in minutest detail. At last, however, he emerged, with an expressionless face. In the little-used sitting-room he sat down at the table and fussed for a while about getting a good point on his quill. Finally he took a form from his pouch, and in a slow, deliberate hand wrote that he officially found the child to be a true female human being, free from any detectable form of deviation. He regarded that thoughtfully for some moments, as though not perfectly satisfied. He let his hand hesitate before he actually dated and signed it, then he sanded it carefully, and handed it to my enraged father, still with a faint air of uncertainty. He had, of course, no real doubt in his mind, or he would have called for another opinion; my father was perfectly well aware of that, too.

And so Petra's existence could at last be admitted. I was formally told that I had a new sister, and presently I was taken to see her where she lay in a crib beside my mother's bed.

She looked so pink and wrinkled to me that I did not see how the Inspector could have been quite sure about her. However, there was nothing obviously wrong with her, so she had got her certificate. Nobody could blame the Inspector for that; she did appear to be as normal as a new-born baby ever looks.

While we were taking turns to look at her somebody started to ring the stable-bell in the customary way. Everyone on the farm stopped work, and very soon we were all assembled in the kitchen for prayers of thanksgiving.

Two, or it may have been three, days after Petra was born I happened upon a piece of my family's history that I would have preferred not to know.

I was sitting quietly in the room next to my parents' bedroom where my mother still lay in bed. It was a matter of chance, and strategy, too. It was the latest place that I had found to stay hidden awhile after the midday meal until the coast was clear and I could slip away without being given an afternoon job. Normally it was very convenient, though just at present its use required caution because the wattle wall between the rooms was cracked and I had to move very cautiously on tiptoe lest my mother should hear me.

On that particular day I was just thinking that I had allowed nearly enough time for people to be busy again when a two-wheeled trap drove up. As it passed the window I had a glimpse of my Aunt Harriet holding the reins.

I had only seen her eight or nine times, for she lived fifteen miles away in the Kentak direction, but what I knew of her I liked. She was some three years younger than my mother. Superficially they were not dissimilar, and yet in Aunt Harriet each feature had been a little softened, so that the effect of them all together was different. I used to feel when I looked at her that I was seeing my mother as she might have been—as, I thought, I would have liked her to be. She was easier to talk to, too; she did not have that somewhat damping manner of listening only to correct.

I edged over carefully on stockinged feet to the window, watched her tether the horse, pick a white bundle out of the trap, and carry it into the house. She cannot have met anyone, for a few seconds later her steps passed the door, and the latch of the next room clicked.

"Why Harriet!" my mother's voice exclaimed in surprise, and not altogether in approval. "So soon! You don't mean to say you've brought a tiny baby all that way!"

"I know," said Aunt Harriet's voice, accepting the reproof in my mother's tone, "—but I had to, Emily, I had to. I heard your baby had come early, so I—— Oh, there she is! Oh, she's lovely, Emily. She's a lovely baby." There was a pause. Presently she added, "Mine's lovely, too, isn't she? Isn't she a lovely darling?"

There was a certain amount of mutual congratulation which did not interest me a lot. I didn't suppose the babies looked much different from other babies, really. My mother said:

"I *am* glad, my dear. Henry must be delighted."

"Of course he is," said Aunt Harriet, but there was something wrong about the way she said it. Even I knew that. She hurried on: "She was born a week ago. I didn't know what to do. Then when I heard your baby had come early and was a girl, too, it was like God answering a prayer." She paused, and then added with a casualness which somehow failed to be casual, "You've got the certificate for her?"

"Of course." My mother's tone was sharp, ready for offense. I knew the expression which went with the tone. When she spoke again there was a disturbing quality in her voice.

"Harriet!" she demanded sharply. "Are you going to tell me that you have *not* got a certificate?"

My aunt made no reply, but I thought I caught the sound of a suppressed sob. My mother said coldly, forcibly:

"Harriet, let me see that child—properly."

For some seconds I could hear nothing but another sob or two from my aunt. Then she said, unsteadily:

"It's such a little thing, you see. It's nothing much."

"*Nothing much!*" snapped my mother. "You have the effrontery to bring your monster into my house, and tell me it's *nothing much!*"

"*Monster!*" Aunt Harriet's voice sounded as though she had been slapped. "Oh!—Oh!—Oh!——" She broke into little moanings.

After a time my mother said:

"No wonder you didn't dare to call the Inspector."

Aunt Harriet went on crying. My mother let the sobs almost die away before she said:

"I'd like to know why you have come here, Harriet? Why did you bring it here?"

Aunt Harriet blew her nose. When she spoke it was in a dull, flat voice:

"When she came—when I saw her—I wanted to kill myself. I knew they would never approve her, although it's such a little thing. But I didn't, because I thought perhaps I could save her somehow. I love her. She's a lovely baby, except for that. She is, isn't she?"

My mother said nothing. Aunt Harriet went on:

"I didn't know how, but I hoped. I knew I could keep her for a little while before they'd take her away—just the month they give you before you *have* to notify. I decided I must have her for that long at least."

"And Henry? What does he say?"

"He—he said we ought to notify at once. But I wouldn't let him—I couldn't, Emily, I *couldn't*. Dear God, not a third time! I kept her, and prayed, and prayed, and hoped. And then when I heard your baby had come early I thought perhaps God had answered my prayers."

"Indeed, Harriet," said my mother coldly, "I doubt whether that had anything to do with it. Nor," she added pointedly, "do I see what you mean."

"I thought," Aunt Harriet went on, spiritlessly now, but forcing herself to the words, "I thought that if I could leave my baby with you, and borrow yours——"

My mother gave an incredulous gasp. Apparently words eluded her.

"It would only be for a day or two; just while I could get the certificate," Aunt Harriet went doggedly on. "You are my sister, Emily, my sister, and the only person in the world who can help me to keep my baby."

She began to cry again. There was another longish pause, then my mother's voice:

"In all my life I have never heard anything so outrageous. To come here suggesting that I should enter into an immoral, a criminal conspiracy to . . . I think you must be mad, Harriet. To think that I should lend——" She broke off at the sound of my father's heavy step in the passage.

"Joseph," she told him as he entered. "Send her away. Tell her to leave the house—and take *that* with her."

"But," said my father, in a bewildered tone, "but it's Harriet, my dear."

My mother explained the situation, fully. There wasn't a sound from Aunt Harriet. At the end he demanded incredulously:

"Is this true? Is this why you've come here?"

Slowly, wearily Aunt Harriet said, "This is the third time. They'll take my baby away again like they took the others. I can't stand that—not again. Henry will turn me out, I think. He'll find another wife, who can give him proper children. There'll be nothing—nothing in the world for me—nothing. I came here hoping for sympathy and help. Emily is the only person who can help me. I—I can see now how foolish I was to hope at all. . . ."

Nobody said anything to that.

"Very well. I understand. I'll go now," she told them, in a dead voice.

My father was not a man to leave his attitude in doubt.

"I do not understand how you dared to come here, to a Godfearing house, with such a suggestion," he said. "Worse still, you don't show an ounce of shame or remorse."

Aunt Harriet's voice was steadier as she answered:

"Why should I? I've done nothing to be ashamed of. I am *not* ashamed. I am only beaten."

"Not ashamed!" repeated my father. "Not ashamed of producing a mockery of your Maker, not ashamed of trying to tempt your own sister into criminal conspiracy!" He drew a breath and launched off in pulpit style. "The enemies of God besiege us. They seek to strike at him through us. Unendingly they work to distort the true image; through our weaker vessels they attempt to defile the race. You have sinned, woman, search your heart, and you will know that you have sinned. You wear the cross on your dress to protect you, but you have not worn it always in your heart. You have not kept constant vigilance for impurity. So there has been a Deviation, and deviation, *any* deviation from the true image is blasphemy—no less. You have produced a defilement."

"One poor little baby!"

"A baby which, if you were to have your way, would grow up to breed, and, breeding, spread pollution until all around us there would be Mutants and

Abominations. Shame on you, woman. Now go! Go home in humility, not defiance. Notify your child, according to law. Then do your penance that you may be cleansed. And pray. You have much to pray for. Not only have you blasphemed by producing a false image, but in your arrogance you have set yourself against the law, and sinned in intent. I am a merciful man; I shall make no charge of that. It will be for you to clean it from your conscience, to go down on your knees and pray—pray that your sin of intention, as well as your other sins, may be forgiven you."

There were two light footsteps. The baby gave a little whimper as Aunt Harriet picked it up. She came toward the door and lifted the latch, then she paused.

"I shall pray," she said. "Yes, I shall pray." She paused, then she went on, her voice steady and harder, "I shall pray God to send charity into this hideous world, and sympathy for the weak, and love for the unhappy and unfortunate. I shall ask him if it is indeed his will that a child should suffer and its soul be damned for a little blemish of the body. And I shall pray him, too, that the hearts of the self-righteous may be broken. . . ."

Then the door closed and I heard her pass slowly along the passage.

I moved cautiously back to the window, and watched her come out and lay the white bundle gently in the trap. She stood looking down on it for a few seconds, then she unhitched the horse, climbed up onto the seat, and took the bundle onto her lap, with one arm guarding it in her cloak.

She turned, and left a picture that is fixed in my mind. The baby cradled in her arm, her cloak half-open showing the upper part of the brown, braid-edged cross on her fawn dress; eyes that seemed to see nothing as they looked toward the house from a face set hard as granite.

Then she shook the reins, and drove off.

I could not help feeling a great curiosity to know what was the "little thing" that had been wrong with the baby—wondering if, perhaps, it was just an extra toe, like Sophie's. But I never found out what it was.

When they broke the news to me next day that my Aunt Harriet's body had been found in the river, no one mentioned a baby.

CHAPTER EIGHT

My FATHER included Aunt Harriet's name in our prayers on the evening of the day the news came, but after that she was never referred to again. It was as though she had been wiped out of every memory but mine. There, however, she remained very clearly, given form at a time when I had only heard her, as an upright figure with a face drained of hope, and a voice saying clearly: "I am *not* ashamed; I am only beaten." And, too, as I had last seen her, looking up at the house.

Nobody told me how she came to die, but somehow I knew that it had not been by accident. There was a great deal that I did not understand in what I had overheard, and yet, in spite of that, it was quite the most disturbing occurrence I had known yet. It alarmed me with a sense of insecurity far greater than I had suffered over Sophie. For several nights I dreamt of Aunt Harriet lying in the river, still clasping the white bundle to her while the water swirled her hair round her pale face, and her wide-open eyes saw nothing. And I was frightened.

This had happened simply because the baby was just a bit different in some way from other babies. It had something or lacked something so that it did not exactly accord with the Definition. There was the "little thing" that made it not quite right, not quite like other people.

A Mutant, my father had called it. A Mutant! I thought of some of the poker-work texts. I recalled the address of a visiting preacher, the detestation there had been in his voice when he thundered from the pulpit: "*Accursed is the Mutant!*"

Accursed is the Mutant. The Mutant, the enemy, not only of the human race, but of all the species God had decreed; the seed of the Devil within, trying unflaggingly, eternally to come to fruition in order that it might destroy the divine order and turn our land, the stronghold of God's will upon Earth, into a lewd chaos like the Fringes; trying to make it a place without the law, like the lands in the South that Uncle Axel had spoken of, where the plants and the animals and the almost-human beings, too, brought forth travesties; where true stock had given place to unnamable creatures, abominable growths flourished, and the spirits of evil mocked the Lord with obscene fantasies.

Just a small difference, the "little thing" was the first step.

I prayed very earnestly those nights.

"Oh, God," I said, "please, please God, let me be like other people. I don't want to be different. Won't you make it so that when I wake up in the morning I'll be just like everyone else, please, God, please!"

But in the morning, when I tested myself I'd soon pick up Rosalind or one of the others, and know that the prayer hadn't altered anything. I had to get up still just the same person who had gone to bed the night before, and I had to go into the big kitchen and eat my breakfast facing the panel which had somehow stopped being just part of the furniture and seemed to stare back at me with the words: ACCURSED IS THE MUTANT IN THE SIGHT OF GOD AND MAN!

And I went on being very frightened.

After about the fifth night that praying hadn't done any good, Uncle Axel caught me leaving the breakfast table and said I'd better come along and help him mend a plow. After we'd worked on that for a couple of hours he declared a rest, so we went out of the forge to sit in the sun, with our backs against a wall. He gave me a chunk of oatcake, and we munched for a minute or two. Then he said:

"Well now, Davie, let's have it."

"Have what?" I said, stupidly.

"Whatever it is that's been making you look as if you were sickening for something the last day or two," he told me. "What's your trouble? Has somebody found out?"

"No," I said. He looked greatly relieved.

"Well, what *is* it, then?"

So I told him about Aunt Harriet and the baby. Before I had finished I was talking through tears, it was such a relief to be able to share it with someone.

"It was her face as she drove away," I explained. "I've never seen anyone look like that before. I keep on seeing it, in the water."

I looked up at him as I finished. His face was as grim as I'd ever seen it, with the corners of his mouth pulled down.

"So that was it," he said, nodding once or twice.

"It was all because the baby was different," I repeated. "And there was Sophie, too. . . . I didn't understand properly before. I—I'm frightened, Uncle Axel. What'll they do when they find out I'm different?"

He put his hand on my shoulder.

"No one else is ever going to know about it," he told me again. "No one but me—and I'm safe."

It did not seem as reassuring now as it had been when he said it before.

"There was that one who stopped," I reminded him, "perhaps they found out about him . . . ?"

He shook his head. "I reckon you can rest easy on that, Davie. I found out there was a boy killed just about the time you said. Walter Brent his name was, about nine years old, he was fooling around when they were felling timber, and a tree got him, poor lad."

"Where?" I asked.

"About nine or ten miles away, on a farm over by Chipping," he said.

I thought back. The Chipping direction certainly fitted, and it was just the kind of accident that would account for a sudden unexplained stop. Without any illwill to the unknown Walter I hoped and thought that was the explanation.

Uncle Axel backtracked a bit.

"There's no reason at all why anyone should find out. There's nothing to show—they can only know if you let them. Learn to watch yourself, Davie, and they'll never find out."

"What *did* they do to Sophie?" I asked once more. But again he refused to be drawn on that. He went on:

"Remember what I told you. They *think* they are the true image, but they can't know for sure. And even if the Old People were the same kind as I am and they are, what of it? Where are they and their wonderful world now?"

" 'God sent Tribulation upon them,' " I quoted.

"Sure, sure. It's easy enough to say, but not so easy to understand, especially when you've seen a bit of the world, and what it has meant. Tribulation wasn't just tempests, hurricanes, floods, and fires like the things they had in the Bible. It was like all of them together, and something a lot worse, too. It made the Black Coasts, and the ruins that glow there at night, and the

56

Badlands. Maybe there's a precedent for that in Sodom and Gomorrah, but what I don't understand is the queer things it did to what was left."

"Except in Labrador," I suggested.

"*Not* except in Labrador, but *less* in Labrador and Newf than any other place," he corrected me. "What can it have been—this terrible thing that must have happened? And why? I can almost understand that God, made angry, might destroy all living things, or the world itself; but I don't understand this instability; these monsters—it makes no sense."

I did not see his real difficulty. After all, God, being omnipotent, could cause anything He liked. I tried to explain this to Uncle Axel, but he shook his head.

"We've got to believe that God is sane, Davie boy. We'd be lost indeed if we didn't do that. But whatever happened out there"—he waved his hand round the horizon at large—"what happened there was *not* sane, not sane at all. It was something vast, yet something beneath the wisdom of God. So what was it? What can it have been?"

"But Tribulation——" I began.

Uncle Axel moved impatiently. "A word," he said, "a rusted mirror, reflecting nothing. It'd do the preachers good to see it for themselves. They'd not understand, but they might begin to think. They might begin to ask themselves: 'What are we doing? What are we preaching? What were the Old People really like? What was it they did to bring this frightful disaster down upon themselves and all the world?' And after a bit they might begin to say: 'Are we right? Tribulation has made the world a different place; can we ever hope to build in it the kind of world the Old People lost? Should we try to? What would be gained if we were to build it up again so exactly that it culminated in another Tribulation?' For it is clear, boy, that however wonderful the Old People were, they were not too wonderful to make mistakes, and nobody knows, or is ever likely to know, where they were wise and where they were mistaken."

Much of what he was saying went right over my head, but I thought I caught its gist. I said:

"But, Uncle, if we don't try to be like the Old People and rebuild the things that have been lost, what *can* we do?"

"Well, we might try being ourselves, and build for the world that is, instead of for one that's gone," he suggested.

"I don't think I understand," I told him. "You mean not bother about the True Line or the True Image? Not mind about Deviations?"

"Not quite that," he said, and then looked sidelong at me. "You heard some heresy from your aunt; well, here's a bit more, from your uncle. What do you think it is that makes a man a man?"

I started on the Definition. He cut me off after five words.

"It is *not!*" he said. "A wax figure could have all that, and he'd still be a wax figure, wouldn't he?"

I supposed he would.

"Well, then, what makes a man a man is something *inside* him."

"A soul?" I suggested.

"No," he said, "souls are just counters for churches to collect, all the same value, like nails. No, what makes man man is mind; it's not a thing, it's a quality, and minds aren't all the same value; they're better or worse, and the better they are, the more they mean. See where we're going?"

"No," I admitted.

"It's this way, Davie. I reckon the church people are more or less right about most deviations—only not for the reasons they say. They're right because most deviations aren't any good. Say they did allow a deviation to live like us, what'd be the good of it? Would a dozen arms and legs, or a couple of heads, or eyes like telescopes give him any more of the quality that makes him a man? They would not. Man got his physical shape—the true image, they call it—before he even knew he was man at all. Like a lot of the animals he was physically pretty nearly as good as he needed to be; but he had this new quality, mind. That was the only thing he could usefully develop. It's the only way open to him now—new qualities of mind." Uncle Axel paused reflectively. "There was a doctor on my second ship who talked that way, and the more I got to thinking it over, the more I reckoned it was the way that made sense. Now, as I see it, some way or another you and Rosalind and the others have got a new quality of mind. To pray God to take it away is wrong. It's like asking him to strike you blind, or make you deaf. I know what you're up against, Davie, but there isn't any easy way out. You have to come to terms with it. You'll have to face it and decide that, since that's the way things *are* with you, what is the best use you can make of it and still keep yourselves safe?"

That evening I told the others about Walter, we were sorry about his accident; nevertheless, it was a relief to all of them to know that it had been simply an accident. One odd thing I discovered was that he was probably some kind of distant relation; my grandmother's name had been Brent.

After that, it seemed wiser for us to find out one another's names in order to prevent such an uncertainty occurring again.

There were now eight of us in all—well, when I say that I mean that there were eight who could talk in thought-shapes. There were some others who sometimes sent traces, but so weak and so limited that they did not count. They were like someone who is not quite blind, but is scarcely able to see more than to know whether it is day or night. The occasional thought-shapes we caught from them were involuntary and too fuzzy and damped to make sense.

The other six were: Michael, who lived about three miles to the north; Sally and Katherine whose homes were on neighboring farms two miles further on, and therefore across the border of the adjoining district; Mark, almost nine miles to the northwest; and Anne and Deborah, a pair of sisters living on a big farm only a mile and a half to the west. Anne, then something over thirteen, was the eldest, Walter Brent had been the youngest by six months.

Knowing who we were was our second stage in gaining confidence. It somehow increased a comforting feeling of mutual support. Gradually I found that the texts and warnings on the walls against Mutants stood out at me less vividly. They toned down and merged once more into the general background. It was not that memories of Aunt Harriet and of Sophie were dulled; it was rather that they did not jump so frighteningly and so often into my mind.

Also, I was soon helped by having a great many new things to think about.

Our schooling, as I have said, was sketchy; mostly writing, reading from a few simple books and the Bible and *Repentances*, which were not at all simple or easy to understand, and a little elementary figuring. It was not much equipment. Certainly it was far too little to satisfy Michael's parents, so they sent him to a school over in Kentak. There, he began to learn a lot of things our old ladies had never thought of. It was natural for him to want the rest of us to know about them, too. At first he was not very clear and the distance being so much more than we were used to gave us all trouble. But, presently, after a few weeks' practice, it became much sharper and better, and he was able to hand on to the rest of us pretty nearly everything he was being taught—even some of the things he did not understand properly himself became clearer when we all thought about them, so that we were able to help him a little, too. And it pleased us to know that he was almost always at the top of his class.

It was a great satisfaction to learn and know more, it helped to ease one over a lot of puzzling matters, and I began to understand many of the things Uncle Axel talked about much better; nevertheless, it brought too, the first taste of complications from which we would never again be free. Quite quickly it became difficult always to remember how much one was supposed to know. It called for conscious restraint to remain silent in the face of simple errors, to listen patiently to silly arguments based on misconceptions, to do a job in the customary way when one knew there was a better way.

There were bad moments, of course: the careless remark that raised some eyebrows, the note of impatience toward those one should respect, the incautious suggestion. But the missteps were few, for the sense of danger now lay closer to the surface in all of us. Somehow, through caution, luck, and quick recoveries we managed to escape direct suspicion and live our two diverging lives for the next six years without the sense of peril becoming sharp.

Until, in fact, the day when we discovered that the eight of us had suddenly become nine.

CHAPTER NINE

IT WAS A FUNNY THING about my little sister, Petra. She seemed so normal. We never suspected, not one of us. She was a happy child, and pretty from infancy, with her close golden curls. I can still see her as a brightly dressed little thing constantly dashing hither and thither at a staggering run, clasping an atrociously crosseyed doll whom she loved with uncritical passion. A toy-like creature herself, prone as any other child to bumps, tears, chuckles, solemn moments, and a very sweet trust. I loved her. Everybody, even my father, conspired to spoil her, with an endearing lack of success. Not even a wandering thought of difference crossed my mind concerning her until her sixth year. Then, abruptly, it happened.

We were harvesting. Up in the twelve-acre there were six men mowing in echelon. I had just given up my scythe to another man, and was helping with the stooking by way of a breather when, without any warning I was struck. I had never known anything like it. One moment I was contentedly, unhurriedly binding and propping up sheaves; the next, it was as if something had hit me physically, inside my head. Very likely I actually staggered under it. Then there was pain, a demand pulling like a fishhook embedded in my mind. There was no question whether or not I should go; I was obeying in a daze. I dropped the sheaf I was holding, and pelted off across the field, past a blur of amazed faces. I kept on running, I did not know why, except that it was urgent; across half the twelve-acre, into the lane, over the fence, down the slope of the East Pasture toward the river.

Pounding across the slope on a slant, I could see the field that ran down to the far side of the river, one of Angus Morton's fields, crossed by a path that led to the footbridge, and on the path was Rosalind, running like the wind.

I kept on, down to the bank, along past the footbridge, downstream toward the deeper pools. I had no uncertainty, I kept right on to the brink of the second pool, and went into a dive without a check. I came up quite close to Petra. She was in the deep water against the steep bank, holding on to a little bush. It was bent over and down, and the roots were on the point of pulling free. A couple of strokes took me near enough to catch her under the arms.

The compulsion ebbed suddenly and faded away. I towed her to an easier landing-place. When I found bottom and could stand up I saw Rosalind's startled face peering anxiously at me over the bushes.

"Who is it?" she asked, in real words, and a shaky voice. She put her hand on her forehead. "Who was able to do that?"

I told her.

"*Petra?*" she repeated, staring incredulously.

I carried my little sister ashore, and laid her on the grass. She was exhausted, and only semi-conscious, but there did not seem to be anything seriously wrong with her.

Rosalind came and knelt on the grass on the other side of her. We looked down at the sopping dress and the darkened, matted curls. Then we gazed across her, at one another.

"I didn't know," I told her. "I'd no idea she was one of us."

Rosalind put her hands to her face, fingertips on her temples. She shook her head slightly and looked at me from disturbed eyes.

"She isn't," she said. "Something like us, but not one of us. None of us could *command*, like that. She's something much more than we are."

Other people came running up then; some who had followed me from the twelve-acre, some from the other side, wondering what had made Rosalind go tearing out of the house as if it were on fire. I picked Petra up to carry her home. One of the men from the field looked at me in a puzzled way:

"But how did you know?" he asked. "I didn't hear a thing."

Rosalind turned an incredulous expression of surprise toward him.

"What! With the way she was yelling! I'd've thought anybody who wasn't deaf would have heard her half-way to Kentak."

The man shook his head doubtfully, but the fact that we had both apparently heard it seemed confirmation enough to make them all uncertain.

I said nothing. I was busy trying to fend off agitated thoughts from the others, telling them to wait until either I or Rosalind was alone and could attend to them without rousing suspicions.

That night, for the first time in years, I had a once-familiar dream, only this time when the knife gleamed high in my father's right hand, the Deviation that struggled in his left was not a calf, it was not Sophie, either; it was Petra. I woke up sweating with fright.

The next day I tried to send thought-shapes to Petra. It seemed to me important for her to know as soon as possible that she must not give herself away. I tried hard, but I could make no contact with her. The rest tried, too, in turn, but there was no response. I wondered whether I should try to warn her in ordinary words, but Rosalind was against that.

"It must have been panic that brought it out," she said. "If she isn't aware of it now, she probably doesn't even know it happened, so it might easily be an unnecessary danger to tell her about it at all. She's only a little over six, remember. I don't think it is fair, or safe, to burden her until it's necessary."

There was general agreement with Rosalind's view. All of us knew that it is not easy to keep on watching each word all the time, even when you've had to practice it for years. We decided to postpone telling Petra until either some occasion made it necessary, or until she was old enough to understand more clearly what we were warning her about; in the meantime we would test occasionally to see whether we could make contact with her, otherwise the matter should rest as it stood at present.

We saw no reason then why it should not continue to stand as it did for all of us—no alternative, indeed. If we did not remain hidden, we should be finished.

In the last few years we had learned more about the people around us, and the way they felt. What had seemed five or six years ago a kind of rather disquieting game, had grown grimmer as we understood more about it. Essentially, it had not changed. Our whole consideration if we were to survive must be to keep our true selves hidden; to walk, talk and live indistinguishably from other people. We had a gift, a sense which, Michael complained bitterly, should have been a blessing, but was little better than a curse. The stupidest Norm was happier; he could feel that he belonged. We did not, and because we did not, we had no positive—we were condemned to negatives, to not revealing ourselves, to not speaking when we would, to not using what we knew, to not being found out, to a life of perpetual deception, concealment, and lying. The prospect stretching out before us chafed Michael more than it did the rest of us. His imagination took him further ahead, giving him a clearer vision of what such frustrations were going to mean, but it was no better at suggesting an alternative than ours were. As far as I was concerned I was only just beginning to perceive the vacancy in our lives. It was my appreciation of danger that had sharpened as I grew up. It had become hardened one afternoon of the summer in the year before we discovered Petra.

It was a bad season, that. We had lost three fields; so had Angus Morton. Altogether there had been twenty-five field-burnings in the district. There had been a higher deviation-rate among the spring births of the stock—not only our own stock, but everyone's, and particularly among the cattle—than had been known for twenty years. There seemed to be more wildcats of various sizes prowling out of the woods by night than there had ever been before. Every week someone was before the court charged with attempted concealment of deviational crops, or the slaughter and consumption of un-declared Offenses among stock, and to cap it all there had been no less than three district alerts on account of raids in force from the Fringes. It was just after the stand-down following the last of these that I happened across Old Jacob grumbling to himself as he forked muck in the yard.

"What is it?" I asked him, pausing beside him.

He jabbed the fork into the muck and leaned one hand on the shaft. He had been an old man forking muck ever since I could remember. I couldn't imagine that he had ever been or would be anything else. He turned to me a lined face mostly hidden in white hair and whiskers which always made me think of Elijah.

"Beans," he said. "Now my bloody beans are wrong. First my potatoes, *then* my tomatoes, *then* my lettuce, *now* my beans. Never knew a year like it. The others I've had before, but who ever heard of beans getting tribulated?"

"Are you sure?" I said.

"Sure? 'Course I am. Think I don't know the way a bean *ought* to look, at my age?"

He glared at me out of the white fuzz.

"It's certainly a bad year," I agreed.

"Bad," he said, "it's ruination. And worse to come, I reckon." He shook his head. "Aye, worse to come," he repeated, with gloomy satisfaction.

"Why?" I inquired.

"It's a judgment," he told me. "*And* they deserve it. No morals, no principles. Look at young Ted Norbat—gets a bit of a fine for hiding a litter of ten and eating all but two before he was found out. Enough to bring his father up out of his grave. Why, if *he'd* done a thing like that— not that he ever would, mind you—but *if* he had, d'you know what he'd have got?" I shook my head. "It'd have been a public shaming on a Sunday, a week of penances, *and* a tenth of all he had," he told me, forcibly.

"But God is not mocked. Bringing Tribulation down on us, again, they are, a season like this is the start; I'm glad I'm an old man and not likely to see the fall of it. But it's coming, you mark my words.

"Government regulations made by a lot of sniveling, weak-hearted, weak-witted babblers in the East. That's what the trouble is. When my father was a young man a woman who bore a child that wasn't in the image was whipped for it. If she bore three out of the image she was uncertified, outlawed, and sold. It made them careful about their Purity and their prayers. My father reckoned there was a lot less trouble with Mutants on account of it, and when there were any, they were burnt, like other Deviations."

"Burnt!" I exclaimed.

He looked at me. "Isn't that the way to cleanse Deviations?" he demanded fiercely.

"But a Mutant isn't responsible for——" I began.

"'Isn't responsible,'" sneered the old man. "Is a tiger-cat responsible for being a tiger-cat? But you kill it. You can't afford to have it around loose. *Repentances* says to keep pure the stock of the Lord by fire, but that's not good enough for the bloody government now.

"Give me the old days when a man was allowed to do his duty and keep the place clean. Heading right for another dose of Tribulation we are now." He went on muttering, looking like an ancient, and wrathful, prophet of doom.

I asked Uncle Axel whether there were a lot of people who really felt the way old Jacob talked. He scratched his cheek, thoughtfully.

"Quite a few of the old ones. They still feel it's a personal responsibility —like it used to be before there were Inspectors. Some of the middle-aged are that way, too, but most of them are willing enough to leave it as it is. They're not so set on the forms as their fathers were. They don't reckon it matters much what way it's done so long as the Mutants don't breed and things go along all right—but give them a run of years with instability as high as it is this year, and I'd not say for certain they'd take it quietly."

"Why should the deviation-rate suddenly get high some years?" I asked him.

He shook his head. "I don't know. Something to do with the weather, they say. Get a bad winter with gales from the southwest, and up goes the deviation-rate—not the next season, but the one after that. Something comes over from the Badlands, they say. Nobody knows what, but it looks as though they're right. The old men look on it as a warning, just a reminder of Tribulation sent to keep us on the right path, and they make the most of it. Next year's going to be a bad one, too. People will listen to them more then. They'll have a sharp eye for scapegoats." He concluded by giving me a long, thoughtful look.

I had taken the hint and passed it on to the others. Sure enough the season had been almost as tribulated as the one before, and there *was* a tendency to look for scapegoats. Public feeling toward concealments was noticeably less tolerant than it had been the previous summer, and it increased the anxiety we should in any case have felt over our discovery of Petra.

For a week after the river incident we listened with extra care for any hint of suspicion about it. We found none, however. Evidently it had been accepted that both Rosalind and I, in different directions, had happened to hear cries for help which must, in any case, have been faint at the distance. We were able to relax again, but not for long. Only about a month went by before we had a new source of misgiving.

Anne announced that she was going to marry.

CHAPTER TEN

THERE WAS a shade of defiance in Anne, even when she told us.

At first we did not take it very seriously. We found it difficult to believe, and we did not want to believe, that she was serious. For one thing, the man was Alan Ervin, the same Alan I had fought on the bank of the stream, and who had informed on Sophie. Anne's parents ran a good farm, not a great deal smaller than Waknuk itself; Alan was the blacksmith's son, his prospects were those of becoming the blacksmith himself in his turn. He had the physique for it, he was tall and healthy, but that was about as far as he went. Quite certainly Anne's parents would be more ambitious for her than that; so we scarcely expected anything to come of it.

We were wrong. Somehow she brought her parents round to the idea, and the engagement was formally recognized. At that point we became alarmed. Abruptly, we were forced to consider some of the implications, and, young though we were, we could see enough of them to make us anxious. It was Michael who put it to Anne, first.

"You can't, Anne. For your own sake you mustn't," he told her. "It'd be like tying yourself for life to a cripple. Do think, Anne, do really think what it is going to mean."

She came back to him angrily. "I'm not a fool. Of course I've thought. I've thought more than you have. I'm a woman—I've a right to marry and have children. There are three of you and five of us. Are you saying that two of us must never marry? Never have any lives or homes of our own? If not, then two of us have got to marry Norms. I'm in love with Alan, and I intend to marry him. You ought to be grateful. It'll help to simplify things for the rest of you."

"That doesn't follow," Michael argued. "We can't be the only ones. There must be others like us—beyond our range, somewhere. If we wait a little . . ."

"Why should I wait? It might be for years, or for always. I've got Alan, and you want me to waste years waiting for someone who may never come, or whom I may hate if he does. You want me to give up Alan, and risk being cheated of everything. Well, I didn't ask to be the way we are; but I've as much right to get what I can out of life as anyone else. It's you who haven't thought, Michael—or any of you. I *know* what I intend to do; the rest of you don't know what you intend to do because you're none of you in love—except David and Rosalind—and so you've none of you faced it."

That was partially true as far as it went; but if we had not faced all the problems before they arose, we were well aware of those that were constantly with us, and of those the main one was the need of dissembling, of leading all the time a suffocating half-life with our families. One of the things we looked forward to most was relief some day from that burden, and though we'd few positive ideas how it could be achieved, we could all realize that marriage to a Norm would become intolerable in a very short while. It could not be anything but a sham of a marriage when the two were separated by something wider than a different language, which had always been hidden by the one from the other. It would be misery, perpetual lack of confidence, and insecurity; there'd be the prospect of a lifetime's guarding against slips —and we knew well enough already that occasional slips were inevitable.

Anne had seen this just as well as the rest of us, but now she pretended to ignore it. She began to defy her differences by refusing to respond to us, though whether she shut her mind off altogether, or continued to listen without taking part we could not tell. We suspected the former as being more in character, but, being unsure, we were not even able to discuss among ourselves what course, if any, we ought to take. Possibly there was no active course. I myself could think of none. Rosalind, too, was at a loss.

Rosalind had grown into a tall, slim young woman, now. She was handsome, with a face one could not help watching, she was attractive, too, in the way she moved and carried herself. Several of the younger men had felt the attraction, and gravitated toward her. She was civil to them, but no more. She would not be entangled with any of them, very likely it was for that reason that she was more shocked than any of us by what Anne proposed to do.

We used to meet, discreetly and not dangerously often. No one but the others, I think, ever suspected anything between us. We had to make love in a snatched, unhappy way when we did meet, wondering miserably whether there would ever be a time when we should not have to hide ourselves. And somehow the business of Anne made us more wretched still. Marriage to a Norm, even the kindest and best of them was unthinkable for both of us.

The only other person I could turn to for advice was Uncle Axel. He knew, as did everyone else, about the forthcoming marriage, but it was news to him that Anne was one of us, and he received it lugubriously. After he had turned it over in his mind, he shook his head.

"No. It won't do, Davie. You're right there. I've been seeing these last five or six years how it wouldn't do, but I've just been hoping that maybe it'd never come to it. I reckon you're all up against a wall, or you'd not be telling me now?"

I nodded. "She wouldn't listen to us," I told him. "Now she's gone further. She won't respond at all. She says that's over. She never wanted to be different from Normals, now she wants to be as like them as she can. I never knew before that anybody could not want anybody else quite like that. She's so fierce and blind about it that she simply doesn't care what may happen later. I don't see what we can do."

"You don't think that perhaps she *can* make herself live like a Norm—cut out the other altogether? It'd be too difficult?" Uncle Axel asked.

"We've thought about that, of course," I told him. "She can refuse to respond. She's doing that now, like somebody refusing to talk. But to go on with it—it'd be like taking a vow of silence for the rest of her life. I mean, she can't just make herself forget, and *become* a Norm. We can't believe that's possible. Michael told her it'd be like pretending to have only one arm because the person one wants to marry has only one arm. It wouldn't be any good—and you couldn't keep it up, either."

Uncle Axel pondered for a bit.

"You're convinced she's crazy about this Alan, quite beyond reason, I mean?" he asked.

"She's not like herself at all. She doesn't think properly any more," I told him. "Before she stopped responding her thought-shapes were all queer with it."

Uncle Axel shook his head disapprovingly again. "Women like to think they're in love when they want to marry; they feel it's a justification which helps their self-respect," he observed. "No harm in that; most of them are going to need all the illusions they can keep up, anyway. But a woman who *is* in love is a different proposition. She lives in a world where all the old perspectives have altered. She is blinkered, single-purposed, undependable in other matters. She will sacrifice anything, including herself, to one loyalty. For her, that is quite logical; for everyone else it looks not quite sane; socially it is dangerous. And when there is also a feeling of guilt to be overcome, and maybe, expiated, it is quite certainly dangerous for someone." He broke off, and reflected in silence awhile. Then he added, "It is *too* dangerous, Davie. Remorse . . . abnegation . . . self-sacrifice . . . the desire for purification . . . all pressing upon her. The sense of burden, the need for help, for someone to share the burden. . . . Sooner or later, I'm afraid, Davie. Sooner or later . . ."

I thought so, too.

"But what can we do?" I repeated, miserably.

He turned steady, serious eyes on me.

"How much are you justified in doing? One of you is set on a course to endanger the lives of all eight. Not altogether wittingly, perhaps, but none the less seriously, for all that. Even if she does intend to be loyal to you, she is deliberately risking you all for her own ends—just a few words in her sleep would be enough. Does she have a moral right to create a constant threat hanging over seven heads just because she wants to live with this man?"

I hesitated. "Well, if you put it like that——" I began.

66

"I *do* put it like that. *Has* she that right?"

"We've done our best to dissuade her," I evaded, inadequately.

"Listen," said Uncle Axel. "I knew a man once who was one of a party who were adrift in a boat after their ship had burnt. They'd not much food and very little water. One of them drank sea water and went mad. He tried to wreck the boat so that they'd all drown together. He was a menace to all of them. In the end they had to throw him overboard, with the result that the other three had just enough food and water to last until they reached land. If they hadn't done it he'd have died anyway, and the rest of them, too, most likely."

I shook my head. "No," I said decisively, "we couldn't do that."

He went on looking at me steadily.

"This isn't a nice cozy world for anyone, especially not for anyone that's different," he said. "Maybe you're not the kind to survive in it, after all."

"It isn't just that," I told him. "If it were Alan you were talking about, if it would help to throw him overboard, we'd do it, but it wouldn't help. She'd understand why, and it'd only make things worse. But it's Anne you're meaning, and we can't do it—not because she's a girl, it'd be the same with any of us; we just couldn't do it. We're all too close together. It's difficult to explain . . ." I broke off, trying to think of a way of showing him what we meant to one another. There didn't seem to be any clear way of putting it, into words. I could only tell him, not very effectively.

"It wouldn't be just murder, Uncle Axel. It'd be something worse, as well; like violating part of ourselves. We couldn't do it."

"The alternative is the sword over your heads," he said.

"I know," I agreed unhappily. "But that isn't the way. A sword inside us would be worse."

I could not even discuss that solution with the others for fear that Anne might catch our thoughts; but I knew with certainty what their verdict on it would be. I knew that Uncle Axel had proposed the only practical solution; and I knew, too, its impossibility meant recognizing that nothing could be done.

Anne now transmitted nothing whatever, we caught no trace of her, but whether she had the strength of will not to receive we were still uncertain. From Deborah, her sister, we learned that she would listen only to words, and was doing her best to pretend to herself that she was a Norm in every way, but that could not give us enough confidence for us to exchange our thoughts with freedom.

And in the following weeks Anne kept it up, so that one could almost believe that she had succeeded in renouncing her difference and becoming a Norm. Her wedding-day passed with nothing amiss, and she and Alan moved into the house which her father gave them on the edge of his own land. Here and there one encountered hints that she might have been unwise to marry beneath her, but otherwise there was little comment.

During the next few months we heard scarcely anything of her. She discouraged visits from her sister as though she was anxious to cut even that last link with us. We could only hope that she was being more successful and happier than we had feared.

One of the consequences, as far as Rosalind and I were concerned, was a more searching consideration of our own troubles. Quite when it was that we had known we were going to marry one another, neither of us was able to remember. It was one of those things that seem ordained, in such proper accord with the law of nature and our own desires, that we felt we had always known it. The prospect colored our thoughts even before we acknowledged it to ourselves. To me, it had never been thinkable that anything else should happen, for when two people have grown up thinking-together as closely as we had, and when they are drawn even closer together by the knowledge of hostility all around them they can feel the need of one another even before they know they are in love.

But when they do know they are in love they suddenly know, too, that there are ways in which they differ not at all from Norms, that some of the same obstacles must be overcome.

The feud between our families which had first come into the open over the matter of the greathorses had now been established for almost a decade. My father and half-uncle Angus, Rosalind's father, had settled down to a regular guerrilla. In their efforts to score points each kept a hawk-like watch upon the other's land for the least Deviation or Offense, and both had been known for some time now to reward the informer who would bring news of irregularities in the other's territory.

It was perfectly clear to us that neither side would be anything but dead set against a union of the families.

For both of us the situation was bound to grow more difficult. Already Rosalind's mother had attempted some matchmaking; and I had seen my mother measuring one or two girls with a calculating, though so far unsatisfied eye.

We were sure that, at present, neither side had an idea of anything between us. There was only acrid communication between the Storms and the Mortons, and the only place they could be found beneath the same roof was church. Rosalind and I met infrequently and very discreetly.

We discussed and explored lengthily for some pacific way out of the dilemma, but even when half a year had passed since Anne's marriage we were no nearer reaching it.

As for the rest of our group, we found that in that six months the first alarm had lost its edge. That is not to say that we were easy in our minds: we had never been that since we discovered ourselves, but once the crisis over Anne had passed we got used to living with a slightly increased degree of threat.

Then, one Sunday at dusk, Alan was found dead in the field-path that led to his home, with an arrow through his neck.

We had the news first from Deborah, and we listened anxiously as she tried to make contact with her sister. She used all the concentration she could manage, but it was useless. Anne's mind remained as firmly closed against us as it had been for the last eight months. Even in distress she transmitted nothing.

"I'm going over to see her," Deborah told us. "She must have someone by her."

We waited expectantly for an hour or more. Then Deborah came through again, very perturbed.

"She won't see me. She won't let me into the house. She's let a neighbor in, but not me. She screamed at me to go away."

"She must think one of us did it," came Michael's response. "Did any of you do it?—or know anything about it?"

Our denials came in emphatically, one after another.

"We've got to stop her thinking that," Michael decided. "She mustn't go on believing it. Try to get through to her."

We all tried. There was no response whatever.

"No good," Michael admitted. "You must get a note to her somehow, Deborah," he added. "Word it carefully so that she'll understand we had nothing to do with it, but so that it won't mean anything to anyone else."

"Very well. I'll try," Deborah agreed doubtfully.

Another hour passed, before we heard from her once more.

"It's no good. I gave the note to the woman who's there, and waited. When the woman came back she said Anne just tore it up without opening it. My mother's in there now, trying to persuade her to come home."

Michael was slow in replying to that. Then he advised:

"We'd best be prepared. All of you make ready to run for it if necessary, but don't rouse any suspicions. Deborah, keep on trying to find out what you can, and let us know at once if anything happens."

I did not know what to do for the best. Petra was already in bed, and I could not rouse her without it being noticed. Besides, I was not sure that it was necessary. She certainly could not be suspected even by Anne of having had any part in the killing of Alan. It was only potentially that she could be considered one of us at all, so I made no move beyond sketching a rough plan in my mind, and trusted that I should have enough warning to get us both clear.

The house had retired for the night before Deborah came through again.

"We're going home, mother and me," she told us. "Anne's turned everyone out, and she's alone there now. Mother wanted to stay, but Anne is beside herself and hysterical. She *made* them go. They were afraid she'd be worse if they insisted on staying. She's told Mother she knows who's responsible for Alan's death, but she wouldn't name anybody."

"You think she means us? After all, it *is* possible that Alan may have had some bitter quarrel of his own that we know nothing about," Michael suggested.

Deborah was more than dubious. "If it were only that, she'd surely have let me in. She wouldn't have screamed at me to go away," she pointed out. "I'll go over early in the morning, and see if she's changed her mind."

With that we had to be content for the moment. We could relax a little for a few hours, at least.

Deborah told us later what happened the following morning.

She had got up an hour after dawn and made her way across the fields to Anne's house. When she reached it she had hesitated a little, reluctant to face the possibility of the same sort of screaming repulse that she had suffered the previous day. However, it was useless simply to stand there looking at the house; she plucked up courage and raised the knocker. The sound of it echoed inside and she waited. There was no result.

She tried the knocker again, more decisively. Still no one answered.

Deborah became alarmed. She hammered the knocker vigorously and stood listening. Then slowly and apprehensively, she lowered her hand from the knocker, and went over to the house of the neighbor who had been with Anne the previous day.

With one of the logs from the woodpile they pushed in a window, and then climbed inside. They found Anne upstairs in her bedroom, hanging from a beam.

They took her down, between them, and laid her on the bed. They were too late by some hours to help her. The neighbor covered her with a sheet.

To Deborah it was all unreal. She was dazed. The neighbor took her by the arm to lead her out. As they were leaving she noticed a folded sheet of paper lying on the table. She picked it up.

"This'll be for you, or maybe your parents," she said, putting it into Deborah's hand.

Deborah looked at it dully, reading the inscription on the outside.

"But it's not——" she began automatically.

Then she checked herself, and pretended to look at it more closely, as it occurred to her that the woman could not read.

"Oh, I see—yes, I'll give it to them," she said, and slipped into the front of her dress the message that was addressed neither to herself, nor to her parents, but to the Inspector.

The neighbor's husband drove her home. She broke the news to her parents. Then, alone in her room, the one that Anne had shared with her before she had married, she read the letter.

It denounced all of us, including Deborah herself, and even Petra. It accused us collectively of planning Alan's murder, and one of us, unspecified, of carrying it out.

Deborah read it through twice, and then carefully burnt it.

The tension eased for the rest of us after a day or two. Anne's suicide was a tragedy, but no one saw any mystery about it. A young wife, pregnant with her first child, thrown off her mental balance by the shock of losing her husband in such circumstances; it was a lamentable result, but understandable.

It was Alan's death that remained unattributable to anyone, and as much of a mystery to us as to the rest. Inquiries had revealed several persons who had a grudge against him, but none with a strong-enough motive for murder, nor any likely suspect who could not convincingly account for himself at the time when Alan must have been killed.

70

Old William Tay acknowledged the arrow to be one of his making, but then, most of the arrows in the district were of his making. It was not a competition shaft, or identifiable in any way; just a plain everyday hunting arrow such as might be found by the dozen in any house. People gossiped, of course, and speculated. From somewhere came a rumor that Anne was less devoted than had been supposed, that for the last few weeks she had seemed to be afraid of him. To the great distress of her parents it grew into a rumor that she had let fly the arrow herself, and then committed suicide out of either remorse, or the fear of being found out. But that, too, died away when, again, no sufficiently strong motive could be discovered. In a few weeks speculation found other topics. The mystery was written off as unsolvable; it might even have been an accident which the culprit dared not acknowledge.

We had kept our ears wide open for any hint of guesswork or supposition that might lead attention toward us, but there was none at all, and as the interest declined we were able to relax.

But although we felt less anxiety than we had at any time for nearly a year, an underlying effect remained, a sense of warning, with a sharpened awareness that we were set apart, with the safety of all of us lying in the hands of each.

CHAPTER ELEVEN

THE SPRING INSPECTIONS that year were propitious. Only two fields in the whole district were on the first cleansing schedule, and neither of them belonged to my father, or to Uncle Angus. The two previous years had been so bad that people who had hesitated during the first to dispose of stock with a tendency to produce deviational offspring had killed them off in the second, with the result that the normality-rate was high on that side, too. Moreover, the encouraging trend was maintained. It put new heart into people, they became more neighborly and cheerful. By the end of May there were quite a lot of bets laid that the deviation figures were going to touch a record low. Even Old Jacob had to admit that divine displeasure was in abeyance for the time being.

For us, as for everyone else, it looked like being a serene, if industrious, summer, and possibly it would have been so, but for Petra.

It was one day early in June that, inspired apparently by a feeling for adventure, she did two things she knew to be forbidden. First, although she was alone, she rode her pony off our own land; and second, she was not content to keep to the open country, but went exploring in the woods.

The woods about Waknuk are, as I have said, considered fairly safe, but it does not do to count on that. Wildcats will seldom attack unless desperate; they prefer to run away. Nevertheless, it is unwise to go into the woods without a weapon of some kind, for it is possible for larger creatures to work their way down the necks of forest which thrust out of the Fringes, almost clear across Wild Country in some places, and then slink from one tract of woodland to another.

Petra's call came as suddenly and unexpectedly as before. Though it did not have the violent, compulsive panic which it had carried last time, it was intense; the degree of distress and anxiety was enough to be highly uncomfortable at the receiving end. Furthermore, the child had no control at all. She simply radiated an emotion which blotted out everything else with a great, amphorous splodge.

I tried to get through to the others to tell them I'd attend to it, but I couldn't make contact even with Rosalind. A blotting like that is hard to describe: something like being unable to make oneself heard against a loud noise, but also something like trying to see through a fog. To make it worse, it gave no picture or hint of the cause. It was—this attempt to explain one sense in terms of others is bound to be misleading—but one might say it was something like a wordless yell of protest. Just a reflex emotion, no thought, or control. I doubted even if she knew she was doing it at all. It was instinctive. All I could tell was that it was a distress signal, and coming from some distance away. . . .

I ran from the forge where I was working, and got the gun—the one that always hung just inside the house door, ready charged and primed for an emergency. In a couple of minutes I had one of the riding horses saddled up, and was away on it. One thing as definite about the call as its quality was its direction. Once I was out on the green lane I thumped my heels and was off at a gallop toward the West Woods.

If Petra had only let up on that overpowering distress-pattern of hers for just a few minutes—long enough to let the rest of us get in touch with one another—the consequences would have been quite different. Indeed, there might have been no consequences at all. But she did not. She kept it up, like a screen, and there was nothing one could do but make for the source of it as quickly as possible.

Some of the going wasn't good. I took a tumble at one point, and lost more time catching the horse again. Once in the woods the ground was harder, for the track was kept clear and fairly well used to save a considerable circuit. I kept on along it until I realized I had overshot. The undergrowth was too thick to allow of a direct line, so I had to turn back and hunt for another track in the right direction. There was no trouble about the direction itself; not for a moment did Petra let up. At last I found a path, a narrow, frustratingly winding affair overhung by branches beneath which I had to crouch as the horse thrust its way along, but its general trend was right. At last the ground became clearer and I could choose my own way. A quarter of a mile farther on I pushed through more undergrowth and reached an open glade.

Petra herself I did not see at first. It was her pony that caught my attention. It was lying on the far side of the glade, with its throat torn open. Working at it, ripping flesh from its haunch with such single-minded intent that it had not heard my approach, was as deviational a creature as I had seen.

The animal was a reddish-brown, dappled with both yellow and darker brown spots. Its huge pad-like feet were covered with mops of fur, matted with blood now on the forepaws, and showing long, curved claws. Fur hung from the tail, too, in a way that made it look like a huge plume. The face was round, with eyes like yellow glass. The ears wide-set and drooping, the nose almost retroussé. Two large incisors projected downward over the lower jaw, and it was using these, as well as the claws, to tear at the pony.

I started to unsling the gun from my back. The movement caught its attention. It turned its head and crouched motionless, glaring at me, with the blood glistening on the lower half of its face. Its tail rose, and waved gently from side to side. I cocked the gun and was in the act of raising it when an arrow took the creature in the throat. It leapt, writhing into the air and landed on all fours, facing me still, with its yellow eyes glaring. My horse took fright and reared, and my gun exploded into the air, but before the creature could spring, two more arrows took it, one in the hindquarters, the other in the head. It stood stock-still for a moment, and then rolled over.

Rosalind rode into the glade from my right, her bow still in her hand. Michael appeared from the other side, a fresh arrow already on his string, and his eyes fixed on the creature, making sure about it. Even though we were so close to one another, we were close to Petra, too, and she was still swamping us.

"Where is she?" Rosalind asked in words.

We looked round and then spotted the small figure twelve feet up a young tree. She was sitting in a fork and clinging round the trunk with both arms. Rosalind rode under the tree and told her it was safe to come down. Petra went on clinging, she seemed unable to let go or to move. I dismounted, climbed the tree and helped her down until Rosalind could reach up and take her. Rosalind seated her astride her saddle in front of her, and tried to soothe her, but Petra was looking down at her own dead pony. Her distress was, if anything, intensified.

"We must stop this," I said to Rosalind. "She'll be bringing all the others here."

Michael, assured that the creature was really dead, joined us. He looked at Petra, worriedly.

"She's no idea she's doing it. It's not intelligent; she's sort of howling with fright inside. It'd be better for her to howl outwardly. Let's start by getting her where she can't see her pony."

We moved off a little, round a screen of bushes. Michael spoke to her quietly, trying to encourage her. She did not seem to understand, and there was no weakening of her distress-pattern.

"Perhaps if we were all to try the same thought pattern on her simultaneously," I suggested. "Soothing-sympathizing-relaxing. Ready?"

We tried, for a full fifteen seconds. There was just a momentary check in Petra's distress, then it crowded us down again.

"No good," said Rosalind, and let up.

The three of us regarded her helplessly. The pattern was a little changed; the incisiveness of alarm had receded, but the bewilderment and distress were still overwhelming. She began to cry. Rosalind put an arm round her and held her close to her.

"Let her have it out. It'll relax the tension," said Michael.

While we were waiting for her to calm down, the thing that I had been afraid of happened. Deborah came riding out of the trees; a moment later a boy rode in from the other side. I'd never seen him until now, but I knew he must be Mark.

We had never met as a group before. It was one of the things that we had known would be unsafe. It was almost certain that the other two girls would be somewhere on the way, too, to complete a gathering that we had decided must never happen.

Hurriedly, we explained in words what had occurred. We urged them to get away and disperse as soon as possible so that they would not be seen together; Michael, too. Rosalind and I would stay with Petra and do our best to calm her.

The three of them appreciated the situation without argument. A moment later they left us, riding off in different directions.

We went on trying to comfort and soothe Petra, with little success.

Some ten minutes later the two girls, Sally and Katherine, came pushing their way through the bushes. They, too, were on horseback, and with their bows strung. We had hoped that one of the others might have met them and turned them back, but clearly they had approached by a different route.

They came closer, staring incredulously at Petra. We explained all over again, in words, and advised them to go away. They were in the act of turning their horses when a large man on a bay mare thrust out of the trees into the open.

He reined in, and sat looking at us.

"What's going on here?" he demanded, with suspicion in his tone.

He was a stranger to me, and I did not care for the look of him. I asked what one usually asked of strangers. Impatiently he pulled out his identity tag, with the current year's punch-mark on it. I showed my own. It was established that we were neither of us outlaws.

"What's all this?" he repeated.

The temptation was to tell him to mind his own damned business, but I thought it more tactful in the circumstances to be placatory. I explained that my sister's pony had been attacked, and that we had answered her calls for help. He wasn't willing to take that at its face value. He looked at me steadily, and then turned to regard Sally and Katherine.

"Maybe. But what brought you here in such a hurry?" he asked them.

"Naturally we came when we heard the child calling," Sally told him.

"I was right behind you, and I heard no calling," he said.

Sally and Katherine looked at one another. Sally shrugged.

"We did," she told him, shortly.

It seemed about time I took a hand.

"I'd have thought everyone for miles around would have heard it," I said. "The pony was screaming too, poor little brute."

I led him round the clump of bushes and showed him the ravaged pony and the dead creature. He looked surprised, as if he'd not expected that evidence, but he wasn't altogether appeased. He demanded to see Rosalind's and Petra's tags.

"What's this all about?" I asked in my turn.

"You didn't know that the Fringes have got spies out?" he said.

"I didn't," I told him. "Anyway, do we *look* like Fringes people?"

He ignored the question. "Well, they have. There's an instruction to watch for them. There's trouble working up, and the clearer you keep of the woods, the less likely you are to meet it before we all do."

He still was not satisfied. He turned to look at the pony again, then at Sally.

"I'd say it's near half an hour since that pony did any screaming. How did you two manage to come straight to this spot?"

Sally's eyes widened a little.

"Well, this was the direction it came from, and then when we got nearer we heard the little girl screaming," she said simply.

"And very good it was of you to follow it up," I put in. "You would have saved her life by doing it if we hadn't happened to be a little nearer. It's all over now, and luckily she wasn't hurt. But she's had a nasty fright and I'd better get her home. Thank you both for wanting to help."

They took that up all right. They congratulated us on Petra's escape, hoped she would soon get over the shock, and then they rode off. The man lingered. He still seemed dissatisfied and a little puzzled. There was, however, nothing for him to take a firm hold of. Presently he gave the three of us a long, searching stare, looking as if he were about to say something more, but he changed his mind. Finally he repeated his advice to keep out of the woods, and then rode off in the wake of the other two. We watched him disappear among the trees.

"Who is he?" Rosalind asked, uneasily.

I could tell her that the name on his tag had been Jerome Skinner, but no more. He was a stranger to me, and our names had not seemed to mean much to him. I would have asked Sally but for the barrier that Petra was still putting up. It gave me a strange, muffled feeling to be cut off from the rest like that, and made me wonder at the strength of purpose which enabled Anne to withdraw herself entirely for those months.

Rosalind, still with her right arm around Petra, started homeward at a walk. I collected the dead pony's saddle and bridle, pulled the arrows out of the creature, and followed them.

They put Petra to bed when I brought her in. During the late afternoon and early evening the disturbance she was making fluctuated from time to time, but it kept up naggingly until almost nine o'clock when it diminished steeply and disappeared.

"Thank goodness for that. She's gone to sleep at last," came from one of the others.

"Who was that man Skinner?" Rosalind and I inquired, anxiously and simultaneously.

Sally answered: "He's fairly new here. My father knows him. He has a farm bordering on the woods near where you were. It was just bad luck his seeing us, and of course he wondered why we were making for the trees at a gallop."

"He seemed very suspicious. Why?" asked Rosalind. "Does he know anything about thought-shapes? I didn't think any of them did."

"He can't make them, or receive them himself—I tried him hard," Sally told her.

Michael's distinctive pattern came in, inquiring what it was all about. We explained. He commented:

"Some of them do have an idea that something of the kind may be possible, but only very roughly of the kind—a sort of emotional transfer of mental impressions. They call it telepathy—at least, those who believe in it do. Most of them are pretty doubtful whether it exists at all."

"Do they think it's deviational, those who do believe it exists, I mean?" I asked.

"It's difficult to say. I don't know that the question has ever been straightly put. But, academically, there's the point that since God is able to read men's minds, the true image ought to be able to do so, too. It might be argued that it is a power that men have temporarily lost as a punishment, part of Tribulation, but I'd not like to risk myself on that argument in front of a tribunal."

"This man had an air of smelling a rat," Rosalind told him. "Has anybody else been inquisitive?"

They all gave her a "no" to that.

"Good," she replied. "But we must be careful this doesn't happen again. David will have to explain to Petra in words and try to teach her to use some self-control. If this distress of hers does occur, you must all of you ignore it, or, anyway, not answer it. Just leave it to David and me. We have to make sure we are not drawn together into a group again. We could easily be a lot less lucky than we were today. Does everybody understand and agree?"

Their assents came in, then presently the rest of them withdrew, leaving Rosalind and me to discuss how I could best tackle Petra.

I woke early the next morning, and the first thing I was aware of was Petra's distress once more. But it was different in quality now; her alarm had quite subsided, but given way to a lament for the dead pony. Nor did it have anything like the intensity of the previous day.

I tried to make contact with her, and, though she did not understand, there was a perceptible check and a trace of puzzlement for some seconds. I got out of bed, and went along to her room. She was glad to have company; the distress-pattern faded a lot as we chatted. Before I left I promised to take her fishing that afternoon.

It is not at all easy to explain in words how one can make intelligent thought-shapes. All of us had first found out for ourselves; a very crude fumbling to begin with, but then more skillful when we had discovered one another and begun to learn by practice. With Petra it was different. Already, at six and a half, she had had a power of projection in a different class from ours, and quite overwhelming—but without realization, and therefore with no control whatever. I did my best to explain to her, but even at her present age of almost eight the necessity of putting it in words that were simple enough presented a difficulty. After an hour of trying to make it clear to her while we sat on the river bank watching our floats, I still had not got anywhere much, and she was growing too bored to try to understand what I said. Another kind of approach seemed to be required.

"Let's play a game," I suggested. "You shut your eyes. Keep them shut tight, and pretend you're looking down a deep, deep well. There's nothing but dark to see. Right?"

"Yes," she said, eyelids tightly clenched.

"Good. Now, don't think of anything at all except how dark it is and how far, far away the bottom is. Just think of that, but look at the dark. Understand that?"

"Yes," she said again.

"Now watch," I told her.

I thought a rabbit for her, and made it twitch its nose. She chuckled. Well, that was one good thing, at least; it made sure that she *could* receive. I abolished the rabbit, and thought a puppy, then some chickens, and then a horse and cart. After a minute or two she opened her eyes, and looked bewildered.

"Where are they?" she asked, looking around.

"They aren't anywhere. They were just think-things," I told her. "That's the game. Now I'll shut my eyes, too. We'll both look down the well and think of nothing but how dark it is. Then it's your turn to think a picture at the bottom of the well, so that I can see it."

I played my part conscientiously and opened my mind to its most sensitive. That was a mistake. There was a flash and a glare and a general impression that I had been struck by a thunderbolt. I staggered in a mental daze, with no idea what her picture had been. The others came in, protesting bitterly. I explained what was going on.

"Well, for heaven's sake be careful, and don't let her do it again. I damned near put an axe through my foot," came aggrievedly from Michael.

"I've scalded my hand with the kettle," from Katherine.

"Lull her. Soothe her down somehow," advised Rosalind.

"She isn't unsoothed. She's perfectly tranquil. That seems to be just the way it is with her," I told them.

"Maybe, but it's a way it can't stay," Michael answered. "She must cut it down."

"I know—I'm doing my best. Perhaps you've got some ideas on how to tackle it?" I suggested.

"Well, next time warn us *before* she tries," Rosalind told me.

I pulled myself together and turned my attention to Petra again.

"You're too rough," I said. "This time make a *little* think-picture; a really little one ever so far away, in soft pretty colors. Do it slowly and gently, as if you were making it out of cobwebs."

Petra nodded, and closed her eyes again.

77

"Here it comes!" I warned the others, and waited, wishing it were the kind of thing one could take cover from.

It was not much worse than a minor explosion this time. It was dazzling, but I did manage to catch the shape of it.

"A fish!" I said. "A fish with a droopy tail."

Petra chuckled delightedly.

"Undoubtedly a fish," came from Michael. "You're doing fine. All you want to do now is to cut her down to about one per cent of the power in that last one before she burns our brains out."

"Now *you* show *me*," demanded Petra, and the lesson proceeded.

The following afternoon we had another session. It was a rather violent and exhausting business, but there was progress. Petra was beginning to grasp the idea of forming thought-shapes—in a childish way, as was only to be expected—but frequently recognizable in spite of distortions. The main trouble still was to keep the power down. When she became excited one was almost stunned by the impact. The rest complained that they could get no work done while we were at it; it was like trying to ignore sudden hammer-bangs inside one's head. Toward the end of the lesson I told Petra:

"Now I'm going to tell Rosalind to give you a think-picture. Just shut your eyes, like before."

"Where's Rosalind?" she asked, looking around.

"She's not here, but that doesn't matter with think-pictures. Now, look at the dark and think of nothing."

"And you others," I added mentally for the benefit of the rest, "just lay off, will you? Keep it all clear for Rosalind and don't interrupt. Go ahead, Rosalind, strong and clear."

We sat silent and receptive.

Rosalind made a pond with reeds round it. She put in several ducks, friendly, humorous-looking ducks of several colors. They swam a kind of ballet, except for one chunky, earnestly trying duck who was always a little late and a little wrong. Petra loved it. She gurgled with enjoyment. Then, abruptly, she projected her delight; it wiped out the whole thing and dazed us all again. It was wearing for everyone, but her progress was encouraging.

In the fourth lesson she learnt the trick of clearing one's mind without closing one's eyes, which was quite a step. By the end of the week we were really getting on. Her thought-shapes were still crude and unstable, but they would improve with practice. Her reception of simple forms was good, though as yet she could catch little of our projections to one another.

"Too difficult to see all at once and too quick," she said. "But I can tell whether it's you, or Rosalind, or Michael, or Sally doing it, but going so fast it gets muddled. The other ones are much *more* muddled, though."

"What other ones—Katherine and Mark?" I asked her.

"Oh, no. I can tell them. It's the other other ones. The long-way-away ones," she said, impatiently.

I decided to take it calmly.

"I don't know," she said. "Can't you hear them? They're over there, but a long, long way." She pointed to the southwest.

I thought that over for a few moments.

"Are they there now?" I asked.

"Yes, but not much," she said.

I tried my best to detect anything, and failed.

"Suppose you try to copy for me what you're getting from them?" I suggested.

She tried. There was something there, and with a quality in it which none of us had. It was not comprehensible and it was very blurred—possibly, I thought, because Petra was trying to relay something she could not understand herself. I could make nothing of it, and called Rosalind in, but she could do no better. Petra was evidently finding it an effort, so after a few minutes we decided to let it rest for the present.

In spite of Petra's continued propensity to slip at any moment into what, in terms of sound, would be a deafening bellow we all felt a proprietorial pride in her progress. There was a sense of excitement, too—rather as if we had discovered an unknown who we knew was destined to become a great singer: only it was something more important than that. . . .

"This," Michael said, "is going to be very interesting indeed—provided she doesn't break us all up before she gets control of it."

At supper, some ten days after the loss of Petra's pony, Uncle Axel asked me to come and give him a hand with truing-up a wheel, while there was still light enough. Superficially the request was casual, but there was something in his eye which made me agree without hesitation. I followed him out, and we went over behind the rick where we should neither be seen nor overheard. He put a straw between his teeth, and looked at me seriously.

"You been careless, Davie boy?" he asked.

There are plenty of ways of being careless, but only one he'd ask me about with the manner he was using.

"I don't think so," I told him.

"One of the others, maybe?" he suggested.

Again, I did not think so.

"H'm," he grunted. "Then why, would you say, has Joe Darley been asking questions about you? Any idea?"

I had no idea why, and told him so. He shook his head.

"I don't like it, boy."

"Just me—or the others, as well?" I asked.

"You and Rosalind Morton."

"Oh," I said, uneasily. "Still, if it's only Joe Darley. . . . Could it be he's heard a rumor about us, and is out to do a bit of scandal-raising?"

"Might be," Uncle Axel agreed, but reservedly. "On the other hand Joe is a fellow that the Inspector has used before now when he wants a few inquiries made on the quiet. I don't like it."

I did not care for it, either. But he had not approached either of us directly, and I did not see where else he was going to get any incriminating information. There was, I pointed out, nothing he could pin on us that brought us within any category of the Scheduled Deviations.

Uncle Axel shook his head. "Those lists are inclusive, not exclusive," he said. "You can't schedule all the million things that *may* happen—only the more frequent ones. There have to be test cases for new ones when they crop up. It's part of the Inspector's job to keep watch and call an inquiry if the information he gets seems to warrant it."

"We've thought about what might happen," I told him. "If there should be any questions they'll not be sure what they're looking for. All we'll have to do is act bewildered, just as a Norm would be. If Joe or anybody has anything it can't be more than suspicion, no solid evidence."

He did not seem reassured.

"There's Deborah," he suggested. "She was pretty much upset by her sister's suicide. Do you think she——?"

"No," I said confidently. "Quite apart from the fact that she couldn't do it without involving herself, we should have known if she were hiding anything."

"Well then, there's young Petra," he said.

I stared at him.

"How did you know about Petra?" I asked. "I never told you."

He nodded in a satisfied way. "So she *is*. I reckoned so."

"How did you find out?" I repeated anxiously, wondering who else might have had a similar idea. "Did she tell you?"

"Oh, no, I kind of came across it." He paused, then he added: "Indirectly it came from Anne. I told you it was a bad thing to let her marry that fellow. There's a type of woman who isn't content until she's made herself some man's slave and doormat—put herself completely in his power. That's the kind she was."

"You're not—you don't mean she *told* Alan about herself?" I protested.

"She did," he nodded. "She did more than that. She told him about all of you."

I stared at him incredulously.

"You can't be sure of that, Uncle Axel!"

"I am, Davie boy. Maybe she didn't intend to. Maybe it was only herself she told him about, being the kind who can't keep secrets in bed. And maybe he had to beat the names of the rest of you out of her, but he knew, all right. He knew."

"But even if he did, how did *you* know he knew?" I asked, with rising anxiety.

He said, reminiscently:

"Awhile ago there used to be a dive down on the waterfront in Rigo. It was run by a fellow called Grouth, and very profitably, too. He had a staff of three girls and two men, and they did as he said—just as he said. If he'd liked to tell what he knew one of the men would have been strung up for mutiny on the high seas, and two of the girls for murder. I don't know what the others had done, but he had the lot of them cold. It was as neat a setup for blackmail as you could find. If the men got any tips he had them. He saw to it that the girls were nice to the sailors who used the place, and whatever they got out of the sailors he had, too. I used to see the way he treated them, and the expression on his face when he watched them, kind of gloating because he'd got them, and he knew it, and they knew it. He'd only got to frown, and they danced."

Uncle Axel paused reflectively.

"You'd never think you'd come across just that expression on a man's face again in Waknuk church, of all places, would you? It made me feel a bit queer when I did. But there it was. It was on Alan's face while he studied first Rosalind, then Deborah, then you, then young Petra. He wasn't interested in anybody else. Just the four of you."

"You could have been mistaken—just an expression. . . ." I said.

"Not *that* expression. Oh, no. I knew that expression, it jerked me right back to the dive in Rigo. Besides, if I wasn't right, how do I come to know about Petra?"

"What did you do?"

"I came home and thought a bit about Grouth, and what a comfortable life he'd been able to lead, and about one or two other things. Then I put a new string on my bow."

"So it was you!" I exclaimed.

"It was the only thing to do, Davie. Of course, I knew Anne would reckon it was one of you that had done it. But she couldn't denounce you without giving herself away and her sister, too. There was a risk there, but I had to take it."

"There certainly was a risk, and it nearly didn't come off," I said, and told him about the letter that Anne had left for the Inspector.

He shook his head. "I hadn't reckoned she'd go as far as that, poor girl," he said. "All the same, it had to be done, and quickly. Alan wasn't a fool. He'd see to it that he was covered. Before he actually began on you he'd have had a written deposition somewhere to be opened in the event of his death, and he'd see that you knew about it, too. It'd have been a pretty nasty situation for all of you."

The more I considered it, the more I realized how nasty it could have been.

"You took a big risk for us yourself, Uncle Axel," I told him.

He shrugged.

"Very little risk for me against a great deal for you," he said.

Presently, we came back to the matter in hand.

"But these inquiries can't have anything to do with Alan. That was weeks ago," I pointed out.

"What's more, it's not the kind of information he'd share with anyone if he wanted to cash in on it," agreed Uncle Axel. "There's one thing," he went on, "they can't know much, or they'd have called an inquiry already, and they'll have to be pretty damn sure of themselves before they do call one. The Inspector isn't going to put himself in a weak spot with your father, if he can help it—nor with Angus Morton, either, for that matter. But that still doesn't get us any nearer to knowing what started it."

I was pressed back again into thinking it must have something to do with the affair of Petra's pony. Uncle Axel knew of its death, of course, but not much more. It would have involved telling him about Petra herself, and we had had a tacit understanding that the less he knew about us, the less he would have to hide in case of trouble. However, now that he did know about Petra, I described the event more fully. It did not look to us to be a likely source, but for lack of any other lead he made a note of the man's name.

"Jerome Skinner," he repeated, not very hopefully. "Very well, I'll see if I can find out anything about him."

We all conferred that night, but inconclusively. Michael put it:

"Well, if you and Rosalind are quite satisfied that there's been nothing to start suspicion in your district, then I don't see that it can be traceable to anybody but that man in the forest." He used a thought-shape rather than bothering to spell out "Jerome Skinner" in letter-forms. "If he *is* the source, then he must have put his suspicions before the Inspector in this district, who will have handed it on as a routine report to the Inspector in yours. That'll mean that several people are wondering about it already, and there'll be questions going on here about Sally and Katherine. I'll see if I can find out anything tomorrow, and let you know."

"But what's the best thing for us to do?" Rosalind put in.

"Nothing at the moment," Michael advised. "If we are right about the source, then you are in two groups: Sally and Katherine in one; you, David, and Petra in the other; and the other three of us aren't involved at all. Don't do anything unusual, or you may cause them to pounce, on suspicion. If it does come to an inquiry we ought to be able to bluff it out by acting simple as we decided. But Petra's the weak spot; she's too young to understand. If they start on her and trick her and trap her, it might end up in sterilization and the Fringes for all of us.

"That makes her the key point. It'll be your job, David, to see that she isn't taken for questioning—at any cost. If you have to kill someone to prevent it, then you must. They'd not think twice about killing us if they had the excuse. Don't forget, if they move at all, they'll be doing it to exterminate us, by the slow method, if not by the fast.

"If the worst comes to the worst, and you can't save Petra, it would be kinder to kill her than let her go to sterilization and banishment to the Fringes—a lot more merciful for a child. You understand? Do the rest of you agree?"

Their agreements came in.

When I thought of little Petra, mutilated and thrust naked into Fringes country, to perish or survive as it should chance, I agreed, too.

"Very well," Michael went on. "Just to be on the safe side, then, it might be best if the four of you and Petra were to make your arrangements to run for it at a moment's notice, if it becomes necessary."

He went on explaining in more detail.

It is difficult to see what other course we could have taken. An overt move by any of us would at once have brought trouble on the rest. Our misfortune lay in our receiving the information regarding the inquiries when we did, and not two or three days earlier.

THE DISCUSSION, and Michael's advice, made the threat of discovery seem both more real and more imminent than it had been when I talked to Uncle Axel earlier in the evening. Michael, I knew, had been increasingly anxious during the last year or so, as if he had a feeling that time was running out, and now I caught some of that sensation, too. I even went as far as making some preparations before I went to bed that night. At least, I put a bow and a couple of dozen arrows handy, and found a sack into which I put several loaves and a cheese. And I decided that next day I would make up a pack of spare clothes and boots and other things that would be useful, and hide it in some dry, convenient place outside. Then we should need some clothing for Petra, and a bundle of blankets, and something to hold drinking water, and it would not do to forget a tinder-box. . . .

I was still listing the desirable equipment in my mind when I fell asleep.

No more than three hours or so could have passed before I was wakened by the click of my latch. There was no moon, but there was starlight enough to show a small, white night-gowned figure by the door.

"David," she said. "Rosalind——"

But she did not need to tell me. Rosalind had already broken in, urgently.

"David," she was telling me, "we must get away at once—just as soon as you can. They've taken Sally and Katherine——"

Michael crowded in on her. "Hurry up, both of you, while there's time. It was a deliberate surprise. If they do know much about us, they'll have tried to time it to send a party for you, too—before you could be warned. They were at Sally's and Katherine's almost simultaneously just over ten minutes ago. Get moving, quick."

"Meet you below the mill. Hurry," Rosalind added.

I told Petra, in words:

"Get dressed as fast as you can. Overalls. And be very quiet."

Very likely she had not understood the thought-shapes in detail, but she had caught the urgency. She nodded, and slipped back into the dark passage.

I pulled on my clothes, and rolled the blankets into a bundle. I groped about in the shadows till I found the bow and arrows and the bag of food, and made for the door.

Petra was almost dressed already. I grabbed some clothes from her cupboard and rolled them in blankets.

"Don't put on your shoes yet," I whispered. "Carry them, and come tiptoe, like a cat."

Outside in the yard I put down the bundle and the sack while we both got our shoes on. Petra started to speak, but I put my finger to my lips, and gave her the thought-shape of Sheba, the black mare. She nodded, and we tiptoed across the yard. I just had the stable-door open when I caught a distant sound, and paused to listen.

"Horses," whispered Petra.

I heard them, too—several sets of hoofs and, faintly, the tinkle of bits. There was no time to find the saddle and bridle for Sheba. We brought her out on the halter, and mounted from the block. With all I was carrying there was no room for Petra in front of me. She got up behind, and hung on round my waist.

Quietly we slipped out of the yard by the far end and started down the path to the riverbank while the hoofbeats on the upper track drew close to the house.

"Are you away?" I asked Rosalind, and let her know what was happening with us.

"I was away ten minutes ago. I had everything ready," she told me reprovingly. "We've all been trying our damnedest to reach you. It was lucky Petra happened to wake up."

Petra caught her own thought-shape, and broke in excitedly to know what was happening. It was like a fountain of sparks.

"Gently, darling. Much more gently," protested Rosalind. "We'll tell you all about it soon." She paused a moment to get over the blinding effect. "Sally? Katherine?" she inquired.

They responded together.

"We're being taken to the Inspector's. We're all innocent and bewildered. Is that best?"

Michael and Rosalind agreed that it was.

"We think," Sally went on, "that we ought to shut our minds to you. It will make it easier for us to act as Normals if we really don't know what is happening. So don't try to reach us, any of you."

"Very well—but we shall be open for you," Rosalind agreed. She diverted her thoughts to me. "Come along, David. There are lights up at the farm now."

"It's all right. We're coming," I told her. "It's going to take them some time in the dark to find which way we went, anyhow."

"They'll know by the stable-warmth that you can't have got far yet," she pointed out.

I looked back. Up by the house I could see a light in a window, and a lantern swinging in someone's hand. The sound of a man's voice calling came to us faintly. We had reached the riverbank now, and it was safe to urge Sheba to a trot. We kept that up for half a mile until we came to the ford, and then for another quarter-mile until we were approaching the mill. It seemed prudent to walk her past there in case anyone was awake. Beyond the wall we heard a dog on the chain, but it did not bark. Presently I caught Rosalind's feeling of relief, coming from somewhere a little ahead.

We trotted again, and a few moments later I noticed a movement under the trees of the track. I turned the mare that way, and found Rosalind waiting for us, and not only Rosalind, but her father's pair of greathorses. The massive creatures towered above us, both saddled with large pannier baskets. Rosalind was standing in one of the baskets, her bow, strung and ready to hand, laid across it.

I rode up close beneath her while she leaned out to see what I had brought.

"Hand me the blankets," she directed, reaching down. "What's in the sack?"

I told her.

"Do you mean to say that's all you've brought?" she said disapprovingly.

"There was some hurry," I pointed out.

She arranged the blankets to pad the saddle-board between the panniers. I hoisted Petra until she could reach Rosalind's hands. With a heave from both of us she scrambled up and perched herself on the blankets.

"We'd better keep together," Rosalind directed. "I've left room for you in the other pannier. You can shoot left-handed from there." She flipped over a kind of miniature rope-ladder so that it hung down the greathorse's left shoulder.

I slid off Sheba's back, turned her head for home, and gave her a smack on the flank to start her off, then I scrambled up awkwardly to the other pannier. The moment my foot was clear of the mounting-rings Rosalind pulled them up and hitched them. She gave the reins a shake, and before I was well settled in the pannier we were off, with the second greathorse following on a lead.

We trotted awhile, and then left the track for a stream. Where that was joined by another we branched off up the lesser. We left that and picked our way across boggy ground to another stream. We held on along the bed of that for perhaps half a mile or more and then turned off onto another stretch of uneven, marshy ground which soon became firmer until presently the hoofs were clinking among stones. We slowed still more while the horses picked a winding way amid rocks. I realized that Rosalind had put in some careful planning to hide our tracks. I must have projected the thought unwittingly, for she came in, somewhat coldly:

"It's a pity *you* didn't do a little more thinking and a little less sleeping."

"I made a start," I protested. "I was going to get everything fixed up today. It didn't seem all that urgent."

"And so when I tried to consult you about it, there you were, swinishly asleep. My mother and I spent two solid hours packing up these panniers and getting the saddles slung up ready for an emergency, while all you did was go on sleeping."

"Your mother?" I asked, startled. "Does she *know?*"

"She's sort of half-known, guessed something, for some time now. I don't know how much she's guessed; she never spoke about it at all. I think she felt that as long as she didn't have to admit it in words it might be all

85

right. When I told her this evening that I thought it very likely I'd have to go, she cried; but she wasn't really surprised. She didn't try to argue, or dissuade me. I think she'd already resolved at the back of her mind that she'd have to help me one day, when the time came, and she did."

I thought that over. I could not imagine my own mother doing such a thing for Petra's sake. And yet she had cried after my Aunt Harriet had been sent away. And Aunt Harriet had been more than ready to break the Purity Laws. So had Sophie's mother. It made one wonder how many mothers there might be who were turning a blind eye toward matters that did not actually infringe the Definition of the True Image—and perhaps to things that did infringe it, if the Inspector could be dodged. I wondered, too, whether my mother would, in secret, be glad or sorry that I had taken Petra away.

We went on by the erratic route that Rosalind had picked to hide the trail. There were more stony places and more streams until finally we urged the horses up a steep bank and into the woods. Before long, we encountered a trackway running southwest. We did not care to risk the spoor of the greathorses there, and so kept along parallel with it until the sky began to show gray. Then we turned deeper into the woods until we found a glade which offered grass for the horses. There we hobbled them and let them graze.

After we had made a meal of bread and cheese Rosalind said:

"Since you slept so well earlier on, you'd better take first watch."

She and Petra settled themselves comfortably in blankets and soon dropped off.

I sat with my strung bow across my knees, and half a dozen arrows stuck handy in the ground beside me. There was nothing to be heard but the birds, occasionally a small animal moving, and the steady munchings of the greathorses. The sun rose into the thinner branches and began to give more warmth. Every now and then I got up and prowled silently round the fringe of the glade, with an arrow ready hooked on the string. I found nothing, but it helped to keep me awake. After a couple of hours of it Michael came through:

"Where are you now?" he inquired.

I explained, as well as I could.

"Where are you heading?" he wanted to know.

"Southwest," I told him. "We thought we'd move by night and lie-up by day."

He approved of that, but:

"The devil of it is that with this Fringes scare there'll be a lot of patrols about. I don't know that Rosalind was wise to take those greathorses—if they're seen at all, word will go round like wildfire, even a hoofmark will be enough."

"Ordinary horses have the speed of them for short bursts," I acknowledged, "but they can't touch them for stamina."

"You may need that. Frankly, David, you're going to need your wits, too. There's hell to pay over this. They must have found out much more about you than we ever guessed, though they aren't on to Mark or Deborah or me yet. But it's got them very worried indeed. They're going to send posses after you. My idea is to volunteer for one of them right away. I'm going to plant a report of your having been seen making southeast. When that peters out, we'll have Mark start up another to take them northwest.

"If anyone does see you, stop him getting away with the news, at all costs. But don't shoot. There's an order going out not to use guns except when necessary, and as signals—all gunshots to be investigated."

"That's all right. We haven't a gun," I told him.

"So much the better. You can't be tempted to use one, but they think you have."

I had deliberately decided against taking a gun, partly on account of the noise, but mostly because they are slow to reload, heavy to carry, and useless if you run out of powder. Arrows haven't the range, but they are silent, and you can get a dozen and more of them off while a man is recharging a gun.

Mark came in: "I heard that. I'll have a northwest rumor ready for when it's needed."

"Good. But don't loose it till I tell you. Rosalind's asleep now, I suppose? Tell her to get in touch with me when she wakes, will you?"

I said I would, and everybody laid off projecting for a while.

I went on keeping my watch for another couple of hours, and then woke Rosalind for her turn. Petra did not stir. I lay down beside her, and was asleep in a minute or two.

Perhaps I was sleeping lightly, or it may have been just coincidence that I woke up to catch an anguished thought from Rosalind.

"I've killed him, Michael. He's quite dead. . . ." Then she slid off into a panicky, chaotic thought-shape.

Michael came in, steady and reassuring.

"Don't be scared, Rosalind. You had to do it. This is a war, between our kind and theirs. We didn't start it—we've just as much right to exist as they have. You mustn't be frightened, Rosalind, dear; you had to do it."

"What's happened?" I asked, sitting up.

They ignored me, or were too much occupied to notice.

I looked round the glade. Petra lay, asleep still, beside me; the greathorses were cropping the grass, undisturbed. Michael came in again:

"Hide him, Rosalind. Try to find a hollow, and pile leaves over him."

A pause. Then Rosalind, her panic conquered now, but with deep distress, agreeing.

I got up, picked up my bow, and walked across the glade in the direction I knew she must be. When I reached the edge of the trees it occurred to me that I was leaving Petra unprotected, so I went no further.

Presently Rosalind appeared among the bushes. She was walking slowly, cleaning an arrow on a handful of leaves as she came.

"What happened?" I repeated.

But she seemed to have lost control over her thought-shapes again, they were muddled and distorted by her emotions. When she got nearer she used words instead:

"It was a man. He had found the trail of the horses. I saw him following them. Michael said . . . oh, I didn't want to do it, David, but what else could I do?"

Her eyes were full of tears. I put my arms around her, and let her cry on my shoulder. There was little I could do to comfort her. Nothing, but assure her as Michael had, that what she had done had been absolutely necessary.

After a little time we walked slowly back. She sat down beside the still-sleeping Petra. It occurred to me to ask:

"What about his horse, Rosalind? Did that get away?"

She shook her head.

"I don't know. I suppose he must have had one, but he was following our tracks on foot when I saw him."

I thought it better to retrace our course and find out whether he had left a horse tethered anywhere along it. I went back half a mile but found no horse, nor was there any trace of recent hoofmarks other than those of the greathorses. When I got back Petra was awake and chattering to Rosalind.

The day wore on. Nothing more came to us from Michael or the rest. In spite of what had happened it seemed better to stay where we were than to move by daylight with the risk of being seen. So we waited.

Then, in the afternoon, something did come, suddenly.

It was not a thought-shape; it had no real form; it was sheer distress, like a cry of agony. Petra gasped, and threw herself whimpering into Rosalind's arms. The impact was so sharp it hurt. Rosalind and I stared at one another, wide-eyed. My hands shook. Yet the shock was so formless that we could not tell which of the others it came from.

Then there was a jumble of pain and shame, overridden with hopeless desolation, and, among it, characteristic glimpses of forms that we knew without doubt were Katherine's. Rosalind put her hand on mine and held it tightly. We endured, while the sharpness dimmed, and the pressure ebbed away.

Presently came Sally, brokenly, in waves of love and sympathy to Katherine, then, in anguish, to the rest of us.

"They've broken Katherine. They've broken her. . . . Oh, Katherine, dear . . . you mustn't blame her, any of you. Please, please don't blame her. They're torturing her. It might have been any of us. She's all clouded now. She can't hear us. . . . Oh, Katherine, darling . . ." Her thoughts dissolved into shapeless distress.

Then there was Michael, unsteadily at first, but hardening into as rigid a form as I had ever received:

"It *is* war. Some day I'll kill them for what they've done to Katherine."

After that there was nothing for an hour or more. We did our rather unconvincing best to soothe and reassure Petra. She understood little of what had passed between us, but she had caught the intensity and that had been enough to frighten her.

Then there was Sally again; dully, miserably forcing herself to it:

"Katherine had admitted it; confessed. I have confirmed it. They would have forced me to it, too, in the end. I——" she hesitated, wavering. "I couldn't face it. Not the hot irons; not for nothing, when she had told them. I couldn't . . . forgive me, all of you . . . forgive us both . . ." She broke off again.

Michael came in unsteadily, anxiously, too.

"Sally, dear, of course we're not blaming you—either of you. We understand. But we must know what you've told them. How much do they know?"

"About thought-shapes—and David and Rosalind. They were nearly sure about them, but they wanted it confirmed."

"Petra, too?"

"Yes. . . . Oh, oh, oh . . . !" There was an unshaped surge of remorse. "We had to—poor little Petra—but they know, really. It was the only reason that David and Rosalind would have taken her with them. No lie would cover it."

"Anyone else?"

"No. We've told them that there isn't anyone else. I think they believe it. They are still asking questions. Trying to understand more about it. They want to know how we make thought-shapes, and what the range is. I'm telling them lies. Not more than five miles, I'm saying, and pretending it's not at all easy to understand thought-shapes even that far away. . . . Katherine's barely conscious. She can't send to you. But they keep on asking us both questions, on and on. . . . If you could see what they've done to her . . . oh, Katherine, darling . . . her feet, Michael—oh, her poor, poor feet . . ."

Sally's patterns clouded in anguish, and then faded away.

Nobody else came in. I think we were all too deeply hurt and shocked. Words have to be chosen, and then interpreted; but thought-shapes you feel, inside you. . . .

The sun was low and we were beginning to pack up when Michael made contact again.

"Listen to me," he told us. "They're taking this very seriously indeed. They're badly alarmed over us. Usually if a Deviation gets clear of a district they let him go. Nobody can settle anywhere without proofs of identity or a very thorough examination by the local Inspector, so he's pretty well bound to end up in the Fringes, anyway. But what's got them so agitated about us is that nothing shows. We've been living among them for nearly twenty years and they didn't suspect it. We could pass for normal anywhere. So a proclamation has been posted describing the three of you and officially classifying you as deviants. That means that you are non-human and therefore not entitled to any of the rights or protections of human society. Anyone who assists you in any way is committing a criminal act; and anyone concealing knowledge of your whereabouts is also liable to punishment.

"In effect, it makes you outlaws. Anyone may shoot you on sight without penalty. There is a small reward if your deaths are reported and confirmed; but there is a very much larger reward for you if you are taken alive."

There was a pause while we took that in.

"I don't understand," said Rosalind. "If we were to promise to go away and stay away . . . ?"

"They're afraid of us. They want to capture you and learn more about us—that's why there's the large reward. It isn't just a question of the true image, though that's the way they're making it appear. What they've seen is that we could be a real danger to them. Imagine if there were a lot more of us than there are, able to think together and plan and coordinate without all their machinery of words and messages. We could outwit them all the time. They find that a very unpleasant thought, so we are to be stamped out before there can be any more of us. They see it as a matter of survival, and they may be right you know."

"Are they going to kill Sally and Katherine?"

That was an incautious question which slipped from Rosalind. We waited for a response from either of the two girls. There was none. We could not tell what that meant; they might simply have closed their minds again, or be sleeping from exhaustion, or perhaps dead already. . . . Michael thought not.

"There's little reason for that when they have them safely in their hands: it would very likely raise a lot of ill-feeling. To declare a new-born baby as non-human on its physical defects is one thing; but this is a lot more delicate. It isn't going to be easy for people who have known them for years to accept the non-human verdict at all. If they were to be killed, it would make a lot of people feel uneasy and uncertain about the authorities—much the same way as a retrospective law does."

"But *we* can be killed quite safely?" Rosalind commented, with some bitterness.

"You aren't already captives, and you aren't among people who know you. To strangers you are just non-humans on the run."

There was not much one could say to that. Michael asked:

"Which way are you traveling tonight?"

"Still southwest," I told him. "We had thought of trying to find some place to stop in Wild Country, but now that any hunter is licensed to shoot us, we shall have to go on into the Fringes, I think."

"That'd be best. If you can find a place to hide-up there for a bit we'll see if we can't fake your deaths. I'll try to think of some way. Tomorrow I shall be with a search party that's going southeast. I'll let you know what it's doing. Meanwhile, if you run into anyone make sure that you shoot first."

On that we broke off. Rosalind finished packing up, and we arranged the gear to make the panniers more comfortable than they had been the previous night. Then we climbed up, I on the left again, Petra and Rosalind together in the right-hand basket this time. Rosalind reached back to give a thump on the huge flank, and we moved ponderously forward once more. Petra, who had been unusually subdued during the packing up, burst into tears, and radiated distress.

She did not, it emerged from her snuffles, want to go to the Fringes, her mind was sorely troubled by thoughts of Old Maggie, and Hairy Jack and his family and the other ominous nursery-threat characters said to lurk in those regions.

It would have been easier to pacify her had we not ourselves suffered from quite a residue of childhood apprehensions, or had we been able to advance some real idea of the region to set against its morbid reputation. As it was, we, like most people, knew too little of it to be convincing, and had to go on suffering her distress again. Admittedly it was less intense than it had been on former occasions, and experience did now enable us to put up more of a barrier against it; nevertheless, the effect was wearing. Fully half an hour passed before Rosalind succeeded in soothing away the obliterating hullabaloo. When she had, the others came in anxiously, Michael inquiring, with irritation:

"What was it this time?"

We explained.

Michael dropped his irritability, and turned his attention to Petra herself. He began telling her in slow clear thought-forms how the Fringes weren't really the bogey place that people pretended. Most of the men and women who lived there were just unfortunate and unhappy. They had been taken away from their homes, often when they were babies, or some of them who were older had had to run away from their homes simply because they didn't look like other people, and they had to live in the Fringes because there was nowhere else people would leave them alone. Some of them did look very queer and funny indeed, but they couldn't help that. It was a thing to be sorry, not frightened, about. If we had happened to have extra fingers or ears by mistake we should have been sent to the Fringes—although we should be just the same people inside as we were now. What people looked like didn't really matter a great deal, one could soon get used to it, and——

But at about this stage Petra interrupted him.

"Who is the other one?" she inquired.

"What other one? What do you mean?" he asked her.

"The somebody else who's making think-pictures all mixed up with yours," she told him.

There was a pause. I opened right out, but could not detect any thought-shapes at all. Then:

"I get nothing," came from Michael, and Mark and Deborah, too. "It must be——"

There was an impetuous strong sign from Petra. In words, it would have been an impatient "Shut up!" We subsided, and waited.

I glanced over at the other pannier. Rosalind had one arm around Petra, and was looking down at her attentively. Petra herself had her eyes shut, as though all her attention were on listening. Presently she relaxed a little.

"What is it?" Rosalind asked her.

Petra opened her eyes. Her reply was puzzled, and not very clearly shaped. "Somebody asking questions. She's a long way, a very long, long way away,

I think. She says she's had my afraid-thoughts before. She wants to know who I am, and where I am. Shall I tell her?"

There was a moment's caution. Then Michael inquiring with a touch of excitement whether we approved. We did.

"All right, Petra. Go ahead and tell her," he agreed.

"I shall have to be very loud. She's such a long way away." Petra warned us.

It was as well she did. If she had let it rip while our minds were wide open she'd have blistered them. I closed mine and tried to concentrate my attention on the way ahead of us. It helped, but it was by no means a thorough defense. The shapes were simple, as one would expect of Petra's age, but they still reached me with a violence and brilliance which dazzled and deafened me.

There was the equivalent of "Phew" from Michael when it let up; closely followed by the repeated equivalent of "Shut up!" from Petra. A pause, and then another briefly blinding interlude. When that subsided:

"Where is she?" inquired Michael.

"Over there," Petra told him.

"For goodness' sake——"

"She's pointing southwest," I explained.

"Did you ask her the name of the place, darling?" Rosalind inquired.

"Yes, but it didn't mean anything except that there were two parts of it and a lot of water," Petra told her, in words and obscurely. "She doesn't understand where I am, either."

Rosalind suggested:

"Tell her to spell it out in letter-shapes."

"But I can't read letters," Petra objected, tearfully.

"Oh, dear, that's awkward," Rosalind admitted. "But at least we can send. I'll give you the letter-shapes one by one, and you can think them on to her. How about that?"

Petra agreed, doubtfully, to try.

"Good," said Rosalind. "Look out, everybody! Here we go again."

She pictured an "L." Petra relayed it with devastating force. Rosalind followed up with an "A" and so on, until the word was complete. Petra told us:

"She understands, but she doesn't know where Labrador is. She says she'll try to find out. She wants to send us her letter-shapes, but I said it's no good."

"But it *is*, darling. You get them from her, then you show them to us—only gently, so that we can read them."

Presently we got the first one. It was "Z." We were disappointed.

"What on earth's that?" everyone inquired at once.

"She's got it back to front. It must be 'S,' " Michael decided.

"It's not 'S,' it's 'Z,' " Petra insisted, tearfully.

"Never mind them. Just go on," Rosalind told her.

The rest of the word built up.

"Well, the others are proper letters," Michael admitted. "Sealand—it must be——"

"*Not* 'S,' it's 'Z,'" repeated Petra, obstinately.

"But, darling, 'Z' doesn't mean anything. Now, Sealand obviously means a land in the sea."

"If that helps," I said doubtfully. "According to my uncle Axel there's a lot more sea than anyone would think possible."

At that point everything was blotted out by Petra conversing indignantly with the unknown. She finished to announce triumphantly: "It *is* 'Z.' She says it's different from 'S'; like the noise a bee makes."

"All right," Michael told her, pacifically, "but ask her if there is a lot of sea."

Petra came back shortly with:

"Yes. There are two parts of it, with lots of sea all around. From where she is you can see the sun shining on it for miles and miles and it's all blue——"

"In the middle of the night?" said Michael. "She's crazy."

"But it isn't night where she is. She showed me," Petra said. "It's a place with lots and lots of houses, different from Waknuk houses, and much, much bigger. And there are funny carts without horses running along the roads. And things in the air, with whizzing things on top of them——"

I was jolted to recognize the picture from the childhood dreams that I had almost forgotten. I broke in, repeating it more clearly than Petra had shown it—a fish-shaped thing, all white and shiny.

"Yes—like that," Petra agreed.

"There's something very queer about this, altogether," Michael put in. David, how on earth did you know——"

I cut him short.

"Let Petra get all she can now," I suggested. "We can sort it out later."

So again we did our best to put up a barrier between ourselves and the apparently one-sided exchange that Petra was conducting in an excited fortissimo.

We made slow progress through the forest. We were anxious not to leave traces on the rides and tracks, so that the going was poor. As well as keeping our bows ready for use we had to be alert enough not to have them swept out of our hands, and to crouch low beneath overhanging branches ourselves. The risk of meeting men was not great, but there was the chance encountering of some hunting beast. Luckily, when we did hear one it was invariably in a hurry to get away. Possibly the bulk of the greathorses was discouraging; if so, it was, at least, one advantage we could set against the distinctive spoor behind us.

The summer nights are not long in those parts. We kept on plodding until there were signs of dawn and then found another glade to rest in. There would have been too much risk in unsaddling the horses. The heavy pack-saddles and panniers would have had to be hoisted off by a pulley on a branch, and that would deprive us of any chance of a quick getaway. We simply had to hobble the horses, as on the previous day.

While we ate our food I talked to Petra about the things her friend had shown her. The more she told me, the more excited I became. Almost everything fitted in with the dreams I had had as a small boy. It was like a sudden inspiration to know that the place must really exist, that I had not simply been dreaming of the ways of the Old People, but that it really was in being now, somewhere in the world. However, Petra was tired, so that I did not question her as much as I would have liked to just then, but let her and Rosalind get to sleep.

Just after sunrise Michael came through in some agitation.

"They've picked up your trail, David. That man Rosalind shot—his dog found him, and they came across the greathorse tracks. Our lot is turning back to the southwest to join in the hunt. You'd better push on. Where are you now?"

All I could tell him was that we had calculated we must be within a few miles of Wild Country by this time.

"Then get moving," he told me. "The longer you delay the more time they'll have to get a party ahead to cut you off."

It sounded like good advice. I woke Rosalind, and explained. Ten minutes later we were on our way again, with Petra still more than half asleep. With speed now more important than concealment we kept on the first southward track that we found, and urged the horses to a ponderous trot.

The way wound somewhat with the lie of the land, but its general direction was right. We followed it for fully ten miles without trouble of any kind, but then, as we rounded a corner, we came face to face with a horseman trotting toward us barely fifty yards ahead.

CHAPTER THIRTEEN

THE MAN cannot have had a moment's doubt who we were, for even as he saw us he dropped his reins and snatched his bow from his shoulder. Before he had a shaft on the string we had both loosed at him.

The motion of the greathorse was unfamiliar, and we both shot wide. He did better. His arrow passed between us, skinning our horse's head, Again I missed, but Rosalind's second shot took his horse in the chest. It reared, almost unseating him, then turned and started to bolt away ahead of us. It leapt sideways, catapulting the man into the bushes, and then sped off down the track as hard as it could go.

We passed the thrown man without checking. He cringed aside as the huge hoofs clumped by within a couple of feet of his head. At the next turn we looked back to see him sitting up, feeling his bruises. The least satisfactory part of the incident was that there was now a wounded riderless horse spreading an alarm ahead of us.

A couple of miles further on, the stretch of forest came to an abrupt end, and we found ourselves looking across a narrow, cultivated valley. There was about a mile and a half of open country before the trees began again on the far side. Most of the land was pasture, with sheep and cattle behind rail and post fences. One of the few arable fields was immediately to our left. The young crop there looked as if it might be oats, but it deviated to an extent which would have caused it to be burnt long ago at home.

The sight of it encouraged us, for it could only mean that we had reached almost to Wild Country where stock could not be kept pure.

The track led at a gentle slope down to a farm which was little better than a cluster of huts and sheds. In the open space among them which served for a yard we could see four or five women and a couple of men gathered round a horse. They were examining it, and we had little doubt what horse it was. Evidently it had only just arrived, and they were still arguing about it. We decided to go on, rather than give them time to arm and come in search of us.

So absorbed were they in their inspection of the horse that we had covered half the distance from the trees before any of them noticed us. Then one glanced up, and the rest, too, turned to stare. They could never have seen a greathorse before, and the sight of two bearing down upon them at a canter with a thunderous rumble of hoofbeats struck them momentarily rigid with astonishment. It was the horse in their midst that broke up the tableau; it reared, whinnied, and made off, scattering them.

There was no need to shoot. The whole group scuttled for the shelter of various doorways, and we pounded through their yard unmolested.

The track bore off to the left, but Rosalind held the greathorse on a straight line ahead, toward the next stretch of forest. The rails flew aside like twigs, and we kept on at a lumbering canter across the fields, leaving a trail of broken fences behind us.

At the edge of the trees, I looked back. The people at the farm emerged from shelter and stood gesticulating and staring after us.

Three or four miles further on we came out into more open country, but not like any region we had seen before. It was dotted with bushes, and brakes, and thickets. Most of the grass was coarse and large-leafed: in some places it was monstrous, growing into giant tufts where the sharp-edged blades stood eight or ten feet high.

We wound our way among them, keeping generally southwest, for another couple of hours. Then we pushed into a copse of queer, but fair-sized trees. It offered a good hiding place, and inside were several open spaces where there grew a more ordinary kind of grass which looked as if it might make suitable fodder. We decided to rest awhile there and sleep.

I hobbled the horses while Rosalind unrolled the blankets, and presently we were eating hungrily. It was pleasantly peaceful there until Petra put out one of her blinding communications so abruptly that I bit my tongue.

Rosalind screwed up her eyes, and put a hand to her head.

"For heaven's sake, child!" she protested.

"Sorry. I forgot," said Petra perfunctorily.

She sat with her head a little on one side for a minute, then she told us:

"She wants to talk to one of you. She says will you all try to hear her while she thinks her loudest."

"All right," we agreed, "but you keep quiet, or you'll blind us."

I tried my very hardest, straining sensitivity to its utmost, but there was nothing—or as near nothing as the shimmer of a heat-haze.

We relaxed again.

"No good," I said, "you'll have to tell her we can't reach her, Petra. Look out, everyone."

We did our best to damp out the exchange they followed, then Petra brought down the force of her thoughts below the dazzle level, and started to relay those she was receiving. They had to be in very simple form so that she could copy them even when she did not understand them; they reached us rather like baby-talk, and with many repeats to make sure that we grasped them. It is scarcely possible to give any idea in words of the way it came across, but it was the over-all impression that mattered, and that reached us clearly enough.

The urgent emphasis was on importance—the importance not of us, but of Petra. At all costs she must be protected. Such a power of projection as she had was unheard-of without special training—she was a discovery of the utmost value. Help was already on the way, but until it could reach us we must play for time and safety—Petra's safety, it seemed, not our own—at all costs.

There was quite a lot more that was less clear, muddled up with it, but that main point was quite unmistakable.

"Did you get it?" I asked of the others, when it had finished.

They had. Michael responded: "This is very confusing. There is no doubt that Petra's power of projection is remarkable, compared with ours, anyway, but what she seemed to me to be putting across was that she was particularly surprised to find it among primitive people, did you notice that? It looked almost as if she were meaning us."

"She was," confirmed Rosalind. "Not a shadow of doubt about it."

"There must be some misunderstanding," I put in. "Probably Petra somehow gave her the impression we were Fringes people. As for——" I was suddenly blotted out for a moment by Petra's indignant denial. I did my best to disregard it, and went on: "As for help, there must be a misunderstanding there, too. She's somewhere southwest, and everybody knows that there are miles and miles of Badlands that way. Even if they do come to an end and she's on the other side of them, how can she possibly help?"

Rosalind refused to argue about that.

"Let's wait and find out," she suggested. "Just now, all I want is sleep."

I felt the same way, and since Petra had slept most of the time in the pannier, we told her to keep a sharp lookout and wake us at once if she heard or saw anything suspicious. Both Rosalind and I fell asleep almost before we laid our heads down.

I awoke with Petra shaking my shoulder, and saw that the sun was not far off setting.

"Michael," she explained.

I cleared my mind for him.

"They've picked up your trail again. A small farm on the edge of Wild Country. You galloped through it. Remember?"

I did. He went on:

"There's a party converging there now. They'll start to follow your tracks as soon as it's light. Better get moving soon. I don't know how it is in front of you, but there may be some men cutting across from the west to head you off. If there are, my bet is that they'll keep in smallish groups for the night. They can't risk a cordon of single sentries because there are known to be Fringes people scouting around. So, with luck, you should be able to sneak through."

"All right," I agreed wearily. Then a question I had meant to ask before occurred to me. "What's happened to Sally and Katherine?"

"I don't know. No answer. The range is getting rather long now. Does anyone know?"

Deborah came in, made faint by the distance.

"Katherine was unconscious. There's been nothing understandable since then. Mark and I are afraid." She faded, in a foggy reluctance to continue.

"Go on," Michael told her.

"Well, Katherine's been unconscious so long we're wondering if she's dead."

"And Sally?"

This time there was even more reluctance.

"We think—we're afraid something queer must have happened to her mind. There've been just one or two little jumbles from her. Very weak, not sensible at all, so we're afraid. . . ." She faded away, in great unhappiness.

There was a pause before Michael started with hard, harsh shapes.

"You understand what that means, David? They *are* afraid of us. Ready to break us down in the attempt to find out more about us, once they can catch us. You mustn't let them get hold of Rosalind or Petra—far better to kill them yourself than let that happen to them. You understand?"

I looked at Rosalind lying asleep beside me, the red of the sunset glistening on her hair, and I thought of the anguish we had felt from Katherine. The possibility of her and Petra suffering that made me shudder.

"Yes," I told him, and the others. "Yes, I understand."

I felt their sympathy and encouragement for a while, then there was nothing.

Petra was looking at me, more puzzled than alarmed. She asked earnestly, in words:

"Why did he say you must kill Rosalind and me?"

I pulled myself together.

"That was only if they catch us," I told her, trying to make it sound as if it were the sensible and usual course in such circumstances. She considered the prospect judicially, then:

"Why?" she asked.

"Well," I tried, "you see we're different from them because they can't

97

make thought-shapes, and when people are different, ordinary people are afraid of them."

"Why should they be afraid of us? We aren't hurting them," she broke in.

"I'm not sure that I know why," I told her. "But they are. It's a feel-thing not a think-thing. And the more stupid they are, the more like everyone else they think everyone ought to be. And once they get afraid they become cruel and want to hurt people who are different."

"Why?" inquired Petra.

"They just do. And they'd hurt us very much if they could catch us."

"I don't see why," Petra persisted.

"It's the way things work. It's complicated and rather nasty," I told her. "You'll understand better when you're older. But the thing is, we don't want you and Rosalind to be hurt. You remember when you spilt the boiling water on your foot? Well, it'd be much worse than that. Being dead's a lot better—it's sort of like being so much asleep that they can't get at you to hurt you at all."

I looked down at Rosalind, at the gentle rise and fall of her breasts as she slept. There was a vagrant wisp of hair on her cheek; I brushed it away gently and kissed her without waking her.

Presently Petra began:

"David, when you kill me and Rosalind——"

I put an arm around her. "Hush, darling. It isn't going to happen, because we aren't going to let them catch us. Now, let's wake her up, but we won't tell her about this. She might be worried, so we'll just keep it to ourselves for a secret, shall we?"

"All right," Petra agreed.

She tugged gently at Rosalind's hair.

We decided to eat again, and then push on when it was a little darker so that there would be stars to steer by. Petra was unwontedly silent over the meal. At first I thought she was brooding upon our recent conversation, but I was wrong, it appeared; after a time she emerged from her contemplations to say, conversationally:

"Zealand must be a funny place. Everybody there can make think-pictures—well, nearly everybody—and nobody wants to hurt anybody for doing it."

"Oh, you've been chatting while we were asleep, have you," remarked Rosalind. "I must say that makes it a lot more comfortable for us."

Petra ignored that. She went on:

"They aren't all of them very good at it, though; most of them are more like you and David," she told us kindly. "But she's much better at it than most of them, and she's got two babies and she thinks they will be good at it, only they're too little yet. But she doesn't think they'll be as good at it as me. She says I can make stronger think-pictures than anybody at all," she concluded, complacently.

"That doesn't surprise me one bit," Rosalind told her. "What you want to learn next is to make *good* think-pictures, instead of just noisy ones," she added, deflatingly.

Petra remained unabashed. "She says I'll get better still if I work at it, and then when I grow up I must have babies who can make strong think-pictures, too."

"Oh, you must, must you," said Rosalind. "Why? My impression of think-pictures up to now is that chiefly they bring trouble."

"Not in Zealand." Petra shook her head. "She says that everybody there *wants* to make them, and people who can't do it much work hard to get better at it."

We pondered that. I recalled Uncle Axel's tales about places beyond the Black Coasts where the Deviations thought that *they* were the true image, and anything else was a Mutant.

"*She* says," Petra amplified, "that people who can only talk with words have something missing. She says we ought to be sorry for them because however old they grow they'll never be able to understand one another much better. They'll have to be one-at-a-times always, never think-togethers."

"I can't say I feel very sorry for them at present," I remarked.

"Well, she says we ought to because they have to live very dull, stupid lives compared with think-picture people," Petra said, somewhat sententiously.

We let her prattle on. It was difficult to make sense of a lot of the things she said, and possibly she had not got them right, anyway, but the one thing that did stand out clearly was that these Zealanders, whoever and wherever they were, thought no small beans of themselves. It began to seem more than likely that Rosalind had been right when she had taken "primitive" to refer to ordinary Labrador people.

In clear starlight we set out again, still winding our way between clumps and thickets in a southwesterly direction. Out of respect for Michael's warning we were traveling as quietly as we could, with our eyes and ears alert for any signs of interception. For some miles there was nothing to be heard but the steady cushioned clumping of the greathorses' hoofs, slight creakings from the girths and panniers, and, occasionally, some small animal scuttling out of our way.

After three hours or more we began to perceive uncertainly a line of deeper darkness ahead, and presently the edge of more forest solidified to loom up like a black wall.

It was not possible in the shadow to tell how dense it was. The best course seemed to be to hold straight on until we came to it and then, if it turned out to be not easily penetrable, to work along the edge until we could find a suitable place to make an entrance.

We had come within a hundred yards of it when without any warning a gun went off to the rear, and shot whistled past us.

Both horses were startled, and plunged. I was all but flung out of my pannier. The rearing horses pulled away and the lead rope parted with a snap. The other horse bolted straight toward the forest, then thought better of it and swerved to the left. Ours pelted after it. There was nothing to be done but wedge oneself in the pannier and hang on as we tore along in a rain of clods and stones flung up by hoofs of the lead horse.

Somewhere behind us a gun fired again, and we speeded up still more. . . .
For a mile or more we hurtled on in a ponderous, earth-shaking gallop.
Then there was a flash ahead and half-left. At the sound of the shot our
horse sprang sideways in mid-stride, swerved right, and raced for the forest.
We crouched still lower in the baskets as we crashed among the trees.

By luck alone we made the entry at a point where the bigger trunks were
well separated, but, for all that, it was a nightmare ride, with branches
slapping and dragging at the panniers. The greathorse simply ploughed ahead,
avoiding the larger trees, thrusting through the rest, smashing its way by
sheer weight while branches and saplings cracked and snapped at the on-
slaught.

Inevitably the horse slowed down, but its panic determination to get
away from the guns abated very little. I had to brace with arms and legs and
whole body to avoid being battered to pieces in the pannier, scarcely daring
to raise my head even for a quick look lest a branch should knock it off.

I could not tell whether there was any pursuit, but it seemed improbable.
Not only was it darker under the trees, but a horse of ordinary size would
most likely have disembowelled itself in any attempt to follow over the
snapped-off stems standing up like stakes behind us.

The horse began to grow calmer; the pace and violence eased, as it started
to pick its way instead of crashing through. Presently the trees on our left
grew thinner. Rosalind, leaning out of her pannier, caught up the reins
again and urged the creature that way. We came out obliquely upon a
narrow open space where we could see the stars overhead again. Whether it
was an artificial track, or a natural opening was impossible to tell in the poor
light. We paused a moment wondering whether to risk it, then decided that
the easier going would offset the disadvantages of easier pursuit, and turned
southward along it. A crackling of branches to one side brought both of us
facing round, with bows ready, but it was only the other greathorse. It came
trotting out of the shadows with a whinny of pleasure, and fell into place
behind us as though the rope still held it.

The country was more broken now. The trail wound, taking us round out-
crops of rock, slanting down the sides of gullies to cross small streams.
Sometimes there were fairly open stretches, at others the trees met overhead.
Our progress was inevitably slow.

We must by now, we reckoned, be truly in the Fringes. Whether or not the
pursuit would risk following us any farther we could not tell. When we tried
to consult Michael there was no response, so we guessed he was asleep. It
was perplexing to know whether the time had not come when we ought to
get rid of the telltale greathorses—perhaps drive them on along the track
while we made off in a different direction on foot. The decision was difficult
to make without more information. It would be foolish to get rid of the
creatures unless we were sure that the pursuit would risk coming right into
Fringes country after us; but, if it did, it would gain on us quickly by making
a great deal faster time in daylight than we were making now. Moreover, we
were tired, and the prospect of starting to travel on foot was far from attrac-

tive. Once more we tried, and failed, to make contact with Michael. A moment later the choice was taken away from us.

We were at one of the stretches where the trees met above us, making a dark tunnel through which the horse chose its way slowly and carefully. Suddenly something dropped full on me, crushing me down in the pannier. I had no warning, no chance to use the bow. There was the weight jolting the breath out of me, then a shower of sparks in my head, and that was the end of it.

CHAPTER FOURTEEN

I CAME BACK SLOWLY, lingering for what seemed a long time only half-aware.

Rosalind was calling me, the real Rosalind, the one who dwelt inside, and showed herself too seldom. The other, the practical, capable one, was her own convincing creation, not herself. I had seen her begin to build it when she was a sensitive, fearful, yet determined child. She became aware by instinct, perhaps sooner than the rest of us, that she was in a hostile world, and deliberately equipped herself to face it. The armor had grown slowly, plate by plate. I had seen her find her weapons and become skilled with them, watched her construct a character so thoroughly and wear it so constantly that for spells she almost deceived herself.

I loved the girl one could see. I loved her tall slim shape, the poise of her neck, her small, pointed breasts, her long slim legs; and the way she moved, and the sureness of her hands, and her lips when she smiled. I loved the bronze-gold hair that felt like heavy silk in one's hand, her satin-skinned shoulders, her velvet cheeks and the warmth of her body, and the scent of her breath.

All these were easy to love—too easy; anyone must love them.

They needed her defenses: the crust of independence and indifference; the air of practical, decisive reliability; the unroused interest; the aloof manner. The qualities were not intended to endear, and at times they could hurt, but no one who had seen the how and why of them could admire them, if only as a triumph of art over nature.

But now it was the under-Rosalind calling gently, forlornly, all armor thrown aside, the heart naked.

And again there are no words.

Words exist that can, used by a poet, achieve a dim monochrome of the body's love, but beyond that they fail clumsily.

My love flowed out to her, hers back to me. Mine stroked and soothed. Hers caressed. The distance—and the difference—between us dwindled and vanished. We could meet, mingle, and blend. Neither one of us existed any more; for a time there was a single being that was both. There was escape from the solitary cell; brief symbiosis, sharing all the world. . . .

No one else knew the hidden Rosalind. Even Michael and the rest caught only glimpses of her. They did not know at what cost the overt Rosalind had been wrought. None of them knew my dear, tender Rosalind longing for escape, gentleness, and love; grown afraid now of what she had built for her own protection, yet more afraid still, of facing life without it.

Duration is nothing. Perhaps it was only for an instant we were together again. The importance of a point is in its existence; it has no dimensions.

Then we were apart, and I was becoming aware of mundane things: a dim gray sky, considerable discomfort, and, presently, Michael, anxiously inquiring what had happened to me. With an effort I raked my wits together.

"I don't know. Something hit me," I told him, "but I think I'm all right now, except that my head aches, and I'm damned uncomfortable."

It was only as I replied that I perceived why I was so uncomfortable. I was still in the pannier, but sort of folded into it, and the pannier itself was still in motion.

Michael did not find that very informative. He applied to Rosalind.

"They jumped down on us from overhanging branches. Four or five of them. One landed right on top of David," she explained.

"They?" asked Michael.

"Fringes people," she told him.

I was relieved. It had occurred to me that we might have been outflanked by the others. I was on the point of asking what was happening now when Michael inquired, "Was it you they fired at last night?"

I admitted that we had been fired at, but there might have been other firing for all I know.

"No. Only one lot," he told us, with disappointment. "I hoped they'd made a mistake and were on a false trail. We've been called together. They think it's too risky to come farther into the Fringes in small groups. We're supposed to be all assembled to move off in four hours or so from now. Round about a hundred they reckon. They've decided that if we do meet any Fringes people and give them a good hiding it'll save trouble later on, anyway. You'd better get rid of those greathorses now, you'll never cover your trail while you have them."

"A bit late for advice," Rosalind told him. "I'm in a pannier on the first horse with my thumbs tied together, and David's all tied up in a pannier on the second."

I tried to move again, and realized for the first time what was wrong, and why I couldn't.

"Where's Petra?" asked Michael anxiously.

"Oh, she's all right. She's in the other pannier of this horse, fraternizing with the man in charge."

"What happened, exactly?" Michael demanded.

"Well, first they dropped on us and then a lot more came out of the trees and steadied up the horses. They made us get down and lifted David down. Then when they'd talked and argued for a bit, they decided to get rid of us. So they loaded us into the panniers again, like this, and put a man on each horse and sent us on, the same way we'd been going."

"Further into the Fringes, that is?"

"Yes."

"Well, at least that's the best direction," Michael commented, "What's the attitude? Threatening?"

"Oh, no. They're just being careful we don't run off. They seemed to have some idea who we were, but weren't quite sure what to do with us. They argued a bit over that, but they were much more interested in the greathorses really, I think. The man on this horse seems to be quite harmless. He's talking to Petra with an odd sort of earnestness. I'm not sure he isn't a little simple."

"Can you find out what they're intending to do with you?"

"I did ask, but I don't think he knows. He's just been told to take us somewhere."

"Well——" Michael seemed at a loss for once. "Well, I suppose all we can do is wait and see, but it'll do no harm to let him know we'll be coming after you."

He left it at that for the moment.

I struggled and wriggled round. My wrists were tied together behind my back, but my feet were free, and with some difficulty I managed to get on to them at last and stand up in the swaying basket. The man in the other pannier looked around at me quite amiably.

"Whoa, there!" he said to the greathorse, and reined in.

I was able to see our surroundings now. It was broken country, no longer thick forest, though well wooded, and even a first look at it assured me that my father had been right about normality being mocked in these parts. I could scarcely identify a single tree with certainty. There were familiar trunks supporting the wrong shape of tree: familiar types of branches growing out of the wrong kind of bark, and bearing the wrong kinds of leaves. For a while our view to the left was cut off by a fantastically woven fence of immense bramble trunks with spines as big as shovels. In another place a stretch of ground looked like a dried out riverbed full of large pebbles, but the pebbles turned out to be globular fungi set as close together as they could grow. There were trees with trunks too soft to stand upright so that they looped over and grew along the ground. Here and there were patches of miniature trees, shrunk and gnarled, and looking centuries old.

I glanced surreptitiously again at the man in the other pannier. There didn't seem to be anything wrong with him except that he was very dirty, as were his ragged clothes and crumpled hat. He caught my eye on him.

"Never been in the Fringes before, boy?" he asked.

"No," I told him. "Is it all like this?"

He grinned, and shook his head.

"None of it's like any other part. That's why the Fringes is the Fringes; pretty near nothing grows true to stock here, yet."

"Yet?" I repeated.

"Sure. It'll settle down though, in time. Wild Country was Fringes once, but it's steadier now; likely the parts you come from were Wild Country once, but they've settled down more. God's little game of patience I reckon it is, but he certainly takes his time over it."

"God?" I said doubtfully. "They've always taught us that it's the Devil that rules in the Fringes."

He shook his head.

"That's what they tell you over there. 'Tisn't so, boy. It's your parts where the old Devil's hanging on and looking after his own. Arrogant, they are. The true image, and all. . . . Want to be like the Old People. Tribulation hasn't taught 'em a thing. . . .

"The Old People thought *they* were the tops, too. Had ideals, they did; knew just how the world ought to be run. All they had to do was get it fixed up comfortable, and keep it that way, then everybody'd be fine, on account of their ideas being a lot more civilized than God's."

He shook his head.

"Didn't work out, boy. Couldn't work out. They weren't God's last word like they thought. God doesn't have any last word. If he did he'd be dead. But he isn't dead; and he changes and grows, like everything else that's alive. So when they were doing their best to get everything fixed and tidy on some kind of eternal lines they'd thought up for themselves, he sent along Tribulation to bust it up and remind 'em that life is change.

"He saw it wasn't going to come out the way things lay, so he shuffled the pack to see if it wouldn't give a better break next time."

He paused to consider that a moment, and went on:

"Maybe he didn't shuffle quite enough. The same sequences seem to have got kind of stuck together some places. Parts where you come from, for instance. There they are, still on the same lines, still reckoning they're the last word, still trying their damnedest to stay as they are and fix up just the same state of affairs that brought Tribulation last time. One day He's going to get pretty tired of the way they can't learn a lesson, and start showing them another trick or two."

"Oh," I said, vaguely, but safely. It was odd, I felt, how many people seemed to have positive, if conflicting, information upon God's views.

The man did not seem altogether satisfied that he had got his point home. He waved his hand at the deviational landscape about us, and I suddenly noticed his own irregularity—the right hand lacked the first three fingers.

"Some day," he proclaimed, "something is going to steady down out of all this. It'll be new, and new kinds of plants mean new creatures. Tribulation was a shake-up to give us a new start."

"But where they can make the stock breed true, they destroy Deviations," I pointed out.

"They try to, they think they do," he agreed. "They're pigheadedly determined to keep the Old People's standards. But do they? Can they? How do you *know* that their crops and their fruit and their vegetables are just the same? Aren't there disputes? And doesn't it nearly always turn out that the breed with the higher yield is accepted in the end? Aren't cattle cross-bred to get hardiness, or milk-yield, or meat? Sure, they can wipe out the obvious Deviations, but are you sure that the Old People would recognize any of the present breeds at all? I'm not, by any means. You can't stop it, you see. You can be obstructive and destructive, and you can slow it all up and distort it for your own ends, but somehow it just keeps on happening. Just look at these horses."

"They're government-approved," I told him.

"Sure. That's just what I mean," he said.

"But if it keeps on anyway, I don't see why there had to be Tribulation," I objected.

"For other forms it keeps on changing," he said, "but not for man, not for kinds like the Old People and your people, if they can help it. They stamp on any change. They close the way and keep the type fixed because they've got the arrogance to think themselves perfect. As they reckon it, they and only they are the true image; very well, then it follows that if the image *is* true, they themselves must be God, and being God they reckon themselves entitled to decree, 'Thus far, and no farther.' That is their great sin: they try to strangle the life out of Life."

There was an air about the last few sentences, rather out of keeping with the rest, which caused me to suspect I had encountered some kind of creed once more. I decided to shift the conversation on to a more practical plane by inquiring why we had been taken prisoner.

He did not seem very sure about that, except to assure me that it was always done when any stranger was found entering Fringes territory.

I thought that over, and then got into touch with Michael again.

"What do you suggest we tell them?" I asked. "I imagine there'll be an examination. When they find we're physically normal we shall have to give some reason for being on the run."

"Best to tell them the truth, only minimize it. Play it right down the way Katherine and Sally did. Just let them know enough to account for it," he suggested.

"Very well," I agreed. "Do you understand that, Petra? You tell them you can just make think-pictures to Rosalind and me. Nothing about Michael, or Zealand people."

"The Zealand people are coming to help. They're not so far away as they were, now," she told us confidently.

Michael received that with skepticism. "All very nice—*if* they can. But don't mention them."

"All right," Petra agreed.

We discussed whether we would tell our two guards about the intended pursuit, and decided it would do no harm.

The man in the other pannier showed no surprise at the news.

"Good. That'll suit us," he said. But he explained no further, and we plodded steadily on.

Petra began to converse with her distant friend again, and there was no doubt that the distance was less. Petra did not have to use such disturbing force to reach her, and for the first time I was able by straining hard to catch bits of the other side of the exchange. Rosalind caught it, too. She put out a question as strongly as she could. The unknown strengthened her projection and came to us clearly, pleased to have made contact, and anxious to know more than Petra could tell.

Rosalind explained what she could of our present situation, and that we did not seem to be in immediate danger. The other advised:

"Be cautious. Agree to whatever they say, and play for time. Be emphatic about the danger you are in from your own people. It is difficult to advise you without knowing the tribe. Some deviational tribes detest the appearance of normality. It can't do any harm to exaggerate how different you are *inside* from your own people. The really important matter is the little girl. Keep her safe at all costs. We have never before known such a power of projection in one so young. What is her name?"

Rosalind spelled it out in letter forms. Then she asked:

"But who are you? What is this Zealand?"

"We are the New People—your kind of people. The people who can think-together. We're the people who are going to build a new kind of world —different from the Old People's world, and from the savages'. "

"The kind of people that God intended, perhaps?" I inquired, with a feeling of being on familiar ground again.

"I don't know about that. Who does? But we do know that we can make a better world than the Old People did. They were only ingenious half-humans, little better than savages; all living shut off from one another, with only clumsy words to link them. Emotions they could sometimes share, but they could not think collectively. When their conditions were primitive they could get along all right, as the animals can; but the more complex they made their world, the less capable they were of dealing with it. They had no means of consensus. They learnt to cooperate constructively in small units; but only destructively in large units. They aspired greedily, and then refused to face the responsibilities they had created. They created vast problems, and then buried their heads in the sands of idle faith. There was, you see, no real communication, no understanding between them. They could, at their best, be near-sublime animals, but not more.

"They could never have succeeded. If they had not brought down Tribulation which all but destroyed them, then they would have bred with the carelessness of animals until they had reduced themselves to poverty and misery, and ultimately to starvation and barbarism. One way or another they were foredoomed because they were an inadequate species."

It occurred to me again that these Zealanders had no little opinion of themselves. To one brought up as I had been this irreverence for the Old People was difficult to take. While I was still wrestling with it Rosalind asked:

"But you? Where do you come from?"

"Our ancestors had the good fortune to live on an island—or, rather, two islands—somewhat secluded. They did not escape Tribulation and its effects even there, though it was less violent there than in most places, but they were cut off from the rest of the world, and sank back almost to barbarism. Then, somehow, the strain of people who could think-together began. In time, those who were able to do it best found others who could do it a little, and taught them to develop it. It was natural for the people who could share thoughts to tend to marry one another, so that the strain was strengthened.

"Later on, they started to discover thought-shape makers in other places, too. That was when they began to understand how fortunate they had been; they found that even in places where physical deviations don't count for much people who have think-together are usually persecuted.

"For a long time nothing could be done to help the same kind of people in other places—though some tried to sail to Zealand in canoes, and sometimes they got there—but later, when we had machines again, we were able to fetch some of them to safety. Now we try to do that whenever we make contact, but we have never before made contact at anything like this distance. It is still a strain for me to reach you. It will get easier, but I shall have to stop now. Look after the little girl. She is unique and tremendously important. Protect her at all costs."

The thought patterns faded away, leaving nothing for a moment. Then Petra came in. Whatever she may have failed to make of the rest, she had caught the last part all right.

"That's me," she proclaimed, with satisfaction and totally unnecessary vigor.

We rocked, and recovered.

"Beware, odious smug child. We haven't met Hairy Jack yet," Rosalind told her, with subduing effect. "Michael," she added, "did all that reach you, too?"

"Yes," Michael responded with a touch of reserve. "Condescending, I thought. Sounded as if she were lecturing to children. Still coming from a devil of a long way away, too. I don't see how they can come fast enough to be any help at all. We shall be starting after you in a few minutes now."

The greathorses clumped steadily on. The landscape was disturbing and alarming to one brought up in respect for the property of forms. Certainly, few things were as fantastic as the growths that Uncle Axel had told of in the South; on the other hand, practically nothing was comfortably familiar, or even orthodox. There was so much confusion that it did not seem to matter any more whether a particular tree was an aberrate or just a miscegenate, but it was a relief to get away from trees and out into open country for a bit, though even there the bushes weren't homogeneal or identifiable, and the grass was pretty queer, too.

We stopped only once for food and drink, and for no more than half an hour before we were on our way again. Two hours or so later, after several more stretches of woodlands, we reached a medium-sized river. On our side the level ground descended in a sharp, steep bank to the water; on the other stood a line of low, reddish cliffs.

We turned downstream, keeping along the top of the bank. A quarter of a mile along, at a place marked by a grossly deviational tree shaped like a huge wooden pear, and with all its branches growing in one big tuft at the top, a runnel cut well back into the bank and made a way for the horses to get down. We forded the river obliquely, making for a gap in the opposite cliffs. When we reached it, it turned out to be little more than a cleft, so narrow in some places that the panniers scraped both walls, and we could scarely squeeze through. There was quite a hundred yards of it before the way widened and began to slope up to normal ground level.

Where the sides diminished to mere banks, seven or eight men stood with bows in their hands. They gaped incredulously at the greathorses, and looked half-inclined to run. Abreast of them, we stopped.

The man in the other pannier scrambled on to the saddle and leaned down to cut the cord on my wrists with a long knife.

"Down you get, boy," he told me.

Petra and Rosalind were already climbing down from the leading great-horse. As I reached the ground the driver gave a thump and both greathorses moved on with stately ponderousness. Petra clasped my hand nervously, but for the moment all the ragged, unkempt bowmen were still more interested in the horses than in us.

There was nothing immediately alarming about the group. One of the hands which held a bow had six fingers; one man displayed a head like a polished brown egg, without a hair on it, or on his face; another had immensely large feet and hands; but whatever was wrong with the rest was hidden under their rags.

Rosalind and I shared a feeling of relief at not being confronted with the kinds of grotesquerie we had half-expected. Petra, too, was encouraged to find that none of them fulfilled the traditional description of Hairy Jack. Presently, when they had watched the horses out of sight up a track that disappeared among trees, they turned their attention to us. A couple of them told us to come along, the rest remained where they were.

A well-used path led downward through woods for a few hundred yards, and then gave on to a clearing. On the right ran a wall of the reddish cliffs again, not more than forty feet high. They appeared to be the reverse side of the ridge which retained the river, and the whole face was pocked by numerous holes, with ladders, roughly made of branches, leading to the higher openings.

The level ground in front was littered with crude huts and tents. One or two small cooking fires smoked among them. A few tattered men and a rather larger number of slatternly-looking women moved around with no great activity.

We wound our way among hovels and refuse-heaps until we reached the largest of the tents. It appeared to be an old rick-cover—the loot, presumably, of some raid—fastened over a framework of lashed poles. A figure seated on a stool just inside the entrance looked up as we approached. The sight of his face jolted me with panic for a moment—it was so like my father's. Then I recognized him—the same "spider-man" I had seen as a captive at Waknuk, seven or eight years before.

The two men who had brought us pushed us forward, in front of him. He looked the three of us over. His eyes traveled up and down Rosalind's slim straight figure in a way I did not care for—nor she, either. Then he studied me more carefully, and nodded to himself, as if satisfied over something.

"Remember me?" he asked.

"Yes," I told him.

He shifted his gaze from my face. He let it stray over the conglomeration of hutches and shacks, and then back again to me.

"Not much like Waknuk," he said.

"Not much," I agreed.

He paused quite lengthily, in contemplation. Then:

"Know who I am?" he inquired.

"I think so. I think I found out," I told him.

He raised an eyebrow, questioningly.

"My father had an elder brother," I said. "He was thought to be normal until he was about three or four years old. Then his certificate was revoked, and he was sent away."

He nodded slowly.

"But not *quite* right," he said. "His mother loved him. His nurse was fond of him, too. So when they came to take him away he was already missing— but they'd hush that up, of course. They'd hush the whole thing up, pretend it never happened." He paused again, reflectively. Presently he added, "The eldest son. The heir. Waknuk should be mine. It would be, except for *this*." He stretched out his long arm, and regarded it for a moment. Then he dropped it and looked at me again.

"Do you know what the length of a man's arm should be?"

"No," I admitted.

"Nor do I. But somebody in Rigo does, some expert on the true image. So, no Waknuk, and I must live like a savage among savages. Are you the eldest son?"

"The only son," I told him. "There was a younger one, but——"

"No certificate, eh?"

I nodded.

"So you, too, have lost Waknuk!"

That aspect of things had never troubled me. I do not think I had ever had any real expectation of inheriting Waknuk. There had always been the sense of insecurity, the expectation, almost the certainty, that one day I should be discovered. I had lived too long with that expectation to feel the resentment that embittered him. Now that it was resolved, I was glad to be safely away, and I told him so. It did not please him. He looked at me thoughtfully.

"You've not the guts to fight for what's yours by right?" he suggested.

"If it's yours by right, it can't be mine by right," I pointed out. "But my meaning was that I've had more than enough of living in hiding."

"We all live in hiding here," he said.

"Maybe," I told him. "But you can be your own selves. You don't have to live a pretense. You don't have to watch yourselves every moment, and think twice whenever you open your mouths."

He nodded slowly.

"We heard about you. We have our ways," he said. "What I don't understand is why they are after you in such strength."

"We think," I explained, "that we worry them more than the usual deviants because they've no way of identifying us. I fancy they must be suspecting that there are a lot more of us that they haven't discovered, and they want to get hold of us to make us tell."

"And even more than usually good reason for not being caught," he said.

I was aware that Michael had come in and that Rosalind was answering him, but I could not attend to two conversations at once, so I left that to her.

"So they are coming right into the Fringes after you? How many of them?" he asked.

"I'm not sure," I said, considering how to play our hand to the best advantage.

"From what I've heard, you should have ways of finding out," he said.

I wondered how much he did know about us, and whether he knew about Michael, too, but that seemed unlikely. With his eyes a little narrowed, he went on:

"It'll be better not to fool with us, boy. It's you they're after, and you've brought trouble this way with you. Why should we care what happens to you? Quite easy to put one of you where they'd find you."

Petra caught the implication of that, and panicked.

"More than a hundred men," she said.

He turned a thoughtful eye on her for a moment.

"So there *is* one of you with them—I rather thought there might be," he observed, and nodded again. "A hundred men is a great many to send after just you three. Too many. . . . I see. . . ." He turned back to me. "There will have been rumors lately about trouble working up in the Fringes?"

"Yes," I admitted.

He grinned.

"So it comes in handy. For the first time they decide that they will take the initiative, and invade us—and pick you up, too, of course. They'll be following your trail, naturally. How far have they got?"

I consulted Michael, and learned that the main body had still some miles to go before they would join the party that had fired on us and bolted the greathorses. The difficulty then was to find a way of conveying the position intelligently to the man in front of me. He appreciated that, and did not seem greatly perturbed.

"Is your father with them?" he asked.

That was a question which I had been careful not to put to Michael before. I did not put it now. I simply paused for a moment, and then told him "No." Out of the corner of my eye I noticed Petra about to speak and felt Rosalind pounce on her.

"A pity," said the spidery man. "It's quite a time now I've been hoping that one day I'd meet your father on equal terms. From what I've heard I should have thought he'd be there. Maybe he's not such a valiant champion of the true image as they say." He went on looking at me with a steady, penetrating gaze. I could feel Rosalind's sympathy, her understanding why I had not put the question to Michael, like a handclasp.

Then, quite suddenly, the man dismissed me from his attention and turned to consider Rosalind. She looked back at him. She stood with her straight, confident air, eyeing him levelly and coldly for long seconds. Then, suddenly, to my astonishment, she broke. Her eyes dropped. She flushed. He smiled slightly.

But he was wrong. It was not surrender to the stronger character, the conqueror. It was loathing, a horror which broke her defenses from within. I had a glimpse of him from her mind, hideously exaggerated. The fears she hid so well burst up and she was terrified; not as a woman weakened by a man, but as a child in terror of a monstrosity. Petra, too, caught the involuntary shape, and it shocked her into a scream.

I jumped full at the man, overturning the stool and sending him sprawling. The two men behind us leaped after me, but I got in at least one good blow before they could drag me off.

The spider-man sat up, and rubbed his jaw. He grinned at me, but not with any amusement.

"Does you credit," he conceded, "but not much more." He got up on his gangling legs. "Not seen much of the women around here, have you, boy? Take a look at 'em as you go. Maybe you'll understand a bit more. Besides, this one can have children. I've had a fancy for some children a long time now, even if they do happen to take after their father a bit." He grinned briefly again, and then frowned at us. "Better take it the way it is, boy. Be a sensible fellow. I don't give second chances."

He looked from me to the men who were holding me.

"Chuck him out," he told them. "And if he doesn't seem to understand that that means stay out, shoot him."

The two of them jerked me round and marched me off. At the edge of the clearing one of them helped me along a path with his boot.

"Keep on going," he said.

I got up and turned around, but one of them had an arrow trained on me. He gave a shake of his head to urge me on. So I did what I was told, kept on going—for a few yards, until the trees hid me. Then I doubled back under cover.

Just what they were expecting. But they didn't shoot me; they just beat me up and slung me back among the undergrowth. I remember flying through the air, but I don't remember landing. . . .

CHAPTER FIFTEEN

I WAS BEING DRAGGED ALONG. There were hands under my shoulders. Small branches were whipping back and slapping me in the face.

"What——?" I began.

"Sh!" whispered a voice behind me.

"Give me a minute. I'll be all right," I whispered back.

The dragging stopped. I lay pulling myself together for a moment, and then rolled over. A woman, a young woman, was sitting back on her heels, looking at me.

The sun was low now, and it was dim under the trees. I could not see her well. There was dark hair hanging down on each side of a sunburnt face, and the glint of dark eyes regarding me earnestly. The bodice of her dress was ragged, a nondescript tawny color, with stains on it. There were no sleeves, but what struck me most was that it bore no cross. I had never before been face to face with a woman who wore no protective cross stitched to her dress. It looked queer, almost indecent. We faced one another for some seconds.

"You don't know me, David," she said sadly.

Until then I had not. It was the way she said "David" that suddenly told me.

"Sophie!" I said, "Oh, Sophie!"

She smiled.

"Dear David," she said. "Have they hurt you badly, David?"

I tried moving my arms and legs. They were stiff and they ached in several places, so did my body and my head. I felt some blood caked on my left cheek, but there seemed to be nothing broken. I started to get up, but she stretched out a hand and put it on my arm.

"No, not yet. Wait a little, till it's dark." She went on looking at me. "I saw them bring you in. You and the little girl, and the other girl. Who is she, David?"

That brought me fully round, with a jolt. Frantically I sought for Rosalind and Petra, and could not reach them. Michael felt my panic and came in steadyingly. Relieved, too.

"Thank goodness for that. We've been worried stiff about you. Take it easy. They're all right, both of them tired out and exhausted; they've fallen asleep."

"Is Rosalind——?"

"She's all right, I tell you. What's been happening to you?"

I told him. The whole exchange only took a few seconds, but long enough for Sophie to be regarding me curiously.

"Who is she, David?" she repeated.

I explained that Rosalind was my cousin. She watched me as I spoke, and then nodded slowly.

"*He* wants her, doesn't he?" she asked.

"That's what he said," I admitted, grimly.

"She could give him babies?" she persisted.

"What are you trying to do to me?" I asked her.

"So, you're in love with her?" she went on.

A word again. . . . When the minds have learned to mingle when no thought is wholly one's own, and each has taken too much of the other ever to be entirely himself alone; when one has reached the beginning of seeing with a single eye, loving with a single heart, enjoying with a single joy; when there can be moments of identity and nothing is separate save bodies that long for one another. . . . When there is that, where is the word? There is only the inadequacy of the word that exists.

"We love one another," I said.

Sophie nodded. She picked up a few twigs, and watched her brown fingers break them. She said:

"He's gone away—where the fighting is. She's safe just now."

"She's asleep," I told her. "They're both asleep."

Her eyes came back to mine, puzzled.

"How do you know?"

I told her briefly, as simply as I could. She went on breaking twigs as she listened. Then she nodded.

"I remember. My mother said there was something . . . something about the way you sometimes seemed to understand her before she spoke. Was that it?"

"I think so. I think your mother had a little of it, without knowing she had it," I said.

"It must be a very wonderful thing to have," she said, half wistfully. "Like more eyes, inside you."

"Something like," I admitted. "It's difficult to explain. But it isn't all wonderful. It can hurt a lot sometimes."

"To be any kind of deviant is to be hurt—always," she said. She continued to sit back on her heels, looking at her hands in her lap, seeing nothing.

"If she were to give him children, he wouldn't want me any more," she said, at last.

There was still enough light to catch a glistening on her cheeks.

"Sophie, dear," I said "Are you in love with him—with this spider-man?"

"Oh, don't call him that—please—we can't any of us help being what we are. His name's Gordon. He's kind to me, David. He's fond of me. You've got to have as little as I have to know how much that means. You've never known loneliness. You can't understand the awful emptiness that's waiting all around us here. I'd have given him babies gladly, if I could. I—oh, why do they do that to us? Why didn't they kill me? It would have been kinder than this."

She sat without a sound. The tears squeezed out from under the closed lids and ran down her face. I took her hand between my own.

I remembered watching. The man with his arm linked in the woman's, the small figure on top of the packhorse waving back to me as they disappeared into the trees. Myself desolate, a kiss still damp on my cheek, a lock tied with a yellow ribbon in my hand. I looked at her now, and my heart ached.

"Sophie," I said. "Sophie, darling. It's not going to happen. Do you understand? It won't happen. Rosalind will never let it happen. I *know* that."

She opened her eyes again, and looked at me through the brimming tears.

"You can't know a thing like that about another person. You're just trying to——"

"I'm not, Sophie. I do know. You and I could only *know* very little about one another. But with Rosalind it is different: it's part of what thinking-together means."

She regarded me doubtfully.

"Is that really true? I don't understand."

"How should you? But it *is* true. I could feel what she was feeling about the spi—about that man."

She went on looking at me, a trifle uneasily.

"You can't see what I think?" she inquired, with a touch of anxiety.

"No more than you can tell what I think," I assured her. "It isn't a kind of spying. It's more as if you could just talk all your thoughts, if you liked—and not talk them if you wanted them private."

It was more difficult trying to explain it to her than it had been to Uncle Axel, but I kept on struggling to simplify it into words until I suddenly became aware that the light had gone, and I was talking to a figure I could scarcely see. I broke off.

"Is it dark enough now?"

"Yes. It'll be safe if we go carefully," she told me. "Can you walk all right? It isn't far."

I got up, well aware of stiffness and bruises, but not of anything worse. She seemed able to see better in the gloom than I could, and took my hand, to lead the way. We kept to the trees, but I could see fires twinkling on my left, and realized that we were skirting the encampment. We kept on round it until we reached the low cliff that closed the northwest side, and then along the base of that, in the shadow, for fifty yards or so. There she stopped, and laid my hand on one of the rough ladders I had seen against the rock face.

"Follow me," she whispered, and suddenly whisked upward.

I climbed more cautiously until I reached the top of the ladder where it rested against a rock ledge. Her arm reached out and helped me in.

"Sit down," she told me.

The lighter patch through which I had come disappeared. She moved about, looking for something. Presently there were sparks as she used a flint and steel. She blew up the sparks until she was able to light a pair of candles. They were short, fat, burnt with smoky flames, and smelled abominable, but they enabled me to see the surroundings.

The place was a cave about fifteen feet deep and nine wide, cut out of the sandy rock. The entrance was covered by a skin curtain hooked across it. In one corner of the inner end there was a flaw in the roof from which water dripped steadily at about a drop a second. It fell into a wooden bucket; the overflow of the bucket trickled down a groove for the full length of the cave, and out of the entrance. In the other inner corner was a mattress of small branches, with skins and a tattered blanket on it. There were a few bowls and utensils. A blackened fire-hollow near the entrance, empty now, showed an ingenious draft-hole drilled to the outer air. The handles of a few knives and other tools protruded from niches in the walls. A spear, a bow, a leather quiver with a dozen arrows in it, lay close to the brushwood mattress. There was nothing much else.

I thought of the kitchen of the Wenders' cottage. The clean, bright room that had seemed so friendly because it had no texts on the walls. The candles flickered, sent greasy smoke up to the roof, and stank.

Sophie dipped a bowl into the bucket, rummaged a fairly clean bit of rag out of a niche, and brought it across to me. She washed the blood off my hair, and examined the cause.

"Just a cut. Not deep," she said, reassuringly.

I washed my hands in the bowl. She tipped the water into the runnel, rinsed the bowl and put it away.

"You're hungry, David?" she said.

"Very," I told her. I had had nothing to eat all day except during our one brief stop.

"Stay here. I won't be long," she instructed, and slipped out under the skin curtain.

I sat looking at the shadows that danced on the rock walls, listening to the plop-plop-plop of the drips. And very likely, I told myself, this is luxury, in the Fringes. "You've got to have as little as I have——" Sophie had said, though it had not been material things that she meant. To escape the forlorn-ness and the squalor I sought Michael's company.

"Where are you? What's been happening?" I asked him. "We've camped for the night," he told me. "Too dangerous to go on in the dark." He tried to give me a picture of the place as he had seen it just before sunset, but it might have been a dozen spots along our route. "It's been slow going all day—tiring, too. They know their woods, these Fringes people. We've been expecting a real ambush somewhere on the way, but it's been sniping and harassing all the time. We've lost three killed, but had seven wounded— only two of them seriously."

"But you're still coming on?"

"Yes. The feeling is that now we do have quite a force here for once, it's a chance to give the Fringes something that will keep them quiet for some time to come. Besides, you three are badly wanted. There's a rumor that there are a couple of dozen, perhaps more, of us scattered about Waknuk and surrounding districts, and you have to be brought back to identify them." He paused a moment there, then he went on in a worried, unhappy mood.

"In point of fact, David, I'm afraid—very much afraid—there is only one."

"One?"

"Deborah managed to reach me, right at her limit, very faintly. She says something has happened to Mark."

"They've caught him?"

"No. She thinks not. He'd have let her know if it were that. He's simply stopped. Not a thing from him in over twenty-four hours now."

"An accident perhaps? Remember Walter Brent—that boy who was killed by a tree? He just stopped like that."

"It might be. Deborah just doesn't know. She's frightened; it leaves her all alone now. She was right at her limit, and I was almost. Another two or three miles, and we'll be out of touch."

"It's queer I didn't hear at least your side of this," I told him.

"Probably while you were knocked out," he suggested.

"Well, when Petra wakes she'll be able to keep touch with Deborah," I reminded him. "She doesn't seem to have any kind of limit."

"Yes, of course. I'd forgotten that," he agreed. "It will help her a bit."

A few moments later a hand came under the curtain, pushing a wooden bowl into the cave mouth. Sophie scrambled in after it, and gave it to me. She trimmed up the disgusting candles and then squatted down on the skin of some unidentifiable animal while I helped myself with a wooden spoon. An odd dish; it appeared to consist of several kinds of shoots, diced meat, and crumbled hard-bread, but the result was not at all bad, and very welcome. I enjoyed it, almost to the last, when I was suddenly smitten in a way that sent a whole spoonful cascading down my shirt. Petra was awake again.

I got in a response at once. Petra switched straight from distress to elation. It was flattering, but almost as painful. Evidently she woke Rosalind, for I caught her pattern among the chaos of Michael asking what the hell? and Petra's Zealand friend anxiously protesting.

Presently Petra got a hold of herself, and the turmoil quietened down. There was a sense of all other parties relaxing cautiously.

"Is she safe now? What was all that thunder and lightning about?" Michael inquired.

Petra told us, keeping it down with an obvious effort; "We thought David was dead. We thought they'd killed him."

Now I began to catch Rosalind's thoughts, firming into comprehensible shapes out of a sort of swirl. I was humbled, bowled over, happy, and distressed all at the same time. I could not think much more clearly in response, for all I tried. It was Michael who put an end to that.

"This is scarcely decent for third parties," he observed. "When you two can disentangle yourselves, there are other things to be discussed." He paused. "Now," he continued, "what is the position?"

We sorted it out. Rosalind and Petra were still in the tent where I had last seen them. The spider-man had gone away, leaving a large, pink-eyed, white-haired man in charge of them. I explained my situation.

"Very well," said Michael. "You say this spider-man seems to be in some sort of authority, and that he has come forward toward the fighting. You've no idea whether he intends to join in the fighting himself, or whether he is simply making tactical dispositions? You see, if it is the latter he may come back at any time."

"I've no idea," I told him.

Rosalind came in abruptly, as near to hysteria as I had known her.

"I'm frightened of him. He's a different kind. Not like us. Not the same sort at all. It would be outrageous—like an animal. I couldn't, ever . . . if he tries to take me I shall kill myself. . . ."

Michael threw himself on that like a pail of ice-water.

"You won't do anything so damned silly. You'll kill the spider-man, if necessary." With an air of having settled that point conclusively he turned his attention elsewhere. At his full range he directed a question at Petra's friend.

"You still think you can reach us?"

The reply came still from a long distance, but clearly and without effort now. It was a calmly confident "Yes."

"When?" Michael asked.

There was a pause before the reply, as if for consultation, then:

"In not more than sixteen hours from now," she told him, just as confidently. Michael's skepticism diminished. For the first time he allowed himself to admit the possibility of her help.

"Then it is a question of insuring that you three are kept safe for that long," he told us, meditatively.

"Wait a minute. Just hold on a bit," I told them.

I looked up at Sophie. The smoky candles gave enough light to show that she was watching my face intently, a little uneasily.

"You were 'talking' to that girl?" she said.

"And my sister. They're awake now," I told her. "They are in the tent, and being guarded by an albino. It seems odd."

"Odd?" she inquired.

"Well, one would have thought a woman in charge of them. . . ."

"This is the Fringes," she reminded me, with bitterness.

"It—oh, I see," I said, awkwardly. "Well, the point is this: do you think there is any way they can be got out of there before he comes back? It seems to me that now is the time. Once he does come back. . . ." I shrugged, keeping my eyes on hers.

She turned her head away and contemplated the candles for some moments. Then she nodded.

"Yes. That would be best for all of us—all of us, except him," she added, half-sadly. "Yes, I think it can be done."

"Straight away?"

She nodded again. I picked up the spear that lay by the couch, and weighed it in my hand. It was somewhat light, but well balanced. She looked at it, and shook her head.

"You must stay here, David," she told me.

"But——" I began.

"No. If you were to be seen, there would be an alarm. No one will take any notice of me going to his tent, even if they do see me."

There was sense in that. I laid the spear down, though with reluctance.

"But can you——?"

"Yes," she said, decisively.

She got up and went to one of the niches. From it she pulled out a knife. The broad blade was clean and bright. It looked as if it might once have been part of the kitchen furnishings of a raided farm. She slipped it into the belt of her skirt, leaving only the dark handle protruding. Then she turned and looked at me for a long moment.

"David——" she began, tentatively.

"What?" I asked.

She changed her mind. In a different tone she said, "Will you tell them no noise? Whatever happens, no sounds at all? Tell them to follow me, and have dark pieces of cloth ready to wrap around themselves. Will you be able to make all that clear to them?"

"Yes," I told her. "But I wish you'd let me——"

She shook her head and cut me short.

"No, David. It'd only increase the risk. You don't know the place."

She pinched out the candles, and unhooked the curtain. For a moment I saw her silhouetted against the paler darkness of the entrance, then she was gone.

I gave her instructions to Rosalind, and we impressed on Petra the necessity for silence. Then there was nothing to do but wait and listen to the steady drip-drip-drip in the darkness.

I could not sit still for long like that. I went to the entrance and put my head out into the night. There were a few cooking fires glowing among the shades, people moving about, too, for the glows blinked occasionally as figures crossed in front of them. There was a murmur of voices, a slight, composite stir of small movements, a night-bird calling harshly a little distance away, the cry of an animal still farther off. Nothing more.

We were all waiting. A small shapeless surge of excitement escaped for a moment from Petra. No one commented on it.

Then from Rosalind a reassuring, "it's-all-right" shape, but with a curious secondary quality of shock to it. It seemed wiser not to distract their attention now by asking about it.

I listened. There was no alarm, no change in the conglomerate murmur. It seemed a long time until I heard the crunch of grit underfoot directly below me. The poles of the ladder scraped faintly on the rock edge as the weight came on them. I moved back into the cave out of the way. Rosalind was asking silently, a little doubtfully:

"Is this right? Are you there, David?"

"Yes. Come along up," I told them.

One figure appeared dimly outlined in the opening. Then another, smaller form, then a third. The opening was blotted out. Presently the candles were alight again.

Rosalind, and Petra, too, watched silently in horrid fascination as Sophie scooped a bowlful of water from the bucket to wash the blood off her arms and clean the knife.

CHAPTER SIXTEEN

THE TWO GIRLS studied one another, curiously and warily. Sophie's eyes traveled over Rosalind, in her russet woolen dress with its brown cross appliqué, and rested anxiously for a moment on her leather shoes. She looked down at her own soft moccasins, then at her short, tattered skirt. In the course of her self-inspection she discovered new stains that had not been on her bodice half an hour before. Without any embarrassment she pulled it off and began to soak them out in the cold water. To Rosalind she said:

"You must get rid of that cross. Hers, as well," she added glancing at Petra. "It marks you. We women in the Fringes do not feel that it has served us very well. The men resent it, too. Here." She took a small, thin-bladed knife from a niche, and held it out.

Rosalind took it, doubtfully. She looked at it, and then down at the cross which had been displayed on every dress she had ever worn. Sophie watched her.

"I used to wear one," she said. "It didn't help me, either."

Rosalind looked at me, still a little doubtfully. I nodded.

"They don't much like insistence on the true image in these parts. Very likely it's dangerous." I glanced at Sophie.

"It is," she said. "It's not only an identification; it's a challenge."

Rosalind lifted the knife and began, half-reluctantly, to pick at the stitches.

I said to Sophie: "What now? Oughtn't we try to get as far away as we can before it's light?"

Sophie, still dabbling her bodice, shook her head.

"No. They may find him any time. When they do, there'll be a search. They'll think that you killed him and then all three of you took to the woods. They'll never think of looking for you here, why should they? But they'll rake the whole neighborhood for you."

"You mean, we stay here?" I asked her. She nodded.

"For two, perhaps three days. Then, when they've called off the search, I'll see you clear."

Rosalind looked up from her unpicking thoughtfully.

"Why are you doing all this for us?" she asked.

I explained to her about Sophie and the spider-man far more quickly than it could have been put into words. It did not seem to satisfy her entirely. She and Sophie went on regarding one another steadily in the flickering light.

Sophie dropped the bodice into the water with a plop. She stood up slowly. She bent toward Rosalind, locks of dark hair dangling down on her naked breasts, her eyes narrowed.

"Damn you," she said viciously. "Leave me alone, damn you."

Rosalind became taut, ready for any movement. I shifted so that I could jump between them if necessary. The tableau held for long seconds. Sophie, uncared for, half-naked in her ragged skirt, dangerously poised; Rosalind, in her brown dress with the unpicked left arm of the cross hanging forward, with her bronze hair shining in the candlelight, her fine features upturned, with eyes alert. The crisis passed, and the tension lost pitch. The violence died out of Sophie's eyes, but she did not move. Her mouth twisted a little and she trembled.

"Damn you!" she said again. "Go on, laugh at me. Laugh at me because I *do* want him, *me!*" She gave a queer, choked laugh herself. "And what's the use? Oh, God, what's the use? If he weren't in love with you, what good would I be to him—like this?"

She clenched her hands to her face and stood for a moment, shaking all over, then she turned and flung herself on the brushwood bed.

We stared into the shadowy corner. One moccasin had fallen off. I could see the brown, grubby sole of her foot, and the line of six toes. I turned to Rosalind. Her eyes met mine, contrite and appalled. Instinctively she made to get up. I shook my head, and, hesitantly she sank back.

The only sounds in the cave were the hopeless, abandoned sobbing, and plop-plop-plop of the drips.

Petra looked at us, then at the figure on the bed, then at us again, expectantly. When neither of us moved she appeared to decide that the initiative lay with her. She crossed to the bedside and knelt down concernedly beside it. Tentatively she put a hand on the dark hair.

"Don't," she said. "Please *don't*."

There was a startled catch in the sobbing. A pause, then a brown arm reached out around Petra's shoulders. The sound became a little less desolate . . . it no longer tore at one's heart; but it left it bruised and aching. . . .

I awoke reluctantly, stiff and cold from lying on the hard rock floor. Almost immediately there was Michael:

"Did you mean to sleep all day?"

I looked up and saw a chink of daylight beneath the skin curtain.

"What's the time?" I asked him.

"About eight, I'd guess. It's been light for three hours, and we've fought a battle already."

"What happened?" I inquired.

"We got wind of an ambush, so we sent an outflanking party. It clashed with the reserve force that was waiting to follow up the ambush. Apparently they thought it was our main body; anyway, the result was a rout, at a cost of two or three wounded, to us."

"So now you're coming on?"

"Yes. I suppose they'll rally somewhere, but they've melted away now. No opposition at all."

That was by no means as one could have wished. I explained our position, and that we certainly could not hope to emerge from the cave in daylight, unseen. On the other hand, if we stayed, and the place were to be captured, it would undoubtedly be searched, and we should be found.

"What about Petra's Zealand friends?" Michael asked. "Can you really count on them, do you think?"

Petra's friend, herself, came in on that, somewhat coolly.

"You *can* count on us."

"Your estimated time is the same? You've not been delayed?" Michael asked.

"Just the same," she assured us. "Approximately eight and a half hours from now." Then the slightly huffy note dropped, a tinge almost of awe colored her thoughts.

"This is a dreadful country indeed. We have seen Badlands before, but none of us has even imagined anything quite so terrible as this. There are stretches of miles across where it looks as if all the ground has been fused into black glass; there is nothing else, nothing but the glass like a frozen ocean of ink . . . then belts of Badlands . . . then another wilderness of black glass. It goes on and on. . . . What did they do here? What can they have done to create such a frightful place? No wonder none of us ever came this way before. It's like going over the rim of the world, into the outskirts of hell. It must be utterly beyond hope, barred to any kind of life for ever and ever . . . but why?—why?—why? There was the power of gods in the hands of children, we know; but were they *mad* children, all of them quite mad? . . . The mountains are cinders and the plains are black glass— still, after centuries! It is so dreary, dreary. A monstrous madness. . . . It is frightening to think that a whole race could go insane. If we did not know that you are on the other side of it we should have turned back and fled——"

Petra cut her off, abruptly blotting everything with distress. We had not known she was awake. I don't know what she had made of most of it, but she had clearly caught that thought of turning back. I went across to soothe her down, so that presently the Zealand woman was able to get through again and reassure her. The alarm subsided, and Petra recovered herself.

Michael came in, asking, "David, what about Deborah?"

I remembered his anxiety the previous night.

"Petra, darling," I said, "we've got too far away now for any of us to reach Deborah. Will you ask her something?"

Petra nodded.

"We want to know if she has heard anything of Mark since she talked to Michael."

Petra put the question. She shook her head.

"No," she said. "She hasn't heard anything. She's very miserable, I think. She wants to know if Michael is all right."

"Tell her he's quite all right—we all are. Tell her we love her, we're ter- ribly sorry she's all alone, but she must be brave—and careful. She must try not to let anyone see she's worried."

"She understands. She says she'll try," Petra reported. She remained thoughtful for a moment. Then she said to me, in words, "Deborah's afraid. She's crying inside. She wants Michael."

"Did she tell you that?" I asked.

Petra shook her head. "No. It was a sort of behind-think, but I saw it."

"We'd better not say anything about it," I decided. "It's not our busi- ness. A person's behind-thinks aren't really meant for other people, so we must just pretend not to have noticed them."

"All right," Petra agreed, equably.

I hoped it was all right. When I thought it over I wasn't at all sure that I cared much for this business of detecting "behind-thinks." It left one a trifle uneasy, and retrospective. . . .

Sophie woke up a few minutes later. She seemed calm, competent again, as though the last night's storm had blown itself out. She sent us to the back of the cave and unhooked the curtain to let the daylight in. Presently she had a fire going in the hollow. The greater part of the smoke from it went out of the entrance; the rest did at least have the compensation that it helped to obscure the interior of the cave from any outside observation. She ladled measures from two or three bags into an iron pot, added some water, and put the pot on the fire.

"Watch it," she instructed Rosalind, and then disappeared down the outside ladder.

Some twenty minutes later her head reappeared. She threw a couple of disks of hard bread over the sill and climbed in after them. She went to the pot, stirred it, and sniffed at the contents.

"No trouble?" I asked her.

"Not about that," she said. "They found him. They think you did it. There was a search—of a sort—early this morning. It wasn't as much of a search as it would have been with more men. But now they've got other things to worry about. The men who went to the fighting are coming back in twos and threes. What happened, do you know?"

I told of the ambush that had failed, and the resulting disappearance of resistance.

"How far have they come now?" she wanted to know.

I inquired of Michael.

"We're just clear of forest for the first time, and into rough country," he told me.

I handed it on to Sophie. She nodded. "Three hours, or a bit less, perhaps, to the riverbank," she said.

She ladled the species of porridge out of the pot into bowls. It tasted better than it looked. The bread was less palatable. She broke a disk of it with a stone, and it had to be dipped in water before one could eat it. Petra grumbled that it was not proper food like we had at home. That reminded her of something. Without any warning she launched a question:

"Michael, is my father there?"

It took him off guard. I caught his "yes" forming before he could suppress it.

I looked at Petra, hoping the implications were lost on her. Mercifully, they were. Rosalind lowered her bowl and stared into it silently.

Suspicion insulated one curiously little against the shock of knowledge. I could recall my father's voice, doctrinaire, relentless. I knew the expression his face would be wearing, as if I had seen him when he spoke.

"A baby—a baby which would grow to breed, and, breeding, spread pollution until all around us there would be Mutants and Abominations. That has happened in places where the will and faith were weak, but here it shall *never* happen."

And then my Aunt Harriet, "I shall pray God to send charity into this hideous world."

Poor Aunt Harriet, with her prayers as futile as her hopes.

A world in which a man could come upon such a hunt, himself! What kind of a man?

Rosalind rested her hand on my arm. Sophie looked up. When she saw my face her expression changed.

"What is it?" she asked.

Rosalind told her. Her eyes widened with horror. She looked from me to Petra, then slowly, bemusedly back to me again. She opened her mouth to speak, but lowered her eyes, leaving the thought unsaid. I looked at Petra, too, then at Sophie, at the rags she wore, and the cave we were in.

"Purity," I said. "The will of the Lord. Honor thy father. . . . Am I supposed to forgive him? Or to try to kill him?"

The answer startled me. I was not aware that I had sent out the thought at large.

"Let him be," came the severe, clear pattern from the Zealand woman. "Your work is to survive. Neither his kind, nor his kind of thinking will survive long. They are the crown of creation, they are ambition fulfilled, they have nowhere more to go. But life is change, that is how it differs from the rocks, change is its very nature.

"The living form defies evolution at its peril, if it does not adapt, it will be broken. The Old People brought down Tribulation, and were broken into fragments by it. Your father and his kind are a part of those fragments. They are determined still that there is a final form to defend. Soon they will attain the stability they strive for, in the only form it is granted— a place among the fossils.

"Whether harsh intolerance and bitter rectitude are the armor worn over fear and disappointment, or whether they are the festival-dress of the sadist, they cover an enemy of the life-force. The difference in kind can be bridged only by self-sacrifice—*his* self-sacrifice, for yours would bridge nothing. So, there is the severance. We have a new world to conquer, they have only a lost cause to lose."

She ceased, leaving me somewhat bemused. Rosalind, too, looked as if she were still catching up on it. Petra seemed bored.

Sophie regarded us curiously. She said, "You give an outsider an uncomfortable feeling. Is it something I could know?"

"Well——" I began, and paused, wondering how to put it.

"She said we're not to bother about my father because he doesn't understand, I think," observed Petra. It seemed a pretty fair summary.

"She . . . ?" Sophie inquired.

I remembered that she knew nothing of the Zealand people.

"Oh, a friend of Petra's," I told her, vaguely.

Sophie was sitting close to the entrance, the rest of us farther back, out of sight from the ground. Presently she looked out and down.

"There are quite a lot of the men back now—most of them, I should think. Some of them are collected around Gordon's tent, most of the others are drifting that way. He must be back, too."

She went on regarding the scene while she finished the contents of her bowl. Then she put it down beside her. "I'll see what I can find out," she said, and disappeared down the ladder.

She was gone fully an hour. I risked a quick look out once or twice, and could see the spider-man in front of his tent. He seemed to be dividing his men up into parties and instructing them by drawing diagrams in the bare earth.

"What's happening?" I asked Sophie, as she returned. "What's the plan?" She hesitated, looking doubtful.

"For goodness' sake," I told her, "we *want* your people to win, don't we? But we don't want Michael to get hurt, if it can be helped."

"We're going to ambush them this side of the river," she said.

"Let them get across?"

"There's nowhere to make a stand on the other side," she explained.

I suggested to Michael that he should hang back at the riverside, or, if he could not do that, he might fall off during the crossing and get carried away downstream. He said he'd bear the proposal in mind, but try to think of a less uncomfortable means of delay.

A few minutes later a voice called Sophie's name from below. She whispered:

"Keep back. It's him," and sped across and down the ladder.

After that nothing happened for more than a hour, when the Zealand woman came through again:

"Reply to me, please. We need a sharper reading on you now. Just keep on sending numbers."

Petra responded energetically, as if she had been feeling left out of things lately.

"Enough," the Zealand woman told her. "Wait a moment." Presently she added: "Better than we hoped. We can cut that estimate by an hour."

Another half-hour went by. I sneaked a few quick glimpses outside. The encampment looked all but deserted now. There was no one to be seen among the shacks but a few older women.

"In sight of the river," Michael reported.

Fifteen or twenty minutes passed. Then Michael again:

"They've muffed it, the fools. We've spotted a couple of them moving on the top of the cliffs. Not that it makes a lot of difference, anyway—that cleft's much too obvious a trap. Council of war now."

The council was evidently brief. In less than ten minutes he was through again:

"Plan. We retreat to cover immediately opposite the cleft. There, at a gap in the cover, we leave half a dozen men occasionally passing and re-passing in view to give the impression of more, and light fires to suggest that we are held up. Rest of the force is splitting to make detours and two crossings, one upstream, and one down. We then pincer-in behind the cleft. Better inform, if you can."

The encampment was no great distance behind the river cliffs. It looked likely that we might be caught within the pincers. I very much wished Sophie would return. An hour passed, then: "We're across the river downstream from you. No opposition," Michael told us.

We went on waiting.

Suddenly a gun went off somewhere in the woods, on the left. Three or four more shots followed, then silence, then another two.

A few minutes later a crowd of ragged men with quite a number of women among them came pouring out of the woods, leaving the scene of their intended ambush and making toward the firing. They were a woebegone, miserable lot, a few of them visibly deviants, but most of them looking simply the wrecks of normal human beings. I could not see more than three or four guns in all. The rest had bows, and a number had short spears scabbarded at their backs, as well. The spider-man stood out among them, taller than the rest, and close beside him I could see Sophie, with a bow in her hand. Whatever degree of organization there may have been had clearly disintegrated.

"What's happening?" I asked Michael. "Was that your lot shooting?"

"No. That was the other party. They're trying to draw the Fringes men across their way so that we can come in from the opposite side and take them in the rear."

"They're succeeding," I told him.

The sound of more firing came from the same direction as before. A clamor and shouting broke out. A few spent arrows dropped into the left-hand end of the clearing. Some men came running back out of the trees.

Suddenly there was a strong, clear question:

"You're still safe?"

We were all three lying on the floor in the front part of the cave now. We had a view of what was going on, and there was little enough chance of anyone noticing our heads, or bothering about us if he did. The way things were going was plain even to Petra. She loosed an urgent, excited flash.

"Steady, child, steady! We're coming," admonished the Zealand woman.

More arrows fell into the left-hand end of the clearing, and more ragged figures appeared in rapid retreat. They ran back, dodging as they came, and took cover among the tents and hovels. Still more followed, with arrows spitting out of the woods after them. The Fringes men crouched behind their bits of cover, bobbing up now and then to take quick shots at figures scarcely visible between the trees.

Unexpectedly a shower of arrows flew in from the other end of the clearing. The tattered men and women discovered themselves to be between two fires, and started to panic. Most of them jumped to their feet and ran for the shelter of the caves. I got ready to push the ladder away if any of them should try to climb into ours.

Half a dozen horsemen appeared, riding out of the trees on the right. I noticed the spider-man. He was standing by his tent, bow in hand, watching the riders. Sophie, beside him, was tugging at his ragged jacket, urging him to run toward the caves. He brushed her back with his long right arm, never taking his eyes from the emerging horsemen. His right hand went back to the string, and held the bow half-drawn. His eyes kept on searching among the horsemen.

Suddenly he stiffened. His bow came up like a flash, bent to its full. He loosed. The shaft took my father in the left of his chest. He jerked, and fell back on Sheba's hindquarters. Then he slithered off sideways and dropped to the ground, his right foot still caught in the stirrup.

The spider-man threw down his bow, and turned. With a scoop of his long arms he snatched up Sophie, and began to run. His spindly legs had not made more than three prodigious strides when a couple of arrows took him simultaneously in the back and side, and he fell.

Sophie struggled to her feet and began to run on by herself. An arrow pierced right through her upper arm, but she held on, with it lodged there. Then another took her in the back of the neck. She dropped in mid-stride, and her body slid along in the dust.

Petra had not seen it happen. She was looking all around, with a bewildered expression.

"What's that?" she asked. "What's that queer noise?"

The Zealand woman came in, calm, confidence-inspiring.

"Don't be frightened. We're coming. It's all right. Stay just where you are."

I could hear the noise now. A strange drumming sound, gradually swelling. One could not place it; it seemed to be filling everywhere, emanating from nowhere.

More men were coming out of the woods into the clearing, most of them on horseback. Many of them I recognized, men I had known all my life, all joined together now to hunt us down.

Suddenly one of the horsemen shouted and pointed upward.

I looked up, too. The sky was no longer clear. Something like a bank of mist, but shot with quick iridescent flashes, hung over us. Above it, as if through a veil, I could make out one of the strange, fish-shaped craft that I had dreamt of in my childhood, hanging in the sky. The mist made it indistinct in detail, but what I could see of it was just as I remembered: a white, glistening body with something half-invisible whizzing around above it. It was growing bigger and louder as it dropped toward us.

As I looked down again I saw a few glistening threads, like cobwebs, drifting past the mouth of the cave. Then more and more of them, giving sudden gleams as they twisted in the air and caught the light.

The shooting fell off. All over the clearing the invaders lowered their bows and guns and stared upward. They goggled incredulously, then those on the left jumped to their feet with shouts of alarm, and turned to run. Over on the right the horses pranced with fright, whinnied, and began to bolt in all directions. In a few seconds the whole place was in chaos. Fleeing men caromed into one another, panic-stricken horses trampled through the flimsy shacks, and tripped on the guy-ropes of tents flinging their riders headlong.

I sought for Michael.

"Here!" I told him. "This way. Come along over here."

"Coming," he told me.

I spotted him then, just getting to his feet beside a fallen horse that was kicking out violently. He looked up toward our cave, found us, and waved a hand. He turned to glance up at the machine in the sky. It was still sinking gently down, perhaps a couple of hundred feet above us now. Underneath it the queer mist eddied in a great swirl.

"Coming," repeated Michael.

He turned toward us and started. Then he paused and picked at something on his arm. His hand stayed there.

"Queer," he told us. "Like a cobweb, but sticky. I can't get my hand——" His thought suddenly became panicky. "It's stuck. I can't move it!"

The Zealand woman came in, coolly advising:

"Don't struggle. You'll exhaust yourself. Lie down if you can. Keep calm. Don't move. Just wait. Keep your back on the ground so that it can't get *around* you."

I saw Michael obey the instruction, though his thoughts were by no means confident. Suddenly, I realized that all over the clearing men were clawing at themselves, trying to get the stuff off, but where their hands touched it they stuck. They were struggling with it like flies in treacle, and all the time more strands were floating down on them. Most of them fought with it for a few seconds and then tried to run for shelter of the trees. They'd take about three steps before their feet stuck together, and they pitched on to the ground. The threads already lying there trapped them further. More threads fell lightly down on them as they struggled and thrashed about until presently they could struggle no more. The horses were no better off. I saw one back into a small bush. When it moved forward it tore the bush out by the roots. The bush swung round and touched the other hind leg. The legs became inseparable. The horse fell over and lay kicking—for a while.

A descending strand wafted across the back of my own hand. I told Rosalind and Petra to get back into the cave. I looked at the strand, not daring to touch it with my other hand. I turned the hand over slowly and carefully and tried to scrape the stuff off on the rock. I was not careful enough. The movement brought the strand, and other strands, looping slowly toward me, and my hand was glued to the rock.

"Here they are," Petra cried, in words and thoughts together.

I looked up to see the gleaming white fish-shape settling into the middle of the clearing. Its descent swirled the floating filaments in a cloud about it and thrust a waft of air outward. I saw some of the strands in front of the cave-mouth hesitate, undulate and then come drifting inward. Involuntarily I closed my eyes. There was a light gossamer touch on my face. When I tried to open my eyes again I found I could not.

It NEEDS a lot of resolution to lie perfectly still while you feel more and more sticky strands falling with a feathery, tickling touch across your face and hands; and still more when you begin to feel those which landed first press on your skin like fine cords and tug gently at it.

I caught Michael wondering with some alarm if this was not a trick, and whether he might not have been better off if he had tried to run. Before I could reply the Zealand woman came in reassuring us again, telling us to keep calm and have patience. Rosalind emphasized that to Petra.

"Has it got you, too?" I asked her.

"Yes," she said. "The wind from the machine blew it right into the cave—Petra, darling, you heard what she said. You must try to keep still."

The throbbing and the whirring that had dominated everything grew less as the machine slowed down. Presently it stopped. The succeeding silence was shocking. There were a few half-muffled calls and smothered sounds, but little more. I understood the reasons for that. Strands had fallen across my own mouth. I could not have opened it to call out if I wanted to.

The waiting seemed interminable. My skin crawled under the touch of the stuff, and the pull of it was becoming painful.

The Zealand woman inquired: "Michael? Keep counting to guide me to you."

Michael started counting, in figure-shapes. They were steady until the one and the two of his twelve wavered and dissolved into a pattern of relief and thankfulness. In the silence that had now fallen I could hear him say in words, "They're in that cave there, that one."

There was a creak from the ladder, a gritting of its poles against the ledge, and presently a slight hissing noise. A dampness fell on my face and hands, and the skin began to lose its puckered feeling. I tried to open my eyes again; they resisted, but gave slowly. There was a sticky feeling about the lids as I raised them.

Close in front of me, standing on the upper rungs of the ladder and leaning inward, was a figure entirely hidden in a shiny white suit. There were still filaments leisurely adrift in the air, but when they fell on the headpiece or shoulders of the white suit they did not stick. They slithered off and wafted gently on their downward way. I could see nothing of the suit's wearer but a pair of eyes looking at me through small, transparent windows. In a white gloved hand was a metal bottle, with a fine spray hissing from it.

"Turn over," came the woman's thought.

I turned, and she played the spray up and down the front of my clothes. Then she climbed the last two or three rungs, stepped over me where I lay, and made her way toward Rosalind and Petra at the back of the cave, spraying as she went.

Michael's head and shoulders appeared above the sill. He, too, was be-dewed with spray, and the few vagrant strands that settle on him lay glisten-ing for a moment before they dissolved. I sat up and looked past him.

The white machine rested in the middle of the clearing. The device on top of it had ceased to revolve, and now that it was observable, seemed to be a sort of conical spiral, built up in a number of spaced sections from some almost transparent material. There were glazed windows in the side of the fish-shaped body, and a door stood open.

The clearing itself looked as if a fantastic number of spiders had spun there with all their might and main. The place was festooned with threads, appearing more white than glossy now; it took a moment or two of feeling something was wrong with them before one perceived that they failed to move in the breeze as webs would. And not only they, but everything, was motionless, petrified.

The forms of a number of men, and horses, too, were scattered among the shacks. They were as unmoving as the rest.

A sudden sharp cracking came from the right. I looked over there, just in time to see a young tree break off a foot from the ground, and fall. Then another movement caught the corner of my eye—a bush slowly leaning over. Its roots came out of the ground as I watched. Another bush moved. A shack crumpled in on itself and collapsed, and another. It was uncanny and alarm-ing.

Back in the cave there was a sigh of relief from Rosalind. I got up and went to her, with Michael following. Petra announced in a subdued, some-what expostulatory tone, "That was *very* horrid."

Her eyes dwelt reprovingly and curiously on the white-suited figure. The woman made a few final, all-encompassing passes with her spray, then pulled off her gloves and lifted back her hood. She regarded us. We frankly stared at her.

Her eyes were large, with irises more brown than green, and fringed with long, deep-gold lashes. Her nose was straight, but her nostrils curved with the perfection of a sculpture. Her mouth was perhaps a little wide; the chin beneath it was rounded, but not soft. Her hair was just a little darker than Rosalind's, and, astonishingly in a woman, it was short. Cut off nearly level with her jaw.

But more than anything it was the lightness of her face that made us stare. It was not pallor, it was simply fairness, like new cream, and with cheeks that might have been dusted with pink petals. There was scarcely a line in its smoothness, it seemed all new and perfect, as if neither wind nor rain had ever touched her. It was hard to believe that any real, living person could look like that, so untouched, so unflawed.

For she was no girl in a first tender blossoming, unmistakably she was a woman—thirty, perhaps; one could not tell. She was sure of herself, with a serenity of confidence which made Rosalind's self-reliance seem almost bravado.

She took us in and then fixed her attention upon Petra. She smiled at her, with just a glimpse of perfect, white teeth.

There was an immensely complex pattern which compounded pleasure, satisfaction, achievement, relief, approval, and most surprisingly to me a touch of something very like awe. The intermixture was subtle far beyond Petra's grasp, but enough of it reached her to give her an unwonted, wide-eyed seriousness for some seconds as she looked up into the woman's eyes, as if she knew in some way, without understanding how or why, that this was one of the cardinal moments in her life.

Then, after a few moments, her expression relaxed. She smiled and chuckled. Evidently something was passing between them, but it was of a quality, or on a level, that did not reach me at all. I caught Rosalind's eye, but she simply shook her head, and watched.

The Zealand woman bent down and picked Petra up. They looked closely into one another's faces. Petra raised her hand and tentatively touched the woman's face, as if to assure herself that it was real. The Zealand woman laughed, kissed her, and put her down again. She shook her head slowly, as if she were not quite believing.

"It was worthwhile," she said, in words, but words so curiously pronounced that I scarcely understood them at first. "Yes. Certainly, it was worthwhile!"

She slipped into thought-forms, much easier to follow than her words.

"It was not simple to get permission to come. Such an immense distance, more than twice as far as any of us has been before. So costly to send the ship. They could scarcely believe it would be worth it. But it will be. . . ." She looked at Petra again, wonderingly. "At her age, and untrained—yet she can throw a thought halfway round the world!" She shook her head once more, as if still unable to believe it entirely. Then she turned to me.

"She has still a great deal to learn, but we will give her the best teachers, and then, one day, she will be teaching them."

She sat down on Sophie's bed of twigs and skins. Against the thrown-back white hood, her beautiful head looked as though it were framed by a halo. She studied each of us thoughtfully in turn, and seemed satisfied. She nodded.

"With one another's help, you have managed to get quite a long way, too; but you'll find that there is a lot more we can teach you." She took hold of Petra's hand. "Well, as you've no possessions to collect, and there's nothing to delay us, we might as well start now."

"For Waknuk?" Michael asked.

It was as much a statement as a question, and she checked herself in the act of rising, to look at him inquiringly.

"There is still Deborah," he explained.

The Zealand woman considered.

"I'm not sure—— Wait a minute," she told him.

She was suddenly in communication with someone on board the machine outside, at a speed and on a level where I could make almost nothing of it. Presently she shook her head, regretfully.

"I was afraid of that," she said. "I am sorry, but we cannot include her."

"It wouldn't take long. It isn't far, not for your flying-machine," Michael insisted.

Again she shook her head.

"I am sorry," she said again. "Of course we would if we could, but it is a technical matter. You see, the journey was longer than we expected. There were some dreadful parts that we dare not cross, even at great height: we had to go far around them. Also, because of what was happening here, we had to come faster than we had intended." She paused, seeming to wonder whether she was attempting an explanation beyond the understanding of such primitives as we. "The machine," she told us, "uses fuel. The more weight it has to carry, and the faster it travels, the more of this fuel it uses, and now we have only just enough of it left to get us back, if we go carefully. If we were to go to Waknuk and make another landing and take-off there, *and* try to carry four of you, as well as Petra, we should use up all our fuel before we could reach home. That would mean that we should fall into the sea, and drown. Three of you from here we can just manage with safety; four and the extra landing, we can't."

There was a pause while we appreciated the situation. She had made it clear enough, and she sat back, a motionless figure in her gleaming white suit, her knees drawn up and her hands clasped around them, waiting sympathetically and patiently for us to accept the facts.

In the pause one became aware of the uncanniness of the silence all about us. There was not a sound to be heard now. Not a movement. Even the leaves on the trees were unable to rustle. A sudden shock of realization brought a question from Rosalind.

"They're not—they're not all—dead? I didn't understand. I thought——"

"Yes," the Zealand woman told her, simply. "They're all dead. The plastic threads contract as they dry. A man who struggles and entangles himself soon becomes unconscious. It is more merciful than your arrows and spears."

Rosalind shivered. Perhaps I did, too. There was an unnerving quality about it—something quite different from the fatal issue of a man-to-man fight, or from the casualty roll of an ordinary battle. We were puzzled, too, by the Zealand woman, for there was no callousness in her mind, nor any great concern, either—just a slight distaste, as if for an unavoidable, but unexceptional, necessity. She perceived our confusion, and shook her head reprovingly.

"It is not pleasant to kill any creature," she agreed, "but to pretend that one can live without doing so is self-deception. There has to be meat in the dish, there have to be vegetables forbidden to flower, seeds forbidden to germinate; even the cycles of microbes must be sacrificed for us to continue our cycles. It is neither shameful nor shocking that it should be so. It is simply a part of the great revolving wheel of natural economy. And just as we have to keep ourselves alive in these ways, so, too, we have to preserve our species against others that wish to destroy it, or else fail in our trust.

"The unhappy Fringes people were condemned through no act of their own to a life of squalor and misery—there could be no future for them. As for those who condemned them—well, that, too, is the way of it. There have been lords of life before, you know. Did you ever hear of the great lizards? When the time came for them to be superseded they had to pass away.

"Sometime there will come a day when we ourselves shall have to give place to a new thing. Very certainly we shall struggle against the inevitable just as these remnants of the Old People do. We shall try with all our strength to grind it back into the earth from which it is emerging, for treachery to one's own species must always seem a crime. We shall force it to prove itself, and when it does, we shall go; as, by the same process, these are going.

"In loyalty to their kind they cannot tolerate our rise; in loyalty to our kind, we cannot tolerate their obstruction.

"If the process shocks you, it is because you have not been able to stand off and, knowing what you are, see what a difference in *kind* must mean. Your minds are confused by your ties and your upbringing, you are still half-thinking of them as the same kind as yourselves. That is why you are shocked. And that is why they have you at a disadvantage, for *they* are not confused. They are alert, corporately aware of danger to their species. They can see quite well that if it is to survive they have not only to preserve it from deterioration, but they must protect it from the even more serious threat of the superior variant.

"For ours *is* a superior variant, and we are only just beginning. We are able to think-together and understand one another as they never could; we are beginning to understand how to assemble and apply the composite team-mind to a problem, and where may that not take us one day? We are not shut away into individual cages from which we can reach out only with inadequate words. Understanding one another, we do not need laws which treat living forms as though they were as indistinguishable as bricks; we could never commit the enormity of imagining that we could mint ourselves into equality and identity, like stamped coins; we do not mechanistically attempt to hammer ourselves into geometrical patterns of society, or policy; we are not dogmatists teaching God how he should have ordered the world.

"The essential quality of life is living; the essential quality of living is change; change is evolution; and we are part of it.

"The static, the enemy of change, is the enemy of life, and therefore our implacable enemy. If you still feel shocked, or doubtful, just consider some of the things that these people who have taught you to think of them as your fellows, have done. I know little about your lives, but the pattern scarcely varies wherever a pocket of the older species is trying to preserve itself. And consider, too, what they intended to do to you, and why."

I found her rhetorical style somewhat overwhelming, but, in general, I was able to follow her line of thought. I did not have the power of detachment that could allow me to think of myself as another species, nor am I sure that I have it yet. In my thinking we were still no more than unhappy minor variants; but I could look back and consider why we had been forced to flee.

I glanced at Petra. She was sitting pretty much bored with all this apologia, watching the Zealand woman's beautiful face with a kind of wistful wonder. A series of memories cut off what my eyes were seeing—my Aunt Harriet's face in the water, her hair gently waving in the current; poor Anne, a limp figure hanging from a beam; Sally, wringing her hands in anguish for Katherine, and in terror for herself; Sophie, degraded to a savage, dying with an arrow in her neck. . . .

Any of those might have been a picture of Petra's future.

I shifted over beside her, and put an arm around her.

During all the Zealand woman's disquisition Michael had been gazing out of the entrance, running his eyes almost covetously over the machine that waited in the clearing. He went on studying it for a minute or two after she had stopped, then he sighed, and turned away. For a few moments he contemplated the rock floor between his feet. Presently he looked up.

"Petra," he asked, "do you think you could reach Deborah for me?"

Petra put out the inquiry, in her forceful way.

"Yes. She's there. She wants to know what's happening," she told him.

"Say first that whatever she may hear, we're all alive and quite all right."

"Yes," said Petra presently. "She understands that."

"Now I want you to tell her this," Michael went on, carefully. "She is to go on being brave—and very careful—and in a little time, three or four days, perhaps, I shall come and fetch her away. Will you tell her that?"

All of us looked at Michael, without open comment.

"Well," he said, defensively, "you two are proscribed as outlaws, so neither of you can go."

"But, Michael——" Rosalind began.

"She's quite *alone*," said Michael. "Would you leave David alone there, or would David leave you?"

There was no answer to that.

"You said 'fetch her away,'" observed Rosalind.

"That's what I meant. We *could* stay in Waknuk for a while, waiting for the day when we, or perhaps our children, would be found out. . . . That's not good enough. Or we could come to the Fringes." He looked around the cave and out across the clearing, with distaste. "That's not good enough, either. Deborah deserves just as well as any of the rest of us. All right, then; since the machine can't take her, someone's got to bring her."

The Zealand woman was leaning forward, watching him. There was sympathy and admiration in her eyes, but she shook her head gently.

"It is a very long way—and there's that awful, impassable country in between," she reminded him.

"I know that," he acknowledged. "But the world is round, so there must be another way to get there."

"It would be hard, and certainly dangerous," she warned.

"No more dangerous than to stay in Waknuk. Besides, how could we stay now, knowing that there is a place for people like us, that there *is* somewhere to go?

"*Knowing* makes all the difference. Knowing that we're not just pointless freaks—a few bewildered Deviations hoping to save their own skins. It's the difference between just trying to keep alive, and having something to live for."

The Zealand woman thought for a moment or two, then she raised her eyes to meet his again.

"When you do reach us, Michael," she told him. "You can be very sure of your place with us."

The door shut with a thud. The machine started to vibrate and blow a great dusty wind across the clearing. Through the windows we could see Michael bracing himself against it, his clothes flapping. Even the deviational trees about the clearing were stirring in their webby shrouds.

The floor tilted beneath us. There was a slight lurch, then the ground began to drop away as we climbed faster and faster into the evening sky. Soon we steadied, pointed toward the southwest.

Petra was excited, and a bit over strength.

"It's awfully wonderful," she announced. "I can see for simply miles and miles and miles. Oh, Michael, you do look funny and tiny down there!"

The lone, miniature figure in the clearing waved its arm.

"Just at present," Michael's thought came up to us, "I seem to be feeling a bit funny and tiny down here, Petra, dear. But it'll pass. We'll be coming after you."

It was just as I had seen it in my dreams. A brighter sun than Waknuk ever knew poured down upon the wide blue bay where the lines of white-topped breakers crawled slowly to the beach. Small boats, some with colored sails, and some with none, were making for a harbor already dotted with craft. Clustered along the shore, and thinning as it stretched back toward the hills, lay the city with its white houses embedded among green parks and gardens. I could even make out the tiny vehicles sliding along the wide, tree-bordered avenues. A little inland, beside a square of green, a bright light was blinking from a tower and a fish-shaped machine was floating to the ground.

It was so familiar that for a swift moment I imagined I should wake to find myself back in my bed in Waknuk. I took hold of Rosalind's hand to reassure myself.

"It *is* real, isn't it? You can see it, too?" I asked her.

"It's beautiful, David. I never thought there could be anything so lovely. . . . And there's something else, too, that you never told me about."

"What?" I asked.

"Listen! Can't you feel it? Open your mind more.—Petra, darling, if you *could* stop bubbling over for a few minutes. . . ."

I did as she told me. I was aware of the engineer in our machine communicating with someone below, but behind that, as a background to it, there was something new and unknown to me. In terms of sound it could be not unlike the buzzing of a hive of bees; in terms of light, a suffused glow.

"What is it?" I said, puzzled.

"Can't you guess, David? It's people. Lots and lots of our kind of people."

I realized she must be right, and I listened to it for a bit, until Petra's excitement got the better of her, and I had to protect myself.

We were over the land now, and looked down at the city coming up to meet us.

"I'm beginning to believe it's real and true at last," I told Rosalind. "You were never with me those other times."

She turned her head. The under-Rosalind was in her face, smiling, shiny-eyed. The armor was gone. She let me look beneath. It was like a flower opening. . . .

"This time, David——" she began.

Then she was blotted out. We staggered, and put our hands to our heads. Even the floor under our feet jerked a little.

Anguished protests came from all directions.

"Oh, sorry," Petra apologized to the ship's crew, and to the city in general, "but it *is* awfully exciting."

"This time, darling, we'll forgive you," Rosalind told her. "It *is*."

THE SHAPE OF THINGS THAT CAME
by Richard Deming

HAD GEORGE BLADE been a scientist like his Uncle Zeke, who invented the time-nightshirt, instead of merely a writer, he would have submitted to the College of Physicists an impersonal report on his trip fifty years into the future. And though in the year 1900 he was but twenty-three and possessed none of the literary fame he was destined to acquire, he probably would have been believed. Not because he was a writer, of course, but because he was the nephew of the late Dr. Ezekiel Herkheimer, the mere mention of whose name was enough to obtain audience with any scientist in the world.

But since he was a professional writer, strange experiences to George were material for fictional stories. It never even occurred to him he should report his trip as fact. He made it a love story about a man from 1900 and a girl from 1950.

He was rather proud of the story. As he waited in the outer office of Mr. Thomas Grayson, his editor, in response to a note from that gentleman, he anticipated nothing but friendly congratulations and a substantial check. When the secretary finally told him he could go in, he smoothed the long sideburns which added so much dash to his appearance, gave his heavy mustache a final tweak and opened the door with a smile of confidence on his face.

The smile died the moment he saw the editor's expression.

"You didn't like it," George said flatly, without waiting to be told.

"Sit down, Mr. Blade," Thomas Grayson invited.

George seated himself on the edge of a chair, leaned forward to grip the head of his stick and resigned himself to the bad news.

Thomas Grayson was a round, cherubic man who looked too kindly to be an editor. As a matter of fact he *was* kindly, a quality he found a handicap in his work, for it caused him to waste much valuable time explaining in detail to disappointed authors just why their manuscripts were unacceptable.

"You obviously put a lot of work into this story, Mr. Blade," the editor said. "And you have quite a fanciful imagination. But, to put it bluntly, your background is entirely implausible."

"Implausible!" George echoed, having expected Mr. Grayson's criticism to center around the story's plot, or perhaps a defective style. "But, sir, I assure you the background is authentic to the last detail."

Mr. Grayson looked puzzled. "We must be talking about two different scripts. I refer to *The Time-Nightshirt*, which I have here before me." He emphasized his statement by rapping the manuscript with his knuckles.

"And so do I, sir."

The editor narrowed his eyes, cleared his throat and said with a touch of impatience, "If you mean that the scientific wonders you describe are theoretically possible, I won't argue with you, for my scientific background is too limited to judge. I am concerned solely with potential reader reaction. The average reader simply won't believe in your year 1950."

George said, "But Mr. Grayson, I meant it literally when I said the background was authentic. I was there."

Mr. Grayson's head snapped up and he stared at the young author in astonishment. Realizing the strange effect of his remarkable statement, George hastened to explain.

"You see, sir, my Uncle Zeke . . . Dr. Ezekiel Herkheimer, the physicist, that is . . . died January twelfth last, and since he died intestate, I inherited his entire belongings. Among them, in one of the trunksful of laboratory equipment, I found the time-nightshirt described in my story."

"You mean," Mr. Grayson asked incredulously, "there actually is such a piece of equipment?"

"Exactly as described, sir. In shape it is a common enough nightshirt, the head opening having the regulation two buttons to hold it snugly against the throat and keep out the night air. But the material seems to be some kind of odd metal . . . a metal so soft and pliable, the garment folds into a bundle small enough to fit a coat pocket. And the two buttons are not merely buttons, but movable dials. I do not understand the pages of technical notes I found with it, explaining my late uncle's theory of time-space travel, but the operation of the nightshirt is very simple. The top dial projects you fifty years into the future, and the bottom dial returns you again."

For a long time Mr. Grayson examined George without saying anything. When he finally spoke, it was in the unnaturally calm voice of a man humoring a maniac. "Why fifty years, particularly?"

George shrugged. "I don't know why. But it has only one speed forward and is entirely incapable of penetrating the past. Something to do with 'areas of limitation' as nearly as I can make out from my uncle's notes. I was rather disappointed when I discovered this, for at first I had visualized trips millions of years into the future and millions of years into the past. But even with its limits, you have to admit it's a remarkable invention."

"Yes, it is that," the editor said nervously. "But now if you will excuse me, Mr. Blade . . ."

It suddenly registered on George that the man did not believe him.

Nettled, he said coldly, "I assure you I am in full possession of my faculties, Mr. Grayson. Nor am I trying to play a practical joke. I actually have the time-nightshirt, and I actually leaped from the year 1900 to the year 1950. I was gone nearly two weeks."

"I'm sure you were," the editor said hastily.

George eyed him with suspicion. In a belligerent tone, he said, "It was the most amazing two weeks I ever spent." He added with less belligerence and more reflectiveness, "And the most embarrassing, in a sense."

"Embarrassing?" Mr. Grayson asked cautiously.

"Embarrassing," George repeated. "In the first place, Uncle Zeke's notes contained no provisions for taking along anything but myself and the nightshirt. Consequently I arrived in the year 1950 a pauper and suitably attired only for bed."

Mr. Grayson emitted a strained laugh.

"Fortunately I was able to remedy this situation almost immediately. But my embarrassment persisted during my entire stay for a different reason."

"What was that?" Mr. Grayson asked, apparently deciding George was a harmless lunatic, and beginning to become interested.

George said, "I have what is supposed to be an excellent education, and always imagined that if I got up against it, I could make a living in any number of genteel ways. But in the year 1950 I was fitted to perform only the most menial tasks. In order to live I had to work, and the only work I could find which I was capable of performing was as a common laborer digging a sewer line."

This time Mr. Grayson's laugh, while still unbelieving, was not even strained. "How did you manage to clothe yourself on arrival?" he asked.

"I'm afraid I stooped to theft," George admitted. "You see, I live in a suite at the Chelsea, and since it is a relatively new building, I assumed it would still be standing in fifty years. I therefore made the time leap in my own bedroom, picking midnight as the best hour to arrive in 1950. Fortunately the tenant occupying the suite which had been mine fifty years before was out when I materialized. Finding his clothing an approximate fit, I shamelessly appropriated what I required. Probably the man is still puzzled, for I returned the clothing two weeks later, when I transmitted myself back to 1900. Incidentally, my second impression of the year 1950 was amazement that aside from boots, trouser widths and cravats, men's styles had remained unchanged for fifty years."

"Your second impression?" Mr. Grayson said. "What was your first?"

"Also a feeling of amazement. The room was dark when I arrived, and I automatically felt for the gas mantle near the door. Instead my hand encountered a flat metal plate from which a tiny switch handle protruded. Experimentally I pushed it, and light sprang into the room."

The editor looked at him blankly.

"They had perfected the incandescent lamp," George explained.

The lamp over Mr. Grayson's desk began to sputter at that moment, distracting the attention of both men until the flow of gas again became even.

"How did you manage to live until you obtained your sewer-digging job?" Mr. Grayson asked finally.

"For the first day I was on charity . . . under false pretenses, I am afraid. After stealing the clothing, I sallied right out into the street. Or rather I 'sallied' as far as the front door of the Hotel Chelsea, after which my mode of progress is perhaps better described as a stagger. The impact of New York City in 1950 was so tremendous on a mind conditioned to 1900 that I could later recall nothing that happened from midnight, when I passed through the hotel's front door, until two A.M. when I stumbled into a Salvation Army Hotel in a state of shock and was shown to bed by a kindly captain who apparently mistook my condition for alcoholism."

A series of small explosions from the street outside interrupted George's story. At the same moment the door flew open and the secretary excitedly burst into the room. She beat the two men to the window.

Along the cobblestoned street rolled an astonishing vehicle. Open-carriaged and high-seated, it was piloted by a creature so begoggled and so encased in a dust-wrapper that its sex was indeterminate. At ten miles an hour it roared past the building, the noise of its exhaust drowning all other sound in the area except the voice of a watching pedestrian who yelled, "Get a horse!"

Long after it had disappeared from sight, the secretary continued to lean out the window and peer after it. Finally she withdrew her head with reluctance.

"That's the third one I've seen," she said in an awed voice.

Shooing her from his office, Mr. Grayson resumed his chair and waved George back to his.

"Frankly, Mr. Blade," he said, "I find your story of visiting 1950 as implausible as the script which you based on it. But I have to admit I find it interesting. What caused the state of shock you were describing when we were interrupted?"

"The same thing that excited your secretary, Mr. Grayson. Suppose when we rushed to the window a moment ago, instead of a single horseless vehicle, we had seen thousands travelling at five times the speed. Wouldn't your eyes bug out?"

"They probably would," Mr. Grayson admitted.

"I have a vague recollection of thousands of glittering metal and glass vehicles roaring along streets on which I was accustomed to seeing only sedately trotting horses; of strident voices, clanging bells, screaming horns, and mingled with all these noises a strange overtone which I can only describe as the drone of a million cogs moving in the complicated machinery of a mechanical city."

"You used that same description in your story," Mr. Grayson remarked.

George said, "After the initial shock, I gradually became sufficiently acclimated to exist in this strange environment, but for the full two weeks of my visit I remained in a constant state of amazement. Some of the mechanical wonders I saw are described in my story, but not nearly all. There seemed to be no end to them. In 1950 nothing was done by people any more . . . except the digging of sewers . . . even the theater having substituted for actors a huge screen upon which by some kind of electrical lighting effect the illusion of real performers was produced, complete with color and sound. But the progress in transportation was the most astounding. I rode great trains through tunnels under the earth, and travelled in horseless carriages at incredible speeds. I even took a ride in one of the streamlined flying machines described in my story."

Mr. Grayson, still obviously unbelieving, brought the conversation back to its original subject.

"This is all very entertaining, Mr. Blade. But even if I conceded your background is based on authentic observation, that is hardly enough to satisfy the reader. Your story has to *sound* plausible. But what have you given us? An incredibly advanced civilization where nearly everything is done by machine. A civilization which travels between continents in spaceships at hundreds of miles an hour, and has warships which move at nearly the speed of sound. The homes of your hyper-civilization are a mass of implausible gadgets run by buttons. Buttons are pushed to bring light, clean rugs, wash clothes, and even to squeeze juice from fruit. Every home has built-in entertainment which picks music, talk and pictures from the air. Heat comes from the walls instead of from stoves, and water, both hot and cold, comes in unlimited amounts from spigots which merely have to have their handles twisted instead of being pumped. And the warfare you describe! A single bomb disintegrates an entire city! Don't you see how implausible it all sounds?"

"But it actually *was* that way," George said sullenly.

The editor smiled indulgently. "Perhaps life will be as you describe it in one million A.D. But no reader would accept such tremendous scientific advance in a mere fifty years. What you seemed to have overlooked, Mr. Blade, is that the children of today will be the leaders of your fantastic future world. You yourself may quite likely still be alive. The whole world has fresh in its mind Andree's balloon attempt, yet you expect your readers to believe such enormous air progress as you describe will take place during their own lifetimes! And your war weapons! Warfare has advanced tremendously in the past few decades—the revolver, the automatic rifle, the ironclad warship—but a Napoleonic marshal could almost instantly master these modern developments. Are we to expect that in fifty years war should take on a shape that Napoleon himself could not comprehend?"

Mr. Grayson's smile became more gentle. "But your worst error in plausibility is related to the first I mentioned. Your leaders of 1950 are living now. Yet in your story they are adjusted to their incredibly mechanized life as though it had always existed. They are not even surprised at civilization's progress. It simply isn't plausible that people *would take such a life for granted.*"

PILLAR OF FIRE
by Ray Bradbury

CHAPTER ONE

HE CAME OUT OF THE EARTH, hating. Hate was his father; hate was his mother.

It was good to walk again. It was good to leap up out of the earth, off of your back, and stretch your cramped arms violently and try to take a deep breath!

He *tried*. He cried out.

He couldn't breathe. He flung his arms over his face and tried to breathe. It was impossible. He walked on the earth, he came out of the earth. But he was dead. He couldn't breathe. He could take air into his mouth and force it half down his throat, with withered moves of long-dormant muscles, wildly, wildly! And with this little air he could shout and cry! He wanted to have tears, but he couldn't make them come, either. All he knew was that he was standing upright, he was dead, he shouldn't be walking! He couldn't breathe and yet he stood.

The smells of the world were all about him. Frustratedly, he tried to smell the smells of autumn. Autumn was burning the land down into ruin. All across the country the ruins of summer lay; vast forests bloomed with flame, tumbled down timber on empty, unleafed timber. The smoke of the burning was rich, blue, and invisible.

He stood in the graveyard, hating. He walked through the world and yet could not taste nor smell of it. He heard, yes. The wind roared on his newly opened ears. But he was dead. Even though he walked he knew he was dead and should expect not too much of himself or this hateful living world.

He touched the tombstone over his own empty grave. He knew his own name again. It was a good job of carving.

WILLIAM LANTRY

That's what the grave stone said.

His fingers trembled on the cool stone surface.

BORN 1898—DIED 1933

Copyright 1948 by Fiction House, Inc.
Reprinted by permission of Harold Matson Company.

141

Born *again* . . . ?

What year? He glared at the sky and the midnight autumnal stars moving in slow illuminations across the windy black. He read the tiltings of centuries in those stars. Orion thus and so, Aurego here! and where Taurus? *There!*

His eyes narrowed. His lips spelled out the year:

"2349."

An odd number. Like a school sum. They used to say a man couldn't encompass any number over a hundred. After that it was all so damned abstract there was no use counting. This was the year 2349! A numeral, a sum. And here he was, a man who had lain in his hateful dark coffin, hating to be buried, hating the living people above who lived and lived and lived, hating them for all the centuries, until today, now, born out of hatred, he stood by his own freshly excavated grave, the smell of raw earth in the air, perhaps, but he could not smell it!

"I," he said, addressing a poplar tree that was shaken by the wind, "am an anachronism." He smiled faintly.

He looked at the graveyard. It was cold and empty. All of the stones had been ripped up and piled like so many flat bricks, one atop another, in the far corner by the wrought iron fence. This had been going on for two endless weeks. In his deep secret coffin he had heard the heartless, wild stirring as the men jabbed the earth with cold spades and tore out the coffins and carried away the withered ancient bodies to be burned. Twisting with fear in his coffin, he had waited for them to come to him.

Today they had arrived at his coffin. But—late. They had dug down to within an inch of the lid. Five o'clock bell, time for quitting. Home to supper. The workers had gone off. Tomorrow they would finish the job, they said, shrugging into their coats.

Silence had come to the emptied tombyard.

Carefully, quietly, with a soft rattling of sod, the coffin lid had lifted.

William Lantry stood trembling now, in the last cemetery on Earth.

"Remember?" he asked himself, looking at the raw earth. "Remember those stories of the last man on earth? Those stories of men wandering in ruins, alone? Well, you, William Lantry, are a switch on the old story. Do you *know* that? You are the last *dead* man in the whole damned world!"

There were no more dead people. Nowhere in any land was there a dead person. Impossible? Lantry did not smile at this. No, not impossible at all in this foolish, sterile, unimaginative, antiseptic age of cleansings and scientific methods! People died, oh my god, yes. But—*dead* people? Corpses? They didn't exist!

What *happened* to dead people?

The graveyard was on a hill. William Lantry walked through the dark burning night until he reached the edge of the graveyard and looked down upon the new town of Salem. It was all illumination, all color. Rocket ships cut fire above it, crossing the sky to all the far ports of earth.

In his grave the new violence of this future world had driven down and seeped into William Lantry. He had been bathed in it for years. He knew all about it, with a hating dead man's knowledge of such things.

Most important of all, he knew what these fools did with dead men.

He lifted his eyes. In the center of the town a massive stone finger pointed at the stars. It was three hundred feet high and fifty feet across. There was a wide entrance and a drive in front of it.

In the town, theoretically, thought William Lantry, say you have a dying man. In a moment he will be dead. What happens? No sooner is his pulse cold when a certificate is flourished, made out, his relatives pack him into a car-beetle and drive him swiftly to—

The Incinerator!

That functional finger, that Pillar of Fire pointing at the stars. Incinerator. A functional, terrible name. But truth is truth in this future world.

Like a stick of kindling your Mr. Dead Man is shot into the furnace.

Flume!

William Lantry looked at the top of the gigantic pistol shoving at the stars. A small pennant of smoke issued from the top.

There's where your dead people go.

"Take care of yourself, William Lantry," he murmured. "You're the last one, the rare item, the last dead man. All the other graveyards of earth have been blasted up. This is the last graveyard and you're the last dead man from the centuries. These people don't believe in having dead people about, much less walking dead people. Everything that can't be used goes up like a match-stick. Superstitions right along with it!"

He looked at the town. All right, he thought, quietly. I hate you. You hate me, or you *would* if you knew I existed. You don't believe in such things as vampires or ghosts. Labels without referents, you cry! You snort. All right, snort! Frankly, I don't believe in *you*, either! I don't *like* you! You and your Incinerators.

He trembled. How very close it had been. Day after day they had hauled out the other dead ones, burned them like so much kindling. An edict had been broadcast around the world. He had heard the digging men talk as they worked!

"I guess it's a good idea, this cleaning up the graveyards," said one of the men.

"Guess so," said another. "Grisly custom. Can you imagine? Being buried, I mean! Unhealthy! All them germs!"

"Sort of a shame. Romantic, kind of. I mean, leaving just this one graveyard untouched all these centuries. The other graveyards were cleaned out, what year was it, Jim?"

"About 2260, I think. Yeah, that was it, 2260, almost a hundred years ago. But some Salem Committee they got on their high horse and they said, 'Look here, let's have just ONE graveyard left, to remind us of the customs of the barbarians.' And the gover'ment scratched its head, thunk it over, and said, 'Okay. Salem it is. But all other graveyards go, you understand, all!'"

"And away they went," said Jim.

"Sure, they sucked out 'em with fire and steam shovels and rocket-cleaners. If they knew a man was buried in a cow-pasture, they fixed him! Evacuated them, they did. Sort of cruel, I say."

"I hate to sound old-fashioned, but still there were a lot of tourists came here every year, just to see what a real graveyard was like."

"Right. We had nearly a million people in the last three years visiting. A good revenue. But—a government order is an order. The government says no more morbidity, so flush her out we do! Here we go. Hand me that spade, Bill."

William Lantry stood in the autumn wind, on the hill. It was good to walk again, to feel the wind and to hear the leaves scuttling like mice on the road ahead of him. It was good to see the bitter cold stars almost blown away by the wind.

It was even good to know fear again.

For fear rose in him now, and he could not put it away. The very fact that he was walking made him an enemy. And there was not another friend, another dead man, in all of the world, to whom one could turn for help or consolation. It was the whole melodramatic living world against one William Lantry. It was the whole vampire-disbelieving, body-burning, graveyard-annihilating world against a man in a dark suit on a dark autumn hill. He put out his pale cold hands into the city illumination. You have pulled the tombstones, like teeth, from the yard, he thought. Now I will find some way to push your damnable Incinerators down into rubble. I will make dead people again, and I will make friends in so doing. I cannot be alone and lonely. I must start manufacturing friends very soon. Tonight.

"War is declared," he said, and laughed. It was pretty silly, one man declaring war on an entire world.

The world did not answer back. A rocket crossed the sky on a rush of flame, like an Incinerator taking wing.

Footsteps. Lantry hastened to the edge of the cemetery. The diggers, coming back to finish up their work? No. Just someone, a man, walking by.

As the man came abreast the cemetery gate, Lantry stepped swiftly out. "Good evening," said the man, smiling.

Lantry struck the man in the face. The man fell. Lantry bent quietly down and hit the man a killing blow across the neck with the side of his hand.

Dragging the body back into shadow, he stripped it, changed clothes with it. It wouldn't do for a fellow to go wandering about this future world with ancient clothing on. He found a small pocket knife in the man's coat; not much of a knife, but enough if you knew how to handle it properly. He knew how.

He rolled the body down into one of the already opened and exhumed graves. In a minute he had shoveled dirt down upon it, just enough to hide it. There was little chance of it being found. They wouldn't dig the same grave twice.

He adjusted himself in his new loose-fitting metallic suit. Fine, fine.

Hating, William Lantry walked down into town, to do battle with the Earth.

CHAPTER TWO

THE INCINERATOR WAS OPEN. It never closed. There was a wide entrance, all lighted up with hidden illumination, there was a helicopter landing table and a beetle drive. The town itself was dying down after another day of the dynamo. The lights were going dim, and the only quiet, lighted spot in the town now was the Incinerator. God, what a practical name, what an unromantic name.

William Lantry entered the wide, well-lighted door. It was an entrance, really; there were no doors to open or shut. People could go in and out, summer or winter, the inside was always warm. Warm from the fire that rushed whispering up the high round flue to where the whirlers, the propellors, the air-jets pushed the leafy grey ashes on away for a ten mile ride down the sky.

There was the warmth of the bakery here. The halls were floored with rubber parquet. You couldn't make a noise if you wanted to. Music played in hidden throats somewhere. Not music of death at all, but music of life and the way the sun lived inside the Incinerator; or the sun's brother, anyway. You could hear the flame floating inside the heavy brick wall.

William Lantry descended a ramp. Behind him he heard a whisper and turned in time to see a beetle stop before the entrance way. A bell rang. The music, as if at a signal, rose to ecstatic heights. There was joy in it.

From the beetle, which opened from the rear, some attendants stepped carrying a golden box. It was six feet long and there were sun symbols on it. From another beetle the relatives of the man in the box stepped and followed as the attendants took the golden box down a ramp to a kind of altar. On the side of the altar were the words, "WE THAT WERE BORN OF THE SUN RETURN TO THE SUN". The golden box was deposited upon the altar, the music leaped upward, the Guardian of this place spoke only a few words, then the attendants picked up the golden box, walked to a transparent wall, a safety lock, also transparent, and opened it. The box was shoved into the glass slot. A moment later an inner lock opened, the box was injected into the interior of the flue and vanished instantly in quick flame.

The attendants walked away. The relatives without a word turned and walked out. The music played.

William Lantry approached the glass fire lock. He peered through the wall at the vast, glowing, never-ceasing heart of the Incinerator. It burned steadily, without a flicker, singing to itself peacefully. It was so solid it was like a golden river flowing up out of the earth toward the sky. Anything you put into the river was borne upward, vanished.

Lantry felt again his unreasoning hatred of this thing, this monster, cleansing fire.

A man stood at his elbow. "May I help you, sir?"

"What?" Lantry turned abruptly. "What did you say?"

"May I be of service?"

"I—that is—" Lantry looked quickly at the ramp and the door. His hands trembled at his sides. "I've never been in here before."

"Never?" The Attendant was surprised.

That had been the wrong thing to say, Lantry realized. But it was said, nevertheless. "I mean," he said. "Not really. I mean, when you're a child, somehow, you don't pay attention. I suddenly realized tonight that I didn't really *know* the Incinerator."

The Attendant smiled. "We never know anything, do we, really? I'll be glad to show you around."

"Oh, no. Never mind. It—it's a wonderful place."

"Yes, it is." The Attendant took pride in it. "One of the finest in the world, I think."

"I—" Lantry felt he must explain further. "I haven't had many relatives die on me since I was a child. In fact, none. So, you see I haven't been here for many years."

"I see." The Attendant's face seemed to darken somewhat.

What've I said now, thought Lantry. What in God's name is wrong? What've I done? If I'm not careful I'll get myself shoved right into that damnable firetrap. What's wrong with this fellow's face? He seems to be giving me more than the usual going over.

"You wouldn't be one of the men who've just returned from Mars, would you?" asked the Attendant.

"No. Why do you ask?"

"No matter." The Attendant began to walk off. "If you want to know anything, just ask me."

"Just one thing," said Lantry.

"What's that?"

"This."

Lantry dealt him a stunning blow across the neck.

He had watched the fire-trap operator with expert eyes. Now, with the sagging body in his arms, he touched the button that opened the warm outer lock, placed the body in, heard the music rise, and saw the inner lock open. The body shot out into the river of fire. The music softened.

"Well done, Lantry, well done."

Barely an instant later another Attendant entered the room. Lantry was caught with an expression of pleased excitement on his face. The Attendant looked around as if expecting to find someone, then he walked toward Lantry. "May I help you?"

"Just looking," said Lantry.

"Rather late at night," said the Attendant.

"I couldn't sleep."

That was the wrong answer, too. Everybody slept in this world. Nobody had insomnia. If you did you simply turned on a hypno-ray, and, sixty seconds later, you were snoring. Oh, he was just *full* of wrong answers. First he had made the fatal error of saying he had never been in the Incinerator before, when he knew damned well that all children were brought here on tours, every year, from the time they were four, to instill the idea of the clean fire death and the Incinerator in their minds. Death was a bright fire, death was warmth and the sun. It was not a dark, shadowed thing. That was important in their education. And he, pale thoughtless fool, had immediately gabbled out his ignorance.

And another thing, this paleness of his. He looked at his hands and realized with growing terror that a pale man also was non-existent in this world. They would suspect his paleness. That was why the first attendant had asked, "Are you one of those men newly returned from Mars?" Here, now, this new Attendant was clean and bright as a copper penny, his cheeks red with health and energy. Lantry hid his pale hands in his pockets. But he was fully aware of the searching the Attendant did on his face.

"I mean to say," said Lantry. "I didn't *want* to sleep. I wanted to think."

"Was there a service held here a moment ago?" asked the Attendant, looking about.

"I don't know, I just came in."

"I thought I heard the fire lock open and shut."

"I don't know," said Lantry.

The man pressed a wall button. "Anderson?"

A voice replied. "Yes."

"Locate Saul for me, will you?"

"I'll ring the corridors." A pause. "Can't find him."

"Thanks." The Attendant was puzzled. He was beginning to make little sniffing motions with his nose. "Do you—*smell* anything?"

Lantry sniffed. "No. Why?"

"I *smell* something."

"I remember once when I was a kid," said the man. "And we found a cow lying dead in the field. It had been there two days in the hot sun. That's what this smell is. I wonder what it's from?"

"Oh, I know what it is," said Lantry quietly. He held out his hand. "Here."

"What?"

"Me, of course."

"You?"

"Dead several hundred years."

"You're an odd joker." The Attendant was puzzled.

"Very." Lantry took out the knife. "Do you know what this is?"

"A knife."

"Do you ever use knives on people any more?"

"How do you mean?"

"I mean—killing them, with knives or guns or poison?"

"You *are* an odd joker!" The man giggled awkwardly.

"I'm going to kill you," said Lantry.

"Nobody kills anybody," said the man.

"Not any more they don't. But they used to, in the old days."

"I know they did."

"This will be the first murder in three hundred years. I just killed your friend. I just shoved him into the fire lock."

That remark had the desired effect. It numbed the man so completely, it shocked him so thoroughly with its illogical aspects that Lantry had time to walk forward. He put the knife against the man's chest. "I'm going to kill you."

"That's silly," said the man, numbly. "People don't do that."

"Like this," said Lantry. "You see?"

The knife slid into the chest. The man stared at it for a moment. Lantry caught the falling body.

CHAPTER THREE

THE SALEM FLUE EXPLODED at six that morning. The great fire chimney shattered into ten thousand parts and flung itself into the earth and into the sky and into the houses of the sleeping people. There was fire and sound, more fire than autumn made burning in the hills.

William Lantry was five miles away at the time of the explosion. He saw the town ignited by the great spreading cremation of it. And he shook his head and laughed a little bit and clapped his hands smartly together.

Relatively simple. You walked around killing people who didn't believe in murder, had only heard of it indirectly as some dim gone custom of the old barbarian races. You walked into the control room of the Incinerator and said, "How do you work this Incinerator?" and the Control Man told you, because everybody told the truth in this world of the future, nobody lied, there was no reason to lie, there was no danger to lie *against*. There was only one criminal in the world, and nobody knew HE existed yet.

Oh, it was an incredibly beautiful set-up. The Control Man had told him just how the Incinerator worked, what pressure gauges controlled the flood of fire gasses going up the flue, what levers were adjusted or readjusted. He and Lantry had had quite a talk. It was an easy free world. People trusted people. A moment later Lantry had shoved a knife in the Control Man also and set the pressure gauges for an overload to occur half an hour later, and walked out of the Incinerator halls, whistling.

Now even the sky was palled with the vast black cloud of the explosion.

"This is only the first," said Lantry, looking at the sky. "I'll tear all the others down before they even suspect there's an unethical man loose in their society. They can't account for a variable like me. I'm beyond their understanding. I'm incomprehensible, impossible, therefore I do not exist. My

God, I can kill hundreds of thousands of them before they even realize murder is out in the world again. I can make it look like an accident each time. Why, the idea is so huge, it's unbelievable!"

The fire burned the town. He sat under a tree for a long time, until morning. Then, he found a cave in the hills, and went in, to sleep.

He awoke at sunset with a sudden dream of fire. He saw himself pushed into the flue, cut into sections by flame, burned away to nothing. He sat up on the cave floor, laughing at himself. He had an idea.

He walked down into the town and stepped into an audio booth. He dialed OPERATOR. "Give me the Police Department," he said.

"I beg your pardon?" said the operator.

He tried again. "The Law Force," he said.

"I will connect you with the Peace Control," she said, at last.

A little fear began ticking inside him like a tiny watch. Suppose the operator recognized the term Police Department as an anachronism, took his audio number, and sent someone out to investigate? No, she wouldn't do that. Why should she suspect? Paranoids were non-existent in this civilization.

"Yes, the Peace Control," he said.

A buzz. A man's voice answered. "Peace Control. Stephens speaking."

"Give me the Homicide Detail," said Lantry, smiling.

"The *what?*"

"Who investigates murders?"

"I beg your pardon, what are you talking about?"

"Wrong number." Lantry hung up, chuckling. Ye gods, there was no such thing as a Homicide Detail. There were no murders, therefore they needed no detectives. Perfect, perfect!

The audio rang back. Lantry hesitated, then answered.

"Say," said the voice on the phone. "Who *are* you?"

"The man just left who called," said Lantry, and hung up again.

He ran. They would recognize his voice and perhaps send someone out to check. People didn't lie. *He* had just lied. They knew his voice. He had lied. Anybody who lied needed a psychiatrist. They would come to pick him up to see why he was lying. For no *other* reason. They suspected him of nothing else. Therefore—he must run.

Oh, how very carefully he must act from now on. He knew nothing of this world, this odd straight truthful ethical world. Simply by looking pale you were suspect. Simply by not sleeping nights you were suspect. Simply by not bathing, by smelling like a—dead cow?—you were suspect. Anything.

He must go to a library. But that was dangerous, too. What were libraries like today? Did they have books or did they have film spools which projected books on a screen? Or did people have libraries at home, thus eliminating the necessity of keeping large main libraries?

He decided to chance it. His use of archaic terms might well make him suspect again, but now it was very important he learn all that could be learned of this foul world into which he had come again. He stopped a man on the street. "Which way to the library?"

The man was not surprised. "Two blocks east, one block north."

"Thank you."

Simple as that.

He walked into the library a few minutes later.

"May I help you?"

He looked at the librarian. May I help you, may I help you. What a world of helpful people! "I'd like to 'have' Edgar Allan Poe." His verb was carefully chosen. He didn't say 'read'. He was too afraid that books were passé, that printing itself was a lost art. Maybe all 'books' today were in the form of fully delineated three-dimensional motion pictures. How in hell could you make a motion picture out of Socrates, Schopenhauer, Nietzsche and Freud?

"What was that name again?"

"Edgar Allan Poe."

"There is no such author listed in our files."

"Will you please check?"

She checked. "Oh, yes. There's a red mark on the file card. He was one of the authors in the Great Burning of 2265."

"How ignorant of me."

"That's all right," she said. "Have you heard much of him?"

"He had some interesting barbarian ideas on death," said Lantry.

"Horrible ones," she said, wrinkling her nose. "Ghastly."

"Yes. Ghastly. Abominable, in fact. Good thing he was burned. Unclean. By the way, do you have any of Lovecraft?"

"Is that a sex book?"

Lantry exploded with laughter. "No, no. It's a man."

She riffled the file. "He was burned, too. Along with Poe."

"I suppose that applies to Machen and a man named Derleth and one named Ambrose Bierce, also?"

"Yes." She shut the file cabinet. "All burned. And good riddance." She gave him an odd warm look of interest. "I bet you've just come back from Mars."

"Why do you say that?"

"There was another explorer in here yesterday. He'd just made the Mars hop and return. He was interested in supernatural literature, also. It seems there are actually 'tombs' on Mars."

"What are 'tombs'?" Lantry was learning to keep his mouth closed.

"You know, those things they once buried people in."

"Barbarian custom. Ghastly!"

"*Isn't* it? Well, seeing the Martian tombs made this young explorer curious. He came and asked if we had any of those authors you mentioned. Of course we haven't even a smitch of their stuff." She looked at his pale face. "You *are* one of the Martian rocket men, aren't you?"

"Yes," he said. "Got back on the ship the other day."

"The other young man's name was Burke."

"Of course. Burke! Good friend of mine!"

"Sorry I can't help you. You'd best get yourself some vitamin shots and some sun-lamp. You look terrible, Mr.——?"

"Lantry. I'll be good. Thanks ever so much. See you next Hallows' Eve!"

"Aren't you the clever one." She laughed. "If there *were* a Hallows' Eve, I'd make it a date."

"But they burned *that*, too," he said.

"Oh, they burned everything," she said. "Good night."

"Good night." And he went on out.

Oh, how carefully he was balanced in this world! Like some kind of dark gyroscope, whirling with never a murmur, a very silent man. As he walked along the eight o'clock evening street he noticed with particular interest that there was not an unusual amount of lights about. There were the usual street lights at each corner, but the blocks themselves were only faintly illuminated. Could it be that these remarkable people were not *afraid of the dark*? Incredible nonsense! *Every* one was afraid of the dark. *Even he* himself had been afraid, as a child. It was as natural as eating.

A little boy ran by on pelting feet, followed by six others. They yelled and shouted and rolled on the dark cool October lawn, in the leaves. Lantry looked on for several minutes before addressing himself to one of the small boys who was for a moment taking a respite, gathering his breath into his small lungs, as a boy might blow to refill a punctured paper bag.

"Here, now," said Lantry. "You'll wear yourself out."

"Sure," said the boy.

"Could you tell me," said the man, "why there are no street lights in the middle of the blocks?"

"Why?" asked the boy.

"I'm a teacher, I thought I'd test your knowledge," said Lantry.

"Well," said the boy, "you don't need lights in the middle of the block, that's why."

"But it gets rather dark," said Lantry.

"So?" said the boy.

"Aren't you afraid?" asked Lantry.

"Of what?" asked the boy.

"The dark," said Lantry.

"Ho ho," said the boy. "Why should I be?"

"Well," said Lantry. "It's black, it's dark. And after all, street lights were invented to take away the dark and take away fear."

"That's silly. Street lights were made so you could see where you were walking. Outside of that there's nothing."

"You miss the whole point—" said Lantry. "Do you mean to say you would sit in the middle of an empty lot all night and not be afraid?"

"Of what?"

"Of what, of what, of what, you little ninny! Of the dark!"

"Ho ho."

"Would you go out in the hills and stay all night in the dark?"

"Sure."

"Would you stay in a deserted house alone?"

"Sure."

"And not be afraid?"

"Sure."

"You're a liar!"

"Don't you call me nasty names!" shouted the boy. Liar was the improper noun, indeed. It seemed to be the worst thing you could call a person.

Lantry was completely furious with the little monster. "Look," he insisted. "Look into my eyes . . ."

The boy looked.

Lantry bared his teeth slightly. He put out his hands, making a clawlike gesture. He leered and gesticulated and wrinkled his face into a terrible mask of horror.

"Ho ho," said the boy. "You're funny."

"*What* did you say?"

"You're funny. Do it again. Hey, gang, c'mere! This man does funny things!"

"Never mind."

"Do it again, sir."

"Never mind, never mind. Good night!" Lantry ran off.

"Good night, sir. And mind the dark, sir!" called the little boy.

Of all the stupidity, of all the rank, gross, crawling, jelly-mouthed stupidity! He had never seen the like of it in his life! Bringing the children up without so much as an *ounce* of imagination! Where was the fun in being children if you didn't imagine things?

He stopped running. He slowed and for the first time began to appraise himself. He ran his hand over his face and bit his finger and found that he himself was standing midway in the block and he felt uncomfortable. He moved up to the street corner where there was a glowing lantern. "That's better," he said, holding his hands out like a man to an open warm fire.

He listened. There was not a sound except the night breathing of the crickets. Faintly there was a fire-hush as a rocket swept the sky. It was the sound a torch might make brandished gently on the dark air.

He listened to himself and for the first time he realized what there was so peculiar to himself. There was not a sound in him. The little nostril and lung noises were absent. His lungs did not take nor give oxygen or carbon-dioxide; they did not move. The hairs in his nostrils did not quiver with warm combing air. That faint purling whisper of breathing did not sound in his nose. Strange. Funny. A noise you never heard when you were alive, the breath that fed your body, and yet, once dead, oh how you missed it!

The only other time you ever heard it was on deep dreamless awake nights when you wakened and listened and heard first your nose taking and gently poking out the air, and then the dull deep dim red thunder of the blood in your temples, in your eardrums, in your throat, in your aching wrists, in your warm loins, in your chest. All of those little rhythms, gone. The wrist beat gone, the throat pulse gone, the chest vibration gone. The sound of the blood coming up down around and through, up down around and through. Now it was like listening to a statue.

And yet he *lived*. Or, rather, moved about. And how was this done, over and above scientific explanations, theories, doubts?

By one thing, and one thing alone.

Hatred.

Hatred was a blood in him, it went up down around and through, up down around and through. It was a heart in him, not beating, true, but warm. He was—what? Resentment. Envy. They said he could not lie any longer in his coffin in the cemetery. He had *wanted* to. He had never had any particular desire to get up and walk around. It had been enough, all these centuries, to lie in the deep box and feel but *not feel* the ticking of the million insect watches in the earth around, the moves of worms like so many deep thoughts in the soil.

But then they had come and said, "Out you go and into the furnace!" And that is the worst thing you can say to any man. You cannot tell him what to do. If you say you are dead, he will want not to be dead. If you say there are no such things as vampires, by God, that man will try to *be* one just for spite. If you say a dead man cannot walk he will test his limbs. If you say murder is no longer occurring, he will make it occur. He was, *in toto*, all the impossible things. They had given birth to him with their damnable practices and ignorances. Oh, how wrong they were. They needed to be shown. He would *show* them! Sun is *good*, so is *night*, there is nothing wrong with dark, *they* said.

Dark is horror, he shouted, silently, facing the little houses. It is *meant* for contrast. You must fear, you hear! That has always been the way of this world. You destroyers of Edgar Allan Poe and fine big-worded Lovecraft, you burner of Halloween masks and destroyer of pumpkin jack-o-lanterns! I will make night what it *once* was, the thing against which man built all his lanterned cities and his many children!

As if in answer to this, a rocket, flying low, trailing a long rakish feather of flame. It made Lantry flinch and draw back.

CHAPTER FOUR

IT WAS BUT TEN MILES to the little town of Science Port. He made it by dawn, walking. But even this was not good. At four in the morning a silver beetle pulled up on the road beside him.

"Hello," called the man inside.

"Hello," said Lantry, wearily.

"Why are you walking?" asked the man.

"I'm going to Science Port."

"Why don't you ride?"

"I *like* to walk."

"*Nobody* likes to walk. Are you sick? May I give you a ride?"

"Thanks, but I like to walk."

The man hesitated, then closed the beetle door. "Good night."

When the beetle was gone over the hill, Lantry retreated into a nearby forest. A world full of bungling helping people. By God, you couldn't even *walk* without being accused of sickness. That meant only one thing. He must not walk any longer, he had to ride. He should have accepted that fellow's offer.

The rest of the night he walked far enough off the highway so that if a beetle rushed by he had time to vanish in the underbrush. At dawn he crept into an empty dry water-drain and closed his eyes.

* * * * *

The dream was as perfect as a rimed snowflake.

He saw the graveyard where he had lain deep and ripe over the centuries. He heard the early morning footsteps of the laborers returning to finish their work.

"Would you mind passing me the shovel, Jim?"

"Here you go."

"Wait a minute, wait a minute!"

"What's up?"

"Look here. We didn't finish last night, did we?"

"No."

"There was one more coffin, wasn't there?"

"Yes."

"Well, here it is, and open!"

"You've got the wrong hole."

"What's the name say on the gravestone?"

"Lantry. William Lantry."

"That's him, that's the one! Gone!"

"What could have happened to it?"

"How do I know. The body was here last night."

"We can't be sure, we didn't look."

"God, man, people don't bury empty coffins. He was in his box. Now he isn't."

"Maybe this box was empty."

"Nonsense. Smell that smell? He was here all right."

A pause.

"Nobody would have taken the body, would they?"

"What for?"

"A curiosity, perhaps."

"Don't be ridiculous. People just don't steal. Nobody steals."

"Well, then there's only one solution."

"And?"

"He got up and walked away."

A pause. In the dark dream, Lantry expected to hear laughter. There was

none. Instead, the voice of the gravedigger, after a thoughtful pause, said,
"Yes. That's it, indeed. He got up and walked away."
"That's interesting to think about," said the other.
"Isn't it, though?"
Silence.

* * * * *

Lantry awoke. It had all been a dream, but God, how realistic. How strangely the two men had carried on. But not unnaturally, oh, no. That was exactly how you expected men of the future to talk. Men of the future. Lantry grinned wryly. That was an anachronism for you. This *was* the future. This was happening *now*. It wasn't 300 years from now, it was now, not then, or any other time. This wasn't the Twentieth Century. Oh, how calmly those two men in the dream had said, "He got up and walked away." "—interesting to think about." "*Isn't* it, though?" With never a quaver in their voices. With not so much as a glance over their shoulders or a tremble of spade in hand. But, of course, with their perfectly honest, logical minds, there was but one explanation; certainly nobody had *stolen* the corpse. "*Nobody* steals." The corpse had simply got up and walked off. The corpse was the only one who could have *possibly* moved the corpse. By the few casual slow words of the gravediggers Lantry knew what they were thinking. Here was a man that had lain in suspended animation, not really dead, for hundreds of years. The jarring about, the activity, had brought him back.

Everyone had heard of those little green toads that are sealed for centuries inside mud rocks or in ice patties, alive, alive oh! And how when scientists chipped them out and warmed them like marbles in their hands the little toads leapt about and frisked and blinked. Then it was only logical that the gravediggers think of William Lantry in like fashion.

But what if the various parts were fitted together in the next day or so? If the vanished body and the shattered, exploded Incinerator were connected? What if this fellow named Burke, who had returned pale from Mars, went to the library again and said to the young woman he wanted some books and she said, "Oh, your friend Lantry was in the other day." And he'd say, "Lantry who? Don't know anyone by that name." And she'd say, "Oh, he *lied*." And people in this time didn't lie. So it would all form and coalesce, item by item, bit by bit. A pale man who was pale and shouldn't be pale had lied and people don't lie, and a walking man on a lonely country road had walked and people don't walk any more, and a body was missing from a cemetery, and the Incinerator had blown up and and and—

They would come after him. They would find him. He would be easy to find. He walked. He lied. He was pale. They would find him and take him and stick him through the open fire lock of the nearest Burner and that would be your Mr. William Lantry, like a Fourth of July set-piece!

There was only one thing to be done efficiently and completely. He arose in violent moves. His lips were wide and his dark eyes were flared and there was a trembling and burning all through him. He must kill and kill and kill and kill and kill. He must make his enemies into friends, into people like himself who walked but shouldn't walk, who were pale in a land of pinks. He must kill and then kill and then kill again. He must make bodies and dead people and corpses. He must destroy Incinerator after Flue after Burner after Incinerator. Explosion on explosion. Death on death. Then, when the Incinerators were all in thrown ruin, and the hastily established morgues were jammed with the bodies of people shattered by the explosion, then he would begin his making of friends, his enrollment of the dead in his own cause.

Before they traced and found and killed him, they must be killed themselves. So far he was safe. He could kill and they would not kill back. People simply do not go around killing. That was his safety margin. He climbed out of the abandoned drain, stood in the road.

He took the knife from his pocket and hailed the next beetle.

It was like the Fourth of July! The biggest damned firecracker of them all. The Science Port Incinerator split down the middle and flew apart. It made a thousand small explosions that ended with a greater one. It fell upon the town and crushed houses and burned trees. It woke people from sleep and then put them to sleep again, forever, an instant later.

William Lantry, sitting in a beetle that was not his own, tuned idly to a station on the audio dial. The collapse of the Incinerator had killed some four hundred people. Many had been caught in flattened houses, others struck by flying metal. A temporary morgue was being set up at—

An address was given.

Lantry noted it with a pad and pencil.

He could go on this way, he thought, from town to town, from country to country, destroying the Burners, the Pillars of Fire, until the whole clean magnificent framework of flame and cauterization was tumbled. He made a fair estimate—each explosion averaged five hundred dead. You could work that up to a hundred thousand in no time.

He pressed the floor stud of the beetle. Smiling, he drove off through the dark streets of the city.

The city coroner had requisitioned an old warehouse. From midnight until four in the morning the grey beetles hissed down the rain-shiny streets, turned in, and the bodies were laid out on the cold concrete floors, with white sheets over them. It was a continuous flow until about four-thirty, then it stopped. There were about two hundred bodies there, white and cold.

The bodies were left alone; nobody stayed behind to tend them. There was no use tending the dead; it was a useless procedure; the dead could take care of themselves.

About five o'clock, with a touch of dawn in the east, the first trickle of relatives arrived to identify their sons or their fathers or their mothers or their uncles. The people moved quickly into the warehouse, made the identification, moved quickly out again. By six o'clock, with the sky still lighter in the east, this trickle had passed on, also.

William Lantry walked across the wide wet street and entered the warehouse.

He held a piece of blue chalk in one hand.

He walked by the coroner who stood in the entranceway talking to two others. ". . . drive the bodies to the Incinerator in Mellin Town, tomorrow . . ." The voices faded.

Lantry moved, his feet echoing faintly on the cool concrete. A wave of sourceless relief came to him as he walked among the shrouded figures. He was among his own. And—better than that, by God! he had *created* these! He had made them dead! He had procured for himself a vast number of recumbent friends!

Was the coroner watching? Lantry turned his head. No. The warehouse was calm and quiet and shadowed in the dark morning. The coroner was walking away now, across the street, with his two attendants; a beetle had drawn up on the other side of the street, and the coroner was going over to talk with whoever was in the beetle.

William Lantry stood and made a blue chalk pentagram on the floor by each of the bodies. He moved swiftly, swiftly, without a sound, without blinking. In a few minutes, glancing up now and then to see if the coroner was still busy, he had chalked the floor by a hundred bodies. He straightened up and put the chalk in his pocket.

Now is the time for all good men to come to the aid of their party, now is the time for all good men to come to the aid of their party, now is the time for all good men to come to the aid of their party, now is the time . . .

Lying in the earth, over the centuries, the processes and thoughts of passing peoples and passing times had seeped down to him, slowly, as into a deep-buried sponge. From some death-memory in him now, ironically, repeatedly, a black typewriter clacked out black even lines of pertinent words:

Now is the time for all good men, for all good men, to come to the aid of—

William Lantry.

Other words—

Arise my love, and come away—

The quick brown fox jumped over . . . *Paraphrase it.* The quick risen body jumped over the tumbled Incinerator . . .

Lazarus, come forth from the tomb . . .

He knew the right words. He need only speak them as they had been spoken over the centuries. He need only gesture with his hands and speak the words, the dark words that would cause these bodies to quiver, rise and walk!

And when they had risen he would take them through the town, they would kill others and the others would rise and walk. By the end of the day there would be thousands of good friends walking with him. And what of the naive, living people of this year, this day, this hour? They would be completely unprepared for it. They would go down to defeat because they would not be expecting war of any sort. They wouldn't believe it possible, it would all be over before they could convince themselves that such an illogical thing could happen.

He lifted his hands. His lips moved. He said the words. He began in a chanting whisper and then raised his voice, louder. He said the words again and again. His eyes were closed tightly. His body swayed. He spoke faster and faster. He began to move forward among the bodies. The dark words flowed from his mouth. He was enchanted with his own formulae. He stooped and made further blue symbols on the concrete, in the fashion of long-dead sorcerers, smiling, confident. Any moment now the first tremor of the still bodies, any moment now the rising, the leaping up of the cold ones!

His hands lifted in the air. His head nodded. He spoke, he spoke, he spoke. He gestured. He talked loudly over the bodies, his eyes flaring, his body tensed. "Now!" he cried, violently. "Rise, *all* of you!"

Nothing happened.

"Rise!" he screamed, with a terrible torment in his voice.

The sheets lay in white blue-shadow folds over the silent bodies.

"Hear me, and act!" he shouted.

Far away, on the street, a beetle hissed along.

Again, again, again he shouted, pleaded. He got down by each body and asked of it his particular violent favor. No reply. He strode wildly between the even white rows, flinging his arms up, stooping again and again to make blue symbols!

Lantry was very pale. He licked his lips. "Come on, get up," he said. "They have, they always have, for a thousand years. When you make a mark— so! and speak a word—so! they always rise! Why not you now, why not you! Come on, come *on*, before *they* come back!"

The warehouse went up into shadow. There were steel beams across and down. In it, under the roof, there was not a sound, except the raving of a lonely man.

Lantry stopped.

Through the wide doors of the warehouse he caught a glimpse of the last cold stars of morning.

This was the year 2349.

His eyes grew cold and his hands fell to his sides. He did not move.

Once upon a time people shuddered when they heard the wind about the house, once people raised crucifixes and wolfbane, and believed in walking dead and bats and loping white wolves. And as long as they believed, then so long did the dead, the bats, the loping wolves exist. The mind gave birth and reality to them.

But . . .

He looked at the white sheeted bodies.

These people did not believe.

They had never believed. They would never believe. They had never imagined that the dead might walk. The dead went up flues in flame. They had never heard superstition, never trembled or shuddered or doubted in the dark. Walking dead people could not exist, they were illogical. This was the year 2349, man, after all!

Therefore, these people could not rise, could not walk again. They were dead and flat and cold. Nothing, chalk, imprecation, superstition, could wind them up and set them walking. They were dead and *knew* they were dead!

He was alone.

There were live people in the world who moved and drove beetles and drank quiet drinks in little dimly illumined bars by country roads, and kissed women and talked much good talk all day and every day.

But he was not alive.

Friction gave him what little warmth he possessed.

There were two hundred dead people here in this warehouse now, cold upon the floor. The first dead people in a hundred years who were allowed to be corpses for an extra hour or more. The first not to be immediately trundled to the Incinerator and lit like so much phosphorous.

He should be happy with them, among them.

He was not.

They were completely dead. They did not know nor believe in walking once the heart had paused and stilled itself. They were deader than dead ever was.

He was indeed alone, more alone than any man had ever been. He felt the chill of his aloneness moving up into his chest, strangling him quietly.

William Lantry turned suddenly and gasped.

While he had stood there, someone had entered the warehouse. A tall man with white hair, wearing a light-weight tan overcoat and no hat. How long the man had been nearby there was no telling.

There was no reason to stay here. Lantry turned and started to walk slowly out. He looked hastily at the man as he passed and the man with the white hair looked back at him, curiously. Had he heard? The imprecations, the pleadings, the shoutings? Did he suspect? Lantry slowed his walk. Had this man seen him make the blue chalk marks? But then, would he interpret them as symbols of an ancient superstition? Probably not.

Reaching the door, Lantry paused. For a moment he did not want to do anything but lie down and be coldly, really dead again and be carried silently down the street to some distant burning flue and there dispatched in ash and whispering fire. If he was indeed alone and there was no chance to collect an army to his cause, what, then, existed as a reason for going on? Killing? Yes, he'd kill a few thousand more. But that wasn't enough. You can only do so much of that before they drag you down.

He looked at the cold sky.

A rocket went across the black heaven, trailing fire.

Mars burned red among a million stars.

Mars. The library. The librarian. Talk. Returning rocket men. Tombs.

Lantry almost gave a shout. He restrained his hand, which wanted so much to reach up into the sky and touch Mars. Lovely red star on the sky. Good star that gave him sudden new hope. If he had a living heart now it would be thrashing wildly, and sweat would be breaking out of him and his pulses would be stammering, and tears would be in his eyes!

He would go down to where ever the rockets sprang up into space. He would go to Mars, one way or another. He would go to the Martian tombs. There, there, by God, were bodies, he would bet his last hatred on it, that would rise and walk and work with him! Theirs was an ancient culture, much different from that of Earth, patterned on the Egyptian, if what the librarian had said was true. And the Egyptian—what a crucible of dark superstition and midnight terror that culture had been! Mars it *was*, then. Beautiful Mars!

But he must not attract attention to himself. He must move carefully. He wanted to run, yes, to get away, but that would be the worst possible move he could make. The man with the white hair was glancing at Lantry from time to time, in the entranceway. There were too many people about. If anything happened he would be outnumbered. So far he had taken on only *one* man at a time.

Lantry forced himself to stop and stand on the steps before the warehouse. The man with the white hair came on onto the steps also and stood, looking at the sky. He looked as if he was going to speak at any moment. He fumbled in his pockets, took out a packet of cigarettes.

CHAPTER FIVE

THEY STOOD OUTSIDE THE MORGUE together, the tall pink, white-haired man, and Lantry, hands in their pockets. It was a cool night with a white shell of a moon that washed a house here, a road there, and further on, parts of a river.

"Cigarette?" The man offered Lantry one.

"Thanks."

They lit up together. The man glanced at Lantry's mouth. "Cool night." "Cool."

They shifted their feet. "Terrible accident."

"Terrible."

"So many dead."

"So many."

Lantry felt himself some sort of delicate weight upon a scale. The other man did not seem to be looking at him, but rather listening and feeling toward him. There was a feathery balance here that made for vast discomfort. He wanted to move away and get out from under this balancing, weighing. The tall white-haired man said, "My name's McClure."

"Did you have any friends inside?" asked Lantry.

"No. A casual acquaintance. Awful accident."

"Awful."

They balanced each other. A beetle hissed by on the road with its seventeen tires whirling quietly. The moon showed a little town further over in the black hills.

"I say," said the man McClure.

"Yes."

"Could you answer me a question?"

"Be glad to." He loosened the knife in his coat pocket, ready.

"Is your name Lantry?" asked the man at last.

"Yes."

"*William* Lantry?"

"Yes."

"Then you're the man who came out of the Salem graveyard day before yesterday, aren't you?"

"Yes."

"Good Lord, I'm glad to meet you, Lantry! We've been trying to find you for the past twenty-four hours!"

The man seized his hand, pumped it, slapped him on the back.

"What, what?" said Lantry.

"Good Lord, man, why did you run off? Do you realize what an instance this is? We want to talk to you!"

McClure was smiling, glowing. Another handshake, another slap. "I *thought* it was you!"

The man is mad, thought Lantry. Absolutely mad. Here I've toppled his Incinerators, killed people, and he's shaking my hand. Mad, mad!

"Will you come along to the Hall?" said the man, taking his elbow.

"Wh-what hall?" Lantry stepped back.

"The Science Hall, of course. It isn't every year we get a real case of suspended animation. In small animals, yes, but in a man, hardly! Will you come?"

"What's the act!" demanded Lantry, glaring. "What's all this talk."

"My dear fellow, what do you mean?" the man was stunned.

"Never mind. Is that the only reason you want to see me?"

"What other reason would there be, Mr. Lantry? You don't know how glad I am to see you!" He almost did a little dance. "I suspected. When we were in there together. You being so pale and all. And then the way you smoked your cigarette, something about it, and a lot of other things, all subliminal. But it is you, isn't it, it *is* you!"

"It is I. William Lantry." Dryly.

"Good fellow! Come along!"

The beetle moved swiftly through the dawn streets. McClure talked rapidly.

Lantry sat, listening, astounded. Here was this fool, McClure, playing his cards for him! Here was this stupid scientist, or whatever, accepting him not as a suspicious baggage, a murderous item. Oh no! Quite the contrary! Only as a suspended animation case was he considered! Not as a dangerous man at all. Far from it!

"Of course," cried McClure, grinning. "You didn't know where to go, whom to turn to. It was all quite incredible to you."

"Yes."

"I had a feeling you'd be there at the morgue tonight," said McClure, happily.

"Oh?" Lantry stiffened.

"Yes. Can't explain it. But you, how shall I put it? Ancient Americans? You had funny ideas on death. And you were among the dead so long, I felt you'd be drawn back by the accident, by the morgue and all. It's not very logical. Silly, in fact. It's just a feeling. I hate feelings but there it was. I came on a, I guess you'd call it a hunch, wouldn't you?"

"You might call it that?"

"And there you were!"

"There I was," said Lantry.

"Are you hungry?"

"I've eaten."

"How did you get around?"

"I hitch-hiked."

"You *what?*"

"People gave me rides on the road."

"Remarkable."

"I imagine it sounds that way." He looked at the passing houses. "So this is the era of space travel, is it?"

"Oh, we've been traveling to Mars for some forty years now."

"Amazing. And those big funnels, those towers in the middle of every town?"

"Those. Haven't you heard? The Incinerators. Oh, of course, they hadn't anything of that sort in your time. Had some bad luck with them. An explosion in Salem and one here, all in a forty-eight hour period. You looked as if you were going to speak; what is it?"

"I was thinking," said Lantry. "How fortunate I got out of my coffin when I did. I might well have been thrown into one of your Incinerators and burned up."

"That would have been terrible, wouldn't it have?"

"Quite."

Lantry toyed with the dials on the beetle dash. He wouldn't go to Mars. His plans were changed. If this fool simply refused to recognize an act of violence when he stumbled upon it, then let him be a fool. If they didn't connect the two explosions with a man from the tomb, all well and good. Let them go on deluding themselves. If they couldn't imagine someone being mean and nasty and murderous, heaven help them. He rubbed his hands with satisfaction. No, no Martian trip for you, as yet, Lantry lad. First we'll see what can be done boring from the inside. Plenty of time. The Incinerators can wait an extra week or so. One has to be subtle, you know. Any more immediate explosions might cause quite a ripple of thought.

McClure was gabbling wildly on.

"Of course, you don't have to be examined immediately. You'll want a rest. I'll put you up at my place."

"Thanks. I don't feel up to being probed and pulled. Plenty of time in a week or so."

They drew up before a house and climbed out.

"You'll want to sleep, naturally."

"I've been asleep for centuries. Be glad to stay awake. I'm not a bit tired."

"Good." McClure let them into the house. He headed for the drink bar. "A drink will fix us up."

"You have one," said Lantry. "Later for me. I just want to sit down."

"By all means sit." McClure mixed himself a drink. He looked around the room, looked at Lantry, paused for a moment with the drink in his hand, tilted his head to one side, and put his tongue in his cheek. Then he shrugged and stirred the drink. He walked slowly to a chair and sat, sipping the drink quietly. He seemed to be listening for something. "There are cigarettes on the table," he said.

"Thanks." Lantry took one and lit it and smoked it. He did not speak for some time.

Lantry thought, I'm taking this all too easily. Maybe I should kill and run. He's the only one that has found me, yet. Perhaps this is all a trap. Perhaps we're simply sitting here waiting for the police. Or whatever in hell they use for police these days. He looked at McClure. No. They weren't waiting for police. They were waiting for something else.

McClure didn't speak. He looked at Lantry's face and he looked at Lantry's hands. He looked at Lantry's chest a long time, with easy quietness. He sipped his drink. He looked at Lantry's feet.

Finally he said, "Where'd you get the clothing?"

"I asked someone for clothes and they gave these things to me. Darned nice of them."

"You'll find that's how we are in this world. All you have to do is ask."

McClure shut up again. His eyes moved. Only his eyes and nothing else. Once or twice he lifted his drink.

A little clock ticked somewhere in the distance.

"Tell me about yourself, Mr. Lantry."

"Nothing much to tell."

"You're modest."

"Hardly. You know about the past. I know nothing of the future, or I should say 'today' and day before yesterday. You don't learn much in a coffin."

McClure did not speak. He suddenly sat forward in his chair and then leaned back and shook his head.

They'll never suspect me, thought Lantry. They aren't superstitious, they simply *can't* believe in a dead man walking. Therefore, I'll be safe. I'll keep putting off the physical checkup. They're polite. They won't force me. Then, I'll work it so I can get to Mars. After that, the tombs, in my own good time, and the plan. God, how simple. How naive these people are."

McClure sat across the room for five minutes. A coldness had come over him. The color was very slowly going from his face, as one sees the color of medicine vanishing as one presses the bulb at the top of a dropper. He leaned forward, saying nothing, and offered another cigarette to Lantry.

"Thanks." Lantry took it. McClure sat deeply back into his easy chair, his knees folded one over the other. He did not look at Lantry, and yet somehow did. The feeling of weighing and balancing returned. McClure was like a tall thin master of hounds listening for something that nobody else could hear. There are little silver whistles you can blow that only dogs can hear. McClure seemed to be listening acutely, sensitively for such an invisible whistle, listening with his eyes and with his half-opened, dry mouth, and with his aching, breathing nostrils.

Lantry sucked the cigarette, sucked the cigarette, sucked the cigarette, and, as many times, blew out, blew out, blew out. McClure was like some lean red-shagged hound listening and listening with a slick slide of eyes to one side, with an apprehension in that hand that was so precisely microscopic that one only sensed it, as one sensed the invisible whistle, with some part of the brain deeper than eyes or nostril or ear. McClure was all chemist's scale, all antennae.

The room was so quiet the cigarette smoke made some kind of invisible noise rising to the ceiling. McClure was a thermometer, a chemist's scales, a listening hound, a litmus paper, an antennae; all these. Lantry did not move. Perhaps the feeling would pass. It had passed before. McClure did not move for a long while and then, without a word, he nodded at the sherry decanter, and Lantry refused as silently. They sat looking but not looking at each other, again and away, again and away.

McClure stiffened slowly. Lantry saw the color getting paler in those lean cheeks, and the hand tightening on the sherry glass, and a knowledge come at last to stay, never to go away, into the eyes.

Lantry did not move. He could not. All of this was of such a fascination that he wanted only to see, to hear what would happen next. It was McClure's show from here on in.

McClure said, "At first I thought it was the finest psychosis I have ever seen. You, I mean. I thought, he's convinced himself, Lantry's convinced himself, he's quite insane, he's told himself to do all these little things." McClure talked as if in a dream, and continued talking and didn't stop.

"I said to myself, he purposely doesn't breathe through his nose. I watched your nostrils, Lantry. The little nostril hairs never once quivered in the last hour. That wasn't enough. It was a fact I filed. It wasn't enough. He breathes through his mouth, I said, on purpose. And then I gave you a cigarette and you sucked and blew, sucked and blew. None of it ever came out your nose. I told myself, well, that's all right. He doesn't inhale. Is that terrible, is that suspect? All in the mouth, all in the mouth. And then, I looked at your chest. I watched. It never moved up or down, it did nothing. He's convinced himself, I said to myself. He's convinced himself about all this. He doesn't move his chest, except slowly, when he thinks you're not looking. That's what I told myself."

The words went on in the silent room, not pausing, still in a dream. "And then I offered you a drink but you don't drink and I thought, he doesn't drink, I thought. Is *that* terrible? And I watched and watched you all this time. Lantry holds his breath, he's fooling himself. But now, yes, now, I understand it quite well. Now I know everything the way it is. Do you know how I know? I do not hear breathing in the room. I wait and I hear nothing. There is no beat of heart or intake of lung. The room is so silent. Nonsense, one might say, but I know. At the Incinerator I know. There is a difference. You enter a room where a man is on a bed and you know immediately whether he will look up and speak to you or whether he will not speak to you ever again. Laugh if you will, but one can tell. It is a subliminal thing. It is the whistle the dog hears when no human hears. It is the tick of a clock that has ticked so long one no longer notices. Something is in a room when a man lives in it. Something is not in the room when a man is dead in it."

McClure shut his eyes a moment. He put down his sherry glass. He waited a moment. He took up his cigarette and puffed it and then put it down in a black tray.

"I am alone in this room," he said.

Lantry did not move.

"You are dead," said McClure. "My mind does not know this. It is not a thinking thing. It is a thing of the senses and the subconscious. At first I thought, this man *thinks* he is dead, risen from the dead, a vampire. Is that not logical? Would not any man, buried as many centuries, raised in a superstitious, ignorant culture, think likewise of himself once risen from the tomb? Yes, that is logical. This man has hypnotized himself and fitted his bodily functions so that they would in no way interfere with his self-delusion, his great paranoia. He governs his breathing. He tells himself, I cannot hear my breathing, therefore I am dead. His inner mind censors the sound of breathing. He does not allow himself to eat or drink. These things he probably does in his sleep, with part of his mind, hiding the evidences of this humanity from his deluded mind at other times."

McClure finished it. "I was wrong. You are not insane. You are not deluding yourself. Nor me. This is all very illogical and—I must admit—almost frightening. Does that make you feel good, to think you frighten me? I have no label for you. You're a very odd man, Lantry. I'm glad to have met you. This will make an interesting report indeed."

"Is there anything wrong with me being dead?" said Lantry. "Is it a crime?"

"You must admit it's highly unusual."

"But, still now, is it a crime?" asked Lantry.

"We have no crime, no criminal court. We want to examine you, naturally, to find out how you have happened. It is like that chemical which, one minute is inert, the next is living cell. Who can say where what happened to what. You are that impossibility. It is enough to drive a man quite insane."

"Will I be released when you are done fingering me?"

"You will not be held. If you don't wish to be examined, you will not be. But I am hoping you will help by offering us your services."

"I might," said Lantry.

"But tell me," said McClure. "What were you doing at the morgue?"

"Nothing."

"I heard you talking when I came in."

"I was merely curious."

"You're lying. That is very bad, Mr. Lantry. The truth is far better. The truth is, is it not, that you are dead and, being the only one of your sort, were lonely. Therefore you killed people to have company."

"How does that follow?"

McClure laughed. "Logic, my dear fellow. Once I *knew* you were really dead, a moment ago, really a—what do you call it—a vampire (silly word!) I tied you immediately to the Incinerator blasts. Before that there was no reason to connect you. But once the one piece fell into place, the fact that you were dead, then it was simple to guess your loneliness, your hate, your envy, all of the tawdry motivations of a walking corpse. It took only an instant then to see the Incinerators blown to blazes, and then to think of you, among the bodies at the morgue, seeking help, seeking friends and people like yourself to work with—"

"You're too damned smart!" Lantry was out of the chair. He was half way to the other man when McClure rolled over and scuttled away, flinging the sherry decanter. With a great despair Lantry realized that, like a damned idiot, he had thrown away his one chance to kill McClure. He should have done it earlier. It had been Lantry's one weapon, his safety margin. If people in a society never *killed* each other, they never *suspected* one another. You could walk up to any one of them and kill him.

"Come back here!" Lantry threw the knife.

McClure got behind a chair. The idea of flight, of protection, of fighting, was still new to him. He had part of the idea, but there was still a bit of luck on Lantry's side if Lantry wanted to use it.

"Oh, no," said McClure, holding the chair between himself and the advancing man. "You want to kill me. It's odd, but true. I can't understand it. You want to cut me with that knife or something like that, and it's up to me to prevent you from doing such an odd thing."

"I *will* kill you!" Lantry let it slip out. He cursed himself. That was the worst possible thing to say.

Lantry lunged across the chair, clutching at McClure.

McClure was very logical. "It won't do you any good to kill me. You *know* that." They wrestled and held each other in a wild, toppling shuffle. Tables fell over, scattering articles. "You remember what happened in the morgue?"

"I don't care!" screamed Lantry.

"You didn't raise *those* dead, did you?"

"I don't care!" cried Lantry.

"Look here," said McClure, reasonably. "There will never be any more like you, ever, there's no use."

"Then I'll destroy all of you, all of you!" screamed Lantry.

"And then what? You'll still be alone, with no more like you about."

"I'll go to Mars. They have tombs there. I'll find more like myself!"

"No," said McClure. "The executive order went through yesterday. All of the tombs are being deprived of their bodies. They'll be burned in the next week."

They fell together to the floor. Lantry got his hands on McClure's throat.

"Please," said McClure. "Do you see, you'll *die*."

"What do you mean?" cried Lantry.

"Once you kill all of us, and you're alone, you'll die! The hate will die. That hate is what moves you, *nothing else!* That envy moves you. Nothing else! You'll die, inevitably. You're not immortal. You're not even alive, you're nothing but a moving hate."

"I don't care!" screamed Lantry, and began choking the man, beating his head with his fists, crouched on the defenseless body. McClure looked up at him with dying eyes.

The front door opened. Two men came in.

"I say," said one of them. "What's going on? A new game?"

Lantry jumped back and began to run.

"Yes, a new game!" said McClure, struggling up. "Catch him and you win!"

The two men caught Lantry. "We win," they said.

"Let me go!" Lantry thrashed, hitting them across their faces, bringing blood.

"Hold him tight!" cried McClure.

They held him.

"A rough game, what?" one of them said. "What do we do *now?*"

The beetle hissed along the shining road. Rain fell out of the sky and a wind ripped at the dark green wet trees. In the beetle, his hands on the half-wheel, McClure was talking. His voice was a susurrant, a whispering, a hypnotic thing. The two other men sat in the back seat. Lantry sat, or rather lay, in the front seat, his head back, his eyes faintly open, the glowing green light of the dash dials showing on his cheeks. His mouth was relaxed. He did not speak.

McClure talked quietly and logically, about life and moving, about death and not moving, about the sun and the great sun Incinerator, about the emptied tombyard, about hatred and how hate lived and made a clay man live and move, and how illogical it all was, it all was, it all was. One was dead, was dead, was dead, that was all, all, all. One did not try to be otherwise. The car whispered on the moving road. The rain spatted gently on the windshield. The men in the back seat conversed quietly. Where were they going, going? To the Incinerator, of course. Cigarette smoke moved slowly up on the air, curling and tying into itself in grey loops and spirals. One was dead and must accept it.

Lantry did not move. He was a marionette, the strings cut. There was only a tiny hatred in his heart, in his eyes, like twin coals, feeble, glowing, fading.

I am Poe, he thought. I am all that is left of Edgar Allan Poe, and I am all that is left of Ambrose Bierce and all that is left of a man named

Lovecraft. I am a grey night bat with sharp teeth, and I am a square black monolith monster. I am Osiris and Bal and Set. I am the Necronomicon, the Book of the Dead. I am the house of Usher, falling into flame. I am the Red Death. I am the man mortared into the catacomb with a cask of Amontillado . . . I am a dancing skeleton. I am a coffin, a shroud, a lightning bolt reflected in an old house window. I am an autumn-empty tree, I am a rapping, flinging shutter. I am a yellowed volume turned by a claw hand. I am an organ played in an attic at midnight. I am a mask, a skull mask behind an oak tree on the last day of October. I am a poison apple bobbling in a water tub for child noses to bump at, for child teeth to snap . . . I am a black candle lighted before an inverted cross. I am a coffin lid, a sheet with eyes, a footstep on a black stairwell. I am Dunsany and Machen and I am the Legend of Sleepy Hollow. I am The Monkey's Paw and I am The Phantom Rickshaw. I am the Cat and the Canary, The Gorilla, the Bat. I am the ghost of Hamlet's father on the castle wall.

All of these things am I. And now these last things will be burned. While I lived *they* still lived. While I moved and hated and existed, *they* still existed. I am *all* that remembers them. I am all of them that *still* goes on, and will *not* go on after tonight. Tonight, all of us, Poe and Bierce and Hamlet's father, we burn together. They will make a big heap of us and burn us like a bonfire, like things of Guy Fawkes' day, gasoline, torch-light, cries and all!

And what a wailing will we put up. The world will be clean of us, but in our going we shall say, oh what is the world like, clean of fear, where is the dark imagination from the dark time, the thrill and the anticipation, the suspense of old October, gone, never more to come again, flattened and smashed and burned by the rocket people, by the Incinerator people, destroyed and obliterated, to be replaced by doors that open and close and lights that go on or off without fear. If only you could remember how once *we* lived, what Halloween was to us, and what Poe was, and how we gloried in the dark morbidities. One more drink, dear friends, of Amontillado, before the burning. All of this, all, exists but in one last brain on earth. A whole world dying tonight. One more drink, pray.

"Here we are," said McClure.

The Incinerator was brightly lighted. There was quiet music nearby. McClure got out of the beetle, came around to the other side. He opened the door. Lantry simply lay there. The talking and the logical talking had slowly drained him of life. He was no more than wax now, with a small glow in his eyes. This future world, how the men *talked* to you, how logically they reasoned away your life. They wouldn't believe in him. The force of their disbelief froze him. He could not move his arms or his legs. He could only mumble senselessly, coldly, eyes flickering.

McClure and the two others helped him out of the car, put him in a golden box and rolled him on a roller table into the warm glowing interior of the building.

I am Edgar Allan Poe, I am Ambrose Bierce, I am Halloween, I am a coffin, a shroud, a Monkey's Paw, a Phantom, a Vampire . . .

"Yes, yes," said McClure, quietly, over him. "I know. I know."

The table glided. The walls swung over him and by him, the music played. You are dead, you are logically dead.

I am Usher, I am the Maelstrom, I am the MS Found In A Bottle, I am the Pit and I am the Pendulum, I am the Telltale Heart, I am the Raven nevermore, nevermore.

"Yes," said McClure, as they walked softly. "I know."

"I am in the catacomb," cried Lantry.

"Yes, the catacomb," said the walking man over him.

"I am being chained to a wall, and there is no bottle of Amontillado here!" cried Lantry weakly, eyes closed.

"Yes," someone said.

There was movement. The flame door opened.

"Now someone is mortaring up the cell, closing me in!"

"Yes, I *know*." A whisper.

The golden box slid into the flame lock.

"I'm being walled in! A very good joke indeed! Let us be gone!" A wild scream and much laughter.

"We know, we understand . . ."

The inner flame lock opened. The golden coffin shot forth into flame.

"For the love of God, Montresor! For the love of God!"

WALDO
by Robert A. Heinlein

THE ACT WAS BILLED as ballet tap—which does not describe it. His feet created an intricate tympany of crisp, clean taps. There was a breath-catching silence as he leaped high into the air, higher than a human being should—and performed, while floating there, a fantastically improbable *entrechat douze.*

He landed on his toes, apparently poised, yet producing a fortissimo of thunderous taps.

The spotlights cut, the stage lights came up. The audience stayed silent a long moment, then realized it was time to applaud, and *gave.*

He stood facing them, letting the wave of their emotion sweep through him. He felt as if he could lean against it; it warmed him through to his bones.

It was wonderful to dance, glorious to be applauded, to be *liked,* to be *wanted.*

When the curtain rang down for the last time he let his dresser lead him away. He was always a little bit drunk at the end of a performance; dancing was a joyous intoxication even in rehearsal, but to have an audience lifting him, carrying him along, applauding him—he never grew jaded to it. It was always new and heartbreakingly wonderful.

"This way, chief. Give us a little smile." The flash bulb flared. "Thanks."

"Thank *you.* Have a drink." He motioned toward one end of his dressing room. They were all such nice fellows, such grand guys—the reporters, the photographers—all of them.

"How about one standing up?" He started to comply, but his dresser, busy with one slipper, warned him:

"You operate in half an hour."

"Operate?" the news photographer said. "What's it this time?"

"A left cerebrectomy," he answered.

"Yeah? How about covering it?"

"Glad to have you—if the hospital doesn't mind."

"We'll fix that."

Such grand guys.

"—trying to get a little different angle on a feature article." It was a feminine voice, near his ear. He looked around hastily, slightly confused. "For example, what made you decide to take up dancing as a career?"

"I'm sorry," he apologized. "I didn't hear you. I'm afraid it's pretty noisy in here."

"I said, why did you decide to take up dancing?"

"Well, now, I don't quite know how to answer that. I'm afraid we would have to go back quite a way——"

James Stevens scowled at his assistant engineer. "What have you got to look happy about?" he demanded.

"It's just the shape of my face," his assistant apologized. "Try laughing at this one: there's been another crash."

"Oh, cripes! Don't tell me—let me guess. Passenger or freight?"

"A Climax duo-freighter on the Chicago-Salt Lake shuttle, just west of North Platte. And, chief——"

"Yes?"

"The Big Boy wants to see you."

"That's interesting. That's very, very interesting. Mac——"

"Yeah, chief."

"How would you like to be Chief Traffic Engineer of North American Power-Air? I hear there's going to be a vacancy."

Mac scratched his nose. "Funny that you should mention that, chief. I was just going to ask you what kind of a recommendation you could give me in case I went back into civil engineering. Ought to be worth something to you to get rid of me."

"I'll get rid of you—right now. You bust out to Nebraska, find that heap before the souvenir hunters tear it apart, and bring back its deKalbs and its control board."

"Trouble with cops, maybe?"

"You figure it out. Just be sure you come back."

" 'With my slipstick, or on it.' "

Stevens's office was located immediately adjacent to the zone power plant; the business offices of North American were located in a hill, a good three quarters of a mile away. There was the usual interconnecting tunnel; Stevens entered it and deliberately chose the low-speed slide in order to have more time to think before facing the boss.

By the time he arrived he had made up his mind, but he did not like the answer.

The Big Boy—Stanley F. Gleason, Chairman of the Board—greeted him quietly. "Come in, Jim. Sit down. Have a cigar."

Stevens slid into a chair, declined the cigar and pulled out a cigarette, which he lit while looking around. Besides the chief and himself, there were present Harkness, head of the legal staff, Dr. Rambeau, Stevens's opposite number for research, and Striebel, the chief engineer for city power.

Us five and no more, he thought grimly—all the heavyweights and none of the middleweights. Heads will roll!—starting with mine.

"Well," he said, almost belligerently, "we're all here. Who's got the cards? Do we cut for deal?"

Harkness looked faintly distressed by the impropriety; Rambeau seemed too sunk in some personal gloom to pay any attention to wisecracks in bad taste. Gleason ignored it. "We've been trying to figure a way out of our troubles, James. I left word for you on the chance that you might not have left."

"I stopped by simply to see if I had any personal mail," Stevens said bitterly. "Otherwise I'd be on the beach at Miami, turning sunshine into vitamin D."

"I know," said Gleason, "and I'm sorry. You deserve that vacation, Jimmie. But the situation has gotten worse instead of better. Any ideas?"

"What does Dr. Rambeau say?"

Rambeau looked up momentarily. "The deKalb receptors can't fail," he stated.

"But they do."

"They can't. You've operated them improperly." He sunk back into his personal prison.

Stevens turned back to Gleason and spread his hands. "So far as I know, Dr. Rambeau is right—but if the fault lies in the engineering department, I haven't been able to locate it. You can have my resignation."

"I don't want your resignation," Gleason said gently. "What I want is results. We have a responsibility to the public."

"And to the stockholders," Harkness put in.

"That will take care of itself if we solve the other," Gleason observed. "How about it, Jimmie? Any suggestions?"

Stevens bit his lip. "Just one," he announced, "and one I don't like to make. Then I look for a job peddling magazine subscriptions."

"So? Well, what is it?"

"*We've got to consult Waldo.*"

Rambeau suddenly snapped out of his apathy. "What! That charlatan? This is a matter of *science*."

Harkness said, "Really, Dr. Stevens——"

Gleason held up a hand. "Dr. Stevens's suggestion is logical. But I'm afraid it's a little late, Jimmie. I talked with him last week."

Harkness looked surprised; Stevens looked annoyed as well. "Without letting me know?"

"Sorry, Jimmie. I was just feeling him out. But it's no good. His terms, to us, amount to confiscation."

"Still sore over the Hathaway patents?"

"Still nursing his grudge."

"You should have let me handle the matter," Harkness put in. "He can't do this to us—there is public interest involved. Retain him, if need be, and let the fee be adjudicated in equity. I'll arrange the details."

"I'm afraid you would," Gleason said dryly. "Do you think a court order will make a hen lay an egg?"

Harkness looked indignant, but shut up.

Stevens continued, "I would not have suggested going to Waldo if I had not had an idea as to how to approach him. I know a friend of his——"

"A friend of *Waldo?* I didn't know he had any."

"This man is sort of an uncle to him—his first physician. With his help I might get on Waldo's good side."

Dr. Rambeau stood up. "This is intolerable," he announced. "I must ask you to excuse me." He did not wait for an answer, but strode out, hardly giving the door time to open in front of him.

Gleason followed his departure with worried eyes. "Why does he take it so hard, Jimmie? You would think he hated Waldo personally."

"Probably he does, in a way. But it's more than that; his whole universe is toppling. For the last twenty years, ever since Pryor's reformulation of the General Field Theory did away with Heisenberg's Uncertainty Principle, physics has been considered an exact science. The power failures and transmission failures we have been suffering are a terrific nuisance to you and to me, but to Dr. Rambeau they amount to an attack on his faith. Better keep an eye on him."

"Why?"

"Because he might come unstuck entirely. It's a pretty serious matter for a man's religion to fail him."

"Hm-m-m. How about yourself? Doesn't it hit you just as hard?"

"Not quite. I'm an engineer—from Rambeau's point of view just a high-priced tinker. Difference in orientation. Not but what I'm pretty upset."

The audio circuit of the communicator on Gleason's desk came to life. "Calling Chief Engineer Stevens—calling Chief Engineer Stevens." Gleason flipped the tab.

"He's here. Go ahead."

"Company code, translated. Message follows: 'Cracked up four miles north of Cincinnati. Shall I go on to Nebraska, or bring in the you-know-what from my own crate?' Message ends. Signed 'Mac.'"

"Tell him to *walk* back!" Stevens said savagely.

"Very well, sir." The instrument cut off.

"Your assistant?" asked Gleason.

"Yes. That's about the last straw, chief. Shall I wait and try to analyze this failure, or shall I try to see Waldo?"

"Try to see Waldo."

"O.K. If you don't hear from me, just send my severance pay care of Palmdale Inn, Miami. I'll be the fourth beachcomber from the right."

Gleason permitted himself an unhappy smile. "If you *don't* get results, I'll be the fifth. Good luck."

"So long."

When Stevens had gone, Chief Stationary Engineer Striebel spoke up for the first time. "If the power to the cities fails," he said softly, "you know where I'll be, don't you?"

"Where? Beachcomber number six?"

"Not likely. I'll be number one in my spot—first man to be lynched."

"But the power to the cities *can't* fail. You've got too many cross-connects and safety devices."

"Neither can the deKalbs fail, supposedly. Just the same—think about Sublevel 7 in Pittsburgh, with the lights out. Or, rather, don't think about it!"

Doc Grimes let himself into the aboveground access which led into his home, glanced at the announcer, and noted with mild, warm interest that someone close enough to him to possess his house combination was inside. He moved ponderously downstairs, favoring his game leg, and entered the lounging room.

"Hi, Doc!" James Stevens got up when the door snapped open and came forward to greet him.

"H'lo, James. Pour yourself a drink. I see you have. Pour me one."

"Right."

While his friend complied, Grimes shucked himself out of the outlandish anachronistic greatcoat he was wearing and threw it more or less in the direction of the robing alcove. It hit the floor heavily, much more heavily than its appearance justified, despite its unwieldy bulk. It clunked.

Stooping, he peeled off thick overtrousers as massive as the coat. He was dressed underneath in conventional business tights in blue and sable. It was not a style that suited him. To an eye unsophisticated in matters of civilized dress—let us say the mythical Man-from-Antares—he might have seemed uncouth, even unsightly. He looked a good bit like an elderly fat beetle.

James Stevens's eye made no note of the tights, but he looked with disapproval on the garments which had just been discarded. "Still wearing that fool armor," he commented.

"Certainly."

"Damn it, Doc—you'll make yourself sick, carrying that junk around. It's unhealthy."

"Danged sight sicker if I don't."

"Rats! *I* don't get sick, and *I* don't wear armor—outside the lab."

"You should." Grimes walked over to where Stevens had reseated himself. "Cross your knees." Stevens complied; Grimes struck him smartly below the kneecap with the edge of his palm. The reflex jerk was barely perceptible. "Lousy," he remarked, then peeled back his friend's right eyelid.

"You're in poor shape," he added after a moment.

Stevens drew away impatiently. "*I'm* all right. It's you we're talking about."

"What about me?"

"Well—— Damnation, Doc, you're throwing away your reputation. They talk about you."

Grimes nodded. "I know. 'Poor old Gus Grimes—a slight touch of cerebral termites.' Don't worry about my reputation; I've always been out of step. What's your fatigue index?"

"I don't know. It's all right."

"It is, eh? I'll wrestle you, two falls out of three."

Stevens rubbed his eyes. "Don't needle me, Doc. I'm run-down. I know that, but it isn't anything but overwork."

"Humph! James, you are a fair-to-middlin' radiation physicist——"

"Engineer."

"—engineer. But you're no medical man. You can't expect to pour every sort of radiant energy through the human system year after year and not pay for it. It wasn't designed to stand it."

"But I wear armor in the lab. You know that."

"Surely. And how about outside the lab?"

"But—— Look, Doc—I hate to say it, but your whole thesis is ridiculous. Sure there is radiant energy in the air these days, but nothing harmful. All the colloidal chemists agree——"

"Colloidal, fiddlesticks!"

"But you've got to admit that biological economy is a matter of colloidal chemistry."

"I've got to admit nothing. I'm not contending that colloids are not the fabric of living tissue—they are. But I've maintained for forty years that it was dangerous to expose living tissue to assorted radiation without being sure of the effect. From an evolutionary standpoint the human animal is habituated to and adapted to only the natural radiation of the sun—and he can't stand that any too well, even under a thick blanket of ionization. Without that blanket—— Did you ever see a solar-X type cancer?"

"Of course not."

"No, you're too young. I have. Assisted at the autopsy of one, when I was an intern. Chap was on the Second Venus Expedition. Four hundred and thirty-eight cancers we counted in him, then gave up."

"Solar-X is whipped."

"Sure it is. But it ought to be a warning. You bright young squirts can cook up things in your labs that we medicos can't begin to cope with. We're behind—bound to be. We usually don't know what's happened until the damage is done. This time you've torn it." He sat down heavily and suddenly looked as tired and whipped as did his younger friend.

Stevens felt the sort of tongue-tied embarrassment a man may feel when a dearly beloved friend falls in love with an utterly worthless person. He wondered what he could say that would not seem rude.

He changed the subject. "Doc, I came over because I had a couple of things on my mind—"

"Such as?"

"Well, a vacation for one. I know I'm run-down. I've been overworked, and a vacation seems in order. The other is your pal, Waldo."

"Huh?"

"Yeah. Waldo Farthingwaite-Jones, bless his stiff-necked, bad-tempered heart."

"Why Waldo? You haven't suddenly acquired an interest in *myasthenia gravis*, have you?"

"Well, no. I don't care what's wrong with him physically. He can have hives, dandruff, or the galloping never-get-overs, for all I care. I hope he has. What I want is to pick his brains."

"So?"

"I can't do it alone. Waldo doesn't help people; he *uses* them. You're his only normal contact with people."

"That is not entirely true——"

"Who else?"

"You misunderstand me. He has *no* normal contacts. I am simply the only person who dares to be rude to him."

"But I thought—— Never mind. D'you know, this is an inconvenient set-up? Waldo is the man we've got to have. Why should it come about that a genius of his caliber should be so unapproachable, so immune to ordinary social demands? Oh, I know his disease has a lot to do with it, but why should *this* man have *this* disease? It's an improbable coincidence."

"It's not a matter of his infirmity," Grimes told him. "Or, rather, not in the way you put it. His weakness *is* his genius, in a way——"

"Huh?"

"Well——" Grimes turned his sight inward, let his mind roam back over his long association—lifelong, for Waldo—with this particular patient. He remembered his subliminal misgivings when he delivered the child. The infant had been sound enough, superficially, except for a slight blueness. But then lots of babies were somewhat cyanotic in the delivery room. Nevertheless, he had felt a slight reluctance to give it the tunk on the bottom, the slap which would shock it into taking its first lungful of air.

But he had squelched his own feelings, performed the necessary "laying on of hands," and the freshly born human had declared its independence with a satisfactory squall. There was nothing else he could have done; he was a young G.P. then, who took his Hippocratic oath seriously. He still took it seriously, he supposed, even though he sometimes referred to it as the "hypocritical" oath. Still, he had been right in his feelings; there *had* been something rotten about that child—something that was not entirely *myasthenia gravis*.

He had felt sorry for the child at first, as well as having an irrational feeling of responsibility for its condition. Pathological muscular weakness is an almost totally crippling condition, since the patient has no unaffected limbs to retrain into substitutes. There the victim must lie, all organs, limbs, and functions present, yet so pitifully, completely weak as to be unable to perform any normal function. He must spend his life in a condition of exhausted collapse, such as you or I might reach at the finish line of a grueling cross-country run. No help for him, and no relief.

During Waldo's childhood he had hoped constantly that the child would die, since he was so obviously destined for tragic uselessness, while simultaneously, as a physician, doing everything within his own skill and the skills of numberless consulting specialists to keep the child alive and cure it.

Naturally, Waldo could not attend school; Grimes ferreted out sympathetic tutors. He could indulge in no normal play; Grimes invented sickbed games which would not only stimulate Waldo's imagination but encourage him to use his flabby muscles to the full, weak extent of which he was capable.

Grimes had been afraid that the handicapped child, since it was not subjected to the usual maturing stresses of growing up, would remain infantile. He knew now—had known for a long time—that he need not have worried. Young Waldo grasped at what little life was offered him, learned thirstily, tried with a sweating tenseness of will to force his undisciplined muscles to serve him.

He was clever in thinking of dodges whereby to circumvent his muscular weakness. At seven he devised a method of controlling a spoon with two hands, which permitted him—painfully—to feed himself. His first mechanical invention was made at ten.

It was a gadget which held a book for him, at any angle, controlled lighting for the book, and turned its pages. The gadget responded to finger tip pressure on a simple control panel. Naturally, Waldo could not build it himself, but he could conceive it, and explain it; the Farthingwaite-Joneses could well afford the services of a designing engineer to build the child's conception.

Grimes was inclined to consider this incident, in which the child Waldo acted in a role of intellectual domination over a trained mature adult neither blood relation not servant, as a landmark in the psychological process whereby Waldo eventually came to regard the entire human race as his servants, his *hands*, present or potential.

"What's eating you, Doc?"

"Eh? Sorry, I was daydreaming. See here, son—you mustn't be too harsh on Waldo. I don't *like* him myself. But you must take him as a whole."

"*You* take him."

"*Shush.* You spoke of needing his genius. He wouldn't have been a genius if he had not been crippled. You didn't know his parents. They were good stock—fine, intelligent people—but nothing spectacular. Waldo's potentialities weren't any greater than theirs, but he had to do more with them to accomplish anything. He had to do everything the hard way. He *had* to be clever."

"Sure. Sure, but why should he be so utterly poisonous? Most big men aren't."

"Use your head. To get anywhere in his condition he had to develop a will, a driving one-track mind, with a total disregard for any other considerations. What would you expect him to be but stinking selfish?"

"I'd—— Well, never mind. We need him and that's that."

"Why?"

Stevens explained.

It may plausibly be urged that the shape of a culture—its mores, evaluations, family organization, eating habits, living patterns, pedagogical methods, institutions, forms of government, and so forth—arise from the economic necessities of its technology. Even though the thesis be too broad and much oversimplified, it is nonetheless true that much which characterized the long peace which followed the constitutional establishment of the United Nations grew out of the technologies which were hothouse-forced by the needs of the belligerents in the war of the forties. Up to that time broadcast and beamcast were used only for commercial radio, with rare exceptions. Even telephony was done almost entirely by actual metallic connection from one instrument to another. If a man in Monterey wished to speak to his wife or partner in Boston, a physical, copper neuron stretched bodily across the continent from one to the other.

Radiant power was then a hop dream, found in Sunday supplements and comic books.

A concatenation—no, a meshwork—of new developments was necessary before the web of copper covering the continent could be dispensed with. Power could not be broadcast economically; it was necessary to wait for the co-axial beam—a direct result of the imperative military shortages of the Great War. Radio telephony could not replace wired telephony until ultra micro-wave techniques made room in the ether, so to speak, for the traffic load. Even then it was necessary to invent a tuning device which could be used by a nontechnical person—a ten-year-old child, let us say—as easily as the dial selector which was characteristic of the commercial wired telephone of the era then terminating.

Bell Laboratories cracked that problem; the solution led directly to the radiant power receptor, domestic type, keyed, sealed, and metered. The way was open for commercial radio power transmission—except in one respect: efficiency. Aviation waited on the development of the Otto-cycle engine; the Industrial Revolution waited on the steam engine; radiant power waited on a really cheap, plentiful power source. Since radiation of power is inherently wasteful, it was necessary to have power cheap and plentiful enough to waste.

The same war brought atomic energy. The physicists working for the United States Army—the United States of North America had its own army then—produced a superexplosive; the notebooks recording their tests contained, when properly correlated, everything necessary to produce almost any other sort of nuclear reaction, even the so-called Solar Phoenix, the hydrogen-helium cycle, which is the source of the sun's power.

Radiant power became economically feasible—and inevitable.

The reaction whereby copper is broken down into phosphorus, $silicon_{29}$ and $helium_3$, plus degenerating chain reactions, was one of the several cheap and convenient means developed for producing unlimited and practically free power.

Of course Stevens included none of this in his explanation to Grimes. Grimes was absent-mindedly aware of the whole dynamic process; he had seen radiant power grow up, just as his grandfather had seen the development of aviation. He had seen the great transmission lines removed from the sky—"mined" for their copper; he had seen the heavy cables being torn from the dug-up streets of Manhattan. He might even recall his first independent-unit radiotelephone with its somewhat disconcerting double dial— he had gotten a lawyer in Buenos Aires on it when attempting to reach his neighborhood delicatessen. For two weeks he made all his local calls by having them relayed back from South America before he discovered that it made a difference which dial he used first.

At that time Grimes had not yet succumbed to the new style in architecture. The London Plan did not appeal to him; he liked a house aboveground, where he could see it. When it became necessary to increase the floor space in his offices, he finally gave in and went subsurface, not so much for the cheapness, convenience, and general all-around practicability of living in a tri-conditioned cave, but because he had already become a little worried about the possible consequences of radiation pouring through the human body. The fused-earth walls of his new residence were covered with lead; the roof of the cave had a double thickness. His hole in the ground was as near radiation-proof as he could make it.

"—the meat of the matter," Stevens was saying, "is that the delivery of power to transportation units has become erratic as the devil. Not enough yet to tie up traffic, but enough to be very disconcerting. There have been some nasty accidents; we can't keep hushing them up forever. I've got to do something about it."

"Why?"

" 'Why?' Don't be silly. In the first place as traffic engineer for NAPA my bread and butter depends on it. In the second place the problem is upsetting in itself. A properly designed piece of mechanism ought to work— all the time, every time. These don't, and we can't find out why not. Our staff mathematical physicists have about reached the babbling stage."

Grimes shrugged. Stevens felt annoyed by the gesture. "I don't think you appreciate the importance of this problem, Doc. Have you any idea of the amount of horsepower involved in transportation? Counting both private and commercial vehicles and common carriers, North American Power-Air supplies more than half the energy used in this continent. We *have* to be right. You can add to that our city-power affiliate. No trouble there—yet. But we don't *dare* think what a city-power breakdown would mean."

"I'll give you a solution."

"Yeah? Well, give."

"Junk it. Go back to oil-powered and steam-powered vehicles. Get rid of these damned radiant-powered deathtraps."

"Utterly impossible. You don't know what you're saying. It took more than fifteen years to make the change-over. Now we're geared to it. Gus, if NAPA closed up shop, half the population of the northwest seaboard would starve, to say nothing of the lake states and the Philly-Boston axis."

"Hrrmph—— Well, all I've got to say is that that might be better than the slow poisoning that is going on now."

Stevens brushed it away impatiently. "Look, Doc, nurse a bee in your bonnet if you like, but don't ask me to figure it into my calculations. Nobody else sees any danger in radiant power."

Grimes answered mildly. "Point is, son, they aren't looking in the right place. Do you know what the high-jump record was last year?"

"I never listen to the sport news."

"Might try it sometime. The record leveled off at seven foot two, 'bout twenty years back. Been dropping ever since. You might try graphing athletic records against radiation in the air—artificial radiation. Might find some results that would surprise you."

"Shucks, everybody knows there has been a swing away from heavy sports. The sweat-and-muscles fad died out, that's all. We've simply advanced into a more intellectual culture."

"Intellectual, hogwash! People quit playing tennis and such because they are tired all the time. Look at you. You're a mess."

"Don't needle me, Doc."

"Sorry. But there has been a clear deterioration in the performance of the human animal. If we had decent records on such things I could prove it, but any physician who's worth his salt can *see* it, if he's got eyes in him and isn't wedded to a lot of fancy instruments. I can't prove what causes it, not yet, but I've a damned good hunch that it's caused by the stuff you peddle."

"Impossible. There isn't a radiation put on the air that hasn't been tested very carefully in the bio labs. We're neither fools nor knaves."

"Maybe you don't test 'em long enough. I'm not talking about a few hours, or a few weeks; I'm talking about the cumulative effects of years of radiant frequencies pouring through the tissues. What does that do?"

"Why, nothing—I believe."

"You believe, but you don't know. Nobody has ever tried to find out. F'rinstance—what effect does sunlight have on silicate glass? Ordinarily you would say 'none,' but you've seen desert glass?"

"That bluish-lavender stuff? Of course."

"Yes. A bottle turns colored in a few months in the Mojave Desert. But have you ever seen the windowpanes in the old houses on Beacon Hill?"

"I've never been on Beacon Hill."

"O.K., then I'll tell you. Same phenomena—only it takes a century or more, in Boston. Now tell me—you savvy physics—could you measure the change taking place in those Beacon Hill windows?"

"Mm-m-m—probably not."

"But it's going on just the same. Has anyone ever tried to measure the changes produced in human tissue by thirty years of exposure to ultra short-wave radiation?"

"No, but——"

"No 'buts.' I see an effect. I've made a wild guess at a cause. Maybe I'm wrong. But I've felt a lot more spry since I've taken to invariably wearing my lead overcoat whenever I go out."

Stevens surrendered the argument. "Maybe you're right, Doc. I won't fuss with you. How about Waldo? Will you take me to him and help me handle him?"

"When do you want to go?"

"The sooner the better."

"Now?"

"Suits."

"Call your office."

"Are you ready to leave right now? It would suit me. As far as the front office is concerned, I'm on vacation; nevertheless, I've got this on my mind. I want to get at it."

"Quit talking and git."

They went topside to where their cars were parked. Grimes headed toward his, a big-bodied, old-fashioned Boeing family landau. Stevens checked him. "You aren't planning to go in that? It 'u'd take us the rest of the day."

"Why not? She's got an auxiliary space drive, and she's tight. You could fly from here to the Moon and back."

"Yes, but she's so infernal slow. We'll use my 'broomstick.'"

Grimes let his eyes run over his friend's fusiformed little speedster. Its body was as nearly invisible as the plastic industry could achieve. A surface layer, two molecules thick, gave it a refractive index sensibly identical with that of air. When perfectly clean it was very difficult to see. At the moment it had picked up enough casual dust and water vapor to be faintly seen—a ghost of a soap bubble of a ship.

Running down the middle, clearly visible through the walls, was the only metal part of the ship—the shaft, or, more properly, the axis core, and the spreading sheaf of deKalb receptors at its terminus. The appearance was enough like a giant witch's broom to justify the nickname. Since the saddles, of transparent plastic, were mounted tandem over the shaft so that the metal rod passed between the legs of the pilot and passengers, the nickname was doubly apt.

"Son," Grimes remarked, "I know I ain't pretty, nor am I graceful. Nevertheless, I retain a certain residuum of self-respect and some shreds of dignity. I am *not* going to tuck that thing between my shanks and go scooting through the air on it."

"Oh, rats! You're old-fashioned."

"I may be. Nevertheless, any peculiarities I have managed to retain to my present age I plan to hang onto. No."

"Look—I'll polarize the hull before we raise. How about it?"

"Opaque?"

"Opaque."

Grimes slid a regretful glance at his own frumpish boat, but assented by fumbling for the barely visible port of the speedster. Stevens assisted him; they climbed in and straddled the stick.

"Atta boy, Doc," Stevens commended, "I'll have you there in three shakes. That tub of yours probably won't do over five hundred, and Wheelchair must be all of twenty-five thousand miles up."

"I'm never in a hurry," Grimes commented, "and don't call Waldo's house 'Wheelchair'—not to his face."

"I'll remember," Stevens promised. He fumbled, apparently in empty air; the hull suddenly became dead black, concealing them. It changed as suddenly to mirror bright; the car quivered, then shot up out of sight.

Waldo F. Jones seemed to be floating in thin air at the center of a spherical room. The appearance was caused by the fact that he was indeed floating in air. His house lay in a free orbit, with a period of just over twenty-four hours. No spin had been impressed on his home; the pseudo gravity of centrifugal force was the thing he wanted least. He had left earth to get away from its gravitational field; he had not been down to the surface once in the seventeen years since his house was built and towed into her orbit; he never intended to do so for any purpose whatsoever.

Here, floating free in space in his own air-conditioned shell, he was almost free of the unbearable lifelong slavery to his impotent muscles. What little strength he had he could spend economically, in movement, rather than in fighting against the tearing, tiring weight of the Earth's thick field.

Waldo had been acutely interested in space flight since early boyhood, not from any desire to explore the depths, but because his boyish, over-trained mind had seen the enormous advantage—to him—in weightlessness. While still in his teens he had helped the early experimenters in space flight over a hump by supplying them with a control system which a pilot could handle delicately while under the strain of two or three gravities.

Such an invention was no trouble at all to him; he had simply adapted manipulating devices which he himself used in combating the overpowering weight of one gravity. The first successful and safe rocket ship contained relays which had once aided Waldo in moving himself from bed to wheelchair.

The deceleration tanks, which are now standard equipment for the lunar mail ships, traced their parentage to a flotation tank in which Waldo habitually had eaten and slept up to the time when he left the home of his parents for his present, somewhat unique, home. Most of his basic inventions had originally been conceived for his personal convenience, and only later adapted for commercial exploitation. Even the ubiquitous and grotesquely humanoid gadgets known universally as "waldoes"—Waldo F. Jones's Synchronous Reduplicating Pantograph, Pat. 296,001,437, new series, et al—passed through several generations of development and private use in Waldo's machine shop before he redesigned them for mass production. The first of them, a primitive gadget compared with the waldoes now to be found in every shop, factory, plant, and warehouse in the country, had been designed to enable Waldo to operate a metal lathe.

Waldo had resented the nickname the public had fastened on them—it struck him as overly familiar—but he had coldly recognized the business advantage to himself in having the public identify him verbally with a gadget so useful and important.

When the newscasters tagged his spacehouse "Wheelchair," one might have expected him to regard it as more useful publicity. That he did not so regard it, that he resented it and tried to put a stop to it, arose from another and peculiarly Waldo-ish fact: Waldo did not think of himself as a cripple.

He saw himself not as a crippled human being, but as something higher than human, the next step up, a being so superior as not to need the coarse, brutal strength of the smooth apes. Hairy apes, smooth apes, then Waldo— so the progression ran in his mind. A chimpanzee, with muscles that hardly bulge at all, can tug as high as fifteen hundred pounds with one hand. This Waldo had proved by obtaining one and patiently enraging it into full effort. A well-developed man can grip one hundred and fifty pounds with one hand. Waldo's own grip, straining until the sweat sprang out, had never reached fifteen pounds.

Whether the obvious inference were fallacious or true, Waldo believed in it, evaluated by it. Men were overmuscled canaille, smooth chimps. He felt himself at least ten times superior to them.

He had much to go on.

Though floating in air, he was busy, quite busy. Although he never went to the surface of the Earth his business was there. Aside from managing his many properties he was in regular practice as a consulting engineer, specializing in motion analysis. Hanging close to him in the room were the paraphernalia necessary to the practice of his profession. Facing him was a four-by-five color-stereo television receptor. Two sets of co-ordinates, rectilinear and polar, crosshatched it. Another smaller receptor hung above it and to the right. Both receptors were fully recording, by means of parallel circuits conveniently out of the way in another compartment.

The smaller receptor showed the faces of two men watching him. The larger showed a scene inside a large shop, hangarlike in its proportions. In the immediate foreground, almost full size, was a grinder in which was being machined a large casting of some sort. A workman stood beside it, a look of controlled exasperation on his face.

"He's the best you've got," Waldo stated to the two men in the smaller screen. "To be sure, he is clumsy and does not have the touch for fine work, but he is superior to the other morons you call machinists."

The workman looked around, as if trying to locate the voice. It was evident that he could hear Waldo, but that no vision receptor had been provided for him. "Did you mean that crack for me?" he said harshly.

"You misunderstand me, my good man," Waldo said sweetly. "I was complimenting you. I actually have hopes of being able to teach you the rudiments of precision work. Then we shall expect you to teach those butter-brained oafs around you. The gloves, please."

Near the man, mounted on the usual stand, were a pair of primary waldoes, elbow length and human digited. They were floating on the line, in parallel with a similar pair physically in front of Waldo. The secondary waldoes, whose actions could be controlled by Waldo himself by means of his primaries, were mounted in front of the power tool in the position of the operator.

Waldo's remark had referred to the primaries near the workman. The machinist glanced at them, but made no move to insert his arms in them.

"I don't take no orders from nobody I can't see," he said flatly. He looked sidewise out of the scene as he spoke.

"Now, Jenkins," commenced one of the two men in the smaller screen.

Waldo sighed. "I really haven't the time or the inclination to solve your problems of shop discipline. Gentlemen, please turn your pickup, so that our petulant friend may see me."

The change was accomplished; the workman's face appeared in the background of the smaller of Waldo's screens, as well as in the larger. "There—is that better?" Waldo said gently. The workman grunted.

"Now . . . your name, please?"

"Alexander Jenkins."

"Very well, friend Alec—the gloves."

Jenkins thrust his arms into the waldoes and waited. Waldo put his arms into the primary pair before him; all three pairs, including the secondary pair mounted before the machine, came to life. Jenkins bit his lip, as if he found unpleasant the sensation of having his fingers manipulated by the gauntlets he wore.

Waldo flexed and extended his fingers gently; the two pairs of waldoes in the screen followed in exact, simultaneous parallelism. "Feel it, my dear Alec," Waldo advised. "Gently, gently—the sensitive touch. Make your muscles work for you." He then started hand movements of definite pattern; the waldoes at the power tool reached up, switched on the power, and began gently, gracefully, to continue the machining of the casting. A mechanical hand reached down, adjusted a vernier, while the other increased the flow of oil cooling the cutting edge. "Rhythm, Alec, rhythm. No jerkiness, no unnecessary movement. Try to get in time with me."

The casting took shape with deceptive rapidity, disclosed what it was—the bonnet piece for an ordinary three-way nurse. The chucks drew back from it; it dropped to the belt beneath, and another rough casting took its place. Waldo continued with unhurried skill, his finger motions within his waldoes exerting pressure which would need to be measured in fractions of ounces, but the two sets of waldoes, paralleled to him thousands of miles below, followed his motions accurately and with force appropriate to heavy work at hand.

Another casting landed on the belt—several more. Jenkins, although not called upon to do any work in his proper person, tired under the strain of attempting to anticipate and match Waldo's motions. Sweat dripped down his forehead, ran off his nose, accumulated on his chin. Between castings he suddenly withdrew his arms from the paralleled primaries. "That's enough," he announced.

"One more, Alec. You are improving."

"No!" He turned as if to walk off. Waldo made a sudden movement—so sudden as to strain him, even in his weight-free environment. One steel hand of the secondary waldoes lashed out, grasped Jenkins by the wrist.

"Not so fast, Alec."

"Let go of me!"

"Softly, Alec, softly. You'll do as you are told, *won't you?*" The steel hand clamped down hard, twisted. Waldo had exerted all of two ounces of pressure.

Jenkins grunted. The one remaining spectator—one had left soon after the lesson started—said, "Oh, I say, Mr. Jones!"

"Let him obey, or fire him. You know the terms of my contract."

There was a sudden cessation of stereo and sound, cut from the Earth end. It came back on a few seconds later. Jenkins was surly, but no longer recalcitrant. Waldo continued as if nothing had happened. "Once more, my dear Alec."

When the repetition had been completed, Waldo directed, "Twenty times, wearing the wrist and elbow lights with the chronanalyzer in the picture. I shall expect the superposed strips to match, Alec." He cut off the larger screen without further words and turned to the watcher in the smaller screen. "Same time tomorrow, McNye. Progress is satisfactory. In time we'll turn this madhouse of yours into a modern plant." He cleared that screen without saying good-by.

Waldo terminated the business interview somewhat hastily, because he had been following with one eye certain announcements on his own local information board. A craft was approaching his house. Nothing strange about that; tourists were forever approaching and being pushed away by his auto-guardian circuit. But this craft had the approach signal, was now clamping to his threshold flat. It was a broomstick, but he could not place the license number. Florida license. Whom did he know with a Florida license?

He immediately realized that he knew no one who possessed his approach signal—that list was *very* short—and who could also reasonably be expected to sport a Florida license. The suspicious defensiveness with which he regarded the entire world asserted itself; he cut in the circuit whereby he could control by means of his primary waldoes the strictly illegal but highly lethal inner defenses of his home. The craft was opaqued; he did not like that.

A youngish man wormed his way out. Waldo looked him over. A stranger—face vaguely familiar perhaps. An ounce of pressure in the primaries and the face would cease to be a face, but Waldo's actions were under cold cortical control; he held his fire. The man turned, as if to assist another passenger. Yes, there was another. Uncle Gus!—but the doddering old fool had brought a stranger with him. He knew better than that. He knew how Waldo felt about strangers!

Nevertheless, he released the outer lock of the reception room and let them in.

Gus Grimes snaked his way through the lock, pulling himself from one handrail to the next, and panting a little as he always did when forced to move weight free. Matter of diaphragm control, he told himself as he always did; can't be the exertion. Stevens streaked in after him, displaying a ground hog's harmless pride in handling himself well in space conditions. Grimes arrested himself just inside the reception room, grunted, and spoke to a man-sized dummy waiting there. "Hello, Waldo."

The dummy turned its eyes and head slightly. "Greetings, Uncle Gus. I do wish you would remember to phone before dropping in. I would have had your special dinner ready."

"Never mind. We may not be here that long. Waldo, this is my friend, Jimmie Stevens."

The dummy faced Stevens. "How do you do, Mr. Stevens," the voice said formally. "Welcome to Freehold."

"How do you do, Mr. Jones," Stevens replied, and eyed the dummy curiously. It was really surprisingly lifelike; he had been taken in by it at first. A "reasonable facsimile." Come to think of it, he had heard of this dummy. Except in vision screen few had seen Waldo in his own person. Those who had business at Wheelchair—no, "Freehold," he must remember that—those who had business at Freehold heard a voice and saw this simulacrum.

"But you *must* stay for dinner, Uncle Gus," Waldo continued. "You can't run out on me like that; you don't come often enough for that. I can stir something up."

"Maybe we will," Grimes admitted. "Don't worry about the menu. You know me. I can eat a turtle *with* the shell."

It had really been a bright idea, Stevens congratulated himself, to get Doc Grimes to bring him. Not here five minutes and Waldo was insisting on them staying for dinner. Good omen!

He had not noticed that Waldo had addressed the invitation to Grimes alone, and that it had been Grimes who had assumed the invitation to be for both of them.

"Where are you, Waldo?" Grimes continued. "In the lab?" He made a tentative movement, as if to leave the reception room.

"Oh, don't bother," Waldo said hastily. "I'm sure you will be more comfortable where you are. Just a moment and I will put some spin on the room so that you may sit down."

"What's eating you, Waldo?" Grimes said testily. "You know I don't insist on weight. And I don't care for the company of your talking doll. I want to see you." Stevens was a little surprised by the older man's insistence; he had thought it considerate of Waldo to offer to supply acceleration. Weightlessness put him a little on edge.

Waldo was silent for an uncomfortable period. At last he said frigidly, "Really, Uncle Gus, what you ask is out of the question. You must be aware of that."

Grimes did not answer him. Instead, he took Stevens's arm. "Come on, Jimmie. We're leaving."

"Why, Doc! What's the matter?"

"Waldo wants to play games. I don't play games."

"But—"

"Ne' mind! Come along. Waldo, open the lock."

"Uncle Gus!"

"Yes, Waldo?"

"Your guest—you vouch for him?"

"Naturally, you dumb fool, else I wouldn't have brought him."

"You will find me in my workshop. The way is open."

Grimes turned to Stevens. "Come along, son."

Stevens trailed after Grimes as one fish might follow another, while taking in with his eyes as much of Waldo's fabulous house as he could see. The place was certainly unique, he conceded to himself—unlike anything he had ever seen. It completely lacked up-and-down orientation. Space craft, even space stations, although always in free fall with respect to any but internally impressed accelerations, invariably are designed with up-and-down; the up-and-down axis of a ship is determined by the direction of its accelerating drive; the up-and-down of a space station is determined by its centrifugal spin.

Some few police and military craft use more than one axis of acceleration; their up-and-down shifts, therefore, and their personnel, must be harnessed when the ship maneuvers. Some space stations apply spin only to living quarters. Nevertheless, the rule is general; human beings are used to weight; all their artifacts have that assumption implicit in their construction—except Waldo's house.

It is hard for a ground hog to dismiss the notion of weight. We seem to be born with an instinct which demands it. If one thinks of a vessel in a free orbit around the Earth, one is inclined to think of the direction toward the Earth as "down," to think of oneself as standing or sitting on that wall of the ship, using it as a floor. Such a concept is completely mistaken. To a person inside a freely falling body there is no sensation of weight whatsoever and no direction of up-and-down, except that which derives from the gravitational field of the vessel itself. As for the latter, neither Waldo's house nor any space craft as yet built is massive enough to produce a field dense enough for the human body to notice it. Believe it or not, that is true. It takes a mass as gross as a good-sized planetoid to give the human body a feeling of weight.

It may be objected that a body in a free orbit around the Earth is not a freely falling body. The concept involved is human, Earth surface in type, and completely erroneous. Free flight, free fall, and free orbit are equivalent terms. The Moon falls constantly toward the Earth; the Earth falls constantly toward the Sun, but the sidewise vector of their several motions prevents them from approaching their primaries. It is free fall nonetheless. Consult any ballistician or any astrophysicist.

When there is free fall there is no sensation of weight. A gravitational field must be opposed to be detected by the human body.

Some of these considerations passed through Stevens's mind as he hand-walked his way to Waldo's workshop. Waldo's home had been constructed without any consideration being given to up-and-down. Furniture and apparatus were affixed to any wall; there was no "floor." Decks and platforms were arranged at any convenient angle and of any size or shape, since they had nothing to do with standing or walking. Properly speaking, they were bulkheads and working surfaces rather than decks. Furthermore, equipment was not necessarily placed close to such surfaces; frequently it was more convenient to locate it with space all around it, held in place by light guys or slender stanchions.

The furniture and equipment was all odd in design and frequently odd in purpose. Most furniture on Earth is extremely rugged, and at least 90 per cent of it has a single purpose—to oppose, in one way or another, the acceleration of gravity. Most of the furniture in an Earth-surface—or sub-surface—house is stator machines intended to oppose gravity. All tables, chairs, beds, couches, clothing racks, shelves, drawers, et cetera, have that as their one purpose. All other furniture and equipment have it as a secondary purpose which strongly conditions design and strength.

The lack of need for the rugged strength necessary to all terrestrial equipment resulted in a fairylike grace in much of the equipment in Waldo's house. Stored supplies, massive in themselves, could be retained in convenient order by compartmentation of eggshell-thin transparent plastic. Ponderous machinery, which on Earth would necessarily be heavily cased and supported, was here either open to the air or covered by gossamer-like envelopes and held stationary by light elastic lines.

Everywhere were pairs of waldoes, large, small, and life-size, with vision pickups to match. It was evident that Waldo could make use of the compartments through which they were passing without stirring out of his easy chair—if he used an easy chair. The ubiquitous waldoes, the insubstantial quality of the furniture, and the casual use of all walls as work or storage surfaces, gave the place a madly fantastic air. Stevens felt as if he were caught in a Disney.

So far the rooms were not living quarters. Stevens wondered what Waldo's private apartments could be like and tried to visualize what equipment would be appropriate. No chairs, no rugs, no bed. Pictures, perhaps. Something pretty clever in the way of indirect lighting, since the eyes might be turned in any direction. Communication instruments might be much the same. But what could a washstand be like? Or a water tumbler? A trap bottle for the last—or would any container be necessary at all? He could not decide and realized that even a competent engineer may be confused in the face of mechanical conditions strange to him.

What constitutes a good ash tray when there is no gravity to hold the debris in place? Did Waldo smoke? Suppose he played solitaire; how did he handle the cards? Magnetized cards, perhaps, and a magnetized playing surface.

"In through here, Jim." Grimes steadied himself with one hand, gesturing with the other. Stevens slid through the manhole indicated. Before he had had time to look around he was startled by a menacing bass growl. He looked up; charging through the air straight at him was an enormous mastiff, lips drawn back, jaws slavering. Its front legs were spread out stiffly as if to balance in flight; its hind legs were drawn up under its lean belly. By voice and manner it announced clearly its intention of tearing the intruder into pieces, then swallowing the pieces.

"Baldur!" A voice cut through the air from some point beyond. The dog's ferocity wilted, but it could not check its lunge. A waldo snaked out a good thirty feet and grasped it by the collar. "I am sorry, sir," the voice added. "My friend was not expecting you."

Grimes said, "Howdy, Baldur. How's your conduct?" The dog looked at him, whined, and wagged his tail. Stevens looked for the source of the commanding voice, found it.

The room was huge and spherical; floating in its center was a fat man—Waldo.

He was dressed conventionally enough in shorts and singlet, except that his feet were bare. His hands and forearms were covered by metallic gauntlets—primary waldoes. He was softly fat, with double chin, dimples, smooth skin; he looked like a great, pink cherub, floating attendance on a saint. But the eyes were not cherubic, and the forehead and skull were those of a man. He looked at Stevens. "Permit me to introduce you to my pet," he said in a high, tired voice. "Give the paw, Baldur."

The dog offered a foreleg, Stevens shook it gravely. "Let him smell you, please."

The dog did so, as the waldo at his collar permitted him to come closer. Satisfied, the animal bestowed a wet kiss on Stevens's wrist. Stevens noted that the dog's eyes were surrounded by large circular patches of brown in contrast to his prevailing white, and mentally tagged it the Dog with Eyes as Large as Saucers, thinking of the tale of the soldier and the flint box. He made noises to it of "Good boy!" and "That's a nice old fellow!" while Waldo looked on with faint distaste.

"Heel, sir!" Waldo commanded when the ceremony was complete. The dog turned in midair, braced a foot against Stevens's thigh, and shoved, projecting himself in the direction of his master. Stevens was forced to steady himself by clutching at a handgrip. Grimes shoved himself away from the manhole and arrested his flight on a stanchion near their host. Stevens followed him.

Waldo looked him over slowly. His manner was not overtly rude, but was somehow, to Stevens, faintly annoying. He felt a slow flush spreading out from his neck; to inhibit it he gave his attention to the room around him. The space was commodious, yet gave the impression of being cluttered because of the assemblage of, well, *junk* which surrounded Waldo. There were half a dozen vision receptors of various sizes around him at different angles, all normal to his line of sight. Three of them had pickups to match. There were control panels of several sorts, some of which seemed obvious enough in their purpose—one for lighting, which was quite complicated, with little ruby telltales for each circuit, one which was the keyboard of a voder, a multiplex television control panel, a board which seemed to be power relays, although its design was unusual. But there were at least half a dozen which stumped Stevens completely.

There were several pairs of waldoes growing out of a steel ring which surrounded the working space. Two pairs, mere monkey fists in size, were equipped with extensors. It had been one of these which had shot out to grab Baldur by his collar. There were waldoes rigged near the spherical wall, too, including one pair so huge that Stevens could not conceive of a use for it. Extended, each hand spread quite six feet from little finger tip to thumb tip.

There were books in plenty on the wall, but no bookshelves. They seemed to grow from the wall like so many cabbages. It puzzled Stevens momentarily, but he inferred—correctly it turned out later—that a small magnet fastened to the binding did the trick.

The arrangement of lighting was novel, complex, automatic, and convenient for Waldo. But it was not so convenient for anyone else in the room. The lighting was, of course, indirect; but, furthermore, it was subtly controlled, so that none of the lighting came from the direction in which Waldo's head was turned. There was no glare—for Waldo. Since the lights behind his head burned brightly in order to provide more illumination for whatever he happened to be looking at, there was glare aplenty for anyone else. An electric eye circuit, obviously. Stevens found himself wondering just how simple such a circuit could be made.

Grimes complained about it. "Damn it, Waldo; get those lights under control. You'll give us headaches."

"Sorry, Uncle Gus." He withdrew his right hand from its gauntlet and placed his fingers over one of the control panels. The glare stopped. Light now came from whatever direction none of them happened to be looking, and much more brightly, since the area source of illumination was much reduced. Lights rippled across the walls in pleasant patterns. Stevens tried to follow the ripples, a difficult matter, since the setup was made *not* to be seen. He found that he could do so by rolling his eyes without moving his head. It was movement of the head which controlled the lights; movement of an eyeball was a little too much for it.

"Well, Mr. Stevens, do you find my house interesting?" Waldo was smiling at him with faint superciliousness.

"Oh—quite! Quite! I believe that it is the most remarkable place I have ever been in."

"And what do you find remarkable about it?"

"Well—the lack of definite orientation, I believe. That and the remarkable mechanical novelties. I suppose I am a bit of a groundlubber, but I keep expecting a floor underfoot and a ceiling overhead."

"Mere matters of functional design, Mr. Stevens; the conditions under which I live are unique; therefore, my house is unique. The novelty you speak of consists mainly in the elimination of unnecessary parts and the addition of new conveniences."

"To tell the truth, the most interesting thing I have seen yet is not a part of the house at all."

"Really? What is it, pray?"

"Your dog, Baldur." The dog looked around at the mention of his name. "I've never before met a dog who could handle himself in free flight."

Waldo smiled; for the first time his smile seemed gentle and warm. "Yes, Baldur is quite an acrobat. He's been at it since he was a puppy." He reached out and roughed the dog's ears, showing momentarily his extreme weakness, for the gesture had none of the strength appropriate to the size of the brute. The finger motions were flaccid, barely sufficient to disturb the coarse fur and to displace the great ears. But he seemed unaware, or unconcerned, by the disclosure. Turning back to Stevens, he added, "But if Baldur amuses you, you must see Ariel."

"Ariel?"

Instead of replying, Waldo touched the keyboard of the voder, producing a musical whistling pattern of three notes. There was a rustling near the wall of the room "above" them; a tiny yellow shape shot toward them—a canary. It sailed through the air with wings folded, bullet fashion. A foot or so away from Waldo it spread its wings, cupping the air, beat them a few times with tail down and spread, and came to a dead stop, hovering in the air with folded wings. Not quite a dead stop, perhaps, for it drifted slowly, came within an inch of Waldo's shoulder, let down its landing gear, and dug its claws into his singlet.

Waldo reached up and stroked it with a finger tip. It preened. "No earth-hatched bird can learn to fly in that fashion," he stated. "I know. I lost half a dozen before I was sure that they were incapable of making the readjustment. Too much thalamus."

"What happened to them?"

"In a man you would call it acute anxiety psychosis. They try to fly; their own prime skill leads them to disaster. Naturally, everything they do is wrong and they don't understand it. Presently they quit trying; a little later they die. Of a broken heart, one might say, poetically." He smiled thinly. "But Ariel is a genius among birds. He came here as an egg; he invented, unassisted, a whole new school of flying." He reached up a finger, offering the bird a new perch, which it accepted.

"That's enough, Ariel. Fly away home."

The bird started the "Bell Song" from *Lakmé*.

He shook it gently. "No, Ariel. Go to bed."

The canary lifted its feet clear of the finger, floated for an instant, then beat its wings savagely for a second or two to set course and pick up speed, and bulleted away whence he had come, wings folded, feet streamlined under.

"Jimmie's got something he wants to talk with you about," Grimes commenced.

"Delighted," Waldo answered lazily, "but shan't we dine first? Have you an appetite, sir?"

Waldo full, Stevens decided, might be easier to cope with than Waldo empty. Besides, his own midsection informed him that wrestling with a calorie or two might be pleasant. "Yes, I have."

"Excellent." They were served.

Stevens was never able to decide whether Waldo had prepared the meal by means of his many namesakes, or whether servants somewhere out of sight had done the actual work. Modern food-preparation methods being what they were, Waldo could have done it alone; he, Stevens, batched it with no difficulty, and so did Gus. But he made a mental note to ask

Doc Grimes at the first opportunity what resident staff, if any, Waldo employed. He never remembered to do so.

The dinner arrived in a small food chest, propelled to their midst at the end of a long, telescoping, pneumatic tube. It stopped with a soft sigh and held its position. Stevens paid little attention to the food itself— it was adequate and tasty, he knew—for his attention was held by the dishes and serving methods. Waldo let his own steak float in front of him, cut bites from it with curved surgical shears, and conveyed them to his mouth by means of dainty tongs. He made hard work of chewing.

"You can't get good steaks any more," he remarked. "This one is tough. God knows I pay enough—and complain enough."

Stevens did not answer. He thought his own steak had been tenderized too much; it almost fell apart. He was managing it with knife and fork, but the knife was superfluous. It appeared that Waldo did not expect his guests to make use of his own admittedly superior methods and utensils. Stevens ate from a platter clamped to his thighs, making a lap for it after Grimes's example by squatting in mid-air. The platter itself had been thoughtfully provided with sharp little prongs on its service side.

Liquids were served in small flexible skins, equipped with nipples. Think of a baby's plastic nursing bottle.

The food chest took the utensils away with a dolorous insufflation. "Will you smoke, sir?"

"Thank you." He saw what a weight-free ash tray necessarily should be: a long tube with a bell-shaped receptacle on its end. A slight suction in the tube, and ashes knocked into the bell were swept away, out of sight and mind.

"About that matter—" Grimes commenced again. "Jimmie here is Chief Engineer for North American Power-Air."

"*What?*" Waldo straightened himself, became rigid; his chest rose and fell. He ignored Stevens entirely. "Uncle Gus, do you mean to say that you have introduced an officer of *that* company into my—home?"

"Don't get your dander up. Relax. Damn it, I've warned you not to do anything to raise your blood pressure." Grimes propelled himself closer to his host and took him by the wrist in the age-old fashion of a physician counting pulse. "Breathe slower. Whatcha trying to do? Go on an oxygen jag?"

Waldo tried to shake himself loose. It was a rather pitiful gesture; the old man had ten times his strength. "Uncle Gus, you—"

"Shut up!"

The three maintained a silence for several minutes, uncomfortable for at least two of them. Grimes did not seem to mind it.

"There," he said at last. "That's better. Now keep your shirt on and listen to me. Jimmie is a nice kid, and he has never done anything to you. And he has behaved himself while he's been here. You've got no right to be rude to him, no matter who he works for. Matter of fact, you owe him an apology."

"Oh, really now, Doc," Stevens protested. "I'm afraid I *have* been here somewhat under false colors. I'm sorry, Mr. Jones. I didn't intend it to be that way. I tried to explain when we arrived."

Waldo's face was hard to read. He was evidently trying hard to control himself. "Not at all, Mr. Stevens. I am sorry that I showed temper. It is perfectly true that I should not transfer to you any animus I feel for your employers . . . though God knows I bear no love for them."

"I know it. Nevertheless, I am sorry to hear you say it."

"I was cheated, do you understand? *Cheated*—by as rotten a piece of quasi-legal chicanery as has ever——"

"Easy, Waldo!"

"Sorry, Uncle Gus." He continued, his voice less shrill. "You know of the so-called Hathaway patents?"

"Yes, of course."

"'So-called' is putting it mildly. The man was a mere machinist. Those patents are mine."

Waldo's version, as he proceeded to give it, was reasonably factual, Stevens felt, but quite biased and unreasonable. Perhaps Hathaway had been working, as Waldo alleged, simply as a servant—a hired artisan, but there was nothing to prove it, no contract, no papers of any sort. The man had filed certain patents, the only ones he had ever filed and admittedly Waldo-ish in their cleverness. Hathaway had then promptly died, and his heirs, through their attorneys, had sold the patents to a firm which had been dickering with Hathaway.

Waldo alleged that this firm had put Hathaway up to stealing from him, had caused him to hire himself out to Waldo for that purpose. But the firm was defunct; its assets had been sold to North American Power-Air. NAPA had offered a settlement; Waldo had chosen to sue. The suit went against him.

Even if Waldo were right, Stevens could not see any means by which the directors of NAPA could, legally, grant him any relief. The officers of a corporation are trustees for other people's money; if the directors of NAPA should attempt to give away property which had been adjudicated as belonging to the corporation, any stockholder could enjoin them before the act or recover from them personally after the act.

At least so Stevens thought. But he was no lawyer, he admitted to himself. The important point was that he needed Waldo's services, whereas Waldo held a bitter grudge against the firm he worked for.

He was forced to admit that it did not look as if Doc Grimes's presence was enough to turn the trick. "All that happened before my time," he began, "and naturally I know very little about it. I'm awfully sorry it happened. It's pretty uncomfortable for me, for right now I find myself in a position where I need your services very badly indeed."

Waldo did not seem displeased with the idea. "So? How does this come about?"

Stevens explained to him in some detail the trouble they had been having with the deKalb receptors. Waldo listened attentively. When Stevens had concluded he said, "Yes, that is much the same story your Mr. Gleason had to tell. Of course, as a technical man you have given a much more coherent picture than that money manipulator was capable of giving. But why do you come to me? I do not specialize in radiation engineering, nor do I have any degrees from fancy institutions."

"I come to you," Stevens said seriously, "for the same reason everybody else comes to you when they are really stuck with an engineering problem. So far as I know, you have an unbroken record of solving any problem you cared to tackle. Your record reminds me of another man——"

"Who?" Waldo's tone was suddenly sharp.

"Edison. He did not bother with degrees either, but he solved all the hard problems of his day."

"Oh, Edison—— I thought you were speaking of a contemporary. No doubt he was all right in his day," he added with overt generosity.

"I was not comparing him to you. I was simply recalling that Edison was reputed to prefer hard problems to easy ones. I've heard the same about you; I had hopes that this problem might be hard enough to interest you."

"It is mildly interesting," Waldo conceded. "A little out of my line, but interesting. I must say, however, that I am surprised to hear you, an executive of North American Power-Air, express such a high opinion of my talents. One would think that, if the opinion were sincere, it would not have been difficult to convince your firm of my indisputable handiwork in the matter of the so-called Hathaway patents."

Really, thought Stevens, the man is impossible. A mind like a weasel. Aloud, he said, "I suppose the matter was handled by the business management and the law staff. They would hardly be equipped to distinguish between routine engineering and inspired design."

The answer seemed to mollify Waldo. He asked, "What does your own research staff say about the problem?"

Stevens looked wry. "Nothing helpful. Dr. Rambeau does not really seem to believe the data I bring him. He says it's impossible, but it makes him unhappy. I really believe that he has been living on aspirin and nembutal for a good many weeks."

"Rambeau," Waldo said slowly. "I recall the man. A mediocre mind. All memory and no intuition. I don't think I would feel discouraged simply because Rambeau is puzzled."

"You really feel that there is some hope?"

"It should not be too difficult. I had already given the matter some thought, after Mr. Gleason's phone call. You have given me additional data, and I think I see at least two new lines of approach which may prove fruitful. In any case, there is always some approach—the correct one."

"Does that mean you will accept?" Stevens demanded, nervous with relief.

"Accept?" Waldo's eyebrows climbed up. "My dear sir, what in the world are you talking about? We were simply indulging in social conversation. I would not help your company under any circumstances whatsoever. I hope to see your firm destroyed utterly, bankrupt and ruined. This may well be the occasion."

Stevens fought to keep control of himself. Tricked! The fat slob had simply been playing with him, leading him on. There was no decency in him. In careful tones he continued, "I do not ask that you have any mercy on North American, Mr. Jones, but I appeal to your sense of duty. There is public interest involved. Millions of people are vitally dependent on the service we provide. Don't you see that the service *must* continue, regardless of you or me?"

Waldo pursed his lips. "No," he said, "I am afraid that does not affect me. The welfare of those nameless swarms of Earth crawlers is, I fear, not my concern. I have done more for them already than there was any need to do. They hardly deserve help. Left to their own devices, most of them would sink back to caves and stone axes. Did you ever see a performing ape, Mr. Stevens, dressed in a man's clothes and cutting capers on roller skates? Let me leave you with this thought: I am not a roller-skate mechanic for apes."

If I stick around here much longer, Stevens advised himself, there will be hell to pay. Aloud, he said, "I take it that is your last word?"

"You may so take it. Good day, sir. I enjoyed your visit. Thank you."

"Good-by. Thanks for the dinner."

"Not at all."

As Stevens turned away and prepared to shove himself toward the exit, Grimes called after him, "Jimmie, wait for me in the reception room."

As soon as Stevens was out of earshot, Grimes turned to Waldo and looked him up and down. "Waldo," he said slowly, "I always did know that you were one of the meanest, orneriest men alive, but—"

"Your compliments don't faze me, Uncle Gus."

"Shut up and listen to me. As I was saying, I knew you were too rotten selfish to live with, but this is the first time I ever knew you to be a four-flusher to boot."

"What do you mean by that? Explain yourself."

"Shucks! You haven't any more idea of how to crack the problem that boy is up against than I have. You traded on your reputation as a miracle man just to make him unhappy. Why, you cheap tinhorn bluffer, if you——"

"*Stop it!*"

"Go ahead," Grimes said quietly. "Run up your blood pressure. I won't interfere with you. The sooner you blow a gasket the better."

Waldo calmed down. "Uncle Gus—what makes you think I was bluffing?"

"Because I know you. If you had felt able to deliver the goods, you would have looked the situation over and worked out a plan to get NAPA by the short hair, through having something they had to have. That way you would have *proved* your revenge."

Waldo shook his head. "You underestimate the intensity of my feeling in the matter."

"I do like hell! I hadn't finished. About that sweet little talk you gave him concerning your responsibility to the race. You've got a head on you. You know damned well, and so do I, that of all people you can least afford to have anything serious happen to the setup down on Earth. That means you don't see any way to prevent it."

"Why, what do you mean? I have no interest in such troubles; I'm independent of such things. You know me better than that."

"Independent, eh? Who mined the steel in these walls? Who raised that steer you dined on tonight? You're as independent as a queen bee, and about as helpless."

Waldo looked startled. He recovered himself and answered, "Oh no, Uncle Gus. I really am independent. Why, I have supplies here for years."

"*How many years?*"

"Why . . . uh, five, about."

"And then what? You may live another fifty—*if* you have regular supply service. How do you prefer to die—starvation or thirst?"

"Water is no problem," Waldo said thoughtfully; "as for supplies, I suppose I could use hydroponics a little more and stock up with some meat animals—"

Grimes cut him short with a nasty laugh. "Proved my point. You don't *know* how to avert it, so you are figuring some way to save your own skin. I know you. You wouldn't talk about starting a truck garden if you knew the answers."

Waldo looked at him thoughtfully. "That's not entirely true. I don't know the solution, but I do have some ideas about it. I'll bet you a half interest in hell that I can crack it. Now that you have called my attention to it, I must admit I am rather tied in with the economic system down below, and"—he smiled faintly—"I was never one to neglect my own interests. Just a moment—I'll call your friend."

"Not so fast. I came along for another reason, besides introducing Jimmie to you. It can't be just any solution; it's got to be a particular solution."

"What do you mean?"

"It's got to be a solution that will do away with the need for filling up the air with radiant energy."

"Oh, *that*. See here, Uncle Gus, I know how interested you are in your theory, and I've never disputed the possibility that you may be right, but you can't expect me to mix that into another and very difficult problem."

"Take another look. You're in this for self-interest. Suppose everybody was in the shape you are in."

"You mean my *physical condition?*"

"I mean just that. I know you don't like to talk about it, but we blamed well need to. If everybody was as weak as you are—presto! No coffee and cakes for Waldo. And that's just what I see coming. You're the only man I know of who can appreciate what it means."

"It seems fantastic."

"It is. But the signs are there for anybody to read who wants to. Epidemic *myasthenia*, not necessarily acute, but enough to raise hell with our mechanical civilization. Enough to play hob with your supply lines. I've been collating my data since I saw you last and drawing some curves. You should see 'em."

"Did you bring them?"

"No, but I'll send 'em up. In the meantime, you can take my word for it." He waited. "Well, how about it?"

"I'll accept it as a tentative working hypothesis," Waldo said slowly, "until I see your figures. I shall probably want you to conduct some further research for me, on the ground—if your data is what you say it is."

"Fair enough. G'by." Grimes kicked the air a couple of times as he absent-mindedly tried to walk.

Stevens's frame of mind as he waited for Grimes is better left undescribed. The mildest thought that passed through his mind was a plaintive one about the things a man had to put up with to hold down what seemed like a simple job of engineering. Well, he wouldn't have the job very long. But he decided not to resign—he'd wait until they fired him; he wouldn't run out.

But he would damn well get that vacation before he looked for another job.

He spent several minutes wishing that Waldo were strong enough for him to be able to take a poke at him. Or kick him in the belly—that would be more fun!

He was startled when the dummy suddenly came to life and called him by name. "Oh, Mr. Stevens."

"Huh? Yes?"

"I have decided to accept the commission. My attorneys will arrange the details with your business office."

He was too surprised to answer for a couple of seconds; when he did so the dummy had already gone dead. He waited impatiently for Grimes to show up.

"Doc!" he said, when the old man swam into view. "What got into him. How did you do it?"

"He thought it over and reconsidered," Grimes said succinctly. "Let's get going."

Stevens dropped Dr. Augustus Grimes at the doctor's home, then proceeded to his office. He had no more than parked his car and entered the tunnel leading toward the zone plant when he ran into his assistant. McLeod seemed a little out of breath. "Gee, chief," he said, "I hoped that was you. I've had 'em watching for you. I need to see you."

"What's busted now?" Stevens demanded apprehensively. "One of the cities?"

"No. What made you think so?"

"Go ahead with your story."

"So far as I know ground power is humming sweet as can be. No trouble with the cities. What I had on my mind is this: *I fixed my heap.*"

"Huh? You mean you fixed the ship you crashed in?"

"It wasn't exactly a crash. I had plenty of power in the reserve banks; when reception cut off, I switched to emergency and landed her."

"But you fixed it? Was it the deKalbs? Or something else?"

"It was the deKalbs all right. And they're fixed. But I didn't exactly do it myself. I got it done. You see——"

"What was the matter with them?"

"I don't know exactly. You see I decided that there was no point in hiring another skycar and maybe having another forced landing on the way home. Besides, it was my own crate I was flying, and I didn't want to dismantle her just to get the deKalbs out and have her spread out all over the countryside. So I hired a crawler, with the idea of taking her back all in one piece. I struck a deal with a guy who had a twelve-ton semitractor combination, and we——"

"For criminy's sake, make it march! What happened?"

"I'm trying to tell you. We pushed on into Pennsylvania and we were making pretty fair time when the crawler broke down. The right lead wheel, ahead of the treads. Honest to goodness, Jim, those roads are something fierce."

"Never mind that. Why waste taxes on roads when 90 per cent of the traffic is in the air? You messed up a wheel. So then what?"

"Just the same, those roads are a disgrace," McLeod maintained stubbornly. "I was brought up in that part of the country. When I was a kid the road we were on was six lanes wide and smooth as a baby's fanny. They ought to be kept up; we might need 'em someday." Seeing the look in his senior's eye, he went on hastily: "The driver mugged in with his home office, and they promised to send a repair car out from the next town. All told, it would take three, four hours—maybe more. Well, we were laid up in the county I grew up in. I says to myself, 'McLeod, this is a wonderful chance to return to the scenes of your childhood and the room where the sun came peeping in the morn.' Figuratively speaking, of course. Matter of fact, our house didn't have any windows."

"I don't care if you were raised in a barrel!"

"Temper . . . temper——" McLeod said imperturbably. "I'm telling you this so you will understand what happened. But you aren't going to like it."

"I don't like it now."

"You'll like it less. I climbed down out of the cab and took a look around. We were about five miles from my home town—too far for me to want to walk it. But I thought I recognized a clump of trees on the brow of a little rise maybe a quarter of a mile off the road, so I walked over to see. I was right; just over the rise was the cabin where Gramps Schneider used to live."

"Gramps Snyder?"

"Not Snyder—*Sch*neider. Old boy we kids used to be friendly with. Ninety years older than anybody. I figured he was dead, but it wouldn't hurt any to walk down and see. He wasn't. 'Hello, Gramps,' I said. 'Come in, Hugh Donald,' he said. 'Wipe the feet on the mat.'

"I came in and sat down. He was fussing with something simmering in a stewpan on his base-burner. I asked him what it was. 'For morning aches,' he said. Gramps isn't exactly a hex doctor."

"Huh?"

"I mean he doesn't make a living by it. He raises a few chickens and garden truck, and some of the Plain People—House Amish, mostly—give him pies and things. But he knows a lot about herbs and such.

"Presently he stopped and cut me a slice of shoo-fly pie. I told him *danke*. He said, 'You've been up-growing, Hugh Donald,' and asked me how I was doing in school. I told him I was doing pretty well. He looked at me again and said, 'But you have trouble fretting you.' It wasn't a question; it was a statement. While I finished the pie I found myself trying to tell him what kind of troubles I had.

"It wasn't easy. I don't suppose Gramps has ever been off the ground in his life. And modern radiation theory isn't something you can explain in words of one syllable. I was getting more and more tangled up when he stood up, put on his hat and said, 'We will see this car you speak about.'

"We walked over to the highway. The repair gang had arrived, but the crawler wasn't ready yet. I helped Gramps up onto the platform and we got into my bus. I showed him the deKalbs and tried to explain what they did—or rather what they were supposed to do. Mind you, I was just killing time.

"He pointed to the sheaf of antennae and asked, 'These fingers—they reach out for the power?' It was as good an explanation as any, so I let it ride. He said, 'I understand,' and pulled a piece of chalk out of his trousers, and began drawing lines on each antenna, from front to back. I walked up front to see how the repair crew were doing. After a bit Gramps joined me. 'Hugh Donald,' he says, 'the fingers—now they will make.'

"I didn't want to hurt his feelings, so I thanked him plenty. The crawler was ready to go; we said good-by, and he walked back toward his shack. I went back to my car, and took a look in, just in case. I didn't think he could hurt anything, but I wanted to be sure. Just for the ducks of it I tried out the receptors. They worked!"

"What!" put in Stevens. "You don't mean to stand there and tell me an old witch doctor fixed your deKalbs?"

"Not witch doctor—*hex* doctor. But you get the idea."

Stevens shook his head. "It's simply a coincidence. Sometimes they come back into order as spontaneously as they go out."

"That's what you think. Not this one. I've just been preparing you for the shock you're going to get. *Come take a look.*"

"What do you mean? Where?"

"In the inner hangar." While they walked to where McLeod had left his broomstick, he continued, "I wrote out a credit for the crawler pilot and flew back. I haven't spoken to anyone else about it. I've been biting my nails down to my elbows waiting for you to show up."

The skycar seemed quite ordinary. Stevens examined the deKalbs and saw some faint chalk marks on their metal sides—nothing else unusual. "Watch while I cut in reception," McLeod told him.

Stevens waited, heard the faint hum as the circuits became activized, and looked.

The antennae of the deKalbs, each a rigid pencil of metal, were bending, flexing, writhing like a cluster of worms. They were *reaching out*, like fingers.

Stevens remained squatting down by the deKalbs, watching their outrageous motion. McLeod left the control saddle, came back, and joined him. "Well, chief," he demanded, "tell me about it. Whaduh yuh make of it?"

"Got a cigarette?"

"What are those things sticking out of your pocket?"

"Oh! Yeah—sure." Stevens took one out, lighted it, and burned it halfway down, unevenly, with two long drags.

"Go on," McLeod urged. "Give us a tell. What makes it do that?"

"Well," Stevens said slowly, "I can think of three things to do next——"

"Yeah?"

"The first is to fire Dr. Rambeau and give his job to Gramps Schneider."

"That's a good idea in any case."

"The second is to just wait here quietly until the boys with the straitjackets show up to take us home."

"And what's the third?"

"The third," Stevens said savagely, "is to take this damned heap out and sink it in the deepest part of the Atlantic Ocean and pretend like it never happened!"

A mechanic stuck his head in the door of the car. "Oh, Dr. Stevens——"

"Get out of here!"

The head hastily withdrew; the voice picked up in aggrieved tones. "Message from the head office."

Stevens got up, went to the operator's saddle, cleared the board, then assured himself that the antennae had ceased their disturbing movements. They had; in fact, they appeared so beautifully straight and rigid that he was again tempted to doubt the correctness of his own senses. He climbed out to the floor of the hangar, McLeod behind him. "Sorry to have blasted at you, Whitey," he said to the workman in placating tones. "What is the message?"

"Mr. Gleason would like for you to come into his office as soon as you can."

"I will at once. And, Whitey, I've a job for you."

"Yeah?"

"This heap here—seal up its doors and don't let anybody monkey with it. Then have it dragged, dragged, mind you; don't try to start it—have it dragged over into the main lab."

"O.K."

Stevens started away; McLeod stopped him. "What do I go home in?"

"Oh yes, it's your personal property, isn't it? Tell you what, Mac—the company needs it. Make out a purchase order and I'll sign it."

"Weeeell, now—I don't rightly know as I want to sell it. It might be the only job in the country working properly before long."

"Don't be silly. If the others play out, it won't do you any good to have the only one in working order. Power will be shut down."

"I suppose there's that," McLeod conceded. "Still," he said, brightening visibly, "a crate like that, with its special talents, ought to be worth a good deal more than list. You couldn't just go out and buy one."

"Mac," said Stevens, "you've got avarice in your heart and thievery in your finger tips. How much do you want for it?"

"Suppose we say twice the list price, new. That's letting you off easy."

"I happen to know you bought that job at a discount. But go ahead. Either the company can stand it, or it won't make much difference in the bankruptcy."

Gleason looked up as Stevens came in. "Oh, there you are, Jim. You seemed to have pulled a miracle with our friend Waldo the Great. Nice work."

"How much did he stick us for?"

"Just his usual contract. Of course his usual contract is a bit like robbery with violence. But it will be worth it if he is successful. And it's on a straight contingent basis. He must feel pretty sure of himself. They say he's never lost a contingent fee in his life. Tell me—what is he like? Did you really get into his house?"

"I did. And I'll tell you about it—sometime. Right now another matter has come up which has me talking to myself. You ought to hear about it at once."

"So? Go ahead."

Stevens opened his mouth, closed it again, and realized that it had to be seen to be believed. "Say, could you come with me to the main lab? I've got something to show you."

"Certainly."

Gleason was not as perturbed by the squirming metal rods as Stevens had been. He was surprised, but not upset. The truth of the matter is that he lacked the necessary technical background to receive the full emotional impact of the inescapable implications of the phenomenon. "That's pretty unusual, isn't it?" he said quietly.

"Unusual! Look, chief, if the sun rose in the west, what would you think?"

"I think I would call the observatory and ask them why."

"Well, all I can say is that I would a whole lot rather that the sun rose in the west than to have this happen."

"I admit it is pretty disconcerting," Gleason agreed. "I can't say that I've ever seen anything like it. What is Dr. Rambeau's opinion?"

"He hasn't seen it."

"Then perhaps we had better send for him. He may not have gone home for the night as yet."

"Why not show it to Waldo instead?"

"We will. But Dr. Rambeau is entitled to see it first. After all, it's his bailiwick, and I'm afraid the poor fellow's nose is pretty well out of joint as it is. I don't want to go over his head."

Stevens felt a sudden flood of intuition. "Just a second, chief. You're right, but if it's all the same to you I would rather that you showed it to him than for me to do it."

"Why so, Jimmie? You can explain it to him."

"I can't explain a damn thing to him I haven't already told you. And for the next few hours I'm going to be very, very busy indeed."

Gleason looked him over, shrugged his shoulders, and said mildly, "Very well, Jim, if you prefer it that way."

Waldo was quite busy, and therefore happy. He would never have admitted—he did not admit even to himself, that there were certain drawbacks to his self-imposed withdrawal from the world and that chief among these was boredom. He had never had much opportunity to enjoy the time-consuming delights of social intercourse; he honestly believed that the smooth apes had nothing to offer him in the way of companionship. Nevertheless, the pleasure of the solitary intellectual life can pall.

He repeatedly urged Uncle Gus to make his permanent home in Freehold, but he told himself that it was a desire to take care of the old man which motivated him. True—he enjoyed arguing with Grimes, but he was not aware how much those arguments meant to him. The truth of the matter was that Grimes was the only one of the human race who treated him entirely as another human and an equal—and Waldo wallowed in it, completely unconscious that the pleasure he felt in the old man's company was the commonest and most precious of all human pleasures.

But at present he was happy in the only way he knew how to be happy—working.

There were two problems: that of Stevens and that of Grimes. Required: a single solution which would satisfy each of them. There were three stages to each problem; first, to satisfy himself that the problems really did exist, that the situations were in fact as they had been reported to him verbally; second, to undertake such research as the preliminary data suggested; and third, when he felt that his data was complete, to invent a solution.

"Invent," not "find." Dr. Rambeau might have said "find," or "search for." To Rambeau the universe was an inexorably ordered cosmos, ruled by unvarying law. To Waldo the universe was the enemy, which he strove to force to submit to his will. They might have been speaking of the same thing, but their approaches were different.

There was much to be done. Stevens had supplied him with a mass of data, both on the theoretical nature of the radiated power system and the deKalb receptors which were the keystone of the system, and also on the various cases of erratic performance of which they had lately been guilty. Waldo had not given serious attention to power radiation up to this time, simply because he had not needed to. He found it interesting but comparatively simple. Several improvements suggested themselves to his mind. That standing wave, for example, which was the main factor in the co-axial beam—the efficiency of reception could be increased considerably by sending a message back over it which would automatically correct the aiming of the beam. Power delivery to moving vehicles could be made nearly as efficient as the power reception to stationary receivers.

Not that such an idea was important at present. Later, when he had solved the problem at hand, he intended to make NAPA pay through the nose for the idea; or perhaps it would be more amusing to compete with them. He wondered when their basic patents ran out—must look it up.

Despite inefficiencies the deKalb receptors should work every time, all the time, without failure. He went happily about finding out why they did not.

He had suspected some obvious—obvious to *him*—defect in manufacture. But the inoperative deKalbs which Stevens had delivered to him refused to give up their secret. He X-rayed them, measured them with micrometer and interferometer, subjected them to all the usual tests and some that were quite unusual and peculiarly Waldo-ish. They would not perform.

He built a deKalb in his shop, using one of the inoperative ones as a model and using the reworked metal of another of the same design, also inoperative, as the raw material. He used his finest scanners to see with and his smallest waldoes—tiny pixy hands, an inch across—for manipulation in the final stages. He created a deKalb which was as nearly identical with its model as technology and incredible skill could produce.

It worked beautifully.

Its elder twin still refused to work. He was not discouraged by this. On the contrary, he was elated. He had proved, proved with certainty, that the failure of the deKalbs was not a failure of workmanship, but a basic failure in theory. The problem was real.

Stevens had reported to him the scandalous performance of the deKalbs in McLeod's skycar, but he had not yet given his attention to the matter. Presently, in proper order, when he got around to it, he would look into the matter. In the meantime he tabled the matter. The smooth apes were an hysterical lot; there was probably nothing to the story. Writhing like Medusa's locks, indeed!

He gave fully half his time to Grimes's problem.

He was forced to admit that the biological sciences—if you could call them science!—were more fascinating than he had thought. He had shunned them, more or less; the failure of expensive "experts" to do anything for his condition when he was a child had made him contemptuous of such studies. Old wives' nostrums dressed up in fancy terminology! Grimes he liked and even respected, but Grimes was a special case.

Grimes's data had convinced Waldo that the old man had a case. Why, this was serious! The figures were incomplete, but nevertheless convincing. The curve of the third decrement, extrapolated not too unreasonably, indicated that in twenty years there would not be a man left with strength enough to work in heavy industries. Button pushing would be all they would be good for.

It did not occur to him that all he was good for was button pushing; he regarded weakness in the smooth apes as an old-style farmer might regard weakness in a draft animal. The farmer did not expect to pull the plow—that was the horse's job.

Grimes's medical colleagues must be utter fools.

Nevertheless, he sent for the best physiologists, neurologists, brain surgeons, and anatomists he could locate, ordering them as one might order goods from a catalogue. He must understand this matter.

He was considerably annoyed when he found that he could not make arrangements, by any means, to perform vivisection on human beings. He was convinced by this time that the damage done by ultra short-wave radiation was damage to the neurological system, and that the whole matter should be treated from the standpoint of electromagnetic theory. He wanted to perform certain delicate manipulations in which human beings would be hooked up directly to apparatus of his own design to find out in what manner nerve impulses differed from electrical current. He felt that if he could disconnect portions of a man's nervous circuit, replace it in part with electrical hookups, and examine the whole matter *in situ*, he might make illuminating discoveries. True, the man might not be much use to himself afterward.

But the authorities were stuffy about it; he was forced to content himself with cadavers and with animals.

Nevertheless, he made progress. Extreme short-wave radiation had a definite effect on the nervous system—a double effect: it produced "ghost" pulsations in the neurons, insufficient to accomplish muscular motor response, but, he suspected, strong enough to keep the body in a continual state of inhibited nervous excitation; and, secondly, a living specimen which had been subjected to this process for any length of time showed a definite, small but measurable, lowering in the efficiency of its neural impulses. If it had been an electrical circuit, he would have described the second effect as a decrease in insulating efficiency.

The sum of these two effects on the subject individual was a condition of mild tiredness, somewhat similar to the malaise of the early stages of pulmonary tuberculosis. The victim did not feel sick; he simply lacked pep. Strenuous bodily activity was not impossible; it was simply distasteful; it required too much effort, too much will power.

But an orthodox pathologist would have been forced to report that the victim was in perfect health—a little run-down, perhaps, but nothing wrong with him. Too sedentary a life, probably. What he needed was fresh air, sunshine, and healthy exercise.

Doc Grimes alone had guessed that the present, general, marked preference for a sedentary life was the effect and not the cause of the prevailing lack of vigor. The change had been slow, at least as slow as the increase in radiation in the air. The individuals concerned had noticed it, if at all, simply as an indication that they were growing a little bit older, "slowing down, not so young as I used to be." And they were content to slow down; it was more comfortable than exertion.

Grimes had first begun to be concerned about it when he began to notice that *all* of his younger patients were "the bookish type." It was all very well for a kid to like to read books, he felt, but a normal boy ought to be out doing a little hell raising too. What had become of the sand-lot football games, the games of scrub, the clothes-tearing activity that had characterized his own boyhood?

Damn it, a kid ought not to spend *all* his time poring over a stamp collection.

Waldo was beginning to find the answer.

The nerve network of the body was not dissimilar to antennae. Like antennae, it could and did pick up electromagnetic waves. But the pickup was evidenced not as induced electrical current, but as nerve pulsation—impulses which were maddeningly similar to, but distinctly different from, electrical current. Electromotive force could be used in place of nerve impulses to activate muscle tissue, but e.m.f. was *not* nerve impulse. For one thing they traveled at vastly different rates of speed. Electrical current travels at a speed approaching that of light; neural impulse is measured in feet per second.

Waldo felt that somewhere in this matter of speed lay the key to the problem.

He was not permitted to ignore the matter of McLeod's fantastic skycar as long as he had intended to. Dr. Rambeau called him up. Waldo accepted the call, since it was routed from the laboratories of NAPA. "Who are you and what do you want?" he demanded of the image.

Rambeau looked around cautiously. "*Ssssh!* Not so loud," he whispered. "They might be listening."

"Who might be? And who are you?"

"'They' are the ones who are doing it. Lock your doors at night. I'm Dr. Rambeau."

"Dr. Rambeau? Oh yes. Well, Doctor, what is the meaning of this intrusion?"

The doctor leaned forward until he appeared about to fall out of the stereo picture. "I've learned how to do it," he said tensely.

"How to do what?"

"Make the deKalbs work. The dear, dear deKalbs." He suddenly thrust his hands at Waldo, while clutching frantically with his fingers. "They go like this: *Wiggle, wiggle, wiggle!*"

Waldo felt a normal impulse to cut the man off, but it was overruled by a fascination as to what he would say next. Rambeau continued. "Do you know why? Do you? Riddle me that."

"Why?"

Rambeau placed a finger beside his nose and smiled roguishly. "Wouldn't you like to know? Wouldn't you give a pretty to know? *But I'll tell you!*"

"Tell me, then."

Rambeau suddenly looked terrified. "Perhaps I shouldn't. Perhaps they are listening. But I will, I will! Listen carefully: Nothing is certain."

"Is that all?" inquired Waldo, now definitely amused by the man's antics.

"'Is that all?' Isn't that enough? Hens will crow and cocks will lay. You are here and I am there. Or maybe not. Nothing is certain. Nothing,

nothing, NOTHING is certain! Around and around the little ball goes, and where it stops nobody knows. Only I've learned how to do it."

"How to do what?"

"How to make the little ball stop where I want it to. Look." He whipped out a penknife. "When you cut yourself, you bleed, don't you? Or do you?" He sliced at the forefinger of his left hand. "See?" He held the finger close to the pickup; the cut, though deep, was barely discernible and it was bleeding not at all.

Capital! thought Waldo. Hysteric vascular control—a perfect clinical case. "Anybody can do that," he said aloud. "Show me a hard one."

"Anybody? Certainly anybody can—if they know how. Try this one." He jabbed the point of the penknife straight into the palm of his left hand, so that it stuck out the back of his hand. He wiggled the blade in the wound, withdrew it, and displayed the palm. No blood, and the incision was closing rapidly. "Do you know why? The knife is only probably there, *and I've found the improbability!*"

Amusing as it had been, Waldo was beginning to be bored by it. "Is that all?"

"There is no end to it," pronounced Rambeau, "for nothing is certain any more. Watch this." He held the knife flat on his palm, then turned his hand over.

The knife did not fall, but remained in contact with the underside of his hand.

Waldo was suddenly attentive. It might be a trick; it probably was a trick—but it impressed him more, much more, than Rambeau's failure to bleed when cut. One was common to certain types of psychosis; the other should not have happened. He cut in another viewphone circuit. "Get me Chief Engineer Stevens at North American Power-Air," he said sharply. "At once!"

Rambeau paid no attention, but continued to speak of the penknife. "It does not know which way is down," he crooned, "for nothing is certain any more. Maybe it will fall—maybe not. I think it will. There—it has. Would you like to see me walk on the ceiling?"

"You called me, Mr. Jones?" It was Stevens.

Waldo cut his audio circuit to Rambeau. "Yes. That jumping jack, Rambeau. Catch him and bring him to me at once. I want to see him."

"But Mr. Jo——"

"Move!" He cut Stevens off, and renewed the audio to Rambeau.

"—uncertainty. Chaos is King, and Magic is loose in the world!" Rambeau looked vaguely at Waldo, brightened, and added, "Good day, Mr. Jones. Thank you for calling."

The screen went dead.

Waldo waited impatiently. The whole thing had been a hoax, he told himself. Rambeau had played a gigantic practical joke. Waldo disliked practical jokes. He put in another call for Stevens and left it in.

When Stevens did call back his hair was mussed and his face was red. "We had a bad time of it," he said.

"Did you get him?"

"Rambeau? Yes, finally."

"Then bring him up."

"To Freehold? But that's impossible. You don't understand. He's blown his top; he's crazy. They've taken him away to a hospital."

"You assume too much," Waldo said icily. "I know he's crazy, but I meant what I said. Arrange it. Provide nurses. Sign affidavits. Use bribery. Bring him to me at once. It is necessary."

"You really mean that?"

"I'm not in the habit of jesting."

"Something to do with your investigations? He's in no shape to be useful to you, I can tell you that."

"That," pronounced Waldo, "is for me to decide."

"Well," said Stevens doubtfully, "I'll try."

"See that you succeed."

Stevens called back thirty minutes later. "I can't bring Rambeau."

"You clumsy incompetent."

Stevens turned red, but held his temper. "Never mind the personalities. He's gone. He never got to the hospital."

"What?"

"That's the crazy part about it. They took him away in a confining stretcher, laced up like a corset. I saw them fasten him in myself. But when they got there he was gone. And the attendants claim *the straps weren't even unbuckled.*"

Waldo started to say, "Preposterous," thought better of it. Stevens went on.

"But that's not the half of it. I'd sure like to talk to him myself. I've been looking around his lab. You know that set of deKalbs that went nuts— the ones that were hexed?"

"I know to what you refer."

"Rambeau's got a second set to doing the same thing!"

Waldo remained silent for several seconds, then said quietly, "Dr. Stevens—"

"Yes."

"I want to thank you for your efforts. And will you please have both sets of receptors, the two sets that are misbehaving, sent to Freehold at once?"

There was no doubt about it. Once he had seen them with his own eyes, watched the inexplicable squirming of the antennae, applied such tests as suggested themselves to his mind, Waldo was forced to conclude that he was faced with new phenomena, phenomena for which he did not know the rules.

If there were rules. . . .

For he was honest with himself. If he saw what he thought he saw, then rules were being broken by the new phenomena, rules which he had considered valid, rules to which he had never previously encountered exceptions. He admitted to himself that the original failures of the deKalbs should have been considered just as overwhelmingly upsetting to physical law as the unique behavior of these two; the difference lay in that one alien phenomenon was spectacular, the other was not.

Quite evidently Dr. Rambeau had found it so; he had been informed that the doctor had been increasingly neurotic from the first instance of erratic performance of the deKalb receptors.

He regretted the loss of Dr. Rambeau. Waldo was more impressed by Rambeau crazy than he had ever been by Rambeau sane. Apparently the man had had some modicum of ability after all; he had found out *something* —more, Waldo admitted, than he himself had been able to find out so far, even though it had driven Rambeau insane.

Waldo had no fear that Rambeau's experience, whatever it had been, could unhinge his own reason. His own self-confidence was, perhaps, fully justified. His own mild paranoid tendency was just sufficient to give him defenses against an unfriendly world. For him it was healthy, a necessary adjustment to an otherwise intolerable situation, no more pathological than a callus, or an acquired immunity.

Otherwise he was probably more able to face disturbing facts with equanimity than 99 per cent of his contemporaries. He had been *born* to disaster; he had met it and had overcome it, time and again. The very house which surrounded him was testimony to the calm and fearless fashion in which he had defeated a world to which he was not adapted.

He exhausted, temporarily, the obvious lines of direct research concerning the strangely twisting metal rods. Rambeau was not available for questioning. Very well, there remained one other man who knew more about it than Waldo did. He would seek him out. He called Stevens again.

"Has there been any word of Dr. Rambeau?"

"No word, and no sign. I'm beginning to think the poor old fellow is dead."

"Perhaps. That witch doctor friend of your assistant—was Schneider his name?"

"Gramps Schneider."

"Yes indeed. Will you please arrange for him to speak with me?"

"By phone, or do you want to see him in person?"

"I would prefer for him to come here, but I understand that he is old and feeble; it may not be feasible for him to leave the ground. If he is knotted up with spacesickness, he will be no use to me."

"I'll see what can be done."

"Very good. Please expedite the matter. And, Dr. Stevens—"

"Well?"

"If it should prove necessary to use the phone, arrange to have a portable full stereo taken to his home. I want the circumstances to be as favorable as possible."

"O.K."

"Imagine that," Stevens added to McLeod when the circuit had been broken. "The Great-I-Am's showing consideration for somebody else's convenience."

"The fat boy must be sick," McLeod decided.

"Seems likely. This chore is more yours than mine, Mac. Come along with me; we'll take a run over into Pennsylvania."

"How about the plant?"

"Tell Carruthers he's 'It.' If anything blows, we couldn't help it anyway."

Stevens mugged back later in the day. "Mr. Jones—"

"Yes, Doctor?"

"What you suggest can't be arranged."

"You mean that Schneider can't come to Freehold?"

"I mean that and I mean that you can't talk with him on the viewphone."

"I presume that you mean he is dead."

"No, I do not. I mean that he will not talk over the viewphone under any circumstances whatsoever, to you or to anyone. He says that he is sorry not to accommodate you, but that he is opposed to everything of that nature—cameras, cinécams, television, and so forth. He considers them dangerous. I am afraid he is set in his superstition."

"As an ambassador, Dr. Stevens, you leave much to be desired."

Stevens counted up to ten, then said, "I assure you that I have done everything in my power to comply with your wishes. If you are dissatisfied with the quality of my co-operation, I suggest that you speak to Mr. Gleason." He cleared the circuit.

"How would you like to kick him in the teeth?" McLeod said dreamily.

"Mac, you're a mind reader."

Waldo tried again through his own agents, received the same answer. The situation was, to him, almost intolerable; it had been years since he had encountered a man whom he could not buy, bully, nor—in extremity—persuade. Buying had failed; he had realized instinctively that Schneider would be unlikely to be motivated by greed. And how can one bully, or wheedle, a man who cannot be seen to be talked with?

It was a dead end—no way out. Forget it.

Except, of course, for a means best classed as a Fate-Worse-Than-Death. No. No, not that. Don't think about it. Better to drop the whole matter, admit that it had him licked, and tell Gleason so. It had been seventeen years since he had been at Earth surface; nothing could induce him to subject his body to the intolerable demands of that terrible field. Nothing!

It might even kill him. He might choke to death, suffocate. No.

He sailed gracefully across his shop, an overpadded Cupid. Give up this freedom, even for a time, for that torturous bondage? Ridiculous! It was not worth it.

Better to ask an acrophobe to climb Half Dome, or demand that a claustrophobe interview a man in the world's deepest mine.

"Uncle Gus?"

"Oh, hello, Waldo. Glad you called."

"Would it be safe for me to come down to Earth?"

"Eh? How's that? Speak up, man. I didn't understand you."

"I said would it hurt me to make a trip down to Earth."

"This hookup," said Grimes, "is terrible. It sounded just like you were saying you wanted to come down to Earth."

"That's what I did say."

"What's the matter, Waldo? Do you feel all right?"

"I feel fine, but I have to see a man at Earth surface. There isn't any other way for me to talk to him, and I've got to talk to him. Would the trip do me any harm?"

"Ought not to, if you're careful. After all, you were born there. Be careful of yourself, though. You've laid a lot of fat around your heart."

"Oh dear. Do you think it's *dangerous*?"

"No. You're sound enough. Just don't overstrain yourself. And be careful to keep your temper."

"I will. I most certainly will. Uncle Gus?"

"Yes?"

"Will you come along with me and help me see it through?"

"Oh, I don't think that's necessary."

"Please, Uncle Gus. I don't trust anybody else."

"Time you grew up, Waldo. However, I will, this once."

"Now remember," Waldo told the pilot, "the absolute acceleration must never exceed one and one tenth gs, *even in landing*. I'll be watching the accelograph the whole time."

"I've been driving ambulances," said the pilot, "for twelve years, and I've never given a patient a rough ride yet."

"That's no answer. Understand me? One and one tenth; and it should not even approach that figure until we are under the stratosphere. Quiet, Baldur! Quit snuffling."

"I get you."

"Be sure that you do. Your bonuses depend on it."

"Maybe you'd like to herd it yourself."

"I don't like your attitude, my man. If I should die in the tank, you would never get another job."

The pilot muttered something.

"What was that?" Waldo demanded sharply.

"Well, I said it might be worth it."

Waldo started to turn red, opened his mouth.

Grimes cut in "Easy, Waldo! Remember your heart."

"Yes, Uncle Gus."

Grimes snaked his way forward, indicated to the pilot that he wanted him to join him there.

"Don't pay any attention to anything he says," he advised the man quietly, "except what he said about acceleration. He really can't stand much acceleration. He *might* die in the tank."

"I still don't think it would be any loss. But I'll be careful."

"Good."

"I'm ready to enter the tank," Waldo called out. "Will you help me with the straps, Uncle Gus?"

The tank was not a standard deceleration type, but a modification built for this one trip. The tank was roughly the shape of an oversized coffin and was swung in gimbals to keep it always normal to the axis of absolute acceleration. Waldo floated in water—the specific gravity of his fat hulk was low—from which he was separated by the usual flexible, gasketed tarpaulin. Supporting his head and shoulders was a pad shaped to his contour. A mechanical artificial resuscitator was built into the tank, the back pads being under water, the breast pads out of the water but retracted out of the way.

Grimes stood by with neoadrenalin; a saddle had been provided for him on the left side of the tank. Baldur was strapped to a shelf on the right side of the tank; he acted as a counterweight to Grimes.

Grimes assured himself that all was in readiness, then called out to the pilot, "Start when you're ready."

"O.K." He sealed the access port; the entry tube folded itself back against the threshold flat of Freehold, freeing the ship. Gently they got under way.

Waldo closed his eyes; a look of seraphic suffering came over his face. "Uncle Gus, suppose the deKalbs fail?"

"No matter. Ambulances store six times the normal reserve."

"You're *sure?*"

When Baldur began to feel weight, he started to whimper. Grimes spoke to him; he quieted down. But presently—days later, it seemed to Waldo— as the ship sank farther down into the Earth's gravitational field, the absolute acceleration necessarily increased, although the speed of the ship had not changed materially. The dog felt the weary heaviness creeping over his body. He did not understand it and he liked it even less; it terrified him. He began to howl.

Waldo opened his eyes. "Merciful heavens!" he moaned. "Can't you do something about that? He must be dying."

"I'll see." Grimes undid his safety belt and swung himself across the tank. The shift in weight changed the balance of the load in the gimbals; Waldo was rocked against the side of the tank.

"Oh!" he panted. "Be careful."

"Take it easy." Grimes caressed the dog's head and spoke to him. When he had calmed down, Grimes grabbed a handful of hide between the dog's shoulders, measured his spot, and jabbed in a hypo. He rubbed the area. "There, old fellow! That will make you feel better."

Getting back caused Waldo to be rocked again, but he bore it in martyred silence.

The ambulance made just one jerky maneuver after it entered the atmosphere. Both Waldo and the dog yelped. "Private ship," the pilot yelled back. "Didn't heed my right-of-way lights." He muttered something about women drivers.

"It wasn't his fault," Grimes told Waldo. "I saw it."

The pilot set them down with exquisite gentleness in a clearing which had been prepared between the highway and Schneider's house. A party of men was waiting for them there; under Grimes's supervision they unslung the tank and carried Waldo out into the open air. The evolution was performed slowly and carefully, but necessarily involved some degree of bumping and uneven movement. Waldo stood it with silent fortitude, but tears leaked out from under his lowered lids.

Once outside he opened his eyes and asked, "Where is Baldur?"

"I unstrapped him," Grimes informed him, "but he did not follow us out."

Waldo called out huskily, "Here, Baldur! Come to me, boy."

Inside the car the dog heard his boss's voice, raised his head, and gave a low bark. He still felt that terrifying sickness, but he inched forward on his belly, attempting to comply. Grimes reached the door in time to see what happened.

The dog reached the edge of his shelf and made a grotesque attempt to launch himself in the direction from which he had heard Waldo's voice. He tried the only method of propulsion he knew; no doubt he expected to sail through the door and arrest his flight against the tank on the ground. Instead he fell several feet to the inner floor plates, giving one agonized yelp as he did so, and breaking his fall most clumsily with stiffened forelegs.

He lay sprawled where he had landed, making no noise, but not attempting to move. He was trembling violently.

Grimes came up to him and examined him superficially, enough to assure him that the beast was not really hurt, then returned to the outside. "Baldur's had a little accident," he told Waldo; "he's not hurt, but the poor devil doesn't know how to walk. You had best leave him in the ship."

Waldo shook his head slightly. "I want him with me. Arrange a litter."

Grimes got a couple of the men to help him, obtained a stretcher from the pilot of the ambulance, and undertook to move the dog. One of the men said, "I don't know as I care for this job. That dog looks vicious. Look't those eyes."

"He's not," Grimes assured him. "He's just scared out of his wits. Here, I'll take his head."

"What's the matter with him? Same thing as the fat guy?"

"No, he's perfectly well and strong; he's just never learned to walk. This is his first trip to Earth."

"Well, I'll be a cross-eyed owl!"

"I knew a case like it," volunteered the other. "Dog raised in Lunopolis —first week he was on Earth he wouldn't move—just squatted down, and howled, and made messes on the floor."

"So has this one," the first said darkly.

They placed Baldur alongside Waldo's tub. With great effort Waldo raised himself on one elbow, reached out a hand, and placed it on the creature's head. The dog licked it; his trembling almost ceased. "There! There!" Waldo whispered. "It's pretty bad, isn't it? Easy, old friend, take it easy."

Baldur thumped his tail.

It took four men to carry Waldo and two more to handle Baldur. Gramps Schneider was waiting for them at the door of his house. He said nothing as they approached, but indicated that they were to carry Waldo inside. The men with the dog hesitated. "Him, too," he said.

When the others had withdrawn—even Grimes returned to the neighborhood of the ship—Schneider spoke again. "Welcome, Mr. Waldo Jones."

"I thank you for your welcome, Grandfather Schneider."

The old man nodded graciously without speaking. He went to the side of Baldur's litter. Waldo felt impelled to warn him that the beast was dangerous with strangers, but some odd restraint—perhaps the effect of that enervating gravitational field—kept him from speaking in time. Then he saw that he need not bother.

Baldur had ceased his low whimpering, had raised his head, and was licking Gramps Schneider's chin. His tail thumped cheerfully. Waldo felt a sudden tug of jealousy; the dog had never been known to accept a stranger without Waldo's specific injunction. This was disloyalty—treason! But he suppressed the twinge and coolly assessed the incident as a tactical advantage to him.

Schneider pushed the dog's face out of the way and went over him thoroughly, prodding, thumping, extending his limbs. He grasped Baldur's muzzle, pushed back his lips, and eyed his gums. He peeled back the dog's eyelids. He then dropped the matter and came to Waldo's side. "The dog is not sick," he said; "his mind confuses. What made it?"

Waldo told him about Baldur's unusual background. Schneider nodded acceptance of the matter—Waldo could not tell whether he had understood or not—and turned his attention to Waldo. "It is not good for a sprottly lad to lie abed. The weakness—how long has it had you?"

"All my life, Grandfather."

"That is not good." Schneider went over him as he had gone over Baldur. Waldo, whose feeling for personal privacy was much more intense than that of the ordinarily sensitive man, endured it for pragmatic reasons. It was going to be necessary, he felt, to wheedle and cajole this strange old creature. It would not do to antagonize him.

To divert his own attention from the indignity he chose to submit to, and to gain further knowledge of the old quack, Waldo let his eyes rove the room. The room where they were seemed to be a combination kitchen-living room. It was quite crowded, rather narrow, but fairly long. A fireplace dominated the kitchen end, but it had been bricked up, and a hole for the flue pipe of the base-burner had been let into the chimney. The fireplace was lopsided, as an oven had been included in its left side. The corresponding space at the right was occupied by a short counter which supported a tiny sink. The sink was supplied with water by a small hand pump which grew out of the counter.

Schneider, Waldo decided, was either older than he looked, which seemed incredible, or he had acquired his house from someone now long dead.

The living room end was littered and crowded in the fashion which is simply unavoidable in constricted quarters. Books filled several cases, were piled on the floor, hung precariously on chairs. An ancient wooden desk, crowded with papers and supporting a long-obsolete mechanical typewriter, filled one corner. Over it, suspended from the wall, was an ornate clock, carved somewhat like a house. Above its face were two little doors; while Waldo looked at it, a tiny wooden bird painted bright red popped out of the left-hand door, whistled *"Th-wu th-woo!"* four times, and popped frantically back into its hole. Immediately thereafter a little gray bird came out of the right-hand door, said *"Cuckoo"* three times in a leisurely manner, and returned to its hole. Waldo decided that he would like to own such a clock; of course its pendulum-and-weight movement would not function in Freehold, but he could easily devise a one-g centrifuge frame to inclose it, wherein it would have a pseudo Earth-surface environment.

It did not occur to him to fake a pendulum movement by means of a concealed power source; he liked things to work properly.

To the left of the clock was an old-fashioned static calendar of paper. The date was obscured, but the letters above the calendar proper were large and legible: New York World's Fair—Souvenir of the World of Tomorrow. Waldo's eyes widened a little and went back to something he had noticed before, sticking into a pincushion on the edge of the desk. It was a round plastic button mounted on a pin whereby it could be affixed to the clothing. It was not far from Waldo's eyes; he could read the lettering on it:

FREE SILVER
SIXTEEN TO ONE

Schneider must be—*old!*

There was a narrow archway, which led into another room. Waldo could not see into it very well; the arch was draped with a fringe curtain of long strings of large ornamental beads.

The room was rich with odors, many of them old and musty, but not dirty.

Schneider straightened up and looked down at Waldo. "There is nought wrong with your body. Up get yourself and walk."

Waldo shook his head feebly. "I am sorry, Grandfather, I cannot."

"You must reach for the power and make it serve you. Try."

"I am sorry. I do not know how."

"That is the only trouble. All matters are doubtful, unless one knows. You send your force into the Other World. You must reach into the Other World and claim it."

"Where is this 'Other World,' Grandfather?"

Schneider seemed a little in doubt as to how to answer this. "The Other World," he said presently, "is the world you do not see. It is here and it is there and it is everywhere. But it is especially *here.*" He touched his forehead. "The mind sits in it and sends its messages through it to the body. Wait." He shuffled away to a little cupboard, from which he removed a small jar. It contained a salve, or unguent, which he rubbed on his hands.

He returned to Waldo and knelt down beside him. Grasping one of Waldo's hands in both of his, he began to knead it very gently. "Let the mind be quiet," he directed. "Feel for the power. The Other World is close and full of power. Feel it."

The massage was very pleasant to Waldo's tired muscles. The salve, or the touch of the old man's hand, produced a warm, relaxing tingle. If he were younger, thought Waldo, I would hire him as a masseur. He has a magnetic touch.

Schneider straightened up again and said, "There—that betters you? Now you rest while I some coffee make."

Waldo settled back contentedly. He was very tired. Not only was the trip itself a nervous strain, but he was still in the grip of this damnable, thick gravitational field, like a fly trapped in honey. Gramps Schneider's ministrations had left him relaxed and sleepy.

He must have dozed, for the last thing he remembered was seeing Schneider drop an eggshell into the coffeepot. Then the old man was standing before him, holding the pot in one hand and a steaming cup in the other. He set them down, got three pillows, which he placed at Waldo's back, then offered him the coffee. Waldo laboriously reached out both hands to take it.

Schneider held it back. "No," he reproved, "one hand makes plenty. Do as I showed. Reach into the Other World for the strength." He took Waldo's right hand and placed it on the handle of the cup, steadying Waldo's hand with his own. With his other hand he stroked Waldo's right arm gently, from shoulder to finger tips. Again the warm tingle.

Waldo was surprised to find himself holding the cup alone. It was a pleasant triumph; at the time he left Earth, seventeen years before, it had been his invariable habit never to attempt to grasp anything with only one hand. In Freehold, of course, he frequently handled small objects one-handed, without the use of waldoes. The years of practice must have improved his control. Excellent!

So, feeling rather cocky, he drank the cupful with one hand, using extreme care not to slop it on himself. It was good coffee, too, he was bound to admit —quite as good as the sort he himself made from the most expensive syrup extract—better, perhaps.

When Schneider offered him coffeecake, brown with sugar and cinnamon and freshly rewarmed, he swaggeringly accepted it with his left hand, without asking to be relieved of the cup. He continued to eat and drink, between bites and sips resting and steadying his forearms on the edges of the tank.

The conclusion of the *Kaffeeklatsch* seemed a good time to broach the matter of the deKalbs. Schneider admitted knowing McLeod and recalled, somewhat vaguely it seemed, the incident in which he had restored to service McLeod's broomstick. "Hugh Donald is a good boy," he said. "Machines I do not like, but it pleasures me to fix things for boys."

"Grandfather," asked Waldo, "will you tell me how you fixed Hugh Donald McLeod's ship?"

"Have you such a ship you wish me to fix?"

"I have many such ships which I have agreed to fix, but I must tell you that I have been unable to do so. I have come to you to find out the right way."

Schneider considered this. "That is difficult. I could show you, but it is not so much what you do as how you think about it. That makes only with practice."

Waldo must have looked puzzled, for the old man looked at him and added, "It is said that there are two ways of looking at everything. That is true and less than true, for there are many ways. Some of them are good ways and some are bad. One of the ancients said that everything either *is*, or *is not*. That is less than true, for a thing can both *be* and *not be*. With practice one can see it both ways. Sometimes a thing which *is* for this world is a thing which *is not* for the Other World. Which is important, since we live in the Other World."

"We live in the Other World?"

"How else could we live? The mind—not the brain, but the mind—is in the Other World, and reaches this world through the body. That is one true way of looking at it, though there are others."

"Is there more than one way of looking at deKalb receptors?"

"Certainly."

"If I had a set which is not working right brought in here, would you show me how to look at it?"

"It is not needful," said Schneider, "and I do not like for machines to be in my house. I will draw you a picture."

Waldo felt impelled to insist, but he squelched his feeling. "You have come here in humility," he told himself, "asking for instruction. Do not tell the teacher how to teach."

Schneider produced a pencil and a piece of paper, on which he made a careful and very neat sketch of the antennae sheaf and main axis of a skycar. The sketch was reasonably accurate as well, although it lacked several essential minor details.

"These fingers," Schneider said, "reach deep into the Other World to draw their strength. In turn it passes down this pillar"—he indicated the axis—"to where it is used to move the car."

A fair allegorical explanation, thought Waldo. By considering the "Other World" simply a term for the hypothetical ether, it could be considered correct if not complete. But it told him nothing. "Hugh Donald," Schneider went on, "was tired and fretting. He found one of the bad truths."

"Do you mean," Waldo said slowly, "that McLeod's ship failed because he was worried about it?"

"How else?"

Waldo was not prepared to answer that one. It had become evident that the old man had some quaint superstitions; nevertheless, he might still be able to show Waldo *what* to do, even though Schneider did not know *why*. "And what did you do to change it?"

"I made no change; I looked for the other truth."

"But how? We found some chalk marks——"

"Those? They were but to aid me in concentrating my attention in the proper direction. I drew them down *so*"—he illustrated with pencil on the sketch—"and thought how the fingers reached out for power. And so they did."

"That is all? Nothing more?"

"That is enough."

Either, Waldo considered, the old man did not know how he had accomplished the repair, or he had had nothing to do with it—sheer and amazing coincidence.

He had been resting the empty cup on the rim of his tank, the weight supported by the metal while his fingers merely steadied it. His preoccupation caused him to pay too little heed to it; it slipped from his tired fingers, clattered and crashed to the floor.

He was much chagrined. "Oh, I'm *sorry*, Grandfather. I'll send you another."

"No matter. I will mend." Schneider carefully gathered up the pieces and placed them on the desk. "You have tired," he added. "That is not good. It makes you lose what you have gained. Go back now to your house, and when you have rested, you can practice reaching for the strength by yourself."

It seemed a good idea to Waldo; he was growing very tired, and it was evident that he was to learn nothing specific from the pleasant old fraud. He promised, emphatically and quite insincerely, to practice "reaching for strength," and asked Schneider to do him the favor of summoning his bearers.

The trip back was uneventful. Waldo did not even have the spirit to bicker with the pilot.

Stalemate. Machines that did not work but should, and machines that did work but in an impossible manner. And no one to turn to but one foggy-headed old man. Waldo worked lackadaisically for several days, repeating, for the most part, investigations he had already made rather than admit to himself that he was stuck, that he did not know what to do, that he was, in fact, whipped and might as well call Gleason and admit it.

The two "bewitched" sets of deKalbs continued to work whenever activated, with the same strange and incredible flexing of each antenna. Other deKalbs which had failed in operation and had been sent to him for investigation still refused to function. Still others, which had not yet failed, performed beautifully without the preposterous fidgeting.

For the umpteenth time he took out the little sketch Schneider had made and examined it. There was, he thought, just one more possibility: to return again to Earth and insist that Schneider actually *do*, in his presence, whatever it was he had done which caused the deKalbs to work. He knew now that he should have insisted on it in the first place, but he had been so utterly played out by having to fight that devilish thick field that he had not had the will to persist.

Perhaps he could have Stevens do it and have the process stereophotoed for a later examination. No, the old man had a superstitious prejudice against artificial images.

He floated gently over to the vicinity of one of the inoperative deKalbs. What Schneider had claimed to have done was preposterously simple. He had drawn chalk marks down each antenna *so*, for the purpose of fixing his attention. Then he had gazed down them and thought about them "reaching out for power," reaching into the Other World, stretching—

Baldur began to bark frantically.

"Shut up, you fool!" Waldo snapped, without taking his eyes off the antennae.

Each separate pencil of metal was wiggling, stretching. There was the low, smooth hum of perfect operation.

Waldo was still thinking about it when the televisor demanded his attention. He had never been in any danger of cracking up mentally as Rambeau had done; nevertheless, he had thought about the matter in a fashion which made his head ache. He was still considerably bemused when he cut in his end of the soundvision circuit. "Yes?"

It was Stevens. "Hello, Mr. Jones. Uh, we wondered . . . that is——"

"Speak up, man!"

"Well, how close are you to a solution?" Stevens blurted out. "Matters are getting pretty urgent."

"In what way?"

"There was a partial breakdown in Great New York last night. Fortunately it was not at peak load and the ground crew were able to install spares before the reserves were exhausted, but you can imagine what it would have been like during the rush hour. In my own department the crashes have doubled in the past few weeks, and our underwriters have given notice. We need results pretty quick."

"You'll get your results," Waldo said loftily. "I'm in the final stages of the research." He was actually not that confident, but Stevens irritated him even more than most of the smooth apes.

Doubt and reassurance mingled in Stevens's face. "I don't suppose you could care to give us a hint of the general nature of the solution?"

No, Waldo could not. Still—it would be fun to pull Stevens's leg. "Come close to the pickup, Dr. Stevens. I'll tell you." He leaned forward himself, until they were almost nose to nose—in effect. "Magic is loose in the world!"

He cut the circuit at once.

Down in the underground labyrinth of North America's home plant, Stevens stared at the blank screen. "What's the trouble, chief?" McLeod inquired.

"I don't know. I don't rightly know. But I *think* that Fatty has slipped his cams, just the way Rambeau did."

McLeod grinned delightedly. "How sweet! I always did think he was a hoot owl."

Stevens looked very sober. "You had better pray that he *hasn't* gone nuts. We're depending on him. Now let me see those operation reports."

Magic loose in the world. It was as good an explanation as any, Waldo mused. Causation gone haywire; sacrosanct physical laws no longer operative. Magic. As Gramps Schneider had put it, it seemed to depend on the way one looked at it.

Apparently Schneider had known what he was talking about, although he naturally had no real grasp of the physical theory involved in the deKalbs.

Wait a minute now! Wait a minute. He had been going at this problem wrongly perhaps. He had approached it with a certain point of view himself, a point of view which had made him critical of the old man's statements— an assumption that he, Waldo, knew more about the whole matter than Schneider did. To be sure he had gone to see Schneider, but he had thought of him as a back-country hex doctor, a man who might possess one piece of information useful to Waldo, but who was basically ignorant and super- stitious.

Suppose he were to review the situation from a different viewpoint. Let it be assumed that everything Schneider had to say was coldly factual and enlightened, rather than allegorical and superstitious—

He settled himself to do a few hours of hard thinking.

In the first place Schneider had used the phrase "the Other World" time and again. What did it mean, literally? A "world" was a space-time-energy continuum; an "Other World" was, therefore, such a continuum, but a different one from the one in which he found himself. Physical theory found nothing repugnant in such a notion; the possibility of infinite numbers of continua was a familiar, orthodox speculation. It was even convenient in certain operations to make such an assumption.

Had Gramps Schneider meant that? A literal, physical "Other World"? On reflection, Waldo was convinced that he must have meant just that, even though he had not used conventional scientific phraseology. "Other World" sounds poetical, but to say an "additional continuum" implies physical meaning. The terms had led him astray.

Schneider had said that the Other World was all around, here, there, and everywhere. Well, was not that a fair description of a space superposed and in one-to-one correspondence? Such a space might be so close to this one that the interval between them was an infinitesimal, yet unnoticed and unreach- able, just as two planes may be considered as coextensive and separated by an unimaginably short interval, yet be perfectly discrete, one from the other.

The Other Space was not entirely unreachable; Schneider had spoken of reaching into it. The idea was fantastic, yet he must accept it for the purposes of this investigation. Schneider had implied—no—*stated* that it was a matter of mental outlook.

Was that really so fantastic? If a continuum were an unmeasurably short distance away, yet completely beyond one's physical grasp, would it be strange to find that it was most easily reached through some subtle and probably subconscious operation of the brain? The whole matter was subtle— and Heaven knew that no one had any real idea of *how* the brain works. No idea at all. It was laughably insufficient to try to explain the writing of a symphony in terms of the mechanics of colloids. No, nobody knew how the brain worked; one more inexplicable ability in the brain was not too much to swallow.

Come to think of it, the whole notion of consciousness and thought was fantastically improbable.

All right, so McLeod disabled his skycar himself by thinking bad thoughts; Schneider fixed it by thinking the correct thoughts. Then what?

He reached a preliminary conclusion almost at once; by extension, the other deKalb failures were probably failures on the part of the operators. The operators were probably run-down, tired out, worried about something, and in some fashion still not clear they infected, or affected, the deKalbs with their own troubles. For convenience let us say that the deKalbs were short-circuited into the Other World. Poor terminology, but it helped him to form a picture.

Grimes's hypothesis! "Run-down, tired out, worried about something!" Not proved yet, but he felt sure of it. The epidemic of crashes through material was simply an aspect of the general *myasthenia* caused by short-wave radiation.

If that were true—

He cut in a sight-sound circuit to Earth and demanded to talk with Stevens.

"Dr. Stevens," he began at once, "there is a preliminary precautionary measure which should be undertaken right away."

"Yes?"

"First, let me ask you this: Have you had many failures of deKalbs in private ships? What is the ratio?"

"I can't give you exact figures at the moment," Stevens answered, somewhat mystified, "but there have been practically none. It's the commercial lines which have suffered."

"Just as I suspected. A private pilot won't fly unless he feels up to it, but a man with a job goes ahead no matter how he feels. Make arrangements for special physical and psycho examinations for all commercial pilots flying deKalb-type ships. Ground any who are not feeling in tiptop shape. Call Dr. Grimes. He'll tell you what to look for."

"That's a pretty tall order, Mr. Jones. After all, most of those pilots, practically all of them, aren't our employees. We don't have much control over them."

"That's your problem," Waldo shrugged. "I'm trying to tell you how to reduce crashes in the interim before I submit my complete solution."

"But—"

Waldo heard no more of the remark; he had cut off when he himself was through. He was already calling over a permanently energized, leased circuit which kept him in touch with his terrestrial business office—with his "trained seals." He gave them some very odd instructions—orders for books, rare books. Books dealing with magic.

Stevens consulted with Gleason before attempting to do anything about Waldo's difficult request. Gleason was dubious. "He offered no reason for the advice?"

"None. He told me to look up Dr. Grimes and get his advice as to what specifically to look for."

"Dr. Grimes?"

"The M.D. who introduced me to Waldo—mutual friend."

"I recall. Mm-m-m . . . it will be difficult to go about grounding men who don't work for us. Still, I suppose several of our larger customers would co-operate if we asked them to and gave them some sort of a reason. What are you looking so odd about?"

Stevens told him of Waldo's last, inexplicable statement. "Do you suppose it could be affecting him the way it did Dr. Rambeau?"

"Mm-m-m. Could be, I suppose. In which case it would not be well to follow his advice. Have you anything else to suggest?"

"No—frankly."

"Then I see no alternative but to follow his advice. He's our last hope. A forlorn one, perhaps, but our only one."

Stevens brightened a little. "I could talk to Doc Grimes about it. He knows more about Waldo than anyone else."

"You have to consult him anyway, don't you? Very well—do so."

Grimes listened to the story without comment. When Stevens had concluded he said, "Waldo must be referring to the symptoms I have observed with respect to short-wave exposure. That's easy; you can have the proofs of the monograph I've been preparing. It'll tell you all about it."

The information did not reassure Stevens; it helped to confirm his suspicion that Waldo had lost his grip. But he said nothing. Grimes continued, "As for the other, Jim, I can't visualize Waldo losing his mind that way."

"He never did seem very stable to me."

"I know what you mean. But his paranoid streak is no more like what Rambeau succumbed to than chicken pox is like mumps. Matter of fact, one psychosis protects against the other. But I'll go see."

"You will? Good!"

"Can't go today. Got a broken leg and some children's colds that'll bear watching. Been some polio around. Ought to be able to make it the end of the week though."

"Doc, why don't you give up G.P. work? It must be deadly."

"Used to think so when I was younger. But about forty years ago I quit treating diseases and started treating people. Since then I've enjoyed it."

Waldo indulged in an orgy of reading, gulping the treatises on magic and related subjects as fast as he could. He had never been interested in such subjects before; now, in reading about them with the point of view that there might be—and even probably was—something to be learned, he found them intensely interesting.

There were frequent references to another world; sometimes it was called the Other World, sometimes the Little World. Read with the conviction that the term referred to an actual, material, different continuum, he could see that many of the practitioners of the forbidden arts had held the same literal viewpoint. They gave directions for using this other world; sometimes the directions were fanciful, sometimes they were baldly practical.

It was fairly evident that at least 90 per cent of all magic, probably more, was balderdash and sheer mystification. The mystification extended even to the practitioners, he felt; they lacked the scientific method; they employed a single-valued logic as faulty as the two-valued logic of the obsolete Spencer determinism; there was no suggestion of modern extensional, many-valued logic.

Nevertheless, the laws of contiguity, of sympathy, and of homeopathy had a sort of twisted rightness to them when considered in relation to the concept of another, different, but accessible, world. A man who had some access to a different space might well believe in a logic in which a thing could *be, not be,* or *be anything* with equal ease.

Despite the nonsense and confusion which characterized the treatments of magic which dated back to the period when the art was in common practice, the record of accomplishment of the art was impressive. There was curare and digitalis, and quinine, hypnotism, and telepathy. There was the hydraulic engineering of the Egyptian priests. Chemistry itself was derived from alchemy; for that matter, most modern science owed its origins to the magicians. Science had stripped off the surplusage, run it through the wringer of two-valued logic, and placed the knowledge in a form in which anyone could use it.

Unfortunately, that part of magic which refused to conform to the neat categories of the nineteenth-century methodologists was lopped off and left out of the body of science. It fell into disrepute, was forgotten save as fable and superstition.

Waldo began to think of the arcane arts as aborted sciences, abandoned before they had been clarified.

And yet the manifestations of the sort of uncertainty which had characterized some aspects of magic and which he now attributed to hypothetical additional continua had occurred frequently, even in modern times. The evidence was overwhelming to anyone who approached it with an *open mind: Poltergeisten,* stones falling from the sky, apportation, "bewitched" persons—or, as he thought of them, persons who for some undetermined reason were loci of uncertainty—"haunted" houses, strange fires of the sort that would have once been attributed to salamanders. There were hundreds of such cases, carefully recorded and well vouched for, but ignored by ortho-dox science as being impossible. They *were* impossible, by known law, but considered from the standpoint of a coextensive additional continuum, they became entirely credible.

He cautioned himself not to consider his tentative hypothesis of the Other World as proved; nevertheless, it was an adequate hypothesis even if it should develop that it did not apply to some of the cases of strange events.

The Other Space might have different physical laws—no reason why it should not. Nevertheless, he decided to proceed on the assumption that it was much like the space he knew.

The Other World might even be inhabited. That was an intriguing thought! In which case anything could happen through "magic." Anything!

Time to stop speculating and get down to a little solid research. He had previously regretfully given up trying to apply the formulas of the medieval magicians. It appeared that they never wrote down *all* of a procedure; some essential—so the reports ran and so his experience confirmed—was handed down verbally from master to student. His experience with Schneider confirmed this; there were things, *attitudes,* which must needs be taught directly. He regretfully set out to learn what he must unassisted.

"Gosh, Uncle Gus, I'm glad to see you!"

"Decided I'd better look in on you. You haven't phoned me in weeks."

"That's true, but I've been working awfully hard, Uncle Gus."

"Too hard, maybe. Mustn't overdo it. Lemme see your tongue."

"I'm O.K." But Waldo stuck out his tongue just the same; Grimes looked at it and felt his pulse.

"You seem to be ticking all right. Learning anything?"

"Quite a lot. I've about got the matter of the deKalbs whipped."

"That's good. The message you sent Stevens seemed to indicate that you had found some hookup that could be used on my pet problem too."

"In a way, yes; but around from the other end. It begins to seem as if it was your problem which created Stevens's problem."

"Huh?"

"I mean it. The symptoms caused by ultra short-wave radiation may have had a lot to do with the erratic behavior of the deKalbs."

"How?"

"I don't know myself. But I've rigged up a working hypothesis and I'm checking it."

"Hm-m-m. Want to talk about it?"

"Certainly—to you." Waldo launched into an account of his interview with Schneider, concerning which he had not previously spoken to Grimes, even though Grimes had made the trip with him. He never, as Grimes knew, discussed anything until he was ready to.

The story of the third set of deKalbs to be infected with the incredible writhings caused Grimes to raise his eyebrows. "Mean to say you caught on to how to do *that?*"

"Yes indeed. Not '*how,*' maybe, but I can do it. I've done it more than once. I'll show you." He drifted away toward one side of the great room where several sets of deKalbs, large and small, were mounted, with their controls, on temporary guys. "This fellow over on the end, it just came in today. Broke down. I'll give it Gramps Schneider's hocus-pocus and fix it. Wait a minute. I forgot to turn on the power."

He returned to the central ring which constituted his usual locus and switched on the beamcaster. Since the ship itself effectively shielded anything in the room from outer radiation, he had installed a small power plant and caster similar in type to NAPA's giant ones; without it he would have had no way to test the reception of the deKalbs.

He rejoined Grimes and passed down the line of deKalbs, switching on the activizing circuits. All save two began to display the uncouth motions he had begun to think of as the Schneider flex. "That one on the far end," he remarked, "is in operation but doesn't flex. It has never broken down, so it's never been treated. It's my control; but this one"—he touched the one in front of him—"needs fixing. Watch me."

"What are you going to do?"

"To tell the truth, I don't quite know. But I'll do it." He did not know. All he knew was that it was necessary to gaze down the antennae, think about them reaching into the Other World, think of them reaching for power, reaching—

The antennae began to squirm.

"That's all there is to it—strictly between ourselves. I learned it from Schneider." They had returned to the center of the sphere, at Grimes's suggestion, on the pretext of wanting to get a cigarette. The squirming deKalbs made him nervous, but he did not want to say so.

"How do you explain it?"

"I regard it as an imperfectly understood phenomenon of the Other Space. I know less about it than Franklin knew about lightning. But I will know—I will! I could give Stevens a solution right now for his worries if I knew some way to get around your problem too."

"I don't see the connection."

"There ought to be some way to do the whole thing through the Other Space. Start out by radiating power into the Other Space and pick it up from there. Then the radiation could not harm human beings. It would never get at them; it would duck around them. I've been working on my caster, but with no luck so far. I'll crack it in time."

"I hope you do. Speaking of that, isn't the radiation from your own caster loose in this room?"

"Yes."

"Then I'll put on my shield coat. It's not good for you either."

"Never mind. I'll turn it off." As he turned to do so there was the sound of a sweet, chirruping whistle. Baldur barked. Grimes turned to see what caused it.

"What," he demanded, "have you got there?"

"Huh? Oh, that's my cuckoo clock. Fun, isn't it?" Grimes agreed that it was, although he could not see much use for it. Waldo had mounted it on the edge of a light metal hoop which spun with a speed just sufficient to produce a centrifugal force of one g.

"I rigged it up," Waldo continued, "while I was bogged down in this problem of the Other Space. Gave me something to do."

"This 'Other Space' business—I still don't get it."

"Think of another continuum much like our own and superposed on it the way you might lay one sheet of paper on another. The two spaces aren't identical, but they are separated from each other by the smallest interval you can imagine—coextensive but not touching—usually. There is an absolute one-to-one, point-for-point correspondence, as I conceive it, between the two spaces, but they are not necessarily the same size or shape."

"Hey? Come again—they would *have* to be."

"Not at all. Which has the larger number of points in it? A line an inch long, or a line a mile long?"

"A mile long, of course."

"No. They have exactly the same number of points. Want me to prove it?"

"I'll take your word for it. But I never studied that sort of math."

"All right. Take my word for it then. Neither size nor shape is any impediment to setting up a full, point-for-point correspondence between two spaces. Neither of the words is really appropriate. 'Size' has to do with a space's own inner structure, its dimensions in terms of its own unique constants. 'Shape' is a matter which happens inside itself—or at least not inside *our* space—and has to do with how it is curved, open or closed, expanding or contracting."

Grimes shrugged. "It all sounds like gibberish to me." He returned to watching the cuckoo clock swing round and round its wheel.

"Sure it does," Waldo assented cheerfully. "We are limited by our experience. Do you know how I think of the Other World?" The question was purely rhetorical. "I think of it as about the size and shape of an ostrich egg, but nevertheless a whole universe, existing side by side with our own, from here to the farthest star. I know that it's a false picture, but it helps me to think about it that way."

"I wouldn't know," said Grimes, and turned himself around in the air. The compound motion of the clock's pendulum was making him a little dizzy. "Say! I thought you turned off the caster?"

"I did," Waldo agreed, and looked where Grimes was looking. The deKalbs were still squirming. "I thought I did," he said doubtfully, and turned to the caster's control board. His eyes then opened wider. "But I *did*. It *is* turned off."

"Then what the devil——"

"*Shut up!*" He had to think—think hard. Was the caster actually out of operation? He floated himself over to it, inspected it. Yes, it was dead, dead as the dinosaurs. Just to make sure he went back, assumed his primary waldoes, cut in the necessary circuits, and partially disassembled it. But the deKalbs still squirmed.

The one deKalb set which had not been subjected to the Schneider treatment was dead; it gave out no power hum. But the others were working frantically, gathering power from—*where?*

He wondered whether or not McLeod had said anything to Gramps Schneider about the casters from which the deKalbs were intended to pick up their power. Certainly he himself had not. It simply had not come into the conversation. But Schneider had said something. "The Other World is close by and full of power!"

In spite of his own intention of taking the old man literally he had ignored that statement. The Other World is full of power. "I am sorry I snapped at you, Uncle Gus," he said.

"'S all right."

"But what do you make of that?"

"Looks like you've invented perpetual motion, son."

"In a way, perhaps. Or maybe we've repealed the law of conservation of energy. Those deKalbs are drawing energy that was never before in this world!"

"Hm-m-m!"

To check his belief he returned to the control ring, donned his waldoes, cut in a mobile scanner, and proceeded to search the space around the deKalbs with the most sensitive pickup for the radio power band he had available. The needles never jumped; the room was dead in the wave lengths to which the deKalbs were sensitive. The power came from Other Space.

The power came from Other Space. Not from his own beamcaster, not from NAPA's shiny stations, but from Other Space. In that case he was not even close to solving the problem of the defective deKalbs; he might never solve it. Wait, now—just what had he contracted to do? He tried to recall the exact words of the contract.

There just might be a way around it. Maybe. Yes, and this newest cock-eyed trick of Gramps Schneider's little pets could have some very tricky aspects. He began to see some possibilities, but he needed to think about it.

"Uncle Gus——"

"Yes, Waldo?"

"You can go back and tell Stevens that I'll be ready with the answers. We'll get his problem licked, and yours too. In the meantime I've got to do some really heavy thinking, so I want to be by myself, please."

"Greetings, Mr. Gleason. *Quiet, Baldur!* Come in. Be comfortable. How do you do, Dr. Stevens."

"How do you do, Mr. Jones."

"This," said Gleason, indicating a figure trailing him, "is Mr. Harkness, head of our legal staff."

"Ah, yes indeed. There will be matters of contract to be discussed. Welcome to Freehold, Mr. Harkness."

"Thank you," Harkness said coldly. "Will your attorneys be present?"

"They are present." Waldo indicated a stereo screen. Two figures showed in it; they bowed and murmured polite forms.

"This is most irregular," Harkness complained. "Witnesses should be present in person. Things seen and heard by television are not evidence."

Waldo drew his lips back. "Do you wish to make an issue of it?"

"Not at all," Gleason said hastily. "Never mind, Charles." Harkness subsided.

"I won't waste your time, gentlemen," Waldo began. "We are here in order that I may fulfill my contract with you. The terms are known—we will pass over them." He inserted his arms into his primary waldoes. "Lined up along the far wall you will see a number of radiant power receptors, commonly called deKalbs. Dr. Stevens may, if he wishes, check their serial numbers——"

"No need to."

"Very well. I shall start my local beamcaster, in order that we may check the efficiency of their operation." His waldoes were busy as he spoke. "Then I shall activate the receptors, one at a time." His hands pawed the air; a little pair of secondaries switched on the proper switches on the control board of the last set in line. "This is an ordinary type, supplied to me by Dr. Stevens, which has never failed in operation. You may assure yourself that it is now operating in the normal manner, if you wish, Doctor."

"I can see that it is."

"We will call such a receptor a 'deKalb' and its operation 'normal.'" The small waldoes were busy again. "Here we have a receptor which I choose to term a 'Schneider-deKalb' because of certain treatment it has received"—the antennae began to move—"and its operation 'Schneider-type' operation. Will you check it, Doctor?"

"O.K."

"You fetched with you a receptor set which has failed?"

"As you can see."

"Have you been able to make it function?"

"No, I have not."

"Are you sure? Have you examined it carefully?"

"Quite carefully," Stevens acknowledged sourly. He was beginning to be tired of Waldo's pompous flubdubbery.

"Very well. I will now proceed to make it operative." Waldo left his control ring, shoved himself over to the vicinity of the defective deKalb, and placed himself so that his body covered his exact actions from the sight of the others. He returned to the ring and, using waldoes, switched on the activating circuit of the deKalb.

It immediately exhibited Schneider-type activity.

"That is my case, gentlemen," he announced. "I have found out how to repair deKalbs which become spontaneously inoperative. I will undertake to apply the Schneider treatment to any receptors which you may bring to me. That is included in my fee. I will undertake to train others in how to apply the Schneider treatment. That is included in my fee, but I cannot guarantee that any particular man will profit by my instruction. Without going into technical details I may say that the treatment is very difficult, much harder than it looks. I think that Dr. Stevens will confirm that." He smiled thinly. "I believe that completes my agreement with you."

"Just a moment, Mr. Jones," put in Gleason. "Is a deKalb foolproof, once it has received the Schneider treatment?"

"Quite. I guarantee it."

They went into a huddle while Waldo waited. At last Gleason spoke for them. "These are not quite the results we had expected, Mr. Jones, but we agree that you have fulfilled your commission—with the understanding that you will Schneider-treat any receptors brought to you and instruct others, according to their ability to learn."

"That is correct."

"Your fee will be deposited to your account at once."

"Good. That is fully understood and agreed? I have completely and successfully performed your commission?"

"Correct."

"Very well then. I have one more thing to show you. If you will be patient——" A section of the wall folded back; gigantic waldoes reached into the room beyond and drew forth a large apparatus, which resembled somewhat in general form an ordinary set of deKalbs, but which was considerably more complicated. Most of the complications were sheer decoration, but it would have taken a skilled engineer a long time to prove the fact.

The machine did contain one novel feature: a built-in meter of a novel type, whereby it could be set to operate for a predetermined time and then destroy itself, and a radio control whereby the time limit could be varied. Furthermore, the meter would destroy itself and the receptors if tampered with by any person not familiar with its design. It was Waldo's tentative answer to the problem of selling free and unlimited power.

But of these matters he said nothing. Small waldoes had been busy attaching guys to the apparatus; when they were through he said, "This, gentlemen, is an instrument which I choose to call a Jones-Schneider-deKalb. And it is the reason why you will not be in the business of selling power much longer."

"So?" said Gleason. "May I ask why?"

"Because," he was told, "I can sell it more cheaply and conveniently and under circumstances you cannot hope to match."

"That is a strong statement."

"I will demonstrate. Dr. Stevens, you have noted that the other receptors are operating. I will turn them off." The waldoes did so. "I will now stop the beamcast and I will ask you to assure yourself, by means of your own instruments, that there is *no* radiant power, other than ordinary visible light, in this room."

Somewhat sullenly Stevens did so. "The place is dead," he announced some minutes later.

"Good. Keep your instruments in place, that you may be sure it remains dead. I will now activate my receptor." Little mechanical hands closed the switches. "Observe it, Doctor. Go over it thoroughly."

Stevens did so. He did not trust the readings shown by its instrument board; he attached his own meters in parallel. "How about it, James?" Gleason whispered.

Stevens looked disgusted. "The damn thing draws power from nowhere!"

They all looked at Waldo. "Take plenty of time, gentlemen," he said grandly. "Talk it over."

They withdrew as far away as the room permitted and whispered. Waldo could see that Harkness and Stevens were arguing, that Stevens was noncommittal. That suited him. He was hoping that Stevens would not decide to take another look at the fancy gadget he had termed a Jones-Schneider-deKalb. Stevens must not learn too much about it—yet. He had been careful to say nothing but the truth about it, but perhaps he had not said all of the truth; he had not mentioned that *all* Schneider-treated deKalbs were sources of free power.

Rather embarrassing if Stevens should discover that!

The meter-and-destruction device Waldo had purposely made mysterious and complex, but it was not useless. Later he would be able to point out, quite correctly, that without such a device NAPA simply could not remain in business.

Waldo was not easy. The whole business was a risky gamble; he would have much preferred to know more about the phenomena he was trying to peddle, but—he shrugged mentally while preserving a smile of smug confidence—the business had dragged on several months already, and the power situation really was critical. This solution would do—if he could get their names on the dotted line quickly enough.

For he had no intention of trying to compete with NAPA.

Gleason pulled himself away from Stevens and Harkness, came to Waldo. "Mr. Jones, can't we arrange this amicably?"

"What have you to suggest?"

It was quite an hour later that Waldo, with a sigh of relief, watched his guests' ship depart from the threshold flat. A fine caper, he thought, and it had worked; he had gotten away with it. He had magnanimously allowed himself to be persuaded to consolidate, provided—he had allowed himself to be quite temperamental about this—the contract was concluded at once, no fussing around and fencing between lawyers. Now or never— put up or shut up. The proposed contract, he had pointed out virtuously, gave him nothing at all unless his allegations about the Jones-Schneider-deKalb were correct.

Gleason considered this point and had decided to sign, had signed.

Even then Harkness had attempted to claim that Waldo had been an employee of NAPA. Waldo had written that first contract himself—a specific commission for a contingent fee. Harkness did not have a leg to stand on; even Gleason had agreed to that.

In exchange for all rights to the Jones-Schneider-deKalb, for which he agreed to supply drawings—wait till Stevens saw, and understood, those sketches!—for that he had received the promise of senior stock in NAPA, nonvoting, but fully paid up and nonassessable. The lack of active participation in the company had been his own idea. There were going to be more headaches in the power business, headaches aplenty. He could see them coming—bootleg designs, means of outwitting the metering, lots of things. Free power had come, and efforts to stop it would in the long run, he believed, be fruitless.

Waldo laughed so hard that he frightened Baldur, who set up an excited barking.

He could afford to forget Hathaway now.

His revenge on NAPA contained one potential flaw; he had assured Gleason that the Schneider-treated deKalbs would continue to operate, would not come unstuck. He believed that to be true simply because he had faith in Gramps Schneider. But he was not prepared to prove it. He knew himself that he did not know enough about the phenomena associated with the Other World to be sure that something would, or would not, happen. It was still going to be necessary to do some hard, extensive research.

But the Other World was a devilishly difficult place to investigate!

Suppose, he speculated, that the human race were blind, had never developed eyes. No matter how civilized, enlightened, and scientific the race might have become, it is difficult to see how such a race could ever have developed the concepts of astronomy. They might know of the Sun as a cyclic source of energy having a changing, directional character, for the Sun is so overpowering that it may be "seen" with the skin. They would notice it and invent instruments to trap it and examine it.

But the pale stars, would they ever notice them? It seemed most unlikely. The very notion of the celestial universe, its silent depths and starlit grandeur, would be beyond them. Even if one of their scientists should have the concept forced on him in such a manner that he was obliged to accept the fantastic, incredible thesis as fact, how then would he go about investigating its details?

Waldo tried to imagine an astronomical phototelescope, conceived and designed by a blind man, intended to be operated by a blind man, and capable of collecting data which could be interpreted by a blind man. He gave it up; there were too many hazards. It would take a subtlety of genius far beyond his own to deal with the inescapably tortuous concatenations of inferential reasoning necessary to the solution of such a problem. It would strain him to invent such instruments *for* a blind man; he did not see how a blind man could ever overcome the difficulties unassisted.

In a way that was what Schneider had done for him; alone, he would have bogged down.

But even with Schneider's hints the problem of investigating the Other World was still much like the dilemma of the blind astronomer. He could not *see* the Other World; only through the Schneider treatment had he been able to contact it. Damnation! how could he design instruments to study it?

He suspected that he would eventually have to go back to Schneider for further instruction, but that was an expedient so distasteful that he refused to think much about it. Furthermore, Gramps Schneider might not be able to teach him much; they did not speak the same language.

This much he did know: the Other Space was there and it could be reached sometimes by proper orientation of the mind, deliberately as Schneider had taught him, or subconsciously as had happened to McLeod and others.

He found the idea distasteful. That thought and thought alone should be able to influence physical phenomena was contrary to the whole materialistic philosophy in which he had grown up. He had a prejudice in favor of order and invariable natural laws. His cultural predecessors, the experimental philosophers who had built up the world of science and its concomitant technology, Galileo, Newton, Edison, Einstein, Steinmetz, Jeans, and their myriad colleagues—these men had thought of the physical universe as a mechanism proceeding by inexorable necessity. Any apparent failure to proceed thus was regarded as an error in observation, an insufficient formulation of hypothesis, or an insufficiency of datum.

Even the short reign of the Heisenberg uncertainty principle had not changed the fundamental orientation toward Order and Cosmos; the Heisenberg uncertainty was one they were certain of! It could be formulated, expressed, and a rigorous statistical mechanics could be built from it. In 1958 Horowitz's reformulation of wave mechanics had eliminated the concept. Order and causation were restored.

But this damned business! One might as well pray for rain, wish on the Moon, go to faith healers, surrender whole hog to Bishop Berkely's sweetly cerebral world-in-your-head. "—the tree's not a tree, when there's no one about on the quad!"

Waldo was not emotionally wedded to Absolute Order as Rambeau had been; he was in no danger of becoming mentally unbalanced through a failure of his basic conceptions; nevertheless, consarn it, it was convenient for things to work the way one expected them to. On order and natural law was based predictability; without predictability it was impossible to live. Clocks should run evenly; water should boil when heat is applied to it; food should nourish, not poison; deKalb receptors should *work*, work the way they were designed to; Chaos was insupportable—it could not be lived with.

Suppose Chaos *were* king and the order we thought we detected in the world about us a mere phantasm of the imagination; where would that lead us? In that case, Waldo decided, it was entirely possible that a ten-pound weight *did* fall ten times as fast as a one-pound weight until the day the audacious Galileo decided in his mind that it was not so. Perhaps the whole meticulous science of ballistics derived from the convictions of a few firm-minded individuals who had sold the notion to the world. Perhaps the very stars were held firm in their courses by the unvarying faith of the astronomers. Orderly Cosmos, created out of Chaos—by Mind!

The world was flat before geographers decided to think of it otherwise. The world was flat, and the Sun, tub size, rose in the east and set in the west. The stars were little lights, studding a pellucid dome which barely cleared the tallest mountains. Storms were the wrath of gods and had nothing to do with the calculus of air masses. A Mind-created animism dominated the world then.

More recently it had been different. A prevalent convention of materialistic and invariable causation had ruled the world; on it was based the whole involved technology of a machine-served civilization. The machines *worked*, the way they were designed to work, because everybody believed in them.

Until a few pilots, somewhat debilitated by overmuch exposure to radiation, had lost their confidence and infected their machines with uncertainty—and thereby let magic loose in the world.

He was beginning, he thought, to understand what had happened to magic. Magic was the erratic law of an animistic world; it had been steadily pushed back by the advancing philosophy of invariant causation. It was gone now—until this new outbreak—and its world with it, except for backwaters of "superstition." Naturally an experimental scientist reported failure when investigating haunted houses, apportations, and the like; his convictions prevented the phenomena from happening.

The deep jungles of Africa might be very different places—when there was no white man around to see! The strangely slippery laws of magic might still obtain.

Perhaps these speculations were too extreme; nevertheless, they had one advantage which orthodox concepts had not: they included Gramps Schneider's hexing of the deKalbs. Any working hypothesis which failed to account for Schneider's—and his own—ability to *think* a set of deKalbs into operation was not worth a continental. This one did, and it conformed to Gramps's own statements: "All matters are doubtful" and "A thing can both *be, not be,* and *be anything.* There are many true ways of looking at the same thing. Some ways are good, some are bad."

Very well. Accept it. Act on it. The world varied according to the way one looked at it. In that case, thought Waldo, he knew how he wanted to look at it. He cast his vote for order and predictability!

He would *set* the style. He would impress his *own* concept of the Other World on the Cosmos!

It had been a good start to assure Gleason that the Schneider-treated deKalbs were foolproof. Good. So let it be. They were foolproof. They would never get out of order.

He proceeded to formulate and clarify his own concept of the Other World in his mind. He would think of it as orderly and basically similar to this space. The connection between the two spaces lay in the neurological system; the cortex, the thalamus, the spinal cord, and the appended nerve system were closely connected with both spaces. Such a picture was consistent with what Schneider had told him and did not conflict with phenomena as he knew it.

Wait. If the neurological system lay in both spaces, then that might account for the relatively slow propagation of nerve impulses as compared with electromagnetic progression. Yes! If the other space had a *c* constant relatively smaller than that of this space, such would follow.

He began to feel a calm assurance that it was *so*.

Was he merely speculating—or creating a universe?

Perhaps he would have to abandon his mental picture of the Other Space as being the size and shape of an ostrich egg, since a space with a slower propagation of light is not smaller, but larger, than the space he was used to. No . . . no, wait a second, the *size* of a space did not depend on its *c* constant, but on its radius of curvature in terms of its *c* constant. Since *c* was a velocity, size was dependent on the notion of time—in this case time as entropy rate. Therein lay a characteristic which could be compared between the two spaces: they exchanged energy; they affected each other's entropy. The one which degenerated the more rapidly toward a state of level entropy was the "smaller."

He need not abandon his picture of the ostrich egg—good old egg! The Other World was a closed space, with a slow *c*, a high entropy rate, a short radius, and an entropy state near level—a perfect reservoir of power at every point, ready to spill over into this space wherever he might close the interval. To its inhabitants, if any, it might seem to be hundreds of millions of light years around; to him it was an ostrich egg, turgid to bursting with power.

He was already beginning to think of ways of checking his hypothesis. If, using a Schneider-deKalb, he were to draw energy at the highest rate he could manage, would he affect the local potential? Would it establish an entropy gradient? Could he reverse the process by finding a way to pump power into the Other World? Could he establish different levels at different points and thereby check for degeneration toward level, maximum entropy?

Did the speed of nerve impulse propagation furnish a clue to the c of the Other Space? Could such a clue be combined with the entropy and potential investigations to give a mathematical picture of the Other Space, in terms of its constants and its age?

He set about it. His untrammeled, wild speculations had produced some definite good: he'd tied down at least one line of attack on that Other Space; he'd devised a working principle for his blind man's telescope mechanism. Whatever the truth of the thing was, it was more than *a* truth; it was a complete series of new truths. It was the very complexity of that series of new truths—the truths, the characteristic laws, that were inherent properties of the Other Space, plus the new truth laws resultant from the interaction of the characteristics of the Other Space with Normal Space. No wonder Rambeau had said anything could happen! Almost anything could, in all probability, by a proper application and combination of the three sets of laws: the laws of Our Space, the laws of Other Space, and the co-ordinate laws of Both Spaces.

But before theoreticians could begin work, new data were most desperately needed. Waldo was no theoretician, a fact he admitted left-handedly in thinking of theory as impractical and unnecessary, time waste for him as a consulting engineer. Let the smooth apes work it out.

But the consulting engineer had to find out one thing: would the Schneider-deKalbs continue to function uninterruptedly as guaranteed? If not, what must be done to assure continuous function?

The most difficult and the most interesting aspect of the investigation had to do with the neurological system in relation to Other Space. Neither electromagnetic instruments nor neural surgery was refined enough to do accurate work on the levels he wished to investigate.

But he had waldoes.

The smallest waldoes he had used up to this time were approximately half an inch across their palms—with microscanners to match, of course. They were much too gross for his purpose. He wished to manipulate living nerve tissue, examine its insulation and its performance *in situ*.

He used the tiny waldoes to create tinier ones.

The last stage was tiny metal blossoms hardly an eighth of an inch across. The helices in their stems, or forearms, which served them as pseudo muscles, could hardly be seen by the naked eye—but, then, he used scanners.

His final team of waldoes used for nerve and brain surgery varied in succeeding stages from mechanical hands nearly life-size down to these fairy digits which could manipulate things much too small for the eye to see. They were mounted in bank to work in the same locus. Waldo controlled them all from the same primaries; he could switch from one size to another without removing his gauntlets. The same change in circuits which brought another size of waldoes under control automatically accomplished the change in sweep of scanning to increase or decrease the magnification so that Waldo always saw before him in his stereo receiver a "life-size" image of his other hands.

Each level of waldoes had its own surgical instruments, its own electrical equipment.

Such surgery had never been seen before, but Waldo gave that aspect little thought; no one had told him that such surgery was unheard-of.

He established, to his own satisfaction, the mechanism whereby short-wave radiation had produced a deterioration in human physical performance. The synapses between dendrites acted as if they were points of leakage. Nerve impulses would sometimes fail to make the jump, would leak off—to where? To Other Space, he was sure. Such leakage seemed to establish a preferred path, a canalization, whereby the condition of the victim became steadily worse. Motor action was not lost entirely, as both paths were still available, but efficiency was lost. It reminded him of a metallic electrical circuit with a partial ground.

An unfortunate cat, which had become dead undergoing the experimentation, had supplied him with much of his data. The kitten had been born and raised free from exposure to power radiation. He subjected it to heavy exposure and saw it acquire a *myasthenia* nearly as complete as his own —while studying in minute detail what actually went on in its nerve tissues.

He felt quite sentimental about it when it died.

Yet, if Gramps Schneider were right, human beings need not be damaged by radiation. If they had the wit to look at it with the proper orientation, the radiation would not affect them; they might even draw power out of the Other World.

That was what Gramps Schneider had told him to do.

That was what Gramps Schneider had told *him* to do!

Gramps Schneider had told him he need not be weak!

That he could be strong——

Strong!

STRONG!

He had never thought of it. Schneider's friendly ministrations to him, his advice about overcoming the weakness, he had ignored, had thrown off as inconsequential. His own weakness, his own peculiarity which made him different from the smooth apes, he had regarded as a basic, implicit fact. He had accepted it as established when he was a small child, a final unquestioned factor.

Naturally he had paid no attention to Schneider's words in so far as they referred to him.

To be strong!

To stand alone—to walk, to run!

Why, he . . . he could, he could go down to Earth surface without fear. He wouldn't mind the field. They *said* they didn't mind it; they even *carried* things—great, heavy things. Everybody did. They *threw* things.

He made a sudden convulsive movement in his primary waldoes, quite unlike his normal, beautifully economical rhythm. The secondaries were oversize, as he was making a new setup. The guys tore loose, a brace plate banged against the wall. Baldur was snoozing nearby; he pricked up his ears, looked around, then turned his face to Waldo, questioning him.

Waldo glared at him and the dog whined. "Shut up!"

The dog quieted and apologized with his eyes.

Automatically he looked over the damage—not much, but he would have to fix it. Strength. Why, if he were strong, he could do anything—anything! No. 6 extension waldoes and some new guys—— Strong! Absent-mindedly he shifted to the No. 6 waldoes.

Strength!

He could even meet women—be stronger than they were!

He could swim. He could ride. He could fly a ship—run, jump. He could handle things with his bare hands. He could even learn to dance!

Strong!

He would have muscles! He could break things.

He could—— He could——

He switched to the great waldoes with hands the size of a man's body. Strong—they were strong! With one giant waldo he hauled from the stock pile a quarter-inch steel plate, held it up, and shook it. A booming rumble. He shook it again. Strong!

He took it in both waldoes, bent it double. The metal buckled unevenly. Convulsively he crumpled it like wastepaper between the two huge palms. The grinding racket raised hackles on Baldur; he himself had not been aware of it.

He relaxed for a moment, gasping. There was sweat on his forehead; blood throbbed in his ears. But he was not spent; he wanted something heavier, *stronger*. Cutting to the adjoining storeroom he selected an L-beam twelve feet long, shoved it through to where the giant hands could reach it, and cut back to them.

The beam was askew in the port; he wrenched it loose, knocking a big dent in the port frame. He did not notice it.

The beam made a fine club in the gross fist. He brandished it. Baldur backed away, placing the control ring between himself and the great hands.

Power! Strength! Smashing, unbeatable strength——

With a spastic jerk he checked his swing just before the beam touched the wall. No—— But he grabbed the other end of the club with the left waldo and tried to bend it. The big waldoes were built for heavy work, but the beam was built to resist. He strained inside the primaries, strove to force the great fists to do his will. A warning light flashed on his control board. Blindly he kicked in the emergency overload and persisted.

The hum of the waldoes and the rasp of his own breath were drowned out by the harsh scrape of metal on metal as the beam began to give way. Exulting, he bore down harder in the primaries. The beam was bending double when the waldoes blew out. The right-hand tractors let go first; the fist flung open. The left fist, relieved of the strain, *threw* the steel from it.

It tore its way through the thin bulkhead, making a ragged hole, crashed and clanged in the room beyond.

But the giant waldoes were inanimate junk.

He drew his soft pink hands from the waldoes and looked at them. His shoulders heaved, and racking sobs pushed up out of him. He covered his face with his hands; the tears leaked out between his fingers. Baldur whimpered and edged in closer.

On the control board a bell rang persistently.

The wreckage had been cleared away and an adequate, neat patch covered the place where the L-beam had made its own exit. But the giant waldoes had not yet been replaced; their frame was uninhabited. Waldo was busy rigging a strength tester.

It had been years since he had paid any attention to the exact strength of his body. He had had so little use for strength; he had concentrated on dexterity, particularly on the exact and discriminating control of his namesakes. In the selective, efficient, and accurate use of his muscles he was second to none; he had control—he *had* to have. But he had had no need for strength.

With the mechanical equipment at hand it was not difficult to jerry-rig a device which would register strength of grip as pounds-force on a dial. A spring-loaded scale and a yoke to act on it sufficed. He paused and looked at the contrivance.

He need only take off the primary waldoes, place his bare hand on the grip, bear down—and he would know. Still he hesitated.

It felt strange to handle anything so large with his bare hand. Now. Reach into the Other World for power. He closed his eyes and pressed. He opened them. Fourteen pounds—less than he used to have.

But he had not really tried yet. He tried to imagine Gramps Schneider's hands on his arm, that warm tingle. Power. Reach out and claim it.

Fourteen pounds, fifteen—seventeen, eighteen, twenty, twenty-one! He was winning! He was winning!

Both his strength and his courage failed him, in what order he could not say. The needle spun back to zero; he had to rest.

Had he really shown exceptional strength—or was twenty-one pounds of grip simply normal for him at his present age and weight? A normally strong and active man, he knew, should have a grip on the order of one hundred and fifty pounds.

Nevertheless, twenty-one pounds of grip was six pounds higher than he had ever before managed on test.

Try, again. Ten, eleven—twelve. Thirteen. The needle hesitated. Why, he had just started—this was ridiculous. Fourteen.

There it stopped. No matter how he strained and concentrated his driving will he could not pass that point. Slowly, he dropped back from it.

Sixteen pounds was the highest he managed in the following days. Twenty-one pounds seemed to have been merely a fluke, a good first effort. He ate bitterness.

But he had not reached his present position of wealth and prominence by easy surrender. He persisted, recalling carefully just what Schneider had said to him, and trying to *feel* the touch of Schneider's hands. He told himself now that he really had been stronger under Schneider's touch, but that he had failed to realize it because of the Earth's heavy field. He continued to try.

In the back of his mind he knew that he must eventually seek out Gramps Schneider and ask his help, if he did not find the trick alone. But he was extremely reluctant to do so, not because of the terrible trip it entailed—though that would ordinarily have been more than enough reason—but because if he did so and Schneider was not able to help him, then there would be no hope, no hope at all.

It was better to live with disappointment and frustration than to live without hope. He continued to postpone it.

Waldo paid little attention to Earth time; he ate and slept when he pleased. He might catch a cat nap at any time; however, at fairly regular intervals he slept for longer periods. Not in a bed, of course. A man who floats in air has no need for a bed. But he did make it a habit to guy himself into place before undertaking eight hours of solid sleep, as it prevented him from casual drifting in random air currents which might carry him, unconscious, against controls or switches.

Since the obsession to become strong had possessed him he had frequently found it necessary to resort to soporifics to insure sleep.

Dr. Rambeau had returned and was looking for him. Rambeau—crazy and filled with hate. Rambeau, blaming his troubles on Waldo. He was not safe, even in Freehold, as the crazy physicist had found out how to pass from one space to another. There he was now! Just his head, poked through from the Other World. "I'm going to get you, Waldo!" He was gone—no, there he was behind him! Reaching, reaching out with hands that were writhing antennae. "You, Waldo!" But Waldo's own hands were the giant waldoes, he snatched at Rambeau.

The big waldoes went limp.

Rambeau was at him, was on him; he had him around the throat.

Gramps Schneider said in his ear, in a voice that was calm and strong, "Reach out for the power, my son. Feel it in your fingers." Waldo grabbed at the throttling fingers, strained, tried.

They were coming loose. He was winning. He would stuff Rambeau back into the Other World and keep him there. There! He had one hand free. Baldur was barking frantically; he tried to tell him to shut up, to bite Rambeau, to help——

The dog continued to bark.

He was in his own home, in his own great room. Baldur let out one more yipe. "Quiet!" He looked himself over.

When he had gone to sleep he had been held in place by four light guys, opposed like the axes of a tetrahedron. Two of them were still fastened to his belt; he swung loosely against the control ring. Of the other two, one had snapped off at his belt; its end floated a few feet away. The fourth had been broken in two places, near his belt and again several feet out; the severed piece was looped loosely around his neck.

He looked the situation over. Study as he might, he could conceive no way in which the guys could have been broken save by his own struggles in the nightmare. The dog could not have done it; he had no way to get a purchase. He had done it himself. The lines were light, being intended merely as stays. Still——

It took him a few minutes to rig a testing apparatus which would test pull instead of grip; the yoke had to be reversed. When it was done he cut in a medium waldo pair, fastened the severed piece of line to the tester, and, using the waldo, pulled.

The line parted at two hundred and twelve pounds.

Hastily, but losing time because of nervous clumsiness, he rerigged the tester for grip. He paused, whispered softly, "Now is the time, Gramps!" and bore down on the grip.

Twenty pounds—twenty-one. Twenty-five!

Up past thirty. He was not even sweating! Thirty-five—forty, -one, -two, -three. Forty-five! And -six! And a half. Forty-seven pounds!

With a great sigh he let his hand relax. He was strong. Strong.

When he had somewhat regained his composure, he considered what to do next. His first impulse was to call Grimes, but he suppressed it. Soon enough when he was sure of himself.

He went back to the tester and tried his left hand. Not as strong as his right, but almost—nearly forty-five pounds. Funny thing, he didn't feel any different. Just normal, healthy. No sensation.

He wanted to try all of his muscles. It would take too long to rig testers for kick, and shove, and back lift, and, oh, a dozen others. He needed a field, that was it, a one-g field. Well, there was the reception room; it could be centrifuged.

But its controls were in the ring and it was long corridors away. There was a nearer one, the centrifuge for the cuckoo clock. He had rigged the wheel with a speed control as an easy way to regulate the clock. He moved back to the control ring and stopped the turning of the big wheel; the clockwork was disturbed by the sudden change; the little red bird popped out, said, "*Th-wu th-woo*" once, hopefully, and subsided.

Carrying in his hand a small control panel radio hooked to the motor which impelled the centrifuge wheel, he propelled himself to the wheel and placed himself inside, planting his feet on the inner surface of the rim and grasping one of the spokes, so that he would be in a standing position with respect to the centrifugal force, once it was impressed. He started the wheel slowly.

Its first motion surprised him and he almost fell off. But he recovered himself and gave it a little more power. All right so far. He speeded it up gradually, triumph spreading through him as he felt the pull of the pseudo gravitational field, felt his legs grow heavy, *but still strong.*

He let it out, one full g. He could take it. He could, indeed! To be sure, the force did not affect the upper part of his body so strongly as the lower, as his head was only a foot or so from the point of rotation. He could fix that; he squatted down slowly, hanging on tight to the spoke. It was all right.

But the wheel swayed and the motor complained. His unbalanced weight, that far out from the center of rotation, was putting too much of a strain on a framework intended to support a cuckoo clock and its counterweight only. He straightened up with equal caution, feeling the fine *shove* of his thigh muscles and calves. He stopped the wheel.

Baldur had been much perturbed by the whole business. He had almost twisted his neck off trying to follow the motions of Waldo.

He still postponed calling Grimes. He wanted to arrange for some selective local controls on the centrifuging of the reception room, in order to have a proper place in which to practice standing up. Then he had to get the hang of this walking business; it looked easy, but he didn't know. Might be quite a trick to learn it.

Thereafter he planned to teach Baldur to walk. He tried to get Baldur into the cuckoo-clock wheel, but the dog objected. He wiggled free and retreated to the farthest part of the room. No matter—when he had the beast in the reception room he would damn well have to learn to walk. Should have seen to it long ago. A big brute like that, and couldn't walk!

He visualized a framework into which the dog could be placed which would force him to stand erect. It was roughly equivalent to a baby's toddler, but Waldo did not know that. He had never seen a baby's toddler.

"Uncle Gus——"

"Oh, hello, Waldo. How you been?"

"Fine. Look, Uncle Gus, could you come up to Freehold—right away?"

Grimes shook his head. "Sorry. My bus is in the shop."

"Your bus is too slow anyhow. Take a taxi, or get somebody to drive you."

"And have you insult 'em when we get there? Huh-uh."

"I'll be sweet as sugar."

"Well, Jimmie Stevens said something yesterday about wanting to see you."

Waldo grinned. "Get him. I'd like to see him."

"I'll try."

"Call me back. Make it soon."

Waldo met them in the reception room, which he had left uncentrifuged. As soon as they came in he started his act. "My, I'm glad you're here. Dr. Stevens—could you fly me down to Earth right away? Something's come up."

"Why—I suppose so."

"Let's go."

"Wait a minute, Waldo. Jimmie's not prepared to handle you the way you have to be handled."

"I'll have to chance it, Uncle Gus. This is urgent."

"But——"

"No 'buts.' Let's leave at once."

They hustled Baldur into the ship and tied him down. Grimes saw to it that Waldo's chair was tilted back in the best approximation of a deceleration rig. Waldo settled himself into it and closed his eyes to discourage questions. He sneaked a look and found Grimes grimly silent.

Stevens made very nearly a record trip, but set them down quite gently on the parking flat over Grimes's home. Grimes touched Waldo's arm. "How do you feel? I'll get someone and we'll get you inside. I want to get you to bed."

"Can't do that, Uncle Gus. Things to do. Give me your arm, will you?"

"Huh?" But Waldo reached for the support requested and drew himself up.

"I'll be all right now, I guess." He let go the physician's arm and started for the door. "Will you untie Baldur?"

"*Waldo!*"

He turned around, grinning happily. "Yes, Uncle Gus, it's true. I'm not weak any more. *I can walk.*"

Grimes took hold of the back of one of the seats and said shakily, "Waldo, I'm an old man. You ought not to do things like this to me." He wiped his eyes.

"Yes," agreed Stevens, "it's a damn dirty trick."

Waldo looked blankly from one face to the other. "I'm sorry," he said humbly. "I just wanted to surprise you."

"It's all right. Let's go downside and have a drink. You can tell us about it then."

"All right. Come on, Baldur." The dog got up and followed after his master. He had a very curious gait; Waldo's trainer gadget had taught him to pace instead of trot.

Waldo stayed with Grimes for days, gaining strength, gaining new reflex patterns, building up his flabby muscles. He had no setbacks; the *myasthenia* was gone. All he required was conditioning.

Grimes had forgiven him at once for his unnecessarily abrupt and spectacular revelation of his cure, but Grimes had insisted that he take it easy and become fully readjusted before he undertook to venture out unescorted. It was a wise precaution. Even simple things were hazards to him.

Stairs, for example. He could walk on the level, but going downstairs had to be learned. Going up was not so difficult.

Stevens showed up one day, let himself in, and found Waldo alone in the living room, listening to a stereo show. "Hello, Mr. Jones."

"Oh—hello, Dr. Stevens." Waldo reached down hastily, fumbled for his shoes, zipped them on. "Uncle Gus says I should wear them all the time," he explained. "Everybody does. But you caught me unawares."

"Oh, that's no matter. You don't have to wear them in the house. Where's Doc?"

"Gone for the day. Don't you, really? Seems to me my nurses always wore shoes."

"Oh yes, everybody does—but there's no law to make you."

"Then I'll wear them. But I can't say that I like them. They feel dead, like a pair of disconnected waldoes. But I want to learn how."

"How to wear shoes?"

"How to act like people act. It's really quite difficult," he said seriously.

Stevens felt a sudden insight, a welling of sympathy for this man with no background and no friends. It must be odd and strange to him. He felt an impulse to confess something which had been on his mind with respect to Waldo. "You really are strong now, aren't you?"

Waldo grinned happily. "Getting stronger every day. I gripped two hundred pounds this morning. And see how much fat I've worked off."

"You're looking fit, all right. Here's a funny thing. Ever since I first met you I've wished to high heaven that you were as strong as an ordinary man."

"You really did? Why?"

"Well . . . I think you will admit that you used some pretty poisonous language to me, one time and another. You had me riled up all the time. I wanted you to get strong so that I could just beat the hell out of you."

Waldo had been walking up and down, getting used to his shoes. He stopped and faced Stevens. He seemed considerably startled. "You mean you wanted to fist-fight me?"

"Exactly. You used language to me that a man ought not to use unless he is prepared to back it up with his fists. If you had not been an invalid I would have pasted you one, oh, any number of times."

Waldo seemed to be struggling with a new concept. "I think I see," he said slowly. "Well—all right." On the last word he delivered a roundhouse swipe with plenty of power behind it. Stevens was not in the least expecting it; it happened to catch him on the button. He went down, out cold.

When he came to he found himself in a chair. Waldo was shaking him. "Wasn't that right?" he said anxiously.

"What did you hit me with?"

"My hand. Wasn't that right? Wasn't that what you wanted?"

"Wasn't that what I——" He still had little bright lights floating in front of his eyes, but the situation began to tickle him. "Look here—is that your idea of the proper way to start a fight?"

"Isn't it?"

Stevens tried to explain to him the etiquette of fisticuffs, contemporary

American. Waldo seemed puzzled, but finally he nodded. "I get it. You have to give the other man warning. All right—get up, and we'll do it over."

"Easy, easy! Wait a minute. You never did give me a chance to finish what I was saying. I *was* sore at you, but I'm not any more. That is what I was trying to tell you. Oh, you were utterly poisonous; there is no doubt about that. But you couldn't help being."

"I don't mean to be poisonous," Waldo said seriously.

"I know you don't, and you're not. I rather like you now—now that you're strong."

"Do you really?"

"Yes, I do. But don't practice any more of those punches on me."

"I won't. But I didn't understand. But, do you know, Dr. Stevens, it's——"

"Call me Jim."

"Jim. It's a very hard thing to know just what people do expect. There is so little pattern to it. Take belching; I didn't know it was forbidden to burp when other people are around. It seems obviously necessary to me. But Uncle Gus says not."

Stevens tried to clear up the matter for him—not too well, as he found that Waldo was almost totally lacking in any notion, even theoretical, of social conduct. Not even from fiction had he derived a concept of the intricacies of *mores*, as he had read almost no fiction. He had ceased reading stories in his early boyhood, because he lacked the background of experience necessary to appreciate fiction.

He was rich, powerful, and a mechanical genius, but he still needed to go to kindergarten.

Waldo had a proposition to make. "Jim, you've been very helpful. You explain these things better than Uncle Gus does. I'll hire you to teach me."

Stevens suppressed a slight feeling of pique. "Sorry. I've got a job that keeps me busy."

"Oh, that's all right. I'll pay you better than they do. You can name your own salary. It's a deal."

Stevens took a deep breath and sighed. "You don't understand. I'm an engineer and I don't hire out for personal service. You can't hire me. Oh, I'll help you all I can, but I won't take money for it."

"What's wrong with taking money?"

The question, Stevens thought, was stated wrongly. As it stood it could not be answered. He launched into a long, involved discussion of professional and business conduct. He was really not fitted for it; Waldo soon bogged down. "I'm afraid I don't get it. But see here—could you teach me how to behave with girls? Uncle Gus says he doesn't dare take me out in company."

"Well, I'll try. I'll certainly try. But, Waldo, I came over to see you about some of the problems we're running into at the plant. About this theory of the two spaces that you were telling me about——"

"It's not theory; it's fact."

"All right. What I want to know is this: When do you expect to go back to Freehold and resume research? We need some help."

"Go back to Freehold? I haven't any idea. I don't intend to resume research."

"You don't? But, my heavens, you haven't finished half the investigations you outlined to me."

"You fellows can do 'em. I'll help out with suggestions, of course."

"Well—maybe we could interest Gramps Schneider," Stevens said doubtfully.

"I would not advise it," Waldo answered. "Let me show you a letter he sent me." He left and fetched it back. "Here."

Stevens glanced through it. "—your generous offer of your share in the new power project I appreciate, but, truthfully, I have no interest in such things and would find the responsibility a burden. As for the news of your new strength I am happy, but not surprised. The power of the Other World is his who would claim it—" There was more to it. It was written in a precise Spencerian hand, a trifle shaky; the rhetoric showed none of the colloquialisms with which Schneider spoke.

"Hm-m-m—I think I see what you mean."

"I believe," Waldo said seriously, "that he regards our manipulations with gadgets as rather childish."

"I suppose. Tell me, what do *you* intend to do with yourself?"

"Me? I don't know, exactly. But I can tell you this: I'm going to have fun. I'm going to have lots of fun. I'm just beginning to find out how much fun it is to be a man!"

His dresser tackled the other slipper. "To tell you just why I took up dancing would be a long story," he continued.

"I want details."

"Hospital calling," someone in the dressing room said.

"Tell 'em I'll be right there, fast. Suppose you come in tomorrow afternoon?" he added to the woman reporter. "Can you?"

"Right."

A man was shouldering his way through the little knot around him. Waldo caught his eye. "Hello, Stanley. Glad to see you."

"Hello, Waldo." Gleason pulled some papers out from under his cape and dropped them in the dancer's lap. "Brought these over myself as I wanted to see your act again."

"Like it?"

"Swell!"

Waldo grinned and picked up the papers. "Where is the dotted line?"

"Better read them first," Gleason cautioned him.

"Oh shucks, no. If it suits you, it suits me. Can I borrow your stylus?"

A worried little man worked his way up to them. "About that recording, Waldo——"

"We've discussed that," Waldo said flatly. "I only perform before audiences."

"We've combined it with the Warm Springs benefit."

"That's different. O.K."

"While you're about it, take a look at this layout." It was a reduction, for a twenty-four sheet:

THE GREAT WALDO
AND HIS TROUPE

with the opening date and theater left blank, but with a picture of Waldo, as Harlequin, poised high in the air.

"Fine, Sam, fine!" Waldo nodded happily.

"Hospital calling again!"

"I'm ready now," Waldo answered, and stood up. His dresser draped his street cape over his lean shoulders. Waldo whistled sharply. "Here, Baldur! Come along." At the door he stopped an instant, and waved. "Good night, fellows!"

"Good night, Waldo."

They were all such grand guys.

THE FATHER-THING
by Philip K. Dick

"Dinner's ready," commanded Mrs. Walton. "Go get your father and tell him to wash his hands. The same applies to you, young man." She carried a steaming casserole to the neatly set table. "You'll find him out in the garage."

Charles hesitated. He was only eight years old, and the problem bothering him would have confounded Hillel. "I—" he began uncertainly.

"What's wrong?" June Walton caught the uneasy tone in her son's voice and her matronly bosom fluttered with sudden alarm. "Isn't Ted out in the garage? For heaven's sake, he was sharpening the hedge shears a minute ago. He didn't go over to the Andersons', did he? I told him dinner was practically on the table."

"He's in the garage," Charles said. "But he's—talking to himself."

"Talking to himself!" Mrs. Walton removed her bright plastic apron and hung it over the doorknob. "Ted? Why, he never talks to himself. Go tell him to come in here." She poured boiling black coffee in the little blue-and-white china cups and began ladling out creamed corn. "What's wrong with you? Go tell him!"

"I don't know which of them to tell," Charles blurted out desperately. "They both look alike."

June Walton's fingers lost their hold on the aluminum pan; for a moment the creamed corn slushed dangerously. "Young man—" she began angrily, but at that moment Ted Walton came striding into the kitchen, inhaling and sniffing and rubbing his hands together.

"Ah," he cried happily. "Lamb stew."

"Beef stew," June murmured. "Ted, what were you doing out there?"

Ted threw himself down at his place and unfolded his napkin. "I got the shears sharpened like a razor. Oiled and sharpened. Better not touch them—they'll cut your hand off." He was a good-looking man in his early thirties; thick blond hair, strong arms, competent hands, square face and flashing brown eyes. "Man, this stew looks good. Hard day at the office—

Friday, you know. Stuff piles up and we have to get all the accounts out by five. Al McKinley claims the department could handle 20 per cent more stuff if we organized our lunch hours; staggered them so somebody was there all the time." He beckoned Charles over. "Sit down and let's go."

Mrs. Walton served the frozen peas. "Ted," she said, as she slowly took her seat, "is there anything on your mind?"

"On my mind?" He blinked. "No, nothing unusual. Just the regular stuff. Why?"

Uneasily, June Walton glanced over at her son. Charles was sitting bolt-upright at his place, face expressionless, white as chalk. He hadn't moved, hadn't unfolded his napkin or even touched his milk. A tension was in the air; she could feel it. Charles had pulled his chair away from his father's; he was huddled in a tense little bundle as far from his father as possible. His lips were moving, but she couldn't catch what he was saying.

"What is it?" she demanded, leaning toward him.

"*The other one,*" Charles was muttering under his breath. "The other one came in."

"What do you mean, dear?" June Walton asked out loud. "What other one?"

Ted jerked. A strange expression flitted across his face. It vanished at once; but in the brief instant Ted Walton's face lost all familiarity. Something alien and cold gleamed out, a twisting, wriggling mass. The eyes blurred and receded, as an archaic sheen filmed over them. The ordinary look of a tired, middle-aged husband was gone.

And then it was back—or nearly back. Ted grinned and began to wolf down his stew and frozen peas and creamed corn. He laughed, stirred his coffee, kidded and ate. But something terrible was wrong.

"The other one," Charles muttered, face white, hands beginning to tremble. Suddenly he leaped up and backed away from the table. "Get away!" he shouted. "Get out of here!"

"Hey," Ted rumbled ominously. "What's got into you?" He pointed sternly at the boy's chair. "You sit down there and eat your dinner, young man. Your mother didn't fix it for nothing."

Charles turned and ran out of the kitchen, upstairs to his room. June Walton gasped and fluttered in dismay. "What in the world—"

Ted went on eating. His face was grim; his eyes were hard and dark. "That kid," he grated, "is going to have to learn a few things. Maybe he and I need to have a little private conference together."

Charles crouched and listened.

The father-thing was coming up the stairs, nearer and nearer. "Charles!" it shouted angrily. "Are you up there?"

He didn't answer. Soundlessly, he moved back into his room and pulled the door shut. His heart was pounding heavily. The father-thing had reached the landing; in a moment it would come in his room.

He hurried to the window. He was terrified; it was already fumbling in the dark hall for the knob. He lifted the window and climbed out on the roof. With a grunt he dropped into the flower garden that ran by the front door, staggered and gasped, then leaped to his feet and ran from the light that streamed out the window, a patch of yellow in the evening darkness.

He found the garage; it loomed up ahead, a black square against the skyline. Breathing quickly, he fumbled in his pocket for his flashlight, then cautiously slid the door up and entered.

The garage was empty. The car was parked out front. To the left was his father's workbench. Hammers and saws on the wooden walls. In the back were the lawnmower, rake, shovel, hoe. A drum of kerosene. License plates nailed up everywhere. Floor was concrete and dirt; a great oil slick stained the center, tufts of weeds greasy and black in the flickering beam of the flashlight.

Just inside the door was a big trash barrel. On top of the barrel were stacks of soggy newspapers and magazines, moldy and damp. A thick stench of decay issued from them as Charles began to move them around. Spiders dropped to the cement and scampered off; he crushed them with his foot and went on looking.

The sight made him shriek. He dropped the flashlight and leaped wildly back. The garage was plunged into instant gloom. He forced himself to kneel down, and for an ageless moment, he groped in the darkness for the light, among the spiders and greasy weeds. Finally he had it again. He managed to turn the beam down into the barrel, down the well he had made by pushing back the piles of magazines.

The father-thing had stuffed it down in the very bottom of the barrel. Among the old leaves and torn-up cardboard, the rotting remains of magazines and curtains, rubbish from the attic his mother had lugged down here with the idea of burning someday. It still looked a little like his father enough for him to recognize. He had found it—and the sight made him sick at his stomach. He hung onto the barrel and shut his eyes until finally he was able to look again. In the barrel were the remains of his father, his real father. Bits the father-thing had no use for. Bits it had discarded.

He got the rake and pushed it down to stir the remains. They were dry. They cracked and broke at the touch of the rake. They were like a discarded snake skin, flaky and crumbling, rustling at the touch. *An empty skin.* The insides were gone. The important part. This was all that remained, just the brittle, cracking skin, wadded down at the bottom of the trash barrel in a little heap. This was all the father-thing had left; it had eaten the rest. Taken the insides—and his father's place.

A sound.

He dropped the rake and hurried to the door. The father-thing was coming down the path, toward the garage. Its shoes crushed the gravel; it felt its way along uncertainly. "Charles!" it called angrily. "Are you in there? Wait'll I get my hands on you, young man!"

His mother's ample, nervous shape was outlined in the bright doorway of the house. "Ted, please don't hurt him. He's all upset about something."

"I'm not going to hurt him," the father-thing rasped; it halted to strike a match. "I'm just going to have a little talk with him. He needs to learn better manners. Leaving the table like that and running out at night, climbing down the roof—"

Charles slipped from the garage; the glare of the match caught his moving shape, and with a bellow the father-thing lunged forward.

"*Come here!*"

Charles ran. He knew the ground better than the father-thing; it knew a lot, had taken a lot when it got his father's insides, but nobody knew the way like *he* did. He reached the fence, climbed it, leaped into the Andersons' yard, raced past their clothesline, down the path around the side of their house, and out on Maple Street.

He listened, crouched down and not breathing. The father-thing hadn't come after him. It had gone back. Or it was coming around the sidewalk.

He took a deep, shuddering breath. He had to keep moving. Sooner or later it would find him. He glanced right and left, made sure it wasn't watching, and then started off at a rapid dog-trot.

"What do you want?" Tony Peretti demanded belligerently. Tony was fourteen. He was sitting at the table in the oak-panelled Peretti dining room, books and pencils scattered around him, half a ham-and-peanut-butter sandwich and a coke beside him. "You're Walton, aren't you?"

Tony Peretti had a job uncrating stoves and refrigerators after school at Johnson's Appliance Shop, downtown. He was big and blunt-faced. Black hair, olive skin, white teeth. A couple of times he had beaten up Charles; he had beaten up every kid in the neighborhood.

Charles twisted. "Say, Peretti. Do me a favor?"

"What do you want?" Peretti was annoyed. "You looking for a bruise?"

Gazing unhappily down, his fists clenched, Charles explained what had happened in short, mumbled words.

When he had finished, Peretti let out a low whistle. "No kidding."

"It's true." He nodded quickly. "I'll show you. Come on and I'll show you."

Peretti got slowly to his feet. "Yeah, show me. I want to see."

He got his b.b. gun from his room, and the two of them walked silently up the dark street, toward Charles' house. Neither of them said much. Peretti was deep in thought, serious and solemn-faced. Charles was still dazed; his mind was completely blank.

They turned down the Anderson driveway, cut through the back yard, climbed the fence, and lowered themselves cautiously into Charles' back yard. There was no movement. The yard was silent. The front door of the house was closed.

They peered through the living room window. The shades were down, but a narrow crack of yellow streamed out. Sitting on the couch was Mrs. Walton, sewing a cotton T-shirt. There was a sad, troubled look on her large face. She worked listlessly, without interest. Opposite her was the father-thing. Leaning back in his father's easy chair, its shoes off, reading the evening newspaper. The TV was on, playing to itself in the corner. A can of beer rested on the arm of the easy chair. The father-thing sat exactly as his own father had sat; it had learned a lot.

"Looks just like him," Peretti whispered suspiciously. "You sure you're not bulling me?"

Charles led him to the garage and showed him the trash barrel. Peretti reached his long tanned arms down and carefully pulled up the dry, flaking remains. They spread out, unfolded, until the whole figure of his father was outlined. Peretti laid the remains on the floor and pieced broken parts back into place. The remains were colorless. Almost transparent. An amber yellow, thin as paper. Dry and utterly lifeless.

"That's all," Charles said. Tears welled up in his eyes. "That's all that's left of him. The thing has the insides."

Peretti had turned pale. Shakily, he crammed the remains back in the trash barrel. "This is really something," he muttered. "You say you saw the two of them together?"

"Talking. They looked exactly alike. I ran inside." Charles wiped the tears away and sniveled; he couldn't hold it back any longer. "It ate him while I was inside. Then it came in the house. It pretended it was him. But it isn't. It killed him and ate his insides."

For a moment Peretti was silent. "I'll tell you something," he said suddenly. "I've heard about this sort of thing. It's a bad business. You have to use your head and not get scared. You're not scared, are you?"

"No," Charles managed to mutter.

"The first thing we have to do is figure out how to kill it." He rattled his b.b. gun. "I don't know if this'll work. It must be plenty tough to get hold of your father. He was a big man." Peretti considered. "Let's get out of here. It might come back. They say that's what a murderer does."

They left the garage. Peretti crouched down and peeked through the window again. Mrs. Walton had got to her feet. She was talking anxiously. Vague sounds filtered out. The father-thing threw down its newspaper. They were arguing.

"For God's sake!" the father-thing shouted. "Don't do anything stupid like that."

"Something's wrong," Mrs. Walton moaned. "Something terrible. Just let me call the hospital and see."

"Don't call anybody. He's all right. Probably up the street playing."

"He's never out this late. He never disobeys. He was terribly upset—afraid of you! I don't blame him." Her voice broke with misery. "What's wrong with you? You're so strange." She moved out of the room, into the hall. "I'm going to call some of the neighbors."

The father-thing glared after her until she had disappeared. Then a terrifying thing happened. Charles gasped; even Peretti grunted under his breath.

"Look," Charles muttered. "What—"

"Golly," Peretti said, black eyes wide.

As soon as Mrs. Walton was gone from the room, the father-thing sagged in its chair. It became limp. Its mouth fell open. Its eyes peered vacantly. Its head fell forward, like a discarded rag doll.

Peretti moved away from the window. "That's it," he whispered. "That's the whole thing."

"What is it?" Charles demanded. He was shocked and bewildered. "It looked like somebody turned off its power."

"Exactly." Peretti nodded slowly, grim and shaken. "It's controlled from outside."

Horror settled over Charles. "You mean, something outside our world?"

Peretti shook his head with disgust. "Outside the house! In the yard. You know how to find?"

"Not very well." Charles pulled his mind together. "But I know somebody who's good at finding." He forced his mind to summon the name. "Bobby Daniels."

"That little colored kid? Is he good at finding?"

"The best."

"All right," Peretti said. "Let's go get him. We have to find the thing that's outside. That made *it* in there, and keeps it going. . . ."

"It's near the garage," Peretti said to the small, thin-faced Negro boy who crouched beside them in the darkness. "When it got him, he was in the garage. So look there."

"In the garage?" Daniels asked.

"*Around* the garage. Walton's already gone over the garage, inside. Look around outside. Nearby."

There was a small bed of flowers growing by the garage, and a great tangle of bamboo and discarded debris between the garage and the back of the house. The moon had come out; a cold, misty light filtered down over everything. "If we don't find it pretty soon," Daniels said, "I got to go back home. I can't stay up much later." He wasn't any older than Charles. Perhaps nine.

"All right," Peretti agreed. "Then get looking."

The three of them spread out and began to go over the ground with care. Daniels worked with incredible speed; his thin little body moved in a blur of motion as he crawled among the flowers, turned over rocks, peered under the house, separated stalks of plants, ran his expert hands over leaves and stems, in tangles of compost and weeds. No inch was missed.

Peretti halted after a short time. "I'll guard. It might be dangerous. The father-thing might come and try to stop us." He posted himself on the back step with his b.b. gun while Charles and Bobby Daniels searched. Charles worked slowly. He was tired, and his body was cold and numb. It seemed impossible, the father-thing and what had happened to his own father, his real father. But terror spurred him on; what if it happened to his mother, or to him? Or to everyone? Maybe the whole world.

"I found it!" Daniels called in a thin, high voice. "You all come around here quick!"

Peretti raised his gun and got up cautiously. Charles hurried over; he turned the flickering yellow beam of his flashlight where Daniels stood. The Negro boy had raised a concrete stone. In the moist, rotting soil the light gleamed on a metallic body. A thin, jointed thing with endless crooked legs was digging frantically. Plated, like an ant; a red-brown bug that rapidly disappeared before their eyes. Its rows of legs scabbled and clutched. The ground gave rapidly under it. Its wicked-looking tail twisted furiously as it struggled down the tunnel it had made.

Peretti ran into the garage and grabbed up the rake. He pinned down the tail of the bug with it. "Quick! Shoot it with the b.b. gun!"

Daniels snatched the gun and took aim. The first shot tore the tail of the bug loose. It writhed and twisted frantically; its tail dragged uselessly and some of its legs broke off. It was a foot long, like a great millipede. It struggled desperately to escape down its hole.

"Shoot again," Peretti ordered.

Daniels fumbled with the gun. The bug slithered and hissed. Its head jerked back and forth; it twisted and bit at the rake holding it down. Its wicked specks of eyes gleamed with hatred. For a moment it struck futilely at the rake; then abruptly, without warning, it thrashed in a frantic convulsion that made them all draw away in fear.

Something buzzed through Charles' brain. A loud humming, metallic and harsh, a billion metal wires dancing and vibrating at once. He was tossed about violently by the force; the banging crash of metal made him deaf and confused. He stumbled to his feet and backed off; the others were doing the same, white-faced and shaken.

"If we can't kill it with the gun," Peretti gasped, "we can drown it. Or burn it. Or stick a pin through its brain." He fought to hold onto the rake, to keep the bug pinned down.

"I have a jar of formaldehyde," Daniels muttered. His fingers fumbled nervously with the b.b. gun. "How do this thing work? I can't seem to—"

Charles grabbed the gun from him. "I'll kill it." He squatted down, one eye to the sight, and gripped the trigger. The bug lashed and struggled. Its force-field hammered in his ears, but he hung onto the gun. His finger tightened . . .

"All right, Charles," the father-thing said. Powerful fingers gripped him, a paralyzing pressure around his wrists. The gun fell to the ground as he struggled futilely. The father-thing shoved against Peretti. The boy leaped away and the bug, free of the rake, slithered triumphantly down its tunnel.

"You have a spanking coming, Charles," the father-thing droned on. "What got into you? Your poor mother's out of her mind with worry."

It had been there, hiding in the shadows. Crouched in the darkness watching them. Its calm, emotionless voice, a dreadful parody of his father's, rumbled close to his ear as it pulled him relentlessly toward the garage. Its cold breath blew in his face, an icy-sweet odor, like decaying soil. Its strength was immense; there was nothing he could do.

"Don't fight me," it said calmly. "Come along, into the garage. This is for your own good. I know best, Charles."

"Did you find him?" his mother called anxiously, opening the back door.

"Yes, I found him."

"What are you going to do?"

"A little spanking." The father-thing pushed up the garage door. "In the garage." In the half-light a faint smile, humorless and utterly without emotion, touched its lips. "You go back in the living room, June. I'll take care of this. It's more in my line. You never did like punishing him."

The back door reluctantly closed. As the light cut off, Peretti bent down and groped for the b.b. gun. The father-thing instantly froze.

"Go on home, boys," it rasped.

Peretti stood undecided, gripping the b.b. gun.

"Get going," the father-thing repeated. "Put down that toy and get out of here." It moved slowly toward Peretti, gripping Charles with one hand, reaching toward Peretti with the other. "No b.b. guns allowed in town, sonny. Your father know you have that? There's a city ordinance. I think you better give me that before—"

Peretti shot it in the eye.

The father-thing grunted and pawed at its ruined eye. Abruptly it slashed out at Peretti. Peretti moved down the driveway, trying to cock the gun. The father-thing lunged. Its powerful fingers snatched the gun from Peretti's hands. Silently, the father-thing mashed the gun against the wall of the house.

Charles broke away and ran numbly off. Where could he hide? It was between him and the house. Already, it was coming back toward him, a black shape creeping carefully, peering into the darkness, trying to make him out. Charles retreated. If there were only some place he could hide . . .

The bamboo.

He crept quickly into the bamboo. The stalks were huge and old. They closed after him with a faint rustle. The father-thing was fumbling in its pocket; it lit a match, then the whole pack flared up. "Charles," it said. "I know you're here, someplace. There's no use hiding. You're only making it more difficult."

His heart hammering, Charles crouched among the bamboo. Here, debris and filth rotted. Weeds, garbage, papers, boxes, old clothing, boards, tin cans, bottles. Spiders and salamanders squirmed around him. The bamboo swayed with the night wind. Insects and filth.

And something else.

A shape, a silent, unmoving shape that grew up from the mound of filth like some nocturnal mushroom. A white column, a pulpy mass that glistened moistly in the moonlight. Webs covered it, a moldy cocoon. It had vague arms and legs. An indistinct half-shaped head. As yet, the features hadn't formed. But he could tell what it was.

A mother-thing. Growing here in the filth and dampness, between the garage and the house. Behind the towering bamboo.

It was almost ready. Another few days and it would reach maturity. It was still a larva, white and soft and pulpy. But the sun would dry and warm it. Harden its shell. Turn it dark and strong. It would emerge from its cocoon, and one day when his mother came by the garage . . .

Behind the mother-thing were other pulpy white larvae, recently laid by the bug. Small. Just coming into existence. He could see where the father-thing had broken off; the place where it had grown. It had matured here. And in the garage, his father had met it.

Charles began to move numbly away, past the rotting boards, the filth and debris, the pulpy mushroom larvae. Weakly, he reached out to take hold of the fence—and scrambled back.

Another one. Another larva. He hadn't seen this one, at first. It wasn't white. It had already turned dark. The web, the pulpy softness, the moistness, were gone. It was ready. It stirred a little, moved its arm feebly.

The Charles-thing.

The bamboo separated, and the father-thing's hand clamped firmly around the boy's wrist. "You stay right here," it said. "This is exactly the place for you. Don't move." With its other hand it tore at the remains of the cocoon binding the Charles-thing. "I'll help it out—it's still a little weak."

The last shred of moist gray was stripped back, and the Charles-thing tottered out. It floundered uncertainly, as the father-thing cleared a path for it toward Charles.

"This way," the father-thing grunted. "I'll hold him for you. When you're fed you'll be stronger."

The Charles-thing's mouth opened and closed. It reached greedily toward Charles. The boy struggled wildly, but the father-thing's immense hand held him down.

"Stop that, young man," the father-thing commanded. "It'll be a lot easier for you if you—"

It screamed and convulsed. It let go of Charles and staggered back. Its body twitched violently. It crashed against the garage, limbs jerking. For a time it rolled and flopped in a dance of agony. It whimpered, moaned, tried to crawl away. Gradually it became quiet. The Charles-thing settled down in a silent heap. It lay stupidly among the bamboo and rotting debris, body slack, face empty and blank.

At last the father-thing ceased to stir. There was only the faint rustle of the bamboo in the night wind.

Charles got up awkwardly. He stepped down onto the cement driveway. Peretti and Daniels approached, wide-eyed and cautious. "Don't go near it," Daniels ordered sharply. "It ain't dead yet. Takes a little while."

"What did you do?" Charles muttered.

Daniels set down the drum of kerosene with a gasp of relief. "Found this in the garage. We Daniels always used kerosene on our mosquitoes, back in Virginia."

"Daniels poured kerosene down the bug's tunnel," Peretti explained, still awed. "It was his idea."

Daniels kicked cautiously at the contorted body of the father-thing. "It's dead, now. Died as soon as the bug died."

"I guess the others'll die, too," Peretti said. He pushed aside the bamboo to examine the larvae growing here and there among the debris. The Charles-thing didn't move at all, as Peretti jabbed the end of a stick into its chest. "This one's dead."

"We better make sure," Daniels said grimly. He picked up the heavy drum of kerosene and lugged it to the edge of the bamboo. "It dropped some matches in the driveway. You get them, Peretti."

They looked at each other.

"Sure," Peretti said softly.

"We better turn on the hose," Charles said. "To make sure it doesn't spread."

"Let's get going," Peretti said impatiently. He was already moving off. Charles quickly followed him and they began searching for the matches, in the moonlit darkness.

THE CHILDREN'S HOUR
by Henry Kuttner and C. L. Moore

HE SAT ON A BENCH in the little grove in front of Administration, watching the clock over the provost marshal's door jerk its long hand toward seven. Presently, when the hour struck, he would be going in that door, and up one flight of stairs, and down the corridor to the room where Lieutenant Dyke sat waiting, as he had waited so many evenings before.

Tonight might be the night that would end it. Lessing thought perhaps it would be. Something was stirring behind the intangible locks of his mind, and tonight that door might open which had resisted the skilled manipulations of hypnosis for so long. The door might swing wide tonight at last, and let the secret out which not even Lessing knew.

Lessing was a good hypnosis subject. Lieutenant Dyke had discovered that early in their class experiments in psychonamics—that astonishing means by which a soldier can learn to desensitize his own body and feel neither pain nor hunger, when pain or hunger would otherwise be intolerable. In the process of learning, dim and untrodden corridors of the mind are sometimes laid bare. But seldom in any mind was such a thing to be encountered as that block in Lessing's.

He responded well to all the usual tests. Immobility and desensitization, the trick of warping the balance center, the familiar routine of posthypnotic commands, all these succeeded without a hitch, as they had succeeded with so many others. But in Lessing's brain one barrier stood up immovable. Three months in his life were locked and sealed behind adamant walls— under hypnosis.

That was the strangest thing of all, for waking, he remembered those three months clearly. Under hypnosis—they did not exist. Under hypnosis he had no recollection that in June, July and August of two years ago he had been living a perfectly normal existence. He was in New York, a civilian then, working in an advertising office and living the patterned life that still existed for a time after December 7, 1941. Nothing had happened to make his hypnotized memory blank out with such stubborn vehemence when asked to remember.

And so began the long sessions of searching, probing, delicately manipulating Lessing's mind as a complicated machine is readjusted, or as muscles wasted and atrophied are gently massaged back to life.

Up to now, the dam had resisted. Tonight—

The first stroke of seven vibrated upon the evening air. Lessing got up slowly, conscious of an unaccustomed touch of panic in his mind. This was the night, he thought. There was a stirring deep down in the roots of his subconscious. He would know the truth tonight—he would look again upon the memory his mind had refused to retain—and he was illogically just a little afraid to face it. He had no idea why.

In the doorway he paused for a moment, looking back. Only the twilight was out there, gathering luminously over the camp, blurring the outlines of barracks, the bulk of the hospital distantly rising. Somewhere a train hooted toward New York an hour away. New York, that held mysteriously the memory his mind rejected.

"Good evening, sergeant," said Lieutenant Dyke, looking up from behind his desk.

Lessing looked at him a little uneasily. Dyke was a small, tight, blond man, sharp with nervous vigor, put together with taut wires. He had shown intense interest in the phenomenon of Lessing's memory, and Lessing had felt a bewildered sort of gratitude until this moment. Now he was not sure.

"Evening, sir," he said automatically.

"Sit down. Cigarette? Nervous, Lessing?"

"I don't know." He took the cigarette without knowing he had done it. This was the flood tide, he thought, and he had no mind for any other awareness than that. The dam was beginning to crumble, and behind it what flood waters, pent up in darkness, waited for release? There were almost inaudible little clicks in his mind as the bolts subconsciously, automatically clicked open. Conditioned reflex by now. His brain, responsive to Dyke's hypnotic probing, was preparing itself.

A bare light swung above Dyke's desk. His eyes turned to it, and everything else began to darken. This, too, was reflexive by now. Dyke, behind him, traced a finger back along his scalp. And Lessing went under very quickly. He heard Dyke's voice, and that changed from a sound to a strong, even suction pulling somewhere in darkness. An indefinable force that drew, and guided as it drew. The dam began to go almost at once. The gates of memory quivered, and Lessing was afraid.

"Go back. Go back. Back to the summer of '41. Summer. You are in New York. When I count ten you will remember. One. Two—" At ten Dyke's voice dropped.

Then again. And again. Until the long, difficult preparation for this moment proved itself, and James Lessing went back through time and . . .

And saw a face, white against the dark, blazing like a flame in the emptiness of the swift temporal current. Whose face? He did not know, but he knew there was a shadow behind it, darker than the blackness, shapeless and watchful.

The shadow grew, looming, leaning over him. A tinkling rhythm beat out. Words fitted themselves to it.

Between the dark and the daylight
When the night is beginning to lower
Comes a pause in the day's occupation
That is known as the children's hour—

It meant nothing. He groped through blindness, searching for reason. And then it began to come back to him, the thing he had forgotten. A minor thing, something hardly worth remembering, surely. Something . . . no, someone— And not quite so minor, after all. Someone rather important. Someone he had met casually in a place he could not quite remember—a bar, or in the park, or at a party somewhere—very casually. Someone—yes, it had been in the park—but who? He could remember now a flickering of green around them, leaves twinkling in sunshine and grass underfoot. A fountain where they had stopped to drink. He could remember the water, clear and colorless, trickling musically away, but he could not quite remember who had . . . who it was— Everything else was coming clear except the person. Forgetfulness clung stubbornly around that figure at his side. That slender figure, smaller than himself—dark? Fair? No, dark.

"Stabbed by a white wench's black eyes."

He caught his breath suddenly, in a violent physical wrench, as memory deluged back with appalling violence. Clarissa! How could he have forgotten? How *could* he? How could even amnesia have erased *her*? He sat stunned, the shining flood all but blinding him. And somewhere under that pouring brightness was grief—but he would not let that break the surface yet.

Clarissa. What words were there to get all that vivid color into speech? When the barrier went down, it collapsed with such a blast of sudden glory that . . . that—

They had walked in the park above the Hudson, blue water marbled with deeper blue and twinkling in the sun, sliding away below them. Clear water in the fountain, tinkling down over pebbles wet and brown in the dappled shadows beneath the trees. And everything as vivid as Creation's first morning, because of Clarissa walking beside him under the shining leaves. *Clarissa*—and he had forgotten.

It was like looking back into a world a little brighter than human. Everything shone, everything glistened, every sound was sweeter and clearer; there was a sort of glory over all he saw and felt and heard. Childhood had been like that, when the newness of the world invested every commonplace with particular glamour. Glamour—yes, that was the word for Clarissa.

Not sveltness and slickness, but *glamour*, the old word for enchantment. When he was with her it had been like stepping back into childhood and seeing everything with an almost intolerable fresh clarity.

But as for Clarissa herself—who had she been? What had she looked like? And above all, how *could* he have forgotten?

He groped backward into the shapeless fog of the past. What phrase was it that had suddenly ripped the curtain? Shock had all but erased it from his mind. It was like a lightning-flash forking through the darkness and vanishing again. Darkness—blackness—black eyes—yes, that was it. "Stabbed by a white wench's black eyes." A quotation, of course, but from what? More groping. Shakespeare? Yes, "Romeo and Juliet." Why, wasn't that what—Mercutio?—had said to Romeo about Romeo's first love? The girl he loved before he met Juliet. The girl he forgot so completely—

Forgot!

Lessing sat back in his chair, letting everything else slide away for a moment in sheer amazement at the complexity of the subconscious. Something had wiped out all recollection of Clarissa from level below level of his memory, but far down in the dark, memory had clung on, disguised, distorted, hiding behind analogy and allegory, behind a phrase written by a wandering playwright three hundred years before.

So it had been impossible, after all, to erase Clarissa entirely from his mind. She had struck so deep, she had glowed so vividly, that nothing at all could quite smudge her out. And yet only Lieutenant Dyke's skill and the chance unburial of a phrase had resurrected the memory. (For one appalling moment he wondered with a shaken mind what other memories lay hidden and shivering behind other allegorical words and phrases and innocent pictures, deep in the submarine gulfs.)

So he had defeated them after all—the bodiless, voiceless people who had stood between them. The jealous god—the shadowy guardians— For a moment the glare of showering gold flashed in his mind's eye blindingly. He was, in that one shutter-flash, aware of strangers in rich garments moving against confused and unfamiliar backgrounds. Then the door slammed in his face again and he sat there blinking.

Them? Defeated *them*? Who? He had no idea. Even in that one magical glimpse before memory blanked out again he thought he had not been sure who *they* were. That much, perhaps, had been a mystery never solved. But somewhere back in the darkness of his mind incredible things lay hidden. Gods and showering gold, and people in bright clothing that blew upon a wind not—surely not—of this earth—

Bright, bright—brighter than normal eyes ever perceive the world. That was Clarissa and all that surrounded her. It had been a stronger glamour than the sheer enchantment of first love. He felt sure about that now. He who walked with Clarissa shared actual magic that shed a luster on all they passed. Lovely Clarissa, glorious world as clear—as *clarissima* indeed—as a child's new, shining world. But between himself and her, the shadowy people—

Wait. Clarissa's—aunt? Had there been an . . . an aunt? A tall, dark, silent woman who damped the glory whenever she was near? He could not remember her face; she was no more than a shadow behind Clarissa's shining presence, a faceless, voiceless nonentity glowering in the background.

His memory faltered, and into the gap flowed the despair which he had been fighting subconsciously since the lustrous flood first broke upon him. *Clarissa, Clarissa*—where was she now with the glory around her?

"Tell me," said Lieutenant Dyke.

"There was a girl," Lessing began futilely. "I met her in a park—"

Clarissa on a glittering June morning, tall and dark and slim, with the waters of the Hudson pouring past beyond her in a smooth, blue, glassy current. *Stabbed by a white wench's black eyes.* Yes, very black eyes, bright and starry with blackness, and set wide apart in a grave face that had the remoteness and thoughtfulness of a child's. And from the moment he met that grave, bright glance they knew one another. He had been stabbed indeed—stabbed awake after a lifetime of drowsiness. (Stabbed—like Romeo, who lost both his loves. . . .)

"Hello," said Clarissa.

"It didn't last very long . . . I think," he told Dyke, speaking distractedly. "Long enough to find out there was something very strange about Clarissa . . . very wonderful . . . but not long enough to find out what it was . . . I *think.*"

(And yet they had been days of glory, even after the shadows began to fall about them. For there were always shadows, just at her elbow. And he thought they had centered about the aunt who lived with her, that grim nonentity whose face he could not remember.)

"She didn't like me," he explained, frowning with the effort of remembering. "Well, no, not quite that. But there was something in the . . . in the air when she was with us. In a minute I may remember— I wish I could think what she looked like."

It probably didn't matter. They had not seen her often. They had met, Clarissa and he, in so many places in New York, and each place acquired a brilliance of its own once her presence made it *clarissima* for him. There was no sensible explanation for that glory about her, so that street noises clarified to music and dust turned golden while they were together. It was as if he saw the world through her eyes when they were together, and as if she saw it with vision clearer—or perhaps less clear—than human.

"I knew so little about her," he said. (She might almost have sprung into existence in that first moment by the river. And so far as he would ever know, now, she had vanished back into oblivion in that other moment in the dim apartment, when the aunt said—now what was it the aunt had said?)

This was the moment he had been avoiding ever since memory began to come back. But he must think of it now. Perhaps it was the most important moment in the whole strange sequence, the moment that had shut him off so sharply from Clarissa and her shining, unreal, better than normal world. . . .

What had the woman said to him?

He sat very still, thinking. He shut his eyes and turned his mind inward and backward to that strangely clouded hour, groping among shadows that slid smoothly away at his touch.

"I can't—" he said, scowling, his eyes still closed. "I can't. They were . . . negative . . . words, I think, but— No, it's no use."

"Try the aunt again," suggested Dyke. "What did she look like?"

Lessing put his hands over his eyes and thought hard. Tall? Dark, like Clarissa? Grim, certainly—or had that only been the connotation of her words? He could not remember. He slumped down in his chair, grimacing with the effort. She had stood before the mirrors, hadn't she, looking down? Had she? What were her outlines against the light? She had no outlines. She had never existed. Her image seemed to slide behind furniture or slip deftly around corners whenever his persistent memory followed it through the apartment. Here, quite clearly, the memory block was complete.

"I don't think I ever can have seen her," he said, looking up at Dyke with strained, incredulous eyes. "She just isn't there."

Yet it was her shadow between him and Clarissa in the last moment before . . . before . . . what was it that cut off all memory between that hour and this? What happened? Well, say before forgetfulness began, then. Before—Lethe.

This much he remembered—Clarissa's face in the shadowed room, grief and despair upon it, her eyes almost unbearably bright with tears, her arms still extended, the fingers curved as they had slipped from his. He could remember the warmth and softness of them in that last handclasp. And then Lethe had poured between them.

"That was it," said Lessing in a bewildered voice. He looked up. "Those were the highlights. None of them mean anything."

Dyke drew on his cigarette, his eyes narrow above its glow. "Somewhere we've missed the point," he said. "The real truth's still hidden, even deeper than all this was. Hard to know yet just where to begin probing. Clarissa, do you think?"

Lessing shook his head. "I don't think she knew." (She had walked through all those enchanted days, gravely and aloofly, a perfectly normal girl except for— What had happened? He could not quite remember yet, but that which did happen had *not* been normal. Something shocking, something terrible, buried deep down under the commonplaces. Something glorious, glimmering far beneath the surface.)

"Try the aunt again," said Dyke.

Lessing shut his eyes. That faceless, bodiless, voiceless woman who maneuvered through his memories so deftly that he began to despair of ever catching her full-face. . . .

"Go back, then," Dyke told him. "Back to the very beginning. When did you first realize that something out of the ordinary was happening?"

Lessing's mind fumbled backward through those unnaturally empty spaces of the past.

He had not even been aware, at the outset, of the one strangeness he could remember now—that wonderful clarifying of the world in Clarissa's presence. It had to come slowly, through many meetings, as if by a sort of induced magnetism he became sensitized to her and aware as she was aware. He had known only that it was delightful simply to breathe the same air as she, and walk the same streets.

The same streets? Yes, something curious had happened on a street somewhere. Street noises, loud voices shouting— An accident. The collision just outside the Central Park entrance at Seventy-second Street. It was coming back clearly now, and with a swelling awareness of terror. They had been strolling up by the winding walk under the trellises toward the street. And as they neared it, the scream of brakes and the hollow, reverberant crash of metal against metal, and then voices rising.

Lessing had been holding Clarissa's hand. At the sudden noise he felt a tremor quiver along her arm, and then very softly, and with a curiously shocking deftness, her hand slipped out of his. Their fingers had been interlocked, and his did not relax, but somehow her hand was smoothly withdrawn. He turned to look.

His mind shrank from the memory. But he knew it had happened. He knew he had seen the circle of shaken air ring her luminously about, like a circle in water from a dropped stone. It was very like the spreading rings in water, except that these rings did not expand, but contracted. And as they contracted, Clarissa moved farther away. She was drawn down a rapidly diminishing tunnel of shining circles, with the park distorted in focus beyond them. And she was not looking at Lessing or at anything around him. Her eyes were downcast and that look of thoughtful quiet on her face shut out the world.

He stood perfectly still, too stunned even for surprise.

The luminous, concentric rings drew together in a dazzle, and when he looked again she was not there. People were running up the slope toward the street now, and the voices beyond the wall had risen to a babble. No one had been near enough to see—or perhaps only Lessing himself could have seen an aberration of his own mind. Perhaps he was suddenly mad. Panic was rising wildly in him, but it had not broken the surface yet. There hadn't been time.

And before the full, stunning realization could burst over him, he saw Clarissa again. She was coming leisurely up the hill around a clump of bushes. She was not looking at him. He stood quite still in the middle of the path, his heart thudding so hard that the whole park shook around him. Not until she reached his side did she look up, smiling, and take his hand again.

And that was the first thing that happened.

"I couldn't talk to her about it," Lessing told Dyke miserably. "I knew I couldn't from the first look at her face I got. Because *she didn't know*. To her it hadn't happened. And then I thought I'd imagined it, of course— but I knew I couldn't have imagined such a thing unless there was something too wrong with me to talk about. Later, I began to figure out a theory." He laughed nervously. "Anything, you know, to keep from admitting that I might have . . . well, had hallucinations."

"Go on," Dyke said again. He was leaning forward across the desk, his eyes piercing upon Lessing's. "Then what? It happened again?"

"Not that, no."

Not that? How did he know? He could not quite remember yet. The memories came in flashes, each complete even to its interlocking foreshadow of events to come, but the events themselves still lay hidden.

Had those shining rings been sheer hallucination? He would have believed so, he was sure, if nothing further had happened. As the impossible recedes into distance we convince ourselves, because we must, that it never really could have been. But Lessing was not allowed to forget. . . .

The memories were unraveling now, tumbling one after another through his mind. He had caught the thread. He relaxed in his chair, his face smoothing out from its scowl of deep concentration. Deep beneath the surface that discovery lay whose astonishing gleam shone up through the murk of forgetfulness, tantalizing, still eluding him, but there to be grasped when he reached it. If he wanted to grasp it. If he dared. He hurried on, not ready yet to think of that.

What had the next thing been?

The park again. Curious how memory-haunted the parks of New York were for him now. This time there had been rain, and something—alarming—had happened. What was it? He did not know. He had to grope back step by step toward a climax of impossibility that his mind shied away from touching.

Rain. A sudden thunderstorm that caught them at the edge of the lake. Cold wind ruffling the water, raindrops spattering down big and noisy around them. And himself saying, "Hurry, we can make it back to the summerhouse."

They ran hand in hand along the shore, laughing, Clarissa clutching her big hat and matching her steps to his, long, easy, running strides so that they moved as smoothly as dancers over the grass.

The summerhouse was dingy from many winters upon the rocks. It stood in a little niche in the black stone of the hillside overlooking the lake, a dusty gray refuge from the spattering drops as they ran laughing up the slope of the rock.

But it never sheltered them. The summerhouse did not wait.

Looking incredulously up the black hills, Lessing saw it glimmer and go in a luminous blurring-out, like a picture on a trick film that faded as he watched.

"Not the way Clarissa disappeared," he told Dyke carefully. "That happened quite clearly, in concentric diminishing rings. This time the thing just blurred and melted. One minute it was there, the next—" He made an expunging gesture in the air.

Dyke had not moved. His clear, piercing gaze dwelt unwavering upon Lessing.

"What did Clarissa say this time?"

Lessing rubbed his chin, frowning. "She saw it happen. I . . . I think she just said something like, 'Well, we're in for it now. Never mind, I like walking in the rain, don't you?' As if she were used to things like that. Of course, maybe she was— It didn't surprise her."

"And you didn't comment this time either?"

"I couldn't. Not when she took it so calmly. It was a relief to know that she'd seen it too. That meant I hadn't just imagined the thing. Not this time, anyhow. But by now—"

Suddenly Lessing paused. Up to this moment he had been too absorbed in the recapture of elusive memory to look objectively at what he was remembering. Now the incredible reality of what he had just been saying struck him without warning and he stared at Dyke with real terror in his eyes. How could there be any explanation for these imaginings, except actual madness? All this could not possibly have happened in the lost months which his conscious mind had remembered so clearly. It was incredible enough that he could have forgotten, but as for *what* he had forgotten, as for the unbelievable theory he had been about to explain to Dyke, and quite matter-of-factly, drawn from hypotheses of sheer miracle—

"Go on," Dyke said quietly. "By now—what?"

Lessing took a long, unsteady breath.

"By now . . . I think . . . I began to discard the idea I was having hallucinations." He paused again, unable to continue with such obvious impossibilities.

Dyke urged him gently. "Go on, Lessing. You've got to go on until we can get hold of something to work from. There must be an explanation somewhere. Keep digging. Why did you decide you weren't subject to hallucinations?"

"Because . . . well, I suppose it seemed too easy an explanation," Lessing said doggedly. It was ridiculous to argue so solidly from a basis of insanity, but he searched through his mind again and came out with an answer of very tenuous logic. "Somehow madness seemed the wrong answer," he said. "As I remember now, I think I felt there was a reason behind what had happened. Clarissa didn't know, but I'd begun to see."

"A reason? What?"

He frowned with concentration. In spite of himself the fascination of the still unknown was renewing its spell and he groped through the murk of amnesia for the answer he had grasped once, years ago, and let slip again.

"It was so natural to her that she didn't even notice. A nuisance, but something to accept with philosophy. You were meant to get wet if you got caught in the rain away from shelter, and if the shelter were miraculously removed—well, that only emphasized the fact that you were meant to get a soaking. *Meant* to, you see." He paused, not at all sure just where this thread was leading, but his memory, dredging among the flotsam, had come up with that one phrase that all but dripped with significance when he saw it in full light. Revelations hovered just beyond the next thought.

"She did get wet," he went on slowly. "I remember now. She went home dripping, and caught cold, and had a high fever for several days—"

His mind moved swiftly along the chain of thoughts, drawing incredible conclusions. Was something, somehow, ruling Clarissa's life with a hand so powerful it could violate every law of nature to keep her in the path its whim selected? Had something snatched her away through a tiny section of time and space to keep the street accident from her? But she had been meant to have that drenching and that fever, so—let the summerhouse be erased. Let it never have been. Let it vanish as naturally as the rain came down, so that Clarissa might have her fever. . . .

Lessing shut his eyes again and ground his palms hard over them. Did he want to remember much farther? What morasses of implausibility was his memory leading him into? Vanishing summerhouses and vanishing girls and . . . and . . . intervention from—outside? He took one horrified mental glance at that thought and then covered it up quickly and went on. Deep down in the murk the gleam of that amazing discovery still drew him on, but he went more slowly now, not at all certain that he wanted to plumb the depths and see it clearly.

Dyke's voice broke in as his mind began to let go and fall slack.

"She had a fever? Go on, what came next?"

"I didn't see her for a couple of weeks. And the . . . the colors began to go out of everything—"

It had to be renewed, then, by her presence, that strange *glamour* that heightened every color, sharpened every outline, made every sound musical when they were together. He began to crave the stimulus as he felt it fade. Looking back now, he remembered the intolerable dullness of that period. It was then, probably, that he first began to realize he had fallen in love.

And Clarissa, in the interval, had discovered it too. Yes, he was remembering. He had seen it shining in her enormous black eyes on the first day he visited her again. A brilliance almost too strong to look upon, as if bright stars were interlacing their rays there until her eyes were a blaze of blackness more dazzling than any light.

He had seen her, alone, in that first meeting after her illness. Where had the aunt been? Not there, at any rate. The strange, windowless apartment was empty except for themselves. Windowless? He looked back curiously. It was true—there had been no windows. But there were many mirrors. And the carpets were very deep and dark. That was his dominant impression of the place, walking upon softness and silence, with the glimmer of reflecting distances all around.

He had sat beside Clarissa, holding her hand, talking in a low voice. Her smile had been tremulous, and her eyes so bright they were almost frightening. They were very happy that afternoon. He glowed a little, even now, remembering how happy they had been. He would not remember, just yet, that nothing was to come of it but grief.

The wonderful clarity of perception came back around him by degrees as they sat there talking, so that everything in the world had seemed gloriously right. The room was the center of a perfect universe, beautiful and ordered, and the spheres sang together as they turned around it.

"I was closer to Clarissa then," he thought to himself, "than I ever came again. That was Clarissa's world, beautiful and peaceful, and very bright. You could almost hear the music of the machinery, singing in its perfection as it worked. Life was always like that to her. No, I never came so close again."

Machinery— Why did that image occur to him?

There was only one thing wrong with the apartment. He kept thinking that eyes were upon him, watching all he thought and did. It was probably only the mirrors, but it made him uncomfortable. He asked Clarissa why there were so many. She laughed.

"All the better to see you in, my darling." But then she paused as if some thought had come to her unexpectedly, and glanced around the reflecting walls at her own face seen from so many angles, looking puzzled. Lessing was used by then to seeing reactions upon her face that had no real origin in the normal cause-and-effect sequence of familiar life, and he did not pursue the matter. She was a strange creature, Clarissa, in so many, many ways. Two and two, he thought with sudden affectionate amusement, seldom made less than six to her, and she fell so often into such disproportionately deep and thoughtful silences over the most trivial things. He had learned early in their acquaintance how futile it was to question her about them.

"By now," he said, almost to himself, "I wasn't questioning anything. I didn't dare. I lived on the fringes of a world that wasn't quite normal, but it was Clarissa's world and I didn't ask questions."

Clarissa's serene, bright, immeasurably orderly little universe. So orderly that the stars in their courses might be forced out of pattern, if need be, to maintain her in her serenity. The smooth machinery singing in its motion as it violated possibility to spare her a street accident, or annihilating matter that she might have her drenching and her fever. . . .

The fever served a purpose. Nothing happened to Clarissa, he was fairly sure now, except things with a purpose. Chance had no place in that little world that circled her in. The fever brought delirium, and in the delirium with its strange, abnormal clarity of vision—suppose she had glimpsed the truth? Or was there a truth? He could not guess. But her eyes were unnaturally bright now, as if the brilliance of fever had lingered or as if . . . as if she were looking ahead into a future so incredibly shining that its reflections glittered constantly in her eyes, with a blackness brighter than light.

He was sure by now that she did not suspect life was at all different for her, that everyone did not watch miracles happen or walk in the same glory *clarissima*. (And once or twice the world reversed itself and he wondered wildly if she could be right and he wrong, if everyone did but himself.)

They moved in a particular little glory of their own during those days. She did love him; he had no doubt of it. But her subtle exaltation went beyond that. Something wonderful was to come, her manner constantly implied, but the most curious thing was that he thought she herself did not know what. He was reminded of a child wakening on Christmas morning and lying there in a delicious state of drowsiness, remembering only that something wonderful waits him when he comes fully awake.

"She never spoke of it?" Dyke asked.

Lessing shook his head. "It was all just beneath the surface. And if I tried to ask questions they . . . they seemed to slide right off. She wasn't consciously evading me. It was more as if she hadn't quite understood—" He paused. "And then things went wrong," he said slowly. "Something—"

It was hard to recapture this part. The bad memories were submerged perhaps a little deeper than the good ones, shut off behind additional layers of mental scar tissue. What had happened? He knew Clarissa loved him; they talked of marriage plans. The pattern of happiness had surely been set out clearly for them to follow.

"The aunt," he said doubtfully. "I think she must have interfered. I think . . . Clarissa seemed to slip out of my hands. She'd be busy when I phoned, or the aunt would say she was out. I was fairly sure she was lying, but what could I do?"

When she did see him, Clarissa had denied her neglect, reassuring him with shining glances and delicate, grave caresses. But she was so preoccupied. She did so little, really, and yet she seemed always absorbingly busy.

"If she was only watching a sparrow pick up crumbs," he told Dyke, "or two men arguing on the street, she gave all her attention to them and had none left over for me. So after awhile—I think about a week had gone by without my even seeing her—I decided to have it out with the aunt."

There were gaps— He remembered clearly only standing in the white hallway outside the apartment door and knocking. He remembered the door creaking softly open a little way. Only a little way. The chain had been on it, and it hung open only that narrow width, the chain glinting slightly from light within. It had been dim inside, light reflecting from wall to wall in the many mirrors, but from no source he could see. He could see, though, that someone was moving about inside, a figure distorted by the mirrors, multiplied by them, flickering quietly as it went about its own enigmatic business within, paying no attention to his ring at the door.

"Hello," he called. "Is that you, Clarissa?"

No answer. Nothing but the silent motion inside, visible now and then in the reflecting walls. He had called the aunt by name, then.

"Is it you, Mrs.—" *What* name? He had no idea, now. But he had called her again and again, getting angrier as the motion flickered on heedlessly. "I can see you," he remembered saying, his face against the jamb. "I know you can hear me. Why don't you answer?"

Still nothing. The motion vanished inside for a moment or two, then wavered twice and was still again. He could not see what figure cast the reflection. Someone dark, moving silently over the thick dark carpets, paying no attention to the voice at the door. What a very odd sort of person the aunt must be. . . .

Abruptly he was struck with the unreality of the situation; that dim, flitting shape in the next room, and the unsatisfactory figure he cut, hesitating there on the threshold calling through the door. Why the devil did the woman insist on this mystery? She was too dominant. Sudden, unexpected reaction. Clarissa's life to please herself—

Hot anger rose in him, a violent, sudden, unexpected reaction. "Clarissa!" he called. Then, as dim motion flickered in the mirrors again, he put his shoulder to the yielding panel, pushing hard.

The safety latch much have been flimsy. It gave with a crackling snap, and Lessing, off balance, staggered forward. The room with its many dark mirrors whirled vertiginously. He did not see Clarissa's aunt except as a swift, enigmatic movement in the glass, but quite suddenly he faced the inexplicable.

Gravity had shifted, both in direction and in force. His motion continued and he fell with nightmare slowness—Alice down the Rabbit Hole—in a spiraling, expanding orbit; it was like anaesthesia in its unlikeliness and the fact that it did not surprise him. The curious *quality* of the motion pushed everything else out of his mind for the moment. There was no one in the room with him; there were no mirrors; there was no room. Bodiless, an equation, a simplified ego, he fell toward—

There was Clarissa. Then he saw a burst of golden light flaming and falling against the white dark. A golden shower that enveloped Clarissa and carried her away.

Distantly, with the underbeat of his mind, he knew he should be surprised. But it was like half-sleep. It was too easy to accept things as they came, and he was too lazy to make the effort of awakening. He saw Clarissa again, moving against backgrounds sometimes only a little unfamiliar, at other times—he thought—wildly impossible—

Then an armored man was dropping down through warm sunlit air to the terrace, and the background was a park, with mountains rising far away. A woman was shrinking from him, two men had moved in front of her. Clarissa was there too. He could understand the language, though he did not know how he understood it. The armored man had a weapon of some sort lifted, and was crying, "Get back, Highness! I can't fire—too close—"

A young man in a long, belted robe of barbaric colors skipped backward, tugging at the coiled scarlet whip which was his belt. But neither of them seemed quite ready to make any aggressive moves, astonishment blanking their faces and staring eyes as they gaped at Lessing. Behind them the tall woman with the commanding, discontented face stood frozen by the same surprise. Lessing glanced around in bewilderment, meeting the incredulous stares of the girls flocking behind her. Clarissa was among them, and beyond her—beyond her—someone he could not quite remember. A dark figure, enigmatic, a little stooped. . . .

All of them stood transfixed. (All but Clarissa, perhaps, and perhaps the figure at her elbow—) The armored man's weapon was poised half lifted, the young robed man's whip unslung but trailing. They wore fantastic garments of a style and period Lessing had never heard of, and all their faces were strained and unhappy beneath the blankness of surprise, as if they had been living under some long-standing pressure of anxiety. He never knew what it was.

Only Clarissa looked as serene as always. And only she showed no surprise. Her black eyes under a strange, elaborate coiffure met his with the familiar twinkling of many lights, and she smiled without saying anything.

A buzzing of excitement rose among the girls. The armored man said uncertainly,

"Who are you? Where did you come from? Stand back or I'll—"

"—Out of thin air!" the robed young man gasped, and gave the crimson whip a flick that made it writhe along the grass.

Lessing opened his mouth to say—well, something. The whip looked dangerous. But Clarissa shook her head, still smiling.

"Never mind," she said. "Don't bother explaining. They'll forget, you know."

If he had meant to say anything, that robbed him of all coherent thought again. It was too fantastically like . . . like . . . something familiar. Alice, that was it. Alice again, in Looking Glass Land, at the Duchess' garden party. The bright, strange costumes, the bright green grass, the same air of latent menace. In a moment someone would scream, "Off with his head!"

The robed man stepped back and braced his feet against the weight of the whip as he swung its long coil up. Lessing watched the scarlet tongue arch against the sky. ("Serpents! Serpents! There's no pleasing them!" he thought wildly.) And then the whole world was spinning with the spin of the whip. The garden was a top, whirling faster and faster under that crimson lash. He lost his footing on the moving grass and centrifugal force flung him off into unconsciousness.

His head ached.

He got up off the hall floor slowly, pushing against the wall to steady himself. The walls were still spinning, but they slowed to a stop as he stood there swaying and feeling the bump on his forehead. His mind took a little longer to stop spinning, but once it came under control again he could see quite clearly what had happened. That chain had never broken at all. He had not fallen into the dark, mirrored room within, where the shadow of the aunt flitted quietly to and fro. The door, actually, had never been opened at all. At least, it was not open now. And the position of the doormat and the long, dark scrape on the floor made it obvious that he had tried to force the door and had slipped. His head must have cracked hard against the knob.

He wondered if such a blow could send hallucinations forward as well as backward through time from the moment of collision. Because he knew he had dreamed—he must have dreamed—that the door was open and the silent shadow moving inside.

When he called Clarissa that night he was fully determined to talk to her this time if he had to threaten the guardian aunt with violence or arrest or whatever seemed, on the spur of the moment, most effective. He knew how humiliatingly futile such threats would sound, but he could think of no other alternative. And the need to see Clarissa was desperate now, after that curious Wonderland dream. He meant to tell her about it, and he thought the story would have some effect. Almost, in his bewilderment, he expected her to remember the part she herself had played, though he knew how idiotic the expectation was.

It was a little disconcerting, after his fiery resolution, to hear not the aunt's voice but Clarissa's on the telephone.

"I'm coming over," he said flatly, frustrated defiance making the statement a challenge.

"Why, of course," Clarissa sounded as if they had parted only a few hours ago.

His eagerness made the trip across town seem very long. He was rehearsing the story he would tell her as soon as they were alone. The dream had been so real and vivid, though it must have passed in the flash of a second between the time his head struck the doorknob and the time his knees struck the floor. What would she say about it? He did not know why at all, but he thought she could give him an answer to his questions, if he told her.

He rang the doorbell impatiently. As before, there was no sound from within. He rang again. No answer. Feeling eerily as if he had stepped back in time, to relive that curious dream all over again, he tried the knob, and was surprised to find the door opening to his push. No chain fastened it this time. He was looking into familiar, many-mirrored dimness as the door swung wide. While he hesitated on the threshold, not sure whether to call out or try the bell again, he saw something moving far back in the apartment, visible only in the mirrors.

For a moment the conviction that he was reliving the past made his head swim. Then he saw that it was Clarissa this time. Clarissa standing quite still and looking up with a glow of shining anticipation upon her face. It was that Christmas morning look he had caught glimpses of before, but never so clearly as now. What she looked at he could not see, but the expression was unmistakable. Something glorious was about to happen, the lovely look implied. Something very glorious, very near, very soon—

About her the air shimmered. Lessing blinked. The air turned golden and began to shower down around her in sparkling rain. This *was* the dream, then, he thought wildly. He had seen it all before. Clarissa standing quietly beneath the golden shower, her face lifted, letting that shining waterfall pour over her slowly. But if it were the dream again, nothing further was to happen. He waited for the floor to spin underfoot—

No, it was real. He was watching another miracle take place, silently and gloriously, in the quiet apartment.

He had seen it in a dream; now it happened before his eyes. Clarissa in a shower of . . . of stars? Standing like Danae in a shower of gold—

Like Danae in her brazen tower, shut away from the world. Her likeness to Danae struck him with sudden violence. And that impossible rain of gold, and her look of rapt delight. What was it that poured down the shining torrent upon her? What was responsible for setting Clarissa so definitely apart from the rest of humanity, sheltering her at the cost of outraging natural laws, keeping the smooth machinery that protected her humming along its inaudible, omnipotent course? Omnipotent—yes, omnipotent as Zeus once was, who descended upon his chosen in that fabulous rain of gold.

Standing perfectly still and staring at the distant reflection in the glass, Lessing let his mind flash swifter and swifter along a chain of reasoning that left him at once gasping with incredulity and stunned with impossible conviction. For he thought at last he had the answer. The wildly improbable answer.

He could no longer doubt that somehow, somewhere, Clarissa's life impinged upon some other world than his. And wherever the two clashed, that other world took effortless precedence. It was difficult to believe that some dispassionate force had focused so solicitously upon her. He thought the few glimpses he had been allowed to catch spoke more of some individual intelligence watching everything she did. Some one being who understood humanity as perfectly as if it were itself very nearly human. Someone in the role of literal guardian angel, shepherding Clarissa along a path toward—what?

Certainly *Someone* had not wanted Clarissa to see the street accident, and had snatched her back through space and time to a safe distance, keeping the veil about her so that she did not even guess it had happened. *Someone* had meant her to experience the delirium of fever, and had erased the summerhouse. *Someone*, he began to realize, was leading her almost literally by the hand through her quiet, thoughtful, shining days and nights, casting *glamour* about her so heavily that it enveloped anyone who came intimately into its range. In her long moments of absorption, when she watched such trivial things so intently, whose voice whispered inaudibly in her ear, repeating what unguessable lessons. . . .

And how did Lessing himself fit into the pattern? Perhaps, he thought dizzily, he had a part to play in it, trivial, but in its way essential. Someone let the two of them amuse themselves harmlessly together, except when that omnipotent hand had to stretch out and push them gently back into their proper course. Clarissa's course, not Lessing's. Indeed, when anything outré had to happen, it was Clarissa who was protected. She did not guess the hiatus at the time of the street accident; she had scarcely noticed the disappearance of the summerhouse. Lessing did know. Lessing was shocked and stunned. But—Lessing was to forget.

At what point in her life, then, had Clarissa stepped into this mirrored prison with the strange aunt for jailor, and turned unknowing and unguessing into the path that *Someone* had laid out for her? Who whispered in her ear as she went so dreamily about her days, who poured down in a golden torrent about this Danae when she stood alone in her glass-walled tower?

No one could answer that. There might be as many answers as the mind could imagine, and many more beyond imagination. How could any man guess the answer to a question entirely without precedent in human experience? Well—no precedent but one.

There was Danae.

It was ridiculous, Lessing told himself at this point, to imagine any connection at all in this chance likeness. And yet—how had the legend of Danae started? Had some interloper like himself, two thousand years ago, unwittingly glimpsed another Clarissa standing rapt and ecstatic under another shower of stars? And if that were possible, what right had Lessing to assume arbitrarily that the first of the Danae legend had been as true as what he was watching, and the last of it wholly false? There were so many, many legends of mortals whom the gods desired. Some of them must have had obvious explanations, but the Greeks were not a naive people, and there might, he thought, have been some basis of fact existing behind the allegory. There *must* have been some basis, to explain those countless stories, pointing so insistently to some definite rock of reality beyond the fantasy.

But why this long preparation which Clarissa was undergoing? He wondered, and then unbidden into his mind leaped the legend of Semele, who saw her Olympian lover in the unveiled glory of his godhood, and died of that terrible sight. Could this long, slow preparation be designed for no other purpose than to spare Clarissa from Semele's fate? Was she being led gently, inexorably from knowledge to knowledge, so that when the god came down to her in his violence and his splendor, she could endure the glory of her destiny? Was this the answer behind that look of shining anticipation he had seen so often on her face?

Sudden, scalding jealousy enveloped him. Clarissa, glimpsing already and without guessing it, the splendor to come in which he himself could have no part . . .

Lessing struck the door a resounding blow and called, *"Clarissa!"*

In the mirror he saw her start a little and turn. The shower wavered about her. Then she moved out of sight, except for a golden flickering among the mirrors, as she approached the door.

Lessing stood there, shaking and sweating with intolerable confusion. He knew his deductions were ridiculous and impossible. He did not really believe them. He was leaping to conclusions too wild to credit, from premises too arbitrary to consider in any sane moment. Granted that inexplicable things were happening, still he had no logical reason to assume a divine lover's presence. But someone, *Someone* stood behind the events he had just been rehearsing, and of that *Someone*, whoever and whatever it might be, Lessing was agonizingly jealous. For those plans did not include himself. He knew they never could. He knew—

"Hello," said Clarissa softly. "Did I keep you waiting? The bell must be out of order—I didn't hear you ring. Come on in."

He stared. Her face was as serene as always. Perhaps a little glow of rapture still shone in her eyes, but the shower of gold was gone and she gave no outward sign of remembering it.

"What were you doing?" he asked, his voice slightly unsteady.

"Nothing," said Clarissa.

"But I saw you!" he burst out. "In the mirrors—I saw you! Clarissa, what—"

Gently and softly a—a hand?—was laid across his mouth. Nothing tangible, nothing real. But the words did not come through. It was silence itself, a thick gag of it, pressing against his lips. There was one appalling, mind-shaking moment of that gag, and then Lessing knew that *Someone* was right, that he must not speak, that it would be cruel and wrong to say what he had meant to say.

It was all over in an instant, so suddenly that afterward he was not sure whether a gag had actually touched his lips, or whether a subtler gag of the mind had silenced him. But he knew he must say nothing, neither of this nor of that strange, vivid dream in which he had met Clarissa. She did not guess. She must not know—yet.

He could feel the sweat rolling down his forehead, and his knees felt shaky and his head light. He said, from a long way off,

"I . . . I don't feel well, Clarissa. I think I'd better go—"

The light above Dyke's desk swung gently in a breeze from the shaded window. Outside a distant train's hooting floated in across the post grounds, made immeasurably more distant by the darkness. Lessing straightened in his chair and looked around a little dizzily, startled at the abrupt transition from vivid memory to reality. Dyke leaned forward above his crossed arms on the desk and said gently,

"And did you go?"

Lessing nodded. He was far beyond any feeling now of incredulity or reluctance to accept his own memories. The things he was remembering were more real than this desk or the soft-voiced man behind it.

"Yes. I had to get away from her and straighten my mind out. It was so important that she should understand what was happening to her, and yet I couldn't tell her about it. She was—asleep. But she had to be wakened before it was too late. I thought she had a right to know what was coming, and I had a right to have her know, let her make her choice between me and—it. Him. I kept feeling the choice would have to be made soon, or it would be too late. *He* didn't want her to know, of course. He meant to come at the right moment and find her unquestioning, prepared for him. It was up to me to rouse her and make her understand before that moment."

"You thought it was near, then?"

"Very near."

"What did you do?"

Lessing's eyes went unfocused in remembrance. "I took her out dancing," he said, "the next night . . ."

She sat across from him at a table beside a little dance floor, slowly twirling a glass of sherry and bitters and listening to the noises of a bad orchestra echoing in the small, smoky room. Lessing was not quite sure why he had brought her here, after all. Perhaps he hoped that though he could not speak to her in words of all he suspected and feared, he could rouse her enough out of her serene absorption so that she might notice for herself how far her own world differed from the normal one. Here in this small, inclosed space shaking with savage rhythms, crowded by people who were deliberately giving themselves up to the music and the liquor, might not that serene and shining armor be pierced a little, enough to show what lay inside?

Lessing was tinkling the ice in his third collins and enjoying the pleasant haze that just enough alcohol lent to the particular, shining haze that always surrounded Clarissa. He would not, he told himself, have any more. He was far from drunk, certainly, but there was intoxication in the air tonight, even in this little, noisy, second-rate nightclub. The soaring music had a hint of marijuana delirium in it; the dancers on the hot, crowded floor exhaled excitement.

And Clarissa was responding. Her great black eyes shone with unbearable brightness, and her laughter was bright and spontaneous too. They danced in the jostling mob, not feeling jostled at all because of the way the music caught them up on its rhythms. Clarissa was talking much more than usual this evening, very gayly, her body resilient in his arms.

As for himself—yes, he was drunk after all, whether on the three drinks or on some subtler, more powerful intoxication he did not know. But all his values were shifting deliciously toward the irresponsible, and his ears rang with inaudible music. Now nothing could overpower him. He was not afraid of anything or anyone at all. He would take Clarissa away—clear away from New York and her jailor aunt, and that shining *Someone* who drew nearer with every breath.

There began to be gaps in his memory after awhile. He could not remember how they had got out of the nightclub and into his car, or just where they intended to go, but presently they were driving up the Henry Hudson Parkway with the river sliding darkly below and the lights of Jersey lying in wreaths upon the Palisades.

They were defying the—the pattern. He thought both of them knew that. There was no place in the pattern for this wild and dizzying flight up the Hudson, with the cross-streets reeling past like spokes in a shining wheel. Clarissa, leaning back in the bend of his free arm, was in her way as drunk as he, on nothing more than two sherries and the savage rhythms of the music, the savage excitement of this strange night. The intoxication of defiance, perhaps, because they were running away. From something— from *Someone*. (That was impossible, of course. Even in his drunkenness he knew that. But they could try—)

"Faster," Clarissa urged, moving her head in the crook of his arm. She was glitteringly alive tonight as he had never seen her before. Very nearly awake, he thought in the haze of his reeling mind. Very nearly ready to be told what it was he must tell her. The warning—

Once he pulled up deliberately beneath a street light and took her in his arms. Her eyes and her voice and her laughter flashed and sparkled tonight, and Lessing knew that if he thought he had loved her before, this new Clarissa was so enchanting that . . . that . . . yes, even a god might lean out from Olympus to desire her. He kissed her with an ardor that made the city whirl solemnly around them. It was delightful to be drunk and in love, and kissing Clarissa under the eyes of the jealous gods . . .

There was feeling of . . . of wrongness in the air as they drove on. The pattern strove to right itself, to force them back into their ordained path. He could feel its calm power pressing against his mind. He was aware of traffic imperceptibly edging him into streets that led back toward the apartment they had left. He had to wrench himself out of it, and then presently the northbound way would be closed off for repairs, and a detour went off along other streets that took them south again. Time after time he found himself driving past descending street numbers toward downtown New York, and swung around the block in bewildered determination not to return.

The pattern must be broken. It *must* be. Hazily he thought that if he could snap one thread of it, defy that smooth, quiet power in even so small a way as this, he would have accomplished his purpose. But alone he could not have done it. The omnipotent machinery humming in its course would have been irresistible—he would have obeyed it without knowing he obeyed —had not Clarissa shared his defiance tonight. There seemed to be a power in her akin to the power of that omnipotence, as if she had absorbed some of it from long nearness to the source.

Or was it that *Someone* stayed his hand rather than strike her forcibly back to her place in the pattern, rather than let her guess—yet—the extent of his power?

"Turn," said Clarissa. "Turn around. We're going wrong again."

He struggled with the wheel. "I can't . . . I can't," he told her, almost breathless. She gave him a dazzling dark glance and leaned over to take the wheel herself.

Even for her it was hard. But slowly she turned the car, while traffic blared irritably behind them, and slowly they broke out of the pattern's grip again and rounded another corner, heading north, the lights of Jersey swimming unfocused in the haze of their delirium.

This was no normal drunkenness. It was increasing by leaps and bounds. This, thought Lessing dimly, is *His* next step. He won't let her see what he's doing, but he knows he's got to stop us now, or we'll break the pattern and prove our independence.

The tall, narrow buildings shouldering together along the streets were like tall trees in a forest, with windows for motionless leaves. No two windows on the same level, or quite alike. Infinite variety with infinitesimal differences, all of them interlacing and glimmering as they drove on and on through the stony forest. Now Lessing could see among the trees, and between them, not transparently but as if through some new dimension. He could see the streets that marked off this forest into squares and oblongs,

and his dazed mind remembered another forest, checkered into squares—
Looking Glass Land.

He was going south again through the forest.

"Clarissa—help me," he said distantly, wrestling again with the wheel.
Her small white hands came out of the dark to cover his.

A shower of light from a flickering window poured down upon them,
enveloping Clarissa as Zeus enveloped Danae. The jealous god, the jealous
god— Lessing laughed and smacked the wheel in senseless triumph.

There was a light glimmering ahead through the trees. He would have
to go softly, he warned himself, and tiptoed forward over the . . . the
cobbled road. Without surprise he saw that he was moving on foot through
a forest in darkness, quite alone. He was still drunk. Drunker than ever, he
thought with mild pride, drunker, probably, than any mortal ever was before.
Any mortal. The gods, now—

People were moving through the trees ahead. He knew they must not
see him. It would shock them considerably if they did; he remembered
the garishly dressed people of his other dream, and the young man with
the whip. No, it would be better to stay hidden this time if he could.
The forest was wheeling and dipping around him behind a haze of ob-
scurity, and nothing had very much coherence. The ringing in his ears was
probably intoxication, not actual sound.

The people were somberly clad in black, with black hoods that covered
their hair and framed pale, intolerant faces. They were moving in a long
column through the trees. Lessing watched them go by for what seemed a
long while. Some of the women carried work bags over their arms and
knitted as they walked. A few of the men read from small books and stumbled
now and then on the cobblestones. There was no laughter.

Clarissa came among the last. She had a gay little face beneath the
black cap, gayer and more careless than he had ever seen her in this . . . this
world. She walked lightly, breaking into something like a dance step occasionally that called down upon her the frowns of those who walked behind. She did not seem to care.

Lessing wanted to call to her. He wanted to call so badly that it seemed
to him she sensed it, for she began to fall behind, letting first one group
pass her and then another, until she walked at the very end of the column.
Several girls in a cluster looked back a few times and giggled a little, but
said nothing. She fell farther back. Presently the procession turned a corner
and Clarissa stopped in the middle of the road, watching them go. Then
she laughed and performed a solemn little pirouette on one toe, her black
skirts swinging wide around her.

Lessing stepped from behind his tree and took a step toward her, ready
to speak her name. But he was too late. Someone else was already nearer
than he. Someone else— Clarissa called out gayly in a language he did not
know, and then there was a flash of crimson through the trees and a figure
cloaked from head to heels in bright red came up to her and took her

into its embrace, the red folds swinging forward to infold them both. Clarissa's happy laughter was smothered beneath the stooping hood.

Lessing stood perfectly still. It might be another woman, he told himself fiercely. It might be a sister or an aunt. But it was probably a man. Or—

He squinted slightly—nothing focused very well in his present state, and things tended to slip sidewise when he tried to fix his eyes upon them—but this time he was almost sure of what he saw. He was almost sure that upon Clarissa's lifted face in the dimness of the woods a light was falling softly—from the hood above her. A light, glowing from within the hood. A shower of light. Danae, in her shower of gold . . .

The woods tilted steeply and turned end for end. Lessing was beyond surprise as he fell away, spinning and whirling through darkness, falling farther and farther from Clarissa in the woods. Leaving Clarissa alone in the embrace of her god.

When the spinning stopped he was sitting in his car again, with traffic pouring noisily past on the left. He was parked, somewhere. Double-parked, with the motor running. He blinked.

"I'll get out here," Clarissa told him matter-of-factly. "No, don't bother. You'll never find a parking place, and I'm so sleepy. Good night, darling. Phone me in the morning."

He could do nothing but blink. The dazzle of her eyes and her smile was a little blinding, and that haze still diffused all his efforts to focus upon her face. But he could see enough. They were exactly where they had started, at the curb before her apartment house.

"Good night," said Clarissa again, and the door closed behind her.

There was silence in the office after Lessing's last words. Dyke sat waiting quietly, his eyes on Lessing's face, his shadow moving a little on the desktop under the swinging light. After a moment Lessing said, almost defiantly,

"Well?"

Dyke smiled slightly, stirring in his chair. "Well?" he echoed.

"What are you thinking?"

Dyke shook his head. "I'm not thinking at all. It isn't time yet for that —unless the story ends there. It doesn't, does it?"

Lessing looked thoughtful. "No. Not quite. We met once more."

"Only once?" Dyke's eyes brightened. "That must be when your memory went, then. That's the most interesting scene of all. Go on—what happened?"

Lessing closed his eyes. His voice came slowly, as if he were remembering bit by bit each episode of the story he told.

"The phone woke me next morning," he said. "It was Clarissa. As soon as I heard her voice I knew the time had come to settle things once and for all—if I could. If I were allowed. I didn't think—He—would let me talk it out with her, but I knew I'd have to try. She sounded upset on the phone. Wouldn't say why. She wanted me to come over right away."

She was at the door when he came out of the elevator, holding it open for him against a background of mirrors in which no motion stirred. She looked fresh and lovely, and Lessing marveled again, as he had marveled on waking, that the extraordinary drunkenness of last night had left no ill effects with either of them this morning. But she looked troubled, too; her eyes were too bright, with a blinding blackness that dazzled him, and the sweet serenity was gone from her face. He exulted at that. She was awakening, then, from the long, long dream.

The first thing he said as he followed her into the apartment was, "Where's your aunt?"

Clarissa glanced vaguely around. "Oh, out, I suppose. Never mind her. Jim, tell me—did we do something wrong last night? Do you remember what happened? Everything?"

"Why I . . . I think so." He was temporizing, not ready yet in spite of his decision to plunge into these deep waters.

"What happened, then? Why does it worry me so? Why can't I remember?" Her troubled eyes searched his face anxiously. He took her hands. They were cold and trembling a little.

"Come over here," he said. "Sit down. What's the matter, darling? Nothing's wrong. We had a few drinks and took a long ride, don't you remember? And then I brought you back here and you said good night and went in."

"That isn't all," she said with conviction. "We were—fighting something. It was wrong to fight—I never did before. I never knew it was there until I fought it last night. But now I do know. What was it, Jim?"

He looked down at her gravely, a tremendous excitement beginning to well up inside him. Perhaps, somehow, they had succeeded last night in breaking the spell. Perhaps *His* grip had been loosened after all, when they defied the pattern even as briefly as they did.

But this was no time for temporizing. Now, while the bonds were slack, was the moment to strike hard and sever them if he could. Tomorrow she might have slipped back again into the old distraction that shut him out. He must tell her now— Together they might yet shake off the tightening coils that had been closing so gently, so inexorably about her.

"Clarissa," he said, and turned on the sofa to face her. "Clarissa, I think I'd better tell you something." Then a sudden, unreasoning doubt seized him and he said irrelevantly, "Are you sure you love me?" It was foolishly important to be reassured just then. He did not know why.

Clarissa smiled and leaned forward into his arms, putting her cheek against his shoulder. From there, unseen, she murmured, "I'll always love you, dear."

For a long moment he did not speak. Then, holding her in one arm, not watching her face, he began.

"Ever since we met, Clarissa darling, things have been happening that —worried me. About you. I'm going to tell you if I can. I think there's something, or someone, very powerful, watching over you and forcing you into some course, toward some end I can't do more than guess at. I'm going to try to tell you exactly why I think so, and if I have to stop without finishing, you'll know I don't stop on purpose. I'll have been stopped."

Lessing paused, a little awed at his own daring in defying that *Someone* whose powerful hand he had felt hushing him before. But no pad of silence was pressed against his lips this time and he went on wonderingly, expecting each word he spoke to be the last. Clarissa lay silent against his shoulder, breathing quietly, not moving much. He could not see her face.

And so he told her the story, very simply and without references to his own bewilderment or to the wild conclusions he had reached. He told her about the moment in the park when she had been drawn away down a funnel of luminous rings. He reminded her of the vanishment of the summerhouse. He told of the dreamlike episode on the hallway here, when he called irrationally into the mirrored dimness, or thought he called. He told her of their strange, bemused ride uptown the night before, and how the pattern swung the streets around under their wheels. He told her of his two vivid dreams through which she—yet not she—had moved so assuredly. And then, without drawing any conclusions aloud, he asked her what she was thinking.

She lay still a moment longer in his arms. Then she sat up slowly, pushing back the smooth dark hair and meeting his eyes with the feverish brilliance that had by now become natural to her.

"So that's it," she said dreamily, and was silent.

"What is?" he asked almost irritably yet suffused now with a sense of triumph because the *Someone* had not silenced him after all, had slipped this once and let the whole story come out into open air at last. Now at last he thought he might learn the truth.

"Then I was right," Clarissa went on. "I *was* fighting something last night. It's odd, but I never even knew it was there until the moment I began to fight it. Now I know it's always been there. I wonder—"

When she did not go on, Lessing said bluntly, "Have you ever realized that . . . that things were different for you? Tell me, Clarissa, what is it you think of when you . . . when you stand and look at something trivial so long?"

She turned her head and gave him a long, grave look that told him more plainly than words that the whole spell was not yet dissolved. She made no answer to the question, but she said,

"For some reason I keep remembering a fairy story my aunt used to tell me when I was small. I've never forgotten it, though it certainly isn't much of a story. You see—"

She paused again, and her eyes brightened as he looked, almost as if lights had gone on behind them in a dark room full of mirrors. The look of expectancy which he knew so well tightened the lines of her face for a moment, and she smiled delightedly, without apparent reason and not really seeming to know she smiled.

"Yes," she went on. "I remember it well. Once upon a time, in a kingdom in the middle of the forest, a little girl was born. All the people in the country were blind. The sun shone so brightly that none of them could see. So the little girl went about with her eyes shut too, and didn't even guess that such a thing as sight existed.

"One day as she walked alone in the woods she heard a voice beside her. 'Who are you?' she asked the voice, and the voice replied, 'I am your guardian.' The little girl said, 'But I don't need a guardian. I know these woods very well. I was born here.' The voice said, 'Ah, you were born here, yes, but you don't belong here, child. You are not blind like the others.' And the little girl exclaimed, 'Blind? What's that?'

"'I can't tell you yet,' the voice answered, 'but you must know that you are a king's daughter, born among these humble people as our king's children sometimes are. My duty is to watch over you and help you to open your eyes when the time comes. But the time is not yet. You are too young—the sun would blind you. So go on about your business, child, and remember I am always here beside you. The day will come when you open your eyes and see.'"

Clarissa paused. Lessing said impatiently, "Well, did she?"

Clarissa sighed. "My aunt never would finish the story. Maybe that's why I've always remembered it."

Lessing started to speak. "I don't think—" But something in Clarissa's face stopped him. An exalted and enchanted look, that Christmas-morning expression carried to fulfillment, as if the child were awake and remembering what many-lighted, silver-spangled glory awaited him downstairs. She said in a small, clear voice,

"It's true. Of course it's true! All you've said, and the fairy tale too. Why, *I'm* the king's child. Of course I am!" And she put both hands to her eyes in a sudden childish gesture, as if half expecting the allegory of blindness to be literal.

"*Clarissa!*" Lessing said.

She looked at him with wide, dazzled eyes that scarcely knew him. And for a moment a strange memory came unbidden into his mind and brought terror with it. Alice, walking with the Fawn in the enchanted woods where nothing has a name, walking in friendship with her arm about the Fawn's neck. And the Fawn's words when they came to the edge of the woods and memory returned to them both. How it started away from her, shaking off the arm, wildness returning to the eyes that had looked as serenely into Alice's as Clarissa had looked into his. "*Why—I'm a Fawn,*" it said in astonishment. "*And you're a Human Child!*"

Alien species.

"I wonder why I'm not a bit surprised?" murmured Clarissa. "I must have known it all along, really. Oh, I wonder what comes next?"

Lessing stared at her, appalled. She was very like a child now, too enraptured by the prospect of—of what?—to think of any possible consequences. It frightened him to see how sure she was of splendor to come, and of nothing but good in that splendor. He hated to mar the look of lovely anticipation on her face, but he must. He had wanted her to help him fight this monstrous possibility if she could bring herself to accept it at all. He had not expected instant acceptance and instant rapture. She *must* fight it—

"Clarissa," he said, "think! If it's true . . . and we may be wrong . . . don't you see what it means? He . . . they . . . won't let us be together, Clarissa. We can't be married."

Her luminous eyes turned to him joyously.

"Of course we'll be married, darling. *They're* only looking after me, don't you see? Not hurting me, just watching. I'm sure they'll let us marry whenever we like. I'm sure they'd never do anything to hurt me. Why darling, for all we know you may be one of us, too. I wonder if you are. It almost stands to reason, don't you think? Or why would They have let us fall in love? Oh, darling—"

Suddenly he knew that someone was standing behind him. *Someone*— For one heart-stopping moment he wondered if the jealous god himself had come down to claim Clarissa, and he dared not turn his head. But when Clarissa's shining eyes lifted to the face beyond his, and showed no surprise, he felt a little reassurance.

He sat perfectly still. He knew he could not have turned if he wanted. He could only watch Clarissa, and though no words were spoken in that silence, he saw her expression change. The rapturous joy drained slowly out of it. She shook her head, bewilderment and disbelief blurring the ecstasy of a moment before.

"No?" she said to that standing someone behind him. "But I thought— Oh, no, you mustn't! You wouldn't! It isn't fair!" And the dazzling dark eyes flooded with sudden tears that doubled their shining. "You can't, you can't!" sobbed Clarissa, and flung herself forward upon Lessing, her arms clasping his neck hard as she wept incoherent protest upon his shoulder.

His arms closed automatically around her while his mind spun desperately to regain its balance. What had happened? Who—

Someone brushed by him. The aunt. He knew that, but with no sense of relief even though he had half-expected that more awesome *Someone* at whose existence he could still only guess.

The aunt was bending over them, pulling gently at Clarissa's shaking shoulder. And after a moment Clarissa's grip on his neck loosened and she sat up obediently, though still catching her breath in long, uneven sobs that wrung Lessing's heart. He wanted desperately to do or say whatever would comfort her most quickly, but his mind and his body were both oddly slowed, as if there were some force at work in the room which he could not understand. As if he were moving against the momentum of that singing machinery he had fancied he sensed so often—moving against it, while the other two were carried effortlessly on.

Clarissa let herself be pulled away. She moved as bonelessly as a child, utterly given up to her grief, careless of everything but that. The tears streaked her cheeks and her body drooped forlornly. She held Lessing's hands until the last, but when he felt her fingers slipping from his the loss of contact told him, queerly, as nothing else quite had power to tell, that this was a final parting. They stood apart over a few feet of carpet, as if inexorable miles lay between them. Miles that widened with every passing second. Clarissa looked at him through her tears, her eyes unbearably bright, her lips quivering, her hands still outstretched and curved from the pressure of his clasp.

This is all. You have served your purpose—now go. Go and forget.

He did not know what voice had said it, or exactly in what words, but the meaning came back to him clearly now. *Go and forget.*

There was strong music in the air. For one last moment he stood in a world that glittered with beauty and color because it was Clarissa's, glittered even in this dark apartment with its many, many mirrors. All about him he could see reflecting Clarissas from every angle of grief and parting, moving confusedly as she let her hands begin to drop. He saw a score of Clarissas dropping their curved hands—but he never saw them fall. One last look at Clarissa's tears, and then . . . and then—

Lethe.

Dyke let his breath out in a long sigh. He leaned back in his creaking chair and looked at Lessing without expression under his light eyebrows. Lessing blinked stupidly back. An instant ago he had stood in Clarissa's apartment; the touch of her fingers was still warm in his hands. He could hear her caught breath and see the reflections moving confusedly in the mirrors around them—

"Wait a minute," he said. "Reflections—Clarissa—I almost remembered something just then—" He sat up and stared at Dyke without seeing him, his brow furrowed. "Reflections," he said again. "Clarissa—lots of Clarissas—but no aunt! I was looking at two women in the mirror, but I didn't see the aunt! I never saw her—not once! And yet I . . . wait . . . the answer's there, you know . . . right there, just in reach, if I could only—"

Then it came to him in a burst of clarity. Clarissa had seen it before him; the whole answer lay in that legend she had told. The Country of the Blind! How could those sightless natives hope to see the king's messenger who watched over the princess as she walked that enchanted wood? How could he remember what his mind had never been strong enough to comprehend? How could he have *seen* that guardian except as a presence without shape, a voice without words, moving through its own bright sphere beyond the sight of the blind?

"Cigarette?" said Dyke, creaking his chair forward.

Lessing reached automatically across the desk. There was no further sound but the rustle of paper and the scratch of a match, for a little while. They smoked in silence, eying one another. Outside feet went by upon gravel. Men's voices called distantly, muffled by the night. Crickets were chirping, omnipresent in the dark.

Presently Dyke let down the front legs of his chair with a thump and reached forward to grind out his unfinished cigarette.

"All right," he said. "Now—are you still too close, or can you look at it objectively?"

Lessing shrugged. "I can try."

"Well, first we can take it as understood—at least for the moment—that such things as these just don't happen. The story's full of holes, of course. We could tear it to pieces in ten minutes if we tried."

Lessing looked stubborn. "Maybe you think—"

"I haven't begun to think yet. We haven't got to the bottom of the thing, naturally. I don't believe it really happened exactly as you remember. Man, how could it? The whole story's still dressed up in a sort of allegory, and we'll have to dig deeper still to uncover the bare facts. But just as it stands—what a problem! Now I wonder—"

His voice died. He shook out another cigarette and scratched a match abstractedly. Through the first cloud of exhaled smoke he went on,

"Take it all as read, just for a minute. Unravel the allegory in the allegory —the king's daughter born in the Country of the Blind. You know, Lessing, one thing strikes me that you haven't noticed yet. Ever think how completely childish Clarissa seems? Her absorption in trivial things, for instance. Her assumption that the forces at work about her must be protective, parental. Yes, even that glow you spoke of that affected everything you saw and heard when you were with her. A child's world is like that. Strong, clear colors. Nothing's ugly because they have no basis for comparison. Beauty and ugliness mean nothing to a child. I can remember a bit from my own childhood— that peculiar enchantment over whatever interested me. Wordsworth, you know— 'Heaven lies about us in our infancy,' and all the rest. And yet she was adult enough, wasn't she? Past twenty, say?"

He paused, eying the tip of his cigarette. "You know," he said, "it sounds like a simple case of arrested development, doesn't it? Now, now, wait a minute! I only said *sounds* like it. You've got sense enough to recognize a moron when you see one. I don't say Clarissa was anything like that. I'm just getting at something—

"I'm thinking about my own little boy. He's eleven now, and getting adjusted, but when he first started school he had an I.Q. away above the rest of the class, and they bored him. He didn't want to play with the other kids. Got to hanging around the house reading until my wife and I realized something had to be done about it. High I.Q. or not, a kid needs other kids to play with. He'll never learn to make the necessary social adjustments unless he learns young. Can't grow up psychically quite straight unless he grows up with his own kind. Later on a high I.Q. will be a fine thing, but right now it's almost a handicap to the kid." He paused. "Well, see what I mean?"

Lessing shook his head. "I can't see anything. I'm still dizzy."

"Clarissa," said Dyke slowly, "might—in the allegory, mind you, not in any real sense—be the king's daughter. She might have been born of . . . well, call it royal blood . . . into a race of inferiors, and never guess it until she began to develop beyond their level. Maybe the . . . the king felt the same as I did about my own child—she needed the company of inferiors . . . of children—while she was growing up. She couldn't develop properly among—adults. Adults, you see, so far developed beyond anything we know that when they're in the same room with you, you can't even remember what they looked like."

It took Lessing a good minute after Dyke stopped speaking to realize just what he meant. Then he sat up abruptly and said, "Oh, no! It can't be that. Why, I'd have known—"

"You ought," Dyke remarked abstractedly, "to watch my kid play baseball. While he's playing, it's the most important thing in life. The other kids never guess he has thoughts that go beyond the game."

"But . . . but the shower of gold, for instance," protested Lessing. "The presence of the god . . . even the—"

"Wait a minute! Just wait, now. You remember yourself that you jumped at conclusions about the god. Made him up completely out of a glimpse of what looked like a golden shower, and the memory of the Danae legend, and the feeling of a presence and a purpose behind what happened. If you'd seen what looked like a burning bush instead of a shower, you'd have come up with a completely different theory involving Moses, maybe. As for the presence and the visions—" Dyke paused and gave him a narrowed look. He hesitated a moment. "I'm going to suggest something about those later on. You won't like it. First, though, I want to follow this . . . this allegory on through. I want to explain fully what *might* lie beyond this obvious theory on Clarissa. Remember, I don't take it seriously. But neither do I want to leave it dangling. It's fascinating, just as it stands. It seems very clearly to indicate—in the allegory—the existence of *homo superior*, here and now, right among us."

"Supermen?" Lessing echoed. With an obvious effort he forced his mind into focus and sat up straighter, looking at Dyke with a thoughtful frown. "Maybe. Or maybe— Lieutenant, do you ever read Cabell? In one of his books somewhere I think he has a character refer to a sort of super-race that impinges on ours with only one . . . one facet. He uses the analogy of geometry, and suggests that the other race might be represented by cubes that show up as squares on the plane geometric surface of our world, though in their own they have a cubic mass we never guess." He frowned more deeply, and was silent.

Dyke nodded. "Something like that, maybe. Fourth dimension stuff— people restricting themselves into our world temporarily, and for a purpose." He pulled at his lower lip and then repeated, "For a purpose. That's humiliating! I'm glad I don't really believe it's true. Even considering the thing academically is embarrassing enough. *Homo superior*, sending his children among us—to play."

He laughed. "Run along, children! I wonder if you see what I'm driving at. I'm not sure myself, really. It's too vague. My mind's human, so it's limited. I'm set in patterns of anthropomorphic thinking, and my habit-patterns handicap me. We have to feel important. That's a psychological truism. That's why Mephistopheles was always supposed to be interested in buying human souls. He wouldn't have wanted them, really—impalpables, intangibles, no use at all to a demon with a demon's powers."

"Where do the demons come in?"

"Nowhere. I'm just talking. *Homo superior* would be another race without any human touching points at all—as adults. Demons, in literature, were given human emotions and traits. Why? Muddy thinking. They wouldn't have them, any more than a superman would. Tools!" Dyke said significantly, and sat staring at nothing.

"Tools?"

"This . . . this world." He gestured. "What the devil do we know about it? We've made atom-smashers and microscopes. And other things. Kid stuff, toys. My boy can use a microscope and see bugs in creek water. A doctor can take the same microscope, use stains, isolate a germ and do something about it. That's maturity. All this world, all this—matter—around us, might be simply tools that we're using like kids. A super-race—"

"By definition, wouldn't it be too super to understand?"

"In toto. A child can't completely comprehend an adult. But a child can more or less understand another child—which is reduced to the same equation as his own, or at least the same common denominator. A superman would have to grow. He wouldn't start out mature. Say the adult human is expressed by x. The adult superman is xy. A superchild—undeveloped, immature—is $\frac{xy}{y}$. Or in other words, the equivalent of a mature specimen of *homo sapiens*. *Sapiens* reaches senility and dies. *Superior* goes on to maturity, the true superman. And that maturity—"

They were silent for awhile.

"They might impinge on us a little, while taking care of their own young," Dyke went on presently. "They might impose amnesia on anyone who came too close, as you did—might have done. Remember Charles Fort? Mysterious disappearances, balls of light, spaceships, Jersey devils. That's a side issue. The point is, a superchild could live with us, right here and now, unsuspected. It would appear to be an ordinary adult human. Or if not quite ordinary—certain precautions might be taken." Again he fell silent, twirling a pencil on the desk.

"Of course, it's inconceivable," he went on at last. "All pure theory. I've got a much more plausible explanation, though as I warned you, you won't like it."

Lessing smiled faintly. "What is it?"

"Remember Clarissa's fever?"

"Of course. Things were different after that—much more in the open. I thought—maybe she saw things in the delirium for the first time that she couldn't be allowed to see head-on, in normal life. The fever seemed to be a necessity. But of course—"

"Wait. Just possibly, you know, you may have the whole thing by the wrong end. Look back, now. You two were caught in a rainstorm, and Clarissa came out of it with a delirium, right? And after that, things got stranger and stranger. Lessing, did it ever occur to you that you were both caught in that storm? Are you perfectly sure that it wasn't *yourself* who had the delirium?"

Lessing sat quite still, meeting the narrowed gaze. After a long moment he shook himself slightly.

"Yes," he said. "I'm sure."

Dyke smiled. "All right. Just thought I'd ask. It's one possibility, of course." He waited.

Presently Lessing looked up.

"Maybe I did have a fever," he admitted. "Maybe I imagined it all. That still doesn't explain the forgetfulness, but skip that. I know one way to settle at least part of the question."

Dyke nodded. "I wondered if you'd want to do that. I mean, right away."

"Why not? I know the way back. I'd know it blindfolded. Why, she may have been waiting for me all this time! There's nothing to prevent me going back tomorrow."

"There's a little matter of a pass," Dyke said. "I believe I can fix that up. But do you think you want to go so soon, Lessing? Without thinking things over? You know, it's going to be an awful shock if you find no apartment and no Clarissa. And I'll admit I won't be surprised if that's just what you do find. I think this whole thing's an allegory we haven't fathomed yet. We may never fathom it. But—"

"I'll have to go," Lessing told him. "Don't you see that? We'll never prove anything until we at least rule out the most obvious possibility. After all, I might be telling the simple truth!"

Dyke laughed and then shrugged faintly.

Lessing stood before the familiar door, his finger hesitating on the bell. So far, his memory had served him with perfect faith. Here was the corridor he knew well. Here was the door. Inside, he was quite sure, lay the arrangement of walls and rooms where once Clarissa moved. She might not be there any more, of course. He must not be disappointed if a strange face answered the bell. It would disprove nothing. After all, two years had passed.

And Clarissa had been changing rather alarmingly when he saw her last. The fever had seemed to speed things up.

Well, suppose it were all true. Suppose she belonged to the super-race. Suppose she impinged upon Lessing's world with only one facet of her four-dimensional self. With that one facet she had loved him—they had that much of a meeting ground. Let her have a deeper self, then, than he could ever comprehend; still she could not yet be fully developed into her world of solid geometry, and while one facet remained restricted into the planar world which was all he knew, she might, he thought, still love him. He hoped she could. He remembered her tears. He heard again the sweet, shy, ardent voice saying, "I'll always love you—"

Firmly he pressed the bell.

The room was changed. Mirrors still lined it, but not—not as he remembered. They were more than mirrors now. He had no time to analyze the change, for a motion stirred before him.

"Clarissa—" he said. And then, in the one brief instant of awareness that remained to him, he knew at last how wrong he had been.

He had forgotten that four dimensions are not the outermost limits of conceivable scope. Cabell had unwittingly led him astray: there are dimensions in which a cube may have many more than six sides. Clarissa's dimension—

Extensions are possible in dimensions not entirely connected with space—or rather, space is merely a medium through which these extensions may be made. And because humans live upon a three-dimensional planet, and because all planets in this continuum are three-dimensional, no psychic tesseract is possible—except by extensions.

That is, a collection of chromosomes and genes, arranged on earth and here conceived, cannot in themselves form the matrix for a superman. Nor can a battery give more than its destined voltage. But if there are three, six, a dozen batteries of similar size, and if they are connected in series—

Until they are connected, until the linkage is complete, each is an individual. Each has its limitations. There are gropings, guided fumblings through the dark, while those in charge seek to help the scattered organism in fulfilling itself. And therefore the human mind can comprehend the existence of a superbeing up to the point that the connection is made and the batteries become one unit, of enormous potential power.

On earth there was Clarissa and her nominal aunt—who could not be comprehended at all.

On a remote planet in Cygnae Taurus, there was a Clarissa too, but her name there was something like Ezandora, and her mentor was a remote and cryptic being who was accepted by the populace as a godling.

On Seven Million Four Twenty Eight of Center Galaxy there was Jandav, who carried with her a small crystal through which her guidance came.

In atmospheres of oxygen and halogen, in lands ringed with the shaking blaze of crusted stars beyond the power of our telescopes—beneath water, and in places of cold and darkness and void, the matrix repeated itself, and by the psychic and utterly unimaginable power and science of *homo superior*, the biological cycle of a race more than human ran and completed itself and began again. Not entirely spontaneously, at the same time, in many worlds, the pattern that was Clarissa was conceived and grew. The batteries strengthened.

Or to use Cabell's allegory, the Clarissa Pattern impinged one facet upon earth, but it was not one facet out of a possible six—but one out of a possible infinity of facets. Upon each face of that unimaginable geometric shape, a form of Clarissa moved and had independent being, and gradually developed. Learned and was taught. Reached out toward the center of the geometric shape that was—or one day would be—the complete Clarissa. One day, when the last mirrorfacet sent inward to the center its matured reflection of the whole, when the many Clarissas, so to speak, clasped hands with themselves and fused into perfection.

Thus far we can follow. But not after the separate units become the complete and tremendous being toward which the immaturity of Clarissa on so many worlds was growing. After that, the destiny of *homo superior* has no common touching point with the understanding of *homo sapiens*. We knew them as children. And they passed. They put away childish things.

"Clarissa—" he said.

Then he paused, standing motionless in silence, looking across that dark threshold into that mirrory dimness, seeing—what he saw. It was dark on the landing. The staircases went up and down, shadowy and still. There was stasis here, and no movement anywhere in the quiet air. This was power beyond the need for expression of power.

He turned and went slowly down the stairs. The fear and pain and gnawing uneasiness that had troubled him for so long were gone now. Outside, on the curb, he lit a cigarette, hailed a taxi, and considered his next movements.

A cab swung in. Further along the street, the liquid, shining blackness of the East River glissaded smoothly down to the Sound. The rumble of an El train came from the other direction.

"Where to, sergeant?" the driver asked.

"Downtown," Lessing said. "Where's a good floorshow?" he relaxed pleasantly on the cushions, his mind quite free from strain or worry now.

This time the memory block was complete. He would go on living out his cycle, complacent and happy as any human ever is, enjoying life to his capacity for enjoyment, using the toys of earth with profound satisfaction.

"Nightclub?" the driver said. "The new Cabana's good—"

Lessing nodded. "O.K. The Cabana." He leaned back, luxuriously inhaling smoke. It was the children's hour.

GOMEZ
by C. M. Kornbluth

Now THAT I'M A CRANKY, constipated old man I can afford to say that the younger generation of scientists makes me sick to my stomach. Short order fry-cooks of destruction, they hear through the little window the dim order: "Atom bomb rare, with cobalt 60!" and sing it back and rattle their stinking skillets and sling the deadly hash—just what the customer ordered, with never a notion invading their smug, too-heated havens that there's a small matter of right and wrong that takes precedence even over their haute cuisine.

There used to be a slew of them who yelled to high heaven about it. Weiner, Urey, Szilard, Morrison—dead now, and worse. Unfashionable. The greatest of them you have never heard of. Admiral MacDonald never did clear the story. He was Julio Gomez, and his story was cleared yesterday by a fellow my Jewish friends call Malach Hamovis, the Hovering Angel of Death. A black-bordered letter from Rosa advised me that Malach Hamovis had come in on runway six with his flaps down and picked up Julio at the age of 39. Pneumonia.

"But," Rosa painfully wrote, "Julio would want you to know he died not too unhappy, after a good though short life with much of satisfaction . . ."

I think it will give him some more satisfaction, wherever he is, to know that his story at last is getting told.

It started twenty-two years ago with a routine assignment on a crisp October morning. I had an appointment with Dr. Sugarman, the head of the physics department at the University. It was the umpth anniversary of something or other—first atomic pile, the test A-bomb, Nagasaki—I don't remember what, and the Sunday editor was putting together a page on it. My job was to interview the three or four University people who were Manhattan District grads.

I found Sugarman in his office at the top of the modest physics building's square gothic tower, brooding through a pointed-arch window at the bright autumn sky. He was a tubby, jowly little fellow. I'd been seeing him around

for a couple of years at testimonial banquets and press conferences, but I
didn't expect him to remember me. He did, though, and even got the name
right.

"Mr. Vilchek?" he beamed. "From the *Tribune?*"

"That's right, Dr. Sugarman. How are you?"

"Fine; fine. Sit down, please. Well, what shall we talk about?"

"Well, Dr. Sugarman, I'd like to have your ideas on the really fundamental
issues of atomic energy, A-bomb control and so on. What in your opinion is
the single most important factor in these problems?"

His eyes twinkled; he was going to surprise me. "Education!" he said, and
leaned back waiting for me to register shock.

I registered. "That's certainly a different approach, doctor. How do you
mean that, exactly?"

He said impressively: "Education—*technical* education—is the key to the
underlying issues of our time. I am deeply concerned over the unawareness
of the general public to the meaning and accomplishments of science. People
underrate me—underrate *science*, that is—because they do not *understand*
science. Let me show you something." He rummaged for a moment
through papers on his desk and handed me a sheet of lined tablet paper
covered with chicken-track handwriting. "A letter I got," he said. I squinted
at the penciled scrawl and read:

October 12

Esteemed Sir:

   *Beg to introduce self to you the atomic Scientist as a youth 17
working with diligence to perfect self in Mathematical Physics. The
knowledge of English is imperfect since am in New-York 1 year only
from Puerto Rico and due to Father and Mother poverty must wash
the dishes in the restaurant. So esteemed sir excuse imperfect English
which will better.*

   *I hesitate intruding your valuable Scientist time but hope you
sometime spare minutes for diligents such as I. My difficulty is with
neutron cross-section absorption of boron steel in Reactor which
theory I am working out. Breeder reactors demand*

$$u = \frac{x}{1} + \frac{x^5}{1} + \frac{x^{10}}{1} + \frac{x^{15}}{1} + \cdots$$

for boron steel, compared with neutron cross-section absorption of

$$v = \frac{x^{1/5}}{1} + \frac{x}{1} + \frac{x^2}{1} + \frac{x^3}{1} + \cdots$$

*for any Concrete with which I familiarize myself. Whence arises
relationship*

$$v^5 = u \, \frac{1 - 2u + 4u^2 - 3u^2 + u^4}{1 + 3u + 4u^2 + 2u^3 + u^4}$$

*indicating only a fourfold breeder gain. Intuitively I dissatisfy with
this gain and beg to intrude your time to ask wherein I neglect. With
the most sincere thanks.*

J. Gomez
% Porto Bello Lunchroom
124th St. & St. Nicholas Ave.
New-York, New-York

I laughed and told Dr. Sugarman appreciatively: "That's a good one. I
wish our cranks kept in touch with us by mail, but they don't. In the newspaper business they come in and demand to see the editor. Could I use it,
by the way? The readers ought to get a boot out of it."

He hesitated and said: "All right—if you don't use my name. Just say 'a
prominent physicist.' I didn't think it was too funny myself though, but I
see your point, of course. The boy may be feeble-minded—and he probably
is—but he believes, like too many people, that science is just a bag of tricks
which any ordinary person can acquire—"

And so on and so on.

I went back to the office and wrote the interview in twenty minutes. It
took me longer than that to talk the Sunday editor into running the Gomez
letter in a box on the atom-anniversary page, but he finally saw it my way.
I had to retype it. If I'd just sent the letter down to the composing room as
was, we would have had a strike on our hands.

On Sunday morning, at a quarter past six, I woke up to the tune of fists
thundering on my hotel-room door. I found my slippers and bathrobe and
lurched blearily across the room. They didn't wait for me to unlatch. The
door opened. I saw one of the hotel clerks, the Sunday editor, a frosty-faced
old man and three hard-faced, hard-eyed young men. The hotel clerk mumbled and retreated and the others moved in. "Chief," I asked the Sunday
editor hazily, "what's going—?"

A hard-faced young man was standing with his back to the door; another
was standing with his back to the window and the third was blocking the
bathroom door. The icy old man interrupted me with a crisp authoritative
question snapped at the editor. "You identify this man as Vilchek?"

The editor nodded.

"Search him," snapped the old man. The fellow standing guard at the
window slipped up and frisked me for weapons while I sputtered incoherently
and the Sunday editor avoided my eye.

When the search was over the frosty-faced old boy said to me: "I am
Rear Admiral MacDonald, Mr. Vilchek. I'm here in my capacity as deputy
director of the Office of Security and Intelligence, U. S. Atomic Energy
Commission. Did you write this?" He thrust a newspaper clipping at my
face.

I read, blearily:

WHAT'S SO TOUGH ABOUT A-SCIENCE?
TEENAGE POT-WASHER DOESN'T KNOW

A letter received recently by a prominent local atomic scientist points up Dr. Sugarman's complaint (see adjoining column) that the public does not appreciate how hard a physicist works. The text, complete with "mathematics" follows:

Esteemed Sir:
Beg to introduce self to you the Atomic Scientist as youth 17 working——

"Yes," I told the admiral. "I wrote it, except for the headline. What about it?"

He snapped: "The letter is purportedly from a New York youth seeking information, yet there is no address for him given. Why is that?"

I said patiently: "I left it off when I copied it for the composing room. That's *Trib* style on readers' letters. *What* is all this about?"

He ignored the question and asked: "Where is the purported original of the letter?"

I thought hard and told him: "I think I stuck it in my pants pocket. I'll get it——" I started for the chair with my suit draped over it.

"*Hold it, mister!*" said the young man at the bathroom door. I held it and he proceeded to go through the pockets of the suit. He found the Gomez letter in the inside breast pocket of the coat and passed it to the admiral. The old man compared it, word for word, with the clipping and then put them both in his pocket.

"I want to thank you for your cooperation," he said coldly to me and the Sunday editor. "I caution you not to discuss, and above all not to publish, any account of this incident. The national security is involved in the highest degree. Good day."

He and his boys started for the door, and the Sunday editor came to life. "Admiral," he said, "this is going to be on the front page of tomorrow's *Trib*."

The admiral went white. After a long pause he said: "You are aware that this country may be plunged into global war at any moment. That American boys are dying every day in border skirmishes. Is it to protect civilians like you who won't obey a reasonable request affecting security?"

The Sunday editor took a seat on the edge of my rumpled bed and lit a cigarette. "I know all that, admiral," he said. "I also know that this is a free country and how to keep it that way. Pitiless light on incidents like this of illegal search and seizure."

The admiral said: "I personally assure you, on my honor as an officer, that you would be doing the country a grave disservice by publishing an account of this."

The Sunday editor said mildly: "Your honor as an officer. You broke into this room without a search warrant. Don't you realize that's against the law? And I saw your boy ready to shoot when Vilchek started for that chair." I began to sweat a little at that, but the admiral was sweating harder.

With an effort he said: "I should apologize for the abruptness and discourtesy with which I've treated you. I do apologize. My only excuse is that, as I've said, this is a crash-priority matter. May I have your assurance that you gentlemen will keep silent?"

"On one condition," said the Sunday editor. "I want the *Trib* to have an exclusive on the Gomez story. I want Mr. Vilchek to cover it, with your full cooperation. In return, we'll hold it for your release and submit it to your security censorship."

"It's a deal," said the admiral, sourly. He seemed to realize suddenly that the Sunday editor had been figuring on such a deal all along.

On the plane for New York, the admiral filled me in. He was precise and unhappy, determined to make the best of a bad job. "I was awakened at three this morning by a phone call from the chairman of the Atomic Energy Commission. *He* had been awakened by a call from Dr. Monroe of the Scientific Advisory Committee. Dr. Monroe had been up late working and sent out for the Sunday *Tribune* to read before going to sleep. He saw the Gomez letter and went off like a 16-inch rifle. The neutron cross-section absorption relationship expressed in it happens to be, Mr. Vilchek, his own work. It also happens to be one of the nation's most closely-guarded—er— atomic secrets. Presumably this Gomez stumbled on it somehow, as a janitor or something of the sort, and is feeding his ego by pretending to be an atomic scientist."

I scratched my unshaved jaw. "Admiral," I said, "you wouldn't kid me? How can three equations be a top atomic secret?"

The admiral hesitated. "All I can tell you," he said slowly, "is that breeder reactors are involved."

"But the letter said that. You mean this Gomez not only swiped the equations but knew what they were about?"

The admiral said grimly: "Somebody has been incredibly lax. It would be worth many divisions to the Soviet for their man Kapitza to see those equations—and realize that they are valid."

He left me to chew that one over for a while as the plane droned over New Jersey. Finally the pilot called back: "E.T.A. five minutes, sir. We have landing priority at Newark."

"Good," said the admiral. "Signal for a civilian-type car to pick us up without loss of time."

"Civilian," I said.

"Of course civilian!" he snapped. "That's the hell of it. Above all we must not arouse suspicion that there is anything special or unusual about this Gomez or his letter. Copies of the *Tribune* are on their way to the Soviet now as a matter of routine—they take all American papers and magazines they can get. If we tried to stop shipment of *Tribunes* that would be an immediate give-away that there was something of importance going on."

We landed and the five of us got into a late-model car, neither drab nor flashy. One of the admiral's young men relieved the driver, a corporal with Signal Corps insignia. There wasn't much talk during the drive from Newark to Spanish Harlem, New York. Just once the admiral lit a cigarette, but he flicked it through the window after a couple of nervous puffs.

The Porto Bello Lunchroom was a store-front restaurant in the middle of a shabby tenement block. Wide-eyed, graceful, skinny little kids stared as our car parked in front of it and then converged on us purposefully. "Watch your car, mister?" they begged. The admiral surprised them—and me—with a flood of Spanish that sent the little extortionists scattering back to their stickball game in the street and their potsy layouts chalked on the sidewalks.

"Higgins," said the admiral, "see if there's a back exit." One of his boys got out and walked around the block under the dull, incurious eyes of black-shawled women sitting on their stoops. He was back in five minutes, shaking his head.

"Vilchek and I will go in," said the admiral. "Higgins, stand by the restaurant door and tackle anyone who comes flying out. Let's go, reporter. And remember that I do the talking."

The noon-hour crowd at the Porto Bello's ten tables looked up at us when we came in. The admiral said to a woman at a primitive cashier's table: "*Nueva York* Board of Health, *señora.*"

"*Ah!*" she muttered angrily. "*Por favor, no aquí!* In back, understand? Come." She beckoned a pretty waitress to take over at the cash drawer and led us into the steamy little kitchen. It was crowded with us, an old cook and a young dishwasher. The admiral and the woman began a rapid exchange of Spanish. He played his part well. I myself couldn't keep my eyes off the kid dishwasher who somehow or other had got hold of one of America's top atomic secrets.

Gomez was seventeen, but he looked fifteen. He was small-boned and lean, with skin the color of bright Virginia tobacco in an English cigarette. His hair was straight and glossy-black and a little long. Every so often he wiped his hands on his apron and brushed it back from his damp forehead. He was working like hell, dipping and swabbing and rinsing and drying like a machine, but he didn't look pushed or angry. He wore a half-smile that I later found out was his normal, relaxed expression and his eyes were far away from the kitchen of the Porto Bello Lunchroom. The elderly cook was making it clear by the exaggerated violence of his gesture and a savage frown that he resented these people invading his territory. I don't think Gomez even knew we were there. A sudden, crazy idea came into my head.

The admiral had turned to him. "*Como se llama, chico?*"

He started and put down the dish he was wiping. "Julio Gomez, *señor. Por que, por favor? Que pasa?*"

He wasn't the least bit scared.

"*Nueva York* Board of Health," said the admiral. "*Con su permiso—*" He took Gomez' hands in his and looked at them gravely, front and back, making *tsk-tsk* noises. Then, decisively: "*Vamanos, Julio. Siento mucho. Usted esta muy enfermo.*" Everybody started talking at once, the woman doubtless objecting to the slur on her restaurant and the cook to losing his dishwasher and Gomez to losing time from the job.

The admiral gave them broadside for broadside and outlasted them. In five minutes we were leading Gomez silently from the restaurant. "*La lotería!*" a woman customer said in a loud whisper. "*O las mutas,*" somebody said back. Arrested for policy or marihuana, they thought. The pretty waitress at the cashier's table looked stricken and said nervously: "Julio?" as we passed, but he didn't notice.

Gomez sat in the car with the half-smile on his lips and his eyes a million miles away as we rolled downtown to Foley Square. The admiral didn't look as though he'd approve of any questions from me. We got out at the Federal Building and Gomez spoke at last. He said in surprise: "This, it is not the hospital!"

Nobody answered. We marched him up the steps and surrounded him in the elevator. It would have made anybody nervous—it would have made *me* nervous—to be herded like that; everybody's got something on his conscience. But the kid didn't even seem to notice. I decided that he must be a half-wit or—there came that crazy notion again.

The glass door said "U. S. Atomic Energy Commission, Office of Security and Intelligence." The people behind it were flabbergasted when the admiral and party walked in. He turned the head man out of his office and sat at his desk, with Gomez getting the caller's chair. The rest of us stationed ourselves uncomfortably around the room.

It started. The admiral produced the letter and asked in English: "Have you ever seen this before?" He made it clear from the way he held it that Gomez wasn't going to get his hands on it.

"*Si, seguro.* I write it last week. This is funny business. I am not really sick like you say, no?" He seemed relieved.

"No. Where did you get these equations?"

Gomez said proudly: "I work them out."

The admiral gave a disgusted little laugh. "Don't waste my time, boy. Where did you get these equations?"

Gomez was beginning to get upset. "You got no right to call me liar," he said. "I not so smart as the big physicists, *seguro,* and maybe I make mistakes. Maybe I waste the *profesór* Soo-har-man his time but he got no right to have me arrest. I tell him right in letter he don't have to answer if he don't want. I make no crime and you got no right!"

The admiral looked bored. "Tell me how you worked the equations out," he said.

"Okay," said Gomez sulkily. "You know the random paths of neutron is expressed in matrix mechanics by *profesór* Oppenheim five years ago, all okay. I transform his equations from path-prediction domain to cross-section domain and integrate over absorption areas. This gives u series and v series. And from there, the u-v relationship is obvious, no?"

The admiral, still bored, asked: "Got it?"

I noticed that one of his young men had a shorthand pad out. He said: "Yes."

The admiral picked up the phone and said: "This is MacDonald. Get me Dr. Mines out at Brookhaven right away." He told Gomez blandly: "Dr.

Mines is the chief of the A.E.C. Theoretical Physics Division. I'm going to ask him what he thinks of the way you worked the equations out. He's going to tell me that you were just spouting a lot of gibberish. And then you're going to tell me where you *really* got them."

Gomez looked mixed up and the admiral turned back to the phone. "Dr. Mines? This is Admiral MacDonald of Security. I want your opinion on the following." He snapped his fingers impatiently and the stenographer passed him his pad. "Somebody has told me that he discovered a certain relationship by taking—" He read carefully. "—by taking the random paths of a neutron expressed in matrix mechanics by Oppenheim, transforming his equations from the path-prediction domain to the cross-section domain and integrating over the absorption areas."

In the silence of the room I could hear the faint buzz of the voice on the other end. And a great red blush spread over the admiral's face from his brow to his neck. The faintly-buzzing voice ceased and after a long pause the admiral said slowly and softly: "No, it wasn't Fermi or Szilard. I'm not at liberty to tell you who. Can you come right down to the Federal Building Security Office in New York? I—I need your help. Crash priority." He hung up the phone wearily and muttered to himself: "Crash priority. Crash." And wandered out of the office looking dazed.

His young men stared at one another in frank astonishment. "Five years," said one, "and—"

"*Nix*," said another, looking pointedly at me.

Gomez asked brightly: "What goes on anyhow? This is damn funny business, I think."

"Relax, kid," I told him. "Looks as if you'll make out all—"

"*Nix*," said the nixer again savagely, and I shut up and waited.

After a while somebody came in with coffee and sandwiches and we ate them. After another while the admiral came in with Dr. Mines. Mines was a white-haired, wrinkled Connecticut Yankee. All I knew about him was that he'd been in mild trouble with Congress for stubbornly plugging world government and getting on some of the wrong letterheads. But I learned right away that he was all scientist and didn't have a phony bone in his body.

"Mr. Gomez?" he asked cheerfully. "The admiral tells me that you are either a well-trained Russian spy or a phenomenal self-taught nuclear physicist. He wants me to find out which."

"Russia?" yelled Gomez, outraged. "He crazy! I am American United States citizen!"

"That's as may be," said Dr. Mines. "Now, the admiral tells me you describe the *u-v* relationship as 'obvious.' I should call it a highly abstruse derivation in the theory of continued fractions and complex multiplication."

Gomez strangled and gargled helplessly trying to talk, and finally asked, his eyes shining: "*Por favor*, could I have piece paper?"

They got him a stack of paper and the party was on.

For two unbroken hours Gomez and Dr. Mines chattered and scribbled. Mines gradually shed his jacket, vest and tie, completely oblivious to the rest of us. Gomez was even more abstracted. He *didn't* shed his jacket, vest and tie. He didn't seem to be aware of anything except the rapid-fire exchange of ideas via scribbled formulae and the terse spoken jargon of mathematics. Dr. Mines shifted on his chair and sometimes his voice rose with excitement. Gomez didn't shift or wriggle or cross his legs. He just sat and scribbled and talked in a low, rapid monotone, looking straight at Dr. Mines with his eyes very wide-open and lit up like searchlights.

The rest of us just watched and wondered.

Dr. Mines broke at last. He stood up and said: "I can't take any more, Gomez. I've got to think it over—" He began to leave the room, mechanically scooping up his clothes, and then realized that we were still there.

"Well?" asked the admiral grimly.

Dr. Mines smiled apologetically. "He's a physicist, all right," he said. Gomez sat up abruptly and looked astonished.

"Take him into the next office, Higgins," said the admiral. Gomez let himself be led away, like a sleepwalker.

Dr. Mines began to chuckle. "Security!" he said. "Security!"

The admiral rasped: "Don't trouble yourself over my decisions, if you please, Dr. Mines. My job is keeping the Soviets from pirating American science and I'm doing it to the best of my ability. What I want from you is your opinion on the possibility of that young man having worked out the equations as he claimed."

Dr. Mines was abruptly sobered. "Yes," he said. "Unquestionably he did. And will you excuse my remark? I was under some strain in trying to keep up with Gomez."

"Certainly," said the admiral, and managed a frosty smile. "Now if you'll be so good as to tell me how this completely impossible thing can have happened—?"

"It's happened before, admiral," said Dr. Mines. "I don't suppose you ever heard of Ramanujan?"

"No."

"*Srinivasa* Ramanujan?"

"*No!*"

"Oh. Well, Ramanujan was born in 1887 and died in 1920. He was a poor Hindu who failed twice in college and then settled down as a government clerk. With only a single obsolete textbook to go on he made himself a very great mathematician. In 1913 he sent some of his original work to a Cambridge professor. He was immediately recognized and called to England where he was accepted as a first-rank man, became a member of the Royal Society, a Fellow of Trinity and so forth."

The admiral shook his head dazedly.

"It happens," Dr. Mines said. "Oh yes, it happens. Ramanujan had only one out-of-date book. But this is New York. Gomez has access to all the mathematics he could hope for and a great mass of unclassified and declassified nuclear data. And—genius. The way he puts things together . . . he seems to have only the vaguest notion of what a proof should be. He *sees* relationships as a whole. A most convenient faculty which I envy him. Where I have to take, say, a dozen painful steps from one conclusion to the next he achieves it in one grand flying leap. Ramanujan was like that too, by the way—very strong on intuition, weak on what we call 'rigor.'" Dr. Mines noted with a start that he was holding his tie, vest and coat in one hand and began to put them on. "Was there anything else?" he asked politely.

"One thing," said the admiral. "Would you say he's—he's a better physicist than you are?"

"Yes," said Dr. Mines. "Much better." And he left.

The admiral slumped, uncharacteristically, at the desk for a long time. Finally he said to the air: "Somebody get me the General Manager. No, the Chairman of the Commission." One of his boys grabbed the phone and got to work on the call.

"Admiral," I said, "where do we stand now?"

"Eh? Oh, it's you. The matter's out of my hands now since no security violation is involved. I consider Gomez to be in my custody and I shall turn him over to the Commission so that he may be put to the best use in the nation's interest."

"Like a machine?" I asked, disgusted.

He gave me both barrels of his ice-blue eyes. "Like a weapon," he said evenly.

He was right, of course. Didn't I know there was a war on? Of course I did. Who didn't? Taxes, housing shortage, somebody's cousin killed in Korea, everybody's kid brother sweating out the draft, prices sky-high at the supermarket. Uncomfortably I scratched my unshaved chin and walked to the window. Foley Square below was full of Sunday peace, with only a single girl stroller to be seen. She walked the length of the block across the street from the Federal Building and then turned and walked back. Her walk was dragging and hopeless and tragic.

Suddenly I knew her. She was the pretty little waitress from the Porto Bello; she must have hopped a cab and followed the men who were taking her Julio away. Might as well beat it, sister, I told her silently. Julio isn't just a good-looking kid any more; he's a military asset. The Security Office is turning him over to the policy-level boys for disposal. When that happens you might as well give up and go home.

It was as if she'd heard me. Holding a silly little handkerchief to her face she turned and ran blindly for the subway entrance at the end of the block and disappeared into it.

At that moment the telephone rang.

"MacDonald here," said the admiral. "I'm ready to report on the Gomez affair, Mr. Commissioner."

Gomez was a minor, so his parents signed a contract for him. The job-description on the contract doesn't matter, but he got a pretty good salary by government standards and a per-diem allowance too.

I signed a contract, too—"Information Specialist." I was partly companion, partly historian and partly a guy they'd rather have their eyes on than not. When somebody tried to cut me out on grounds of economy, Admiral

MacDonald frostily reminded him that he had given his word. I stayed, for all the good it did me.

We didn't have any name. We weren't Operation Anything or Project Whoozis or Task Force Dinwiddie. We were just five people in a big fifteen-room house on the outskirts of Milford, New Jersey. There was Gomez, alone on the top floor with a lot of books, technical magazines and blackboards and a weekly visit from Dr. Mines. There were the three Security men, Higgins, Dalhousie and Leitzer, sleeping by turns and prowling the grounds. And there was me.

From briefing sessions with Dr. Mines I kept a diary of what went on. Don't think from that that I knew what the score was. War correspondents have told me of the frustrating life they led at some close-mouthed commands. Soandso-many air sorties, the largest number since January fifteenth. Casualties a full fifteen per cent lighter than expected. Determined advance in an active sector against relatively strong enemy opposition. And so on— all adding up to nothing in the way of real information.

That's what it was like in my diary because that's all they told me. Here are some excerpts: "On the recommendation of Dr. Mines, Mr. Gomez today began work on a phase of reactor design theory to be implemented at Brookhaven National Laboratory. The work involves the setting-up of thirty-five pairs of partial differential equations . . . Mr. Gomez announced tentatively today that in checking certain theoretical work in progress at the Los Alamos Laboratory of the A.E.C. he discovered a fallacious assumption concerning neutron-spin which invalidates the conclusions reached. This will be communicated to the Laboratory . . . Dr. Mines said today that Mr. Gomez has successfully invoked a hitherto-unexploited aspect of Minkowski's tensor analysis to crack a stubborn obstacle towards the control of thermonuclear reactions . . ."

I protested at one of the briefing sessions with Dr. Mines against this gobbledygook. He didn't mind my protesting. He leaned back in his chair and said calmly: "Vilchek, with all friendliness I assure you that you're getting everything you can understand. Anything more complex than the vague description of what's going on would be over your head. And anything more specific would give away exact engineering information which would be of use to foreign countries."

"This isn't the way they treated Bill Lawrence when he covered the atomic bomb," I said bitterly.

Mines nodded, with a pleased smile. "That's it exactly," he said. "Broad principles were being developed then—interesting things that could be told without any great harm being done. If you tell somebody that a critical mass of U-235 or Plutonium goes off with a big bang, you really haven't given away a great deal. He still has millions of man-hours of engineering before him to figure out how much is critical mass, to take only one small point."

So I took his word for it, faithfully copied the communiques he gave me and wrote what I could on the human-interest side for release some day.

So I recorded Gomez' progress with English, his taste for chicken pot pie and rice pudding, his habit of doing his own housework on the top floor and his old-maidish neatness. "You live your first fifteen years in a tin shack, Beel," he told me once, "and you find out you like things nice and clean." I've seen Dr. Mines follow Gomez through the top floor as the boy swept and dusted, talking at him in their mathematical jargon.

Gomez worked in forty-eight-hour spells usually, and not eating much. Then for a couple of days he'd live like a human being grabbing naps, playing catch on the lawn with one or another of the Security people, talking with me about his childhood in Puerto Rico and his youth in New York. He taught me a little Spanish and asked me to catch him up on bad mistakes in English.

"But don't you ever want to get out of here?" I demanded one day.

He grinned: "Why should I, Beel? Here I eat good, I can send money to the parents. Best, I find out what the big professors are up to without I have to wait five-ten years for damn de-classifying."

"Don't you have a girl?"

He was embarrassed and changed the subject back to the big professors.

Dr. Mines drove up then, with his chauffeur who looked like a G-man and almost certainly was. As usual, the physicist was toting a bulging briefcase. After a few polite words with me, he and Julio went indoors and upstairs.

They were closeted for five hours—a record. When Dr. Mines came down I expected the usual briefing session. But he begged off. "Nothing serious," he said. "We just sat down and kicked some ideas of his around. I told him to go ahead. We've been—ah—using him very much like a sort of computer, you know. Turning him loose on the problems that were too tough for me and some of the other men. He's got the itch for research now. It would be very interesting if his forte turned out to be creative."

I agreed.

Julio didn't come down for dinner. I woke up in darkness that night when there was a loud bump overhead, and went upstairs in my pyjamas.

Gomez was sprawled, fully dressed, on the floor. He'd tripped over a footstool. And he didn't seem to have noticed. His lips were moving and he stared straight at me without knowing I was there.

"You all right, Julio?" I asked, and started to help him to his feet.

He got up mechanically and said: "—real values of the zeta function vanish."

"How's that?"

He saw me then and asked, puzzled: "How you got in here, Beel? Is dinnertime?"

"Is four A.M., *por dios*. Don't you think you ought to get some sleep?" He looked terrible.

No; he didn't think he ought to get some sleep. He had some work to do. I went downstairs and heard him pacing overhead for an hour until I dozed off.

This splurge of work didn't wear off in forty-eight hours. For a week I brought him meals and sometimes he ate absently, with one hand, as he scribbled on a yellow pad. Sometimes I'd bring him lunch to find his breakfast untouched. He didn't have much beard, but he let it grow for a week—too busy to shave, too busy to talk, too busy to eat, sleeping in chairs when fatigue caught up with him.

I asked Leitzer, badly worried, if we should do anything about it. He had a direct scrambler-phone connection with the New York Security and Intelligence office, but his orders didn't cover anything like a self-induced nervous breakdown of the man he was guarding.

I thought Dr. Mines would do something when he came—call in an M.D., or tell Gomez to take it easy, or take some of the load off by parcelling out whatever he had by the tail.

But he didn't. He went upstairs, came down two hours later and absently tried to walk past me. I headed him off into my room. "What's the word?" I demanded.

He looked me in the eye and said defiantly: "He's doing fine. I don't want to stop him."

Dr. Mines was a good man. Dr. Mines was a humane man. And he wouldn't lift a finger to keep the boy from working himself into nervous prostration. Dr. Mines liked people well enough, but he reserved his love for theoretical physics. "How important can this thing be?"

He shrugged irritably. "It's just the way some scientists work," he said. "Newton was like that. So was Sir William Rowan Hamilton—"

"Hamilton-Schmamilton," I said. "What's the sense of it? *Why* doesn't he sleep or eat?"

Mines said: "*You* don't know what it's like."

"Of course," I said, getting good and sore. "I'm just a dumb newspaper man. Tell me, Mr. Bones, what is it like?"

There was a long pause, and he said mildly: "I'll try. That boy up there is using his brain. A great chess player can put on a blindfold and play a hundred opponents in a hundred games simultaneously, remembering all the positions of his pieces and theirs and keeping a hundred strategies clear in his mind. Well, that stunt simply isn't in the same league with what Julio's doing up there.

"He has in his head some millions of facts concerning theoretical physics. He's scanning them, picking out one here and there, fitting them into new relationships, checking and rejecting when he has to, fitting the new relationships together, turning them upside-down and inside-out to see what happens, comparing them with known doctrine, holding them in his memory while he repeats the whole process and compares—and all the while he has a goal firmly in mind against which he's measuring all these things." He seemed to be finished.

For a reporter, I felt strangely shy. "What's he driving at?" I asked.

"I think," he said slowly, "he's approaching a unified field theory."

Apparently that was supposed to explain everything. I let Dr. Mines know that it didn't.

He said thoughtfully: "I don't know whether I can get it over to a layman—no offense, Vilchek. Let's put it this way. You know how math comes in waves, and how it's followed by waves of applied science based on the math. There was a big wave of algebra in the middle ages—following it came navigation, gunnery, surveying and so on. Then the renaissance and a wave of analysis—what you'd call calculus. That opened up steam power and how to use it, mechanical engineering, electricity. The wave of *modern* mathematics since say 1875 gave us atomic energy. That boy upstairs may be starting off the next big wave."

He got up and reached for his hat.

"Just a minute," I said. I was surprised that my voice was steady. "What comes next? Control of gravity? Control of personality? Sending people by radio?"

Dr. Mines wouldn't meet my eye. Suddenly he looked old and shrunken. "Don't worry about the boy," he said.

I let him go.

That evening I brought Gomez chicken pot pie and a non-alcoholic egg nog. He drank the egg nog, said "Hi, Beel," and continued to cover yellow sheets of paper.

I went downstairs and worried.

Abruptly it ended late the next afternoon. Gomez wandered into the big first-floor kitchen looking like a starved old rickshaw coolie. He pushed his lank hair back from his forehead, said: "Beel, what is to eat—" and pitched forward onto the linoleum. Leitzer came when I yelled, expertly took Gomez' pulse, rolled him onto a blanket and threw another one over him. "It's just a faint," he said. "Let's get him to bed."

"Aren't you going to call a doctor, man?"

"Doctor couldn't do anything we can't do," he said stolidly. "And I'm here to see that security isn't breached. Give me a hand."

We got him upstairs and put him to bed. He woke up and said something in Spanish, and then, apologetically: "Very sorry, fellows. I ought to taken it easier."

"I'll get you some lunch," I said, and he grinned.

He ate it all, enjoying it heartily, and finally lay back gorged. "Well," he asked me, "what it is new, Beel?"

"What *is* new. And you should tell me. You finish your work?"

"I got it in shape to finish. The hard part it is over." He rolled out of bed.

"Hey!" I said.

"I'm okay now," he grinned. "Don't write this down in your history, Beel. Everybody will think I act like a woman."

I followed him into his work room where he flopped into an easy chair, his eyes on a blackboard covered with figures. He wasn't grinning any more.

"Dr. Mines says you're up to something big," I said.

"*Si.* Big."

"Unified field theory, he says."

"That is it," Gomez said.

"Is it good or bad?" I asked, licking my lips. "The application, I mean."

His boyish mouth set suddenly in a grim line. "That, it is not my business," he said. "I am American citizen of the United States." He stared at the blackboard and its maze of notes.

I looked at it too—*really* looked at it for once—and was surprised by what I saw. Mathematics, of course, I don't know. But I had soaked up a very little *about* mathematics. One of the things I had soaked up was that the expressions of higher mathematics tend to be complicated and elaborate, involving English, Greek and Hebrew letters, plain and fancy brackets and a great variety of special signs besides the plus and minus of the elementary school.

The things on the blackboard weren't like that at all. The board was covered with variations of a simple expression that consisted of five letters and two symbols: a right-handed pothook and a left-handed pothook.

"What do they mean?" I asked, pointing.

"Somethings I made up," he said nervously. "The word for that one is 'enfields.' The other one is 'is enfielded by.' "

"What's *that* mean?"

His luminous eyes were haunted. He didn't answer.

"It looks like simple stuff. I read somewhere that all the basic stuff is simple once it's been discovered."

"Yes," he said almost inaudibly. "It is simple, Beel. Too damn simple, I think. Better I carry it in my head, I think." He strode to the blackboard and erased it. Instinctively I half-rose to stop him. He gave me a grin that was somehow bitter and unlike him. "Don't worry," he said. "I don't forget it." He tapped his forehead. "I *can't* forget it." I hope I never see again on any face the look that was on his.

"Julio," I said, appalled. "Why don't you get out of here for a while? Why don't you run over to New York and see your folks and have some fun? They can't keep you here against your will."

"They told me I shouldn't—" he said uncertainly. And then he got tough. "You're damn right, Beel. Let's go in together. I get dressed up. Er— You tell Leitzer, hah?" He couldn't quite face up to the hard-boiled security man.

I told Leitzer, who hit the ceiling. But all it boiled down to was that he sincerely wished Gomez and I wouldn't leave. We weren't in the Army, we weren't in jail. I got hot at last and yelled back that we were damn well going out and he couldn't stop us. He called New York on his direct wire and apparently New York confirmed it, regretfully.

We got on the 4:05 Jersey Central, with Higgins and Dalhousie tailing us at a respectful distance. Gomez didn't notice them and I didn't tell him. He was having too much fun. He had a shine put on his shoes at Penn Station and worried about the taxi fare as we rode up to Spanish Harlem.

His parents lived in a neat little three-room apartment. A lot of the furniture looked brand-new, and I was pretty sure who had paid for it. The mother and father spoke only Spanish, and mumbled shyly when "*mi amigo Beel*" was introduced. I had a very halting conversation with the father while the mother and Gomez rattled away happily and she poked his ribs to point up the age-old complaint of any mother anywhere that he wasn't eating enough.

The father, of course, thought the boy was a janitor or something in the Pentagon and, as near as I could make out, he was worried about his Julio being grabbed off by a man-hungry government girl. I kept reassuring him that his Julio was a good boy, a very good boy, and he seemed to get some comfort out of it.

There was a little spat when his mother started to set the table. Gomez said reluctantly that we couldn't stay, that we were eating somewhere else. His mother finally dragged from him the admission that we were going to the Porto Bello so he could see Rosa, and everything was smiles again. The father told me that Rosa was a good girl, a very good girl.

Walking down the three flights of stairs with yelling little kids playing tag around us, Gomez asked proudly: "You not think they in America only a little time, hey?"

I yanked him around by the elbow as we went down the brownstone stoop into the street. Otherwise he would have seen our shadows for sure. I didn't want to spoil his fun.

The Porto Bello was full, and the pretty little girl was on duty as cashier at the table. Gomez got a last-minute attack of cold feet at the sight of her. "No table," he said. "We better go someplace else."

I practically dragged him in. "We'll get a table in a minute," I said.

"Julio," said the girl, when she saw him.

He looked sheepish. "Hello, Rosa. I'm back for a while."

"I'm glad to see you again," she said tremulously.

"I'm glad to see you again too—" I nudged him. "Rosa, this is my good friend Beel. We work together in Washington."

"Pleased to meet you, Rosa. Can you have dinner with us? I'll bet you and Julio have a lot to talk over."

"Well, I'll see . . . look, there's a table for you. I'll see if I can get away."

We sat down and she flagged down the proprietress and got away in a hurry.

All three of us had *arróz con pollo*—rice with chicken and lots of other things. Their shyness wore off and I was dealt out of the conversation, but I didn't mind. They were a nice young couple. I liked the way they smiled at each other, and the things they remembered happily—movies, walks, talks. It made me feel like a benevolent uncle with one foot in the grave. It made me forget for a while the look on Gomez' face when he turned from the blackboard he had covered with too-simple math.

Over dessert I broke in. By then they were unselfconsciously holding hands. "Look," I said, "why don't you two go on and do the town? Julio, I'll be at the Madison Park Hotel." I scribbled the address and gave it to him. "And I'll get a room for you. Have fun and reel in any time." I rapped his knee. He looked down and I slipped him four twenties. I didn't know whether he had money on him or not, but anything extra the boy could use he had coming to him.

"Swell," he said. "Thanks." And looked shame-faced while I looked paternal.

I had been watching a young man who was moodily eating alone in a corner, reading a paper. He was about Julio's height and build and he wore a sports jacket pretty much like Julio's. And the street was pretty dark outside.

The young man got up moodily and headed for the cashier's table. "Gotta go," I said. "Have fun."

I went out of the restaurant right behind the young man and walked as close behind him as I dared, hoping we were being followed.

After a block and a half of this, he turned on me and snarled: "Wadda you, mister? A wolf? Beat it!"

"Okay," I said mildly, and turned and walked the other way. Higgins and Dalhousie were standing there, flat-footed and open-mouthed. They sprinted back to the Porto Bello, and I followed *them*. But Julio and Rosa had already left.

"Tough, fellows," I said to them as they stood in the doorway. They looked as if they wanted to murder me. "He won't get into any trouble," I said. "He's just going out with his girl." Dalhousie made a strangled noise and told Higgins: "Cruise around the neighborhood. See if you can pick them up. I'll follow Vilchek." He wouldn't talk to me. I shrugged and got a cab and went to the Madison Park Hotel, a pleasantly unfashionable old place with big rooms where I stay when business brings me to New York. They had a couple of adjoining singles; I took one in my own name and the other for Gomez.

I wandered around the neighborhood for a while and had a couple of beers in one of the ultra-Irish bars on Third Avenue. After a pleasant argument with a gent who thought the Russians didn't have any atomic bombs and faked their demonstrations and that we ought to blow up their industrial cities tomorrow at dawn, I went back to the hotel.

I didn't get to sleep easily. The citizen who didn't believe Russia could maul the United States pretty badly or at all had started me thinking again —all kinds of ugly thoughts. Dr. Mines who had turned into a shrunken old man at the mention of applying Gomez' work. The look on the boy's face. My layman's knowledge that present-day "atomic energy" taps only the smallest fragment of the energy locked up in the atom. My layman's knowledge that once genius has broken a trail in science, mediocrity can follow the trail.

But I slept at last, for three hours.

At four-fifteen A.M. according to my watch the telephone rang long and hard. There was some switchboard and long-distance-operator mumbo-jumbo and then Julio's gleeful voice: "Beel! Congratulate us. We got marriage!"

"Married," I said fuzzily. "You got *married*, not marriage. How's that again?"

"We got *married*. Me and Rosa. We get on the train, the taxi driver takes us to justice of peace, we got *married*, we go to hotel here."

"Congratulations," I said, waking up. "Lots of congratulations. But you're under age, there's a waiting period—"

"Not in this state," he chuckled. "Here is no waiting periods and here I have twenty-one years if I say so."

"Well," I said. "Lots of congratulations, Julio. And tell Rosa she's got herself a good boy."

"Thanks, Beel," he said shyly. "I call you so you don't worry when I don't come in tonight. I think I come in with Rosa tomorrow so we tell her mama and my mama and papa. I call you at the hotel, I still have the piece of paper."

"Okay, Julio. All the best. Don't worry about a thing." I hung up, chuckling, and went right back to sleep.

Well, sir, it happened again.

I was shaken out of my sleep by the strong, skinny hand of Admiral MacDonald. It was seven-thirty and a bright New York morning. Dalhousie had pulled a blank canvassing the neighborhood for Gomez, got panicky and bucked it up to higher headquarters.

"Where is he?" the admiral rasped.

"On his way here with his bride of one night," I said. "He slipped over a couple of state lines and got married."

"By God," the admiral said, "we've got to do something about this. I'm going to have him drafted and assigned to special duty. This is the last time—"

"Look," I said. "You've got to stop treating him like a chess piece. You've got duty-honor-country on the brain and thank God for that. Somebody has to; it's your profession. But can't you get it through your head that Gomez is a kid and that you're wrecking his life by forcing him to grind out science like a machine? And I'm just a stupe of a layman, but have you professionals worried once about digging too deep and blowing up the whole shebang?"

He gave me a piercing look and said nothing.

I dressed and had breakfast sent up. The admiral, Dalhousie and I waited grimly until noon, and then Gomez phoned up.

"Come on up, Julio," I said tiredly.

He breezed in with his blushing bride on his arm. The admiral rose automatically as she entered, and immediately began tongue-lashing the boy. He spoke more in sorrow than in anger. He made it clear that Gomez wasn't treating his country right. That he had a great talent and it belonged to the United States. That his behavior had been irresponsible. That Gomez would have to come to heel and realize that his wishes weren't the most important thing in his life. That he could and would be drafted if there were any more such escapades.

"As a starter, Mr. Gomez," the admiral snapped, "I want you to set down, immediately, the enfieldment matrices you have developed. I consider it almost criminal of you to arrogantly and carelessly trust to your memory alone matters of such vital importance. Here!" He thrust pencil and paper at the boy, who stood, drooping and disconsolate. Little Rosa was near crying. She didn't have the ghost of a notion as to what it was about.

Gomez took the pencil and paper and sat down at the writing table silently. I took Rosa by the arm. She was trembling. "It's all right," I said. "They can't do a thing to him." The admiral glared briefly at me and then returned his gaze to Gomez.

The boy made a couple of tentative marks. Then his eyes went wide and he clutched his hair. "*Dios mio!*" he said. "*Esta perdido! Olvidado!*"

Which means: "My God, it's lost! Forgotten!"

The admiral turned white beneath his tan. "Now, boy," he said slowly and soothingly. "I didn't mean to scare you. You just relax and collect yourself. Of course you haven't forgotten, not with that memory of yours. Start with something easy. Write down a general biquadratic equation, say."

Gomez just looked at him. After a long pause he said in a strangled voice: "*No puedo.* I can't. It too I forget. I don't think of the math or physics at all since—" He looked at Rosa and turned a little red. She smiled shyly and looked at her shoes.

"That is it," Gomez said hoarsely. "Not since then. Always before in the back of my head is the math, but not since then."

"My God," the admiral said softly. "Can such a thing happen?" He reached for the phone.

He found out that such things can happen.

Julio went back to Spanish Harlem and bought a piece of the Porto Bello with his savings. I went back to the paper and bought a car with *my* savings. MacDonald never cleared the story, so the Sunday editor had the satisfaction of bulldozing an admiral, but didn't get his exclusive.

Julio and Rosa sent me a card eventually announcing the birth of their first-born: a six-pound boy, Francisco, named after Julio's father. I saved the card and when a New York assignment came my way—it was the National Association of Dry Goods Wholesalers; dry goods are important in our town—I dropped up to see them.

Julio was a little more mature and a little more prosperous. Rosa—alas! —was already putting on weight, but she was still a pretty thing and devoted to her man. The baby was a honey-skinned little wiggler. It was nice to see all of them together, happy with their lot.

Julio insisted that he'd cook *arróz con pollo* for me, as on the night I practically threw him into Rosa's arms, but he'd have to shop for the stuff. I went along.

In the corner grocery he ordered the rice, the chicken, the garbanzos, the peppers and, swept along by the enthusiasm that hits husbands in groceries, about fifty other things that he thought would be nice to have in the pantry.

The creaking old grocer scribbled down the prices on a shopping bag and began painfully to add them up while Julio was telling me how well the Porto Bello was doing and how they were thinking of renting the adjoining store.

"Seventeen dollars, forty-two cents," the grocer said at last.

Julio flicked one glance at the shopping bag and the upside-down figures. "Should be seventeen thirty-nine," he said reprovingly. "Add up again."

The grocer painfully added up again and said. "Is seventeen thirty-nine. Sorry." He began to pack the groceries into the bag.

"Hey," I said.

We didn't discuss it then or ever. Julio just said: "Don't tell, Beel." And winked.

THE [WIDGET], THE [WADGET], AND BOFF

by Theodore Sturgeon

THROUGHOUT THE CONTINUUM TIN as we know it (and a good deal more, as we don't know it) there are cultures that fly and cultures that swim; there are boron folk and fluorine fellowships, cupro-coprophages and (roughly speaking) immaterial lifeforms which swim and swirl around each other in space like so many pelagic shards of metaphysics. And some organize into super-entities like a beehive or a slime-mold so that they live plurally to become singular, and some have even more singular ideas of plurality.

Now, no matter how an organized culture of intelligent beings is put together or where, regardless of what it's made of or how it lives, there is one thing all cultures have in common, and it is the most obvious of traits. There are as many names for it as there are cultures, of course, but in all it works the same way—the same way the inner ear functions (with its contributory synapses) in a human being when he steps on Junior's roller skate. He doesn't think about how far away the wall is, some wires or your wife, or in which direction: he *grabs*, and, more often than not, he *gets*—accurately and without analysis. Just so does an individual reflexively adjust when imbalanced in his sociocultural matrix: he experiences the reflex of reflexes, a thing as large as the legendary view afforded a drowning man of his entire past, in a single illuminated instant wherein the mind moves, as it were, at right angles to time and travels high and far for its survey.

And this is true of every culture everywhere, the cosmos over. So obvious and necessary a thing is seldom examined: but it was once, by a culture which called this super-reflex "Synapse Beta sub Sixteen."

What came out of the calculator surprised them. They were, after all, expecting an answer.

Human eyes would never have recognized the device for what it was. Its memory bank was an atomic cloud, each particle of which was sealed away from the others by a self-sustaining envelope of force. Subtle differences in nuclei, in probability shells, and in internal tensions were the coding, and fields of almost infinite variability were used to call up the particles in the desired combinations. These were channeled in a way beyond description in earthly mathematics, detected by a principle as yet unknown to us, and translated into language (or, more accurately, an analog of what we understand as language). Since this happened so far away, temporally, spatially, and culturally, proper nouns are hardly proper; it suffices to say that it yielded results, in this particular setting, which were surprising. These were correlated into a report, the gist of which was this:

Prognosis positive, or prognosis negative, depending upon presence or absence of Synapse Beta sub Sixteen.

The pertinent catalog listed the synapse in question as "indetectible except by field survey." Therefore an expedition was sent.

All of which may seem fairly remote until one realizes that the prognosis was being drawn for that youthful and dangerous aggregate of bubbling yeasts called "human culture," and that when the term "prognosis negative" was used it meant *finis*, the end, zero, *ne plus ultra* altogether.

It must be understood that the possessors of the calculator, the personnel of the expedition to Earth, were not Watchers in the Sky and Arbiters of Our Fate. Living in our midst, here and now, is a man who occupies himself with the weightgain of amebae from their natal instant to the moment they fission. There is a man who, having produced neurosis in cats, turns them into alcoholics for study. Someone has at long last settled the matter of the camel's capacity for, and retention of, water. People like these are innocent of designs on the destinies of *all* amebae, cats, camels and cultures; there are simply certain things they want to *know*. This is the case no matter how unusual, elaborate, or ingenious their methods might be. So—an expedition came here for information.

EXCERPT FROM FIELD EXPEDITION [NOTEBOOK]. [VOLUME] ONE: CONCLUSION.
. . . to restate the obvious, [we] have been on Earth long enough and more than long enough to have discovered anything and everything [we] [wished] about any [sensible-predictible-readable] culture anywhere. This one, however, is quite beyond [understanding-accounting-for]. At first sight, [one] was tempted to conclude immediately that it possesses the Synapse, because no previously known culture has advanced to this degree without it, ergo . . . And then [we] checked it with [our] [instruments] [! ! !] [Our] [gimmick] and our [kickshaw] gave [us] absolutely negative readings, so [we] activated a high-sensitivity [snivvy] and got results which approximate nonsense: the Synapse is scattered through the population randomly, here non-existent or dormant, there in brief full activity at [unheard-of] high levels. [I] thought [Smith] would go [out of [his] mind] and as for [myself], [I] had a crippling attack of the [   ]s at the very concept. More for [our] own protection than for the furtherance of the Expedition, [we] submitted all our data to [our] [ship]'s [computer] and got what appeared to be even further nonsense: the conclusion that this species possesses the Synapse but to all intents and purposes does not use it.

How can a species possess Synapse Beta sub Sixteen and not use it? Nonsense, nonsense, nonsense!

So complex and contradictory are [our] data that [we] can only fall back on a microcosmic analysis and proceed by its guidance. [We] shall therefore isolate a group of specimens under [laboratory] control, even though it means using a [miserable] [primitive] [battery]-powered [wadget]. [We]'ll put our new-model [wadget] on the job, too. [We]'ve had enough of this [uncanny, uncomfortable] feeling of standing in the presence of [apology-for-obscenity] paradox.

CHAPTER ONE

THE TOWN WAS OLD ENOUGH to have slums, large enough to have no specific "tracks" with a right and a wrong side. Its nature was such that a boarding house could, without being unusual, contain such varied rungs on the social ladder as a young, widowed night-club hostess and her three-year-old son; a very good vocational guidance expert; a young law clerk; the librarian from the high school; and a stage-struck maiden from a very small small town. They said Sam Bittelman, who nominally owned and operated the boarding house, could have been an engineer, and if he had been, a marine architect as well, but instead he had never risen higher than shop foreman. Whether this constituted failure or success is speculative; apply to a chief petty officer or top sergeant who won't accept a commission, and to the president of your local bank, and take your pick of their arguments. It probably never occurred to Sam to examine the matter. He had other things to amuse him. Tolerant, curious, intensely alive, old Sam had apparently never retired from anything but his job at the shipyards back east.

He in turn was owned and operated by his wife, whom everyone called "Bitty" and who possessed the harshest countenance and the most acid idiom ever found in a charter member of the Suckers for Sick Kittens and Sob Stories Society. Between them they took care of their roomers in that special way possible only in boarding houses which feature a big dining table and a place set for everyone. Such places are less than a family, or more if you value your freedom. They are more than a hotel, or less if you like formality. To Mary Haunt, who claimed to be twenty-two and lied, the place was the most forgettable and soon-to-be-forgotten of stepping stones; to Robin it was home and more: it was the world and the universe, an environment as ubiquitous, unnoticed, and unquestioned as the water around a fish; but Robin would, of course, feel differently later. He was only three. The only other one of the Bittelmans' boarders who breathed what was uniquely the Bittelman quality as if it were air was Phil Halvorsen, a thoughtful young man in the vocational guidance field, whose mind was on food and housing only when they annoyed him, and since the Bittelmans made him quite comfortable, in effect they were invisible. Reta Schmidt appreciated the Bittelmans for a number of things, prime among which was the lengths to which her dollar went with them, for Miss Schmidt's employers were a Board of Education. Mr. Anthony O'Banion permitted himself a genuine admiration of almost nothing in these parts. So it remained for Sue Martin to be the only one in the place who respected and admired them, right from the start, with something approaching their due. Sue was Robin's widowed mother and worked in a night club as hostess and sometime entertainer. She had done, in the past, both better and worse. She still might do better for herself, but only that which would be worse for Robin. The Bittelmans were her godsend. Robin adored them, and the only thing they would not do for him was to spoil him. The Bittelmans were there to give him breakfast in the mornings, to dress him when he went out to play, to watch over him and keep him amused and content until Sue rose at 11. The rest of the day was for Sue and Robin together, right up to his bedtime, when she tucked him in and storied him to sleep. And when she left for work at 9 P.M., the Bittelmans were there, safe and certain, ready and willing to cope with anything from a bladder to a blaze. They were like insurance and fire extinguishers, hardly ever used but comforting by their presence. So she valued them . . . but then, Sue Martin was different from most people. So was Robin; however, this is a truism when speaking of three-year-olds.

Such was the population of Bittelmans' boarding house, and if they seem too many and too varied to sort out all at once, have patience and remember that each of them felt the same way on meeting all the others.

CHAPTER TWO

A PAWNSHOP is a dismal place.

A pawnshop in the rain. A closed pawnshop in the rain, on a Sunday.

Philip Halvorsen did not object. He had a liking for harmony, and the atmosphere suited him well just now, his thoughts, his feelings. A sunbeam would have been an intrusion. A flower shop could not have contributed so much. People, just now, would have been intolerable.

He leaned his forehead against the wet black steel of the burglar-proof gate and idly inventoried the contents of the window and his thoughts about them. Like the window and its contents, and the dark recesses inside, his thoughts were miscellaneous, cluttered, captured in that purgatory of uselessness wherein things are not dead, only finished with what they have been and uncaring of what will happen to them and when. His thoughts were binoculars without eyes, cameras without film, silent guitars and unwound watches.

He found himself approving more of the guitars than the two dirty violins hanging in the window. He almost wondered why this should be, almost let the question disappear into lethargy, and at last sighed and ran the matter down because he knew it would bother him otherwise and he was in no mood to be bothered. He looked at the instruments lazily, one, the other, analyzing and comparing. They had a great deal in common, and some significant differences. Having a somewhat sticky mind, to which windblown oddments of fact had been adhering for nearly 30 years now, he knew of the trial-and-error evolution of those resonance-chambers and of the high degree of perfection they had come to. Given that design followed function in both the violin and the guitar, and aside from any preference in the sounds they made (actually Halvorsen was completely indifferent to music anyway), then why should he intuitively prefer the guitars he saw over the violins? Size, proportion, number of strings, design of bridge, frets or lack of them, finish, peg and tailpiece mechanics—all these had their differences and all were perfect for the work they did.

Suddenly, then, he saw it, and his mind swiftly thumbed through the mental pictures of all the violins he had ever seen. They all checked out. One flickering glance at the guitars in the window settled the matter.

All violins have a scroll carved at the end of the neck—*all* of them. There is scrollwork on some guitars, none on others; it's obviously optional. The back-bending spiral at the end of a violin's neck is not optional, but traditional, and it has no function. Halvorsen nodded slightly and permitted his mind to wander away from the matter. It wasn't important—not in itself; only settling it was important. His original, intuitive approval of guitars over violins was not a matter of moment either; his preference for the functional over the purely traditional was just that—a preference.

None of this required much of Halvorsen's conscious effort or attention. The survey, the sequence, was virtually reflexive, and his thoughts moved as fish in some deep clear pool might move, hanging and hanging, fanning, then suddenly darting about with a swirl and a splash, to hang again fanning, alive and waiting.

He stood motionless, the fine rain soaking into the back of his collar and his eyes unseeking but receptive. Binoculars with mother-of-pearl; binoculars without. A watch with glass rubies in the face. Display cards: cheap combs, cheap wallets, cheap pens. An electric steam iron with a frayed cord. A rack of second-hand clothing.

Guns.

He felt again that vague dissatisfaction, set up a certain amount of lethargic resistance to it, and when it came through anyway he patiently gave it its head. He looked at the guns. What bothered him about the guns?

One had a pearl handle and rococo etching along the barrel, but that wasn't it. He glanced down the row and settled on a .38 automatic, about as functional an artifact as could be imagined—small, square, here knurled and there polished, with the palm safety and lock-safety just where they should be. And still he felt that faint disapproval, that dissatisfaction that spelt criticism. He widened his scan to all the guns, and felt it just as much. Just as little.

It was categorical then. It had to do with all these guns, or with all guns. He looked again, and again, and within this scope found no crevice for the prying of his reason, so he turned the problem on its back and looked again: what would a gun be like if it satisfied this fastidious intuition of his?

It came in a flash, and he hardly believed it: a flimsy structure of rolled sheet metal with a simple firing pin on a piece hinged and sprung like the business part of a rattrap. There was no butt, there were no sights. No trigger either; just a simple catch and—what was that?—and a piece of string. He visualized it sitting on a polished surface on a wire stand, its thin barrel angled upwards about 45°, like a toy cannon. Its caliber was about .38. The feature which struck him most was the feeling of fragility, lightness, in the whole design. Design! What would an object like that be designed *for*?

He looked again at the pawned guns. Among the things they had in common was massiveness. Breeches were cast steel, muzzles thick-walled, probably all rifled; parts were tempered, hardened, milled, designed and built to contain and direct repeated explosions, repeated internal assaults by hot hurtling metal.

It was as if a little red signal-light flickered on the concept *repeated*. Was that it, that all these guns were designed for repeated use? Was he dissatisfied with that? Why?

He conjured up the image of a single-shot dueling pistol he had once handled: long-barreled, muzzle-loading, with a powder-pan for priming and a chip of flint fixed to the hammer. To his surprise he found the little mental red light still aflicker; this was a design that displeased him too, somewhere in the area labeled *repeated*.

Even a single-shot pistol was designed to be used over again; that must be it. Then to him, a gun satisfied its true function only if it was designed to be used only once. *Enough* is the criterion of optimum design, and in this case once was enough.

Halvorsen snorted angrily. He disliked being led by rational means to a patently irrational conclusion. He cast back over his reasoning, looking for the particular crossroads where he must have taken a wrong turning.

There was none.

At this point his leisurely, almost self-powered curiosity was replaced by an incandescent ferocity of examination. Logic burned in Halvorsen as fury did in other men, and he had no tolerance for the irrational. He attacked it as a personal indignity, and would not let up until he had wrapped it up, tied it down, in the fabric of his understanding.

He let himself visualize the "gun" of his satisfied imagination, with its mousetrap firing mechanism, its piece of string, its almost useless flimsiness, and for a moment pictured police, cattlemen, Army officers handling such a ridiculous object. But the vision dissolved and he shook his head; the guns ordinarily used by such people satisfied his sense of function perfectly. He slipped (hypothetically) into the consciousness of such a man and regarded his gun—*a* gun—any gun with satisfaction. No, this seemed a personal matter, unlike the dissatisfaction everyone should feel (if they cared) about the extraordinary fact that automobiles are streamlined only where they show, and are powered by a heat-engine which is inoperable without a cooling system.

What's so special about my mousetrap gun? he demanded of himself, and turned his eye inward to look at it again. There it sat, on a polished surface—table-top, was it?—with its silly piece of string leaning forward toward him and its muzzle tilted upward, unabashedly showing off its sleazy construction.

Why could he see how thin the metal of that muzzle was?

Because it was aimed right at the bridge of his nose.

Make a statement, Halvorsen, and test it. Statement: Other guns satisfy other men because they can be used over and over again. This gun satisfies me because it goes off once, and once is enough.

Test: A dueling pistol goes off only once; yet it can be reloaded and used again. Why not this? Answer: Because whoever uses a dueling pistol expects to be able to use it again. Whoever sees it used expects it will be used again, because the world goes on.

After Halvorsen's mousetrap gun went off, the world wouldn't go on. Not for Halvorsen—which of course is the same thing. "I am the core and center of the universe" is a fair statement for anyone.

So restate, and conclude: The optimum gun design is that which, having shot Halvorsen between the eyes, need no longer exist. Since *optimum* carried with it the flavor of *preferred performance*, it is fair to state that within himself Halvorsen found a preference for being shot to death. More specifically, for dying. Correction: for being dead—gladly.

Momentarily, Halvorsen felt such pleasure at having solved his problem that he neglected to look at the solution, and when he did, it chilled him far more than the fine rain could.

Why should he want to be dead?

He glanced at the racked guns in the pawnshop and saw them as if for the first time, each one very real and genuinely menacing. He shuddered, clung for a moment to the wet black steel of the gate, then abruptly turned away.

In all his thoughtful—thought-*filled*—life he had never consciously entertained such a concept. Perhaps this was because he was a receptive person rather than a transmissive one. What he collected he used on his external world—his job—rather than on himself. He had no need for the explanations and apologies, the interpretations and demands-to-be-heard of the outgoing person, so he had no need to indulge in self-seeking and the complicated semantics of ego-translation. He was rather a clearing-house for the facts he found, taking knowledge and experience from *here* and storing them virtually untouched until they could be applied *there*.

He walked slowly homeward, in a state that would be numbness except for the whirling, wondering core which turned and poked and worried at this revelation. Why should he want to be dead?

Philip Halvorsen loved being alive. Correction: He enjoyed being alive. (Question: Why the correction? File for later.) He was a vocational guidance worker employed by a national social service organization. He was paid what he should be, according to his sense of values, and thanks to the Bittelmans he lived a little better on it than he might otherwise. He did not work for money, anyway; his work was a way of thinking, a way of life. He found it intriguing, engrossing, deeply satisfying. Each applicant was a challenge, each placement a victory over one or more of the enemies that plague mankind—insecurity, inferiority, blindness and ignorance. Each time he looked up from his desk and saw a new applicant entering his cubicle, he experienced a strange silent excitement. It was a pressure, a power, like flicking on the master switch of a computing machine; he sat there with all relays open and all circuits blank, waiting for the answers to those first two questions: "What are you doing now?" and "What do you want to do?" Just that; it was enough for that indefinable sense of satisfaction or dissatisfaction to make itself known to him. And just as he had analyzed its source in the matter of guns, so he analyzed his clients. That flickering light signaling wrongness, misapplication, malfunction, misevaluation—all the flaws in design, the false goals, the frustrations and hurts of those who wonder if they have chosen the right vocation—that light burned on while he worked on each case, and would not go out until he found an answer. Once or twice he had wished, whimsically, that his imagined signal light would illuminate a sign for the client which said *Steeplejack* and for that one which said *Frog Farmer*, but it refused to be so obliging. It only told him when he was wrong. Being right involved laborious and meticulous work, but he did it gladly. And when at last he was satisfied, he frequently found that his work had just begun: to tell an eighty-dollar-a-week bank clerk that his proper niche is in freight-handling with a two-year apprenticeship at 50 is initially a thankless task. But Halvorsen knew how to be quiet and wait, and had become a past master at the art of letting a client fight himself, defeat himself, reconstruct himself, and at last persuade himself that the vocational counsellor was right. And all of it, Halvorsen liked, from the challenge to the accomplishment. Why, why should there be a wish in him to have this cease, to end the world in which all these intriguing problems existed? And to be glad of its ending?

What would he advise a client, a stranger, if that stranger blurted out such a desire?

Well, he wouldn't. It would depend. He would simply throw that in with everything else about the client—age, education, temperament, marital status, I.Q., and all the rest of it, and let the deathwish throw its weight along with all the other factors. It would, however, predispose him to conclude that the man was intolerably misplaced in some area: in a marriage, a family situation, a social beartrap of some kind . . . or his job. His job. Was he, Halvorsen, judge and arbiter of occupations—was he in the wrong job?

He slouched along in the rain, huddled down into himself to escape a far more penetrating chill than this drenching mist. So uncharacteristically wrapped in his inward thought was he that he had taken three steps on dry pavement before he became aware of it. He stopped and took his bearings.

He stood under the marquee of the smallest and cheapest of the town's four theaters. It was closed and dark, this being Sunday in a "blue-law" district, but dead bulbs and locked doors did not modify the shrillness of its decorations. Over the main entrance were two groups of huge letters, one for each of the two features on the bill. SIN FOR SALE, one shrieked, and the other blared back SLAVES OF THE HELLFLOWER. Under these was a third sign, offering as a special added attraction *Love Rites of a South Sea Eden*. From the sidewalk on the far left, up to the marquee, across and down the other side was an arch of cardboard cutouts of women, wilting and wet, unnaturally proportioned and inhumanly posed, with scraps of ribbon and drape, locks of hair and induced shadows performing a sort of indicative concealment on their unbelievable bodies. Over the box office was the stern advice: *Adults only! ! !* and papering the supporting pillars just inside the mirrored cavern of a lobby were still photographs of high-lights of the pictures: A bare-backed female with her hands trussed to a high tree-branch, being whipped; a man standing, gun in hand, over a delectable corpse whose head hung back and down over the edge of a bed so that her carefully arranged hair swept the floor, and some flyblown sam-ples of the South Sea Eden with the portraits of its inhabitants smeared strategically with rubber-stamp ink in angry and careless obedience to some local by-law.

At the best of times this sort of display left Phil Halvorsen cold. At the worst of times (up to now) he would have felt a mild disgust leavened by enough amusement at the out-house crudity of it to make it supportable— and forgettable. But at the moment things were a little worse than the worst had ever been before. It was as if his earlier unpleasant revelation had in some obscure way softened him up, opened a seam in a totally unex-pected place in his armor. The display smote him like a blast of heat. He blinked and stepped back a pace, half-raising his hands and screwing his eyes shut. Behind the lids the picture of his ridiculous one-shot cannon rose up roaring. He thought he could see a bullet emerging from its smoking muzzle like the tip of a hot black tongue. He shuddered away from the mil-lisecond nightmare and opened his eyes, only to get a second and even more overwhelming reaction from the theater-front.

My God, what's happening to me? he silently screamed to himself. He pounded his forehead with his fists twice, then put his head down and ran up the street, up the hill. His photographic eye had picked up the banner inside the lobby, and as he ran, part of him coldly read it:

SEE (in flaming scarlet) the big-city orgies
SEE the temptation of a teenager
SEE lust run riot
SEE the uncensored rites of an island cult
SEE . . . . SEE . . . . There was more. As he ran, he moaned.

And then he thought, at the Bittelmans there are people, it is light, it is warm, it is almost home.

He began to run to something instead of away.

316

CHAPTER THREE

THE BITTELMANS' KITCHEN was a vague "backstairs" area to O'Banion and a functional adjunct of the boarding house to Halvorsen; to Miss Schmidt it was forbidden ground which excited no special interest for that—almost all the world was forbidden ground to Miss Schmidt. In it Sue Martin was as content as she was anywhere, and among the torments of Mary Haunt, the kitchen was a special hell. But in Robin's world it was central, more so than the bedroom he shared with his mother, more so than his crib. He ate in the kitchen, played there when it was raining or especially cold. When he went outdoors it was through the kitchen door, and it was a place to come back to with a bruised knee, with a hollow stomach, with a sudden flood of loneliness or of a three-year-old's wild manic passion. It was big and warm and full of friends.

The most resourceful of these friends was, of course, Bitty, who without ever losing her gruffness knew the right time to apply a cookie or a story (usually about a little boy with a beautiful mother) or a swat on the bottom. Sam was a friend, too, mostly as something safe to climb on. Of late, O'Banion had carved a rather special niche for himself, and Robin had always liked a limited amount of Miss Schmidt's self-conscious passiveness; she was a wonderful listener. He treated Halvorsen with cheerful respect, and Mary Haunt as if she did not exist. There were other people, too, every bit as much so as anyone who ate and had a job and occupied rooms elsewhere in the house. There was the electric mixer and the washing machine—in Robin's economical language "Washeen"—the blendor and the coffeepot; in short, everything which had a motor in it. (The presence or absence of motors in percolators is arguable only by those with preconceptions.) To him they were all alive, responsive and articulate, and he held converse with them all. He showed them his toys and he told them the news, he bade them goodby and good morning, hello, what's the matter, and happy birthday.

And besides all these people, there were Boff and Googie, who, though by no means limited to the kitchen, were often there.

They were not there on that dark Sunday while the sky grieved and Halvorsen fought his personal devils outdoors. "Mits-ter, Boff an' Googie gone for ride," Robin informed the electric mixer. Its name, Mits-ter, was identical in his vocabulary with "Mister" and was a clear link between the machine and the males he heard spoken of, and just another proof of the living personality he assigned to it. He got a kitchen chair and carried it effortlessly over to the work-table, where he put it down and climbed on it. He tilted the mixer up and back and turned its control-cowling, and it began to hum softly. Bitty kept the beaters in a high drawer well out of his reach and let him play with the therefore harmless machine to his heart's content. "Ats right, Mitster," he crooned. "Eat your yunch. Hey, Washeen!" he called to the washing machine, "Mitster's eatin' his yunch all up, I go' give him a cookie, he's a *good* boy." He revved the control up and down, the machine whining obediently. He spun the turntable, turned the motor off, listened to the ball-bearings clicking away in the turntable, stopped it and turned on the motor again. He turned suddenly at the nudge of some sixth sense and saw O'Banion in the doorway. "Goo' morning Tonio," he called, beaming. "Go picnic now?"

"Not today, it's raining," said O'Banion. "and it's 'good afternoon' now." He crossed to the table. "What you up to, fellow?"

"Mitster eatin' his yunch."

"Your mother asleep?"

"Yis."

O'Banion stood watching the child's complete preoccupation with the machine. Little son of a gun, he thought, how did you do it?

The question was all he could express about the strangely rewarding friendship which flowered between him and Robin. He had never liked (nor, for that matter, disliked) a child in his life. He had never been exposed to one before; his only sibling was an older sister and he had never associated with anyone but contemporaries since he was a child himself.

Robin had caught him alone one day and had demanded to know his name. "Tony O'Banion," he had growled reluctantly. "Tonio?" "Tony O'Banion," he had corrected distinctly. "Tonio," Robin had said positively, and from then on that was inalterably that. And surprisingly, O'Banion had come to like it. And when, on the outskirts of town, someone had set up something called a Kiddie Karnival, a sort of miniature amusement park, and he had been assigned to handle land rentals there for his firm, he found himself thinking of Robin every time he saw the place, and of the Karnival every time he saw Robin, until one warm Sunday he startled himself and everyone else concerned by asking Sue Martin if he could take the boy there. She had looked at him gravely for a moment and said, "Why?"

"I think he might like it."

"Well, thanks," she had said warmly, "I think that's wonderful." And so he and Robin had gone.

And they'd gone again, several times, mostly on Sunday when Sue Martin was taking her one luxurious afternoon nap of the week, but a couple of times during the week too, when O'Banion had business out there and could conveniently pick the child up on the way out from the office and drop him again on the way back. And then, just for a change, a picnic, Robin's very first, by the bank of a brook where they had watched jewel-eyed baby frogs and darting minnows and a terrifying miniature monster that he later identified as a dragonfly nymph; and Robin had asked so many questions that he had gone to a bookstore the next day and bought a bird book and a wildflower guide.

Occasionally he asked himself *why*? What was he getting out of it? and found the answers either uncomfortable or elusive. Perhaps it was the re-laxation: for the first time he could have communion with another human being without the cautious and watchful attention he usually paid to

"Where did you go to school?" and "Who are your people?" Perhaps it was the warmth of friendship radiating from a face so disturbingly like the one which still intruded itself between his eyes and his work once in a while, and which was so masked and controlled when he encountered it in the flesh.

And there had been the Sunday when Sue Martin, after having given her permission for one of these outings, had suddenly said, "I haven't much to do this afternoon. Are these excursions of yours strictly stag?" "Yes," he had said immediately, "they are." He'd told *her*. But—it didn't feel like a victory, and she had not seemed defeated when she shrugged and smiled and said, "Let me know when you go coeducational." After that she didn't put a stop to the picnics, either, which would have pleased him by permitting him to resent her. He found himself wishing she would ask again, but he knew she would not, not ever. And if he should ask her to come, and she should refuse . . . he could not bear the thought. Sometimes he thought the whole business of amusing the child was done to impress the mother; he had overheard Mary Haunt make a remark to Miss Schmidt once that intimated as much, and had furiously sworn off for all of six hours, which was when Robin asked him where they would go next. As long as it was simple, a matter between him and the child, it required no excuses or explanations. As soon as he placed the matter in any matrix, he became confused and uncertain. He therefore avoided analyses, and asked himself admiringly and academically, little son of a gun, how did you do it? while he watched Robin's animated conversation with the electric mixer.

He rumpled Robin's hair and went to the stove, where he picked up the coffeepot and swirled it. It was almost full, and he lit the gas under it.

"Wha' you do, Tonio? Make coffee?"

"Yea bo."

"Okay," said Robin, as if granting permission. "Boff doesn't drink coffee, Tonio," he confided. "Oh no."

"He doesn't, hm?" O'Banion looked around and up. "Is Boff here?"

"No," said Robin. "He not here."

"Where'd he go? Out with the Bittlemans?"

"Yis." The coffeepot grumbled and Robin said, "*Hello*, Coffeepot."

Halvorsen came in and stood blindly in the doorway. O'Banion looked up and greeted him, then said under his breath, "My God!" and crossed the room. "You all right, Halvorsen?"

Halvorsen directed blind eyes at the sound of his voice, and O'Banion could watch seeing enter them slowly, like the fade-in on a movie screen. "What?" His face was wet with the rain, fish-belly pale, and he stood slumping like a man with a weight on his back, raising his face to look up rather than lifting his head.

"You'd better sit down," said O'Banion. He told himself that this unwonted concern for the tribulations of a fellow-human was purely a selfish matter of not wanting to shovel the stunned creature up off the floor. Yet as Halvorsen turned toward the ell with its wooden chairs, O'Banion caught at the open front of Halvorsen's coat. "Let me take this, it's sopping."

"No," said Halvorsen. "No." But he let O'Banion take the coat; rather, he walked out of it, leaving O'Banion with it foolishly in his hands. O'Banion cast about him, then hung it up on the broom-hook and turned again to Halvorsen, who had just fallen heavily back into a chair.

Again Halvorsen went through that slow transition from blindness to sight, from isolation to awareness. He made some difficult, internal effort and then said, "Supper ready?"

"We roll our own," said O'Banion. "Bitty and Sam are taking their once-a-month trip to the fleshpots."

"Fleshpots," said Robin, without turning his head.

Carefully controlling his face and his voice, O'Banion continued, "They said to raid the refrigerator, only hands off the leg o' lamb, that's for tomorrow." Motioning toward Robin with his head, he added, "He doesn't miss a trick," and at last released a broad grin.

Halvorsen said, "I'm not hungry."

"I've got some coffee going."

"Good."

O'Banion dropped a round asbestos mat on the table and went for the coffeepot. On the way back he got a cup and saucer. He put them on the table and sat down. Sugar was already there; spoons were in a tumbler, handles down, country-style. He poured and added sugar and stirred. He looked across at Halvorsen, and saw something on that reserved face that he had read about but had never seen before; the man's lips were blue. Only then did it occur to him to get a cup for Halvorsen. He went for it, and remembered milk, too, just in case. He brought them back, hesitated, and then poured the second cup. He put a spoon in the saucer, and with sudden shyness pushed it and the milk toward the other man. "Hey!"

"What?" Halvorsen said in the same dead, flat tone, and "Oh. Oh! Thanks, O'Banion, thanks very I'm sorry." Suddenly he laughed forcefully and without mirth. He covered his eyes and said plaintively, "What's the *matter* with me?"

It was a question neither could answer, and they sat sipping coffee uncomfortably, a man who didn't know how to unburden himself and a man who had never taken up another's burden. Into this tableau walked Mary Haunt. She had on a startling yellow hostess gown and had a magazine tucked under her arm. She threw one swift gaze around the room and curled her lip.

"Grand Central Station," she growled and walked out.

O'Banion's anger came as a great relief to him at just that moment; he was almost grateful to the girl. "One of these days someone's going to grab that kid by the scruff of the neck and housebreak her," he snorted.

Halvorsen found a voice, too, and probably was as grateful for the change in focus. "It won't last," he said.

"What do you mean?"

"I mean she can't go on that way much longer," said Halvorsen thoughtfully. He paused and closed his eyes; O'Banion could see him pulling himself hand over hand out of his personal swamp, moving to dry ground, high ground, where he could look with familiarity at a real world again. When he opened his eyes he gave O'Banion a strange little smile and said, as if in parenthesis, "Thanks for the coffee, O'Banion," and went on: "She's waiting for the Big Break. She thinks she deserves it and that it will come to her if she only waits. She really believes that. You've heard of high-school kids who perch on drugstore stools hoping for a movie scout to come along and discover them. That's harmless as long as they do it an hour or two a day. But Mary Haunt does it every minute she's out of this house. None of us here could help her, so she treats us the way anyone treats useless things. But you ought to see her down at the station."

"What station?"

"She types continuities at the radio station," said Halvorsen. "From what I hear, she's not very good, but on the other hand they don't pay her much money, so nobody kicks. But to her a radio station is the edge of the world she wants to crash—it starts there and goes to TV and to the movies. I'll bet you anything you like she has a scene all rehearsed in her mind, where a big producer or director stops here and drops in at the radio station to see someone, and *bang!* our Mary's a starlet being groomed for the top."

"She'd better learn some manners," grumbled O'Banion.

"Oh, she's got manners when she thinks they'll do her some good."

"Why doesn't she use them on you, for example?"

"Me?"

"Yes. Don't you get people better jobs. That sort of thing?"

"I see a lot of people, a lot of different kinds of people," said Halvorsen, "but they have one thing in common: they aren't sure what they want to do, to be." He pointed his spoon at the doorway. "She is. She may be wrong, but she's certain."

"Well, what about Sue Martin?" said O'Banion. He pursued the subject quickly, almost thoughtlessly, because of a vague feeling that if he didn't, Halvorsen would slip back into that uncomfortable introspective silence. "Surely there's a lot about show business Mary Haunt could learn from her."

Halvorsen gave the nearest thing yet to a grin and reached for the coffeepot. "Mrs. Martin's a nightclub entertainer," he said, "and as far as Mary Haunt's concerned, night clubs are slums."

O'Banion blushed violently and cursed himself for it. "Why that little— no background, no—no—how could *she* look down on . . . I mean, she's a little *nobody!*" Conscious that he was spluttering under the direct and passionless gaze of Halvorsen's dark eyes, he reached for the first thing he could think of that was not an absolute non sequitur: "One night a couple of months ago Mrs. Martin and I saw her throw a fit of hysterics over something . . . oh, Miss Schmidt had a magazine she wanted . . . anyway, after it was all over, Mrs. Martin said something about Mary Haunt that could have been a compliment. I mean, to some people. I can't think of Mary Haunt ever doing as much for her."

"What did she say?"

"Mrs. Martin? Oh, she said anybody who gets between Mary Haunt and what she wants is going to have a Mary-sized hole through them."

"It wasn't a compliment," said Halvorsen immediately. "Mrs. Martin knows as well as you or I do what's between that girl and her Big Break."

"What is?"

"Mary Haunt."

O'Banion thought about that for a moment and then chuckled. "A Mary-sized hole wouldn't leave much." He looked up. "You're quite a psychologist."

"Me?" said Halvorsen in genuine surprise. At that moment Robin, who had all this while been murmuring confidences to the mixer, switched off the machine and looked up. "Boff!" he cried joyously. "Hello, *Boff!*" He watched something move toward him, turning slightly to follow it with his eyes until it settled on the spice shelf over his table. "Wash you doin', Boff? Come for dinner?" Then he laughed, as if he had thought of something pleasant and very funny.

"I thought Boff was out with the Bittelmans, Robin," O'Banion called.

"No, he hide," said Robin, and laughed uproariously. "Boff right here. He come back."

Halvorsen watched this with a dazed smile. "Who on earth is Boff?" he asked O'Banion.

"Imaginary playmate," said O'Banion knowledgeably. "I'm used to it now but I don't mind telling you it gave me the creeps at first. Lots of kids have them. My sister did, or so Mother says—Sister doesn't remember it now. A little girl called Ginny who used to live in the butler's pantry. You laugh off this 'Boff' and the other one—her name's Googie—until you see Robin holding the door open to let them in, or refusing to go out to play until they get downstairs. And he isn't kidding. That's a nice little kid most of the time, Halvorsen, but some things will make him blow up like a little bottle of nitro, and one of 'em is to deny that Boff and Googie are real. I know. I tried it once and it took half a day and six rides on a merry-go-round to calm him down." He emphasized with a forefinger: "Six rides for Boff and Googie too."

Halvorsen watched the child. "I'll be darned." He shook his head slightly. "Is that—uh—healthy?"

"I bought a book," said O'Banion, and, unaccountably, found himself blushing again, "and it says no, long as the child has good contact with reality, and believe me, he has. They grow out of it. Nothing to worry about."

Just then Robin cocked his head up to the spice shelf, as if he had heard a sound. Then he said, "Okay, Boff," climbed down from his chair, carried the chair across the kitchen to its place against the wall, and said cheerfully, "Tonio, Boff wan see cars. Okay. Shall we?"

O'Banion rose, laughing. "My master's voice. I got the *Popular Electrics* special issue on this year's automobiles and Boff and Robin can't get enough of it."

"Oh?" Halvorsen smiled. "What do they like this year?"

"Red ones. Come on, Robin. See you, Halvorsen."

"See you."

Robin trotted after O'Banion, paused near the door. "Come *on*, Boff!"

He waved violently at Halvorsen. "See you, Have-sum-gum."

Halvorsen waved back, and they were gone.

Halvorsen sat numbly for a while, his hand still raised. The presence of the other man and the child had been a diversion from his strange inner explosion and its shock-waves. Now they were gone, but he would not permit himself to sink into that welter of approaching bullet, rain-dampened torsos, *why do I want to be dead?* So he hung motionless for a moment between disturbance and diversion. He thought of following O'Banion into the parlor. He thought of sinking back into his panic, facing it, fighting it. But he wasn't ready to fight, not yet, and he didn't want to run . . . and he couldn't stay like this. It was like not breathing. Anyone can stop breathing, but not for long.

"Mr. Halvorsen?"

Soft-footed, soft-voiced, timidly peering about her to be sure she was not intruding, Miss Schmidt came in. Halvorsen could have hugged her. "Come in, come in!" he cried warmly.

The half-alive smile brightened like fanned embers at his tone. "Good afternoon, Mr. Halvorsen. I was looking, that is, wondering, you know, if Mr. Bittelman was back yet, and I thought perhaps that . . ." She wet her lips and apparently thought it was worth another try. "I wanted to see him about—I mean to say, ask him if he—about something." She exhaled, took a breath, and would surely have come out with more of the same, but Halvorsen broke in.

"No, not yet. Sure picked a miserable day for a joy-ride."

"It doesn't seem to matter to the Bittelmans. Every fourth week, like clockwork." She suddenly uttered a soft little bleat of a laugh. "I'm sure I don't mean clockwork, Mr. Halvorsen, I mean, four weeks."

He laughed politely, for her sake. "I know what you mean." He saw her drop her eyes to her kneading hands, divined that her next movement would be toward the door. He felt he couldn't bear that, not just now. "How about—uh—a cup of tea or something. Sandwich. I was just going to—" He rose.

She went pink and smiled again. "Why, I—"

There was a short, sibilant sound in the doorway, a sniff, a small snort of anger. Mary Haunt stood there glowering. Miss Schmidt said, faintly, "No, no thank you, I'd better, I mean, just go and . . . I only wanted to see if Mr. Bittelman was—" She faded out altogether and tiptoed apologetically to the door. Mary Haunt swung her shoulders but did not move her feet. Miss Schmidt slid out and escaped past her.

Halvorsen found himself standing, half angry, half foolish. His own last words echoed in his mind: "Sandwich. I was just going to—" and he let them push him to the other end of the kitchen. He was furious, but why? Nothing had happened; a lot had happened. He would have liked to rear back on his hind legs and blast her for persecuting a little defenseless rabbit like Miss Schmidt; yet what had she actually done? Couldn't she say with absolute truth, "Why, I never said a word to her!"? He felt ineffectual, unmanned; and the picture of the flimsy gun flickered inside his eyelids and shocked him. He trembled, pulled himself together, painfully aware of the bright angry eyes watching his back from the doorway. He fumbled into the breadbox and took out half a loaf of Bitty's magnificent home-baked bread. He took down the breadboard and got a knife from the drawer, and began to saw. Behind him he heard a sharp slap as Mary Haunt tossed her magazine on the table beside the coffeepot, and then he was conscious of her at his elbow. If she had said one word, she would have faced a blaze of anger out of all proportion to anything that had happened. But she didn't, and didn't: she simply stood there and watched him. He finished cutting the first slice, started on the second. He almost swung to face her but checked the motion, whereupon the knife bit into the first joint of his thumb. He closed his eyes, finished cutting the bread, and turned away to the refrigerator. He opened it and then bent over the shelves, holding his cut thumb in his other hand.

"What do you think you're doing?" asked the girl.

"What's it look like?" he growled. His cut suddenly began to hurt.

"I couldn't say," said Mary Haunt. She stepped to the breadboard, picked up the knife and with it whisked the bread he had cut into the sink.

"Hey!"

"You better push that cut up against the freezer coils for a second," she said with composure. She put a hand on the loaf and with one sweep straightened its hacked end. "Sit down," she said as he filled his lungs to roar at her. "If there's anything I hate it's to see someone clumsy paddling around in food." One, two, three, four even slices fell to the board as she spoke. And again she interrupted him just as he was forming a wounded-bear bellow, "You want a sandwich or not? Just sit down over there and stay out from underfoot."

Slackjawed, he watched her. Was she doing him a kindness? Mary Haunt doing someone a *kindness*?

He found himself obeying her, pressing his cut against the freezer coils. It felt good. He withdrew his hand just as she came toward the refrigerator, and dodged out of the way. He backed to the table, sat down, and watched her.

She was something to watch. The pale, over-manicured hands flew. She set out mayonnaise, cream cheese, a platter of cold-cuts, parsley, radishes. With almost a single motion she put a small frying pan and a butter-melter on the stove and lit the fire under them. Into the frying pan went a couple of strips of bacon; into the other, two tablespoons of water and half the fluid from a jar of capers. She added spices, "by ear"—a shake, a pinch: poultry seasoning, oregano, garlic salt. The tiny pan began to hiss, and suddenly the kitchen smelt like the delivery entrance to paradise. She snatched it off, scraped the contents into a bowl, added cream cheese and mayonnaise, and thrust it under the electric mixer. She turned the bacon, shoved two of the bread slices into the toaster, and busied herself with a paring knife and the radishes.

Halvorsen shook his head unbelievingly and muttered an exclamation. The girl threw him a look of such intense scorn that he dropped his eyes. He found them resting on her magazine. It was called *Family Day* and was a home-making publication from a chain supermarket—in no way a movie magazine.

Out of the frying pan came the bacon, crackling. She drained it on a paper towel and crumbled it into the bowl where the mixer was working. As if some kitchen choreographer was directing the work, the toast popped up as she reached out her hand for it. She dropped in the other two slices and went back to her alchemy with the radishes. In a moment she turned off the mixer and spread the contents of the bowl on the toast. On this she laid cold-cuts, narrow strips of various kinds, deftly weaving them so they formed a beautiful basket pattern. As she finished the first two, the second pair popped out of the toaster; it was a continuous thing, the way she did all the different things she did; it was like music or a landscape flowing by a train window.

She did something swift with the knife, and set the results out on two plates: bite-sized sandwiches arranged like a star, and in the center what looked like a tiny bouquet of rosebuds—the radishes, prepared with curled petals and nested in a neat bed of parsley, its stems all drawn together by one clever half-hitch in one of them. The whole amazing performance had taken perhaps six minutes. "You can make your own coffee," she snapped.

He came over and picked up one of the plates. "Why, this is—is—well, *thanks!*" He looked at her and smiled. "Come on, let's sit down."

"With *you?*" She stalked to the table, carrying the other plate, and scooped up the magazine as if it were a guilty secret. She went to the door. "You can clean up," she said, "and if you ever tell anyone about this I'll snatch you bald-headed."

Staring after her, stunned, he absently picked up one of the sandwiches and bit into it, and for a moment forgot even his amazement, it was so delicious. He sat down slowly, and for the first time since he had started comparing violins with guitars in the pawn-shop, he gave himself up completely to his senses and forgot his troubles. He ate the sandwiches slowly and appreciatively and let them own him.

EXCERPT FROM FIELD EXPEDITION [NOTEBOOK]: *So [weary-irritated] [I] can barely [write]. As if this kind of research wasn't arduous enough at the best of times, which this is not, with the best of equipment, which [we] lack, [I] am plagued by a [partner-teammate] with insuperable enthusiasm and a quality [I] can only describe as headlong stubbornness. [Smith] means well, of course, but the universe is full of well-meaning [individuals] [who] have succeeded only in making [   ]s of themselves.*
All during the tedious and infuriating process of re[charging] the [wadget] [Smith] argued that purely objective observation would get [us] nowhere and would take [forever]; that [we] have sufficient data now to apply stimuli to these specimens and determine once and for all if a reliable, functional condition of Synapse Beta sub Sixteen is possible to them. [I] of course objected that it is against [our] highest [ethic] to apply [force]

to alien species; [Smith] then argued that it would not really be [force], but only the [magnification-amplification-increased efficiency] of that which they already possessed. [I] then pointed out that even if [we] succeed, [we] can only test the final result by means which may readily kill some or all of the specimens. This [Smith] is willing to worry about only when the time comes. [I] pointed out further that in order to supply the necessary stimuli [we] shall have to re[wire] not only the [widget], but that [ ]ed, inefficient, [stone] age excuse for a [mechanism], the [wadget]. [Smith] readily agreed, and while [I] went on arguing [he] began re[wiring], and [I] argued, and [he] [wired], and by the time [I]'d [made my point] [he] was practically finished and [I] found [myself] holding the [light] as well.

[I] forgot to ask [Smith] what [he] planned to do if one of the specimens finds out what [we]'re up to. Kill it? Kill them all? It wouldn't [surprise] [me]. In the name of [research] [Smith] would happily [watch] [his] [elderly forebear]'s [knuckles] being [knurled].

CHAPTER FOUR

MISS SCHMIDT, muffled up to the pharynx in a quilted robe, bedsocked, slippered and shawled, half-dozed in her easy chair. When she heard the sounds she had waited for, she jumped up, went to her door, which was ajar, and stood a moment to listen and be sure. Then she tightened her sash, checked the hooks-and-eyes under her chin, tugged her voluminous robe downward at the hips, and pulled the shawl a little higher on her shoulders. She crossed her arms at the wrists and pressed her hands modestly against her collarbones and scurried silently past the bathroom, down the long hall to the foyer. Bitty was in the kitchen and Sam Bittelman was hanging up a damp trench coat on the hall tree.

"Mr. Bittelman—"

"Sam," he corrected jovially. "Top of the morning to you, Miss Schmidt. It turned morning, y'know, ten minutes ago."

"Oh dear yes, I know it's late," she whispered. "And I'm terribly sorry, really I am, I wouldn't for the world trouble you. I mean, I *am* sorry, I don't want to be a nuisance. Oh *dear!*" Her perennially frightened face crinkled with her small explosion of distress.

"Now you just tell me what's troubling you, lady, and we'll get it fixed," he said warmly.

"You're very kind. Very kind. It happens there is something. I mean, something to fix. In . . . in my *room*." She bent forward with this, as with a deep confidence.

"Well, let's go have a look. Bitty!" Miss Schmidt put a shocked hand over her lips as he raised his voice. "I'm going to fix something for the lady. Be right with you." He turned back to Miss Schmidt and made a jocular bow. "Lead on."

"We mustn't wake the . . . anybody," she reproved him, then blushed because she had. He only grinned, and followed her back to her room. She entered, opened the door as wide as it would go, and self-consciously picked up the wastepaper basket and set it to hold the door open. She looked up from this task right into Sam's twinkling eyes, and sent up a prayer that he wouldn't tease her about it. One never knew what Sam was going to say; sometimes he was beyond understanding and sometimes he was just— *awful*. "The window," she said. "The blind."

He looked at it. "Oh, that again. Durn things are always getting the cords frayed." The venetian blind hung askew, the bottom slats almost vertical, leaving a lower corner of the window exposed. Sam tugged at the raising-cord. It was double; one part was jammed tight and the other ran free. He pulled it all the way out and ruefully exhibited the broken end. "See? That's it, all right. Have to see if I can't put in a new cord for you in the morning, if I can find one."

"In the morning? But—I mean, well, Mr. uh—Sam, what about now? That is, what am I going to *do?*"

"Why, just don't worry your pretty little head about it! Get your beauty-sleep, little lady, and by the time you're back from school tomorrow I'll have it—"

"You don't understand," she wailed softly, "I can't go to bed with it like that. That's why I waited up for you. I've tried everything. The drapes won't go across it and there's nothing to hang a towel to and the chair-back isn't high enough to cover it and—and—oh, *dear!*"

"Oh-h-h."

Struck by something in his single, slow syllable, she looked sharply at him. There was something—what was it? like a hum in the room. But it wasn't a sound. He hadn't changed . . . and yet there was something in his eyes she had never seen before. She had never seen it in anyone's eyes. About Sam Bittelman there had always been a leisurely strength, and it was there now, but easier, stronger, more comforting than ever. To her, with her multiple indecisions, unsurenesses, his friendly certitude was more wondrous than a halo might have been. He said, "Just what bothers you about that window?"

Her usual self moved quite clearly to indicate, indignantly, that part of the window was uncovered and surely that spoke for itself; yet her usual self was unaccountably silent, and she gave him his answer: "Somebody might look *in!*"

"You know what's outside that window?"

"Wh— Oh. Oh, the back of the garage."

"So nobody's going to see in. Well now, suppose there was no garage, and you turned out your lights. Could anybody see in?"

"N-no . . ."

"But it still bothers you."

"Yes, of course it does." She looked at the triangle of exposed glass, black with night outside, and shuddered. He leaned against the doorpost and scratched his head. "Let me ask you something," he said, as if her permission might make a difference. "S'pose we took away the garage, and you forgot and left your light on, *and* somebody saw you?"

She squeaked.

"Really bothers you, don't it?" He laughed easily, and instead of infuriating her, the sound flooded her with comfort. "What exactly is bothersome about that, aside from the fact that it's bothersome?"

"Why . . . why," she said breathlessly, "I know what I'*d* think of a hussy that would parade around that way with the lights on and—"

"I didn't say parade. Nor 'prance,' either, which is the other word people use, I don't know why. So what really bothers you is what some peepin' Tom might think, hm? Now, Miss Schmidt, is that really anything to worry about? What do you care what he thinks you are? Don't you know what you are?" He paused, but she had nothing to say. "You ever sleep naked?"

She gasped, and, round-eyed, shook her head.

"Why not?" he demanded.

"Why I—I—" She had to answer him; she had to. Fear rose like a thin column of smoke within her, and then a swift glance at his open, friendly face dispelled it completely. It was extraordinary, uncomfortable, exhilarating, disturbing, exciting all at once. He compelled her and comforted her at the same time.

She found her voice and answered him. "I just couldn't sleep . . . like that. Suppose there was a fire?"

"Who said that?" he snapped.

"I beg your—"

"Who said 'suppose there's a fire'? Who told you that?"

"Why, I suppose it—yes, it was my mother."

"Not your idea then. Figured as much. 'Thou shalt not kill.' Do you believe that?"

"Of course!"

"You do. How old were you when you learned that?"

"I don't—know. All children—"

"Children seven, eight, nine? All right. How old were you when you were taught not to unpin your diapers? Not to let anyone *see* you?"

She did not answer but the answer was there.

"Wouldn't you say you'd learned 'thou shalt not expose thy body' earlier, better, more down-deep than 'thou shalt not kill'?"

"I—yes."

"Do you realize it's a deeper commandment with you than any of the Ten? And aside from right-'n-wrong, isn't it deeper than the deepest, strongest one of all—save thyself? Can't you see yourself dying under a bush rather than walk naked out on the road and flag a car? 'Suppose there's a fire?' Can't you see yourself burn to death rather'n jump out a window without your bathrobe?"

She didn't answer except from her round eyes and her whole heart.

"Does that make any *sense*, to believe a thing like that?"

"I don't know," she whispered. "I—have to think."

328

Surprisingly, he said, "Retroactive." He pointed to the window. "What can we do about that?" he asked.

Absently she glanced at it. "Never mind it tonight, Mr. Bittelman."

"Sam. Okay. Good night, little lady."

She felt herself, abruptly, tottering on the edge of a bottomless pit. He had walked in here and disoriented her, ripped into shreds a whole idea-matrix which had rested undisturbed in the foundations of her thinking, like a cornerstone. Just at this startled second she had not made the admission, but she would have to admit to herself soon that she must think "retroactive," as he had put it, and that when she did she would find that the clothes convention was not the only one she would have to reappraise. The inescapable, horizonless, unfamiliar task loomed over her like a black cloud—her only comfort, her only handhold was Sam Bittelman, and he was leaving. "No!" she cried. "No! No! No!"

He turned back, smiling, and that magic happened again, his sureness and ease. She stood gasping as if she had run up a hill.

"It's all right, little lady."

"Why did you tell me all this? Why?" she asked pathetically.

"You know something? I didn't tell you a thing," he said gently. "I just asked questions. They were all questions you could've asked yourself. And what's got you scared is answers—answers that came from here—" He put a gentle knuckle against her damp forehead. "—and not from me. You've lived with it all quite a while; you got nothing to fear from it now." And before she could answer he had waved one capable hand, winked, and was gone.

For a long time she stood there, trembling and afraid to think. At last she let her open eyes see again, and although they saw nothing but the open door, it was as if some of Sam's comfort slipped in with vision. She turned around, and around again, taking in the whole room and reaping comfort and more comfort from the walls, as if Sam had hung it for her to gather like ripe berries. She put it all in the new empty place within her, not to fill, but at least to be there and to live with until she could get more. Suddenly her gaze met the silly little wastebasket sitting against the door, holding it open, and to her utter astonishment she laughed at it. She picked it up, shook her head at it as if it had been a ridiculous puppy which had been eating her talcum powder; she even spanked it lightly, once, and put it down, and closed the door. She got into bed and put out the light without even looking at the window.

CHAPTER FIVE

"Aw, you shouldn't!" cried Bitty with a joyous sort of chagrin as she pushed open Sue Martin's door. "Here I've got all your fresh linen and you've went and made the bed!"

Sue Martin, sleep-tousled and lovely in a dark negligee, rose from the writing desk. "I'm sorry, Bitty. I forgot it was Thursday."

"Well Thursday it is," the older woman scolded, "and now I'll have to do it up all over again. Young lady, I've told you and *told* you I'll take care of the room."

"You have plenty to do," Sue smiled. "Here, I'll help. What's Robin up to?"

Together they took down the spread, the light blanket, then the sheets from the big double bed. "Kidnaped by that young idiot O'Banion again. He's driving out to the new project over Huttonville way and thought Robin might want to see the bulldozers."

"Robin loves bulldozers. He's not an idiot."

"He's an idiot," said Bitty gruffly, apparently needing no translation of the two parts of Sue's statement. "Time this was turned, since we're both here," she said, swatting the mattress.

"All right." Sue Martin loosely folded the spread and blanket and carried them to the chest. "Robin just loves him."

"So do you."

Sue's eyes widened. She shot a look at the other woman, but Bitty's back was turned as she bent over the bed. When she spoke, her voice was perfectly controlled. "Yes, for some time." She went to stand beside Bitty and they laid hold of the mattress straps. "Ready?" Together they heaved and the mattress rose up, teetered for a moment on edge, and fell back the other way. They pulled it straight.

"Well, what are you doing about it?" Bitty demanded.

Sue found her eyes captured by Bitty's for a strange moment. She saw herself, in a flash of analog, walking purposefully away from some tired, dark place toward something she wanted; and as she walked there appeared running softly behind her, around her, something like a moving wall. She had a deep certainty that she could not stop nor turn aside; but that as long as she kept moving at the same speed, in the same direction, the moving wall could not affect her. She—and it—were moving toward what she wanted, just as fast as she cared to go. While this was the case, she was not being restrained or compelled, helped nor hindered. So she would not fear this thing, fight it or even question it. It could not possibly change anything. In effect, irresistible as it might be, it need not and therefore did not exist for her. Here and now, some inexplicable something had happened to make it impossible not to answer Bitty's questions—and this compulsion was of no moment at all for her as long as Bitty asked questions she wanted to answer. "What are you doing about it?" was such a question.

"Everything I should do," said Sue Martin. "Nothing at all."

Bitty grunted noncommittally. She took a folded sheet from the top of the highboy and shook it out across the bed. Sue Martin went round to the other side and caught it. She said, "He has to know why, that's all, and he can't do anything or say anything until he does know."

"Why what?" Bitty asked bluntly.

"Why he loves me."

"Oh—you know that, do you?"

This was one question, compulsion or no, that Sue Martin did not bother to answer. It was on the order of "Is this really a bed?" or "Is it Thursday?" So Bitty asked another: "And you're just waiting, like a little edelweiss on an Alp, for him to climb the mountain and pick you?"

"Waiting?" Sue repeated, puzzled.

"You're not doing anything about it, are you?"

"I'm being myself," said Sue Martin. "I'm living my life. What I have to give him—anyone who's *right* for me—is all I am, all I do for the rest of my life. As long as he wants something more, or something different, nothing can happen." She closed her eyes for a moment. "No, I'm not waiting, exactly. Put it this way: I know how to be content with what I am and what I'm doing. Either Tony will knock down that barrier he's built, or he won't. Either way I know what's going to happen, and it's good."

"That wall—why don't you take a pickax and beat it down?"

She flashed the older woman a smile. "He'd defend it. Men get very fond of the things they defend, especially when they find themselves defending something stupid."

Bitty shook out the second sheet. "And don't you have any of his kind of trouble—wondering *why* you love him?"

Sue Martin laughed. "Wouldn't we live in a funny world if we had to understand everything that was real, or it wouldn't exist? It's always good to know *why*. It isn't always necessary. Tony'll find that out one day." She sobered. "Or he won't. Hand me a pillowslip."

They finished their task in silence. Bitty bundled up the old linen and trudged out. Sue Martin stood looking after her. "I hope she wasn't disappointed," she murmured, and, "I don't think so . . . and what did I mean by that?"

CHAPTER SIX

ONE MORNING Mary Haunt opened her eyes and refused to believe them. For a moment she lay still looking at the window numbly; there was something wrong with it, and a wrong feeling about the whole room. Then she identified it: there was sunlight streaming in and down through the venetian blind where no sunlight should be at her rising time. She snatched her watch off the night table and squinted at it, and moaned. She reared up in bed and peered at the alarm clock, then turned and punched furiously at the pillow. She bounded out of bed, struggled into her yellow robe, and flew out of the room with her bare feet slapping angrily down the long corridor. Sam Bittelman was sitting at the kitchen table peering at the morning paper over the tops of his black-rimmed reading-glasses. Bitty was at the sink. "What 'm I, the forgotten man or something?" Mary Haunt demanded harshly.

Sam put down his paper and only then began to remove his gaze from it. "M-m-m? Oh, good morning, gal." Bitty went on with her business.

"Good *nothing!* Don't you know what time it is?"

"Sure do."

"What's the big fat idea leaving me to sleep like this? You know I got to get to work in the morning."

"Who called you four times?" said Bitty without turning around or raising her voice. "Who went in and shook you, and got told *get out of my room* for it?"

Mary Haunt poised between pace and pace, between syllables. Now that Bitty mentioned it, she *did* half-remember a vague hammering somewhere, a hand on her shoulder . . . but that was a dream, or the middle of the night or—or had she really chased the old lady out? "*Arrgh*," she growled disgustedly. She stamped out into the foyer and snatched up the phone. She dialed. "Get me Muller," she snapped at the voice that answered.

"Muller," said the phone.

"Mary Haunt here. I'm sick today. I'm not coming in."

"So with this phone call," said the telephone, "I'll notice."

"Why you lousy Heinie, without me you couldn't run a yo-yo, let alone a radio station!" she shouted, but she had hung up before she started to shout.

She padded back into the kitchen and sat down at the table. "Got coffee?"

Bitty, still with her back turned, nodded in the appropriate direction and said, "On the stove," but Sam folded his paper and got up. He went to the stove, touched the pot briefly with the back of his hand, and carried it back, picking up a cup and saucer on the way. "You'll want milk."

"You know better than that," she said, arching her lean body. While she poured herself a cup, Sam sat down at the other end of the table. He leaned his weight on his elbows, his forearms and worn hands flat on the table. Something like the almost-silent whisper from a high-speed fan made her look up. "What are you looking at?"

He didn't answer her question. "Why do you claim to be twenty-two?" he asked instead, and quick as the rebound of billiard ball from cue ball, propelled by hostility, inclusive as buckshot, her reply jetted up: "*What's it to you?*" But it never reached her lips; instead she said "I have to," and then sat there astounded. Once she had worn out a favored phonograph record, knew every note, every beat of it, and she had replaced it; and for once the record company had made a mistake and the record was not what the label said it was. The first half-second of that new record was like this, a moment of expectation and stunned disbelief. This was even more immediate and personal, however; it was like mounting ten steps in the dark and finding, shockingly, that there were only nine in the flight. From this moment until she left the kitchen, she was internally numb and frightened, yet fascinated, as her mind formed one set of words and others came out.

"You have to," asked Sam mildly, "the way you have to be in the movies? You just *have* to?"

The snarl, *have I kept it a secret?* came out, "It's what I want."

"Is it?"

There didn't seem to be any answer to that, on any level. She waited, tense.

"What you're doing—the job at the radio station—living here in this town instead of someplace else—all of it; is what you're doing the best way to get what you want?"

Why else would I put up with it all—the town, the people—you? But she said, "I think so." Then she said, "I've thought so."

"Why don't you talk to young Halvorsen? He might be able to find something you'd do even better'n going to Hollywood."

"I don't *want* to find anything better!" This time there was no confusion.

From the other end of the room, Bitty asked, "Were you always so all-fired pretty, Mary Haunt? Even when you were a little girl?"

"Everyone always said so."

"Ever wish you weren't?"

Are you out of your mind? "I . . . don't think so," she whispered.

Gently, Sam asked her, "Did they throw you out, gal? Make you leave home?"

Defiantly, defensively, *They treated me like a little princess at home, like a piece of fine glassware. They carried my books and felt good all day if I smiled. They did what I wanted, what they thought I wanted, at home or in town. They acted as if I was too good to walk that ground, breathe that air, they jumped at the chance to take advantage of being at the same place at the same time; they did everything for me they could think of doing, as if they had to hurry or I'd be gone. Throw me out? Why, you old fool!* "I left home my own self," she said. "Because I had to, like—" But here words failed her, and she determined not to cry, and she cried.

"Better drink your coffee."

She did, and then she wanted something to eat with it, but couldn't bear to sit with these people any longer. She sniffed angrily. "I don't know what's the matter with me," she said. "I never overslept before."

"Long as you know what you want," said Sam, and whether that was the stupid, non-sequitur remark of a doddering dotard, or something quite different, she did not know. "Well," she said, rising abruptly; and then felt foolish because there was nothing else to say. She escaped back to her room and to bed, and huddled there most of the day dully regarding the two coddled ends of her life, pampering in the past and pampering in the future, while trying to ignore today with its empty stomach and its buzzing head.

CHAPTER SEVEN

DURING PROHIBITION it had been a restaurant, in that category which is better than just "nice" but not as good as "exclusive"; the town was too small then to have anything exclusive. Now it was a bar as well, and although there was imitation Carrara on some walls, and a good deal of cove-lighting, the balcony had never been altered and still boasted the turned-spoke railing all the way around, looking like a picket fence that had gone to heaven. There was a little service bar up there, and a man could stay all evening watching what went on down below without being seen. This was what Tony O'Banion was doing, and he was doing it because he had felt like a drink and had never been to the club before, and he wanted to see what kind of place it was and what Sue Martin did there; and every one of these reasons were superficial—if he preceded them with "why," he felt lost. Within him were the things he believed, about the right sort of people, about background, breeding and blood. Around him was this place, as real as the things he believed in. Why he was here, why he wanted a drink just now, why he wanted to see the place and what happened in it—this was a bridge between one reality and the other, and a misty, maddening, nebulous bridge it was. He drank, and waited to see her emerge from the small door by the bandstand, and when she did he watched her move to the piano and help the pianist, a disheveled young man, stack and restack and shuffle his music, and he drank. He drank, and watched her go to the cashier and spend a time over a ledger and a pile of checks. She disappeared through the swinging doors into the kitchen, and he drank; he drank and she came out talking to a glossy man in a tuxedo, and he winced when they laughed.

At length the lights dimmed and the glossy man introduced her and she sang in a full, pleasant voice something about a boy next door, and someone else played an accordion which was the barest shade out of tune with the piano. Then the piano had a solo, and the man sang the last chorus, after which the lights came up again and he asked the folks to stick around for the main show at ten sharp. Then the accordion and the piano began to make dance music. It was all unremarkable, and Tony didn't know why he stayed. He stayed, though: "Waiter! Do it again."

"Do it twice."

Tony spun around. "Time someone else bought, hm?" said Sam Bittelman. He sat down.

"Sam! Well, sit down. Oh, you *are*." Tony laughed embarrassedly. His tongue was thick and he was immeasurably glad to see the old man. He was going to wonder why until he remembered that he'd sworn off wondering why just now. He was going to ask what Sam was doing there and then decided Sam would only ask him the same, and it was a question he didn't want to fool with just now. Yes he did.

"I'm down here slumming in the fleshpots and watching the lower orders cavorting and carousing," he blurted, making an immense effort to be funny. He wasn't funny. He sounded like a little snob, and a tight little snob at that.

Sam regarded him gravely, not disapproving, not approving. "Sue Martin know you're here?"

"No."

"Good."

The waiter came just in time; Sam's single syllable had given him a hard hurt; but for all the pain, it was an impersonal thing, like getting hit by a golfer on his backswing. When the waiter had gone Sam asked quietly, "Why don't you marry the girl?"

"What're ya—kidding?"

Sam shook his head. O'Banion looked into his eyes and away, then down at Sue Martin where she leaned against the piano, leafing through some music. *Why don't you marry the girl?* "You mean if she'd have me?" It was not the way he felt, but it was something to say. He glanced at Sam's face, which was still waiting for a real answer. All right then. "It wouldn't be right."

" 'Right'?" Sam repeated.

O'Banion nipped his thick tongue in the hope it might wake his brains up. The rightness of it . . . vividly he recalled his Mother's words on the subject: "Aside from the amount of trouble you'll save yourself, Anthony, you must remember that it's not only your right, it's your *duty* not to marry beneath your class. Fine hounds, fine horses, fine humans, my dear; it's breeding that matters." That was all very well, but how to say it to this kind old man, himself obviously a manual worker all his life? O'Banion was not a cruel man, and he was well aware that coarse origins did not always mean dull sensibilities. Actually, some of these people were very sensitive. So he made a genuinely noble try at simultaneous truth and kindness: "I've always felt it's wiser to form relationships like that with—uh—people of one's own kind."

"You mean, people with as much money as you got?"

"No!" O'Banion was genuinely shocked. "That's no longer a standard to go by, and it probably never was, not by itself." He laughed ruefully and added, "Besides, there hasn't been any money in my family since I can remember. Not since 1929."

"Then what's your kind of people?"

How? How? "It's . . . a way of life," he said at length. That pleased him. "A way of life," he repeated, and took a drink. He hoped Sam wouldn't pursue the subject any further. Why examine something when you're content with it the way it is?

"Why are you here anyway, boy?" Sam asked. "I mean, in this town instead of in the city, or New York or some place?"

"I'm good for a junior partnership in another year or so. Then I can transfer as a junior partner to a big firm. If I'd gone straight to the city it would take me twice as long to get up there."

Sam nodded. "Pretty cute. Why the law? I always figured lawyer's work was pretty tough and pretty dusty for a young man."

His Mother had said, "Of course the law field's being invaded by all sorts of riffraff now—but what isn't? However, it's still possible for a gentleman to do a gentleman's part in law." Well, that wouldn't do. He'd have to go deeper. He averted his eyes from old Sam's casual penetration and said, "Tough, yes. But there's something about law work . . ." He wondered if the old man would follow this. "Look, Sam, did it ever occur to you that the law is the biggest thing ever built? It's bigger'n bridges, bigger'n buildings—because they're all built *on* it. A lawyer's a part of the law, and the law is part of everything else—everything we own, the way we run governments, everything we make and carry and use. Ever think of that?"

"Can't say I did," said Sam. "Tell me something—the law, is it finished?"

"Finished?"

"What I mean, this rock everything's built on, how solid is it? Is it going to change much? Didn't it change a whole lot to get the way it is?"

"Well sure! Everything changes a lot while it's growing up."

"Ah. It's grown up."

"Don't you think it has?" O'Banion asked with sudden truculence.

Sam grinned easily. "Shucks, boy, I don't think. I just ask questions. You were saying about 'your sort of people'; you think you-all *belong* in the law?"

"Yes!" said O'Banion, and saw immediately that Sam would not be satisfied with so little. "We do in this sense," he said earnestly. "All through the ages men have worked and built and—and owned. And among them there rose a few who were born and bred and trained to—to—" He took another drink, but it and the preceding liquor seemed not to be helping him. He wanted to say *to rule* and he wanted to say *to own*, but he had wit enough about him to recognize that Sam would misunderstand. So he tried again. "Born and bred to—live that—uh—way of life I mentioned before. It's to the interest of those few people to invest their lives in things as they are, to keep them that way; in other words, to work for and uphold the law." He leaned back with a flourish that somehow wasn't as eloquent as he had hoped and very nearly upset his glass to boot.

"Don't the law contradict itself once in a while?"

"Naturally!" O'Banion's crystallizing concept of the nobility of his work was beginning to intoxicate him more than anything else. "But the very nature of our courts is a process of refinement, constant purification." He leaned forward excitedly. "Look, laws are dreams, when they're first thought of—inspirations! There's something . . . uh . . . holy about that, something beyond the world of men. And that's why when the world of men comes into contact with it, the wording of the inspiration has to be redone in the books, or interpreted in the courtroom. That's what we mean by 'precedents'— that's what the big dusty books are for, to create and maintain consistency under the law."

"What about justice?" murmured Sam, and then quickly, as if he hadn't meant to change the subject, "That's not what I meant by contradictin', counsellor. I meant all laws that all men have dreamed up and lived by and got theirselves killed over. Tell me something, counsellor, is there even one single law so right for men that it shows up in every country that is or was?"

O'Banion made a startled sound, as half a dozen excellent examples flashed into his mind at once, collided, and, under the first examination, faded away.

"Because," said Sam in a voice which was friendly and almost apologetic, "if there ain't such a law, you might say every set of laws ever dreamed up, even the sets that were bigger and older and lasted longer than the one you practice, even any set you can imagine for the future—they're all goin' to contradict one another some way or other. So, who's really to say whose set of laws are right—or fit to build anything on, or breed up a handful of folks fit to run it?"

O'Banion stared at his glass without touching it. For an awful moment he was totally disoriented; a churning pit yawned under his feet and he must surely topple into it. He thought wildly, you can't leave me here, old man! You'd better say something else, and fast, or I . . . or I . . .

There was a sort of pressure in his ears, like sound too high-pitched for humans. Sam said softly, "You really think Sue Martin ain't good enough for you?"

"I didn't say that, I didn't say that!" O'Banion blurted, hoarse with indignation, and fright, and relief as well. He shuddered back and away from the lip of this personal precipice and looked redly at the composed old face. "I said different, too different, that's all. I'm thinking of her as well as—"

For once Sam bluntly interrupted, as if he had no patience with what O'Banion was saying. "What's different?"

"Background, I told you. Don't you know what that is?"

"You mean the closer a girl's background is to yours, the better chance you'd have bein' happy the rest of your life?"

"Isn't it obvious?" The perfect example popped into his mind, and he speared a finger out and downward toward the piano. "Did you hear what she was singing just before you got here? 'The boy next door.' Don't you understand what that really means, why that song, that idea, hits home to so many people? Everybody understands that; it's the appeal of what's familiar, close by—the similar background I'm talking about!"

"You have to shout?" chuckled Sam. Sobering, he said, "Well, counsellor, if you're goin' to think consistently, like you said, couldn't you dream up a background even more sim'lar than your next-door neighbor?"

O'Banion stared at him blankly, and old Sam Bittelman asked, "Are you an only child, counsellor?"

O'Banion closed his eyes and saw the precipice there waiting; he snapped them open in sheer self-defense. His hands hurt and he looked down, and slowly released them from the edge of the table. He whispered, "What are you trying to tell me?"

His bland face the very portrait of candor, Sam said, "Shucks, son, I couldn't tell you a thing, not a blessed thing. Why, I don't know anything you don't know to tell you! I ain't asked you a single question you couldn't've asked yourself, and the answers were all yours, not mine. Hey . . ." he breathed, "you better come along home. You wouldn't want Miz Martin to see you looking the way you do right now."

Numbly, Anthony Dunglass O'Banion followed him out.

IT WAS HOT, so hot that apparently even Bitty felt it, and after supper went to sit on the verandah. It was very late when at last she came in to do the dishes, but she went ahead without hurrying, doing her usual steady, thorough job. Sam had gone to bed, Mary Haunt was sulking in her room after yet another of those brief, violent brushes with Miss Schmidt. O'Banion was crouching sweatily over some law-books in the parlor, and Halvorsen—

Halvorsen was standing behind her, just inside the kitchen. On his face was a mixture of expressions far too complicated to analyze, but simple in sum—a sort of anxious wistfulness. In his hands was a paper sack, the mouth of which he held as if it were full of tarantulas. His stance was peculiar, strained and off-balance, one foot advanced, his shoulders askew; his resolution had equated with his diffidence and immobilized him, and there he stayed like a bee in amber.

Bitty did not turn. She went right on working steadily, her back to him, until she had finished the pot she was scouring. Still without turning, she reached for another and said, "Well, come on in, Philip."

Halvorsen literally sagged as her flat, matter-of-fact voice reached him, shattering with its exterior touch his interior deadlock. He grinned, or just bared his teeth, and approached her. "You *do* have eyes in the back of your head."

"Nup." She rapped once with her knuckle on the window-pane over the sink. Night had turned it to black glass. Halvorsen watched the little cone of suds her hand had left, then refocused his eyes on the image in the glass —vivid, the kitchen and everything in it. Hoarsely, he said, "I'm disappointed."

"I don't keep things I don't need," she said bluntly, as if they'd been talking about apple-corers. "What's on your mind? Hungry?"

"No." He looked down at his hands, tightened them still more on the bag. "No," he said again, "I have, I wanted . . ." He noticed that she had stopped working and was standing still, inhumanly still, with her hands in the dishwater and her eyes on the window-pane. "Turn around, Bitty."

When she would not, he supported the bottom of the paper bag with one hand and with the other scrabbled it open. He put his hand down inside it. "Please," he tried to say, but it was only a hiss.

She calmly shook water off her hands, wiped them on a paper towel. When she turned around her face was eloquent—as always, and only because it always was. Its lines were eloquent, and the shape of her penetrating eyes, and the light in them. As a photograph or a painting such a face is eloquent. It is a frightening thing to look into one and realize for the first time that behind it nothing need be moving. Behind the lines of wisdom and experience and the curved spoor of laughter, something utterly immobile could be waiting. Only waiting.

Halvorsen said, "I think all the time." He wet his lips. "I never stop thinking, I don't know how. It's . . . there's something wrong."

Flatly, "What's wrong?"

"You. Sam," said Halvorsen with difficulty. He looked down at the bag over his hand. She did not. "I've had the . . . feeling . . . for a long time now. I didn't know what it was. Just something wrong. So I talked to O'Banion. Miss Schmidt too. Just, you know, talk." He swallowed. "I found out. What's wrong, I mean. It's the way you and Sam talk to us, all of us." He gestured with the paper bag. "*You never say anything!* You only ask questions!"

"Is that all?" asked Bitty good-humoredly.

"No," he said, his eyes fixed on hers. He stepped back a pace.

"Aren't you afraid that paper bag'll spoil your aim, Philip?"

He shook his head. His face turned the color of putty.

"You didn't go out and buy a gun just for me, did you?"

"You see?" he breathed. "Questions. You see?"

"You already had it, didn't you, Philip? Bought it for something else?"

"Stay away from me," he whispered, but she had not moved. He said, "Who are you? What are you after?"

"Philip," she said gently—and now she smiled. "Philip—*why do you want to be dead?*"

SPECIAL ENTRY IN FIELD EXPEDITION [NOTEBOOK]: *Since it is not* [my] *intention to prefer charges against* [my] [partner-teammate] [Smith] *and to use these* [notes] *as a formal* [document] *in the matter,* [I] *shall now summarize in detail the particulars of the case:* [We] *have been on Earth for* [expression of time-units] *on a field expedition to determine whether or not the dominant species here possesses the Synapse known to our* [catalog] *as Beta sub Sixteen, the master* [computer] [at home] *having concluded that without the Synapse, this Earth culture must become extinct. Needless to* [say] [we] *are here to observe and not to interfere; to add to the* [memory-banks] *of the master* [computer] *only, it being a matter of no significance otherwise.*

On arrival [we] *set up the usual* [detectors], *expecting to get our information in a* [expression of very short time-unit] *or so; but to our* [great astonishment] *the readings on the* [kickshaw], *the* [gimmick] *and our high-sensitivity* [snivvy] *were mixed; it appeared that this culture possessed the Synapse but did not use it.* [! ! !]

[We] *therefore decided to conduct a* [microcosmic] *observation on each of the specimens in a small group, under* [laboratory] *conditions, to discover to what extent the Synapse exists in them, and under what circumstances it might become functional.*

We have set up for this purpose [the analog of] *a* [ ], *or* [residence], *called, in Terrestrial terms, small town boarding house, and have attracted to it:*

PHILIP HALVORSEN, *a young vocational guidance expert, who has a cease-lessly active analytical mind, and a kind of instinct for illogic: he knows when a person or situation is, in some way, wrong, and will not rest until he finds out why. He has recently followed his own logic to the conclusion that he wants to be dead—and he can't find out why!* . . . MARY HAUNT, *a beautiful girl who claims to be twenty-two (and lies), and who wants to be a movie star with an ambition transcending all reason. She is employed in a very minor capacity at the local radio station, and is always angry at everyone.* . . . ANTHONY DUNGLASS O'BANION, *young lawyer, deeply con-vinced that his family background, "breeding," "culture" and occupation set him apart from everyone else in town; he is desperately fighting a growing conviction that he is in love with* . . . SUE MARTIN, *young wid-owed night-club hostess (whom O'Banion's Mother, if she were here, would certainly refer to as a "woman of that sort"). Sue Martin, a woman of un-usual equilibrium, loves O'Banion but will not submit herself to his snob-bery and therefore keeps her feelings very much to herself.* . . . *Her young son* ROBIN, *who is three, and is friends with everyone everywhere including his invisible, "imaginary" playmates Boff and Googie. Robin's special friend is the lawyer O'Banion; they get along very well indeed.* . . . *Finally,* MISS SCHMIDT, *the high-school librarian, who is a soft-voiced, timid little rabbit of a woman, afraid of the world and abjectly obedient to propriety.*
The retired couple who run the boarding house are SAM *and* BITTY BITTEL-MAN, *wise, relaxed, helpful, observant. They are available always except for one day a month when they go out "for a ride."*
That, in Terrestrial terms, is [our] laboratory setup. [We] installed a [widget] and [rigged-up] a [wadget] as complementary [observation-and-control] even though it meant using a [miserable] [inefficient] [old-fash-ioned] power supply on the [wadget], which has to be re[charged] every [equivalent of Earth month]. Everything proceeded satisfactorily until [Smith], plagued by what [I] can only, in the most cosmic breadth of generosity, call an excess of enthusiasm, insisted that [we] speed up our research by stimulating the Synapse in these specimens. In spite of [my] warnings and [caution], he [bulled] ahead giving [me] no choice but to assist [him] in re[wiring] the [machines] for this purpose. But let it be on the [record] that [I] specifically warned [him] of the dangers of re-vealing [our] presence here. [I] for [one] dread the idea of being re-sponsible for the destruction of organized life. Even if only one of the specimens should detect [us], there is so much intercommunication in this small group that it would be virtually impossible to remove or destroy one without alerting and disturbing all. The least effect would be to negate all [our] efforts so far; the most is something [I] cannot [ethically] live with. Under these [unhappy] circumstances [we] proceeded with the stimula-tion: Old Sam Bittelman went to Miss Schmidt's room when she reported her venetian blind broken and unable to close. She suddenly found it im-possible not to answer Sam's questions, which probed at the very roots of her timidity. Shocked to these roots, but more thoughtful than she had ever been in her life before, she went to bed forgetting the blind and thinking

about the fact that her conditioning to keep her body covered was more deeply instilled into her than Thou shalt not kill—*and other, equally unsettling concepts.*

Mary Haunt overslept, for the very first time, and went into the kitchen, furious. Sam and Bitty were there, and suddenly the girl had to answer the questions they shot at her. She escaped quickly, but spent the rest of the day in bed, miserable and disoriented, wondering if, after all, she did want Hollywood. . . .

Anthony O'Banion went down to the night club where Sue Martin worked, and sat out of sight on the balcony. Suddenly Sam Bittelman was at the table with him, asking him deeply troubling questions about the law and why he practiced it, about his convictions of blood and breeding, and about his feelings for Sue Martin. Dizzied and speechless, O'Banion was led home by kind old Sam.

Bitty found Sue Martin alone in her room one morning, and asked her some pointed questions, all of which Sue answered with ease, quite undisturbed, quite willing. Yes, she loved O'Banion. No, she wouldn't do anything about it; that was O'Banion's problem. Sue Martin was no trouble at all to Bitty. . . .

Late one hot evening Halvorsen walked into the kitchen with a gun in his hand, saying there was something wrong, something he couldn't name . . . but "Who are you and what do you want?" Bitty calmly asked him why he had bought a gun: "It was for yourself, wasn't it, Philip? Why do you want to be dead?"

[I] submit that [Smith] is guilty of carelessness and [unethical] conduct. [I] see no solution but to destroy this specimen and perhaps the others. [I] declare that this situation has arisen only because [Smith] ignored [my] clearly [stated] warning. As [I] [write], this alerted, frightened specimen stands ready to commit violence on [our] [equipment] and thereby itself. [I] hereby serve notice on [Smith] that [he] got [us] into this and [he] can [   ]ing well get [us] out.

CHAPTER NINE

"Why do you want to be dead?"

Phil Halvorsen stood gaping at the old woman, and the gun, still shrouded in its silly paper bag, began whispering softly as he trembled. The butt fitted his hand as his hand fitted the butt; *It's holding me,* he thought hysterically, knowing clearly that his hysteria was a cloud, a cloak, a defense against that which he was not equipped to think about . . . well, maybe not ready to think about; but how had she known?

For nearly two days he had been worrying and gnawing at this sense of wrongness about him. Back and back he would come to it, only to reach bafflement and kick it away angrily; not eating enough, hardly sleeping at all; *let me sleep first!* something wailed within him, and as he sensed it he kicked it away again: more hysteria, not letting him think. And then a word from O'Banion, a phrase from Miss Schmidt, and his own ragbag memory: The Bittelmans never said—they always asked. It was as if they could reach into a man's mind, piece together questions from the unused lumber stored there, and from it build shapes he couldn't bear to look at. *How many terrible questions have I locked away?* And has she broken the lock? He said, "Don't . . . ask me that . . . why did you ask me that?"

"Well, why ever not?"

"You're a . . . you can read my mind."

"Can I?"

"*Say* something!" he shouted. The paper bag stopped whispering. He thought she noticed it.

"Am I reading your mind," she asked reasonably, "if I see you walk in here the way you did looking like the wrath o' God, holding that thing out in front of you and shying away from it at the same time, and then tell you that if you accidentally pull the trigger you might have to die for it? Read minds? Isn't it enough to read the papers?"

Oh, he thought. . . . Oh-h. He looked at her sharply. She was quite calm, waiting, leaving it to him. He knew, suddenly and certainly, that this woman could outthink him, outtalk him, seven ways from Sunday without turning a hair. This meant either that he was completely and embarrassingly wrong, or that her easy explanations weren't true ones . . . which was the thing that had been bothering him in the first place. "Why did you say I bought the gun for something else?" he snapped.

She gave him that brief, very warm smile. "Didn't say; I asked you, right? How could I really know?"

For one further moment he hesitated, and it came to him that if this flickering doubt about her was justified, the chances were that a gun would be as ineffective as an argument. And besides . . . it was like a silent current in the room, a sort of almost-sound, or the aural pressure he could feel sometimes when a car was braking near him; but here it came out feeling like comfort.

He let the bag fall until it swung from its mouth. He twisted it closed. "Will you—I mean," he bumbled, "I don't want it."

"Now what would I do with a gun?" she asked.

"I don't know. I just don't want it around. I can't throw it away. I don't want to have anything to do with it. I thought maybe you could put it away somewhere."

"You know, you'd better sit down," said Bitty. She didn't exactly push him but he had to move back to get out of her way as she approached, and when the back of his knees hit a chair he had to sit down or fall down. Bitty continued across the kitchen, opened a high cupboard and put the bag on the topmost shelf. "Only place in the house Robin can't climb into."

"Robin. Oh yes," he said, seeing the possibilities. "I'm sorry. I'm sorry."

"You'd better talk it out, Philip," she said in her flat, kind way. "You're fixing to bust wide open. I won't have you messing up my kitchen."

"There's nothing to talk about."

She paused on her way back to the sink, in a strange hesitation like one listening. Suddenly she turned and sat down at the table with him. "What did you want with a gun, Philip?" she demanded; and just as abruptly, he answered her, as if she had hurled something at him and it had bounced straight back into her waiting hands, "I was thinking about killing myself."

If he thought this would elicit surprise, or an exclamation, or any more questions, he was disappointed. She seemed only to be waiting, so he said, with considerably more care, "I don't know why I told you that but it came out right. I said I was thinking about doing it. I didn't say I was going to do it." He looked at her. Not enough? Okay then: "I couldn't be sure exactly what I was thinking until I bought a gun. Does that make any sense to you?"

"Why not?"

"I don't ever know exactly what I think unless I try it out. Or get all the pieces laid out ready to try."

"Or tell somebody?"

"I couldn't tell anybody about this."

"Did you try?"

"*Damn* it!" It was a whisper, but it emerged under frightening pressure. Then normally, "I'm sorry, Bitty, I'm real sorry. I suddenly got mad at the language, you know what I mean? You say something in words of one syllable and it comes out meaning something you never meant. I told you, 'I couldn't tell anybody about this.' That sounds as if I knew all about it and was just shy or something. So you ask me, 'Did you try?' But what I really mean was that this whole thing, everything about it, is a bunch of—of feelings and—well, crazy ideas *that I couldn't tell anyone about.*"

Bitty's rare smile flickered. "Did you try?"

"Well I'll be. You're worse than ever," he said, this time without anger. "You *do* know what I'm thinking."

"So what were you thinking?"

He sobered immediately. "Things . . . all crazy. I think all the time, Bitty, like a radio was playing all day, all night, and I can't turn it off. Wouldn't want to; wouldn't know how to live without it. Ask me is it going to rain and off I go, thinking about rain, where it comes from, about clouds, how many different kinds there are; about air-currents and jet-streams and everything else you pick up reading those little paragraphs at the bottom of newspaper columns; about—"

"About why you bought a gun?"

"Huh? Oh . . . all right, all right, I won't ramble." He closed his eyes to hear his thoughts, and frowned at them. "Anyway, at the tail end of these run-downs is always some single thing that stops the chain—for the time. It might be the answer to some question I asked myself, or someone asks me, or it might just be as far as the things I know will take me.

"So one day a few weeks ago I got to thinking about guns, and never mind the way I went, but what I arrived at was the idea of a gun killing me, and then just the idea of being dead. And the more I thought, the more scared I got."

After waiting what seemed to be long enough, Bitty said, "Scared."

"It wasn't kil—being dead that scared me. It was the feeling I had about it. I was glad about it. I wanted it. That's what scared me."

"Why do you want to be dead?"

"That's what I don't know." His voice fell. "Don't know, I just don't know," he mumbled. "So I couldn't get it out of my head and I couldn't make any sense out of it, and I thought the only thing I could do was to get a gun and load it and—get everything ready, to see how I felt then." He looked up at her. "That sounds real crazy, I bet."

Bitty shrugged. Either she denied the statement or it didn't matter. Halvorsen looked down again and said to his clenched hands, "I sat there in my room with the muzzle in my mouth and all the safeties off, and hooked my thumb around the trigger."

"Learn anything?"

His mouth moved but he couldn't find words to fit the movement.

"Well," said Bitty sharply, "why didn't you pull it?"

"I just—" He closed his eyes in one of those long, inward-reading pauses. "—couldn't. I mean, *didn't*. I wasn't afraid, if that's what you want to know." He glanced at her and couldn't tell what she wanted to know. "Sitting there, that way, I came to realize that this wasn't the way it should happen," he said with some difficulty.

"What is the way?"

"Like this: if ever there was an earthquake, or I looked up and saw a safe falling on me, or some other thing like that, something from outside myself—I wouldn't move aside. I'd let it happen."

"Is there a difference between that and shooting yourself?"

"Yes!" he said, with more animation than he had shown so far. "Put it like this: there's part of me that's dead, and wants the rest of me dead. There's part of me that's alive, and wants all of me alive." He looked that over and nodded at it. "My hand, my arm, my thumb on the trigger—they're alive. All the live parts of me want to help me go on living, d'you see? No live part should help the dead part get what it wants. The way it'll happen, the way it should happen, is not when I do something to make it happen. It'll be when I don't do something. I won't get out of the way, and that's it, and thanks for keeping the gun for me, it's no use to me." He stood up and found his eyes locked with hers, and sat right down again, breathing hard.

"Why do you want to be dead?" she asked flatly.

He put his head down on his hands and began to rock it slowly to and fro.

"Don't you want to know?"

Muffled, his voice came up from the edge of the table. "No." Abruptly he sat up, staring. "No? What made me say no? Bitty," he demanded, "what made me say that?"

344

She shrugged. He jumped up and began pacing swiftly up and down the kitchen. "I'll be dogged," he murmured once, and "Well, what d'ye kn—"

Bitty watched him, and catching him on a turn when their eyes could meet, she asked, "Well—why do you want to—"

"Shut up," he said. He said it, not to her, but to any interruption. His figmentary signal-light, which indicated dissatisfaction, unrightness, was casting its glow all over his interior landscape. To be hounded half to death by something like this, then to discover that basically he didn't want to investigate it. . . . He sat down and faced her, his eyes alight. "I don't know yet," he said, "but I will, I will." He took a deep breath. "It's like being chased by something that's gaining on you, and you duck into an alley, and then you find it's blind, there's only a brick wall; so you sit down to wait, it's all you can do. And all of a sudden you find a door in the wall. Been there all the time. Just didn't look."

"Why do you want to be dead?"

"B-because I—I shouldn't be alive. Because the average guy— Different, that's what I am, different, unfit."

"Different, unfit." Bitty's eyebrows raised slightly. "They the same thing, Philip?"

"Well, sure."

"You can't jump like a kangaroo, you can't eat grass raw like a cow— different. You unfit because you can't do those things?"

He made an annoyed laugh. "Not that, not that. People, I mean."

"You can't fly a plane. You can't sing like Sue Martin. You can't spout law like Tony O'Banion. That kind of different?"

"No," he said, and in a surge of anguish, "No, no! I can't talk about it, Bitty!" He looked at her and again saw that rare, deep smile. He answered it in kind, but weakly, remembering that he had said that to her before. "This time I mean I can't talk about such things to you. To a lady," he said in abrupt, unbearable confusion.

"I'm no lady," said Bitty with conviction. Suddenly she punched his forearm; he thought it was the first time she had ever touched him. "To you I'm not even a human being. Not even another person. I mean it," she said warmly. "Have I asked you a single question you couldn't've asked yourself? Have I told you anything you didn't know?"

His peculiar linear mind cast rapidly back and up again. He felt an odd instant of disorientation. It was not unpleasant. Bitty said gently, "Go on talking to yourself, boy. Who knows—you might find yourself in good company."

"Aw . . . thanks, Bitty," he mumbled. His eyes stung and he shook his head. "All right, all *right*, then . . . it just came to me, one big flash, and I guess I couldn't sit here—here," he said, waving his arm to include the scrubbed, friendly kitchen, "and look at you, and think about these—uh this—all at once." He swallowed heavily. "Well, that time I told you about, that day I found out I wanted to be dead, it was like getting hit on the head. Right after that, only a couple of minutes, I got hit on the head just as hard by something else. I didn't know—want to know till now that they

345

were connected, some way." He closed his eyes. "It was a theater, that rathole down across the Circle. You know. It—it hit out at me when I wasn't looking. It was all covered with . . . pictures and—and it said SEE this and SEE that and SEE some dirty other thing, adults only, you know what I mean." He opened his eyes to see what Bitty was doing, but Bitty was doing nothing at all. Waiting. He turned his face away from her, and said indistinctly into his shoulder, "All my life those things meant nothing to me. *There!*" he shouted, "you see? Different, different!"

But she wouldn't see. Or she wouldn't see until he did, himself, more clearly. She still waited.

He said, "Down at work, there's a fellow, Scodie. This Scodie, he's a good man, really can turn out a day's work. I mean, he likes what he's doing, he cares. Except every time a girl goes by, everything stops. He snaps up out of what he's doing, he watches her. I mean, *every* time. It's like he can't help himself. He does it the way a cadet salutes an officer on the street. He does it like that crossing-guard on the toy train, that pops out of his little house every time his little light goes on. He watches until the girl's gone by, and then he says 'mmm*yuh!*' and looks over at me and winks."

"What do you do, every time?"

"Well, I—" He laughed uncertainly. "I guess I wink back at him and I say, mm-*hm!* But I know why I do it, it's because he expects me to; he'd think it was sort of peculiar if I didn't. But he doesn't do it for me; I don't expect anything of him one way or the other. He does it—" Words failed him, and he tried again. "Doing that, he's part of—everybody. What he does is the same thing every song on every radio says every minute. Every ad in every magazine does it if it possibly can, even if it means a girl in her underwear with stillson wrenches for sale." He leapt to his feet and began to pace excitedly. "You got to back off a little to see it," he told Bitty, who smiled behind his back. "You got to look at the whole thing all at once, to see how *much* there is of it, the jokes people tell—yeah, you got to laugh at them, whatever, you even have to know a couple, or they'll . . . The window displays, the television, the movies . . . somebody's writing an article about transistors or termites or something, and every once in a while he figures he's been away from it long enough and he has to say something about the birds and the bees and 'Gentlemen prefer.' Everywhere you turn the whole world's at it, chipping and chipping away at it—"

He stamped back to the table and looked into Bitty's face intently. "You got to back away and look at it all at once," he cautioned again. "I'm not in kindergarten, I know what it's all about. I'm not a woman-hater. I've been in love. I'll get married, some day. Go ahead and tell me I'm talking about one of the biggest, strongest, down-deep urges we have—I'll buy that. That's what I *mean*, that's what I'm *talking* about." His forehead was pink and shiny; he took out a crumpled handkerchief and batted at it. "So *much* of it, all around you, all the time, filling a big hungry need in average people. I don't mean the urge itself; I mean all this *reminding*, this what do you call it, indoctrination. It's a need or folks wouldn't stand for so much of it, comic books, lipstick, that air-jet in the floor at the funnyhouse at the

Fair." He thumped into his chair, panting. "Do you begin to see what I mean about 'different'?"

"Do you?" asked Bitty, but Halvorsen didn't hear her; he was talking again. "Different, because I don't feel that hunger to be reminded, I don't need all that high-pressure salemanship, I don't want it. Every time I tell one of my jokes, every time I wink back at old Scodie, I feel like a fool, like some sort of a liar. But you got to protect yourself; you can't ever let anyone find out. You know why? Because the average guy, the guy-by-the-millions that needs all that noise so much, he'll let you be the way he is, or he'll let you be . . . I'm sorry, Bitty. Don't make me go into a lot of dirty details. You see what I mean, don't you?"

"What do you mean?"

Irritated, he blew a single sharp blast from his nostrils. "Well, what I mean is, they'll let you be the way they are, or you have to be . . . sick, crippled. You can't be anything else! You can't be Phil Halvorsen who isn't sick and who isn't crippled but who just doesn't naturally go around banging his antlers against the rocks so the whole world can hear it."

"So—that's what you mean by unfit?"

"That's why I wanted to be dead. I just don't think the way other people do; if I act the way other people do I feel . . . feel guilty. I guess I had this piling up in me for years, and that day with the guns, when I found out what I wanted to do . . . and then that theater-front, yawping over me like a wet mouth full of dirty teeth . . ." He giggled foolishly. "Listen to me, will you . . . Bitty, I'm sorry."

She utterly ignored this. "High-pressure salesmanship," she said.

"What?"

"You said it, I didn't. . . . Isn't hunger one of those big deep needs, Philip? Suppose you had a bunch of folks starving on an island and dropped them a ton of food—would they need high-pressure salesmanship?"

It was as if he stood at the edge of a bottomless hole—more, the very outer edge of the world, so close his very toes projected over the emptiness. It filled him with wonder; he was startled, but not really afraid, because it might well be that to fall down and down into that endless place might be a very peaceful thing. He closed his eyes and slowly, very slowly, came back to reality, the kitchen, Bitty, Bitty's words. "You mean . . . the av— the ordin—you mean, people aren't really interested?"

"Not that interested."

He blinked; he felt as if he had ceased to exist in his world and had been plunked down in a very similar, but totally new one. It was far less lonely here.

He hit the table and laughed into Bitty's calm face. "I'm going to sleep," he said, and got up; and he knew she had caught his exact shade of meaning when she said gently, "Sure you can."

EXCERPT FROM FIELD EXPEDITION [NOTEBOOK]: [*I*] *had thought up to now that in* [*Smith*]*'s* [*immorally*] *excessive enthusiasm and* [*bullheadedness*] [*I*] *had encountered the utmost in* [*irritants*]. [*I*] *was in* [*error*]; [*he*] *now surpasses*

*these, and without effort. In the first place, having placated and outwitted
the alerted specimen, [he] has destroyed [my] preliminary detailed [report]
on him; this is [irritat]ing not only because it was done without consulting
[me], not only because of the trouble [I] went to to [write] it all up, but
mostly because [he] is technically within [his] [ethics-rights]—the emergency
created by [his] [bumbling mismanagement] no longer exists. [I] have [force]-
fully pointed out to [him] that it was only by the application of [my] kind
of cautious resourcefulness that [he] succeeded, but [he] just [gloats]. [I]
[most strongly affirm-and-bind-myself], the instant [we] get back home and
are released from Expeditionary [ethic-discipline], [I] shall [bend] [his] [   ]s
over [his] [   ] and [tie a knot in] them.*

*[We] have now, no [credit-thanks] to [Smith], reached a point where all our
specimens are in a state of [heavy] preconditioning of their unaccountably
random Synapse Beta sub Sixteen. Being a synapse, it will of course come into
full operation only on a reflexive level and in an extreme emergency, which
[we] are now setting up.*

*Unless [Smith] produces yet more [stupidities], the specimens should live
through this.*

CHAPTER TEN

IT HAD BECOME impossibly hot, and very still. Leaves dropped at impossible angles, and still the dust lay on them. Sounds seemed too enervated
to travel very far. The sky was brass all day, and at night, for want of ambition, the overcast was no more than a gauzy hood of haze.

It was the Bittelmans' "day off" again, and without them the spine had
been snatched out of the household. The boarders ate pokily, lightly, at
random, and somehow got through the time when there was nothing to
do but sit up late enough to get tired enough to get whatever rest the
temperature would permit. It was too hot, even, to talk, and no one attempted it. They drifted to their rooms to wait for sleep; they slumped in front
of fans and took cold showers which generated more heat than they dis-
sipated. When at last darkness came, it was a relief only to the eyes. The
household pulse beat slowly and slower; by eight o'clock it was library-quiet,
by nine quite silent, so that the soft brushing of knuckles on Miss Schmidt's
door struck her like a shout.

"Wh-who is it?" she quavered, when she recovered her breath.

"Sue."

"Oh—oh. Oh, do come in." She pulled the damp sheet tight up against
her throat.

"Oh, you're in bed already. I'm sorry."

"*I'm* sorry. It's all right."

Sue Martin swung the door shut and came all the way in. She was wearing
an off-the-shoulder peasant blouse and a pleated skirt with three times more

filmy nylon in it than one would guess until she turned, when it drifted like smoke. "My," said Miss Schmidt enviously. "You look cool."

"State of mind," Sue smiled. "I'm about to go to work and I wish I didn't have to."

"And Bitty's out. I'm honorary baby-sitter again."

"You're an angel."

"No, oh, no!" cried Miss Schmidt. "I wish everything I had to do was that easy. Why, in all the time I've known you, every time I've done it, I— I've had nothing to do!"

"He sleeps pretty soundly. Clear conscience, I guess."

"I think it's because he's happy. He smiles when he sleeps."

"Smiles? Sometimes he laughs out loud," said Sue Martin. "I was a little worried tonight, for a while. He was so flushed and wide-awake—"

"Well, it's *hot*."

"It wasn't that." Sue chuckled. "His precious Boff was all over the place, 'fixin' things,' Robin said. What he was fixing all over the walls and ceiling, Robin didn't say. Whatever it was, it's finished now, though, and Robin's sound asleep. I'm sure you won't even have to go in. And Bitty ought to be home soon."

"You'll leave your door open?"

Sue Martin nodded and glanced up at the large open transom over Miss Schmidt's door. "You'll hear him if he so much as blinks. . . . I've got to run. Thanks *so* much."

"Oh, really, Mrs. M—uh, Sue. Don't thank me. Just run along."

"Good night."

Sue Martin slipped out, silently closing the door behind her. Miss Schmidt sighed and looked up at the transom. After Sue's light footsteps had faded away, she listened, listened as hard as she could, trying to pour part of herself through the transom, across the hall, through Sue Martin's open door. A light sleeper at any time, she knew confidently that she was on guard now and would wake if anything happened. If she slept at all in this sticky heat.

She might sleep, at that, she thought after a while. She shifted herself luxuriously, and edged to a slightly cooler spot on the bed. "That wicked Sam," she murmured, and blushed in the dark. But he had been right. A *nightgown* in weather like this?

Suddenly, she slept.

In O'Banion's room, there was a soft sound. He had put off taking a shower until suddenly he had used up his energy, and could hardly stir. I'll just rest my eyes, he thought, and bowed his head. The soft sound was made by his forehead striking the book.

Halvorsen lay rigid on his bed, staring at the ceiling. There, almost as if it was projected, was the image of a flimsy cylinder vomiting smoke. Go ahead, he thought, detachedly. Or go away. I don't care which. Before I talked to Bitty, I wanted you. Now, I don't care. Is that better? He closed his eyes, but the image was still there. He lay very quietly, watching the insides of his eyelids. It was like being asleep. When he was asleep the thing was there too.

Mary Haunt sat by her window, pretending it was cooler there than in bed. There was no anger in her, just now as she lay back and dreamed. The Big Break, the pillars of light at her première, her name two stories tall over a Broadway marquee—these had no place in this particular favorite dream. I'll do over Mom's room, she thought, dimity, this time, and full, full skirts on the vanity and the night table. She closed her eyes, putting herself in Mom's room with such vividness that she could almost smell the cool faint odor of lavender sachets and the special freshness of sheets dried in the sun. Yes, and something else, outside the room, barely, just barely she knew bread was baking, so that the kitchen would be heavenly with it; the bread would dominate the spice-shelf for a while, until it was out of the oven and cooled. "Oh, Mom . . ." she whispered. She lay still in her easychair, holding and holding to the vision until this room, this house, this town didn't matter any more.

Some hours went by.

Robin floated in a luminous ocean of sleep where there was nothing to fear and where, if he just turned to look, there were love and laughter waiting for him. His left hand uncurled and he thrust the second and third fingers together into his mouth. Somehow he was a big bulldozer with a motor that sounded like Mitster and tracks that clattered along like Coffeepot, and Boff and Googie were riding along with him and laughing. Then without effort he was a glittery ferris-wheel, but he could watch himself too in one of the cars, screaming his delight and leaning against Tonio's hard arm. All this, yet he was still afloat in that deep bright place where there was no fear, where love and laughter hid around some indescribable corner, waiting. Bright, brighter. Warm, warm, warmer . . . oh, hot, *hot!*

CHAPTER ELEVEN

MISS SCHMIDT OPENED HER EYES to an impossible orange glare and a roar like the end of the world. For one full second she lay still, paralyzed by an utter disbelief; no light could have become so bright, no sound could have risen to this volume, without waking her as it began. Then she found a way to focus her eyes against that radiance, and saw the flames, and in what was left to her of her immobile second, she explained the whole thing to herself and said relievedly, of course, of course: it's only a nightmare and *suppose there's a fire?*—and that's so *silly,* Sam—

And then she was out of bed in a single bound, standing in the center of the room, face to flaming face with reality. Everything was burning— everything! The drapes had already gone and the slats of the venetian blind, their cords gone, were heaped on the floor, going like a campfire. Even as she watched the screen sagged and crumpled, its pine frame glaring and spitting pitch through blistering paint. It fell outside.

Outside, outside! The window's open, you're on the ground floor; yes, and there on the chair, not burning yet, your bathrobe; take the robe and jump, quick!

Then, beyond belief, there was a sound louder than the earth-filling roar, and different; fine hot powder and a hot hail of plaster showered on her shoulders; she looked up to see the main beam, right over her head, sag toward her and hang groaning, one part reaching to the other with broken flat fingers of splintered wood which gloved themselves in flame as she saw them. She cowered, and just then the handle of the door turned and a gout of smoke slammed it open and whisked out of sight in the updraft; and there in the hall stood Robin, grinding a fat little fist into one abruptly wakened eye. She could see his lips move, though she could hear nothing in this mighty bellow of sound. She knew it, though, and heard it clearly in her mind: "What's 'at noice?"

The beam overhead grumbled and again she was showered with plaster. She batted it off her shoulders, and whimpered. A great flame must have burst from the roof above her just then, for through the window she saw a brilliant glare reflected from the white clapboards of the garage wall outside. The glare tugged at her—*jump!*—and besides, her robe . . .

The beam thundered and began to fall. Now she must make a choice, in microseconds. The swiftest thought would not be fast enough to weigh and consider and decide; all that could matter now was what was inside her, throwing switches (some so worn and easy to move!). A giant was throwing them, and he was strong; his strength was a conditioning deeper than *thou shalt not kill*; he was a lesson learned before she had learned to love God, or to walk, or to talk. He was her mother's authority and the fear of all the hairy, sweaty, dangerous mysteries from which she had shielded herself all her life; and his name and title were Cover Thyself! With him, helping him, was the reflexive Save Thyself! and against these—Robin, whom she loved (but love is what she felt, once, for a canary, and once for a Raggedy Ann doll) and her sense of duty to Sue Martin (but so lightly promised, and at the time such a meaningless formality). There could be no choice in such a battle, though she must live with the consequences for all her years.

Then—

—it was as if a mighty voice had called *Stop!*, and the very flames froze. Half a foot above her hung the jagged end of the burning beam, and chunks of plaster, splinters and scraps of shattered lath and glowing joist stopped in midair. Yet during this sliver of a fraction of time, she knew that the phenomenon was a metal something, a figment, and the idea of time-cessation only a clumsy effort of her mind's to account for what was happening.

Save Thyself was still there, hysterical hands clutching for the controls, but *Cover Thyself* disappeared into the background. Save herself she would, but it would be on new terms. She was in the grip of a reflex of reflexes, one which took into consideration all the factors a normal reflex would, to the end goal of survival. But along with these, it called up everything Reta Schmidt had ever done, everything she had been. In a single soundless flash, a new kind of light was thrown into every crevice and cranny of her existence. It was her total self now, reacting to a total situation far wider than that which obtained here in this burning room. It illuminated even the future—that much of it which depended upon these events, between them and the next probable major "crossroads." It canceled past misjudgments and illogics and replaced them with rightness, even for the times she had known what was right and had done otherwise. It came and was gone even while she leaped, while she took two bounding steps across the floor and the beam crashed and crushed and showered sparks where she had been standing.

She scooped up the child and ran down the hall, through the foyer, into the kitchen. It was dark there, thick with swirling smoke, but the glass panels on the kitchen door glared with some unfamiliar light from outdoors. She began to cough violently, but grimly aimed at that light and drove ahead. It was eclipsed suddenly by a monstrous shadow, and suddenly it exploded inward. There were lights out there she had never seen before, and half-silhouetted in the broken doorway was a big man with a gleaming helmet and an axe. She tried to call, or perhaps it was only a scream, but instead she went into a spasm of coughing.

"Somebody in here?" asked the man. A beam of light, apparently from the street, lit up the shield on the front of his helmet as he leaned forward. He stepped inside. "Whew! Where are you?"

She went blindly to him and pushed Robin against his coat. "The baby," she croaked. "Get him out of this smoke."

He grunted and suddenly Robin was gone from her arms. "You all right?" He was peering into the black and the smoke.

"Take him out," she said. "Then I'll want your coat."

He went out. Miss Schmidt could hear Robin's clear voice: "You a fireman?"

"I sure am," rumbled the man. "Want to see my fire engine? Then sit right there on the grass and wait one second. Okay?"

"Okay."

The coat flew through the doorway.

"Got it?"

"Thank you." She put the huge garment on and went out. The fireman waited there, again holding Robin in his arms. "You all right, ma'am?"

Her lungs were an agony and she had burns on her feet and shoulders. Her hair was singed and one of her hands was flayed across its back. "I'm just fine," she said.

They began to walk up the road. Robin squirmed around in the man's arms and popped his head out to look back at the brightly burning house.

"'By, Boff," he said happily, and then gave his heart to the fire engine.

CHAPTER TWELVE

"Mother, the bread's burning!"

Mary Haunt opened her eyes to an impossible glare and a great roaring. She shrieked and flailed out blindly, as if she could frighten it away, whatever it was; and then she came enough to her senses to realize that she still sat in her chair by the window, and that the house was on fire. She leaped to her feet, sending the heavy chair skittering across the room where it toppled over against the clothespress. As it always did when it was bumped, the clothespress calmly opened its doors.

But Mary Haunt didn't wait for that or anything else. She struck the screen with the flat of her hand. It popped out easily, and she hit the ground almost at the same time as it did. She ran off a few steps, and then, like Lot's wife, curiosity overtook her and she stopped. She turned around in fascination.

Great wavering flames leapt fifty and sixty feet in the air and all the windows were alight. From the town side she could hear the shriek and clang of fire engines, and windows and doors opening, and running feet. But the biggest sound of all was the roar of the fire, like a giant's blowtorch.

She looked back at her own window. She could see into the room easily, the chair on its side, the bed with its chenille top-spread sprouting measles of spark and char, and the gaping doors of the—"My clothes! My clothes!"

Furiously she ran back to the window, paused a moment in horror to see fire run along the picture-molding of the inside wall like a nightmare caterpillar. "My clothes," she whispered. She didn't make much money at her job, but every cent that wasn't used in bed and board went on her back. She mouthed something, and from her throat came that animal growl of hers; she put both hands on the sill and leaped, and tumbled back into the house.

She was prepared for the heat but not for that intensity of light, and the noise was worst of all. She recoiled from it and stood for a moment with her hands over her eyes, swaying with the impact of it. Then she ground her teeth and made her way across to the clothespress. She swept open the bottom drawer and turned out the neatly folded clothes. Down at the bottom was a cotton print dress, wrapped carefully around a picture frame. She lifted it out and hugged it, and ran across to the window with it. She leaned far out and dropped it gently on the grass, then turned back in again.

The far wall, by the door, began to buckle high up, and suddenly there was fire up there. The corner near the ceiling toppled into the room with a crash and a cloud of white dust and greasy-looking smoke, and then the whole wall fell, not toward her, but away, so that her room now included a section of the corridor outside. As the dust settled somebody, a man, came roaring inarticulately and battering through the rubble. She could not know who it was. He apparently meant to travel the corridor whether it was all there or not, and he did, disappearing again into the inferno.

She staggered back toward the clothespress. She felt mad, drunk, crazy. Maybe it was the de-oxygenated atmosphere and maybe it was fear and reaction, but it was sort of wonderful, too; she felt her face writhing and part of her was numb with astonishment at what the rest of her was doing: she was laughing. She slammed into the clothespress, gasping for breath, filled her lungs and delivered up a shrill peal of laughter. Almost helpless from it, she fumbled down a dull satin evening gown with a long silver sash. She held it up in front of her and laughed again, doubling over it, and then straightened up, rolling the dress up into a ball as she did so. With all her might she hurled it into the rubble of the hallway. Next was a simple black dress with no back and a little bolero; with an expression on her face that can only be described as cheerful, she threw it after the evening gown. Then the blue, and the organdy with the taffeta underskirt, and the black and orange one she used to call her Hallowe'en dress; each one she dragged out, held up, and hurled: "You," she growled between her convulsions of laughter, "you, and you, and *you*." When the press was empty, she ran to the bureau and snatched open her scarf drawer, uncovering a flowerbed of dainty, filmy silk and nylon and satin shawls, scarves, and kerchiefs. She whipped out an oversized babushka, barely heavier than the air that floated it, and ran with it to the flaming mass where her door once was. She dipped and turned like a dancer, fluttering it through flame, and when it was burning she bounded back to the bureau and put it in the drawer with the others. Fire streamed out of the drawer and she laughed and laughed . . .

And something nipped her sharply on the calves; she yelped and turned and found the lace of her black negligee was on fire. She twisted back and gathered the cloth and ripped it away. The pain had sobered her and she was bewildered now, weak and beginning to be frightened. She started for the window and tripped and fell heavily, and when she got up the smoke was suddenly like a scalding blanket over her head and shoulders and she didn't know which way to go. She knelt and peered and found the window in an unexpected direction, and made for it. As she tumbled through, the ceiling behind her fell, and the roof after it.

On her belly she clawed away from the house, sobbing, and at last rose to her knees. She smelt of smoke and burned hair and all her lovely fingernails were broken. She squatted on the ground, staring at the flaming shell of the house, and cried like a little girl. But when her swollen eyes rested on that square patch in the grass, she stopped crying and got up and limped over to it. Her cotton print, and the picture . . . she picked the tidy package up and went tiredly away with it into the shadows where the hedge met the garage.

CHAPTER THIRTEEN

O'BANION RAISED HIS HEAD groggily from the flyleaf of his *Blackstone* and the neat inscription written there:

The law doth punish man or woman
That steals the goose from off the common,
But let the greater felon loose,
That steals the common from the goose,

—a piece of Eighteenth Century japery which O'Banion deplored. However, it had been written there by Opdycke when he was in law school, and the Opdyckes were a darn fine family. Princeton people, of course, but nobody minded.

All this flickered through his mind as he swam up out of sleep, along with "What's the matter with my head?" because any roaring that loud must be in his ears; it would be too incredible anywhere else, and "What's the matter with the light?"

Then he was fully awake, and on his feet. "My *God!*"

He ran to the door and snatched it open. Flame squirted at him as if from a hose; in a split second he felt his eyebrows disappear. He yelled and staggered back from it, and it pursued him. He turned and dove out the window, landing clumsily on his stomach with his fists clenched over his solar plexus. His own weight drove the fists deep, and for a full minute he lay groaning for air. At last he got up, shook himself, and pelted around the house to the front. One fire engine was already standing by the curb. There was a police car and the knot of bug-eyed spectators who spring apparently out of the ground at the scene of any accident anywhere at any hour. At the far end of the Bittelman lot, there was a sharp scream of rubber and a glare of lights as a taxicab pulled in as close to the police barrier as it could get. The door was already open; a figure left it, half running, half thrown out by the sudden stop.

"*Sue!*" But no one heard him—everyone else was yelling too: "Look!" "Somebody stop her!" "Hey!" "Hey, you!"

O'Banion backed off a little to cup his hands and yell again, when directly over his head a cheerful small voice said, "Mommy runs *fast!*"

"Robin! You're all right—" He was perched on top of the fire engine with one arm around the shining brass bell, looking like a Botticelli seraph. Someone beside him—good heavens, it was Miss Schmidt, disheveled and bright-eyed, wrapped up in some tentlike garment—Miss Schmidt screamed, "Stop her, stop her, I've got the baby here!"

Robin said to Miss Schmidt, "Tonio runs fast too, shall we?"

Now they were all yelling at O'Banion, but in four paces he could hear nothing but the roar ahead of him. He had never seen a house burn like this, all over, all at once. He took the porch steps in one bound and had just time to turn his shoulder to the door. It was ajar, but couldn't swing fast enough under such an impact. It went down flat and slid, and for one crazy moment O'Banion was riding it like an aquaplane in a sea of fire, for the foyer floor was ablaze. Then the leading edge of the door caught on something and spilled him off. He rolled over twice in fuming débris and then got his feet under him. It was like a particularly bad dream, so familiar, so confusing. He turned completely around to orient himself, found the corridor, and started up it, yelling for Sue at the top of his voice. He saw a left-hand wall lean down toward him and had to scamper back out of the way. It had barely poured its rubble down when he was on, in, and through it. Over the crash and roar, over his own hoarse bellowing, he thought he heard a crazy woman laughing somewhere in the fire. Even in his near-hysteria, he could say, "Not Sue, that's not Sue Martin. . . ." And he was, before he knew it, at and past Sue Martin's room. He flung out a hand and caught the door-jamb, which immediately came off in his hand. He bounced off the end wall and turned as he did so, like a sprint swimmer, and swung into Sue Martin's room. "Sue! Sue!"

Was he mistaken? Did someone call, "Robin—Robin honey . . ."?

He dropped to his knees, where he could see in relatively clearer air. "Sue, oh Sue!"

She lay half buried in rubble from the fallen ceiling. He threw off scorched and broken two-by-fours and burning lath, took her by the shoulders and lifted her out of the heap of broken plaster—thank the powers for that! it had protected her to some degree. "Sue?"

"Robin," she croaked.

He shook her. "He's all right, he's outside, I saw him."

She opened her eyes and frowned at him. Not at him; at what he had said. "He's here somewhere."

"I saw him. Come on!" He lifted her to her feet, and as she dragged, "It's the truth; do you think I would lie to you?"

He felt strength surge into her body. "You forgot to say, 'I, an O'Banion,'" she said, but it didn't hurt. They stumbled to the window and he pushed her through it and leaped after her. For two painful breaths they lay gulping clean air, and then O'Banion got to his feet. His head was spinning and he almost lay down again. He set his jaw and helped Sue Martin up. "Too close!" he shouted. Holding her up, he half-dragged her no more than a step when she suddenly straightened, and with unexpected and irresistible strength leapt back toward the burning wall, pulling him with her. He caught at her to regain his balance, and she put her arms tight around him. "The wall!" he screamed as it leaned out over them. She said nothing, but her arms tightened even more, and he could have moved more easily if he had been bound to a post with steel chains. The wall came down then, thunder and sparks, like the end of the world; madly, it occurred to him just then that he could solve one of his problem cases by defining the unorthodox contract under suit as a stock certificate.

But instead of dying he took a stinging blow on his right shoulder, and that was all. He opened his eyes. He and Sue Martin still stood locked together, and all around them was flame like a flower-bed with the rough outline of the house wall and its peaked roof. Around their feet was the four-foot circular frame of the attic vent, which had ringed them like a quoit.

The woman slumped in his arms, and he lifted her and picked his way, staggering, into the friendly dark and the welcome hands of the firemen. But when they tried to lift her away from him she held his arm and would not let go. "Put me down, just put me down," she said. "I'm all right. Put me down."

They did and she leaned against O'Banion. He said, "We're okay now. We'll go up to the road. Don't mind about us." The firemen hesitated, but when they began to walk, they were apparently reassured, and ran back to their work. Hopeless work, O'Banion amended. But for a few sagging studs and the two chimneys, the house was little more than a pit of flames.

"Is Robin really—"

"Shh. He's really. Miss Schmidt got him out, I think. Anyway, he's sitting on the fire engine enjoying every minute. He watched you going in. He approves of your speed."

"You—"

"I saw you too. I yelled."

"And then you came after me." They walked a slow pace or so. "Why?"

Robin was safe, of course, he was about to say, so you didn't have to— and then there was within him a soundless white flash that lit up all he had ever done and been, everything he had read, people and places and ideas. Where he had acted right, he felt the right proven; where he had been wrong, he could see now the right in full force, even when for years he had justified his wrong. He saw fully now what old Sam Bittelman had almost convinced him of intellectually with his searching questions. He had fought away Sam's suggestion that there was something ludicrous, contradictory about the law and its pretensions to permanence. Now he saw that the law, as he knew it, was not under attack at all. As long as a man treated the body of law like a great stone buttress, based in bedrock and propping up civilization, he was fortifying a dead thing which could only kill the thing it was built to uphold. But if he saw civilization as an intricate, *moving* entity, the function of law changed. It was governor, stabilizer, inhibitor, *control* of something dynamic and progressive, subject to the punishments and privileges of evolution like a living thing. His whole idea of the hair-splitting search for "precedent" as a refining process in law was wrong. It was an adaptive process instead. The suggestion that not one single law is common to all human cultures, past and present, was suddenly no insult to law at all, but a living compliment; to nail a culture to permanent laws now seemed as ridiculous a concept as man conventionally refusing to shed his scales and his gills.

And with this revelation of the viability of man and his works, O'Banion experienced a profound realignment in his (or was it really his) attitude toward himself, his effortful preoccupation to defend and justify his blood and breeding and his gentleman's place in the world. It came to him now that although the law may say here that men are born equal, and there that they must receive equal treatment before the law, no one but a complete fool would insist that men *are* equal. Men, whatever they came from, whatever they claim for themselves, are only what's in their heads and what's in their hearts. The purest royal blood that yields a weak king will yield a failure; a strong peasant can rise higher and accomplish more, and if what he accomplishes is compatible with human good, he is surely no worse than a beneficent king. Over and above anything else, however, shone the fact that a good man needs least of all to prove it by claiming that he comes from a line of good men. And for him to assume the privileges and postures of the landed gentry after the land is gone is pure buffoonery. Time enough for sharp vertical differentiations between men when the differences become so great that the highest may not cross-breed with the lowest; until then, in the broad view, differences are so subtle as to be negligible, and the concept "to marry out of one's class" belongs with the genesis of hippogriffs and gryphons—in mythology.

All this, and a thousand times more, unfolded and was clear to O'Banion in this illuminated instant, so short it took virtually no time at all, so bright it lit up all the days of his past and part of his future as well. And it had happened between pace and pace, when Sue Martin said, "You followed me. Why?"

"I love you," he said instantly.

"Why?" she whispered.

He laughed joyously. "It doesn't matter."

Sue Martin—*Sue Martin!*—began to cry.

CHAPTER FOURTEEN

PHIL HALVORSEN OPENED HIS EYES and saw that the house was on fire. He lay still, watching the flames feed, and thought, isn't this what I was waiting for?

Now there can be an end to it, he thought peacefully. Now I never need worry again that I'm wrong to be as I am, and other people's needs, the appetites and rituals of the great Average will no longer accuse me. I cannot be excluded unless I exist, so here's an end to being excluded. I cannot be looked down on when I can no longer be seen.

The ceiling began to develop a tan patch, and hot white powder fell from it to his face. He covered it with the pillow. He was resigned to later, final agonies because they would be final, but he saw no reason to put up with the preliminaries. Just then most of the plaster came down on him. It didn't hurt much, and it meant the thing would be over sooner than he had thought.

He heard faintly, over the colossal roaring, a woman scream. He lay still. As much as anyone—perhaps more—he would ordinarily be concerned about the others. But not now. Not now. Such concern is for a man who expects to live with a conscience afterward.

Something—it sounded like an inside wall—went down very near. It jolted the foot of his bed and he felt its hot exhalation and the taste of its soot, but otherwise it did not reach him. "So come on," he said tightly, "get it over with, will you?" and hurled the pillow away.

As if in direct and obedient answer the ceiling over him opened up—*up*; apparently a beam had broken and was tipping down into an adjoining room, upward here. Then the tangle of stringers it carried fell away and started down. High above was blackness, suddenly rent by smoky orange light—the inside of the roof, a section of which was falling in with the stringers.

"All right," said Halvorsen, as if someone had asked him a question. He closed his eyes.

He closed his eyes on a flash of something like an inner and unearthly light, and time stood still . . . or perhaps it was only that subjectively he had all the time in the world to examine this shadowless internal cosmos.

Most immediately, it laid out before him the sequence of events which had brought him here, awaiting death on a burning bed. In this sequence a single term smote him with that "well, of *course!*" revelation that rewarded his plodding, directive thoughts when they were successful for him. The term was "Average," and his revelation came like a burst of laughter: for anyone else this would have been a truism, an inarguable axiom; like a fool he had let his convoluted thinking breeze past "Average," use "Average," worry about "Average" without ever looking at it.

But "Average"—Average Appetite—was here for him to see, a line drawn from side to side on a huge graph. And all over the graph were spots— millions of them. (He was in a place where he could actually see and comprehend "millions".) On that line lived this creation, this demigod, to whom he had felt subservient for so long, whose hungers and whose sense of fitness ought to have been—*had* been—Halvorsen's bench-mark, his reference point. Halvorsen had always felt himself member of a minority—a minority which shrank as he examined it, and he was always examining it. All the world catered to Average Man and his "normal" urges, and this must be proper, for he was aware of the reciprocities: Average Man got these things because these things were what Average Man wanted and needed.

Want and need . . . and there was the extraordinary discovery he had made when Bitty asked him: if people really needed it, would there have to be so much high-pressure salesmanship?

This he threw on the graph like a transparent overlay; it too bore a line from side to side, but much lower down, indicating with much more accuracy just how interested Average Man was in the specific appetite about which he made so much noise. Now bend close and look at those millions of spots—individual people all, each with his true need for the kind of cultural pressure which was driving a man, here, to his death from guilt.

The first thing Halvorsen saw was that the dots were scattered so widely that the actual number falling on the line Average Man was negligible: there were countless millions more un-average people. It came to him that those who obey the gospel of Average Man are, in their efforts to be like the mass of humanity, obeying the dictates of one of the smallest minorities of all. The next thing to strike him was that it took the presence of *all* these dots to place that line just where it was; there was no question of better, or worse, or more or less fit. Except for the few down here and their opposite numbers up there, the handful of sick, insane, incomplete or distorted individuals whose sexual appetites were non-existent or extreme, the vast majority above and below the true average were basically "normal." And here where he, Halvorsen might appear on the graph—he had plenty of company.

He'd never known that! The magazine covers, the advertisements, the dirty jokes—they hadn't let him know it.

He understood, now, the mechanism of this cultural preoccupation; it came to him in the recollection that he had appeared at work for three hundred consecutive working days and nobody noticed his ears. And then one day a sebaceous cyst in his left lobe had become infected, and the doctor removed it and he showed up at work with a bandage covering his ear. *Everybody began to think about Halvorsen's ear!* Every interview had to begin with an explanation of his ear or the applicant would keep straying his attention to it. And he'd noticed, too, that after he explained about the cyst, the interviewee would always glance at Halvorsen's other ear before he got back to business. Now, in this silver place where all interrelationships were true ones, he could equate his covered and noticeable ear with a Bikini bathing suit, and see clearly how normal interest-disinterest—acceptance—can be put under forced draft.

It came to him also *why* this particular cultural matrix did this to itself. In its large subconscious, it probably knew quite clearly the true status of its sensual appetites. It must reason, then, that unless it kept these appetites whipped up to a froth at all times, it might not increase itself, and it felt it must increase. This was not a pretty thought, but neither is the pounce of a cat on a baby bird; yet one cannot argue with the drive behind it.

So it was that Halvorsen's reasons for not living ceased to be reasons; with the purest of truth he could say I am not unmanned; I am not unfit; I am not abnormal . . . I am not alone.

All this in no-time, as he closed his eyes to await the mass even now falling on him. And the reflex of reflexes acted just as eyelids met; he spun off the bed, bounced out of the nearby window, and was on the grass outside as the ceiling and walls together met the floor in a gout of flame.

CHAPTER FIFTEEN

THE GIRL CLIMBED up to the front seat of the fire engine. "Move over."

Miss Schmidt swung her worried gaze away from the burning house, and said in a preoccupied tone, "I don't think you'd be allowed to, little girl. We're from that hou—why, it's Mary Haunt!"

"Didn't recognize me, huh?" said Mary Haunt. She swung a hip and shunted Miss Schmidt over. "Can't say I blame you. What a mess!" she said, indicating the house.

"Mr. O'Banion is in there; he went after Mrs. Martin. And have you seen Mr. Halvorsen?"

"No."

"Tonio! Tonio!" Robin suddenly cried.

"Shh, dear. He'll be along."

"Dare he *iss!* Dare he *iss!* Mom*ee!*" he shrieked, "Come and see my fire engine, shall we?"

"Oh, thank God, thank God they're safe," said Miss Schmidt. She hugged Robin until he grunted.

"I'm all choked up," growled Mary Haunt. Again she made the angry gesture at the house. "W*hat* a mess. Everything I own—the warpaint, the clothes, all my magazines—everything, gone. You know what that means. I—"

I've got to go home now. And it was here, on the slightest matter of phrasing that the strange flash of silver suffused Mary Haunt; not under the descending scythe of Death, nor under the impact of soul found, heart found: just for the nudge of a word, she had her timeless instant.

All her life and the meaning of her life and all the things in it: the dimity curtains and home-baked bread, Jackie and Seth whamming away at each other for the privilege of carrying her books, the spice-shelf and the daffodils under the parlor windows. She'd loved it so, and reigned over it; and mostly, she'd been a gentle princess and ruled kindly.

Did they throw you out, gal?

She'd never known where it started, how it came about, until now. Now, with astonishment, she did. Daddy started it, before she was old enough to walk, Daddy one of the millions who had applauded a child actress called Shirley Temple, one of the thousand who had idolized her, one of the hundreds who had deified her. "Little Mary Hollywood," he'd called his daughter, and it had been "When you're in pictures, honey—" Every morning was a fountain to empty the reservoir of his dreams; every night he filled again from the depthless well of his ambition for her.

And everyone believed him. Mom came to believe him, and her kid brother, and finally everyone in town. They had to; Daddy's unswerving, undoubting conviction overrode any alternatives, and she herself clinched it, just by being what she was, an exquisite child exquisitely groomed, who grew more beautiful (by Hollywood standards) every year. She wanted what every child wants: loving attention. She got it in fullest measure. She wanted to do what every child wants to do: gain the approval of her elders. She tried; and indeed, no other course was open to her.

Did they throw you out, gal?

Perhaps Daddy might have outgrown it; or if not, perhaps he'd have known, or found out, how to accomplish his dream in a real world. But Daddy died when she was six, and Mom took over his dream as if it had been a flower from his dead hand. She did not nourish it; she pressed it between the leaves of her treasured memories of him. It was a live thing, true, but arrested at the intensity and the formlessness of his hopes for her when she was six. She encouraged the child only to want to be in pictures, and to be sure she would be; it never occurred to her that there might be things for the child to learn. Her career was coming; it was coming like Christmas.

But no one knew when.

And when she cleaned house, they all thought it was sweet, so pretty to watch, but they'd rather take the broom away from her; and when she baked, it was pretty too but not what she was really *for*; and when she read the diet sections in the grocery magazines, that was all right, but the other features—how to make tangerine gravy for duck, how to remove spots from synthetic fibers—"Why, Mary! you'll have a little army worrying about those things for you!"

Movie magazines then, and movies, and waiting, until the day she left.

Did they throw you out, gal?

Screen Society had a feature on Hollywood High School, and it mentioned how many stars and starlets had come from there, and the ages some of them had been when they signed contracts. And suddenly she wasn't the Shirley Temple girl at all, she was older, years older than two girls in the article, the same age as five of them. Yet here she was still, while the whole town waited . . . suppose she never made it? Suppose nothing happened here? And she began to interpret this remark, that look, the other silence, in ways that troubled her, until she wanted to hide, or to drop dead, or leave.

Just like that, leaving was the answer. She told no one, she took what clothes she had that were good, she bought a ticket for just anywhere and wrote thrilling, imaginative, untrue letters at wider and wider intervals. Naïvely she got a job which might mean her Big Break and which actually never would. And at last she reached a point where she would not look back, for wanting home so much; she would not look forward, for knowing there was nothing there; she held herself in a present of futility and purposive refusal to further the ambition she insisted she had; and she had no pleasure and no outlet but anger. She took refuge in her furies; she scorned people and what they did and what they wanted, and told them all so. And she took the picture of Mom standing in front of the house in the spring, with the jonquils all about and the tulips coming, and she wrapped it up in the cotton print Mom had made for her fourteenth birthday and never given her because *Screen Society* had said princess-style for teeners was corny.

Did they throw you out, gal?

Old Sam had asked her that; he knew, even when she didn't. But now, in this strange silver moment, she knew; she knew it all. Yes, they had thrown her out. They had let her be a dead man's dream until she was nearly dead herself. They never let her be Mary Haunt who wanted to fix the new curtains and bake a berry pie, and have a square hedge along the Elm Street side and go to meeting on Sundays. They had marked her destiny on her face and body and on the clothes she wore, and stamped it into her speech and fixed her hair the way they wanted it, and to the bottom of her heart she was angry.

And now, all of a sudden, and for the very first time, it occurred to her that she could, if she wanted, be Mary Haunt her own self, and be it right there at home; that home was the best place to be that very good thing, and she could replace their disappointment with a very real pride. She could be home before the Strawberry Festival at the church; she would wear an apron and get suds on her forehead when she pushed her hair back, the way Bitty did sometimes.

So Mary Haunt sat on a fire engine, next to the high-school librarian who was enveloped in a tremendous raincoat, saying that everything was burned up, lost; and about to say, "I've got to go home now." But she said, "I can go home now." She looked into Miss Schmidt's eyes and smiled a smile the older woman had never seen before. "I can, I can! I can go home now!" Mary Haunt sang. Impulsively she took Miss Schmidt's hand and squeezed it. She looked into her face and laughed, "I'm not mad any more, not at you or anybody . . . and I've been a little stinker and I'm sorry; I'm going *home!*" And Miss Schmidt looked at the smudged face, the scorched hair drawn back into a childish pony-tail and held by a rubber band, the spotless princess dress. "Why," said Miss Schmidt, "you're beautiful, just beautiful!" "I'm not. I'm seventeen, only seventeen," Mary Haunt said out of a wild happiness, "and I'm going home and bake a cake." And she hugged her mother's picture and smiled; even the ruined house did not glow quite this way.

EXCERPT FROM FIELD EXPEDITION [NOTEBOOK]: [*!!!*] *Did it ever work!* [You]'d *think these specimens had used Synapse Beta sub Sixteen all their lives! If* [we] *had a* [tenth] *as much stamina* [we] *could* [lie down] *in a* [bed] *of paradoxes and go to* [sleep].
[We] *will observe for a* [short period] *longer, and then pack up and leave. This is a* [fascinating] *place to visit, but* [I] *wouldn't want to* [live] *here.*

CHAPTER SIXTEEN

It was october, and possibly the last chance they'd have for a picnic, and the day agreed and was beautiful for them. They found a fine spot where a stand of birch grew on both sides of an old split-rail fence, and a brook went by just out of sight. After they were finished O'Banion lay on his stomach in the sun, and thoughtfully scratched his upper lip with a bit of straw.

His wife laughed softly.

"Hm?"

"You're thinking about the Bittelmans again."

"How'd you know?"

"Just used to it. When you go off into yourself and look astonished and mystified and annoyed all at once, it's the Bittelmans again."

"Harmless hobby," said Halvorsen, and smiled.

"Is it? Tonio, how would you like me to go all pouty and coy and complain that you've spent more time thinking about them than about me?"

"Do by all means go all pouty and coy. I'll divorce you."

"Tony!"

"Well," he said lazily, "I had so much fun marrying you in the first place that it might be worth doing again. Where's Robin?"

"Right h— Oh dear. *Robin!*"

Down in the cleft, where the brook gurgled, Robin's voice answered instantly. "Frogs here, Mommy. Deelicious!"

"Does he eat 'em raw?" asked Halvorsen mildly.

Sue laughed. "That just means 'pretty' or 'desirable' or even 'bright green.' Robin, don't you dare get wet, you promise me?"

"I promise me," said the voice.

"And don't go away!"

"I don't."

"Why don't they show up?" demanded O'Banion. "Just once, that's all I'd ever want. Just show their faces and answer two questions."

"Why don't who—oh, Sam and Bitty. What two questions?"

"What they did to us, how and why."

"That's one question, counsellor?" asked Halvorsen.

"Yes. Two: What they are."

"Now, why'd you say 'what' instead of 'who'?"

"It comes to that." He rolled over and sat up. "Honey, would you mind if I ran down everything we've found out so far, just once more?"

"Summarize and rest your case?"

"I don't know about resting it . . . reviewing the brief."

"I often wonder why you call it a brief," Halvorsen chuckled.

O'Banion rose and went to the fence. Putting one hand on a slender birch trunk, he hopped upward, turning, to come to rest sitting on the top rail.

"Well, one thing I'm sure of: Sam and Bitty could *do* things to people, and they did it to all of us. And I refuse to believe that they did it with logic and persuasion."

"They could be pretty persuasive."

"It was more than that," O'Banion said impatiently. "What they did to me changed everything about me."

"How very intriguing."

"Everything about the way I *think*, hussy. I can look back on that now and realize that I was roped, thrown and notched. When he wanted me to answer questions I had to answer them, no matter what I was thinking. When he was through with me he turned me loose and made me go back to my business as if nothing had happened. Miss Schmidt told me the same thing." He shifted his weight on the rail and said excitedly, "Now there's our prize exhibit. All or us were—changed—by this thing, but Reta—she's a *really* different person."

"She wasn't more changed than the others," said Sue soberly. "She's thirty-eight years old. It's an interesting age because when you're there and look five years older, and then spruce up the way she did and look five years younger, it looks like twenty years' difference, not ten. That's all cosmetics and clothes, though. The real difference is as quiet and deep as—well, Phil here."

Again Halvorsen found a smile. "Perhaps you're right. She shifted from the library to teaching. It was a shift from surrounding herself with other people's knowledge to surrounding other people with hers. She's alive."

"I'll say. Boyfriend too."

"Quiet and deep," said O'Banion thoughtfully, swinging his feet. "That's right. All you get out of Halvorsen when you ask him about it is a smile like a light going on and, 'Now it's right for me to be me.'"

"That's it—all of it," chuckled Halvorsen happily.

"And Mary Haunt, bless her. Second happiest child I ever saw. *Robin! Are you all right?*"

"Yis!" came the voice.

"I'm still not satisfied," said O'Banion. "I have the feeling we're staring at very petty and incidental results of some very important cause. In a moment of acute stress I made a decision which affected my whole life."

"*Our.*"

He blew her a kiss. "Reta Schmidt says the same thing, though she wouldn't go into detail. And maybe that's what Halvorsen means when he says, 'Now it's right for me . . .' You annoy me."

"Sir!" she cried with mock horror.

He laughed. "You know what I mean. Only you got exposed to the Bittelmans and didn't change. Everybody else got wonderful," he smiled, "You just stayed wonderful. Now what's so special about you?"

"Must I sit here and be—"

"Shush. Think back. Was there any *different* kind of thing that happened to you that night, some kind of emergency thinking you did that was above and beyond anything you thought you could do?"

"Not that I remember."

Suddenly he brought his fist down on his thigh. "There *was!* Remember right after we got out of the house, the wall fell on us? You dragged me back and held me still and that attic vent dropped right around us?"

"That. Yes, I remember. But it wasn't special. It just made sense."

"*Sense?* I'd like to put a computer on that job—after scorching it half through and kicking it around a while. Somehow you calculated how fast that thing was falling and how much ground it would cover when it hit. You computed that against our speed outward. You located the attic vent opening and figured where it would land, and whether or not it could contain us both. Then you estimated our speed *if* we went toward the safe spot and concluded that we could make it. *Then* you went into action, more or less over my dead body to boot. All that in—" He closed his eyes to relive the moment. "—all of one and a half seconds absolute tops. It wasn't special?"

"No, it wasn't," she said positively. "It was an emergency, don't you see? A real emergency, not only because we might get hurt, but in terms of all we were to each other and all we could be if only you—"

"Well, I did," he smiled. "But I still don't understand you. You mean you think more, not less—widen your scope instead of narrowing your focus when it's that kind of emergency? You can think of all those things at once, better and faster and more accurately?"

Halvorsen suddenly lunged and caught O'Banion's foot, pulling it sharply upward. He shouted "*Yoop!*" His right hand whipped up and back and scrabbled at the tree-trunk; his torso twisted and his left hand shot straight down. His legs flailed and straightened; for a moment he seesawed on the rail on his kidneys. At last he got his left hand on the rail and pulled himself upward to sit again. "Hey! What do you think you're—"

"Proving a point," said Halvorsen. "Look, Tony: without warning you were thrown off balance. What did you do? You reached out for that tree-trunk without looking—got it, too; you knew just how fast and how far to go. But at the same time you put your left hand straight down, ready to catch your weight if you went down to the ground. Meantime you banged around with your legs and shifted your weight this way just enough to make a new balance on top. Now tell me: did you sit there after I pushed you and figure all those things out, one by one?"

"By golly no. Snop—snap—synapses."

"What?"

"Synapses. Sort of pathways in the brain that get paved better and better as you do something over and over. After a while they happen without conscious thought. Keeping your balance is that kind of thing, on the motor level. But don't tell me you have a sort of . . . personal-cultural inner ear— something that makes you react reflectively in terms of your past and your future and . . . but that's what happened to me that night!" He stared at Halvorsen. "You figured that out long ago, you and your IBM head!"

"It always happens if the emergency's a bad one," Sue said composedly. "Sometimes when you don't even know it is an emergency. But what's remarkable? Aren't drowning men supposed to see their whole lives pass before them?"

"Did you say that always happens with your emergencies?"

"Well, doesn't it?"

Suddenly he began to chuckle softly, and at her questioning look he said, "You remind me of something a psychologist told me once. A man was asked to describe his exact sensations on getting drunk. 'Just like anybody else,' he says. 'Well, describe it,' says the doctor. The man says, 'Well, first your face gets a little flushed and your tongue gets thick, and after a while your ears begin to wiggle—' Sue, honey, I've got news for you. Maybe you react like that in important moments, a great big shiny flash of truth and proportional relationships, but believe me, other people don't. I never did until that night. *That's it!*" he yelled at the top of his voice.

From down the slope came a clear little voice, "Wash 'at noice?"

Sue and Halvorsen smiled at one another and then O'Banion said earnestly, "That's what Bitty and Sam gave us—a synaptic reflex like the equilibrium mechanisms, but bigger—much bigger. A human being is an element in a whole culture, and the culture itself is alive . . . I suppose the species could be called, as a whole, a living thing. And when we found ourselves in a stress situation which was going to affect us signally—dangerously, or just importantly—we reacted to it in the way I did just now when you pushed me— only on a cultural level. It's as if Sam and Bitty had found a way to install or develop that 'balancing' mechanism in us. It resolved some deep personal conflict of Halvorsen's; it snapped Mary out of a dangerous delusion and Miss Schmidt out of a dangerous retreat. And, well, you know about me."

"I can't believe people don't think that way in emergencies!" she said, dazed.

"Maybe some do," said Halvorsen. "Come to think of it, people do some remarkable things under sudden stress; they make not-obvious but very right choices under pressure, like the man who cracks a joke and averts a panic or the boy who throws himself on a grenade to save his squad. They've surveyed themselves in terms of all they are and measured that against their surroundings and all it is—all in a split fraction of a second. I guess everyone has it. Some of it."

"Whatever this synapse is, the Bittelmans gave it to us . . . yes, and maybe set the house on fire too . . . why? Testing? Testing what—just us, or human beings? *What are they?*" demanded the lawyer.

"Gone, that's what," said Halvorsen.

For a very brief time, he was wrong to say that.

EXCERPT FROM FIELD EXPEDITION [NOTEBOOK]: [*Our*] *last* [*hour*] *here, so* [*we*] [*induced*] *three of the test specimens to* [*locus B*] *for final informal observation.* [*Smith*] *pretends to a certain* [*chagrin*]. *After all,* [*he*] [*says*] *all* [*we*] *did was to come* [*sizable abstract number*] *of* [*terrestrially immeasurable distance unit*]*s, foregoing absolutely the company of* [*our*] [ ] *and the pleasures of the* [ ]; *strain* [*our*] *ingenuity and our* [*technical equipment*] *to the* [*break*]*ing point, even getting trapped into using that* [*miserable impractical*]

power supply and [charge]ing it up every [month]—all to detect and analyze the incidence of Synapse Beta sub Sixteen. And here these specimens sit, locating and defining the Synapse during a brief and idle conversation! Actually, [I] [think] [Smith] is [pleased] with them for it.
We shall now [dismantle] the [widget] and the [wadget] and [take off].

Robin was watching a trout.

"Tsst! Tsst!"

He was watching more than the trout, really; he was watching its shadow. It had occurred to him that perhaps the shadow wasn't a shadow, but another and fuzzier kind of fish which wouldn't let the more clear-cut one get away from over it, so maybe that was why the trout kept hanging into the current, hanging and *zoom!* darting forward. But he never was fast enough for the fuzzy one, which stayed directly under him no matter what.

"Tsst! Robin!"

He looked up, and the trout was forgotten. He filled his powerful young lungs with air and his face with joy, and then made a heroic effort and stifled his noisy delight in obedience to that familiar finger-on-lips and its explosive "*Shh!*"

Barely able to contain himself, he splashed straight across the brook, shoes and all, and threw himself into Bitty's arms. "Ah Robin!" said the woman, "wicked little boy. Are you a wicked little boy?"

"Yis. Bitty-bitty-BITTY!"

"Shh. Look who's with me." She put him down, and there stood old Sam. "Hey-y-y-y, boy?"

"Ah Sam!" Robin clasped his hands together and got them between his knees, bending almost double in delight. "Ware you *been*, Sam?"

"Around," said Sam. "Listen, Robin, we came to say goodby. We're going away now."

"Don't go 'way."

"We have to," said Bitty. She knelt and hugged him. "Goodby, darling."

"Shake," said Sam gravely.

"Shake, rattle an' roll," said Robin with equal sobriety.

"Ready, Sam?"

"All set."

Swiftly they took off their bodies, folded them neatly and put them in two small green plastic cases. On one was lettered [WIDGET] and on the other [WADGET], but of course Robin was too young to read. Besides, he had something else to astonish him. "Boff!" he cried. "Googie!"

Boff and Googie [waved] at him and he waved back. They picked up the plastic cases and threw them into a sort of bubble that was somehow there, and [walked] in after them. Then they [went].

Robin turned away and without once looking back, climbed the slope and ran to Sue. He flung himself into her lap and uttered the long, whistle-like wail that preceded his rare bouts with bitter tears.

"Why *darling*, whatever happened? What *is* it? Did you bump your—"

He raised a flushed and contorted face to her. "Boff gone," he said wetly. "Oh, oh-h-h, Boff an' Googie gone."

He cried most of the way home, and never mentioned Boff again.

INCIDENTAL [NOTES] ON FIELD REPORT: *The discovery of total incidence and random use of Synapse Beta sub Sixteen in a species is unique in the known [cosmos]; yet introduction of the mass of data taken on the Field Expedition into the [master] [computer] alters its original [dictum] not at all: the presence of this Synapse in a species ensures its survival.*

In the particular case at hand, the species undoubtedly bears, and will always bear, the [curse] of interpersonal and intercultural frictions, due to the amount of paradox possible. Where so many actions, decisions, and organizational activities can occur uncontrolled by the Synapse and its [universal-interrelational] modifying effect, paradox must result. On the other [hand], any species with such a concentration of the Synapse, even in partial use, will not destroy itself and very probably cannot be destroyed by anything. Prognosis positive.

Their young are delightful. [I] [feel good]. [Smith], [I] [forgive] [you].

SANDRA
by George P. Elliott

A FEW YEARS AGO I inherited a handsome neo-Spanish house in a good neighborhood in Oakland. It was much too large for a single man, as I knew perfectly well; if I had behaved sensibly I would have sold it and stayed in my bachelor quarters; I could have got a good price for it. But I was not sensible; I liked the house very much; I was tired of my apartment-house life; I didn't need the money. Within a month I had moved in and set about looking for a housekeeper.

From the moment I began looking, everyone assured me that I should get a domestic slave. I was reluctant to get one, not so much because of the expense as because of my own inexperience. No one in my family had ever had one, and among my acquaintances there were not more than three or four who had any. Nevertheless, the arguments in favor of my buying a slave were too great to be ignored. The argument that irritated me most was the one used by the wives of my friends. "When you marry," they would say, "think how happy it will make your wife to have a domestic slave." Then they would offer, zealously, to select one for me. I preferred to do my own selecting. I began watching the classified ads for slaves for sale.

Some days there would be no slaves listed for sale at all; on Sundays there might be as many as ten. There would be a middle-aged Negro woman, 22 years experience, best recommendations, $4500; or a 35-year-old Oriental, speaks English, excellent cook, recommendations, $5000; or a middle-aged woman of German descent, very neat, no pets or vices . . . sensible choices, no doubt, but none of them appealed to me. Somewhere in the back of my mind there was the notion of the slave I wanted. It made me restless, looking; all I knew about it was that I wanted a female. I was hard to satisfy. I took to dropping by the Emeryville stores, near where my plant is located, looking for a slave. What few there were in stock were obviously of inferior quality. I knew that I would have to canvass the large downtown stores to find what I wanted. I saw the ads of Oakland's Own Department Store, announcing their January white sale; by some quirk, they had listed seven white domestic slaves at severely reduced prices. I took off a Wednesday, the first day of the sale, and went to the store at opening time, 9:45, to be sure to have the pick of the lot.

Oakland's Own is much the largest department store in the city. It has seven floors and two basements, and its quality runs from $1498 consoles to factory-reject cotton work socks. It has a good solid merchandising policy, and it stands behind its goods in a reassuring, old-fashioned way. The wives of my friends were opposed to my shopping in Oakland's Own, because, they said, secondhand slaves were so much better trained than new, and cost so little more. Nevertheless, I went.

I entered the store the moment the doors were opened, and went straight up to the sixth floor on the elevator. All the same I found a shapeless little woman in the slave alcove ahead of me picking over the goods—looking at their teeth and hair, telling them to bend over, to speak so she could hear the sound of their voices. I was furious at having been nosed out by the woman, but I could not help admiring the skill and authority with which she inspected her merchandise. She told me something about herself. She maintained a staff of four, but what with bad luck, disease and her husband's violent temper she was always having trouble. The Federal Slave Board had ruled against her twice—against her husband, really, but the slaves were registered in her name—and she had to watch her step. In fact she was on probation from the FSB now. One more adverse decision and she didn't know what she'd do. Well, she picked a strong, stolid-looking female, ordered two sets of conventional domestic costumes for her, signed the charge slip, and left. The saleswoman came to me.

I had made my decision. I had made it almost the moment I had come in, and I had been in agonies for fear the dumpy little shopper would choose my girl. She was not beautiful exactly, though not plain either, nor did she look especially strong. I did not trouble to read her case-history card; I did not even find out her name. I cannot readily explain what there was about her that attracted me. A certain air of insouciance as she stood waiting to be looked over—the bored way she looked at her fingernails and yet the fearful glance she cast from time to time at us shoppers—the vulgarity of her make-up and the soft charm of her voice—I do not know. Put it down to the line of her hip as she stood waiting, a line girlish and womanly at once, dainty and strong, at ease but not indolent. It's what I remember of her best from that day, the long pure line from her knee to her waist as she stood staring at her nails, cocky and scared and humming to herself.

I knew I should pretend impartiality and indifference about my choice. Even Oakland's Own permits haggling over the price of slaves; I might knock the price down as much as $300, particularly since I was paying for her cash on the line. But it wasn't worth the trouble to me. After three weeks of dreary looking I had found what I wanted, and I didn't feel like waiting to get it. I asked the saleswoman for the card on my slave. She was the sixth child of a carpenter in Chico. Chico is a miserable town in the plains of the San Joaquin Valley; much money is spent each year teaching the people of Chico how to read and write; *chico* means greasewood. Her father had put her up for sale, with her own consent, at the earliest legal age, eighteen, the year of graduation from high school. The wholesaler had taught her the rudiments of cooking, etiquette, and housecleaning. She was listed as above average in cleanliness, intelligence and personality, superb in copulation, and fair in versatility and sewing. But I had known as much from just looking at her, and I didn't care. Her name was Sandra, and in a way I had known that too. She had been marked down from $3850 to $3299. As the saleswoman said, how could I afford to pass up such a bargain? I got her to knock the price down the amount of the sales taxes, wrote out my check, filled out the FSB forms, and took my slave Sandra over to be fitted with clothes.

And right there I had my first trouble as a master, right on the fifth floor of Oakland's Own in the Women's Wear department. As a master, I was supposed to say to Sandra, or even better to the saleswoman about Sandra, "Plain cotton underwear, heavy-weight nylon stockings, two dark-blue maid's uniforms and one street dress of conservative cut," and so on and so on. *The slave submits to the master*: I had read it in the FSB manual for domestic slave owners. Now I find it's all very well dominating slaves in my office or my factory. I am chief engineer for the Jergen Calculating Machine Corp., and I have had no trouble with my industrial and white-collar slaves. They come into the plant knowing precisely where they are, and I know precisely where I am. It's all cut and dried. I prefer the amenities when dealing with, say, the PBX operator. I prefer to say, "Miss Persons, will you please call Hoskins of McKee Steel?" rather than "Persons, get me Hoskins of McKee." But this is merely a preference of mine, a personal matter, and I know it and Persons knows it. No, all that is well set, but this business of Sandra's clothes quite threw me.

I made the blunder of asking her her opinion. She was quick to use the advantage I gave her, but she was very careful not to go too far. "Would you like a pair of high heels for street wear?" I asked her. "If it is agreeable with you, sir." "Well, now, let's see what they have in your size. —Those seem sturdy enough and not too expensive. Are they comfortable?" "Quite comfortable, sir." "There aren't any others you'd rather have?" "These are very nice, sir." "Well, I guess these will do quite well, for the time being at least." "I agree with you, sir."

I agree with you: that's a very different matter from I submit to you. And though I didn't perceive the difference at the moment, still I was anything but easy in my mind by the time I had got Sandra installed in my house. Oh, I had no trouble preserving the proper reserve and distance with her, and I could not in the slightest detail complain of her behavior. It was just that I was not to the manner bred; that I was alone in the house with her, knowing certain external things to do, but supported by no customs and precedents as I was at the plant; that I found it very uncomfortable to order a woman, with whom I would not eat dinner at the same table, to come to my bed for an hour or so after she had finished washing the dishes. Sandra was delighted with the house and with her quarters, with the television set I had had installed for her and with the subscription to *Cosmopolitan* magazine that I had ordered in her name. She was delighted and I was glad she was delighted. That was the bad thing about it—I was glad. I should have provided these facilities only as a heavy industry provides half-hour breaks and free coffee for its workers—to keep her content and to get more work out of her. Instead I was as glad at her pleasure in them as though she were an actual person. She was so delighted that tears came to her eyes and she kissed my feet; then she asked me where the foot basin was kept. I told her I had none. She said that the dishpan would do until we got one. I told her to order a foot basin from Oakland's Own the next day, along with any other utensils or supplies she felt we needed. She thanked me, fetched the dishpan and washed my feet. It embarrassed me to have her do it; I knew it was often done, I enjoyed the sensuous pleasure of it, I admired the grace and care with which she bent over my feet like a shoeshine, but all the same I was embarrassed. Yet she did it every day when I came home.

I do not think I could describe more economically the earlier stages of my connection to Sandra than by giving an account of the foot washing.

At first, as I have said, I was uneasy about it, though I liked it too. I was not sure that as a slave she had to do it, but she seemed to think she had to and she certainly wanted to. Now this was all wrong of me. It is true that domestic slaves usually wash their masters' feet, but this is not in any sense one of the slave's rights. It is a matter about which the master decides, entirely at his own discretion. Yet, by treating it as a set duty, a duty like serving me food in which she had so profound an interest as to amount to a right, Sandra had from the outset made it impossible for me to will not to have her wash my feet. She did it every day when I came home; even when I was irritable and told her to leave me alone, she did it. Of course, I came to depend upon it as one of the pleasures and necessary routines of the day. It was, in fact, very soothing; she spent a long time at it and the water was always just lukewarm, except in cold weather when it was quite warm; she always floated a slice of lemon in the water. The curve of her back, the gesture with which she would shake the hair out of her eyes, the happy, private smile she wore as she did it, these were beautiful to me. She would always kiss, very lightly, the instep of each foot after she had dried them—always, that is, when we were alone.

If I brought a friend home with me, she would wash our feet all right, but matter-of-factly, efficiently, with no little intimacies as when I was alone. But if it was a woman who came with me, or a man and wife, Sandra would wash none of our feet. Nor did she wash the feet of any callers. I thought this was probably proper etiquette. I had not read my *Etiquette for Slaves* as well as Sandra obviously had. I let it go. During the first few weeks, all my friends, and particularly all my women friends, had to come to observe Sandra. She behaved surely and with complete consistency towards them all. I was proud of her. None of the women told me that Sandra was anything less than perfect, not even Helen who would have been most likely to, being an old friend and sharp-tongued. After the novelty had worn off, I settled down with her into what seemed to be a fine routine. To be sure, it was not long before I would think twice about bringing someone home for dinner with me; if there was much doubt in my mind about it, the difference in Sandra's foot washing alone would sway me not to bring my friend along, especially if my friend was a woman.

When I would come home late at night she would be waiting for me, with a smile and downcast eyes. I went, in October, to a convention in St. Louis for a week. When I came back, I think she spent an hour washing my feet, asking me to tell her about the physical conditions of my trip, nothing personal or intimate but just what I had eaten and what I had seen and how I had slept; but the voice in which she asked it— One night I came home very late, somewhat high, after a party. I did not want to disturb her, so I tried to go to my room noiselessly. But she heard me and came in in her robe to wash my feet; she helped me to bed, most gently. Not by a glance did she reproach me for having disturbed her sleep. But then, she never reproached me.

I did not realize fully how much I had come to depend on her until she fell sick. She was in the hospital with pneumonia for three days and spent six days convalescing. It was at Thanksgiving time. I declined invitations out to dinner, in order to keep Sandra company—to tend to her, I said to myself, though she tended to herself very nicely. I was so glad to have her well again that the first time she could come to me I kept her in my bed all night—so that she might not chill herself going back to her own bed, I told myself. That was the first time, yet by Christmas we were sleeping together regularly, though she kept her clothes in her own room. She still called me sir, she still washed my feet; according to the bill of sale I owned her: I thought her a perfect slave. I was uneasy no longer.

In fact, of course, I was making a fool of myself, and it took Helen to tell me so.

"Dell," she said over the edge of her cocktail glass, "you're in love with this creature."

"In love with Sandra!" I cried. "What do you mean?"

And I was about to expostulate hotly against the notion, when I bethought me that too much heat on my part would only confirm her in her opinion. Therefore, seeming to study the problem, I relapsed into a brown study— under Helen's watchful eye—and tried to calculate the best out for myself.

I rang for Sandra.

"More manhattans," I said to her.

She bowed, took the shaker on her tray, and left. She was impeccable.

"No, Helen," I said finally, "she does not make my pulses race. The truth is, I come a lot closer to being in love with you than with Sandra."

This threw her considerably off balance, as I had hoped it would.

"How absurd. You've never even made a pass at me."

"True."

But Sandra returned with the drinks, and after she had left we talked about indifferent matters.

As I was seeing Helen to the door, she said to me, "All the same, Dell, watch out. You'll be marrying this creature next. And who will drop by to see you then?"

"If I ever marry Sandra," I said, "it will not be for love. If I have never made a pass at you, my dear, it has not been for lack of love."

I looked at her rather yearningly, squeezed her hand rather tightly, and with a sudden little push closed the door behind her. I leaned against the wall for a moment and offered up a short prayer that Helen would never lose her present husband and come looking in my part of the world for another. I could have managed to love her all right, but she scared me to death.

I thought about what she had told me. I knew that I was not in love with Sandra—there were a thousand remnants of Chico in her that I could not abide—but I could not deny that I needed her very much. What Helen had made me see clearly was the extent to which I had failed to keep Sandra a slave. I did not know whether it was her scheming that had brought it about, or my slackness, or whether, as I suspected, something of both. Some of the more liberal writers on the subject say, of course, that such development is intrinsic in the situation for anyone in our cultural milieu. It is a problem recognized by the FSB in its handbook. But the handbook advises the master who finds himself in my predicament to trade his slave for another, preferably some stodgy, uninteresting number or one who is deficient in the proper qualities—in my case, as I thought, copulating. The trouble with this sound advice was that I didn't want to get rid of Sandra. She made me comfortable.

In fact, she made me so comfortable that I thought I was happy. I wanted to show my gratitude to her. After she had straightened up the kitchen that evening I called her into the living room where I was sitting over the paper.

"Yes, sir?" she said, standing demurely on the other side of the coffee table.

"Sandra," I began, "I'm very fond of you. I would like to do something for you."

"Yes, sir."

"Sit down."

"Thank you, sir."

As she sat, she took a cigarette from the box, without asking my permission, and lighted it. The way she arched her lips to smoke it, taking care not to spoil her lipstick, annoyed me, and the coy way she batted her eyelids made me regret I had called her in. "Still," I thought, "the Chico in her can be trained out. She's sound."

"What can I give you, Sandra?"

She did not answer for a moment. Every slave knows the answer to that question, and knows it is the one answer for which he won't be thanked.

"Whatever you wish to give me, sir, would be deeply appreciated."

I couldn't think of a thing to buy for her. Magazines, movies, television, clothes, jewelry, book club books, popular records, a permanent wave every four months, what else could I get her? Yet I had started this offer; I had to follow up with something. In my uneasiness and annoyance with myself, and knowing so well what it was she wanted, I went too far.

"Would you like freedom, Sandra?"

She dropped her eyes and seemed to droop a little. Then tears rolled down her cheeks, real mascara-stained tears of sadness.

"Oh yes, sir," she said. "Oh, my God, yes. Don't tease me about it. Please don't tease me."

So I promised her her freedom. I myself was moved, but I did not want to show it.

"I'm going for a short walk," I said. "You may go to your room."

I went for my walk, and when I came back she had prepared my foot bath. She had burned two pine boughs in the fireplace so that the room smelled wonderful. She had put on her loveliest dress, and had brushed her hair down as I liked it best. She did not speak as she washed my feet, nor even look up at my face. All her gratitude she expressed in the tenderness with which she caressed my feet and ankles. When she had finished drying them, she kissed them and then pressed them for a time against her breast. I do not think either of us, during these past years, has ever been happier than at that moment.

Well, I had my lawyer draw up a writ of substantial manumission, and Sandra took the brass ring out of her left ear, and that was that. And that was about all of that, so far as I could see. She was free to go as she wanted, but she didn't want. She got wages now, it is true, but all she did with them was to buy clothes and geegaws. She continued to take care of my house and me, to sleep in my bed and keep her own possessions in her own room, and to wash my feet as before. The manumission was nothing in itself, only a signpost that there had been some changes made. Continually and slowly changes kept being made.

For one thing, we began to eat together, unless I had guests in to dinner. For another, she began to call me Mr. Oakes. It seemed strange to have her go where she wanted, without asking me about it, on her nights out. I became so curious about what she could be doing that finally I asked her where she went. To night school, she said, learning how to type. I was delighted to hear that she had not been wasting her time at public dances, but I could not imagine why she wanted to learn typing. She had even bought a portable typewriter which she practiced on in her room when I was away. "Why?" she said. "My mother always said to me, 'Sandra, they can't fire slaves.' Well, I'm not a slave any longer. That was one nice thing about it, I wasn't ever afraid you'd fire me." "But, my darling," I cried, "I'm never going to fire you. I couldn't possibly get along without you." "I know it," she replied, "and I never want to leave either. All the same, I'm going to learn how to type." She had her own friends in to visit her; she even gave a bridge party one evening when I was not at home. But she never called me by my first name, she never checked up on me, she never asked me the sort of intrusive, prying question which a man hates answering. She kept her place.

Then she discovered she was pregnant. I immediately said I would assume all the financial responsibilities of her pregnancy and of rearing the child. She thanked me, and did not mention the subject again. But she took to sleeping in her own bed most of the time. She would serve breakfast while still in her robe and slippers. Her eyes were often red and swollen, though she always kept some sort of smile on her face. She mentioned something about going back to Chico. She began serving me canned soup at dinner. I drove her off to Reno and married her.

Helen had been right, I had married Sandra; but I had been right too, it wasn't for love. Oh, I loved her, some way or other, I don't know just how. But I had married her simply because it was the next thing to do; it was just another milestone.

Nothing much happened for a while after we were married, except that she called me Dell and didn't even take the curlers out of her hair at breakfast. But she hadn't got to be free and equal overnight. That was to take some months of doing.

First of all, as a wife, she was much frailer than she had been as a slave. I had to buy all sorts of things for her, automatic machines to wash the clothes and the dishes, a cooking stove with nine dials and two clocks, an electric ironer that could iron a shirt in two minutes, a vacuum cleaner, one machine to grind the garbage up and another to mix pancake batter, a thermostatic furnace, an electric floor waxer, and a town coupe for her to drive about to do her errands in. She had to get other people to wash her hair now, and shave her legs and armpits, and polish her toenails and fingernails for her. She took out subscriptions to five ladies' magazines, which printed among them half a million words a month for her to read, and she had her very bathrobe designed in Paris. She moved the television set into the living room and had a tear-drop chandelier hung from the center of the ceiling. When she had a miscarriage in her sixth month, she had a daily bouquet of blue orchids brought to her room; she had to rest, and pale blue orchids are so restful. She became allergic to the substances of which my mattress and pillows were composed, and I had to get a foam rubber mattress and foam rubber pillows, which stank. She finally insisted that we go to visit her family in Chico, so we finally did, and that we go visit my family in Boston, so we finally did. The visits were equally painful. We began to go to musical comedies and night clubs. Helen had been right: my friends did not drop by to see us, and they were apt to be sick when I invited them to dinner. Still we weren't all the way.

One night I came home late from work, tired and hungry. Dinner was not yet started, because Sandra had been delayed by her hairdresser. She fixed pork chops, frozen green beans, and bread and butter, with canned apricots for dessert. I could have done better myself. After dinner, after the machine had washed the dishes, I asked her if she would bathe my feet. I was so tired, I told her, my feet were so tired; it would be very soothing to me. But she said, in an annoyed voice, that she was feeling nervous herself. She was going to go to bed early. Besides, the silence she left behind her said, besides I am your wife now. She went to bed and I went to bed. She was restless; she twisted and turned. Every time I would shift my position or start to snore a little, she would sigh or poke me. Finally she woke me clear up and said it was impossible for her to sleep like this. Why didn't I go sleep in her former room? She couldn't because of her allergy, she had to stay in the foam rubber bed. So I moved into her room. And then I knew that she was equal, for most of the equal wives of my friends lived like this.

Another night, I came home wanting very much to make love to her. She had avoided my embrace for a long while. She was always too nervous, or too tired, for the less she worked the tireder she became; or she was busy, or simply not in the mood. But tonight I would admit of no evasion. She was beautiful and desirable, and I knew how well she had once made love with me. Finally, I held her in my arms. She knew I wanted her, and in a way as odd as mine she loved me too. But there was no sensuous pressure of her body against mine, no passion in her kiss. She put her arms about my neck not to caress me but to hang like an albatross against me. She pressed her head against my shoulder not for amorous affection but to hide her face, to shelter it, in loneliness and fear and doubt. She did not resist me, or yield to me, or respond to me, or try to overcome me. She only went away and left me her body to do with as I pleased. And then I knew that she was free, for most of the free wives of my friends were like this with their husbands.

I had four choices, as I saw it: divorce her, have her psychoanalyzed, kill her, or return her to slavery. I was strongly tempted to kill her, but I was an optimist, I thought she was salvageable. Besides, who would do my housework for me? I made her a slave again.

It is a wise provision of the law that says no slave may be completely manumitted. Even substantial manumission provides for a five-year probationary period. Sandra had not passed probation. I had the necessary papers drawn up, told her, an hour before the men came, what was happening, and had her sent to the FSB Rehabilitation School in Colorado for a month.

She came back with the ring in her ear, saying sir to me, and the very first night she washed my feet. Furthermore she made love better than she had done for a year. I thought we were to be happy again, and for a week we seemed to be. But the machines are still there to do most of the work, and she still has her allergy. She does what a slave is supposed to do, but she is depressed about it. She has tasted the fruit of freedom; though it is a bitter fruit it is habit-forming. She does what she is supposed to do, but it is an effort, she has to will it, it exhausts her.

One evening six months ago, I came home to find no dinner cooking, no foot bath waiting for me, no sign of Sandra in her room. I found her lying on my bed reading *McCall's* and smoking with a jewel-studded holder I had given her when she was my wife. She flicked an ash onto the rug when I entered the room, waved a langorous *Hi!* at me, and kept on reading. I had my choice; she had clearly set it up for me. I hesitated only a moment. I went down to the basement where I had stored away the three-thronged lash which had been provided along with the manual of instructions when I had first bought her, and I beat her on the bed where she lay.

I think I was more upset by the beating than Sandra was. But I knew I had had to do it. I knew I had neglected my duty as a master not to have done it long ago. I think, now, that all this trouble could have been avoided if formerly I had only kept a firm hand, that is to say, had beaten her when she had risen too presumptuously. For the truth is, Sandra is happiest as a slave.

But the beatings I should have given her formerly would simply have hurt; she would simply have avoided them. Now, I am not so sure.

For she repeated the offense, exactly, within a month, and I repeated the punishment. It wasn't so bad for me the second time. She began seeing just how far she could go before I would bring out the lash. She cooked more and more badly till I gave her warning one evening. When I had finished speaking, she sank to the floor, pressed her forehead against my foot, looked at me, and said, "Your wish is my command." The irony was all in the act and words, if irony there was, for there was none in the voice or face. The truth was, as she discovered the next evening when she served me corned beef hash and raw carrots for dinner, my lash is her command. She seems happier, in a way, after these distasteful blow-ups, comes to my bed voluntarily and with the welts still on her back, does her work well, hums sometimes. Yet she falls back into her old stubborn mood, again and again. There seems to be nothing else for me to do but beat her. The FSB manual supports me. Yet I find it repugnant, and it cannot be good for Sandra's skin. I had to lash her a week ago, and already, from the dirt she is allowing to collect on the living room rug, it looks as though I'll have to do it again.

It seems a pity to have to resort to this, when it was all quite unnecessary. It's my own fault of course; I lacked the training, the matter-of-fact experience of being a master, and I did not set about my duties as a master so conscientiously as I should have. I know all this, but knowing it doesn't help matters a bit. Sometimes I think I should have killed her: it would have been better for both of us; but then she will do some little act of spontaneous love, as now bringing me a cup of hot chocolate and kissing me lightly on the back of the neck, which makes me glad to have her around. Yet tomorrow I shall have to beat her again. This is not what I had wanted, and it cannot be what she wants, not really. We were uneasy and felt something lacking when she was a slave before, though we were happy too. We were altogether miserable when she was free. Yet, this is not what either of us had ever wanted, though we are both of us doing what we must.

BEYOND SPACE AND TIME
by Joel Townsley Rogers

WE MADE THE ROCKET (said Gunderson) to penetrate beyond the earth's atmosphere, out of the sun's orbit, and out of the galaxy, if possible. The conception and the mathematical formulae were Hartley's, the details of the construction mine. It was our purpose to explore outer space, to investigate the mystery of the cosmos, to solve the riddle of the fourth dimension, Time, and to reach that roof of heaven where, eighteen million light-years or more away, according to the best available data of mathematics, infinity curves and returns upon itself in a parabolic trajectory—to find the answer to the last question, in short, and the solution of the ultimate equation. An unparalleled venture, yes. But it was time, as Hartley said, that it be done.

At no time ever before in the world's history had there existed contemporaneously two men whose capabilities and geniuses so complemented and dovetailed each other as did our own; and it might well happen that there would not be again two men like us for fifty thousand years, if ever.

Consider briefly who we were: Hartley, the greatest mathematician and theoretical physicist that the world has ever known, the perfect exponent of completely idealistic and abstract thought, a man beside whom Galileo was only an ignorant schoolboy and Archimedes no more than a primitive barbarian; and myself, Helver Gunderson, of Gunderson Laboratories, the developer of the make-and-break ray, of the spinning wing, the watch-type televisor, the roadless sky pavement, and the atom engine, to speak of only a few—a man with an intellect on a far lower and humbler plane than Hartley's (I would be the last to dispute it), but still a man who at the very least has shown himself the greatest pragmatic inventor since Edison.

There we were. The combination might never happen again. Perhaps we had been put here for something, by a distant Mind which had controlled our conception. If for no purpose, still we must milk the blind cow, Chance, and obtain some nourishment from the circumstance.

To probe the final mystery. There could be no venture greater. Only the two of us knew anything about our plan and purpose, and, of course, Nivea, my wife—Hartley himself was unmarried, except to his science and his mind. We worked on the blueprints nine months together, after Hartley had brought me his calculations and equations, which had taken him ten years to produce. The actual building of the rocket was done in one of my own plants, the Gunderson, Engineering Three, at Bridgeport, which was specialized for experimental work of the most confidential sort and staffed with a picked corps of super-skilled and loyal technicians.

Even so, we had to go carefully. Each workman, working on his individual part, did not know the purpose of the whole. It was rumored that it was a great new submarine, that it was an invention for boring toward the center of the earth into that great core of compressed and adamantine gold on which all the continents float. I let them think as they wished to think. If they had known the real purpose of that unprecedented ship, they would have thought I was insane.

The building of it took six months, and I was with it night and day, hardly sleeping in all that time more than two hours at a stretch, and frequently neglecting to eat for days, working in an increasing tension as it neared completion. There were many problems to be met, many seemingly insuperable difficulties to be overcome. There were times when I almost despaired, when my inventive skill seemed to have run up against a blank and impenetrable wall. As if there were a Hand which stood pushed out against me, and said: Thus far, and no farther!

Yet who could say that to me, Gunderson? One by one I broke down and overcame those problems, solved the last difficulty. There came the dawn when the last rivet had been driven, the last delicate instrument tested and installed, and the machine was trundled onto the cradle prepared for its christening and launching on the shore of the Sound in front of the factory, on—what day is this?—on May the 7, 1968.

We stood there beside it on its launching platform, Hooker Hartley and I, in that stupendous moment before its take-off into the distances of ultimate space, while Nivea prepared to christen it with champagne, and the dazed and uncomprehending workmen, who had trucked it forth and set it there, clustered bewilderedly on the ground a hundred feet below. It was a ship capable of accomplishing the great thing that Hartley had conceived and I had planned, I knew without a doubt. It was the greatest of all my inventions, the most stupendously conceived, the most perfectly wrought in every detail. I put my hand on it and stroked its welded sides as if it had been a living bird. A thing of midnight blue and silver, shaped like a great tear, ready for the stars.

"Will it do it, really?" said Hartley, standing there bareheaded with me, hunched and shivering, with his hands jammed in his topcoat pockets, staring at it with his great luminous eyes. "Beyond the orbit, Helver?"

"Beyond the orbit?" I said. "Beyond the drift! Beyond the galaxy!"

"Beyond the galaxy!" he said. "To the outer-galactic void?"

"Beyond! Beyond the utmost nebula!" I said. "To the ultimate limits of space, Hooker!"

He shivered beside me on the launching platform, standing there, soft, plump, and delicately boned, with his head pulled down between his shoulders, the black curly hair growing thin on top of the great skull above the mighty brain. His full lips were pursed together and a little twisted, with one eye half shut. His topcoat collar was pulled up around his ears, and still he shivered a little in the cold thin dawn. The elevation of the platform perhaps affected him. He had always been a little squeamish about heights.

And even he was awed.

"I made it," I told him. "I am Helver Gunderson. If I say that it will do it, it will do it."

Perhaps I was a little irritated. Every nerve in my body was a hot wire. There was burning sand upon my brain. I looked down at him with my red glaring eyes, and he seemed to shrink away from me a little. He had not really doubted me, of course. He knew that I was Helver Gunderson. He knew that if I had made it, it would do it. His question had just been a demand for reiteration of a true but astonishing fact.

"I use atomic energy for the take-off, Hooker," I explained to him more patiently. "And plenty of it. An adaptation of the neutron-deutron principle, stepped up to the ratio of omega-pi. We take off with an initial speed of five thousand m.p.m., accelerating with geometric progression. She travels by cosmic energy after the first nine minutes, by which time we should be well beyond Mars, I think.

"The problem of power was not too hard to solve, you see—the problem of shape was somewhat more difficult. It is probably that which stumps you. The hull's apparent contour is obvious, of course, but it is merely for the minimum of friction in the atmosphere. Atmospheric pressure keeps it up. Beyond a hundred miles, in half a second, she collapses into her true shape of a ten-pointed star, the only conceivable one, naturally, for maximum efficiency in interstellar space. The way I worked the mechanical problem of the change of shape was this——"

But he was paying no attention, I realized; he was immersed in those vaster, more splendid thoughts of his own. Shivering, with pursed lips, and with one eye blinking.

"But mechanics bore you," I said a little lamely. "The point is, it will do it. It will work. Do you want to look inside?"

"What?" he said. "Oh, no. No, thanks. I'll take your word for it. I wouldn't understand it, anyway."

I felt a little baffled by him. A little humilated and regretful that he should not find sufficiently interesting the mechanical problems which I had faced and conquered. But who was he to waste his mind on things like engines?

"To the ultimate limits of space!" he repeated, catching his breath.

He had a picture of it, I knew, in his mind. "And back," I said.

But he did not hear me. His teeth chittered, while he shivered. Suddenly he began to laugh, with the breathless gasping laughter which some men get in moments of intense excitement. All his formulae, all his dreams!

The ship I had made that would prove them all. That picture of infinity which he could see. Shivering and laughing, with tight lips, with a gasping in his throat, as if he were strangling from something deep inside him, and for his life he could not stop.

"I knew that you could make it," he gasped. "To ultimate space! My God, what a man you are!"

It rested there beside us in its lofty cradle, the great rocket, silver and midnight blue. "I christen thee Viking!" said Nivea in her cold clear ringing voice, breaking the bottle of champagne across its nose.

Nivea! The dawn light shone on her smooth brushed golden hair, upon her eyes like the sparkle of beautiful blue ice, upon her small clear-cut face, so cold and proud. She wore silver fox furs around her soft white throat. There was a bunch of violets at her slender supple waist, which no motherhood had ever spoiled. "I christen thee Viking!" she said, Nivea. "May you beach on the ultimate stars!"

There were only the three of us there and the uncomprehending workmen staring up from below. No newsreel men or photographers. They would not have believed it if they saw it. The dawn wind was cold. The blue Sound sparkled. The moon was a pale ghost. The remnants of the wine bottle had dropped to the ground below. Nivea turned to me with her proud eyes. I polished my goggles and put on my helmet, and I got into the ship after a last handshake with Hartley and a kiss on Nivea's cheek.

"Good-by, old man!" said Hartley.

"Good-by, darling!" said Nivea. "Good luck!"

I battened down the hatch, waved a farewell through the porthole, flipped my controls a couple of times, and took off.

So it was launched without fanfare that morning (said Gunderson), the greatest invention of my career, the culmination of all my mechanical genius and adaptability, upon its course into outer space according to the formulae of Hartley.

I shall never forget—though for years I did let myself forget in Mara's arms—the sight of Nivea there upon the platform, with a last wave and cry to me as my swift cruiser of galactic space took off. How many years ago! What day is this? May 7, 1968—yes, of course, that must be right. It was this year, this day, and this moment, at six o'clock in the morning. The same hour as when I left. . . .

CHAPTER TWO

You wonder (said Gunderson) why a man like me should have been interested at all in a project so theoretical, a quest so unrelated to any practical value or prospect of commercial profit, so unearthly and so abstract. You see in me no more than a super-mechanic—oh, a man with an inexplicable and unparalleled genius for machines, and with a pragmatic grasp and understanding of matter in every form, which has enabled me to produce those various inventions which have changed in the course of a few years the whole aspect of man's civilization. But still only a mechanic underneath, for all of that—a big-shouldered, heavy-faced fellow, with big broken-nailed hands a little grimy with engine oil, with low brow and unkempt hair, with dull eyes and no dreams behind them—a man with a cogwheel brain. A big apelike lout of a man for all his millions, not quick of wit or speech in any way, a man whose very handclasp is curved to the clutch of a wrench. A man who but for the accident of half a dozen incomprehensible brain cells might be lying with his shoulder blades on the floor of any garage draining out the oil from your car at twenty-two dollars a week. A man, at the best, whose every purpose and accomplishment has been practical and commercially profitable, an unimaginative hard-headed, realistic man, with his feet upon the earth, his eye to the dollar. And that is true, no doubt.

It is true, like everything else, in part. I was born to the bitterest poverty; I knew terrific toil as a boy; acute hunger was a daily and constant companion to me for the first twenty years of my life; and I have had to keep my feet on the earth, to think of profit and values and commercial utility in everything in order to climb up out of that slough which otherwise would have swallowed me.

I wanted millions, and I made them. At first, to keep away from me the specter of starvation which I had known too well. After I had married Nivea, to take care of her, to maintain for her the background of great houses, jewels, clothes, society, travel, yachts, servants that she needed and deserved—to make her ever more proud and loving of me, because of the power of money that I could shower on her.

And to such a need of money it takes a long time to reach an end. For years there had been no time for me to taste the pleasures of pure science and abstract thinking, no time for dreams. But that did not mean that the dreams were not there. I, Helver Gunderson, super-mechanic, engineer, multimillionaire industrialist, Swedish wizard, cogwheel freak, I too had my dreams. Of outer space. Of infinity. Of the vast dark blue voids which lie between the nebulae. Of adventures in those realms of pure and immaculate mathematics which lie beyond space and time, wherein Hartley's great mind ranged as mine did among my electrons and differential gears.

It was the racial adventuresomeness of my blood, perhaps, that was aroused and stirred when Hartley first broached his magnificent proposition to me. The Norse blood. The old seafarers who were my ancestors, driven by an unappeasable urge in their quest for the unknown. By a thing within their hearts which cried, Go on! Go on, till the last shore is reached and the world's rim!

The days of the dragon boats and the thin frail sails and the howl and lash of the spindrift in a man's teeth and the glorious lightning wrack and the chartless seas are done. But if a man has that thing in his blood, this earth will not suffice him. And the sons of those men will be faring till the world shall end. Education, civilization—but still the call of the blood is there—

and still I must always be aware of that adventure-cry. It was that thing in me, born in my blood, which no doubt was one of the impulses which drew me on.

A second, no doubt, was Nivea. For she, too, felt the great splendor of that quest. The time had come when there was no more money I could make, since taxes on increased gains would actually decrease my revenue, while what was already flowing in from royalties and contracts was more than even she could spend. So that I was free from pressure and Nivea's future was forever secured, as far as money could do it.

The thought of that unprecedented voyage into the void, that great quest conceived by Hartley, inspired her intellect with a lofty enthusiasm such as I had never known her to show before, and she spurred me on with her cold and passionless fire.

Nivea, my wife—you know her, gentlemen. She was a Saltonstall of Boston, highborn, with a lofty mind, cold, but beautiful as ice. And God knows that I loved her, humbly and worshipfully, with all the power of my soul and brain. Yes, I loved her, and wanted her respect and admiration.

She had never thought a great deal of the inventions, you understand— those things had always seemed a little dirty and beneath her, and though she endured them because of the money they brought in, in her heart she had always despised them. Dirt and machines, test tubes and stinking chemicals, she often told me, curling the edges of her thin fine nostrils as she drew back from me; I had only wheels in my brain; there was a stink about me which would not wash off. Who could blame her? She was so highborn, you see. She had married far beneath her; there was no secret in that. Her father had been a gentleman; he had never worked in his life. Me—me, Gunderson, the Swede, with my great awkward hands, my uncouth manners; an ignorant miner's son, born in the dirt—it could be understood how much she had sacrificed, how much she had lowered herself, by marrying me. What had I ever done to make her proud of me? But this was a project perhaps not unworthy of her, this great forthfaring into outer space.

This was something of pure science, such as even a gentleman might be honored to attempt, and to which, if successful, sufficient honor would be attached. So to warm her cold proud eyes, to do something great and splendidly worthy of her—that was another reason that I undertook the venture, gentlemen.

And yet beyond the Viking blood, and beyond the desire I had to glorify Nivea, there was most of all the necessity I had to carry through the quest, because Hartley had brought it to me. Hartley, the greatest scientific intelligence that ever lived! In my far humbler sphere of endeavor and achievement I had always looked up to him as the man of hands must always look up, I suppose, to the man of mind. Ever since I had first known him Hartley had been my god, since I had none other. And so he had come to me with this great conception of investigating outer space, with the formulae which he had worked out to the ultimate decimal of perfection. He had called on me for help, had Hartley, as to an equal. And I tell you, it made me proud. Only that stupendous brain of his could have worked out the ineffable equation. And yet only these hands of mine could have made the ship.

I shall always swagger a little through the eternities of hell because of that, gentlemen. He came to me, Hooker Hartley, and he said that never before in the world's history had there been two men such as he and I, and likely there would never be again. He said it was time the thing be done. To make a ship to fly beyond the orbit, and beyond the galaxy, if possible. And he said, "Can you, Helver?" And I said, "I can." And he said, "Will you, Helver?" And I said, "I will." And so I did.

With these hands ...

I first knew Hartley (said Gunderson) in college ten years ago. I knew him, but there was no reason he should know me. Even as a sophomore he was by far the most famous man in college, the leader in everything. Not merely because of his intellect—though even then, at nineteen years old, he was already confounding all the professors and had started work on his epochal thesis destroying the speculations of Einstein—but also because of the other things which he represented: Groton prep-school training, Newport family, wealth, breeding, generations of gentlemen behind him. A member of the best clubs, the quarterback and captain of the football team, handsome as a faun, with dark curly hair and the tilt of his head, his amazingly attractive smile, his elegant manner of wearing clothes. He knew art, wine, clothes, literature. The best restaurants to go to, how to order a dinner for a chorus girl, and how to treat a servant.

He had everything; he knew everything; he was all the things that a man envies and wishes he might be. Picture me, on the other hand, clumsy, uncouth, badly dressed, friendless and poor. I was only Gunderson, the big dumb ugly Swede, taciturn and alone, who lived in a little attic room up on the fourth floor. A grind, working his way through by waiting on table, by tending furnaces, and by running a shoeshine stand for the rich men's sons. I was twenty-six, too, much older than the rest, for it had taken me time to save to go to college at all.

There was nothing to recommend me. I didn't even have an overcoat to my name. My only shoes, a pair of cheap work-brogans, had holes in their soles as big as a dollar, and I remember how the fellows used to laugh behind my back as I went clumping through the Yard from class to class, with the mud and water squishing between my toes like the sound of an elephant in muck, with the rain or snow falling on me, and my big red-knuckled hands clutching my books.

I wasn't even brilliant in studies, for while I might know the answers in most courses, still I had to plug for them, and if I did one or two things with atoms in the lab that made the professors lift their brows, why, that was only a kind of trick, and no one could mistake me for an intellectual. I was just one of those queer shabby earnest nondescript bugs that crawl out from behind cracks in the plaster at a big college, that don't really belong at all and never will, whose names nobody ever knows.

I was in my back room after supper one night when the door opened, and there was Hartley. I dropped everything and stood up. I didn't know he knew I was alive. I couldn't swallow. My brain was a blank at sight of him.

"Sit down," he said easily, dropping into a chair. He looked at me through cigarette smoke. "Gunderson," he said, "you and I are the greatest minds in our class, without a question, and in all college. I suspect, in fact, that we are the greatest minds in all the world. There should be a confraternity of genius. I think we should get acquainted."

"Mr. Hartley," I managed to say—I found it was all I could do to speak— "Mr. Hartley, do not make fun of me, please. I am not worthy to be mentioned in the same breath with you by anyone, nor by you at all. And you know it very well. I have no intelligence at all. Or at the best, a very slow and heavy intelligence. I have only a cogwheel brain. Beside you, I am only a mechanic."

His bright little faun's eyes danced in approval.

"I know," he said, nodding negligently. "I know. You are a grind. Still, there is something in you, Gunderson. Don't be too modest. The way you made that atom bounce like a jumping bean in lab the other day rather amused me. There's no one before who's ever done it. It was near."

"Merely a pragmatic experiment in augmenting the molecular cohesion of air," I hastened to tell him, "to be used by planes in flight to build themselves a solid roadway under wing, and so obviate the greatest present handicap to air flight, which is the risk of falling. A mechanical invention purely, and of no theoretical scientific importance."

"There you are, damn it," said Hartley, nodding. "An invention for practical use. I can do rings around you theoretically, Gunderson. But you have a hard practicality in your mind that I lack. You can see the application, where I can see only the idea. You will be a millionaire someday, while after I've lost in the market what's left to me, I shan't know how to make an honest dime. You've got the money-making gift, Gunderson, as sure as fate, and I'm not such a fool as not to see it. So I say there's something in you. You ought to be developed. I think that I am going to take you under my wing."

"Under your wing, Mr. Hartley?" I said.

"Socially. Bring out your better points, my boy. Teach you the art of knowing how to live and spend the money when you make it. I'll bet you don't even know what a woman is. I'll bet you never even had a drink."

"Never," I said, "Mr. Hartley."

"Don't call me Mr. Hartley, call me Hooker, Helver," he said. "We're classmates, equals, aren't we, and we're friends? Do you know what I'm going to do with you tonight?" he said thoughtfully. "I'm going to take you around to Nivea Saltonstall's party, the biggest brawl of the season. Nivea, poor girl," he said. "There's no doubt she's a living beauty. I'd marry her myself, maybe, if I was the marrying kind, or if she had the dough. But that's no dice. Her old man's Cabot Saltonstall, and he's down to his last dime. He's throwing this big party for Nivea to give her a chance to hook some guy with dough. But unfortunately there are more beautiful gals on the market than guys with a hundred grand or so to buy them with. But it'll be a good party while it lasts. White tie, Helver. And do you have to wrap your hands around your wrists and your feet around your ankles like that?"

"I don't know how to dance, Mr. Hartley—Hooker," I told him.

"Just drape yourself around the punch bowl and you won't have to. No one's going to want you to anyway, after one look at your feet."

"But I haven't got a dress suit," I said.

"I wish I could lend you one of mine, but you couldn't get your feet into the pants," he said. "You'll simply have to rent one, Helver—shoes to silk hat. You can do it for fifteen bucks at Moe's on Washington Street, which keeps open all night."

"Fifteen dollars to rent a suit!" I said. "I haven't got fifteen cents."

"Hell," he said, "you've got a million."

And he pulled a letter out of his pocket and tossed it to me, a little excitedly. "I saw it in the mail rack in the transept," he said. "My old man is a director of the company. I saw the envelope and thought it must be for me and opened it without bothering particularly with the address."

I fumbled with the envelope. For the moment my fingers were too thick to feel. I unfolded the letter, with the thick bond paper shaking and crackling in my hand. It was from Amalgamated Air, offering me a million cash and a royalty for the rights of the flying wheel which I had developed.

"A million!" I said. "A million! I can eat whenever I want to now! I can have a three-course dinner every day!"

"And you can go to Nivea's party tonight," said Hartley heartily. "Isn't it a fortunate coincidence that my determination to take you under my social wing happened to hit at the same time as this? I was just telephoning Nivea about you. Don't be bashful. She will like you, Helver, I'm sure."

I went with him to Nivea's party that night and met her. Within a week we were engaged; I don't know yet how it happened. It was such a dream. I remember Hartley drank with us to our betrothal the night it happened, and how smiling he looked and contented, and Nivea's cold proud eyes, over the rim of the wineglass from which she did not sip, drifting from him to me.

"Luck to us!" said Hartley. "Don't forget old friends, Nivea, my darling. A night beneath the moon. To you, Helver, millions, more and more."

Nivea's lips were pressed white at her wineglass rim, and she looked from him to me and closed her eyes. Upon her shy tears, no doubt. Women, Hartley told me, are like that.

We were married in the spring after I quit college to devote myself to business. I had conditions in history and had flunked philosophy, and even my chemistry wasn't what they were looking for, quite, so it was probably just as well. Being a married man, of course, I had to work hard, to make money to compensate for the things she had given up.

Mr. Saltonstall, her father, kindly allowed me to advance him two hundred thousand dollars, with which he went to Paris. The climate of Paris, it seemed, had always agreed with him. And Nivea began the building of her first house. When she started buying the gold bathroom fixtures she was very happy. It was wonderful to see her so happy, when I had time to see her. I was working night and day.

The next year Hartley's father lost his money, and I sold Roadless Skyways for five million and ten per cent of the profits—it still pays the biggest dividends after the pocket television which I developed in two years more and put on the market myself.

So I had been close to Hartley in his youth. I had basked humbly in the shadow of his greatness, and as he grew in fame he did not grow away from me. Nivea's home and mine was always his. It was my pride to erect the Hartley Hall of Science for him at Cambridge, the most completely equipped workshop that money could procure, with ten-thousand dollar rugs and books and paintings, and to endow the Hartley Professorship of Physics, which he accepted. When he won the Nobel prize, five years out of college, Nivea and I went with him to Stockholm to receive it. He had even allowed me to aid in a humble way in the mechanical side of the problem which had won the prize for him. He was cited for it, as you recall, for developing a technic for filtering starlight rays through radium. I devised the apparatus for doing it one evening in my spare time, though the idea of course was his. All this time, of course, he was devoting himself to his major problem, to the working out of those abstruse and perfect formulae on the curve of space and the parabolic declivity of infinity which he had set as his lifework, and while I was burying my nose in the grimy business of commercial invention, he was working on those equations reducing the cosmos to the nth root, which is the theoretical ultimate conceivable by the mind of man or God. He worked on his formulae and his equations ten years. . . .

CHAPTER THREE

I REMEMBER THE EVENING when he came to me with his final equations. I had been out in Chicago at Gunderson Production Five, my biggest plant, where we were turning out televisors on the belt, ironing out a few small kinks of mass production. I was very tired. Suddenly, because the night was hot and I felt lonely, and the making of money alone cannot altogether suffice for a man, and because I had not seen Nivea for two months, I decided to come home to her. I hopped my plane, took Skyway Route 3 all the way, with the road mostly clear of traffic and no red lights at that hour, and arrived home at the house on Long Island in an hour and a half.

A butler met me at the door. "Madam has a guest," he said, "and cannot be disturbed. If you would tell me what it is you wish . . ."

"You fool!" I said, "I am your master! And I don't like you, nor your smug smirking face!" And I pushed him away from me like a sack of wheat, and I went leaping up the great marble stairs three at a time, calling "Nivea! Nivea!" Below me the butler was bleating, "It's Gunderson!" as if I had come to burn the house down or were some kind of crazy tiger.

I remember the shadowy fox-footed servants running in the halls, and I called to them, "Which is Madame's room? Show me Madame's room!" But they would not answer. It was a new house, new servants.

There were always new houses; there were always servants like weasels. But this night there seemed to me, perhaps because I was red-eyed and tired, more and more. And I was sick of new houses. I was sick of servants. I wanted Nivea. To kiss her hand, to throw myself on my knees before her, Nivea, my wife. My cold, proud, highborn wife.

"Nivea! Nivea! Show me her bedroom. I'm Gunderson, your master! Where is she? What's going on here?"

Then I saw one face that I knew. It was Nivea's personal maid, Jeanne. She was standing with her back to a door, with her arms stretched out in a cross, and her mustache was trembling with her breathing and her lips were gray and her eyes were locked with terror.

"Non! Non!" she said. "Mais non! Madame is sick! M'sieu' must not go in!"

But I was in a frenzy of terror by then. I thought she might be dying. I took Jeanne by the shoulder and hurled her to the opposite wall. I lunged against the door, and it was locked. I lunged again, and it burst in before me.

"Nivea!"

But it was Hartley in the room. He stared at me as I came bursting in. He had a highball glass in his hand, and his hand shook a little, spilling it down on the soft bulge of his waist, as he stared at me numbly.

"Helver!" he said heartily after a moment, while his face creased in a plump and happy smile. "Just the man I wanted to see!"

I slapped him on the back and asked about his health. He seemed a little pale, and there was a clammy sweat upon his forehead. But he gulped his highball down, and the color came back into his cheeks.

"What are you doing here?" I said. "I wanted you to join me in Chicago. I thought you were in Cambridge working. What's the news?"

"I've finished the formulae!" he said. "I couldn't wait to tell you. I thought you might come home."

"Clairvoyance!" I told him with warm admiration. "What a mind you have! Even I didn't have an idea that I'd be back until two hours ago. Perhaps I heard you calling me, old friend. Where's Nivea, have you seen her?"

"Oh yes, at dinner."

"Where is she now?"

I looked around the room. I saw some of her things upon the bureau. Some of her frocks at the edge of the closet door, which had been closed upon them. She had given him her own room, then. She must have moved to some other.

"Where is she?" I said.

But he didn't hear me, or at least paid no attention, he was so excited with his great success.

"The formulae, Helver!" he repeated. "I have finished them! Don't you want to look them over?"

"What formulae?" I said.

Stupidly, for the instant I had forgot. "What formulae?" I repeated, a little harshly, a little nerve-worn and tired.

He drew back from me. "You know, the space-time formulae that I have been working on for ten years! The thing that you built the Hall of Science for me for, and established the professorship for!"

"You've finished them at last?"

"I thought that would knock your eye out!" he said, with a pleased quiet laugh. "Sit down, and look them over."

He poured me a stiff drink. I sat down and looked at them. My mind was tired. I was a little slow. I could not concentrate. Figures and graphs.

"What do they mean?" I said.

"They mean the way is ready!" he said. "For the great adventure, Helver!"

I drank the whisky, and the warmth seeped through my blood. I heard far off the singing of the spheres. The great blue voids called to me with a song of winds. Beyond the orbit, beyond the drift, beyond the galaxy! With my breast bared to the hurricane, and the spindrift in my face. Go on! Go on, to the ultimate shore! There are strange lands to be discovered, beyond the trackless sea! And my heart lifted in my breast; it sang; and I clenched and unclenched my hands.

"What a dream!" I said.

And Nivea was there; I don't know where she came from, but she was there on the floor at my feet. With her smooth golden hair about her shoulders, her supple slender form in her silk gown.

"Oh, Helver," she said, stroking my knee. "How proud I would be of you! Unknown shores to conquer!"

"The unknown seas!" I said.

I stroked her head. But there was no feeling in me. Neither a feeling of heat nor cold. My head was back; my heart roared in my breast; and there was a great calm within my spirit; I heard the calling of the spheres and the singing of the sea.

"Let's launch the dragon boat!" I said. "Why are we sitting here? Let's get it launched, and go! Do we want to rot and grow fat on the dull and deadly shore, when there is a wind upon the sea? Do we want to live forever to stroke a woman's golden hair, and grub like slaves for the soft pap we eat? To rot and die while still alive! Let's launch the dragon boat, by God, and we'll put out to sea!"

I held my glass out, and Hartley filled it to the brim again.

I stood up. I took my hand from Nivea. The drink was strong and deep and good. "Let's go!" I said, crashing down the glass. "The unknown sea! The lightning wrack and the world's rim! Forever and forever. Beyond the gates of Hercules lies Italy! Beyond the going-down-of-the-sun sea lie golden sands and copper women, and things such as no man has felt or seen! Get out the dragon boat, by God, and we'll put out to sea!"

And Nivea was laughing and choking and gasping. Laughing with pride for the glory of me.

"My Viking!" she said.

"Can you make the ship, Helver?" said Hartley, looking at me with his great luminous eyes.

"Can I make the ship?" I said.

"Do you dare do it?" said Hartley.

"Do I dare!" I said.

"What a man you are!" he said.

"What a man I am!" I said. "To the roof of the world and back! Let's go!" I said. "Why are we rotting here, when we hear the calling of the sea?"

So we worked together on the blueprints. Many months. Hartley remained installed in the house, to lend me any theoretical advice, as needed. I was at the shops much still, for I had a million men to feed, men and their families depending on me, and I could not leave things just at loose ends for my own selfish quest. But I gave every moment that I could to going over the plans with Hartley on Sundays and nights when I could get home.

There came this day when the ship was launched. I remember the day well. By the shore of the blue salt water, in the dawn, the great ship that I had made, all midnight blue and silver, standing in its cradle with its bow pointed to the faded stars.

"I christen thee Viking!" said Nivea. And I shook hands with Hartley; I kissed Nivea upon her cold proud cheek; I got into the hatchway of the ship. Oh, I was tired, tired. With the sleepless nights and the months of effort and the brain-shattering problems to be solved. But there was a singing in my heart, and I heard the roaring of the spheres.

"Have you forgotten anything, old man?" said Hartley.

"If I have, I have my hands."

"The wrench to tighten your inside lugs and batten down your hatch?"

"I have that, all right," I said.

"Oh, Helver!" said Nivea.

For the moment her cold controlled voice seemed to break. Perhaps she was remembering many things, the clumsy awkward youngster whom Hartley had brought to her party many years before, in his cheap rented dress suit, loutish and inarticulate, and his eyes which had lit with a humble and eternal light at sight of her. Perhaps that boy upon his knees, kissing her hand and the hem of her skirt when she said she would be his wife.

And the inventions, the conquests he had brought her, eager to have her know about them first of all, hungry for her praise. The fame and money, the millions rolling in, the great houses he had given her, his clumsy hands fumbling with her hair. Perhaps she remembered that, and many things. The boy, the man, the work, the dreams, the years.

I shall never really know.

And for the moment her voice had seemed to break. But she got control of it. She smiled at me with a brave warm smile, the warmest from her that I had ever known. Oh, but I wished in that moment with a blind and frustrate longing that I had had sons by her, to grow to strong manhood during the years when I should be gone. To find them waiting on the shore when I came back, sons of her body, and of the Viking blood. To throw their arms about me and cling to me with pride, when I came back from the ultimate sea.

But that was not to be, and never in this life to be.

Still, her smile was on me warm, and the warmest I had ever known. And I knew that nothing I had ever done before for her had so pleased her as this. Nor anything, in her eyes, was so becoming for me.

"Good luck! Don't forget to come back, Helver!" she said, with her warm smile, almost gaily.

"Nor that," I said.

I could see her pride and happiness shining in her eyes, and her cold face seemed suddenly warm, intoxicated.

I closed the hatch and tightened the lugs. I saw her through the thick glass porthole, clasping the arm of Hartley beneath the armpit, drawing him close to her, as I settled to the controls. The dawn sun shone on her smooth gold hair. Her eyes like the blue of inmost fire, the passionless fire of ice.

And the wind stirred Hartley's dark curly hair. It had grown a little thin, I saw. He was a little plump. The soft years had put it on him. In that moment somehow, I do not know why it was, he looked no more to me than a fat and greasy worm, a man with pouch eyes too young, a soft and squashy thing, with a great hollow skull in which no more than empty formulae rattled, and greedy eyes—Hartley, the greatest brain that ever lived! Oh, it was only the distortion of the thick glass which made him seem so, made seem malevolent and vile the smile that was painted on Nivea's cold face.

They smiled at me. His arm was around Nivea, supporting her, there on the lofty platform beside me, and she blew a kiss at me, and waved. She shouted something, but I could not hear.

There was no need of prolonging it. I pushed the electronizer, and I zoomed off. Beyond the orbit, beyond the drift, beyond the limits of the galaxy! Toward the universe's end, if possible! Toward the answer to the last question, and the sealed books of God.

Upon that unknown sea . . .

CHAPTER FOUR

THE ROCKET WENT OFF with a speed faster than light, as I had calculated (said Gunderson). I turned around in the take-off instant to wave farewell, in my last glimpse of earth, at them on the high launching platform, the men upon the ground, the chimney stacks, the blue waters of the

Sound. I turned, but before I had got my eyes focused, the whole earth was no more than a fading planet far down the sparkling steel-blue sky. I had shot from the atmosphere in half a breath. In five minutes I was beyond the moon. Her speed increased as she caught the cosmic rays, which began to beat upon her hull like hail. Mars went whipping past like a great red ball of fire.

In two hours I was shooting past the high frozen mountains of Neptune, and the sun, far down within the wheeling sky at the center of the orbit, was no bigger than the largest star, blue as a diamond. In the bright blue light of outer space the other suns went hurtling past. We gathered speed.

The parsecs passed like clicking telegraph poles, and each one of them was nineteen trillion miles. Before noon I was streaking upward past the Pleiades, and well upon my way. I curved my bow outward from the drift, past there, steering course 205. As night fell, Betelgeuse, hotter and bigger than ten thousand suns, was dropping like a pumpkin seed far down the sky. I set the controls and slept. It was noon when I woke up. I had slept the clock around, and more, after those exhausting months of sleepless strain. A sleep so long and deep that I sang in every bone, and there was a great restfulness in my soul. Still the weather had grown stormy, and the rocket was pitching in great waves as she sped. My wrist watch was stopping, as though time itself was growing more motionless. There was not a star around. We had passed clear from the galaxy; the Milky Way was only a thin spot of smoke far down the sky; and in the terrific emptiness of inter-galactic space a hurricane was blowing up.

The ion spray leaped against my porthole with a gleam like St. Elmo's fire. I saw the crests of great white billows rushing, and they were nebulae. The wind howled in the eternal void; I felt the battering and straining of my hull-plates; lightning went flashing past; and we were caught in the grip of a terrific current. I gripped the shivering controls with my great hands and laughed. Ah, ah, the thin sails and the lightning wrack, and the dragon boat upon the trackless sea! And so, with controls locked in both fists and my eyes ahead, in the grip of an electronic current which went rushing toward a notch ahead, I shot toward the dimensionless point where space and time come to an end in nothingness, and reverse in minus quantity.

There is this about space and time (explained Gunderson, making a gesture carefully with his great heavy hands), they are shaped like a pair of inverted cones, lying point to point. Like an hourglass, roughly, let us say, or like the torso of a woman in a cubistic dream. They are not illimitable and all plus, as the astronomers think, with distance piled on distance, and time on time. Nor are they curved, like the inside of an egg, returning on themselves in a parabola, according to the concept of the mathematicians.

In whatever direction a man goes, they narrow to a point at the end of the cone, and beyond that there is an inverted cone of minus space and minus time, and the stars rotate from east to west, and time moves backward from its end to its beginning, and all vacuums are solid, and there is a dark light. You understand. That is the secret of eternity. Once explained, it is quite obvious, and even a child could grasp it. Whereas—that is, upon this earth—within this cone of plus and forward, of west-to-east and outside-out, time moves forward from the past into the future, and dimensions move outward from the center into the infinite; beyond the end of the cone it is all just the other way. That is the reason for the stars which seem millions of light-years away.

They are old and are going backward to their beginnings, and by the measure of their seeming distance they are near. It is an obvious and a simple thing, yet there is no man who has understood this before me. I passed this point; I shot forward into minus space and minus time. The speed went out of my ship with geometric deceleration, in ratio as it had gathered. I landed on the other earth, which is called Threa.

There is only one other earth (said Gunderson), and from here to there is the distance from plus to minus and no more. It is an earth that once was old and now is growing young. The people there are like frozen flame. There I met Mara.

(He paused, Gunderson.) She was like nothing ever dreamed of, a soul of light, a body of fire. Growing younger and lovelier hour by hour. What is there to say of her that you could understand? All that men upon this earth do not yet know. Behind her the million years of the race's future, of wisdom, beauty, and love. Ahead of her the simplicity, the loveliness of the child. With her I dreamed the golden years away.

With her (he said), with Mara, and with the seven strong sons she bore me! Those sons which upon this earth I shall never have. I can see them yet; I can feel their arms about my neck; I can hear their valiant young voices shouting and laughing even now in my ear, running about at their play—Loar, Lrac, Cire, Feil, Zral, Rednug, and Ollor, my sons! My strong Viking sons of flame, upon that earth, with Mara! I can hear them calling yet! The golden years going backward into youth! Life, love, peace, strength, and beauty! Threa, the other earth! Beyond the cone. Within the reverse of the future. Ah, Mara! I lived with her fourteen years on Threa. My eldest son was just thirteen, the littlest one was toddling at my knee.

But you would not understand. What is there to say? One day she took me with her to look through the telescope, which looks into the future, which is their past. I turned it on the earth. I saw Nivea in the arms of Hartley, beside the cradle where their youngest child lay. I got into my ship, and I came back. . . .

I shot back through minus space and minus time, and the years I had spent had been less than nothing, and through the telescope which I had mounted on my bow I watched the years upon the earth roll back like a swift film, as I sped toward it, swifter than light.

I was entering the galaxy when I saw them laughing, drinking in the bedchamber, and it was but the morning of tomorrow. I was passing the Pleiades when I saw them at the bedroom door, and—as I sped toward them—

going backward from it, and backward outward from the house, and it was but the evening of today. I was making the swift turn into the drift, and they were at dinner together, saluting each other over their highballs' rims with hot and fusing eyes.

And as I shot onward, through the hours, they went backward, backward, back through the afternoon and back through lunch, and back into the morning. And then there was dawn light around me, and the small blue sun was there ahead, and I was passing past Neptune, and I was in the orbit once again. And they were back there by the Sound's shore; they were back there on the high platform beside the great empty cradle of my rocket, still watching, clasped in each other's arms, with their eyes focused on me while I shot off into space. Still watching, with the greed and hope and old evil treacherous lust within their faces; she with her warm look beside him that had never warmed for me, he with his sly fat lips and greasy, greedy eyes. They were there, watching me far off, and in an instant more the wind of my departure was blowing in their faces, and they were bent with their arms across their eyes.

I landed, and they were standing there, just waving me good-by through the porthole, and Nivea shouting some word that I could not hear. And the golden, golden years had rolled backward and away, and plus and minus together added had become a sum of nothingness.

I took the wrench and undid the hatch's lugs and I rose up through the hatch door, tired, tired. . . .

"Don't forget to come back, Helver, darling!" said Nivea.

But there was a blank unearthly terror in her eyes, as if she had suddenly awakened from a dream that had rolled away.

"I haven't," I said, "my darling."

"You haven't forgotten your wrench, have you, old man?" said Hartley.

"Nor that!" I said.

And his face, too, as fixed with terror, as if he, too, had dreamed a dream.

"Why, what's the matter?" he said.

I got out upon the platform. With my red, red eyes and my great hands. Oh, she was beginning to moan softly with terror then, deep in her white throat. And Hartley's knees were like jelly beneath him, and his breath was wheezing up his windpipe, and the veins throbbed on his great smooth thin-haired skull, and the dawn wind blew cold, and high up there, and his face was a green and moldy paste. The whole scene was some insanity of anger I had dreamed in that other world. . . .

"I've been," I said. "I came back."

"Don't! Don't!" he screamed. "In God's name, Helver!"

He backed toward the edge of the high platform, with his arms swinging and the terror in his face. But I lifted the wrench in my great hand, and I crushed in his eggshell skull with it. I crushed it in, like rotten pulp, the greatest brain that ever lived, with one great swinging blow upon it, and he was dead with the awful horror on his face before he crashed backward through the platform railing and fell to the ground far, far below.

And Nivea was screaming; she was screaming, upon her knees there at my feet. She had always loved me, she was screaming to me. She would bear me sons; she would forever love me; she would always be true. But I strangled her with my two hands, and with her golden hair about her soft white throat.

What day is this? May 7, 1968? Yes, yes, that is right. The golden years that have rolled away. It is six o'clock in the morning. That is Dr. Hooker Hartley, the eminent physicist, gentlemen, lying there. That is Nivea, my wife. . . .

(He paused, Gunderson, rubbing his red eyes with his hands.)

"Take him away!" said the police sergeant grimly. "He is utterly insane!"

But Gunderson did not hear the grim-faced trooper in blue. Still in his ears was the great roaring of the spheres. He was still thinking of the woman of flame.

CHAPTER FIVE

Report of Sergeant J. K. Billings, Flying Troop G, Connecticut State Police, May 7, 1968:
WHILE FLYING on traffic patrol Skyway 1A, between Bridgeport and Norwalk, at altitude 1000 feet, today at 6:00 A.M., Sergeant Billings observed a large crowd of several hundred men on the ground in front of the Gunderson Plant, Engineering Three, on the shore between Bridgeport and Fairfield, and a high towerlike structure built of new planking, on which there rested, in a cradle, a large torpedo-shaped device of blue and silver.

Looking down, Billings observed three figures, two men and a woman, on a platform at the top of the tower beside the torpedo-shaped device, which apparently was undergoing some kind of a christening ceremony. As Billings cut his skyway pavement from beneath him and spiraled down, he saw one of the men get into the hatchway of the torpedo and close down the lid.

A cloud passed over the sun in that instant. Or at least for the instant, as near as Billings can describe it, he was struck with an attack of vertigo and a momentary lapse of the time sense. He had a feeling as if a streak of gray and invisible lightning had shot up from the earth and in the same instant as if it had shot back again.

He wishes to mention this in reference to his request for sick leave with pay which has lain untouched on the lieutenant's desk for the past month, as proof that the complaint of overwork, which he therein respectfully alleges, was not just a stall, but medically sound and legitimate, and someday he will faint in the air maybe in spite of looking so healthy, unless he is allowed said leave, and then where would he be?

Anyway, this time fortunately Billings' attack of vertigo was of short duration, lasting approximately one hundredth of a second, as near as he could estimate, or about the time of two lightning streaks. He shook his head, and his vision cleared. Looking down, he saw the man who had climbed into the torpedo climbing out of it again, with a wrench in his hand, and suddenly attack the other man upon the platform. Forcing said victim of his assault to the edge of the platform, he struck him on the head with violent force, causing said victim to fall off. Immediately he attacked the woman, who was fighting and screaming for her life.

The crowd of mechanics were swarming up the stairs to the platform. Billings spiraled down to a landing. He mounted to the platform, and found the mechanics already there surrounding the attacker.

This man identified himself, and was identified by them, as Helver Gunderson, the millionaire inventor. Gunderson was crouched on the floor of the platform beside the body of the woman, who was identified as his wife, and at Billings' demand he made a long and rambling statement in which there was no sense, except a confession that he had attacked and killed Dr. Hooker Hartley and likewise said wife of his.

To an inquiry as to whether he regretted his act he did not reply. Billings took Gunderson into custody with the help of a squad of troopers who had been summoned.

From various witnesses, whose names are appended, Billings obtained the following general information. That Mr. Gunderson had shown some signs of mental strain and aberration for the past number of months, working on the production of a device whose purpose they did not know, and which he kept to himself with more than usual taciturnity. That this morning Dr. Hartley, who had been summoned by Mr. Gunderson, together with Mrs. Gunderson, to come down to the plant, as the work was finished, informed various of the employees privately that Gunderson had delusions that he had made a space-rocket, and was afraid for his sanity.

He was merely going through with it, said Dr. Hartley, to humor Gunderson.

Moreover, while on the platform at the purported launching of the ship, Dr. Hartley was seen to make various gestures behind Gunderson's back whenever he had the opportunity, such as tapping his skull, spinning his hand around beside his ear, winking to the men below, and so on, emphasizing his sad conviction that Gunderson was insane. The men said that Mrs. Gunderson, likewise, seemed convinced of her husband's insanity, and was laughing constantly and hysterically almost all through the performance. However, she did not care for her husband, having been in love with Hartley for many years.

"And he couldn't have been so dumb as not to know it himself, either, the old Swede," said J. Koliawsky, superintendent of construction, whose address for further questioning is appended. "He just pulled this bug act to get away with it. There wasn't anything ever to that machine, and he knew it. Lots of times while we've been working on it I've heard him stop and chuckle to himself, 'The greatest brain that ever lived!' and things like that."

The question as to whether Gunderson deliberately plotted and carefully planned an alibi of insanity, preliminary to murdering Dr. Hartley and Mrs. Gunderson, as Koliawsky intimates, is for the courts to determine.

It is the opinion of Sergeant Billings, however, that he is as bughouse as they come. He was whimpering and weeping for someone called Mara when we took him away, and talking about his sons, when the men tell me he is childless, and no one to inherit all his money.

Billings set a guard over the rocket before taking Gunderson away. The men insisted that they had hauled it out of the shop only this dawn, new and fresh with paint. But they must be wrong in that, since its paint, Billings observed, had an old weathered look as if it had been exposed to the elements for many years, and there were streaks upon it of a grayish powder which burned Billings when he touched them.

When Gunderson was asked as to what they were, in the hope that he might be induced to make some final and more coherent statement, he only said that they were star dust, and the spume of the Milky Way. Billings therefore reiterates his belief, as an officer of old experience, that Gunderson is crazy.

In view of the attack of vertigo and the simultaneous gray lightning flashes going and coming, which Billings was subjected to, he respectfully repeats his request for leave, for otherwise he feels that some of the rambling and incoherent things which Gunderson told to him this morning might start him off, too, looking for this land called Threa.

THE MARTIAN CROWN JEWELS
by Poul Anderson

THE SIGNAL WAS PICKED UP when the ship was still a quarter million miles away, and recorded voices summoned the technicians. There was no haste, for the ZX28749, otherwise called the *Jane Brackney*, was right on schedule; but landing an unmanned spaceship is always a delicate operation. Men and machines prepared to receive her as she came down, but the control crew had the first order of business.

Yamagata, Steinmann, and Ramanowitz were in the GCA tower, with Hollyday standing by for an emergency. If the circuits *should* fail—they never had, but a thousand tons of cargo and nuclear-powered vessel, crashing into the port, could empty Phobos of human life. So Hollyday watched over a set of spare assemblies, ready to plug in whatever might be required.

Yamagata's thin fingers danced over the radar dials. His eyes were intent on the screen. "Got her," he said. Steinmann made a distance reading and Ramanowitz took the velocity off the Dopplerscope. A brief session with a computer showed the figures to be almost as predicted.

"Might as well relax," said Yamagata, taking out a cigarette. "She won't be in control range for a while yet."

His eyes roved over the crowded room and out its window. From the tower he had a view of the spaceport: unimpressive, most of its shops and sheds and living quarters being underground. The smooth concrete field was chopped off by the curvature of the tiny satellite. It always faced Mars, and the station was on the far side, but he could remember how the planet hung enormous over the opposite hemisphere, soft ruddy disc blurred with thin air, hazy greenish-brown mottlings of heath and farmland. Though Phobos was clothed in vacuum, you couldn't see the hard stars of space: the sun and the floodlamps were too bright.

There was a knock on the door. Hollyday went over, almost drifting in the ghostly gravity, and opened it. "Nobody allowed in here during a landing," he said. Hollyday was a stocky blond man with a pleasant, open countenance, and his tone was less peremptory than his words.

"Police." The newcomer, muscular, round-faced, and earnest, was in plain clothes, tunic and pajama pants, which was expected; everyone in the tiny settlement knew Inspector Gregg. But he was packing a gun, which was not usual, and looked harried.

Yamagata peered out again and saw the port's four constables down on the field in official spacesuits, watching the ground crew. They carried weapons. "What's the matter?" he asked.

"Nothing . . . I hope." Gregg came in and tried to smile. "But the *Jane* has a very unusual cargo this trip."

"Hm?" Ramanowitz's eyes lit up in his broad plump visage. "Why weren't we told?"

"That was deliberate. Secrecy. The Martian crown jewels are aboard." Gregg fumbled a cigarette from his tunic.

Hollyday and Steinmann nodded at each other. Yamagata whistled. "On a robot ship?" he asked.

"Uh-huh. A robot ship is the one form of transportation from which they could not be stolen. There were three attempts made when they went to Earth on a regular liner, and I hate to think how many while they were at the British Museum. One guard lost his life. Now my boys are going to remove them before anyone else touches that ship and scoot 'em right down to Sabaeus."

"How much are they worth?" wondered Ramanowitz.

"Oh . . . they could be fenced on Earth for maybe half a billion UN dollars," said Gregg. "But the thief would do better to make the Martians pay to get them back . . . no, Earth would have to, I suppose, since it's our responsibility." He blew nervous clouds. "The jewels were secretly put on the *Jane*, last thing before she left on her regular run. I wasn't even told till a special messenger on this week's liner gave me the word. Not a chance for any thief to know they're here, till they're safely back on Mars. And that'll be *safe!*"

Ramanowitz shuddered. All the planets knew what guarded the vaults at Sabaeus.

"Some people did know, all along," said Yamagata thoughtfully. "I mean the loading crew back at Earth."

"Uh-huh, there is that." Gregg smiled. "Several of them have quit since then, the messenger said, but of course, there's always a big turnover among spacejacks—they're a restless bunch." His gaze drifted across Steinmann and Hollyday, both of whom had last worked at Earth Station and come to Mars a few ships back. The liners went on a hyperbolic path and arrived in a couple of weeks; the robot ships followed the more leisurely and economical Hohmann A orbit and needed 258 days. A man who knew what ship was carrying the jewels could leave Earth, get to Mars well ahead of the cargo, and snap up a job here—Phobos was always shorthanded.

"Don't look at me!" said Steinmann, laughing. "Chuck and I knew about this—of course—but we were under security restrictions. Haven't told a soul."

"Yeah. I'd have known it if you had," nodded Gregg. "Gossip travels fast here. Don't resent this, please, but I'm here to see that none of you boys leaves this tower till the jewels are aboard our own boat."

"Oh, well. It'll mean overtime pay."

"If I want to get rich fast, I'll stick to prospecting," added Hollyday.

"When are you going to quit running around with that Geiger in your free time?" asked Yamagata. "Phobos is nothing but iron and granite."

"I have my own ideas about that," said Hollyday stoutly.

"Hell, everybody needs a hobby on this God-forsaken clod," declared Ramanowitz. "I might try for those sparklers myself, just for the excitement—" He stopped abruptly, aware of Gregg's eyes.

"All right," snapped Yamagata. "Here we go. Inspector, please stand back out of the way, and for your life's sake don't interrupt us."

The *Jane* was drifting in, her velocity on the carefully precalculated orbit almost identical with that of Phobos. Almost, but not quite—there had been the inevitable small disturbing factors, which the remote-controlled jets had to compensate, and then there was the business of landing her. The team got a fix and were frantically busy.

In free fall, the *Jane* approached within a thousand miles of Phobos— a spheroid 500 feet in radius, big and massive, but lost against the incredible bulk of the satellite. And yet Phobos is an insignificant airless pill, negligible even beside its seventh-rate planet. Astronomical magnitudes are simply and literally incomprehensible.

When the ship was close enough, the radio directed her gyros to rotate her, very, very gently, until her pickup antenna was pointing directly at the field. Then her jets were cut in, a mere whisper of thrust. She was nearly above the spaceport, her path tangential to the moon's curvature. After a moment Yamagata slapped the keys hard, and the rockets blasted furiously, a visible red streak up in the sky. He cut them again, checked his data, and gave a milder blast.

"Okay," he grunted. "Let's bring her in."

Her velocity relative to Phobos's orbit and rotation was now zero, and she was falling. Yamagata slewed her around till the jets were pointing vertically down. Then he sat back and mopped his face while Ramanowitz took over; the job was too nerve-stretching for one man to perform in its entirety. Ramanowitz sweated the awkward mass to within a few yards of the cradle. Steinmann finished the task, easing her into the berth like an egg into a cup. He cut the jets and there was silence.

"Whew! Chuck, how about a drink?" Yamagata held out unsteady fingers and regarded them with an impersonal stare.

Hollyday smiled and fetched a bottle. It went happily around. Gregg declined. His eyes were locked to the field, where a technician was checking for radioactivity. The verdict was clean, and he saw his constables come soaring over the concrete, to surround the great ship with guns. One of them went up, opened the manhatch, and slipped inside.

It seemed a very long while before he emerged. Then he came running. Gregg cursed and thumbed the tower's radio board. "Hey, there! Ybarra! What's the matter?"

The helmet set shuddered a reply: "Señor . . . Señor Inspector. . . . the crown jewels are gone."

Sabaeus is, of course, a purely human name for the old city nestled in the Martian tropics, at the juncture of the "canals" Phison and Euphrates. Terrestrial mouths simply cannot form the syllables of High Chlannach, though rough approximations are possible. Nor did humans ever build a town exclusively of towers broader at the top than the base, or inhabit one for twenty thousand years. If they had, though, they would have encouraged an eager tourist influx; but Martians prefer more dignified ways of making a dollar, even if their parsimonious fame has long replaced that of Scotchmen. The result is that though interplanetary trade is brisk and Phobos a treaty port, a human is still a rare sight in Sabaeus.

Hurrying down the avenues between the stone mushrooms, Gregg felt conspicuous. He was glad the airsuit muffled him. Not that the grave Martians stared; they varkled, which is worse.

The Street of Those Who Prepare Nourishment in Ovens is a quiet one, given over to handicrafters, philosophers, and residential apartments. You won't see a courtship dance or a parade of the Lesser Halberdiers on it: nothing more exciting than a continuous four-day argument on the relativistic nature of the null class or an occasional gunfight. The latter are due to the planet's most renowned private detective, who nests here.

Gregg always found it eerie to be on Mars, under the cold deep-blue sky and the shrunken sun, among noises muffled by the thin oxygen-deficient air. But for Syaloch he had a good deal of affection, and when he had gone up the ladder and shaken the rattle outside the second-floor apartment and had been admitted, it was like escaping from nightmare.

"Ah, Krech!" The investigator laid down the stringed instrument on which he had been playing and towered gauntly over his visitor. "An unexbectet bleassure to see hyou. Come in, my tear chab, to come in." He was proud of his English—but simple misspellings will not convey the whistling, clicking Martian accent. Gregg had long ago fallen into the habit of translating it into a human pronunciation as he listened.

The Inspector felt a cautious way into the high, narrow room. The glow-snakes which illuminated it after dark were coiled asleep on the stone floor, in a litter of papers, specimens, and weapons; rusty sand covered the sills of the Gothic windows. Syaloch was not neat except in his own person. In one corner was a small chemical laboratory. The rest of the walls were taken up with shelves, the criminological literature of three planets—Martian books, Terrestrial micros, Venusian talking stones. At one place, patriotically, the glyphs representing the reigning Nestmother had been punched out with bullets. An Earthling could not sit on the trapezelike native furniture, but Syaloch had courteously provided chairs and tubs as well; his clientèle was also triplanetary. Gregg found a scarred Duncan Phyfe and lowered himself, breathing heavily into his oxygen tubes.

"I take it you are here on official but confidential business." Syaloch got out a big-bowled pipe. Martians have happily adopted tobacco, though in their atmosphere it must include potassium permanganate. Gregg was thankful he didn't have to breathe the blue fog.

He started. "How the hell do you know that?"

"Elementary, my dear fellow. Your manner is most agitated, and I know nothing but a crisis in your profession would cause that in a good stolid bachelor. Yet you come to me rather than the Homeostatic Corps . . . so it must be a delicate affair."

Gregg laughed wryly. He himself could not read any Martian's expression—what corresponds to a smile or a snarl on a totally nonhuman face? But this overgrown stork—

No. To compare the species of different planets is merely to betray the limitations of language. Syaloch was a seven-foot biped of vaguely storklike appearance. But the lean, crested, red-beaked head at the end of the sinuous neck was too large, the yellow eyes too deep; the white feathers were more like a penguin's than a flying bird's, save at the blue-plumed tail; instead of wings there were skinny red arms ending in four-fingered hands. And the overall posture was too erect for a bird.

Gregg jerked back to awareness. God in Heaven! The city lay gray and quiet; the sun was slipping westward over the farmlands of Sinus Sabaeus and the desert of the Aeria; he could just make out the rumble of a treadmill cart passing beneath the windows—and he sat here with a story which could blow the Solar System apart!

His hands, gloved against the chill, twisted together. "Yes, it's confidential, all right. If you can solve this case, you can just about name your own fee." The gleam in Syaloch's eyes made him regret that, but he stumbled on: "One thing, though. Just how do you feel about us Earthlings?"

"I have no prejudices. It is the brain that counts, not whether it is covered by feathers or hair or bony plates."

"No, I realize that. But some Martians resent us. We do disrupt an old way of life—we can't help it, if we're to trade with you—"

"K'teh. The trade is on the whole beneficial. Your fuel and machinery—and tobacco, yesss—for our kantz and snull. Also, we were getting too . . . stale. And of course space travel has added a whole new dimension to criminology. Yes, I favor Earth."

"Then you'll help us? And keep quiet about something which could provoke your planetary federation into kicking us off Phobos?"

The third eyelids closed, making the long-beaked face a mask. "I give no promises yet, Gregg."

"Well . . . damn it, all right, I'll have to take the chance." The policeman swallowed hard. "You know about your crown jewels, of course."

"They were lent to Earth for exhibit and scientific study."

"After years of negotiation. There's no more priceless relic on all Mars—and you were an old civilization when we were hunting mammoths. All right. They've been stolen."

Syaloch opened his eyes, but his only other movement was to nod.

"They were put on a robot ship at Earth Station. They were gone when that ship reached Phobos. We've damn near ripped the boat apart trying to

404

find them—we did take the other cargo to pieces, bit by bit—and they aren't there!"

Syaloch rekindled his pipe, an elaborate flint-and-steel process on a world where matches won't burn. Only when it was drawing well did he suggest: "Is it possible the ship was boarded en route?"

"No. It isn't possible. Every spacecraft in the System is registered, and its whereabouts are known at any time. Furthermore, imagine trying to find a speck in hundreds of millions of cubic miles, and match velocities with it . . . no vessel ever built could carry that much fuel. And mind you, it was never announced that the jewels were going back this way. Only the UN police and the Earth Station crew *could* know till the ship had actually left—by which time it'd be too late to catch her."

"Most interesting." Syaloch puffed hard.

"If word of this gets out," said Gregg miserably, "you can guess the results. I suppose we'd still have a few friends left in your Parliament—"

"In the House of Actives, yesss . . . a few. Not in the House of Philosophers, which is of course the upper chamber."

"It could mean a twenty-year hiatus in Earth-Mars traffic—maybe a permanent breaking off of relations. Damn it, Syaloch, you've *got* to find those stones!"

"Hm-m-m. I pray your pardon. This requires thought." The Martian picked up his crooked instrument and plucked a few tentative chords. Gregg sighed and attempted to relax. He knew the Chlannach temperament; he'd have to listen to an hour of minor-key caterwauling.

The colorless sunset was past, night had fallen with the unnerving Martian swiftness, and the glowsnakes were emitting blue radiance when Syaloch put down the demifiddle.

"I fear I shall have to visit Phobos in person," he said. "There are too many unknowns for analysis, and it is never well to theorize before all the data have been gathered." A bony hand clapped Gregg's shoulder. "Come, come, old chap. I am really most grateful to you. Life was becoming infernally dull. Now, as my famous Terrestrial predecessor would say, the game's afoot . . . and a very big game indeed!"

A Martian in an Earthlike atmosphere is not much hampered, needing only an hour in a compression chamber and a filter on his beak to eliminate excess oxygen and moisture. Syaloch walked freely about the port clad in filter, pipe, and *tirstokr* cap, grumbling to himself at the heat and humidity. He noticed that all the humans but Gregg were reserved, almost fearful, as they watched him—they were sitting on a secret which could unleash red murder.

He donned a spacesuit and went out to inspect the *Jane Brackney*. The vessel had been shunted aside to make room for later arrivals, and stood by a raw crag at the edge of the field, glimmering in the hard spatial sunlight. Gregg and Yamagata were with him.

"I say, you *have* been thorough," remarked the detective. "The outer skin is quite stripped off."

The spheroid resembled an egg which had tangled with a waffle iron: an intersecting grid of girders and braces above a thin aluminum hide. The jets, hatches, and radio mast were the only breaks in the checkerboard pattern, whose depth was about a foot and whose squares were a yard across at the "equator."

Yamagata laughed in a strained fashion. "No, the cops fluoroscoped every inch of her, but that's the way these cargo ships always look. They never land on Earth, you know, or any place where there's air, so streamlining would be unnecessary. And since nobody is aboard in transit, we don't have to worry about insulation or airtightness. Perishables are stowed in sealed compartments."

"I see. Now where were the crown jewels kept?"

"They were supposed to be in a cupboard near the gyros," said Gregg. "They were in a locked box, about six inches high, six inches wide, and a foot long." He shook his head, finding it hard to believe that so small a box could contain so much potential death.

"Ah . . . but *were* they placed there?"

"I radioed Earth and got a full account," said Gregg. "The ship was loaded as usual at the satellite station, then shoved a quarter mile away till it was time for her to leave—to get her out of the way, you understand. She was still in the same free-fall orbit, attached by a light cable—perfectly standard practice. At the last minute, without anyone being told beforehand, the crown jewels were brought up from Earth and stashed aboard."

"By a special policeman, I presume?"

"No. Only licensed technicians are allowed to board a ship in orbit, unless there's a life-and-death emergency. One of the regular station crew—fellow named Carter—was told where to put them. He was watched by the cops as he pulled himself along the cable and in through the manhatch." Gregg pointed to a small door near the radio mast. "He came out, closed it, and returned on the cable. The police immediately searched him and his spacesuit, just in case, and he positively did not have the jewels. There was no reason to suspect him of anything—good steady worker—though I'll admit he's disappeared since then. The *Jane* blasted a few minutes late and her jets were watched till they cut off and she went into free fall. And that's the last anyone saw of her till she got here—without the jewels."

"And right on orbit," added Yamagata. "If by some freak she had been boarded, it would have thrown her off enough for us to notice as she came in. Transference of momentum between her and the other ship."

"I see." Behind his faceplate, Syaloch's beak cut a sharp black curve across heaven. "Now then, Gregg, were the jewels actually in the box when it was delivered?"

"At Earth Station, you mean? Oh, yes. There are four UN Chief Inspectors involved, and HQ says they're absolutely above suspicion. When I sent back word of the theft, they insisted on having their own quarters and so on searched, and went under scop voluntarily."

"And your own constables on Phobos?"

"Same thing," said the policeman grimly. "I've slapped on an embargo—

nobody but me has left this settlement since the loss was discovered. I've had every room and tunnel and warehouse searched." He tried to scratch his head, a frustrating attempt when one is in a spacesuit. "I can't maintain those restrictions much longer. Ships are coming in and the consignees want their freight."

"*Hnachla.* That puts us under a time limit, then." Syaloch nodded to himself. "Do you know, this is a fascinating variation of the old locked room problem. A robot ship in transit is a locked room in the most classic sense." He drifted off into a reverie.

Gregg stared bleakly across the savage horizon, naked rock tumbling away under his feet, and then back over the field. Odd how tricky your vision became in airlessness, even when you had bright lights. That fellow crossing the field there, under the full glare of sun and floodlamps, was merely a stipple of shadow and luminance . . . what the devil was he doing, tying a shoe of all things? No, he was walking quite normally—

"I'd like to put everyone on Phobos under scop," said Gregg with a violent note, "but the law won't allow it unless the suspect volunteers—and only my own men have volunteered."

"Quite rightly, my dear fellow," said Syaloch. "One should at least have the privilege of privacy in his own skull. And it would make the investigation unbearably crude."

"I don't give a fertilizing damn how crude it is," snapped Gregg. "I just want that box with the crown jewels safe inside."

"Tut-tut! Impatience has been the ruin of many a promising young police officer, as I seem to recall my spiritual ancestor of Earth pointing out to a Scotland Yard man who—hm—may even have been a physical ancestor of yours, Gregg. It seems we must try another approach. Are there any people on Phobos who might have known the jewels were aboard this ship?"

"Yes. Two men only. I've pretty well established that they never broke security and told anyone else till the secret was out."

"And who are they?"

"Technicians, Hollyday and Steinmann. They were working at Earth Station when the *Jane* was loaded. They quit soon after—not at the same time—and came here by liner and got jobs. You can bet that *their* quarters have been searched!"

"Perhaps," murmured Syaloch, "it would be worthwhile to interview the gentlemen in question."

Steinmann, a thin redhead, wore truculence like a mantle; Hollyday merely looked worried. It was no evidence of guilt—everyone had been rubbed raw of late. They sat in the police office, with Gregg behind the desk and Syaloch leaning against the wall, smoking and regarding them with unreadable yellow eyes.

"Damn it, I've told this over and over till I'm sick of it!" Steinmann knotted his fists and gave the Martian a bloodshot stare. "I never touched the things and I don't know who did. Hasn't any man a right to change jobs?"

"Please," said the detective mildly. "The better you help the sooner we can finish this work. I take it you were acquainted with the man who actually put the box aboard the ship?"

"Sure. Everybody knew John Carter. Everybody knows everybody else on a satellite station." The Earthman stuck out his jaw. "That's why none of us'll take scop. We won't blab out all our thoughts to guys we see fifty times a day. We'd go nuts!"

"I never made such a request," said Syaloch.

"Carter was quite a good friend of mine," volunteered Hollyday.

"Uh-huh," grunted Gregg. "And he quit too, about the same time you fellows did, and went Earthside and hasn't been seen since. HQ told me you and he were thick. What'd you talk about?"

"The usual." Hollyday shrugged. "Wine, women, and song. I haven't heard from him since I left Earth."

"Who says Carter stole the box?" demanded Steinmann. "He just got tired of living in space and quit his job. He *couldn't* have stolen the jewels—he was searched, remember?"

"Could he have hidden it somewhere for a friend to get at this end?" inquired Syaloch.

"Hidden it? Where? Those ships don't have secret compartments." Steinmann spoke wearily. "And he was only aboard the *Jane* a few minutes, just long enough to put the box where he was supposed to." His eyes smoldered at Gregg. "Let's face it: the only people anywhere along the line who ever had a chance to lift it were our own dear cops."

The Inspector reddened and half rose. "Look here, you—"

"We've got *your* word that you're innocent," growled Steinmann. "Why should it be any better than mine?"

Syaloch waved both men back. "If you please. Brawls are unphilosophic." His beak opened and clattered, the Martian equivalent of a smile. "Has either of you, perhaps, a theory? I am open to all ideas."

There was a stillness. Then Hollyday mumbled: "Yes. I have one."

Syaloch hooded his eyes and puffed quietly, waiting.

Hollyday's grin was shaky. "Only if I'm right, you'll never see those jewels again."

Gregg sputtered.

"I've been around the Solar System a lot," said Hollyday. "It gets lonesome out in space. You never know how big and lonesome it is till you've been there, all by yourself. And I've done just that—I'm an amateur uranium prospector, not a lucky one so far. I can't believe we know everything about the universe, or that there's only vacuum between the planets."

"Are you talking about the cobblies?" snorted Gregg.

"Go ahead and call it superstition. But if you're in space long enough . . . well, somehow, you *know*. There are beings out there—gas beings, radiation beings, whatever you want to imagine, there's *something* living in space."

"And what use would a box of jewels be to a cobbly?"

Hollyday spread his hands. "How can I tell? Maybe we bother them, scooting through their own dark kingdom with our little rockets. Stealing

408

the crown jewels would be a good way to disrupt the Mars trade, wouldn't it?"

Only Syaloch's pipe broke the inward-pressing silence. But its burbling seemed quite irreverent.

"Well—" Gregg fumbled helplessly with a meteoric paperweight. "Well, Mr. Syaloch, do you want to ask any more questions?"

"Only one." The third lids rolled back, and coldness looked out at Steinmann. "If you please, my good man, what is your hobby?"

"Huh? Chess. I play chess. What's it to you?" Steinmann lowered his head and glared sullenly.

"Nothing else?"

"What else is there?"

Syaloch glanced at the Inspector, who nodded confirmation, and then replied gently:

"I see. Thank you. Perhaps we can have a game sometime. I have some small skill of my own. That is all for now, gentlemen."

They left, moving like things of dream through the low gravity.

"Well?" Gregg's eyes pleaded with Syaloch. "What next?"

"Very little. I think . . . yesss, while I am here I should like to watch the technicians at work. In my profession, one needs a broad knowledge of all occupations."

Gregg sighed.

Ramanowitz showed the guest around. The *Kim Brackney* was in and being unloaded. They threaded through a hive of spacesuited men.

"The cops are going to have to raise that embargo soon," said Ramanowitz. "Either that or admit why they've clamped it on. Our warehouses are busting."

"It would be politic to do so," nodded Syaloch. "Ah, tell me . . . is this equipment standard for all stations?"

"Oh, you mean what the boys are wearing and carrying around? Sure. Same issue everywhere."

"May I inspect it more closely?"

"Hm?" *Lord, deliver me from visiting firemen!* thought Ramanowitz. He waved a mechanic over to him. "Mr. Syaloch would like you to explain your outfit," he said with ponderous sarcasm.

"Sure. Regular spacesuit here, reinforced at the seams." The gauntleted hands moved about, pointing. "Heating coils powered from this capacitance battery. Ten-hour air supply in the tanks. These buckles, you snap your tools into them, so they won't drift around in free fall. This little can at my belt holds paint that I spray out through this nozzle."

"Why must spaceships be painted?" asked Syaloch. "There is nothing to corrode the metal."

"Well, sir, we just call it paint. It's really gunk, to seal any leaks in the hull till we can install a new plate, or to mark any other kind of damage. Meteor punctures and so on." The mechanic pressed a trigger and a thin, almost invisible stream jetted out, solidifying as it hit the ground.

"But it cannot readily be seen, can it?" objected the Martian. "I, at least, find it difficult to see clearly in airlessness."

"That's right, Light doesn't diffuse, so . . . well, anyhow, the stuff is radioactive—not enough to be dangerous, just enough so that the repair crew can spot the place with a Geiger counter."

"I understand. What is the halflife?"

"Oh, I'm not sure. Six months, maybe? It's supposed to remain detectable for a year."

"Thank you." Syaloch stalked off. Ramanowitz had to jump to keep up with those long legs.

"Do you think Carter may have hid the box in his paint can?" suggested the human.

"No, hardly. The can is too small, and I assume he was searched thoroughly." Syaloch stopped and bowed. "You have been very kind and patient, Mr. Ramanowitz. I am finished now, and can find the Inspector myself."

"What for?"

"To tell him he can lift the embargo, of course." Syaloch made a harsh sibilance. "And then I must get the next boat to Mars. If I hurry, I can attend the concert in Sabaeus tonight." His voice grew dreamy. "They will be premiering Hanyech's *Variations on a Theme by Mendelssohn*, transcribed to the Royal Chlannach scale. It should be most unusual."

It was three days afterward that the letter came. Syaloch excused himself and kept an illustrious client squatting while he read it. Then he nodded to the other Martian. "You will be interested to know, sir, that the Estimable Diadems have arrived at Phobos and are being returned at this moment."

The client, a Cabinet Minister from the House of Actives, blinked. "Pardon, Freehatched Syaloch, but what have you to do with that?"

"Oh . . . I am a friend of the Featherless police chief. He thought I might like to know."

"*Hraa.* Were you not on Phobos recently?"

"A minor case." The detective folded the letter carefully, sprinkled it with salt, and ate it. Martians are fond of paper, especially official Earth stationery with high rag content. "Now, sir, you were saying—?"

The parliamentarian responded absently. He would not dream of violating privacy—no, never—but if he had X-ray vision he would have read:

"Dear Syaloch,

"You were absolutely right. Your locked room problem is solved. We've got the jewels back, everything is in fine shape, and the same boat which brings you this letter will deliver them to the vaults. It's too bad the public can never know the facts—two planets ought to be grateful to you—but I'll supply that much thanks all by myself, and insist that any bill you care to send be paid in full. Even if the Assembly had to make a special appropriation, which I'm afraid it will.

"I admit your idea of lifting the embargo at once looked pretty wild to me, but it worked. I had our boys out, of course, scouring Phobos with

410

Geigers, but Hollyday found the box before we did. Which saved us a lot of trouble, to be sure. I arrested him as he came back into the settlement, and he had the box among his ore samples. He has confessed, and you were right all along the line.

"What was that thing you quoted at me, the saying of that Earthman you admire so much? 'When you have eliminated the impossible, whatever remains, however improbable, must be true.' Something like that. It certainly applies to this case.

"As you decided, the box must have been taken to the ship at Earth Station and left there—no other possibility existed. Carter figured it out in half a minute when he was ordered to take the thing out and put it aboard the *Jane*. He went inside, all right, but still had the box when he emerged. In that uncertain light nobody saw him put it 'down' between four girders right next to the hatch. Or as you remarked, if the jewels are not *in* the ship, and yet not *away* from the ship, they must be *on* the ship. Gravitation would hold them in place. When the *Jane* blasted off, acceleration pressure slid the box back, but of course the waffle-iron pattern kept it from being lost; it fetched up against the after rib and stayed there. All the way to Mars! But the ship's gravity held it securely enough even in free fall, since both were on the same orbit.

"Hollyday says that Carter told him all about it. Carter couldn't go to Mars himself without being suspected and watched every minute once the jewels were discovered missing. He needed a confederate. Hollyday went to Phobos and took up prospecting as a cover for the search he'd later be making for the jewels.

"As you showed me, when the ship was within a thousand miles of this dock, Phobos gravity would be stronger than her own. Every spacejack knows that the robot ships don't start decelerating till they're quite close; that they are then almost straight above the surface; and that the side with the radio mast and manhatch—the side on which Carter had placed the box—is rotated around to face the station. The centrifugal force of rotation threw the box away from the ship, and was in a direction toward Phobos rather than away from it. Carter knew that this rotation is slow and easy, so the force wasn't enough to accelerate the box to escape velocity and lose it in space. It would have to fall down toward the satellite. Phobos Station being on the side opposite Mars, there was no danger that the loot would keep going till it hit the planet.

"So the crown jewels tumbled onto Phobos, just as you deduced. Of course Carter had given the box a quick radioactive spray as he laid it in place, and Hollyday used that to track it down among all those rocks and crevices. In point of fact, its path curved clear around this moon, so it landed about five miles from the station.

"Steinmann has been after me to know why you quizzed him about his hobby. You forgot to tell me that, but I figured it out for myself and told him. He or Hollyday had to be involved, since nobody else knew about the cargo, and the guilty person had to have some excuse to go out and look for the box. Chess playing doesn't furnish that kind of alibi. Am I right? At least, my deduction proves I've been studying the same canon you go by. Incidentally, Steinmann asks if you'd care to take him on the next time he has planet leave.

"Hollyday knows where Carter is hiding, and we've radioed the information back to Earth. Trouble is, we can't prosecute either of them without admitting the facts. Oh, well, there are such things as blacklists.

"Will have to close this now to make the boat. I'll be seeing you soon— not professionally, I hope!"

Admiring regards,
Inspector Gregg

But as it happened, the Cabinet minister did not possess X-ray eyes. He dismissed unprofitable speculation and outlined his problem. Somebody, somewhere in Sabaeus, was farniking the krats, and there was an alarming zaksnautry among the hyukus. It sounded to Syaloch like an interesting case.

THE WEAPON SHOPS OF ISHER
by A. E. van Vogt

PROLOGUE

MAGICIAN BELIEVED TO
HAVE HYPNOTIZED CROWD

June 11, 1951—Police and newspapermen believe that Middle City will shortly be advertised as the next stopping place of a master magician and they are prepared to extend him a hearty welcome if he will condescend to explain exactly how he fooled hundreds of people into believing they saw a strange building, apparently a kind of gunshop.

The building seemed to appear on the space formerly, and still, occupied by Aunt Sally's Lunch and Patterson Tailors. Only employees were inside the two aforementioned shops, and none noticed any untoward event. A large, brightly shining sign featured the front of the gunshop, which had been so miraculously conjured out of nothingness; and the sign constituted the first evidence that the entire scene was nothing but a masterly illusion. For from whichever angle one gazed at it, one seemed to be staring straight at the words, which read:

FINE WEAPONS
THE RIGHT TO BUY WEAPONS IS THE
RIGHT TO BE FREE

The window display was made up of an assortment of rather curiously shaped guns, rifles as well as small arms; and a glowing sign in the window stated:

THE FINEST ENERGY WEAPONS IN
THE KNOWN UNIVERSE

Inspector Clayton of the Investigation Branch attempted to enter the shop, but the door seemed to be locked. A few moments later, C. J. (Chris)

McAllister, reporter of the *Gazette-Bulletin*, tried the door, found that it opened, and entered.

Inspector Clayton attempted to follow him, but discovered that the door was again locked. It is believed that McAllister went through to the back, as several spectators reported seeing him. Immediately after his reappearance, the strange building vanished as abruptly as it had appeared.

Police state they are baffled as to how the master magician created so detailed an illusion for so long a period before so large a crowd. They are prepared to recommend his show, when it comes, without reservations.

(Author's Note: The foregoing account did not mention that the police, dissatisfied with the affair, attempted to contact McAllister for a further interview, but were unable to locate him. Weeks have passed; and he has still not been found.

What *did* happen to McAllister from the instant that he found the door of the gunshop unlocked?)

There was a curious quality about the gunshop door. It was not so much that it opened at his first touch as that, when he pulled, it came away like a weightless thing. McAllister had the impression that the knob had freed itself into his palm.

He stood very still, startled. The thought that came finally had to do with Inspector Clayton who, a minute earlier, had found the door locked. The thought was like a signal. From behind him boomed the voice of the inspector:

"Ah, McAllister, I'll handle this now."

It was dark inside the shop beyond the door, too dark to see anything, and somehow, his eyes wouldn't accustom themselves to the intense gloom. Pure reporter's instinct made him step forward toward the blackness that pressed from beyond the rectangle of door. Out of the corner of one eye, he saw Inspector Clayton's hand reaching for the door handle that his own fingers had let go a moment before. And he knew instantly that if the inspector could prevent it, no reporter would get inside that building. His head was still turned, his gaze more on the police officer than on the darkness in front; and it was as he began another step forward that the remarkable thing happened.

The door handle would not allow Inspector Clayton to touch it. It twisted in some queer way, in some *energy* way, for it was still there, a strange, blurred shape. The door itself, without visible movement it was so swift, was suddenly touching McAllister's heel. Light, almost weightless, was that touch; and then, before he could think or react to what had happened, the momentum of his forward movement had carried him inside. As he breasted the darkness, there was a sudden, agonized tensing along his nerves. Then the door shut tight, the brief, unexpected agony faded. Ahead was a brightly-lit shop; behind—were unbelievable things!

For McAllister, the moment that followed was one of blank impression. He stood, body twisted awkwardly, only vaguely conscious of the shop's interior, but tremendously aware in the brief moment before he was interrupted of what lay beyond the transparent panels of the door through which he had just come.

There was no unyielding blackness anywhere, no Inspector Clayton, no muttering crowd of gaping spectators, no dingy row of shops across the way. It was not even the same street. There was *no* street. Instead, a peaceful park was visible. Beyond it, brilliant under a noon sun, was the skyline of a vast city. From behind him, a husky, musical, woman's voice said:

"You will be wanting a gun?"

McAllister turned. The movement was automatic reaction to a sound. And because the affair was still like a dream, the city scene faded almost instantly; his mind focused on the young woman who was advancing slowly from the rear section of the store. Briefly, his thought wouldn't come clear. A conviction that he ought to say something was tangled with first impressions of the girl's appearance. She had a slender well-shaped body; her face was creased with a pleasant smile. She had brown eyes, and wavy brown hair. Her simple frock and sandals seemed so normal at first glance that he gave them no further thought. He was able to say:

"What I can't understand is why the police officer, who tried to follow me, couldn't get in. And where is he now?"

To his surprise, the girl's smile became faintly apologetic: "We know that people consider it silly of us to keep harping on that ancient feud." Her voice grew firmer. "We even know how clever the propaganda is that stresses the silliness of our stand. Meanwhile, we never allow any of *her* men in here. We continue to take our principles very seriously."

She paused as if she expected comprehension from him. But McAllister saw from the slow puzzlement creeping into her eyes that his face must look as blank as the thoughts behind it. *Her men!* The girl had spoken the words as if she were referring to some personage, and in direct reply to his use of the word, police officer. That meant *her* men, whoever she was, were policemen; and they weren't allowed in this gunshop. So the door was hostile, and wouldn't admit them. And emptiness struck into McAllister's mind, matching the hollowness that was beginning to afflict the pit of his stomach, a sense of unplumbed depths, the first staggering conviction that all was not as it should be. The girl was speaking in a sharper tone:

"You mean you know nothing of all this, that for generations the gunmaker's guild has existed in this age of devastating energies as the common man's only protection against enslavement? The right to buy guns—" She stopped, her narrowed eyes searching him; then: "Come to think of it, there's something very peculiar about you. Your outlandish clothes—you're not from the northern farm plains are you?"

He shook his head dumbly, more annoyed with his reactions every passing second. But he couldn't help it. A tightness was growing in him now, becoming more unbearable instant by instant, as if somewhere a vital mainspring was being wound to the breaking point.

The young woman went on more swiftly: "And come to think of it, it is astounding that a policeman should have tried the door, and there was no alarm."

Her hand moved. Metal flashed in it, metal as bright as steel in blinding sunlight. There was not the slightest hint of an apology in her voice as she said: "You will stay where you are, sir, until I have called my father. In our business, with our responsibilities, we never take chances. Something is very wrong here."

Curiously, it was at that point that McAllister's mind began to function clearly. The thought that came paralleled hers. How had this gunshop appeared on a 1951 street? How had he come here into the fantastic world? Something was very wrong indeed.

It was the gun that held his attention. It was a tiny thing, shaped like a pistol, but with three cubes projecting in a half circle from the top of the slightly-bulbous firing chamber. He began to feel shaken, looking at it, for that wicked little instrument, glittering there in her browned fingers, was as real as herself.

"Good Heaven," he whispered. "What the devil kind of a gun is it. Lower that thing and let's try to find out what all this is about."

She seemed not to be listening. He noticed that her gaze was flicking to a point on the wall somewhat to his left. He followed her look in time to see seven miniature white lights flash on. Curious lights! He was fascinated by the play of light and shade, the waxing and waning from one tiny globe to the next, a rippling movement of infinitesimal increments and decrements, an incredibly delicate effect of instantaneous reaction to some supersensitive barometer. The lights steadied; his gaze reverted to the girl. To his surprise, she was putting away her gun. She must have noticed his expression.

"It's all right," she said coolly. "The automatics are on you now. If we're wrong about you, we'll be glad to apologize. Meanwhile, if you're still interested in buying a gun, I'll be happy to demonstrate."

So the automatics were on him, McAllister thought. He felt no relief at the information. Whatever the automatics were, they wouldn't be working in his favor. The young woman putting away her gun in spite of her suspicions spoke volumes for the efficiency of the new watchdogs. He'd have to get out of this place, of course. Meanwhile, the girl was assuming that a man who came into a gunshop would, under ordinary circumstances, want to buy a gun. It struck him, suddenly, that of all the things he could think of, what he most wanted to see was one of those strange guns. There were incredible implications in the very shape of the instruments. Aloud he said:

"Yes, by all means show me." A thought occurred to him. He added, "I have no doubt your father is somewhere in the background making some sort of study of me."

The young woman made no move to bring out any weapons. Instead, she stared at him in puzzlement.

"You may not realize it," she said slowly, "but you have already upset our entire establishment. The lights of the automatics should have gone on the moment father pressed the buttons, as he did when I called him. They didn't! That's unnatural, and yet—" her frown deepened—"if you were one of *them*, how did you get through that door? Is it possible that *her scientists* have discovered human beings who do not affect the sensitive energies? And that you are but one of many such, sent as an experiment to determine whether or not entrance could be gained? Yet that isn't logical either. If they had even a hope of success, they wouldn't risk the chance of throwing away an overwhelming surprise. In that case, you would be the entering wedge of an attack on a vast scale. She is ruthless, she's brilliant; and she craves complete power over poor fools like you who have no more sense than to worship her and the splendor of the Imperial Court."

The young woman paused, with the faintest of smiles. "There I go again, making a political speech. But you can see that there are at least a few reasons why we should be careful about you."

There was a chair in one corner. McAllister started for it. His mind was calmer. "Look," he began, "I don't know what you're talking about. I don't even know how I came to be in this shop. I agree with you that the whole thing requires explanation, but I mean that differently than you do."

His voice trailed. He had been half lowered over the chair, but instead of sinking into it, he came erect, slowly, like an old, old man. His eyes fixed on lettering that shone above a glass case of guns behind her. He said hoarsely:

"Is that—a calendar?"

She followed his gaze, puzzled: "Yes, it's June 3rd. What's wrong?"

"I don't mean that. I mean—" He caught himself with an effort. "I mean those figures above that: I mean—what year is this?"

The girl looked surprised. She started to say something, then stopped and backed away. Finally: "Don't look like that! There's nothing wrong. This is eighty-four of the four thousand seven hundredth year of the Imperial House of the Isher. It's quite all right."

II

Very deliberately McAllister sat down, and the conscious wonder came: Exactly how *should* he feel? Not even surprise came to his aid. The events were beginning to fall into a kind of distorted pattern. The building front superimposed on those two 1951 shops; the way the door had acted. The great exterior sign with its odd linking of freedom with the right to buy weapons. The actual display of weapons in the window, the finest energy weapons in the known universe! . . . He grew aware that the girl was talking earnestly with a tall, gray-haired man who was standing on the threshold of the door through which she had originally come. There was a tenseness in the way they were talking. Their low-spoken words made a blur of sound in his ears, strange and unsettling. McAllister could not quite analyze the meaning of it until the girl turned, and said:

"What is your name?"

McAllister gave it.

The girl hesitated, then: "Mr. McAllister, my father wants to know what year you're from!"

The gray-haired man stepped forward. "I'm afraid," he said gravely, "that there is no time to explain. What has happened is what we gunmakers have feared for generations: that once again would come one who lusted for unlimited power; and who, to attain tyranny, must necessarily seek first to destroy us. Your presence here is a manifestation of the energy force that she has turned against us—something so new that we did not even suspect it was being used against us. But I have no time to waste. Get all the information you can, Lystra, and warn him of his own personal danger." The man turned. The door closed noiselessly behind his tall figure.

McAllister asked: "What did he mean—personal danger?"

He saw the girl's brown eyes were uneasy as they rested on him. "It's hard to explain," she began in an uncomfortable voice. "First of all, come to the window and I'll try to make everything clear. It's all very confusing to you, I suppose."

McAllister drew a deep breath. "Now we're getting somewhere."

His alarm was gone. The gray-haired man seemed to know what it was all about. That meant there should be no difficulty getting home again. As for all this danger to the gunmaker's guild, that was their worry, not his. He stepped forward, closer to the girl. To his amazement, she cringed away as if he had threatened her. As he stared blankly, she laughed humorlessly; and finally she said:

"Don't think I'm being silly; don't be offended—but for your life's sake, don't touch any human body you might come in contact with."

McAllister was conscious of a chill. Then, suddenly, he felt a surge of impatience at the fear that showed in the girl's face. "Now look," he began, "I want to get things clear. We can talk here without danger, providing I don't touch, or come near you. Is that right?"

She nodded. "The floor, the walls, every piece of furniture—in fact the entire shop is made of non-conducting material."

McAllister had a sense of being balanced on a tight rope over a bottomless abyss. He forced calm onto his mind. "Let's start," he said, "at the beginning. How did you and your father know that I was not of—" he paused before the odd phrase, then went on—"of this time?"

"Father photographed you," the girl said. "He photographed the contents of your pockets. That was how he first found out what was the matter. You see, the sensitive energies themselves become carriers of the energy with which you're charged. That's what was wrong. That's why the automatics wouldn't focus on you, and—"

"Energy—charged?" said McAllister.

The girl was staring at him. "Don't you understand?" she gasped. "You've come across seven thousand years of time. And of all the energies in the universe, time is the most potent. You're charged with trillions of trillions of time-energy units. If you should step outside this shop, you'd blow up Imperial City and half a hundred miles of land beyond.

"You—" she finished on an unsteady, upward surge of her voice— "you could conceivably destroy the Earth!"

He hadn't noticed the mirror before. Funny, too, because it was large enough, at least eight feet high, and directly in front of him on the wall where, a minute before (he could have sworn) had been solid metal.

"Look at yourself," the girl was saying soothingly. "There's nothing so steadying as one's own image. Actually, your body is taking the mental shock very well."

He stared at his image. There was a paleness in the lean face that stared back at him. But his body was not actually shaking as the whirling in his mind had suggested. He grew aware again of the girl. She was standing with a finger on one of a series of wall switches. Abruptly, he felt better. "Thank you," he said quietly. "I certainly needed that."

She smiled encouragingly; and he was able now to be amazed at her conflicting personality. There had been on the one hand her inability a few minutes earlier to get to the point of the danger, an incapacity for explaining things with words. Yet obviously her action with the mirror showed a keen understanding of human psychology. He said: "The problem now is, from your point of view, to circumvent this Isher woman and get me back to 1951 before I blow up the Earth of . . . of whatever year this is."

The girl nodded. "Father says that you can be sent back, but as for the rest, watch!"

He had no time for relief at the knowledge that he could be returned to his own time. She pressed another button. Instantly, the mirror was gone into metallic wall. Another button clicked. The wall vanished. Before him stretched a park similar to the one he had already seen through the front door, obviously an extension of the same garden-like vista. Trees were there, and flowers, and green, green grass in the sun.

One vast building, as high as it was long, towered massively dark against the sky and dominated the entire horizon. It was a good quarter mile away; and incredibly, it was at least that long and that high. Neither near that monstrous building, nor in the park, was a living person visible. Everywhere was evidence of man's dynamic labor, but no men, no movement. Even the trees stood motionless in that breathless sunlit day.

"Watch!" said the girl again, more softly.

There was no click this time. She made an adjustment on one of the buttons, and the view was no longer so clear. It wasn't that the sun had dimmed its bright intensity. It wasn't even that glass was visible where a moment before there had been nothing. There was still no apparent substance between them and that gemlike park. But the park was no longer deserted.

Scores of men and machines swarmed out there. McAllister stared in amazement; and then as the sense of illusion faded, and the dark menace of those men penetrated, his emotion changed to dismay.

"Why," he said at last, "those men are soldiers, and the machines are—"

"Energy guns!" she said. "That's always been their problem. How to get their weapons close enough to our shops to destroy us. It isn't that the guns are not powerful over a very great distance. Even the rifles we sell can kill unprotected life over a distance of miles, but our gunshops are so heavily fortified that, to destroy us, they must use their biggest cannon at point-blank range. In the past, they could never do that because we own the surrounding park, and our alarm system was perfect—until now. The new energy they're using affects none of our protective instruments; and, what is infinitely worse, affords them a perfect shield against our own guns. Invisibility, of course, has long been known, but if you hadn't come, we would have been destroyed without ever knowing what happened."

"But," McAllister exclaimed sharply, "what are you going to do? They're still out there, working—"

Her brown eyes burned with a fierce, yellow flame. "My father has warned the guild. And individual members have now discovered that similar invisible guns are being set up by invisible men outside their shops. The council will meet shortly to discuss defences."

Silently, McAllister watched the soldiers connecting what must have been invisible cables that led to the vast building in the background; foot thick cables that told of the titanic power that was to be unleashed on the tiny weapon shop. There was nothing to be said. The reality out there overshadowed sentences and phrases. Of all the people here, he was the most useless, his opinion the least worth while. He must have said so, but he did not realize that until the familiar voice of the girl's father came from one side of him.

"You're quite mistaken, Mr. McAllister. Of all the people here you are the *most* valuable. Through you, we discovered that the Isher were actually attacking us. Furthermore, our enemies do not know of your existence, therefore have not yet realized the full effect produced by the new blanketing energy they have used. You, accordingly, constitute the unknown factor. We must make immediate use of you."

The man looked older, McAllister thought. There were lines of strain in his lean, sallow face as he turned to his daughter, and his voice, when he spoke, was edged with sharpness: "Lystra, No. 7!"

As the girl's fingers touched the seventh button, her father explained swiftly to McAllister, "The guild supreme council is holding an immediate emergency session. We must choose the most likely method of attacking the problem, and concentrate individually and collectively on that method. Regional conversations are already in progress, but only one important idea has been put forward as yet and—ah, gentlemen!"

He spoke past McAllister, who turned with a start. Men were coming out of the solid wall, lightly, easily, as if it were a door and they were stepping across a threshold. One, two, three—thirty.

They were grim-faced men, all except one who glanced at McAllister, started to walk past, and then stopped with a half-amused smile.

"Don't look so blank. How else do you think we could have survived these many years if we hadn't been able to transmit material objects through space? The Isher police have always been only too eager to blockade our sources of supply. Incidentally, my name is Cadron—Peter Cadron!"

McAllister nodded in a perfunctory manner. He was no longer genuinely impressed by the new machines. Here were the end-products of the machine age; science and invention so advanced that men made scarcely a move that did not affect, or was not affected by, a machine. A heavy-faced man near him said: "We have gathered here because it is obvious that the source of the new energy is the great building just outside this shop—"

He motioned toward the wall which had been a mirror and then the window through which McAllister had gazed at the monstrous structure in question. The speaker went on: "We've known, ever since the building was completed five years ago, that it was a power building aimed against us; and now from it new energy has flown out to engulf the world, immensely potent energy so strong that it broke the very tensions of time, fortunately only at this nearest gunshop. Apparently, it weakens when transmitted over distance."

"Look, Dresley," came a curt interruption from a small, thin man, "what good is all this preamble? You have been examining the various plans put forward by regional groups. Is there, or isn't there, a decent one among them?"

Dresley hesitated. To McAllister's surprise, the man's eyes fixed doubtfully on him, his heavy face worked for a moment, then hardened. "Yes, there is a method, but it depends on compelling our friend from the past to take a great risk. You all know what I'm referring to. It will gain us the time we need."

"Eh!" said McAllister, and stood stunned as all eyes turned to stare at him.

IV

It struck McAllister that what he needed again was the mirror to prove to himself that his body was putting up a good front. His gaze flicked over the faces of the men. The gunmakers made a confusing pattern in the way they sat, or stood, or leaned against glass cases of shining guns; and there seemed to be fewer than he had previously counted. One, two—twenty-eight, including the girl. He could have sworn there had been thirty-two. His eyes moved on, just in time to see the door of the back room closing. Four of the men had gone to whatever lay beyond that door.

He shook his head, puzzled. And then, consciously drawing his attention back, stared thoughtfully at the faces before him. He said: "I can't understand how any one of you could even think of compulsion. According to you, I'm loaded with energy. I may be wrong, but if any of you should try to thrust me back down the chute of time, or even touch me, that energy in me would do devastating things—"

"You're damned right!" chimed in a young man. He barked irritably at

Dresley: "How the devil did you ever come to make such a psychological blunder? You know that McAllister will have to do as we want to save himself; and he'll have to do it fast!"

Dresley grunted. "Hell," he said, "the truth is that we have no time to waste in explanation and I just figured that he might scare easily. I see, however, that we're dealing with an intelligent man."

McAllister's eyes narrowed over the group. This was phony. He said sharply, "And don't give me any soft soap about being intelligent. You fellows are sweating blood. You'd shoot your own grandmothers and trick me into the bargain, because the world you think right is at stake. What's this plan of yours that you were going to compel me to participate in?"

It was the young man who replied. "You are to be given insulated clothes and sent back to your own time—"

He paused. McAllister said: "That sounds okay so far. What's the catch?"

"There is no catch!"

McAllister stared. "Now, look here," he began, "don't give me any of that. If it's as simple as that, how the devil am I going to be helping you against the Isher energy?"

The young man scowled blackly at Dresley. "You see," he said, "you've made him suspicious with that talk of yours about compulsion." He faced McAllister. "What we have in mind is an application of a sort of an energy lever and fulcrum principle. You are to be the weight at the long end of a kind of energy 'crowbar,' which lifts the greater weight at the short end. You will go back five thousand years in time; the machine in the great building, to which your body is tuned and which has caused all this trouble, will move ahead in time several months."

"In that way," interrupted another man before McAllister could speak, "we should have time to find another counter agent. There must be a solution, else our enemies would not have acted so secretly. Well, what do you think?"

McAllister walked slowly over to the chair that he had occupied previously. His mind was turning at furious speed, but he knew with a grim foreboding that he hadn't the technical knowledge necessary to safeguard himself. He said slowly:

"As I see it, this is supposed to work something like a pump handle. The lever principle, the old idea that if you had a lever long enough, and a suitable fulcrum, you could move the Earth out of its orbit."

"Exactly!" It was the heavy-faced Dresley who spoke. "Only this works in time. You go five thousand years, the building goes—"

His voice faded, his eagerness drained from him as he caught the expression in McAllister's face.

"Look!" said McAllister. "There's nothing more pitiful than a bunch of honest men engaged in an act of dishonesty. You're strong men, the intellectual type, who've spent your lives enforcing an idealistic conception. You've always told yourselves that if the occasion should ever require it, you would not hesitate to make drastic sacrifices. But you're not fooling anybody. *What's the catch?*"

V

It was startling to have the suit thrust at him. He had noticed the men emerge from the back room; and it came as a shock to realize that they had gone for the insulated clothes before they could have known that he would use them. McAllister stared grimly at Peter Cadron, who held the dull, grayish, limp thing toward him, and said in a tight voice:

"Get into this, and get going! It's a matter of minutes, man! When those guns out there start spraying energy, you won't be alive to argue about our honesty."

Still he hesitated. The room seemed insufferably hot. Perspiration streaked down his cheeks and he felt sick with uncertainty. Somewhere in the background a man was saying:

"Our first purpose must be to gain time, then we must establish new shops in communities where they cannot be easily attacked. Simultaneously, we must contact every Imperial potential who can help us directly or indirectly, and finally we must—"

The voice went on, but McAllister heard no more. His frantic gaze fell on the girl, standing silent and subdued near the front door. He strode toward her; and either his glare or presence was frightening, for she cringed and turned white.

"Look!" he said. "I'm in this as deep as hell. What's the risk in this thing? I've got to feel that I have some chance. Tell me, what's the catch?"

The girl was gray now, almost as gray and dead looking as the suit Peter Cadron was holding. "It's the friction," she mumbled finally, "you may not get all the way back to 1951. You see, you'll be a sort of 'weight' and—"

McAllister whirled away from her. He climbed into the soft almost flimsy suit, crowding the overall-like shape over his neatly pressed clothes. "It comes tight over the head, doesn't it?" he asked.

"Yes!" It was Lystra's father who answered. "As soon as you pull that zipper shut, the suit will become completely invisible. To outsiders, it will seem just as if you have your ordinary clothes on. The suit is fully equipped. You could live on the moon inside it."

"What I don't get," complained McAllister, "is why I have to wear it. I got here all right without it." He frowned. His words had been automatic, but abruptly a thought came. "Just a minute," he said, "what becomes of the energy with which I'm charged when I'm bottled up in this insulation?"

He saw by the stiffening expressions of those around him that he had touched on a vast subject.

"So that's it!" he snapped. "The insulation is to prevent me losing any of that energy. That's how it can make a 'weight.' I have no doubt there is a connection from this suit to that other machine. Well, it's not too late."

With a desperate twist, he tried to jerk aside, to evade the clutching hands of the four men who leaped at him. But they had him instantly, and their

423

grips on him were strong beyond his power to break. The fingers of Peter Cadron jerked the zipper tight, and Peter Cadron said:

"Sorry, but when we went into that back room, we also dressed in insulated clothing. That's why you couldn't hurt us. And remember this: There's no certainty that you are being sacrificed. The fact that there is no crater in *our* Earth proves that you did not explode in the past, and that you solved the problem in some other way. *Now, somebody open the door, quick!*"

Irresistibly, he was carried forward. And then—

"Wait!"

It was the girl. Her eyes glittered like dark jewels and in her fingers was the tiny, mirror-bright gun she had pointed in the beginning at McAllister. The little group hustling McAllister stopped as if they had been struck. He was scarcely aware. For him there was only the girl, and the way the muscles of her lips were working and the way her voice suddenly cried: "This is utter outrage. Are we such cowards—is it possible that the spirit of liberty can survive only through a shoddy act of murder and gross defiance of the rights of the individual? I say no! Mr. McAllister must have the protection of the hypnotism treatment; surely so brief a delay will not be fatal."

"Lystra!" It was her father; and McAllister realized by his swift movement how quickly the older man grasped every aspect of the situation. He stepped forward and took the gun from his daughter's fingers—the only man in the room, McAllister thought, who could dare approach her in that moment with the certainty she would not fire. For hysteria was in every line of her face; and the tears that followed showed how dangerous her stand might have been against the others.

Strangely, not for a moment had hope come. The entire action seemed divorced from his life and his thought; there was only the observation of it. He stood there for a seeming eternity, and, when emotion finally came, it was surprise that he was not being hustled to his doom. With the surprise came awareness that Peter Cadron had let go of his arm, and stepped clear of him.

The man's eyes were calm, his head held proudly erect. He said, "Your daughter is right, sir. At this point we rise above our fears, and we say to this unhappy young man: 'Have courage! You will not be forgotten. We can guarantee nothing, cannot even state exactly what will happen to you. But we say, if it lies in our power to help you, that help you shall have.' And now—we must protect you from the devastating psychological pressures that would otherwise destroy you, simply but effectively."

Too late, McAllister noticed that the others had turned their faces away from that extraordinary wall—the wall that had already displayed so vast a versatility. He did not even see who pressed the activating button for what followed.

There was a flash of dazzling light. For an instant he felt as if his mind had been laid bare; and against that nakedness the voice of Peter Cadron pressed like some engraving stamp: "To retain your self-control and your sanity— this is your hope; this you will do in spite of everything! And, for your own sake, speak of your experience only to scientists or to those in authority whom you feel will understand and help. Good luck!"

So strong remained the effect of that brief flaring light that he felt only vaguely the touch of their hands on him, propelling him.

He felt himself falling.

CHAPTER ONE

THE VILLAGE AT NIGHT made a curiously timeless picture. Fara walked contentedly beside his wife along the street. The air was like wine; and he was thinking dimly of the artist who had come up from Imperial City, and made what the telestats called—he remembered the phrase vividly—"a symbolic painting reminiscent of a scene in the electrical age of seven thousand years ago."

Fara believed that utterly. The street before him with its weedless, automatically tended gardens, its shops set well back among the flowers, its perpetually hard, grassy sidewalks, and its street lamps that glowed from every pore of their structure—this was a restful paradise where time had stood still.

And it was like being a part of life that the great artist's picture of this quiet, peaceful scene before him was now in the collection of the empress herself. She had praised it, and naturally the thrice-blest artist had immediately and humbly begged her to accept it. What a joy it must be to be able to offer personal homage to the glorious, the divine, the serenely gracious and lovely Innelda Isher, one hundred eightieth of her line.

As they walked, Fara half turned to his wife. In the dim light of the nearest street lamp, her kindly, still youthful face was almost lost in shadow. He murmured softly, instinctively muting his voice to harmonize with the pastel shades of night: "She said—our empress said—that our little village of Glay seemed to her to have in it all the wholesomeness, the gentleness, that constitutes the finest qualities of her people. Wasn't that a wonderful thought, Creel? She must be a marvelously understanding woman."

They had come to a side street, and what he saw about a hundred and fifty feet along it stopped his words. "Look!" Fara said hoarsely.

He pointed with rigid arm and finger at a sign that glowed in the night, a sign that read:

FINE WEAPONS

THE RIGHT TO BUY WEAPONS IS THE

RIGHT TO BE FREE

Fara had a strange, empty feeling as he stared at the blazing sign. He saw that other villagers were gathering. He said finally, huskily, "I've heard of these shops. They're places of infamy against which the government of the empress will act one of these days. They're built in hidden factories and then transported whole to towns like ours and set up in gross defiance of property rights. That one wasn't there an hour ago." His face hardened. His voice had a harsh edge in it as he said, "Creel, go home."

He was surprised when Creel did not move off at once. All their married life, she had had a pleasing habit of obedience that had made life a wonderful thing. He saw that she was looking at him wide-eyed, and that it was a timid alarm that held her there. She said, "Fara, what do you intend to do? You're not thinking of—"

"Go home!" Her fear brought out all the determination in his nature. "We're not going to let such a monstrous thing desecrate our village. Think of it—" his voice shivered before the appalling thought—"this fine, old-fashioned community, which we had resolved always to keep exactly as the empress has it in her picture gallery, debauched now, ruined by this . . . this thing— But we won't have it; that's all there is to it."

Creel's voice came softly out of the half-darkness of the street corner, the timidity gone from it: "Don't do anything rash, Fara. Remember it is not the first new building to come into Glay—since the picture was painted."

Fara was silent. This was a quality of his wife of which he did not approve, this reminding him unnecessarily of unpleasant facts. He knew exactly what she meant. The gigantic, multitentacled corporation, Automatic Atomic Motor Repair Shops, Inc., had come in under the laws of the State with their flashy building, against the wishes of the village council, and had already taken half of Fara's repair business.

"That's different!" Fara growled finally. "In the first place people will discover in good time that these new automatic repairers do a poor job. In the second place it's fair competition. But this weapon shop is a defiance of all the decencies that make life under the House of Isher such a joy. Look at the hypocritical sign: 'The right to buy weapons—' Aaaaahh!" He broke off with, "Go home, Creel. We'll see to it that they sell no weapons in this town."

He watched the slender woman-shape move off into the shadows. She was halfway across the street when Fara called after her: "And if you see that son of ours hanging around some street corner, take him home. He's got to learn to stop staying out so late at night."

The shadowed figure of his wife did not turn; and after watching her for a moment moving against the dim background of softly glowing street lights, Fara twisted on his heel and walked swiftly toward the shop. The crowd was growing larger every minute, and the night air pulsed with excited voices. Beyond doubt, here was the biggest thing that had ever happened to the village of Glay.

The sign of the weapon shop was, he saw, a normal-illusion affair. No matter what his angle of view, he was always looking straight at it. When he paused in front of the great display window, the words had pressed back against the store front, and were staring unwinkingly down at him. Fara sniffed once more at the meaning of the slogan, then turned to the sign in the window. It read:

THE FINEST ENERGY WEAPONS IN THE KNOWN
UNIVERSE

A spark of interest struck fire inside Fara. He gazed at the brilliant display of guns, fascinated in spite of himself. The weapons were of every size, ranging from tiny little finger pistols to express rifles. They were made of every one of the light, hard, ornamental substances: glittering glassein, the colorful but opaque Ordine plastic, viridescent magnesitic beryllium. And others. It was the deadly extent of the destructive display that brought a chill to Fara. So many weapons for the little village of Glay, where not more than two people to his knowledge had guns, and those only for hunting. Why, the thing was absurd, fantastically mischievous, and threatening.

Somewhere behind Fara a man said: "It's right on Lan Harris' lot. Good joke on that old scoundrel. Will he raise a row!"

There was a titter from several men, that made an odd patch of sound on the warm, fresh air. And Fara saw that the man had spoken the truth. The weapon shop had a forty-foot frontage. And it occupied the center of the green, gardenlike lot of tight-fisted old Harris. Fara frowned. Clever, these weapon shop people, selecting the property of the most disliked man in town, giving everybody an agreeable titillation. But the cunning of it made it vital that the trick should not succeed. He was still scowling anxiously when he saw the plump figure of Mel Dale, the mayor. Fara edged toward him hurriedly, touched his hat respectfully, and said, "Where's Jor?"

"Here." The village constable elbowed his way through a little crowd of men. "Any plans?" he said.

"There's only one plan," said Fara boldly. "Go in and arrest them."

The two men looked at each other, then at the ground. It was the big constable who answered shortly, "Door's locked. And nobody answers our pounding. I was just going to suggest we let the matter ride until morning."

"Nonsense!" Astonishment made Fara impatient. "Get an axe and we'll break down the door. Delay will only encourage such riffraff to resist. We don't want their kind in our village for a single night. Isn't that so?"

There was a hasty nod of agreement from everybody in his immediate vicinity. Too hasty. Fara looked around puzzled at eyes that lowered before his level gaze. He thought: "They are all scared. And unwilling." Before he could speak, Constable Jor said:

"I guess you haven't heard about those doors or these shops. From all accounts, you can't break into them."

It struck Fara with a sudden pang that it was he who would have to act here. He said, "I'll get my atomic cutting machine from my shop. That'll fix them. Have I your permission to do that, Mr. Mayor?"

In the glow of the weapon shop window, the plump man was sweating visibly. He pulled out a handkerchief, and wiped his forehead. He said: "Maybe I'd better call the commander of the Imperial garrison at Ferd, and ask them."

"No!" Fara recognized evasion when he saw it. Suddenly, the conviction came that all the strength in this village was in him. "We must act ourselves. Other communities have let these people get in because they took no decisive action. We've got to resist to the limit. Beginning this minute. Well?"

The mayor's "All right!" was scarcely more than a sigh of sound. But it was all Fara needed. He called out his intention to the crowd, and then, as he pushed his way out of the mob, he saw his son standing with some other young men staring at the window display.

Fara called: "Cayle, come and help me with the machine."

Cayle neither stirred nor turned. Fara paused, half inclined to make an issue of it, then hurried on, seething. That wretched boy! One of these days he'd have to take firm action there. Or he'd have a no-good on his hands.

The energy was soundless and smooth. There was no sputter, no fireworks. It glowed with a soft, pure white light, almost caressing the metal panels of the door. But after a minute it had still not affected the material. Fara refused to believe the failure, and played the boundlessly potent energy on that resisting wall. When he finally shut off his machine, he was perspiring freely. "I don't understand it," he gasped. "Why—no metal is supposed to stand up against a steady flood of atomic force. Even the hard metal plates used inside the blast chamber of a motor take the explosions in what is called infinite series, so that each one has unlimited rest. That's the theory, but actually steady running crystallizes the whole plate after a few months."

"It's as Jor told you," said the mayor. "These weapon shops are—big. They spread right through the empire, *and they don't recognize the empress*."

Fara shifted his feet on the hard grass, disturbed. He didn't like this kind of talk. It sounded sacrilegious. And besides it was nonsense. It must be. Before he could speak, a man in the crowd said, "I've heard it said that that door will open only to those who cannot harm the people inside."

The words shocked Fara out of his daze. His failure had had a bad psychological effect. He said sharply, "That's ridiculous! If there were doors like that, we'd all have them. We—"

What stopped his words was the sudden realization that *he* had not seen anybody try to open the door; and with all this reluctance around him it was quite possible that no one had tried. He stepped forward, grasped at the doorknob, and pulled. The door opened with an unnatural weightlessness that gave him the fleeting impression that the knob had come loose into his hand. With a gasp, Fara jerked the door wide open.

"Jor," he yelled, "get in!"

The constable made a distorted movement—distorted by what must have been a will to caution, followed by the instant realization that he could not hold back before so many. He leaped awkwardly toward the open door. And it closed in his face.

Fara stared stupidly at his hand, which was still clenched. And then, slowly, a thrill coursed along his nerves. The knob had withdrawn. It had twisted, become viscous, and slipped amorphously from his straining fingers. Even the memory of the sensation gave him a feeling of unnormal things. He grew aware that the crowd was watching with silent intentness. Fara reached angrily for the knob, but this time the handle neither turned nor yielded in any way. The obstacle brought his determination back in force. He motioned to the constable.

"Go back, Jor, while I pull."

The man retreated, but it did no good. And tugging did not help. The door would not open. Somewhere in the crowd, a man said darkly, "It decided to let you in, then it changed its mind."

"What foolishness are you talking!" Fara spoke violently. "*It* changed its mind. Are you crazy? A door has no sense."

Fear put a quaver into his voice. Shame at his alarm made him bold beyond his normal caution. Fara faced the shop grimly. The building loomed there under the night sky, in itself bright as day, alien and menacing, and no longer easily conquerable. He wondered what the soldiers of the empress would do if they were invited to act. And, suddenly, he foresaw flashingly that even they would be able to do nothing. Fara was conscious of horror that such an idea could enter his mind. He shut his brain tight.

"The door opened for me once," he said wildly. "It will open again."

It did. Gently, without resistance, *with* that same sensation of weightlessness, the strange, sensitive door followed the tug of his fingers. Beyond the threshold was dimness, a wide, darkened alcove. Behind him, Mayor Dale said:

"Fara, don't be a fool. What will you do inside?"

Fara was amazed to realize that he had stepped across the threshold. He turned, startled, and stared at the blur of faces. "Why—" he began blankly; then he brightened—"Why, I'll buy a gun, of course."

The brilliance of his reply, the cunning implicit in it, dazzled him for half a minute longer. The mood yielded slowly as he found himself in the dimly lighted interior of the weapon shop.

CHAPTER TWO

IT WAS PRETERNATURALLY QUIET INSIDE. No sound penetrated from the night out of which he had come. Fara walked forward gingerly on a carpeted floor that deadened his footsteps. His eyes accustomed themselves to the soft lighting, which came like a reflection from the walls and ceiling. He had expected ultranormalness. The ordinariness of the atomic lighting acted like a tonic to his tensed nerves. He glanced around with gathering confidence. The place looked normal enough. It was a shop, scantily furnished. There were showcases on the walls and on the floor, lovely things, but nothing unusual, and not many of them—a dozen. There was in addition a double door leading to a back room.

Fara tried to keep one eye on that door as he examined several showcases, each with three or four weapons either mounted or arranged in boxes or holsters. With narrowed eyes, he estimated his chances of grabbing one of the weapons from a case, and then, the moment someone came, force him outside where Jor would perform the arrest. Behind him, a man said quietly, "You wish to buy a gun?"

Fara turned with a jump. Brief rage flooded him at the way his plan had been wrecked by the arrival of the clerk. The anger died as he saw that the clerk was a fine looking, silver-haired man, older than himself. That was disconcerting. Fara had an immense and almost automatic respect for age. He said at last, lamely, "Yes, yes, a gun."

"For what purpose?" said the man in his quiet voice. Fara could only look at him. He wanted to get mad. He wanted to tell these people what he thought of them.

But the age of this representative locked his tongue. He managed speech with an effort of will. "For hunting." The plausible words stiffened his mind. "Yes, definitely for hunting. There is a lake to the north of here," he went on more fulsomely, "and—"

He stopped, scowling at the extent of his dishonesty. He was not prepared to go so deeply into prevarication. He said curtly, "For hunting."

Fara was himself again. He hated the man for having put him so completely at a disadvantage. With smoldering eyes he watched the old fellow click open a showcase and take out a green-shining rifle. As the man faced him, weapon in hand, Fara was thinking: "Pretty clever, having an old man as a front." It was the same kind of cunning that had made them choose the property of Miser Harris. He reached for the gun; but the man held it out of his reach.

"Before I can even let you test this," he said, "I am compelled by the by-laws of the weapon shops to inform you under what circumstances you may purchase a gun."

So they had private regulations. What a system of psychological tricks to impress the gullible.

"We weapon makers," the clerk was saying mildly, "have evolved guns that can, in their particular range destroy any machine or object made of what is called matter. Thus whoever possesses one of our weapons is more than a match for any soldier of the empress. I say more because each gun is the center of a field of force which acts as a perfect screen against immaterial destructive forces. That screen offers no resistance to clubs or spears or bullets, or other material substances, but it would require a small atomic cannon to penetrate the superb barrier it creates around its owner.

"You will readily comprehend," the man went on, "that such a potent weapon could not be allowed to fall, unmodified, into irresponsible hands. Accordingly, no gun purchased from us may be used for aggression or murder. In the case of the hunting rifle, only such specified game birds and animals as we may from time to time list in our display windows may be shot. Finally, no weapon can be resold without our approval. Is that clear?"

Fara nodded. For the moment, speech was impossible to him. He wondered if he ought to laugh out loud, or curse the man for daring to insult his intelligence. So the gun mustn't be used for murder or robbery. So only certain birds and animals could be shot. And as for reselling it, suppose— suppose he bought this thing, took a trip of a thousand miles, and offered it to some wealthy stranger for two credits—who would ever know? Or suppose he held up a stranger. Or shot him. How would the weapon shop ever find out? He grew aware that the gun was being held out to him stock first. He took it, and had to fight the impulse to turn the muzzle directly on the old man.

"How does it work?" he asked.

"You simply aim it, and pull the trigger. Perhaps you would like to try it on a target we have."

Fara swung the gun up. "Yes," he said triumphantly, "and you're it. Now, just get over there to the front door, and then outside." He raised his voice, "And if anybody's thinking of coming through the back door, I've got that covered, too." He motioned jerkily at the clerk. "Quick now, move! I'll shoot! I swear I will."

The man was cool, unflustered. "I have no doubt you would. When we decided to attune the door so that you could enter despite your hostility, we assumed the capacity for homicide. However, this is our party. You had better adjust yourself accordingly, and look behind you."

There was silence. Finger on trigger, Fara stood moveless. Dim thoughts came of all the *half-things* he had heard in his days about the weapon shops; that they had secret supporters in every district, that they had a private and ruthless hidden government, and that once you got into their clutches, the only way out was death. But what finally came clear was a mind picture of himself, Fara Clark, family man, faithful subject of the empress, standing here in this dimly-lighted store, deliberately fighting so vast and menacing an organization. He forced courage into his sagging muscles. He said, "You can't fool me by pretending there's someone behind me. Now, get to that door."

The firm eyes of the old man were looking past him. The man said quietly, "Well, Rad, have you all the data?"

"Enough for a primary," said a young man's voice behind Fara. "Type A-7 conservative. Good average intelligence, but a Monaric development peculiar to small towns. One-sided outlook fostered by the Imperial schools present in exaggerated form. Extremely honest. Reason would be useless. Emotional approach would require extended treatment. I see no reason why we should bother. Let him live his life as it suits him."

"If you think," Fara said shakily, "that that trick voice is going to make me turn, you're crazy. That's the left wall of the building. I know there's no one there."

"I'm all in favor, Rad," said the old man, "of letting him live his life. But he was the prime mover of the crowd outside. I think he should be discouraged."

"We'll advertise his presence," said Rad. "He'll spend the rest of his life denying the charge."

Fara's confidence in the gun had faded so far that, as he listened in puzzled uneasiness to the incomprehensible conversation, he forgot it completely.

The old man said persistently: "I think a little emotion might have a long-run effect. Show him the palace."

Palace! The word tore Fara out of his paralysis. "See here," he began, "I can see now that you lied to me. This gun isn't loaded at all. It's—"

His voice failed him. His body went rigid. There was no gun in his hand.

"Why, you—" he began wildly. And stopped again. His mind heaved with imbalance. He fought off the spinning sensation, thought finally, tremblingly: Somebody must have sneaked the gun from him. That meant there was someone behind him. The voice was no mechanical thing. He started to turn. And couldn't. He struggled, pushing with his muscles. And couldn't turn, couldn't move, couldn't budge. The room was growing curiously dark. He had difficulty seeing the old man. He would have shrieked then if he could. Because the weapon shop was gone.

He was standing in the sky above an immense city. Standing in the sky, and nothing around him but air, and blue summer heaven, and the city a mile, two miles below. His breath seemed solidly embedded in his lungs. Sanity came back as the remote awareness impinged on his mind that he was actually standing on a hard floor, and that the city must be a picture somehow focussed directly into his eyes.

For the first time, with a start, Fara recognized the metropolis below. It was the city of dreams, Imperial City, Capital of the glorious Empress Isher. From his great height he could see the grounds of the silver palace, the Imperial residence itself. The last tendrils of his fear were fading now before a gathering fascination and wonder. The fear vanished as he recognized with a thrill that the palace was drawing nearer at tremendous speed. "Show him the palace!" they had said. The glittering roof flashed straight at his face. The solid metal of it passed through him.

His first sense of imminent and mind shaking desecration came as the picture paused in a huge room, where a score of men sat around a table at the head of which sat a young woman. The inexorable, sacrilegious, limitlessly powered cameras that were doing the photographing swung across the table and caught the woman full face.

It was a handsome face, but there was passion twisting it now, as she leaned forward and said in a voice at once familiar—how often Fara had heard its calm, measured tones on the telestats—and distorted. Distorted by anger and an insolent certainty of command. That caricature of a beloved voice slashed across the silence as clearly as if he were there in the great room:

"I want that traitor killed, do you understand? I don't care how you do it, but I want to hear by tomorrow night that he is dead."

The picture snapped off and instantly Fara was back in the weapon shop. He stood for a moment, swaying, fighting to accustom his eyes to the dimness. His first emotion was contempt at the simpleness of the trickery. A motion picture. What kind of a fool did they think he was, to swallow something as transparently unreal as that? Abruptly, the appalling depravity of the scheme, the indescribable wickedness of what was being attempted here brought red rage.

"Why, you scum!" he flared. "So you've got somebody to act the part of the empress, trying to pretend that— Why, you—"

"That will do," said the voice of Rad. Fara shook as a big young man walked into his line of vision. The alarmed thought came that people who

432

would besmirch so vilely the character of her imperial majesty would not hesitate to do physical damage to Fara Clark. The young man went on in a steely tone, "We do not pretend that what you saw was taking place this instant in the palace. That would be too much of a coincidence. But it was taken two days ago. The woman is the empress. The man whose death she ordered is a former adviser whom she considered a weakling. He was found dead in his apartment last night. His name, if you care to look it up in the news files, was Banton Vickers. However, let that pass. We're finished with you."

"But I'm not finished," Fara said in a thick voice. "I've never heard or seen so much infamy in all my life. If you think this town is through with you, you're crazy. We'll have a guard on this place day and night, and nobody will get in or out."

"That will do." It was the silver-haired man. "The examination has been most interesting. As an honest man, you may call on us if you are ever in trouble. That is all. Leave through the side door."

It was all. Impalpable forces grabbed him, and he was shoved at a door that appeared miraculously in the wall, where seconds before had been the palace. He found himself standing in a flower garden, and there was a crowd to his left. He recognized his fellow townsmen, and that he was outside.

The nightmare was over. As he entered his house half an hour later, Creel said, "Where's the gun?"

"The gun?" Fara stared at his wife.

"It said over the 'stat a few minutes ago that you were the first customer of the new weapon shop."

Fara stood, remembering what the young man had said: "We'll advertise his presence." He thought in agony: His reputation! Not that his was a great name, but he had long believed with a quiet pride that Fara Clark's motor repair shop was widely known in the community and countryside. First, his private humiliation inside the shop. And now this lying to people who didn't know why he had gone into the store.

He hurried to the telestat, and called Mayor Dale. His hopes crashed as the plump man said:

"I'm sorry, Fara. I don't see how you can have free time on the telestat. You'll have to pay for it. They did."

"They did!" Fara wondered if he sounded as empty as he felt.

"And they've paid Lan Harris for his lot. The old man asked top price, and got it. He phoned me to transfer the title."

"Oh!" Fara's world was shattering. "You mean nobody's going to do anything? What about the Imperial garrison at Ferd?"

Dimly, he was aware of the mayor mumbling something about the empress' soldiers refusing to interfere in civilian matters. "Civilian matters!" Fara exploded. "You mean these people are just going to be allowed to come here whether we want them or not, illegally forcing the sale of lots by first taking possession of them?" A thought struck him. "Look," he said breathlessly, "you haven't changed your mind about having Jor keep guard in front of the shop?"

433

The plump face in the telestat plate grew impatient. "Now, see here, Fara, let the constituted authorities handle this matter."

"But you're going to keep Jor there," Fara said doggedly.

The mayor looked annoyed. "I promised, didn't I? So he'll be there. And now, do you want to buy time on the telestat? It's fifteen credits for one minute. Mind you, as a friend, I think you're wasting your money. No one has ever caught up with a false statement."

Fara said grimly, "Put two on, one in the morning, one in the evening."

"All right. We'll deny it completely. Good night."

The telestat went blank; and Fara sat there. A new thought hardened his face. "That boy of ours—there's going to be a showdown. He either works in my shop or he gets no more allowance."

Creel said, "You've handled him wrong. He's twenty-three, and you treat him like a child. Remember, at twenty-three you were a married man."

"That was different," said Fara. "I had a sense of responsibility. Do you know what he did tonight?"

He didn't quite catch her answer. For a moment he thought she said: "No. In what way did you humiliate him first?"

Fara felt too impatient to verify the improbable words. He rushed on, "He refused in front of the whole village to give me help. He's a bad one, all bad."

"Yes," said Creel in a bitter tone. "He's all bad. I'm sure you don't realize how bad. He's as cold as steel, but without steel's strength or integrity. He took a long time, but he hates even me now because I stood up for you for so long when I knew you were wrong."

"What's that?" said Fara, startled; then gruffly: "Come, come, my dear, we're both upset. Let's go to bed."

He slept poorly.

CHAPTER THREE

THERE WERE DAYS when the conviction that this was a personal fight between himself and the weapon shop lay heavily on Fara. Though it was out of his way, he made a point of walking past the weapon shop on his way to and from work, always pausing to speak to Constable Jor. On the fourth day, the policeman wasn't there.

Fara waited patiently at first, then angrily. He walked finally to his shop and called Jor's house. Jor wasn't home. He was, according to his wife, guarding the weapon store. Fara hesitated. His own shop was piled with work, and he had a guilty sense of having neglected his customers for the first time in his life. It would be simple to call up the mayor and report Jor's dereliction. And yet he didn't want to get the man into trouble.

Out in the street, he saw that a large crowd was gathering in front of the weapon shop. Fara hurried. A man he knew greeted him excitedly: "Jor's been murdered, Fara!"

"Murdered!" Fara stood very still, and at first he was not clearly conscious of the thought that was in his mind: Satisfaction! Now, even the soldiers would have to act. He realized the ghastly tenor of his thoughts, but pushed the sense of shame out of his mind. He said slowly, "Where's the body?"

"Inside."

"You mean those . . . scum—" In spite of himself, he hesitated over the epithet. It was difficult to think of the silver-haired weapon shop man in such terms. His mind hardened. "You mean, those scum killed him, then pulled his body inside?"

"Nobody saw the killing," said another man, "but he's gone and hasn't been seen for three hours. The mayor got the weapon shop on telestat, but they claim they don't know anything about him. They've done away with him, that's what, and now they're pretending innocence. Well, they won't get out of it as easily as that. Mayor's gone to phone the soldiers at Ferd to bring up some big guns."

Something of the excitement that was in the crowd surged through Fara, the feeling that big things were brewing. It was the most delicious sensation that had ever tingled along his nerves, and it was all mixed with a strange pride that he had been so right about this, that he at least had never doubted that here was evil. He did not recognize the emotion as the full-flowering joy that comes to a member of a mob. But his voice shook as he said, "Guns? Yes, that will be the answer, and the soldiers will have to come, of course."

Fara nodded to himself in the immensity of his certainty that the Imperial soldiers would now have no excuse for not acting. He started to say something about what the empress would do if she found out that a man had lost his life because the soldiers had shirked their duty, but the words were drowned in a shout:

"Here comes the mayor! Hey, Mr. Mayor, when are the atomic cannons due?"

There was more of the same general meaning as the mayor's car landed lightly. Some of the questions must have reached his honor, for he stood up in the open two-seater, and held up his hand for silence. To Fara's astonishment, the plump-faced man gazed at him with accusing eyes. He looked around him, but he was almost alone; everybody else had crowded forward. Fara shook his head, puzzled by that glare, and then flinched as Mayor Dale pointed a finger at him and said in a voice that trembled, "There's the man who's responsible for the trouble that has come upon us. Stand forward, Fara Clark, and show yourself. You've cost this town seven hundred credits that we could ill afford to spend."

Fara couldn't have moved or spoken to save his life. The mayor went on, with self-pity in his tone, "We've all known that it wasn't wise to interfere with these weapon shops. So long as the Imperial government leaves them alone, what right have we to set up guards, or act against them? That's what I've thought from the beginning, but this man . . . this . . . this Fara Clark

435

kept after all of us, forcing us to move against our wills, and so now we've got a seven-hundred credit bill to meet and—"

He broke off with, "I might as well make it brief. When I called the garrison, the commander laughed and said that Jor would turn up. And I had barely disconnected when there was a money call from Jor. He's on Mars." He waited for the shouts of amazement to die down. "It'll take four weeks for him to come back by ship, and we've got to pay for it, and Fara Clark is responsible."

The shock was over. Fara stood cold, his mind hard. He said finally, scathingly, "So you're giving up, and trying to blame me all in one breath. I say you are all fools."

As he turned away, he heard Mayor Dale saying that the situation was not completely lost as he had learned that the weapon shop had been set up in Glay because the village was equidistant from four cities, and that it was the city business the shop was after. This would mean tourists, and accessory trade for the village stores.

Fara heard no more. Head high, he walked back to his shop. There were one or two catcalls from the mob, but he ignored them. The worst of it, as the days passed, was the realization that the people of the weapon shop had no personal interest in him. They were remote, superior, undefeatable. When he thought of it, he felt a vague fear at the way they had transferred Jor to Mars in a period of less than three hours, when all the world knew that the trip by fastest spaceship could never be made in less than 24 days.

Fara did not go to the express station to see Jor arrive home. He had heard that the council had decided to charge Jor with half of the expense of the trip, on the threat of losing his job if he objected. On the second night after Jor's return, Fara slipped down to the constable's house, and handed the officer one hundred and seventy-five credits. He returned home with a clearer conscience.

It was on the third day after that the door of his shop banged open and a man came in. Fara frowned as he saw who it was: Castler, a village hanger-on. The man was grinning. "Thought you might be interested, Fara. Somebody came out of the weapon shop today."

Fara strained deliberately at the connecting bolt of a hard plate of the atomic motor he was fixing. He waited with a gathering annoyance that the man did not volunteer further information. Asking questions would be a form of recognition of the worthless fellow. A developing curiosity made him say finally, grudgingly, "I suppose the constable promptly picked him up?"

He supposed nothing of the kind; but it was an opening.

"It wasn't a man. It was a girl."

Fara knitted his brows. He didn't like the idea of making trouble for women. But the cunning devils! Using a girl, just as they had used an old man as a clerk. It was a trick that deserved to fail; the girl was probably a hussy who needed rough treatment. Fara said harshly, "Well, what's happened?"

"She's still out, bold as you please. Pretty thing, too."

The bolt off, Fara took the hard plate over to the polisher, and began patiently the long, careful task of smoothing away the crystals that heat had seared on the once shining metal. The soft throb of the polisher made the background to his next words, "Has anything been done?"

"Nope. The constable's been told, but he says he doesn't fancy being away from his family for another month or so, and paying the cost into the bargain."

Fara contemplated that for a minute, as the polisher throbbed on. His voice shook with suppressed fury when he said firmly, "So they're letting them get away with it. It's all been as clever as hell. Can't they see that they mustn't give an inch before these . . . these transgressors? It's like giving countenance to sin."

From the corner of his eye, he noticed that there was a grin on the face of the other. It struck Fara suddenly that the man was enjoying his anger. And there was something else in that grin—a secret knowledge. Fara pulled the engine plate away from the polisher. He faced the ne'er-do-well. "Naturally, that sin part wouldn't worry you much."

"Oh," said the man nonchalantly, "the hard knocks of life make people tolerant. For instance, after you know the girl better, you yourself will probably come to realize that there's good in all of us."

It was not so much the words, as the I've-got-secret-information tone that made Fara snap, "What do you mean—after I get to know the girl better! I won't even speak to the brazen creature."

"One can't always choose," the other said with enormous casualness. "Suppose he brings her home."

"Suppose who brings who home?" Fara spoke irritably. "Castler, you—" He stopped. A dead weight of dismay plumped into his stomach; his whole being sagged. "You mean—" he said.

"I mean," replied Castler with a triumphant leer, "that the boys aren't letting a beauty like her be lonesome. And, naturally, your son was the first to speak to her." He finished: "They're walkin' together now on Second Avenue, comin' this way."

"Get out of here!" Fara roared. "And stay away from me with your gloating. Get out!"

The man hadn't expected such an ignominious ending. He flushed scarlet, then went out, slamming the door. Fara stood for a moment, stiffly. Then, with jerky movements, he shut off his power and went out into the street. The time to put a stop to that kind of thing was—now!

He had no clear plan, simply a determination to end an impossible situation. It was all mixed up with his anger against Cayle. How could he have had such a worthless son, he who paid his debts and worked hard, and tried to be decent and live up to the highest standards of the empress?

He wondered if there mightn't be bad blood on Creel's side, not from her mother, of course—Fara added the qualification hastily. There was a fine, hard-working woman, who would leave Creel a tidy sum one of these days. But Creel's father had disappeared when she was a child.

And now, Cayle with this weapon shop girl, who had let herself be picked up—he saw them as he turned the corner onto Second Avenue. They were heading away from Fara. As he came up, the girl was saying:

"You have the wrong idea about us. A person like you can't get a job in our organization. You belong in the Imperial service, where they can use young men of good appearance and ambition."

Fara was too intent for her words to mean anything. He said harshly, "Cayle!"

The couple turned, Cayle with the measured unhurriedness of a young man who had gone a long way on the road to acquiring steel-like nerves; the girl was quicker, but dignified.

Fara had a feeling that his anger was self-destroying, but the violence of his emotions ended that thought even as it came. He said thickly, "Cayle, get home at once."

He was aware of the girl looking at him curiously from strange, gray-green eyes. No shame, he thought, and his rage mounted, driving away the alarm that came at the sight of the flush that was creeping into Cayle's cheeks.

The flush faded into a pale, tight-lipped anger as Cayle half-turned to the girl and said, "This is the childish old fool I've got to contend with. Fortunately, we seldom see each other. We don't even eat our meals at the same table. What do you think of him?"

The girl smiled impersonally, "Oh, we know Fara Clark. He's the mainstay of the empress in Glay."

"Yes," the boy sneered. "You ought to hear him. He thinks we're living in heaven, and the empress is the divine power. The worst part of it is that there's no chance of his ever getting that stuffy look wiped off his face."

They walked off; and Fara stood there. The extent of what had happened drained anger from him as if it had never been. There was the realization that he had made a mistake. But he couldn't quite grasp it. For long now, since Cayle had refused to work in his shop, he had felt this building up to a climax. Suddenly, his own uncontrollable ferocity stood revealed as a partial product of that deeper problem. Only, now that the smash was here, he didn't want to face it.

All through the day in his shop, he kept pushing it out of his mind, kept thinking: Would this go on now, as before, Cayle and he living in the same house, not even looking at each other when they met, going to bed at different times, getting up, Fara at 6:30, Cayle at noon? Would *that* go on through all the days and years to come?

Creel was waiting for him when he arrived home. She said: "Fara, he wants you to loan him five hundred credits, so that he can go to Imperial City."

Fara nodded wordlessly. He brought the money back to the house the next morning, and gave it to Creel, who took it into Cayle's bedroom.

She came out a minute later. "He says to tell you goodbye."

When Fara came home that evening, Cayle was gone. He wondered whether he ought to feel relieved. But the only sensation that finally came was a conviction of disaster.

CHAPTER FOUR

HE HAD BEEN CAUGHT in a trap. Now he was escaping.

Cayle did not think of his departure from the village of Glay as the result of a decision. He had wanted to leave for so long that the purpose seemed part of his body hunger, like the need to eat or drink. But the impulse had grown dim and undefined. Baffled by his father, he had turned an unfriendly eye on everything that was of the village. And his obstinate defiance was matched at every turn by the obdurate qualities of his prison— until now.

Just why the cage had opened was obscure. There was the weapon shop girl, of course. Slender, her gray-green eyes intelligent, her face well-formed and carrying about her an indefinable aura of a person who had made many successful decisions, she had said—he remembered the words as if she were still speaking them—"Why, yes, I'm from Imperial City. I'm going back there Thursday afternoon."

This Thursday afternoon *she* was going to the great city, while he remained in Glay. He couldn't stand it. He felt ill, savage as an animal in his desire to go also. It was that, more than his quarrel with his father, which made him put pressure on his mother for money. Now, he sat on the local carplane to Ferd, dismayed to find that the girl was not aboard.

At the Ferd Air Center, waiting for the Imperial City plane, he stood at various vantage points and looked for Lucy Rall. But the crowds jamming toward the constant stream of interstate planes defeated even his alert eyes. All too soon his own vast machine glided in for a landing. That is, it seemed too soon until he saw the plane coming toward him. A hundred feet high at the nose, absolutely transparent, it shimmered like a jewel as it drew up in the roadstead.

To Cayle there came a tremendous excitement. Thought of the girl faded. He clambered aboard feverishly. He did not think of Lucy again until the plane was hurtling along over the evergreen land far below. He leaned back in his comfortable chair then, and wondered: What kind of a person was she, this girl of the weapon shops? Where did she live? What was her life as a member of an almost rebel organization? . . . There was a man in a chair about ten feet along the aisle. Cayle suppressed an impulse to ask him all the questions that bubbled inside him. Other people might not realize as clearly as he himself did that, though he had lived all his life in Glay, he wasn't really village. He'd better not risk a rebuff.

A man laughed. A woman said, "But, darling, are you sure we can afford a tour of the planets?" They passed along the aisle, Cayle assessing the casualness with which they were taking the trip.

He felt enormously self-conscious at first, but he also gradually grew casual. He read the news on his chair 'stat. With idle glances he watched the scenery speeding by below, adjusting his chair scope for enlarged vision. He felt quite at home by the time the three men seated themselves opposite him and began to play cards.

It was a small game for tiny stakes. And, throughout, two of the men were never addressed by name. The third one was called "Seal". Unusual name, it seemed to Cayle. And the man was as special as his name. He looked about thirty. He had eyes as yellow as a cat's. His hair was wavy, boyish in its unruliness. His face was sallow, though not unhealthy-looking. Jeweled ornaments glittered from each lapel of his coat. Multiple rings flashed colored fire from his fingers. When he spoke it was with slow assurance. And it was he who finally turned to Cayle and said:

"Noticed you watching us. Care to join us?"

Cayle had been intent, automatically accepting Seal as a professional gambler, but not quite decided about the others. The question was, which one was the sucker?

"Make the game more interesting," Seal suggested.

Cayle was suddenly pale. He realized now that these three were a team. And he was their selected victim. Instinctively, he glanced around to see how many people were observing his shame. To his relief, nobody at all was looking. The man who had been sitting ten feet away was not in sight. A stout, well-dressed woman paused at the entrance of the section but turned away. Slowly the color trickled back into his face. So they thought they had found someone who would be an easy mark, did they. He stood up, smiling.

"Don't mind if I do," he said.

He sat down in the vacant chair across from the yellow-eyed man. The deal fell to Cayle. In quick succession and honestly, he dealt himself a king down and two kings up. He played the hand to the limit and, even with the low stakes, eventually raked in about four credits in coins.

He won three out of the next eight games, which was below average for him. He was a callidetic, with temporary emphasis on automatic skill at cards, though he had never heard the word. Once, five years before when he was seventeen, while playing with four other boys for credit twentieths, he won nineteen out of twenty games of showdown. Thereafter, his gambling luck, which might have rescued him from the village, was so great that no one in Glay would play with him.

In spite of his winning streak now, he felt no sense of superiority. Seal dominated the game. There was a commanding air about him, an impression of abnormal strength, not physical. Cayle began to be fascinated.

"I hope you won't be offended," he said finally, "but you're a type of person who interests me."

The yellow eyes studied him thoughtfully, but Seal said nothing.

"Been around a lot, I suppose?" said Cayle.

He was dissatisfied with the question. It was not what he wanted. It sounded less than mature. Seal, mere gambler though he was, towered above such a naive approach. But he replied this time. "A bit," he said noncommittally.

His companions seemed to find that amusing. They both guffawed. Cayle flushed, but there was a will in him to know things. "To the planets?" he asked.

No answer. Seal carefully studied the cards that were down, then raised a credit-fortieth. Cayle struggled against the feeling that he was making a fool of himself. Then, "We all hear things," he said apologetically, "and it's sometimes hard to know what's true and what isn't. Are any of the planets worth going to?"

The yellow eyes studied him now with amusement. "Listen, fella," said Seal impressively, "don't go near them. Earth is the heaven of this system and if anybody tells you that wonderful Venus is beckoning, tell 'em to go to hell—that's Venus. Hell, I mean. Endless sandstorms. And one day, when I was in Venusburg, the temperature rose to eighty-four Centigrade." He finished, "They don't tell you things like that in the ads, do they?"

Cayle agreed hastily that they didn't. He was taken aback by the volubility of the reply. It sounded boastful like—he couldn't decide. But the man was abruptly less interesting. He had one more question.

"Are you married?" he asked.

Seal laughed. "Married! Listen, my friend, I get married every place I go. Not legally, mind you." He laughed again, significantly. "I see I'm giving you ideas."

Cayle said, "You don't have to get ideas like that from other people."

He spoke automatically. He hadn't expected such a revelation of character. No doubt Seal was a man of courage. But the glamour was gone from him. Cayle recognized that it was his village morality, his mother's ethics, that were assessing the other. But he couldn't help it. For years he had had this conflict between his mother's credos and his instinctive awareness that the world outside could not be compressed into the mores that encompassed village life.

Seal was speaking again, heartily. "This boy is really going to be somebody in ever-glorious Isher, eh, boys? And I'm not over-stating, either." He broke off. "Where do you get all those good cards?"

Cayle had won again. He raked in the pot, and hesitated. He had won forty-five credits, and knew he had better quit before he caused irritation. "I'm afraid I'll have to stop," he said. "I've some things to do. It's been a pleas—"

He faltered, breathless. A tiny, glittering gun peered at him over the edge of the table. The yellow-eyed man said in a monotone, "So you think it's time to quit, eh?" His head did not turn, but his voice reached out directly at his companions. "He thinks it's time to quit, boys. Shall we let him?" It must have been a rhetorical question, for the henchmen merely grimaced.

"Personally," the leader went on, "I'm all in favor of quitting. Now, let me see," he purred. "According to the transparency his wallet is in his upper right hand breast pocket and there are some fifty-credit notes in an envelope pinned into his shirt pocket. And then, of course, there's the money he won from us in his trouser pocket."

He leaned forward and his strange eyes were wide open and ironic. "So you thought we were gamblers who were going to take you, somehow. No, my friend, we don't work that way. Our system is much simpler. If you refused to hand over, or tried to attract somebody's attention, I'd fire this energy gun straight into your heart. It works on such a narrow beam that no one would even notice the tiny hole in your clothing. You'd continue to sit right there, looking a little sleepy perhaps, but who would wonder about that on this big ship, with all its busy, self-centered people?" His voice hardened. "Hand it over! Quick! I'm not fooling. I'll give you ten seconds."

It took longer than that to turn over the money but apparently the continuity of acquiescence was all that was required. He was allowed to put his empty pocketbook back into his pocket and several coins were ignored. "You'll need a bite before we land," Seal said generously.

The gun disappeared under the table and Seal leaned back in his chair with an easy relaxation. "Just in case," he said, "you decide to complain to the captain, let me tell you that we would kill you instantly without worrying about the consequences. Our story is simple. You've been foolish and lost all your money at cards." He laughed and climbed to his feet, once more imperturbable and mysterious. "Be seeing ya, fellow. Better luck next time."

The other men were climbing to their feet. The three sauntered off and, as Cayle watched, they disappeared into the forward cocktail bar. Cayle remained in his chair, hunched and devastated.

His gaze sought the distant clock—July 15, 4784 Isher—two hours and fifteen minutes out of Ferd and an hour still to Imperial City.

With closed eyes Cayle pictured himself arriving in the old city as darkness fell. His first night there, that was to have been so thrilling, would now be spent on the streets.

CHAPTER FIVE

HE COULDN'T SIT STILL. And three times, as he paced through the ship, he paused before full length energy mirrors. His bloodshot eyes glared back at him from the lifelike image of himself. And over and above the desperate wonder of what to do now, he thought: How had they picked him for victim? What was there about him that had made the gang of three head unerringly toward him?

As he turned from the third mirror he saw the weapon shop girl. Her gaze flicked over him without recognition. She wore a soft blue tailored dress, and a strand of creamy pearls around her tanned neck. She looked so smart and at ease that he didn't have the heart to follow her. Hopelessly, Cayle moved out of her line of vision and sank into a seat.

A movement caught his distracted gaze. A man was slumping into a chair at the table across the aisle. He wore the uniform of a colonel in Her Imperial Majesty's Army. He was so drunk he could hardly sit, and how he had walked to the seat was a mystery rooted deep in the laws of balance. His head came around, and his eyes peered blearily at Cayle.

"Spying on me, eh?" His voice went down in pitch, and up in volume. "*Waiter!*"

A steward hurried forward. "Yes, sir?"

"The finest wine for my shadow n'me." As the waiter rushed off, the officer beckoned Cayle. "Might as well sit over here. Might as well travel together, eh?" His tone grew confidential. "I'm a wino, y'know. Been trying to keep it from the Empress for a long time. She doesn't like it." He shook his head sadly. "Doesn't like it at all. *Well, what're you waiting for? C'mon over here.*"

Cayle came hastily, cursing the drunken fool. But hope came too. He had almost forgotten, but the weapon shop girl had suggested he join the Imperial forces. If he could obtain information from this alcoholic and join up fast, then the loss of the money wouldn't matter. "I've got to decide," he told himself. He distinctly thought of himself as making a decision.

He sipped his wine presently, more tense than he cared to be, eyeing the older man with quick, surreptitious glances. The man's background emerged slowly out of a multitude of incoherent confidences. His name was Laurel Medlon. Colonel Laurel Medlon, he would have Cayle understand, confidant of the Empress, intimate of the palace, head of a tax collecting district.

"Damned, hic, good one, too," he said with a satisfaction that gave more weight to his words than the words themselves.

He looked sardonically at Cayle. "Like to get in on it, eh?" He hiccoughed. "Okay, come to my office—tomorrow."

His voice trailed. He sat mumbling to himself. And, when Cayle asked a question, he muttered that he had come to Imperial City ". . . when I was your age. Boy, was I green!" He quivered in a spasm of vinous indignation. "Y'know, those damned clothing monopolies have different kinds of cloth they send out to the country. You can spot anybody from a village. I was sure spotted fast . . ."

His voice trailed off into a series of curses. His reminiscent rage communicated itself to Cayle.

So that was it—his clothes!

The unfairness of it wracked his body. His father had consistently refused to let him buy his suits even in nearby Ferd. Always Fara had protested, "How can I expect the local merchants to bring their repair work to me if my family doesn't deal with them?" And having asked the unanswerable question, the older man would not listen to further appeals.

"And here I am," Cayle thought, "stripped because that old fool—" The futile anger faded. Because large towns like Ferd probably had their own special brand of cloth, as easily identifiable as anything in Glay. The unfairness of it, he saw with reaching clarity, went far beyond the stubborn stupidity of one man.

But it was good to know, even at this eleventh hour.

The colonel was stirring. And, once more, Cayle pressed his question.

"But how did you get into the Army? How did you become an officer in the first place?"

The drunken man said something about the Empress having a damned nerve complaining about tax money. And then there was something about the attack on the weapon shops being a damned nuisance, but that wasn't clear. Another remark about some two-timing dames who had better watch out made Cayle visualize an officer who maintained several mistresses. And then, finally came the answer to his question.

"I paid five thousand credits for my commission—damn crime . . ." He gabbled again for a minute, then, "Empress insists on giving them out for nothing right now. Won't do it. A man's got to have his graft." Indignantly, "I sure paid plenty."

"You mean," Cayle urged, "commissions are available now without money? Is that what you mean?" In his anxiety, he grabbed the man's sleeve.

The officer's eyes, which had been half closed, jerked open. They glared at Cayle suspiciously. "Who are you?" he snapped. "Get away from me." His voice was harsh, briefly almost sober. "By God," he said, "you can't travel these days without picking up some leech. I've a good mind to have you arrested."

Cayle stood up, flushing. He staggered as he walked away. He felt shaken and on the verge of panic. He was being hit too hard and too often.

The blur faded slowly from his mind. He saw that he had paused to peer into the forward cocktail bar. Seal and his companions were still there. The sight of them stiffened him and he knew why he had come back to look at them. There was a will to action growing in him, a determination not to let them get away with what they had done. But first he'd need some information.

He spun on his heel and headed straight for the weapon shop girl, who sat in one corner reading a book, a slim, handsome young woman of twenty years or so. Her eyes studied his face as he described how his money had been stolen. Cayle finished. "Here's what I want to know. Would you advise me to go to the captain?"

She shook her head. "No," she said, "I wouldn't do that. The captain and the crew receive a forty percent cut on most of these ships. They'd help dispose of your body."

Cayle leaned back in his seat. He felt drained of vitality. The trip, his first beyond Ferd, was taking toll of his strength. "How is it," he asked finally, straightening, "that they didn't pick you? Oh, I know you probably aren't wearing village type clothes, but how do they select?"

The girl shook her head. "These men," she said, "go around surreptitiously using transparencies. The first thing they discover is, if you're wearing a weapon shop gun. Then they leave you strictly alone."

Cayle's face hardened. "Could I borrow yours?" he asked tautly. "I'll show those skunks."

The girl shrugged. "Weapon shop guns are tuned to individuals," she said. "Mine wouldn't work for you. And, besides, you can use it only for defense. It's too late for you to defend yourself."

Cayle stared gloomily down through the myradel floor. The beauty below mocked him. The splendor of the towns that appeared every few minutes merely deepened his depression. Slowly the desperation came back. It seemed to him suddenly that Lucy Rall was his last hope and that he had to persuade her to help him. He said, "Isn't there anything that the weapon shops do besides sell guns?"

The girl hesitated. "We have an information center," she said finally.

"What do you mean—information? What kind of information?"

"Oh, everything. Where people were born. How much money they have. What crimes they've committed or are committing. Of course, we don't interfere."

Cayle frowned at her, simultaneously dissatisfied and fascinated. He had not intended to be distracted but for years there had been questions in his mind about the weapon shops.

And here was somebody who knew.

"But what do they do?" He said insistently. "If they've got such wonderful guns why don't they just take over the government?"

Lucy Rall smiled and shook her head. "You don't understand," she said. "The weapon shops were founded more than two thousand years ago by a man who decided that the incessant struggle for power of different groups was insane and the civil and other wars must stop forever. It was a time when the world had just emerged from a war in which more than a billion people had died and he found thousands of people who agreed to follow him. His idea was nothing less than that whatever government was in power should not be overthrown. But that an organization should be set up which would have one principal purpose—to ensure that no government ever again obtained complete power over its people. A man who felt himself wronged should be able to go somewhere to buy a defensive gun. You cannot imagine what a great forward step that was. Under the old tyrannical governments it was frequently a capital offense to be found in possession of a blaster or a gun."

Her voice was taking on emotional intensity now. It was clear that she believed what she was saying. She went on earnestly. "What gave the founder the idea was the invention of an electronic and atomic system of control which made it possible to build indestructible weapon shops and to manufacture weapons that could only be used for defense. That last ended all possibility of weapon shop guns being used by gangsters and other criminals and morally justified the entire enterprise. For defensive purposes a weapon shop gun is superior to an ordinary or government weapon. It works on mind control and leaps to the hand when wanted. It provides a defensive screen against other blasters, though not against bullets but since it is so much faster, that isn't important."

She looked at Cayle and the intentness faded from her face. "Is that what you wanted to know?" she asked.

"Suppose you're shot from ambush?" Cayle asked.

She shrugged. "No defense." She shook her head, smiling faintly. "You really don't understand. We don't worry about individuals. What counts is that many millions of people have the knowledge that they can go to a weapon shop if they want to protect themselves and their families. And, even more important, the forces that would normally try to enslave them are restrained by the conviction that it is dangerous to press people too far. And so a great balance has been struck between those who govern and those who are governed."

Cayle stared at her in bitter disappointment. "You mean that a person has to save himself? Even when you get a gun you have to nerve yourself to resist? Nobody is there to help you?"

It struck him with a pang that she must have told him this in order to show him why she couldn't help him.

Lucy spoke again. "I can see that what I've told you is a great disappointment to you. But that's the way it is. And I think you'll realize that's the way it has to be. When a people lose the courage to resist encroachment on their rights, then they can't be saved by an outside force. Our belief is that people always have the kind of government they want and that individuals must bear the risks of freedom, even to the extent of giving their lives."

There must have been an expression on his face, a reflection of the strain that was in him. For she broke off. "Look," she urged, "let me alone for a while to think over what you've told me. I won't promise anything. But I'll give you my decision before we reach our destination. All right?"

He thought it was a nice way of getting rid of him. He stood up, smiling wryly, and took an empty seat in an adjoining salon. Later, when he glanced in the doorway, the corner where she had been sitting was unoccupied.

It was that that decided him. She was evading the problem. He had been tensing again and now he climbed to his feet and headed for the forward bar.

He came upon Seal from behind and struck him a cruel blow on the side of the face. The smaller man was plummeted out of his stool and knocked to the floor. His two companions jumped to their feet. Cayle kicked the nearer man in the groin, mercilessly. The fellow moaned, and staggered, clutching his stomach.

Ignoring him, Cayle dived at the third man who was trying to get his gun from a shoulder holster. He struck the gambler with the full weight of his body and from that moment the advantage was his. It was he who secured the gun, struck savagely with it at the man's groping hand and drew blood and a cry of pain, followed by a mad scramble to break free.

Cayle whirled, in time to see Seal climb to his feet. The man rubbed his jaw and they stood staring at each other.

"Give me back my money," said Cayle. "You picked the wrong man."

Seal raised his voice. "Folks, I'm being robbed. This is the most bare-faced—"

He stopped. He must have realized that this was not a matter of being clever or reasonable. He must have realized it for he suddenly held up his hands and said quickly, "Don't shoot, you fool! After all, we didn't shoot you."

Cayle, finger on trigger, restrained himself. "My money?" he snapped.

There was an interruption. A loud voice said, "What's going on here? Put up your hands, you with the gun."

Cayle turned and backed toward the near wall. Three ship's officers with portable blasters stood just inside the door, covering him. Not once during the argument that followed did Cayle lower his own gun.

He told his story succinctly and refused to surrender. "I have reason to believe," he said, "that the officers of a ship on which such incidents can occur are not above suspicion. Now, quick, Seal, my money."

There was no answer. He sent a swift look to where Seal had been—and felt a sense of emptiness.

The gambler was gone. There was no sign of the two henchmen.

"Look," said the officer who seemed to be in command, "put up your gun and we'll forget the whole matter."

Cayle said, "I'll go out of that door." He motioned to his right. "When I'm through there I'll put up my gun."

That was agreeable and Cayle wasted no time. He searched the ship, then, from stem to stern, but found no sign of Seal or his companions. In a fury, he sought out the Captain. "You scum, you," he said coldly, "you let them get away in an airboat."

The officer stared at him coolly. "Young man," he said finally, satirically, "you are discovering that the ads are right. Travel is very educational. As a result of being aboard our ship, you have become more alert. You have discovered within yourself qualities of courage hitherto unsuspected. Within the space of a few hours, in short, you've grown up a little. The value of that in terms of survival cannot be estimated. In terms of money, you've paid a small amount. If you should desire, at some future date to pay an additional gratuity, I shall be happy to give you my address."

Cayle said, "I'll report you to your firm."

The officer shrugged. "Complaint forms are available in the lounge. You'll have to attend a hearing at our Ferd office at your own expense."

"I see," said Cayle grimly. "It works out very nicely for you, doesn't it?"

"I didn't make the rules," was the reply. "I just live under them."

Quivering, Cayle walked back to the salon where he had last seen the weapon shop girl. But she was still not in sight. He began to tense himself for the landing, now less than half an hour away. Below he could see that the shadows of approaching darkness were lengthening over the world of Isher. The whole eastern sky looked dark and misty as if out there, beyond the far horizon, night had already come.

A few minutes after Cayle had walked away from her, the girl closed her book and strolled in a leisurely fashion into a private telestat booth. She locked the door, then pulled the switch that disconnected the instrument from the main board in the captain's cabin.

She took one of the rings from her finger, manipulated it into a careful integration with the government 'stat. A woman's face took shape on the screen, said matter-of-factly, "Information Center."

"Connect me with Robert Hedrock."

"One moment, please."

The man's face that came almost immediately onto the screen was rugged rather than handsome but it looked sensitive as well as strong and there was a pride and vitality in every muscular quirk, in every movement, that was startling to see. The personality of the man poured forth from the image of him in a ceaseless, magnetic stream. His voice, when he spoke, was quiet though resonant:

"Coordination department."

"This is Lucy Rall, guardian of Imperial Potential, Cayle Clark." She went on to describe briefly what had happened to Cayle. "We measured him as a callidetic giant and are watching him in the hope that his rise will be so rapid that we can use him in our fight to prevent the empress from destroying the weapon shops with her new time weapon. This is in accord with the directive that no possibility be neglected provided there is someone available to do something about it. I think he should be given some money."

"I see." The virile face was thoughtful. "What is his village index?"

"Middling. He may have a hard time in the city for a while. But he'll get over his small town attitudes quickly. The trouble he is involved in now will toughen him. But he needs help."

There was decision on Hedrock's face. "In such cases as this the smaller the amount of money the greater the subsequent gratitude—" he smiled— "we hope. Give him fifteen credits and let him regard it as a personal loan from you. Provide no other protection of any kind. He's on his own completely. Anything else?"

"Nothing."

"Goodbye then."

It required less than a minute for Lucy Rall to restore the 'stat to its full government status.

CHAPTER SIX

CAYLE WATCHED the face of the landlady as she looked him over. *This* decision was out of his hands.

He actually thought of it as that—a decision. The question was, would she spot him as village? He couldn't be sure. Her expression, when she nodded, was enigmatic. The room she rented him was small but it cost only a credit-fourth a day.

Cayle lay down on the bed and relaxed by the rhythm system. He felt amazingly well. The theft of his money still stung but it was no longer a disaster. The fifteen credits the weapon shop girl had given him would tide him over for a few weeks. He was safe. He was in Imperial City. And the very fact that the girl had loaned him money and given him her name and address must prove something. Cayle sighed with pleasure, finally, and went out to get some supper.

He had noticed an automat at the corner. It was deserted except for a middle-aged man. Cayle bought a steak from the instantaneous cooking machine, and then deliberately sat down near the other diner.

"I'm new here," he said conversationally. "Can you give me a picture of the city? I'd appreciate it."

It was a new tack, for him, admitting naivete. But he felt very sure of himself, and very convinced that he needed data more than he needed to protect his own self-conscious pride. He was not too surprised when the stranger cleared his throat importantly and then said:

"New to the big city, eh? Been anywhere yet?"

"No. Just arrived."

The man nodded, half to himself, a faint gleam of interest in his gray eyes. Cayle thought cynically: "He's wondering how he can take advantage of me."

The other spoke again, his tone half-ingratiating now. "My name is Gregor. I live just around the corner in a skytel. What do you want to know?"

"Oh," Cayle spoke quickly, "where's the best residential district? Where's the business section? Who's being talked about?"

Gregor laughed. "That last—the empress, of course. Have you ever seen her?"

"Only on the 'stats."

"Well, you know then that she's just a kid trying hard to be tough."

Cayle knew nothing of the kind. Despite his cynicism, he had never thought of any member of the ruling family of Isher except in terms of their titles. Automatically, he rejected this man's attempt to make a human being out of Imperial Innelda.

He said, "What about the empress?"

"They've got her trapped in the palace—a bunch of old men who don't want to give up power."

Cayle frowned, dissatisfied with the picture. He recalled the last time he had seen the empress on the 'stats. It was a wilful face as he remembered it; and her voice had had in it great pride as well as determination. If any group was trying to use her as a tool, then they had better watch out. The young empress had a mind of her own.

Gregor said, "You'll want to try the games. That's on the Avenue of Luck. And then there's the theatres, and the restaurants, and—"

Cayle was losing interest. He should have known better than to expect that a casual acquaintance in a cheap residential district would be able to tell him what he wanted to know. This man had a small mind. What he had to say would not be important.

The man was continuing: "I'll be very happy to take you around. I'm a little short myself right now but—"

Cayle smiled wryly. So that was the extent of this man's machinations. It was part of the corrupt pattern of Isher life, but in this case such a mean and miserable part that it didn't matter. He shook his head and said gently:

"I'll be happy to go out some other time. Tonight, I'm kind of tired— you know, long trip—just got in."

He applied himself to his food, not at all unhappy. The conversation had done him no harm, in fact, he felt slightly better. Without ever having been in Imperial City, he had a better idea than Gregor as to what was, and what was not, sensible.

The meal cost more than he had expected. But even that he decided not to regret. After his experiences on the plane he needed sustenance. He went out onto the street contentedly. The neighborhood swarmed with children, and though it was already dark the play went on relentlessly.

Cayle paused for a moment to watch them. Their ages seemed to vary from about six to twelve years. Their play was of the group-rhythm type taught in all the schools, only this was heavily overlaid with a sex-motif that he had never seen before. He was startled, then rueful.

"Good heavens!" he thought. "I had the reputation for being a devil of a fellow. To these kids I'd be just plain naive."

He went up to his room, conscious that the young man over whom the elders of Glay had many times shaken their heads was really a simple, honest soul. He might come to a bad end but it would be because he was too innocent, not the other way around.

It disturbed him. In Glay there had been a certain pleasure in defying the conventions. In Glay he had thought of himself as being "city". Lying on the bed he knew that was true up to a point only. He lacked experience and knowledge, automatic response and awareness of dangers. His immediate plans must include remedies for these weaknesses. The vagueness of the purpose disturbed him. He had an uneasy feeling that he was making stop-gap decisions, that somehow he was not comprehending the main decision he must make one of these days.

He drifted into sleep, worrying about it. Twice, when he stirred on the edge of wakening, the thought was still there, unpleasant, urgent, a jarring background to his first night in the city of dreams. He awoke tired and unhappy. Only gradually did the uneasiness wear off.

He avoided the expensive automat, eating breakfast for a credit-eighth in a restaurant that offered personal service and featured "home" cooking. He regretted his miserliness. The weight of the indigestible meal on his stomach did not lighten until he was in the Penny Palace, an ornate gambling establishment on the world famous Avenue of Luck.

According to a guidebook which dealt exclusively with the avenue and its games, the Penny Palace owners "have put up glitter signs which modestly claim that it is possible for anyone to come in with a penny and walk out with a million, meaning, of course, a million credits." Whether or not this good fortune has ever been achieved the signs do not indicate.

The write-up concluded generously, "The Penny Palace has the distinction of having more fifty-fifty games for the number of machines it has in operation than any other establishment on the Avenue of Luck."

It was that plus the low stakes that interested Cayle. His immediate plans did not include walking out "with a million." He wanted five hundred credits to begin with. After that—well, then he could afford to enlarge his horizon.

He laid his first bet on a machine that pumped the words *odd* and *even* into a swirling pool of light. When ten of each had been pumped into the pool the liquid-looking stuff suffered a chemical change, after which it would support only one of the words on its surface. All the others sank through a screen and vanished.

The winning words floated easily face up and somehow set in motion the paying mechanism or the collecting mechanism. The bettors either saw their bets vanish with a click or else their winnings would slide automatically to the square before which they stood. Cayle heard the click of defeat.

He doubled his bet and this time won. He withdrew his original stake, and played with the coin he had won. The intricate lights fused, the pump squished, then up floated the word *even*. The pleasant sound of money sliding softly toward him assailed Cayle's ears. It was a sound that he was to hear often during the next hour and a half for, despite the fact that he played cautiously and only with pennies, he won just over five credits.

Tired at last he retreated to a connecting restaurant. When he came back into the "treasure room", as it was called, he noticed a game that was played in an even more intimate fashion by the player himself.

The money went into a slot, releasing a lever, and when this was pulled a light sequence was set up. The movement was very rapid but it resolved swiftly into red or black. The game was thus but another variation of the odd and even sequence, since the player had the same fifty-fifty chance of winning.

Cayle slipped a half credit coin into the proper slot, pulled the activating lever—and lost. His second guess was equally wrong, and his third, also. The fourth time his color shimmered into place and he had his first win. He won the next ten straight, lost four, then won seven out of another ten series. In two hours, by playing carefully, limiting his luck rather than forcing it, he won seventy-eight credits.

He withdrew to one of the bars for a drink, and pondered his next move. So many things to do—buy a new suit, protect his winnings, prepare for another night and pay back the money Lucy Rall had loaned him.

His mind poised, titillated. He felt comfortable and very sure of himself. A moment later he was putting through a 'stat call to the weapon shop girl.

Making more money could wait.

She came in almost immediately. "I'm out on the street now," she answered his request.

Cayle could see what she meant. Her face almost filled the screen. Extens-stats magnified from a tiny image. People used them on the street, keeping them connected with their home 'stats. One of the fellows in Glay had one.

Before Cayle could speak, the girl said, "I'm on my way to my apartment. Wouldn't you like to meet me there?"

Would he!

Her apartment turned out to be a four room affair, unique only in the abundance of automatic devices. After a quick look around, it was clear to Cayle that Lucy Rall never did a stroke of housework. What puzzled him, however, was that the place seemed unprotected. The girl came out of her bedroom dressed for the street and shrugged at his comment.

"We weapon shop people," she said, "live just like anyone else, usually in the nicer residential districts. Only our shops and—" she hesitated—"a few factories and, of course, the Information Center are protected from interference."

She broke off. "You said something about buying a suit. If you wish I'll help you select it. I've only two hours, though."

Cayle held the door open for her, exhilarated. The invitation to her apartment must have a personal meaning. Whatever her duties for the weapon shops, they couldn't possibly include inviting obscure Cayle Clark to her apartment, even if only for a few moments. He decided to assume that she was interested in him as an individual.

They took a carplane, Lucy pushing the button that brought the machine down to pick them up.

"Where are we going?" Cayle asked.

The girl smiled, and shook her head. "You'll see," she said. When they were in the plane, she pointed up. "Look," she said.

An artificial cloud was breaking out in the sky above. It changed colors several times, then vividly through it shone the letters: HABERDASHERY PARADISE.

Cayle said, "Why, I saw their ad last night."

He had forgotten but now he remembered. The streamers of lights had soared aloft the night before as he walked from the automat to his rooming house. Advertising Paradise. Informing males of every age that here was the place to buy, here the retail establishment that could furnish anything in men's clothing any hour of the day or night, anywhere on earth, Mars or Venus and, for a trifling extra cost, anywhere in the inhabited Solar System.

The ad had been one of hundreds—and so, in spite of his need for clothes, the name didn't remain in his memory.

"It's a store worth seeing," Lucy said.

It seemed to Cayle that she was enjoying his enjoyment. It made him feel a little naive—but not too much. What was important was that she was going with him. He ventured, "It's so kind of you to help me."

Haberdashery Paradise turned out to be more impressive than its ads. The building was three blocks long and eighty stories high. So Lucy told him; and added, "We'll go to the main sections quickly, then buy your suit."

The entrance to Paradise was a hundred yards wide, and thirty stories high. An energy screen kept the weather out but its doorless vastness was otherwise without barriers. It was easy to press through the harmless screen into the domed anteroom. The Paradise not only supplied beach clothing—it supplied a beach with a quarter of a mile of surging water tumbling from a misty horizon onto acres of sand, complete with seashells, complete with the rich, tangy smell of the sea itself. Paradise not only supplied ski outfits, it supplied startlingly lifelike mountains with a twisting half-mile of snow-covered slope.

"Paradise is a COMPLETE STORE", said one flashing sign to which Lucy called his attention. "If there is anything you do not see that fits in with our slogan, 'Everything for the Man', ask for it. We have it at a price."

"That includes women," Lucy said matter-of-factly. "They charge the same for women as they do for their suits, anywhere from five credits to fifty thousand. You'd be surprised how many women of good family register when they need money. It's all very discreet, of course."

Cayle saw that she was looking at him thoughtfully. And that he was expected to make a comment. It was so direct that he was startled. He said hastily, "I shall never pay money for a woman."

It seemed to satisfy her, for they went from there to the suits. There were thirty floors of suits but each floor had its own price range. Lucy took him to the twenty-thirty credit floor and pointed out to him the difference in weave between "city" cloth and the cloth of his own suit. For thirty-two credits he bought a suit, shirt, tie, socks and shoes.

"I don't think," said Lucy practically, "you should go any higher than that yet."

She refused his offer of the credits he owed her. "You can pay me that later on. I'd rather you put it in the bank now, as a reserve fund."

It meant he would see her again. It seemed to mean she wanted to see him again.

"Better hurry and change," said Lucy. "I'll wait."

It was that that decided him to try to kiss her before they separated. But when he came out, her first words dashed this determination. "I didn't realize how late it was," she said. "It's three o'clock."

She paused to look at him, smiled. "You're a big, strong, handsome man," she said. "Did you know? But now, let's hurry."

They separated at the Gargantuan entrance, Lucy hurrying to a carplane stop, leaving him empty behind her. The feeling departed slowly. He began to walk at a quickening pace.

By the time he came to where the Fifth Interplanetary Bank sat heavily on the base from which its ethereal spires soared to a height of sixty-four stories, ambition was surging in him again. It was a big bank in which to depost the tiny sum of fifteen credits but the money was accepted without comment, though he was required to register his fingerprints.

Cayle left the bank, more relaxed than he had been at any time since the robbery. He had a savings account. He was suitably dressed. There remained one more thing before he proceeded to the third phase of his gambling career.

From one of the public carplanes he had located the all-directional sign of a weapon shop, nestling in its private park near the bank. He walked briskly up the beflowered pathway, and he was almost at the door when he noticed the small sign, which he had never seen before in a weapon shop. The sign read:

ALL METROPOLITAN WEAPON SHOPS
TEMPORARILY CLOSED
NEW AND OLD RURAL SHOPS OPEN AS USUAL

Cayle retreated reluctantly. It was one possibility he had not expected, the fabulous weapon shops being closed. He turned as a thought came. But there was no indication as to when the shops would reopen, no date, nothing at all but the one simple announcement. He stood frowning, experiencing a sense of loss, shocked by the silence. Not, he realized that that last should be bothering him. In Glay it was always silent around the weapon shop.

The feeling of personal loss, the what-ought-he-to-do-now bewilderment grew. On impulse, he tried the door. It was solid and immovable. His second retreat began, and this time he carried through to the street.

He stood on a safety isle undecided as to what button to push. He thought back over the two and a half hours with Lucy and it seemed a curious event in space-time. He felt appalled, remembering how drab his conversation had been. And yet, except for a certain directness, a greater decisiveness, her own conversation left no dazzling memories.

"This is it," he thought. "When a girl puts up with a dull fellow for an afternoon, she's felt something."

The pressures inside him grew stronger, the will to action telescoping his plans, impelling him to swift activity. He had thought—weapon shop, more gambling, then Army District Headquarters commanded by Colonel Med-lon—over a period of a week. The weapon shop had to be first because weapon shops did not open for Imperial agents, whether soldiers or merely government employees.

But he couldn't wait for that now. He pressed the button that would bring down the first carplane going toward District Number 19.

A minute later he was on his way.

CHAPTER SEVEN

DISTRICT 19 HEADQUARTERS was an old style building of the waterfall design. The pattern was overdone, the design renewing itself at frequent intervals. Stream after marble stream poured forth from hidden crevices and gradually merged one with another.

It was not a big building, but it was big enough to give Cayle pause. Its fifteen stories and its general offices, filled with clucking file machines and clerks, were impressive. He hadn't pictured such a field of authority behind the drunken man on the plane.

The building directory listed civil functions and military functions.

Cayle presumed that he would find Colonel Medlon somewhere behind the heading: STAFF OFFICES, PENTHOUSE.

A note in brackets under the listing said: *Secure pass to penthouse elevator at reception desk on 15th floor.*

The reception department took his name, but there was a subdued consultation before a man attached it to a relayer and submitted it for the examination of an inner office authority. A middle-aged man in captain's uniform emerged from a door. He scowled at Cayle. "The colonel," he said, "doesn't like young men." He added impatiently, "Who are you?"

It didn't sound promising. But Cayle felt his own stubbornness thickening in his throat. His long experience at defying his father made it possible for him to say in a level voice, "I met Colonel Medlon on a plane to Imperial City yesterday and he insisted I come to see him. If you will please inform him that I am here—"

The captain looked at him for a full half minute. Then, without a word, he went back into the inner sanctum. He emerged, shaking his head but more friendly. "The colonel says that he does not remember you but that he will give you a minute." He lowered his voice to a whisper. "Was he—uh—under the influence?"

Cayle nodded. He did not trust himself to speak. The captain said in a low, urgent voice, "Go inside and push him for all he's worth. A very important personage has called him twice today and he wasn't in. And now you've got him nervous. He's frightened of what he says when he's under. Doesn't dare touch a drop when he's in town, you know."

Cayle followed the backstabbing captain, with one more picture of the Isher world taking form in his mind. Here was a junior officer who appeared to be maneuvering for his superior's job.

He forgot that as he stepped out of the penthouse elevator. He wondered tensely if he were capable of handling this situation. The gloomy feeling came that he wasn't. He took one look at the man who sat behind a great desk in the corner of a large room and the fear that he would be thrown bodily out of the 19th District Headquarters evaporated.

It was the same man as on the ship, but somehow shrunken. His face, which had seemed bloated when he was drunk, looked smaller. His eyes were thoughtful, and he drummed nervously on his desk.

"You may leave us alone, captain." His voice was quiet and authoritative. The captain departed with a set look on his face. Cayle sat down.

"I seem to recall your face now," said Medlon. "Sorry, I guess I had been drinking a little." He laughed hollowly.

Cayle was thinking that what the other had said about the empress must be highly dangerous for a man of his position. Aloud, he said, "I did not receive the impression of anything unusual, sir." He hesitated. "Though, when I think of it, you were perhaps too free with your confidences." Once more he paused. "I thought it was your position that made it possible for you to speak so strongly and so freely."

There was silence. Cayle had time for cautious self-congratulation but he did not delude himself. This man had not risen to his present position by being afraid or simple-minded.

"Uh—" said Colonel Medlon finally, "what did we—uh—agree on?"

"Among other things, sir," said Cayle, "you told me that the government was in need of officers and you offered me a commission."

"I do not," said Colonel Medlon, "recall the offer." He seemed to be bracing himself. "However, if I did so far forget myself as to make such an offer I have very regretfully to inform you that I have no authority to make you an officer. There is a regular procedure with regard to commissions, completely out of my hands. And since the positions are held in great esteem, the government has long regarded them as a source of financial return. For instance, a lieutenancy would cost you five thousand credits even with my influence behind you. A captaincy would disturb you to the extent of fifteen thousand credits, which is quite a sum for a young fellow to raise and—"

Cayle had been listening with a developing wryness. Looking back over his words it seemed to him that he had done his best with the material. He just wasn't in a position to make use of Medlon's indiscretions. He said with a twisted smile, "How much is a colonelcy?"

The officer guffawed. "Young fella," he said jovially, "it is not paid for in money. The price comes out of your soul, one black spot at a time."

He broke off, earnestly, "Now, look," he said. "I'm sorry if I was a little free with Her Majesty's commissions yesterday, but you understand how these things are. And just to show you I'm not a welsher, even when I'm not responsible, tell you what I'll do. You bring five thousand credits here at your convenience in, say—well, two weeks, and I'll practically guarantee you a commission. How's that?"

For a man who owned less than forty credits, it was a fairly futile attempt at a solution. If the empress had actually ordered that commissions not be sold in future, the command was being ignored by corrupt henchmen. Cayle had his second insight into the Imperial Innelda's situation.

She and her advisers were not all-powerful. He had always thought that only the weapon shops restrained her government. But the net she was caught in was more intangible than that. The vast mass of individuals who served her will had their own schemes, their own desires, which they pursued with more ardor than they served the woman to whom they had sworn allegiance.

The colonel was rustling papers on his desk. The interview was over. Cayle was about to say some final word, when the telestat on the wall behind Medlon lighted up. The face of a young woman came onto the screen.

"Colonel," she said curtly, "where the hell have you been?"

The officer stiffened. Then turned slowly. But Cayle did not need the uneasy reaction of the other man to realize who the woman was.

He was looking at the Empress of Isher.

CAYLE, WHO HAD BEEN SITTING DOWN, climbed to his feet. It was an automatic movement. Motivating it was an awareness that he was an intruder. He was halfway to the door when he saw that the woman's eyes were watching him.

"Colonel," he mumbled, "thank you for the privilege—"

His voice was a sick sound in his ears and he stopped in shame. And then he felt a surge of doubt, a disbelief that such an event could be happening to him. He looked at the woman with eyes that momentarily questioned her identity. At that moment Medlon spoke.

"That will be all, Mr. Clark," he said, too loudly.

It was the loudness that brought Cayle out of his blur of emotional reaction. He was still ashamed of himself but it was a shame of something that had happened, not of what was happening. He had a sudden picture of himself, tall and well-dressed, and not too bad looking, standing here before a drink-wrecked caricature of a man, and before *the* woman of Isher. His gaze touched her face in the 'stat without flinching. He bowed slightly, an instinctive gesture that made him feel even better.

He had no doubt now of her identity. At twenty-five the Empress Innelda was not the world's most beautiful woman. But there was no mistaking her long, distinctive face and green eyes. It was the face of the Isher family of emperors and empresses. Her voice, when she spoke again, was her 'stat voice, familiar to anyone who had ever listened to her anniversary greetings—so different, though, to have her speaking directly at him.

"What is your name, young man?"

It was Medlon who answered, quickly, his voice tense but calm. "An acquaintance of mine, Your Majesty." He turned to Cayle. "Goodbye, Mr. Clark. I enjoyed our conversation."

"I said, *what is your name?*" The woman ignored the interruption.

It was spoken so straight at him that Cayle shrank. But he gave his name.

"And why are you in Medlon's office?"

Cayle caught Medlon's eye. A tense eye, it was, striving to attract his attention. A remote part of his brain had admired Medlon's skillful earlier words. His admiration faded. The man was in a panic. Deep inside Cayle a hope started. He said, "I was inquiring about the possibility of obtaining a commission in Your Majesty's armed forces."

"I thought so," said the empress in a level voice. She paused. She looked thoughtfully from Cayle to Medlon, then back to Cayle. Her skin was a smooth, light tan in color. Her head was proudly held. She looked young and alive and gloriously confident. And something of her experience in handling men showed then. Instead of asking Cayle the next question, she gave Medlon a way out.

"And may I ask, Colonel, what your answer was?"

The officer was rigid, perspiring. But in spite of that his voice was calm and there was even an edge of joviality in it as he said, "I informed him, Your Majesty, that his commission would require about two weeks to put through." He laughed deprecatingly. "As you know, there is a certain amount of red tape."

Cayle felt himself riding a tide that was lifting him higher and higher. Because the benefits of this were for him. He felt an unnatural admiration for the Empress—she was so different from what he had expected. It amazed him that she would restrain herself so as not to embarrass one of her officers virtually caught in a misdemeanor.

The restraint did not keep the sarcasm out of her voice, however, as she said, "Yes, Colonel, I know but too well. This whole rigmarole is only too familiar to me." Passion replaced the sarcasm. "Somehow or other, the young men who normally buy their way into the army have heard that something is up and so they remain away in droves. I am beginning to suspect there is a pro-weapon shop conspiracy to put off the few likely prospects who do turn up."

Her eyes flashed with green fires. It was apparent that she was angry and that the restraints were off. She turned to Cayle.

"Cayle Clark," she said in a ringing voice, "how much were you asked to pay for your commission?"

Cayle hesitated. Medlon's eye was a terrible thing to see, it was so dark. His half-turned head seemed unnatural in the way it was twisted. The message in that abnormal eye needed no words. The colonel was regretting everything he had said to the prospective lieutenant of Her Majesty's Imperial Army.

The appeal was so great that Cayle felt repelled. He had never before experienced the sensation of having a man completely at his mercy. It made him cringe. Abruptly, he didn't want to look. He said, "Your Majesty, I met Colonel Medlon on the Inter-State yesterday and he offered me a commission without any strings attached."

He felt better for the words. He saw that the officer was relaxing and that the woman was smiling with pleasure.

"Well, Colonel," she said, "I'm glad to hear that. And, since it answers in a satisfactory fashion what I was going to talk to you about, you have my felicitations. That is all."

The screen clicked into blankness. Colonel Medlon sank slowly back into his chair. Cayle walked forward, smiling. The colonel said in a level voice, "It has been a pleasure to meet you, young man. But now, I am very busy. I certainly hope I shall be hearing from you in the next two weeks with the five thousand. Goodbye."

Cayle did not move immediately, but the bitterness of the defeat was already upon him. Out of the darkness of his thoughts came the consciousness that to him had come an improbable opportunity. And he had nullified it by being weak. He had believed that an amoral wretch would be grateful for being saved from exposure. He saw that the colonel, looking quite jaunty, was eyeing him with amusement.

"The Empress doesn't understand the problem involved in ending a system of paid commissions." Medlon shrugged. "I have nothing to do with it myself. I can no more alter it that I can cut my throat. One man would destroy himself bucking it." He hesitated. A sneer came into his face. "My friend," he said, "I hope this has been a lesson to you in the economics of personal advancement." He finished curtly. "Well, good day."

Cayle decided against attacking the man physically. This was a military building, and he had no intention of being arrested for assault where he could not properly defend himself. In his mind he marked the colonel down for further attention at a later date.

Darkness was settling over the city of the Ishers when he finally emerged from District 19 Headquarters. He looked up at the cold fixed stars through a mist of ads, and felt much more at home than he had the night before. He was beginning to see his way through the maze of existence on this world. And it seemed to him that he had come through very well, considering his ignorance. All around him, the sidewalks began to give off the sunlight they had absorbed during the day. The night waxed brighter as the heavens above grew darker. He became more confident as he walked. He had been right to attack Seal regardless of risks, and he had been right to hold back on Medlon. Seal was an individual out in the open as he was, and basically no one cared what happened to him. But the colonel could call on the power of Isher law.

He had not intended to return to the Avenue of Luck until morning. But now having, it seemed to him, resolved his inner doubts, he changed his mind. If he could win five thousand credits and buy a commission, the treasures of Isher would start pouring in his direction. And Lucy Rall—he mustn't forget Lucy.

Even one day was too long to wait.

CHAPTER NINE

CAYLE HAD TO PUSH HIS WAY through throngs of human beings in order to enter the Penny Palace. The size of the crowds encouraged him. In this mass of money-hungry humanity he would be like a piece of driftwood in a vast ocean.

He did not hesitate. He had looked over the games earlier and he headed straight toward the one he wanted for his final bid for fortune. It would be important, he thought, to gain a playing position and stick to it.

The new game paid odds as high as a hundred to one and as low as five to one. It worked in a comparatively simple fashion, though Cayle, who knew something of the energies, having worked in his father's shop since before he was fifteen, realized there was electronic intricacy behind the deceptive appearance of artlessness. A ball of force was the core. It was about an inch in diameter and it rolled erratically inside a larger plastic ball. Faster, faster, faster it darted over the inner surface, until its speed transcended the resistance of matter. Then, like the pure force it was, it burst the limitations of its prison. Through the plastic it plunged, as if there were nothing there, as if it were a beam of light that had been imprisoned by an unnatural physical law in an almost invisible cage.

And yet, the moment it was free, it grew afraid. It changed color, subtly, swiftly, and it slowed. Its speed of escape must have been miles a second but so great was its fear that it stopped completely after traveling less than three feet.

It began to fall. And until that moment of fall, until it almost touched the table, it gave an illusion of being everywhere. It was an illusion entirely inside the minds of the players, a product of enormous velocity and mental hallucination. Each player had the conviction that the ball was flying straight toward him, that when it fell it would fall into the channel he had activated with a number. It was inevitable that the majority of the gamblers were due for disappointment when the ball, its mission accomplished, dropped into a channel and activated the odds mechanism.

The very first game in which Cayle participated paid him thirty-seven credits for his one. He raked in his winnings with an attempt at casualness but the shock of victory overflowed along his nerves in spasms of excitement. He placed a credit each in four channels, lost, then bet the same numbers again and won ninety credits. During the next hour he won on an average once in five times. He recognized that this luck was phenomenal even for him—and long before the hour was up he was risking ten credits in each channel that he played.

At no time did he have an opportunity to count his money. At intervals, he would thrust a handful of credits into the automatic changer and receive large bills, which he would press into an inner pocket. Not once did he draw on his reserves. After awhile, he thought in a curious panic, "I must have three or four thousand credits. It's time to quit. It's not necessary to win the whole five thousand in one night. I can come back tomorrow and the day after and day after that."

It was the speed of the game that confused him. Each time the impulse came, that it was time to think of stopping his play, the ball would start to whirl and he would hastily drop money into several channels. If he lost, irritation would come, and a greedy determination not to leave behind even a penny of his winnings.

If he won, it seemed ridiculous to stop in the middle of the most amazing streak of luck that he could ever hope to have. Wait, he told himself, till he lost ten in a row . . . ten in a row . . . ten . . . Somewhere along there he had a glimpse of a wad of forty or fifty one-thousand credit notes which he had put in his side pocket. There was more money in other pockets—and again and again, without being more than blurrily aware of the fact, he would strew large bills at random in various channels. How much he couldn't remember. Nor did it matter. The machine always counted accurately and paid him the right odds.

He was swaying now like a drunken man. His body seemed to be floating above the floor. He played on in an emotional mist almost oblivious of others. He did become conscious that more and more players were riding his luck, calling up his numbers in their own channels. But that was unimportant and personally meaningless. He did not come out of his daze until the ball plunked down like a dead thing in its cage. He stood stolid, waiting for the game to begin again, unaware that he had anything to do with its stopping until a plump, dark man came forward.

The stranger said with an oily smile, "Congratulations, young man, we welcome your patronage. We are happy for you—but for these other ladies and gentlemen we have bad news. The rules of this house, which are conspicuously posted in our fine establishment, do not permit luck riders, as we call them. This fortunate young man's trend of luck has been definitely established. Henceforth, all other bets must be placed before the 'winner' makes his choice. The machine has been set to react accordingly. So do not cause yourself disappointment by making a last-second wager. It will not work. And now, good luck to all of you and especially to you, young man."

He waddled off, still smiling. A moment later, the ball was whirling again.

It was during the third game that Cayle thought out of nothingness: "Why, I'm the center of attention." It startled him. He had come out of that oblivion on which he had counted to maintain his security. "I'd better slip out of here as quietly as possible," he thought.

He turned from the table—and a pretty girl threw her arms around him, pressed tightly against him and kissed him.

"Oh, please, let me have some of your luck. Please, please."

He disentangled himself blankly, the original impulse forgotten. "I was going to do something," he remembered and laid several bets while he frowned over the elusive memory. He was aware that newcomers were jostling up to the table, sometimes forcibly crowding out the less resourceful and determined of those who had been there first. Once, when he noticed a particularly violent ejection of a vociferously protesting player, the warning thought ticked again in his head that he and this table were now plainly marked by a thousand avid eyes.

He couldn't recall just what it was he wanted to do about that. There seemed to be a lot of women around, plucking at him with their fingers, kissing him if he turned his head, and he had a sense of an over-abundance of their perfume.

He couldn't move his hands without a woman's bare skin being available for his touch—naked arms, naked backs, and dresses cut so low in front that he was constantly having his head drawn down into soft, daintily perfumed bosoms. When he bent an inch for a natural reason the ever-present hands pulled him the rest of the way.

And still the night and his luck did not end. He had a sense of too much pleasure, too much applause at every spin, at every win. And whether he won or not women flung themselves into embraces with him and either kissed him commiseratingly or in a frenzy of delight. Wild music played in the background. He was twenty-three years old and the attack on every sense of his body overwhelmed his caution. When he had won uncountable thousands of credits the doors of the Penny Palace closed and the roly-poly man came over and spoke curtly.

"All right," he said, "that's enough. The place is cleared of strangers and we can stop this nonsense."

Cayle stared at him, and the clock of danger was ticking so loudly that his whole brain hummed with the sound. "I think," he mumbled, "I'll go home."

Somebody slapped his face—hard. "Again," said the plump man. "He's still riding an emotional jag." The second blow was harder. Cayle came out of his haze with a sharp comprehension that he was in deadly peril.

"What's going on here?" he stammered. His eyes appealed to the people who had been cheering him only minutes before. The people whose presence had lulled him . . . It was impossible that anything would be done against him while they were around.

He whirled on the plump man. And then stood rigid as rough hands grabbed him and rougher hands probed in the pockets of his clothes relieving him of his winnings. As from a great distance he heard the plump man speak again.

"Don't be naive. There is nothing unusual about what has happened. All the regular players have been squeezed out. Not only out of the game, but out of the building. The thousand people in here now are hired for such occasions and cost us ten credits each. That's only ten thousand altogether, and you won from fifty to a hundred times as much as that." He shrugged. "People don't realize the economics of such things. Next time, don't be so greedy." He smiled an oily smile. "That is, if there is a next time."

Cayle found his voice. "What are you going to do?"

"You'll see." His voice went up. "All right, men, take him to the truck-plane and we'll open up again."

Cayle felt himself irresistibly hustled across the room and into a dark corridor. He was thinking in despair that, once again, he had put himself into a position where other men decided his fate.

INTERLUDE

McAllister, reported from 1951, realized that he was lying on a sidewalk. He climbed to his feet. A group of curious faces gawked at him; and there was no park, no magical city of the future. Instead, a bleak row of one-story shops made a dull pattern on either side of the street.

A man's voice floated toward him out of a blur of other sounds: "I'm sure it's the reporter who went into that weapon shop."

So he was back in his own time. Perhaps even the same day. As he moved slowly away, the same penetrating voice said, "He looks kind of sick. I wonder what—"

He heard no more. But he thought, "Sick!" These people would never understand how sick. But somewhere on earth must be a scientist who could help him. The record was that he hadn't exploded.

He was walking rapidly now, and clear of the crowd. Once, he looked back, and saw that the people were dispersing in the aimless fashion of folk who had lost their center of interest. McAllister turned a corner, and forgot them.

"I've got to decide."

The words were loud, close. It took a moment to realize that he had spoken them.

Decide? He hadn't thought of his position as requiring a decision. Here he was. Find a scientist . . . If that was a decision, he had already made it. The question was, who? Memory came of his old physics professor at City College. Automatically, he turned into a phone booth and fumbled for a nickel. With a sickening sense of disaster, he remembered that he was dressed in an all-enclosing, transparent suit, and that his money was inside. He drew back, then stopped, shaken. *What was happening?*

It was night, in a brilliant, glowing city. He was standing on the boulevard of an avenue that stretched jewel-like into remote distance. It was a street that flamed with a soft light gleaming up from its surface—a road of light, like a river flowing under a sun that shone nowhere else, straight and smooth.

He walked along for uncomprehending minutes, fighting a wild hope, but at last the thought forced through to his consciousness: Was this again the age of Isher and the gunmakers? It could be. It looked right, and it meant they had brought him back. After all, they were not evil, and they would save him if they could. For all he knew, weeks had passed in their time.

He began to hurry. Find a weapon shop. A man walked by him, and McAllister turned and called after him. The man paused curiously, and looked back, then continued on his way. McAllister had a brief picture of dark, intense eyes, and a visualization of a person on his way to a marvellous home of the future. It was that that made him suppress his impulse to run after the man.

Afterwards, he realized he should have. It was the last person he saw on all those quiet, deserted streets. It must have been the in-between hour before the false dawn, and no one was abroad. Oddly, it was not the absence of human life that disturbed. It was the fact that not once did he see a weapon shop.

In spite of that, his hope mounted. Soon it would be morning. Men would come out of these strange, glowing homes. Great scientists of an age of wizard scientists would examine him, not in a frenzy of haste, with the fear of destruction hanging over their heads. But quietly, in the sanity of super-laboratories.

The thought ended. He felt the *change.*

He was in the center of a blinding snow storm. He staggered from the first mighty, unexpected blow of that untamed wind. Then, bracing himself, he fought for mental and physical calm.

The shining, wondrous night city was gone. Gone also the glowing road. Both vanished, transformed into this deadly, wilderness world. He peered through the driving snow. It was daylight, and he could make out the dim shadows of trees that reared up through the white mist of blizzard less than fifty feet away. Instinctively, he pressed toward their shelter and stood finally, out of that blowing, pressing wind. He thought: "One minute in the distant future; the next—where?"

There was certainly no city. Only trees, and uninhabited forest and a bitter, primeval winter. How long he stood there, while those winds blew and that storm raged, he had no idea. He had time for a thousand thoughts, time to realize that the suit protected him from the cold as if there was no cold; and then—

The blizzard was gone. And the trees. He stood on a sandy beach. Before him stretched a blue, sunlit sea that rippled over broken, white buildings. All around, scattered far into that shallow, lovely sea, far up into the weed-grown hills, were the remnants of a once tremendous city. Over all clung an aura of incredible age, and the silence of the long-dead was broken only by the gentle, timeless lapping of the waves.

Again came that instantaneous transition. More prepared this time, he nevertheless sank twice under the surface of the vast, swift river that carried him on and on. It was hard swimming, but the insulated suit was buoyant with the air it manufactured each passing second. And, after a moment, he began to struggle purposely toward the tree-lined shore a hundred feet to his right. A thought came, and he stopped swimming. "What's the use!" The truth was as simple as it was terrible. He was being shunted from the past to the future. He was the "weight" on the long end of an energy seesaw; and in some way he was slipping further ahead and further back each time. Only that could explain the catastrophic changes he had already witnessed. In an hour would come another change.

It came. He was lying face downward on green grass. When he looked up, he saw a half dozen low-built buildings on the horizon of grass. They looked alien, unhuman. But his curiosity was not about them. A thought had come: How long, actually, did he remain in one particular time?

He kept an eye on his watch; and the time was two hours and forty minutes. That was his last curiosity. Period after period, as the seesaw jerked on, he remained in his one position, water or land, it made no difference to him. He did not fight it. He neither walked nor ran nor swam nor even sat up . . . Past—future—past—future—

His mind was turned inward. He had a vague feeling that there was something he ought to do, inside his skin, not outside. Something about a decision he had believed he must make. Funny, he couldn't recall what it was.

Beyond doubt, the gunmakers had won their respite. For at the far end of this dizzy teeter-totter was the machine that had been used by the Isher soldiers as an activating force. It too teetered past, then future, in this mad seesaw.

But that decision. He'd really have to try to think about it . . .

CHAPTER TEN

AT TEN MINUTES OF MIDNIGHT, July 16, 4748 Isher, the door of the coordination department of the weapon makers, in the Hotel Royal Ganeel, opened. Robert Hedrock came out and strode along a wide bright corridor that stretched off into the distance ahead of him. He moved with an almost catlike alertness but actually his attention was not on his surroundings.

Little more than a year ago he had applied for weapon shop membership, his given reason being that he expected a crisis between government and weapon shop forces and that he desired to be on the weapon shop side. His papers were in order, the Pp machine gave him so high a rating in every mental, physical and moral category that his file was immediately brought to the attention of the weapon shop executive council. From the beginning he was on special duty and his assignment to the coordination department during an emergency was merely a normal step in his metric rise to weapon shop power.

Hedrock was aware that a few members of the council and a number of the top executives considered his ascent too rapid and not in the best interests of the weapon shops. That he was even regarded by some as a mysterious figure, though no sinister connotations were intended by the critics. No one actually questioned the verdict of the Pp machine in his favor, which puzzled him at times. At some later date, he decided, he would investigate the machine much more carefully and discover just why normally skeptical men accepted its judgements without question.

It had proved inordinately simple for him to fool it, lie to it, tell it his carefully doctored story.

True, he had special control of his mind and abnormal technical knowledge of machine reaction to biological processes. There was also the overruling fact of his friendliness to the weapon shops—which undoubtedly helped. The Pp machine, he had been told, had the weapon shop door's unique sensitivity for recognizing hidden hostility. And its basic structure included the ability, also built into every gun, to recognize and react within limitations. Like the weapons that would not kill except in self-defense, or under other restrictions, its intricately acute electronic senses perceived minute differences in the reactions of every part of the examined body. It was an invention that had been developed since the last time he had been a member of the weapon shops a hundred-odd years before. It was new to him. And their dependence on it made it necessary for Robert Hedrock,

Earth's one immortal man, friend of the weapon shops, to make sure it was as effective a safeguard as they thought.

But that was for later. It was the least of the problems confronting him. He was a man who had to make up his mind, how soon was not yet clear— but all too soon it seemed to him. The first great attack of the youthful Empress had already closed the weapon shops in every large city on Earth. But even that was secondary compared to the problem of the endless see-saw. He could not escape the conviction that only he, of all the human beings on earth, was qualified to make the decision about *that*. And he still had not an idea of what to do.

His thought reached that point, as he came to the door marked *Private— Executives Only*, his destination. He knocked; waited the necessary seconds, then entered without further preliminary.

It was a curiously arranged room in which he found himself. Not a large room, by Isher standards, but large enough. It was so close to being a 200-foot cube that Hedrock's eyes could not detect the difference. Its most curious feature was that the door, through which he entered, was about a hundred feet above the floor with the ceiling an equal distance higher. There was a platform just inside the door. From it projected an energy plane. Hedrock stepped into one of the pairs of insulators on the platform. The moment he felt them grip his shoes he walked out onto the vaguely glowing lattice-work of force.

In the center of the room (center on height-depth as well as length-width level) seven weapon shop councilors were standing around a machine that floated in a transparent plastic case. They greeted Hedrock briefly, then returned their attention to the machine. Hedrock watched them silently, conscious of their intense, unnormal depression. Beside him Peter Cadron whispered, "It's almost time for another swing."

Hedrock nodded. And slowly, as he gazed at the wizard mechanism floating in its vacuumized case, their absorption communicated itself to him. It was a map of time. A map of inter-crossed lines so finely drawn that they seemed to waver like heat waves on a torrid day.

Theoretically the lines extended from a central point into the infinite past and the infinite future (with the limitation that in the mathematics employed, infinity was almost zero). But after several trillion years the limitation operated to create a blurred effect, which was enhanced by the unwillingness of the eyes to accept the image. On that immense ocean of time, the shadowy shapes, one large and very near the center, one a mere speck on the curving vastness of the map, lay moveless. Hedrock knew that the speck was a magnified version of the reality, which was too small to make out with the naked eye. The image had been so organized that its every movement was followed by a series of magnifiers. These instruments were attuned to separate sensitive energies and adjusted automatically to the presence of additional onlookers.

As Hedrock watched with pitying eyes both shadows moved. It was a movement that had no parallel in macrocosmic space—a movement so alien that the vision could not make an acceptable image. It was not a particularly swift process but, in spite of that, both shadows—withdrew. Where? Even the weapon shop scientists had never quite decided that. They withdrew and then slowly reappeared, but now their positions were reversed, with variations.

They were farther out. The large shadow, which had been wavering one month and three days from the center in the *past*, was suddenly a month and three days and a few hours in the *future*. The tiny speck, which had been 97 billion years in the future, reversed to about 106 billion years in the past.

The time distance was so colossal that Hedrock shrank in spite of himself and half turned to Cadron. "Have they figured out his energy potential?"

Cadron nodded wearily. "Enough to destroy the planet." He groaned. "Where in the name of space are we going to release it?"

Hedrock tried to picture that. He had not been among those who talked to McAllister, the reporter from the twentieth century. His understanding of what had happened had been pieced together from fragmentary accounts. And one of his purposes in coming to this room now was to learn the details.

He drew Cadron aside and frankly asked for information. Cadron gazed at him with a wry smile. "All right," he said, "I'll tell you. The truth is, all of us are ashamed of the way we acted."

Hedrock said. "Then you feel that McAllister should not have been sacrificed?"

Cadron shook his head. "No, that isn't exactly what I mean." His frown deepened. "I guess the best method is to tell you the whole story—briefly, of course."

He began. "The girl attendant of the Greenway shop heard someone come and went out to attend to him. The customer was a queer looking chap in outlandish clothes. It turned out that he was a newspaper reporter from the twentieth century A.D. He was so obviously disconcerted, so fascinated by the showcases with their energy guns. And he gave an account of a weapon shop having appeared in a street in the little city in which he lived. I can imagine the sensation it caused but the truth is that everybody thought it was an illusion of some kind.

"It seemed solid, of course. But when the police tried to open the door, naturally it wouldn't open. McAllister, with a reporter's curiosity, finally tried the door himself. For him, of course—he not being a police or government official—it opened immediately. He went inside.

"He admitted to the attendant experiencing a sense of tension as he crossed the threshold and, though he didn't know it, it was at that moment that he picked up the first measure of time-energy, the equivalent of approximately seven thousand years—his weight being the other factor. When the attendant told her father—who was in charge of the shop—what had occurred, he realized immediately that something was wrong. In a few minutes he had verified that the shop was being subjected to titanic energy pressure. He discovered that the source of the energy was the huge government building on an adjoining street. He immediately called the weapon makers into council.

"By the time we arrived on the scene a swift decision was necessary.

McAllister had enough time energy locked up in his body to destroy the entire city—that is if he ever stepped outside our insulated shop without himself being insulated. Meanwhile, the pressure from the government building against our shop continued unabated. At any moment it might succeed in precipitating the shop itself into the time stream, and there was reason to believe that other attacks would be made at any moment on our shops everywhere. No one could guess what the result would be. To cut a long story short we saw a way to gain time by focussing the energy of the building upon McAllister and tossing him back into his own time. We could do this by putting him into an insulated space suit which would prevent him from exploding until we could develop a mechanism for that purpose.

"We knew that he would seesaw back and forth in time, shifting the government building and its energies out of this space-time area."

Cadron shook his head gloomily. "I still don't see what else we could have done. We were compelled to act swiftly in a field where no great knowledge is available, and the fact that we merely got out of the frying pan and into the fire was just our hard luck. But personally I feel very badly about the whole thing."

"Do you think McAllister is still alive?" Hedrock asked.

"Oh yes. The suit into which we put him was one of our supers, complete with an eight ring food-making device, and there's a cup in it that's always full of water. The other facilities are equally automatic."

He smiled a twisted smile. "We had an idea, completely false as it turned out, that we could save him at some later date."

"I see," said Hedrock. He felt depressed. It was unfortunate but all the decisions had been made before he had even heard of the danger.

The newsman was now the juggernaut of juggernauts. In all the universe there had never been anything like the power that was accumulating, swing by swing, in his body. Released, the explosion would rock the fabric of space. All time would sigh to its echoes and the energy tensions that created the illusion of matter might collapse before the strain.

"What's the latest about the building?" Hedrock asked.

Cadron was more cheerful. "It's still within its critical limits. We've got to make our decision before it reaches the danger stage."

Hedrock was silent. The matter of what the decision should be was a sore point with him, who was obviously not going to be asked. He said finally. "What about the men who are working on the problem of slowing the swings and bringing the seesaw back this way?"

Another man answered that. "The research is abandoned. Science four thousand seven hundred and eighty-four has no answer. We're lucky enough to have made one of our shops the fulcrum. We can set off the explosion anywhere in the past or future. But which? And when? Particularly when?"

The shadows on that cartograph made no movement, gave no sign. *Their* time of action was not yet.

THE STRAIN ATTENDANT on watching another swing faded. The men were turning away from the map, and there was a murmur of conversation. Somebody said something about using the opportunity to acquire all the possible data on time travel. Councilor Kendlon remarked that the body's accumulation of energy was fairly convincing proof that time travel would never be popular.

It was Dresley, the precise, the orderly, who finally remarked, "Gentlemen, we are here as delegates of the Council to listen to Mr. Hedrock's report of the counterattack against the Empress. In his report some weeks ago he was able to give us administrative details. And you will recall that we found his organization set-up to be efficient in the extreme. Mr. Hedrock, will you now bring us up to date?"

Hedrock glanced from person to person thoughtfully. He saw that they were watching him, and that raised his necessity level. His problem, it seemed to him, was to make up his own mind about the seesaw, then carry out his decision without regard for the attitude of his nominal superiors. It would be difficult.

He began succinctly, "Since the first directive was given me, we have set up one thousand two hundred and forty-two new shops, primarily in small villages, and three thousand eight hundred and nine contacts have been established, however tenuous in some cases, with imperial government personnel, both military and civil."

He explained briefly his system of classifying the various individuals into groups on the basis of vocation, degree of importance and, what was more important, pitch of enthusiasm for the venture into which the Empress had precipitated her adherents.

"From three scientists," Hedrock went on, "who regard the weapon shops as an integral part of Isher civilization, we gained in the first ten days the secret of the science behind the time-energy machine in so far as that science is known to the government. We discovered that, of the four generals in charge of the enterprise, two were opposed to it from the beginning, a third was won over when the building disappeared—but the fourth, General Doocar, the man in charge, unfortunately will not abandon the attack until she does. He is an Empress man in the sense of personal loyalty transcending his own feelings and opinions.

He paused, expecting them to comment. But no one said anything. Which was actually the most favorable response of all. Hedrock continued, "Some thousands of officers have deserted the Imperial forces, but only one member of the Imperial Council, Prince del Curtin, openly opposed the attack after the execution of Banton Vickers who, as you know, criticized the whole plan.

And the prince's method of disapproval has been to withdraw from the palace while the attack is in progress.

"Which brings us," said Hedrock, "to the Empress herself." He summarized her character for them. The glorious Innelda, an orphan since her eleventh birthday, had been crowned when she was eighteen and was now twenty-five. "An age," said Hedrock grimly, "which is an in-between stage in the development of the animal man to human man levels."

He saw that they were puzzled by his reiteration of facts they all knew. But he had no intention of condensing his account. He had his own formula for defeating the Empress and he wanted to state it at least once in as skilful a fashion as possible. "At twenty-five," he said, "our Innelda is emotional, unstable, brilliant, implacable, impatient of restrictions on her desires and just a bit unwilling to grow up. As the thousands of reports came in, it seemed to me finally that our best method of dealing with such a person was to leave channels along which she could withdraw gracefully when the crises came."

He looked around, questioningly. He was keenly aware that, with these men he dared not try to put his ideas over in a disguised form. He said frankly, "I hope that Council members will not take it amiss if I recommend for their consideration the following basic tactic. I am counting on some opportunity occurring of which we can take advantage and so bring her whole war machine to a stop. My assumption is that once it has stopped the Empress will busy herself with other matters and conveniently forget all about the war she started."

Hedrock paused in order to give weight to his next words. "My staff and I will watch anxiously for the opportunity and will call your attention to anything that seems to have possibilities. And now, are there any questions?"

The first few were minor. Then a man said, "Have you any notion as to what form this so-called opportunity will take?"

Hedrock said carefully, "It would be difficult to go into all the avenues that we are exploring. This young woman is open on many fronts to persuasion and to pressure. She is having a hard time with recruits for the army. She is still subject to the connivances and intrigues of a group of older people who are reluctant to accept her as an adult. They withhold information from her. Despite her efforts to keep in touch with what is going on, she is caught in an old, old net: Her communication with the real world is snarled up." Hedrock finished, "In one way or another we are trying to take advantage of these various weaknesses."

The man who had already spoken said, "This is only a formula."

"It is a formula," said Hedrock, "based on my study of the character of the Empress."

"Don't you think you had better leave such studies to the Pp machine experts and to the No-men?"

"I examined all the weapon shop data on the lady before offering my suggestion."

"Still," said the man, "it is up to the elected Council to make decisions in such matters."

Hedrock did not back down. "I have made a suggestion," he said, "not a decision."

The man said nothing more. But Hedrock had his picture of a Council of very human members, jealous of their prerogatives. These people would not easily accept his decision, when he finally made it, on the problem of the seesaw drama that was being played to its still undetermined conclusion in ever remoter bends of time.

He saw that his audience was becoming restless. Eyes turned involuntarily toward the time map and several men glanced anxiously at their watches. Hastily Hedrock withdrew from the room with its almost invisible energy floors. Watching that pendulum could become a drug. The brain itself would be weakened by the strain of attending a mechanism which recorded the spasms of real bodies in their movements through time itself.

It was bad enough to know that the building and the man were swinging steadily back and forth.

He arrived back in his office just in time to catch a 'stat call-up from Lucy. ". . . in spite of my efforts," she said, "I was forced out of the Penny Palace. And when the doors shut I knew what was going to happen. I'm afraid he was taken to one of the houses of illusion, and you know what that means."

Hedrock nodded thoughtfully. He noted sharply that the girl seemed disturbed by her experience. "Among other things," he said slowly, "the illusion energies have some qualifying effect on callidity. The nature of the modification cannot be determined without subsequent measurement but it can be stated with reasonable certainty that his luck will never again take the direction of success at gambling."

He had delayed his reaction while he examined her face. Now he said with decision, "It is unfortunate that Clark has fallen prey to all these pitfalls of the city so easily. But since he was never more than a long-run possibility we can let him go without regret, particularly—and this cannot be stressed too often—as even the slightest interference in the natural progression of his life would cause later suspicion that would nullify any good he might do us.

"You may accordingly consider yourself detached from him. Further instructions will be given you in due course." He paused. "What's the matter, Lucy? Got an emotional fixation on him?"

Her expression left no doubt of it. Hedrock pressed on quietly, "When did you discover it?"

Whatever resistance had been in her, whatever fear of discovery, was gone. "It was when those other women were kissing him. You mustn't think," she added hastily, "that disturbed me. He'll go through quite a lot of it before he settles down."

"Not necessarily," said Hedrock earnestly. "You'll have to resign yourself to the house of illusion but it has been my observation that a fair percentage of men emerge from such an experience hard as steel in some respects but rather weary of worldliness."

He realized from her face that he had said enough. The groundwork for her future action was established. Results would follow in the natural course of events. He smiled a friendly smile. "That's all for now, Lucy. Don't let it get you down."

Her image and his faded from the screen in a flash.

Robert Hedrock glanced out of the door of his office several times during the next hour. At first the corridors seemed very busy. Gradually the activity died down and at last the corridor was clear.

He acted now with decision but without haste. From a wall safe he took the micro-film plans of the time control machine—the one in the room where he had talked to the weapon shop councilors a little more than two hours before. He had requested Information Center to send them to him and they had done so without comment. There was nothing unusual in their compliance. As head of the coordination department he had access to all the scientific knowledge of the weapon shops. He even had an explanation as to why he wanted the plans in the event that he were asked. He wanted to study them, so his story would go, in the hope that some solution would suggest itself. But his reasons were private and his purpose personal.

With the films in his pocket he headed along the corridor toward the nearest stairway. He went down five flights and came to a section of the Hotel Royal Ganeel that was not occupied by the weapon shops. He unlocked an apartment door, went inside, and locked the door behind him.

It was an imposing suite, as befitted an executive of the weapon shops— five rooms and a tremendous library. He went straight to the library, closed and locked the door, then carefully examined the place for spying devices. There were none, which was what he expected. As far as he knew he was not under suspicion. But he never took unnecessary chances.

Swiftly he held one of the rings on his finger against an ordinary looking electric socket. A loop of metal slid out. He inserted his finger into the loop and pulled. What happened in that moment was an ordinary enough weapon shop phenomenon. He was transmitted by a weapon shop matter transmitter a distance of about eleven hundred miles into one of his numerous laboratories. What was out of the ordinary about the action was that the presence of the transmitter was not known to the weapon shop council. The laboratory had for centuries been one of his many closely-guarded secret retreats.

He decided that he could safely remain an hour. But that all he could hope to do in one night was to make another print of the microfilm. Building a duplicate machine would require many visits such as this. As it turned out he had time to make an extra print of the plans. Very carefully he put the additional copy into a vault filing case, there to join the tens of thousands of other diagrams and plans to which, over a period of several thousand years, he had given an AA priority.

At the end of the hour, Earth's one immortal man, founder of the weapon shops, possessor of secrets unknown to any other living human being, returned to the library of his apartment in the Hotel Royal Ganeel.

Presently he was back in his office, five flights farther up.

Lucy rall emerged from the government 'stat booth, and she was hurrying through an alcove when she caught a glimpse of herself in an energy mirror. She stopped. The outside lights beckoned. The sidewalks were aglow with a brightness that defied the night. But she stood there in front of the reverse image of herself and stared at her pale face and tensed eyes.

She had always thought of herself as goodlooking, but the face that confronted her was too drawn to be pretty. She thought, "Is *that* what Mr. Hedrock saw?"

Out on the street, finally, she walked uncertainly along. She had made her call from a booth in one of the gambling palaces and the flashing brilliance of the famous Avenue of Luck was unabated. Magic street still, alive with swarms of human moths fluttering from one light source to another. The lights themselves blazed day and night, but the crowds would gradually fade away as the darkness of the upper skies waned. It was time for her also to go home. But she lingered in an unnatural indecision, knowing she could do nothing, wondering what she could do. The inner conflict drained her strength and twice within an hour she paused for energy drinks.

There was something else, also, a sense of personal disaster. She had always taken it for granted that she would eventually marry a weapon shop man. All through school and college, when her own application for membership was already approved, she had considered all others—the ordinary people—as outsiders. She thought with a piercing comprehension, "It was that moment on the ship when he was in trouble. I was sorry for him."

He was in deeper trouble now. If she could possibly locate the house he had been taken to, she would—what? Her mind paused. She felt astounded at the forcefulness of the idea that came. Why, it was ridiculous. If she went to one of those places she would have to go through with an illusion, mentally *and* physically.

It seemed to her, shakily, that the weapon shops would separate her from their organization for even considering such a thing. But when her mind automatically flashed back over the fine print of the documents she had signed, she couldn't recall any prohibition. In fact, some of the sentences, as she remembered them, were positively sensational when examined in her present situation:

". . . Weapon Shop people may marry according to their desire . . . participate in, or partake of, any vice or pleasure of Isher for personal reasons . . . There are no restrictions on the use made of a member's spare time by the member . . .

"It is, of course, taken for granted that no member will wish to do anything that might harm his or her standing with the Pp machine . . . as everyone has been clearly told . . . periodic examinations by the *Pp* will determine the status of a member's continuance with the shops . . .

"In the event that a member is discovered to have fallen below the requirements in any vital degree, the weapon shops will relieve the individual of all weapon shop memories and information the possession of which by unauthorized persons might be dangerous to the shops . . .

"The following vices and pleasures, when pursued with too much ardor, have proven in the past to be initial steps in the severance of relations . . ."

Among those she remembered as being mildly dangerous for women was "Houses of illusions." She couldn't recall clearly but it seemed to her there had been a footnote in connection with that listing. Something about the danger not being in the pleasure itself but in the knowledge that the men in such places were nearly always unwilling slaves. Repeated experiences caused penetration of the ego with the result that what began as a search for a comparatively normal sensual adventure ended with the ever bolder participation of the ego.

She came out of her intent memory reverie to realize that she was walking rapidly toward the special flash signal of a 'stat station. Within a minute she had her connection with the Weapon Shop Information Center. A few seconds later she tucked a 'stat duplicate of the 2108 addresses of houses of Illusion in her purse, and headed for the Penny Palace.

Her decision was made and from that moment she had not a thought of drawing back.

Inside the Penny Palace she saw things that Cayle could not possibly have observed without having the knowledge that she had. The play, she saw, was almost back to normal. A few of the hired people were still ostentatiously playing at games that would otherwise have been bare of players. The moment enough legitimate pleasure seekers were risking money on a machine the hirelings withdrew casually. Lucy headed toward the rear of the great room, pausing frequently and pretending to watch the play at various games. She carried a weapon shop nullifier in her purse. So she opened and shut doors leading to the manager's office without setting off the Imperial-type alarms.

Inside she depended entirely on her ring alarm to warn her of the approach of anyone. Coolly but swiftly she searched the office. First she pressed the machine-file activator, pecking out the key word *illusion*. The file screen remained blank. She clicked off the word *house*. No response.

Surely he had the address of the house or houses with which he dealt. In a fury she snatched up the 'stat book and operated its activators. But there, too, *house* and *illusion* produced no response. Was it possible this man Martin—she had found his name on various documents—had connections with only a few houses and had their numbers in his head? Grimly, she realized it was very possible indeed.

She had no intention of leaving before she had exhausted all the possibilities of her position. She made a quick examination of the contents of the desk. Finding nothing she settled into the comfortable chair and waited. Not for long. Her finger tingled as the ring-alarm went off. She turned it, first toward one of the two doors, then the other. The active response came from the same door through which she had entered nearly fifteen minutes earlier. Whoever it was would now be in the corridor, his hand reaching for the office door.

The door opened, and the roly-poly man came in. He was humming softly to himself. The big desk and the chair in which she was sitting were so placed that he was inside before he saw that he had a visitor. He blinked at her with sea-blue eyes, a fatty little man who had somehow, long ago, conquered all fear. The pig-like eyes switched to the gun in her fingers, then back to her face, greedily.

"Pretty girl," he said at last.

It was obviously not a complete reaction. Lucy waited. And finally it came, a purring question with an overtone of snarl. "What do you want?"

"My husband."

From all angles that seemed to Lucy the best identification to make of herself. It was natural that there might be a Mrs. Cayle Clark in the background.

"Husband?" echoed the man blankly. He looked genuinely puzzled.

Lucy said in a monotone, "He was winning. I waited in the background, keeping an eye on him. Then I was forced out by a pushing crowd. When I tried to get back in the doors were locked. And when they opened he wasn't there. I put two and two together and here I am."

It was a long speech, but it covered the subject. It gave the picture of a worried, determined wife. And that was very important. It would be unfortunate if he suspected that the weapon shops were interested in Cayle Clark. She saw that understanding had come to the pig-like man.

"Oh, you mean him." He laughed curtly, his eyes watchful. "Sorry, young lady, I merely called a truckplane service that had contacts. What they do with the people they pick up I don't know."

Lucy said precisely, "What you mean is you don't know the address to which they took him but you know the kind of place. Is that correct?"

He stared at her thoughtfully, as if trying to make up his mind about something. Finally, he shrugged. "House of Illusion," he said.

The fact that she had guessed that did not make the confirmation less valuable. Just as his apparent frankness did not mean that he was telling the truth. Lucy said, "I notice there's a Lambeth in the corner over there. Bring it here."

He brought it instantly. "You'll notice," he said, "I'm not resisting."

Lucy made no reply. She picked up the Lambeth cone and pointed it at the fat man. "What is your name?"

"Harj Martin."

The Lambeth needles remained stationary. Martin it was.

Before she could speak, the man said, "I'm prepared to give you all the information you want." He shrugged. "Doesn't mean a thing to me. We're protected. If you can locate the house your husband was taken to, go ahead. But you should know the houses have their own methods of getting rid of men when the police are called in."

There was a nervousness in his manner that interested Lucy. She looked at him with bright eyes. "You must be making plans," she said. "You would like to reverse our positions." She shook her head deprecatingly. "Don't try it. I would shoot."

"It's a weapon shop gun," Martin said, pointedly.

"Exactly," said Lucy. "It won't shoot unless you attack me."

That wasn't strictly true. Weapon shop members had special guns, that would shoot under fewer restrictions than the guns sold to consumers.

Martin sighed. "Very well," he said. "The name of the firm is Lowery Truckplanes."

The Lambeth needles indicated the name was correct. Lucy backed toward the door. "You're getting off easy," she said. "I hope you realize that."

The fat man nodded, licking his lips. She had a final mental picture of his blue eyes watching her warily, as if he still hoped to catch her off guard.

No further words were spoken. She opened the door, slipped through, and half a minute later was safely out on the street.

Anton Lowery was a blond giant who lifted himself sleepily from his pillow and stared stupidly at Lucy. He made no attempt to get up. He said finally, "I don't know where they would have taken him. It's just transportation business with us, you understand. The driver calls up houses at random, until he finds one that can use a man. We don't keep records."

He sounded vaguely indignant. Like an honest trucker whose business ethics were being questioned for the first time. Lucy wasted no time arguing the matter.

"Where can I locate the driver?" she asked.

It seemed the driver had gone off duty at 2 A.M. and was not due back for another 66 hours. "It's these unions," said Mr. Lowery. "Short hours, big pay and plenty of time off." Giving her the information seemed to bring him a satisfaction, a sense of victory over her that detracted considerably from the indignation in his tone.

"Where does he live?" Lucy asked.

He hadn't the faintest idea. "Might get that from the union," he suggested. "They don't give us addresses."

It turned out that he couldn't remember the name of the union. The Lambeth, which she had brought with her from the Penny Palace, verified his statements one by one. Lucy sagged. In three days Cayle would be initiated into the sordid life of the houses of illusion. The dark thought aroused her to abrupt anger.

"Damn you!" she said savagely. "When the driver reports back to work, you get the address of the house from him. I'll call you ten minutes after he's due back and you'd better have the information."

Her tone and manner must have been convincing. For Anton Lowery assured her hastily that he had no objection to her gaining the information and would personally see to it that she got it. He was still protesting as she left his bedroom.

Outside Lucy had another energy drink at a corner automat—and realized it wasn't enough. Her watch showed a few minutes to 5 A.M. And her tense body told her it was time to go home to bed.

She reached her apartment without incident. Wearily, she undressed, and heavily climbed between the sheets. Her last conscious thought was: "Three days . . . would the time pass more slowly for the man who was enduring continuous pleasure? Or for herself who knew that pleasure prolonged was the greatest pain of all?

She slept on that thought like an overtired child.

CHAPTER THIRTEEN

As soon as she had the address of the house she called up Hedrock. He listened thoughtfully to her account, then nodded.

"Good work," he said. "We'll back you up. I'll send a warship over, very high up. And if we don't hear from you in a reasonable time we'll raid." He hesitated. "I hope you realize that the only way we can justify such action is if you leave no doubt in Clark's mind that your reasons are purely personal. Are you prepared to go that far?"

He didn't need to ask the question. The haggard face that stared at him from the 'stat screen left no doubt of the extent of her fixation. This girl was emotionally wrought up. He felt a qualm of pity, and yet, he realized, he was not responsible for her feelings. He had merely recognized them, and used his knowledge of psychology to intensify her pursuit. A callidetic of the measurement of Cayle Clark would yet make himself felt in Isher. The chance that the impact would affect the war itself was not impossible. Once started on the right path, the pace of activity, the pattern of callidity, would be a direct moving cube, piling up so fast that no human brain would grasp the extent of what was happening until afterwards.

If only there were some way of discovering what form it would take— Hedrock shook himself inwardly. He was not given to wishful thinking. They would simply have to watch Clark's movements and hope that they would recognize the moment when it arrived. He saw that the girl was waiting for him to speak again. His thoughts grew instantly sharp. He said, "What time is your appointment? Tonight or tomorrow?"

"Tonight at ten-thirty." She managed a grim smile. "The receptionist insisted I be on time. Apparently, they can hardly handle the business they get."

"Supposing he isn't among those available at that time—what will you say?"

"I gather that there is a complete illusion break at that time. The men and women are then allowed to select partners. However, if he shouldn't be available, I shall not be either. I shall be very finicky."

"Do you think Clark will recognize you?" He saw that she didn't understand what he meant. He explained. "The illusions leave after-image hallucinations which interfere with visual perception."

Lucy said, "I'll make him recognize me."

She described several methods she would use. Hedrock considered them, then shook his head. "It's obvious," he said, "that you've never been in a house. These people are perpetually, endlessly, suspicious. Until you are actually in a state of illusion your chances of saying anything that is not overheard are dim. Once the automatic machines begin radiating stimuli they don't worry about you any more. Bear that in mind and adjust yourself to any situation that may come up."

Lucy was recovered from her shock. After the afternoon she and Cayle had spent together she had felt sure of him. "He'll recognize me," she said firmly.

Hedrock said nothing to that. He had merely wanted to point out the problem. Three days and nights of illusions was a long time. Even if there were no after images, the brain was dulled, the body's capacity for life temporarily at low ebb, no energy for memory.

Lucy was speaking again. "I'd better get ready. Goodbye, Mr. Hedrock."

"All the luck in the world, Lucy," said Hedrock. "But don't call for help unless it's absolutely necessary."

Hedrock did not leave the 'stat the moment the connection was broken. During this period of emergency he lived in an apartment adjoining the coordination office. His work was his life. Virtually all his waking hours were spent at his desk. Now he called the weapon shop naval headquarters and ordered them to dispatch a protective warship. And still he was not satisfied. Frowning, he considered the potentialities of Lucy's position and finally called for her secret file. In two minutes, by weapon shop interspatial transportation, the remote Information Center precipitated the plate onto the table in front of him. First, he checked the facts—comprehension 110, horizon 118, plethora 105, dominance 151, ego 120, emotional index 150—

Hedrock paused there. Compared to the norm of 100, not forgetting the average of 85, Lucy was a fine, intelligent girl with a somewhat high-category emotional capacity. It was that that had brought her into the affair. After Cayle Clark was identified (by a routine check-up on the crowds that gathered before a new weapon shop) as a callidetic giant it was decided to contact him through the medium of an unmarried woman with a high emotion index.

Deliberately, the weapon makers' Council anticipated that the callidetic would excite fixation in Lucy. There were other factors involved in her selection, mostly sanity safeguards for a young woman who was going to be subjected to unnatural stresses. For one thing it was desirable, from the point of view of the girl's happiness, that the attraction be mutual for the time being. Permanency, of course, could not be guaranteed in a changing world.

One by one Hedrock examined the factors applicable to the present situation. At last he sighed. He felt sorry for Lucy. The weapon shops did not normally interfere with the private lives of their members or of anyone.

Only the unparalleled emergency justified using an individual human being as a pawn.

Thought of the emergency drew his mind. He returned the file to Information Center, then switched on the 'stat again. He manipulated it intently, rejected several images that resulted from the "draw" of energy in the room he was aiming at and finally had what he wanted, the map of time. He had no difficulty locating the large shadow. It was lying six weeks and a day in the future. The tiny shadow was harder to find. He saw it then, a minute black point on the curving vastness of the map. It seemed to be approximately a million million years in the past. Hedrock closed his eyes, and strove to visualize the span of time. He couldn't. The energy locked up in McAllister was too great now for planetary comparisons. The problem of exploding it was a logic nightmare.

When at last he shut off the 'stat, he experienced a great weariness, and an incredulous wonder that, after all this time he still didn't have even a tentative solution to the deadliest danger that had ever confronted the entire Solar System.

He spent the next hour studying précis of reports that had been filed by other agents throughout the day. Lucy didn't know that she was among the few dozen agents who obtained immediate and direct access to him at any time of the day or night. Those not so favored talked to machines or to any one of a dozen executives who alternated on a three-shift basis.

Again and again the condensed accounts required more thorough investigation. Not once did he begrudge the time. Not once did he let himself feel rushed. Each report was examined in the detail that he considered necessary.

Ten-thirty came and, though he was aware that Lucy must now have arrived at the house, he paused only briefly and called the weapon shop warship, which was hovering high above the place. For a moment he examined the house itself as it showed through a telescope, a toylike structure in a suburban estate that seemed all garden. Then, the picture of it clear in his mind, he returned to his work.

CHAPTER FOURTEEN

As SHE PUSHED OPEN THE GATE, Lucy felt a warm glow sweep through her. She stopped, almost in mid-stride.

The sensation of warmth, she knew, had been artificially induced. This was the first step of pleasure leading up to the strange heights of sensory joys offered by a House of Illusion. There would be scarcely a moment from now until she left the grounds that some new, perhaps insidious and unsuspected manipulation of her nervous system would not be occurring.

The brief indecisiveness yielded to her purpose. Slowly, she walked forward, studying the house as she did so. The House of Illusion was set well back from the street in grounds that were beautifully landscaped. Flowers and shrubs protruded cunningly from a score of breaks in the abundant stone that made up the larger part of the yard. A massive screen of gigantic green-fronded plants started about a hundred feet from the entrance of the building, and almost hid it from view.

She walked under them, and came presently to an entrance that built up gradually, beginning as a low fence that soon towered higher than her head, and finally curved up above her to form a gleaming roof. She could see the end of it nearly fifty yards ahead.

Twice, involuntarily, she slowed. The first time, something soft seemed to caress her face. It was almost as if a loving hand reached out and delicately touched her, with affectionate fingers. The second time, the result was more dramatic. She caught her breath suddenly. A flush burned her face and spread warmly down her body. She felt embarrassed yet happy, a little shy but excited. She couldn't help wondering if this could be how a young girl might feel on her wedding night.

It was in just such nuances that the Houses of Illusion excelled. Here, tired old roues—men and women both—could recapture for a price otherwise lost emotions of their abused bodies.

She reached the turning of the corridor, and found herself confronted by an alcove fitted with scores of mirrors. She moved toward them hesitantly, wondering if they could be doors, disturbed by the possibility that she might choose the wrong one. She paused finally, and waited for one of the doors to open. But after a minute or so, nothing had happened; so she began to push against the face of first one mirror, then another.

The first six were solid, as if there was unmoveable wall behind them. The seventh opened easily, and proved to be a swinging door. She went through it into a corridor that was only a little wider than her body. Her shoulders kept brushing the walls, and she had an uneasy feeling of being closed in, a distinct sensation of the space being too narrow for comfort. It was more than a physical feeling. It was in her mind, associated with fears of confined places, somehow connected with all the unknown things that could happen to a person who, if anything went wrong, could only move forward or backward.

She wondered if the uneasiness might possibly derive from her own tension, the knowledge that she was here for a purpose that had nothing to do with the normal business of the establishment. She was against what went on in such a place. She intended to disrupt at least a part of their organization. Her anxiety might well derive from the possibility that her motives could be discovered before she could do what she wanted to do. It seemed reasonable that the regular customers of this abode would not be alarmed by a narrow passageway, knowing as they undoubtedly did where it ended.

Her fears faded as quickly as they had begun. She felt a sudden anticipation of immeasurable joy about to be experienced. Breathlessly, she came to the end of the corridor, and pushed at the narrow wall-end that was there. It opened easily, and this time, to her relief, she saw that she had come to a small though nicely furnished room. As she entered, she saw that a woman sat behind a desk just left of the door. Lucy stopped, and the woman said:

"Sit down, please. Naturally, there has to be an interview the first time someone visits our establishment."

She was a woman of forty or so, with classically good-looking face, except that her eyes were narrowed and her lips drawn into a thin line. Silently she indicated a chair, and Lucy sat down without a word. The woman began:

"You understand, my dear, that everything you tell me will be kept confidential. In fact—" Her lips made the motions of a smile, and she touched her forehead with a manicured finger—"it never gets beyond here. But I must tell you that I have a perfect memory. Once I hear somebody talk, or see someone, I never forget them."

Lucy said nothing. She had met a number of individuals with eidetic memories; and she accepted the woman's statement that she had such a memory. From all the accounts she herself had heard of the houses of illusion, no record had ever been found of the customers. Apparently, this house kept its records inside the mind of someone who could remember such things.

The woman went on, "This means, of course, that we operate on a strictly cash basis. What is your annual income?"

"Five thousand credits." Lucy did not hesitate.

"Where do you work?"

Lucy named a firm well-known in the city. All this was simple, and long prepared for by the Weapon Shops. Every weapon shop member was listed as a worker in an organization which was either secretly owned by the shops or else owned by a weapon shop supporter. Thus, if a member was questioned in the normal routine of Isher commercial life, legitimate and checkable answers could be given.

"How much rent do you pay?" asked the woman.

"One hundred credits a month."

"And your food bills come to what?"

"Oh, fifty, sixty—something like that."

The woman said thoughtfully, half to herself, "Transportation, ten; clothes, twenty-five; miscellaneous, ten—that leaves you a good twenty-five hundred a year for extras. If you wanted to come here once a week, you could do it at fifty credits each. However, we'll make you a discount for emergencies. Thirty-five credits, please."

Lucy counted out the money, startled by the ruthlessness of the calculations involved. Actually, her income had other charges on it—a thousand credits' income tax, for instance. Her clothes bill was much higher than twenty-five credits. And yet—and yet, she could, if necessary, if her craving for pleasure over-reached her caution, get by on even less than the woman had indicated. Inherent in the other's calculations was the obvious fact that a person on the downward path would want to come oftener than once a week. In such an event, she could move to cheaper quarters, buy less expensive clothes, eat less—there were many short cuts possible, and all of them as old as human corruption.

The woman placed the money in a drawer, and stood up. "Thank you, my dear. I hope we have a long and mutually satisfying association. Through this door, please."

It was another concealed door, and it led to a broad corridor with an open doorway at the end of it. As she approached it, Lucy saw that it was a large and luxurious bedroom. The size of it was apparent even before she reached it. Several things about it made her suspicious, and so she did not enter immediately, but paused instead on the threshold, and studied the interior. She must, she told herself, remember that this was a house of *illusion*. Here, what would normally seem real, might be nothing but fantasy. She recalled the clues Hedrock had given her as to how to detect the mechanically-induced delusions. And presently she saw that if she let herself look at the room out of the corners of her eyes, the scene blurred curiously, particularly at the very edge of her vision. She seemed to see the figure of a woman, and there was a suggestion of the room being larger than it appeared now.

Lucy smiled, walked toward the far wall, straight through it—solid though it seemed—and found herself in an enormous room that glittered with mirrors along three of its walls. A woman attendant hurried toward her, and bowed apologetically. "You will please pardon us, Miss. But since this is your first visit to our establishment, it was necessary to assume that you knew nothing of our little bag of tricks. Did you learn about this particular illusion from a friend, or have you been to other houses?"

It was a pointed question; and Lucy knew better than to evade it. "I heard a friend describe it," she said truthfully.

The answer seemed satisfactory. The woman, a small, vivacious looking blonde, led the way to what turned out to be a mirror door. "Please change your clothes," she said, "and then go through the door on the far side."

Lucy found herself in a small dressing room. An attractive white dress hung on a hanger against one wall. A pair of sandals were on the floor. Nothing else. She undressed slowly, beginning suddenly to feel committed. It was going to be difficult indeed to get out of this situation. If she failed to contact Cayle during the time that would be available, then she might find herself experiencing what this house had to offer whether she wanted to or not.

The white dress was wonderfully soft to her touch; and, as she slipped it over her head, the feel of it on her skin brought a gasp of delight from her lips. The creation was made of a special costly cloth that was designed to affect only the pleasure nerves of the body. Its cost was more than a hundred credits a yard.

She stood for a long moment, letting the sensation of pleasure creep over her. Abruptly, excitement swept her. She swayed dizzily, and thought: "It really doesn't matter. Whatever happens here tonight, I'm going to have some fun."

She slipped her feet cosily into the sandals, staggered a little as she fumbled for the catch of the door; and then, steady again, opened it, and stood blinking at a vista-like room where men sat at tables along one wall and women along the opposite wall. The walls glittered with colorful plastic designs. A great liquor bar spread all across the side of the room facing her. Lucy made a half-hearted attempt to test for illusion by looking at the scene out of the corners of her eyes. But she didn't worry about it. This was it. Here was the concourse room. In a few minutes she would have her chance to get Cayle. If she didn't make contact—well, it didn't matter. There were other nights. So she told herself hazily.

She walked out into the room, swaggering a little. Scornfully, she surveyed the other women, sitting at their little tables, drinking from tiny glasses. Most were older than she was, older by a great deal. Abruptly bored by her competition, she glanced toward the men on the far side of the room. She saw with momentary interest that what had seemed one room was in reality two. A transparent barrier ran the full length of the room from ceiling to floor, dividing the men from the women. It was possible, of course, that the barrier also was an illusion. And that it would disappear either for individuals or for the entire group at the right moment. Lucy, who knew something of the energies involved in the processes by which the houses achieved their effects, guessed that such a joining of the two sections would eventually occur.

The thought faded from her mind, as she ran her gaze rapidly along the line of men. Without exception, they were relatively young people. Her eyes were past Cayle before she recognized him. She started to bring them back for a second look, but just in time a basic pattern of caution stopped her. Already beginning to sober up after her brief emotional intoxication, she turned toward one of the small tables, and walked to it carrying with her the mental image of him.

She sat down, the high exhilaration gone out of her. She felt miserable with a remembrance of the disaster she had seen on his face. Haggard, worn-out, unhappy Cayle Clark—that was the vision she had. She wondered doubtfully if by any chance his glazed eyes had seen her. She thought finally: "I'll look again in a minute. And this time, I'll try to attract his attention."

She looked steadily at her watch, determined not to be rushed. The hands showed five seconds of the end of the minute when a slim little man came out of the alcove, and raised his hand. Lucy glanced hastily toward Cayle, saw with a sudden lift that he was watching her, and then heard the little man say in a cheerful tone:

"Down goes the barrier, folks. Now's the time to get acquainted."

There were different reactions to the signal. Most of the women remained seated. Several, however, got up hastily and hurried across the room. Lucy, seeing that Cayle was coming toward her, stayed where she was. He sank down into the chair opposite her, and said steadily, "I think you're very attractive, miss."

She nodded her acceptance of the compliment, not trusting herself to speak. An attendant bent down beside her. "Satisfactory, Miss?" The question was softly spoken.

Lucy inclined her head again. The attendant said, "This way."

She stood up, thinking: "As soon as we're alone, we can start to plan."

There was a sudden flurry of excitement at one of the doors. The woman who had originally interviewed Lucy rushed in, and spoke in a low tone to the little man. A moment later, a bell began to ring. Lucy half-turned; and, doing so, in some curious fashion lost her balance. She felt herself falling into darkness . . .

Hedrock was still in his office at five minutes after eleven when the 'stat buzzed, and Lucy's face came on the screen. She shook her head in bewilderment. "I don't know what happened. Things seemed to be going along all right. He recognized me without giving away that he knew me, and we were apparently about to be led to some private room, when everything went black. The next thing I knew I was here in my apartment."

"Just a moment," Hedrock said.

He broke the connection, and called the warship. The commander shook his head. "I was just about to call you. There was a police raid, and the warning must have been very short, because they loaded the women into carplanes—half a dozen to a machine—and carted them off to their homes."

"What about the men?" Hedrock was tense. In emergencies the house sometimes had nasty habits.

"That's why I didn't call you immediately. I saw them pile the men into a truckplane, and cart them off. I followed, but they used the usual method."

"I see," said Hedrock. He covered his eyes with one shielding hand, and groaned inwardly. The problem of Cayle Clark was becoming complex again, and there was nothing to do but to let him go. "Okey, captain," he said gloomily. "Good work."

He clicked off, called Lucy again, and gave her the news. "I'm sorry," he said, "but that eliminates him from the picture. We don't dare interfere."

"What'll I do?" she asked.

"Just wait," he said. "Wait."

That was all there was to say.

CHAPTER FIFTEEN

FARA WORKED. He had nothing else to do, and the thought was often in his mind that now he would be doing it till the day he died. Fool that he was—he told himself a thousand times how big a fool—he kept hoping that Cayle would walk into the shop and say:

"Father, I've learned my lesson. If you can ever forgive me, teach me the business, and then you retire to a well-earned rest."

It was on August 26th that the telestat clicked on just after Fara had finished lunch. "Money call," it sighed. "Money call."

Fara and Creel looked at each other. "Eh," said Fara finally, "money call for us."

He could see from the gray look in Creel's face the thought that was in her mind. He said under his breath: "Damn that boy!"

But he felt relieved. Amazingly, relieved! Cayle was beginning to appreciate the value of parents. He switched on the viewer. "Come and collect," he said.

The face that came on the screen was heavy-jowled beetle-browed and strange. The man said: "This is Clerk Pearton of the Fifth Bank of Ferd. We have received a sight draft on you for ten thousand credits. With carrying charges and government tax, the sum required will be twelve thousand one hundred credits. Will you pay it now or will you come in this afternoon and pay it?"

"B-but . . . b-but—" said Fara. "W-who—" He stopped, conscious of the heavy-faced man saying something about the money having been paid out to Cayle Clark, that morning, on emergency call. At last Fara found his voice:

"But the bank had no right," he expostulated, "to pay out the money without my authority."

The voice cut him off coldly. "Are we then to inform our central that the money was obtained under false pretenses? Naturally, an order will be issued immediately for the arrest of your son."

"Wait . . . wait—" Fara spoke blindly. He was aware of Creel beside him, shaking her head at him. She was white, and her voice was a sick, stricken thing, as she said:

"Fara, let him go. He's through with us. We must be as hard. Let him go."

The words rang senselessly in Fara's ears. They didn't seem to fit into any normal pattern. He was saying: "I . . . I haven't got— How about my paying . . . installments?"

"If you wish a loan," said Clerk Pearton, "naturally we will be happy to go into the matter. I might say that when the draft arrived, we checked up your status, and we are prepared to loan you eleven thousand credits on indefinite call with your shop as security. I have the form here, and if you are agreeable, we will switch this call through the registered circuit, and you can sign at once."

"Fara, no!"

The clerk went on: "The other eleven hundred credits will have to be paid in cash. Is that agreeable?"

"Yes, yes, of course. I've got twenty-five hund—" He stopped his chattering tongue with a gulp; then: "Yes, that's satisfactory."

The deal completed, Fara whirled on his wife. Out of the depths of his hurt and bewilderment, he raged: "What do you mean, standing there and talking about not paying it? You said several times that I was responsible for him being what he is. Besides, we don't know why he needed the money. He said it was an emergency."

Creel said in a low, dead voice, "In one hour he's stripped us of our savings. He must have done it deliberately, thinking of us as two old fools who wouldn't know any better than to pay it."

"All I see," Fara interrupted, "is that I have saved our name from disgrace."

His high sense of duty rightly done lasted until mid-afternoon, when the bailiff from Ferd came to take over the shop.

"But what—" Fara began.

The bailiff said, "The Automatic Atomic Repair Shops, Limited, took over your loan from the bank and are foreclosing."

"It's unfair," said Fara. "I'll take it to court." He was thinking dazedly: If the empress ever learned of this, she'd . . . she'd—

The courthouse was a big, gray building; and Fara felt emptier and colder every second, as he walked along the gray corridors. In Glay, his decision not to give himself into the hands of a lawyer had seemed a wise act. Here, in these enormous halls and palatial rooms, it seemed the sheerest folly.

He managed, nevertheless, to give an account of the criminal act of the bank in first giving Cayle the money, then turning over the note to his chief competitor, apparently within minutes of his signing it. He finished with, "I'm sure, sir, the empress would not approve of such goings-on against honest citizens."

"How dare you," said the cold-voiced person on the bench, "use the name of her holy majesty in support of your own gross self-interest?"

Fara shivered. The sense of being intimately a member of the empress' great human family yielded to a sudden chill and a vast mind-picture of the ten million icy courts like this, and the myriad malevolent and heartless men—like this—who stood between the empress and her loyal subject, Fara. He thought passionately: If the empress knew what was happening here, how unjustly he was being treated, she would—

Or would she?

He pushed the terrible doubt out of his mind—came out of his reverie with a start, to hear the Cadi saying: "Plaintiff's appeal dismissed, with costs assessed at seven hundred credits, to be divided between the court and the defense solicitor in the ratio of five to two. See to it that the appellant does not leave until the costs are paid. Next case."

Fara went alone the next day to see Creel's mother. He called first at "Farmer's Restaurant" on the outskirts of the village. The place was, he noted with satisfaction in the thought of the steady stream of money flowing in, half full, though it was only mid-morning. But madame wasn't there. Try the feed store.

He found her in the back of the feed store, overseeing the weighing out of grain into cloth measures. The hard-faced old woman heard his story without a word. She said finally, curtly:

"Nothing doing, Fara. I'm one who has to make loans often from the bank to swing deals. If I tried to set you up in business, I'd find the Automatic Atomic Repair people getting after me. Besides, I'd be a fool to turn money over to a man who lets a bad son squeeze a fortune out of him. Such a man has no sense about worldly things. And I won't give you a job because I don't hire relatives in my business." She finished, "Tell Creel to come and live at my house. I won't support a man, though. That's all."

He watched her disconsolately for a while, as she went on calmly superintending the clerks who were manipulating the old, no longer accurate measuring machines. Twice her voice echoed through the dust-filled interior, each time with a sharp: "That's overweight, a gram at least. Watch your machine."

Though her back was turned, Fara knew by her posture that she was still aware of his presence. She turned at last with an abrupt movement, and said, "Why don't you go to the weapon shop? You haven't anything to lose, and you can't go on like this."

Fara went out then, a little blindly. At first the suggestion that he buy a gun and commit suicide had no real personal application. But he felt immeasurably hurt that his mother-in-law should have made it. Kill himself? It was ridiculous. He was still a young man, just going on fifty. Given the proper chance, with his skilled hands, he would wrest a good living even in a world where automatic machines were encroaching everywhere. There was always room for a man who did a good job. His whole life had been based on that credo.

He went home to find Creel packing. "It's the common sense thing to do," she said. "We'll rent the house and move into rooms."

He told her about her mother's offer to take her in, watching her face as he spoke. Creel shrugged. "I told her 'No' yesterday," she said thoughtfully. "I wonder why she mentioned it to you."

Fara walked swiftly over to the great front window overlooking the garden with its flowers, its pool, its rockery. He tried to think of Creel away from this garden of hers, this home of two thirds a lifetime, Creel living in rooms. And knew what her mother had meant. There was one more hope. He waited until Creel went upstairs, then called Mel Dale on the telestat. The mayor's plump face took on an uneasy expression as he saw who it was. But he listened pontifically, said finally, "Sorry, the council does not loan money; and I might as well tell you, Fara—I have nothing to do with this, mind you—but you can't get a license for a shop any more."

"W-what?"

"I'm sorry!" The mayor lowered his voice. "Listen, Fara, take my advice and go to the weapon shop. These places have their uses."

There was a click, and Fara sat staring at the blank face of the viewing screen.

So it was to be death!

CHAPTER SIXTEEN

IT TOOK TWO MONTHS of living in one room to make up his mind. He waited until the street was deserted, then slipped across the boulevard, past a design of flower gardens, and so to the door of the weapon shop. The brief fear came that the door wouldn't open, but it did, effortlessly. As he emerged from the dimness of the alcove into the shop proper, he saw the silver-haired old man sitting in a corner chair, reading under a softly bright light. The old man looked up, put aside his book, then rose to his feet.

"It's Mr. Clark," he said quietly. "What can we do for you?"

A faint flush crept into Fara's cheeks. He had hoped that he would not suffer the humiliation of being recognized. But now that his fear was realized, he stood his ground stubbornly. The important thing about killing himself was that there be nobody for Creel to bury at great expense. Neither knife nor poison would satisfy that basic requirement. "I want a gun," said Fara, "that can be adjusted to disintegrate a body six feet in diameter in a single shot. Have you that kind?"

The old man turned to a showcase and brought forth a sturdy revolver that glinted with all the soft colors of the inimitable Ordine plastic. The man said in a precise voice, "Notice the flanges on this barrel are little more than bulges. This made the model ideal for carrying in a shoulder holster under the coat. It can be drawn very swiftly because, when properly attuned, it will leap toward the reaching hand of its owner. At the moment it is attuned to me. Watch while I replace it in its holster and—"

The speed of the draw was amazing. The old man's fingers moved; and the gun, four feet away, was in them. There was no blur of movement. It was like the door the night that it had slipped from Fara's grasp, and slammed noiselessly in Constable Jor's face. *Instantaneous!*

Fara, who had parted his lips, as the old man was explaining, to protest the needlessness of illustrating any quality of the weapon except what he had asked for, closed them again. He stared in fascination. And something of the wonder that was here held his mind and his body. He had seen and handled the guns of soldiers, and they were simply ordinary metal or plastic things that one used clumsily like any other material substance, not like this at all, not possessed of a dazzling life of their own, leaping with an intimate eagerness to assist with all their superb power the will of their master.

With a start, Fara remembered his purpose. He smiled wryly, and said, "All this is very interesting. But what about the beam that can fan out?"

The old man said calmly, "At pencil thickness, this beam will pierce any body except certain alloys of lead up to four hundred yards. With proper adjustment of the firing nozzle, you can disintegrate a six-foot object at fifty yards or less. This screw is the adjuster."

He indicated a tiny device in the muzzle itself. "Turn it to the left to spread the beam, to the right to close it."

Fara said, "I'll take the gun. How much is it?"

He saw that the old man was looking at him thoughtfully. The oldster said finally, slowly, "I have previously explained our regulations to you, Mr. Clark. You recall them, of course?"

"Eh!" said Fara, and stopped, wide-eyed. "You mean," he gasped, "those things actually apply. They're not—" Tense and cold, he finished, "All I want is a gun that will shoot in self-defense, but which I can turn on myself if I have to—or want to."

"Oh, suicide!" said the old man. He looked as if a great understanding had dawned on him. "My dear sir, we have no objection to you killing yourself at any time. That is your personal privilege in a world where privileges grow scanter every year. As for the price of this revolver, it's four credits."

"Four . . . only four credits!" said Fara.

He stood astounded, his mind snatched from its dark purpose. Why, the plastic alone was—and the whole gun with its fine, intricate workmanship—twenty-five credits would have been cheap. He felt a thrill of interest. The mystery of the weapon shops suddenly loomed as vast and important as his own black destiny. But the old man was speaking again:

"And now, if you will remove your coat, we can put on the holster."

Automatically, Fara complied. It was vaguely startling to realize that, in a few seconds, he would be walking out of here, equipped for self-murder, and that there was now not a single obstacle to his death. Curiously, he was disappointed. He couldn't explain it, but somehow there had been in the back of his mind a hope that these shops might, just might—what?

What indeed? Fara sighed. And grew aware again of the old man's voice:

"Perhaps you would prefer to step out of our side door. It is less conspicuous than the front."

There was no resistance in Fara. He was conscious of the man's fingers on his arm, half guiding him; and then the old man pressed one of several buttons on the wall—so that's how it was done—and there was the door. He could see flowers beyond the opening. Without a word he walked toward them. He was outside almost before he realized it.

CHAPTER SEVENTEEN

Fara stood for a moment in the neat little pathway, striving to grasp the finality of his situation. But nothing would come except awareness of many men around him. His mind was like a log drifting along a stream at night. Through that darkness grew a consciousness of something wrong. The wrongness was there in the back of his mind as he turned leftward to go to the front of the weapon shop. Vagueness transformed to a startled sense of shock. For he was not in Glay, and the weapon shop was not where it had been.

A dozen men brushed past Fara to join a long line of men farther along. But Fara was immune to their presence, their strangeness. His mind, his vision, his very being was concentrating on the section of machine that stood where the weapon shop had been. His brain lifted up, up in his effort to grasp the tremendousness of the dull-metaled immensity of what was spread here under a summer sun beneath a sky as blue as a remote southern sea.

The machine towered into the heavens, five great tiers of metal, each a hundred feet high; and the superbly streamlined five hundred feet ended in a peak of light, a spire that tilted straight up a sheer two hundred feet farther, and matched the sun for brightness.

And it *was* a machine, not a building, because the whole lower tier was alive with shimmering lights, mostly green, but sprinkled colorfully with red and occasionally blue and yellow. Twice, as Fara watched, green lights directly in front of him flashed unscintillating into red.

The second tier glowed with white and red lights, although there were only a fraction as many lights as on the lowest tier. The third section had on its dull-metal surface lights of blue and yellow; they twinkled softly here and there over the vast area.

The fourth tier was a series of signs, that brought the beginning of comprehension. The whole sign was:

WHITE—BIRTHS
RED—DEATHS
GREEN—LIVING
BLUE—IMMIGRATION TO EARTH
YELLOW—EMIGRATION

The fifth tier was all sign, finally explaining:

POPULATIONS

SOLAR SYSTEM	11,474,463,747
EARTH	11,193,247,361
MARS	97,298,604
VENUS	141,053,811
MOONS	42,863,971

The numbers changed, even as he looked at them, leaping up and down, shifting below and above what they had first been. People were dying, being born, moving to Mars, to Venus, to the moons of Jupiter, to Earth's moon, and others coming back again, landing minute by minute in the scores of spaceports. Life went on in its gigantic fashion—and here was the record.

"Better get in line," said a friendly voice beside Fara. "It takes quite a while to put through an individual case, I understand."

Fara stared at the man. He had the impression of having had senseless words flung at him. "In line?" he started, then stopped himself with a jerk that hurt his throat.

He was moving forward, blindly, ahead of the younger man, thinking a jumble about this having been the way that Constable Jor was transported to Mars, when another of the man's words penetrated.

"Case?" said Fara violently. "Individual case!"

The man, a heavy-faced, blue-eyed young chap of around thirty-five, looked at him curiously: "You must know why you're here," he said. "Surely, you wouldn't have been sent through here unless you had a problem of some kind that the weapon shop courts will solve for you; there's no other reason for coming to Information Center."

Fara walked on because he was in the line now, a fast-moving line that curved him inexorably around the machine; and seemed to be heading him toward a door that led into the interior of the great metal structure.

So it was a building as well as a machine.

A problem, he was thinking, why of course, he had a problem. A hopeless, insoluble, completely tangled problem so deeply rooted in the basic structure of Imperial civilization that the whole world would have to be overturned to make it right.

With a start, he saw that he was at the entrance. He thought with awe: In seconds he would be committed irrevocably—to what?

CHAPTER EIGHTEEN

INSIDE THE WEAPON SHOP information center, Fara moved along a wide, shining corridor. Behind him, the young man said:

"There's a side corridor, practically empty. Let's go."

Fara turned into it, trembling. He noticed that at the end of the hallway were a dozen young women sitting at desks interviewing men. He stopped in front of one of the girls. She was older than she had looked from a distance, over thirty, but goodlooking, alert. She smiled pleasantly but impersonally, and said:

"Your name, please?"

He gave it, and added a mumble about being from the village of Glay. The woman said:

"Thank you. It will take a few minutes to get your file. Won't you sit down?"

He hadn't noticed the chair. He sank into it, and his heart was beating so wildly that he felt choked. There was scarcely a thought in his head, nor a real hope; only an intense, almost mind-wrecking excitement. He realized, suddenly, that the girl was speaking to him, but only snatches of what she said came through that screen of tension in his mind:

"—Information Center is . . . in effect . . . a bureau of statistics. Every person born . . . registered here . . . their education, change of address . . . occupation . . . and the highlights of their life. The whole is maintained by . . . combination of . . . unauthorized and unsuspected liaison with . . . Imperial Chamber of Statistics and . . . through medium of agents . . . every community—"

It seemed to Fara that he was missing vital information, and that if he could only force his attention and hear more— He strained, but it was of no use. His nerves were jumping too madly for him to focus his mind on what she was saying. He tried to speak, but before he could force words out of his trembling lips, there was a click, and a thin, dark plate slid onto the woman's desk. She took it up and examined it. After a moment, she said something into a mouthpiece, and in a short time two more plates precipitated out of the empty air onto her desk. She studied them impassively, looked up finally.

"You will be interested to know," she said, "that your son, Cayle, is on Mars."

"Eh?" said Fara. He half rose from his chair, but before he could say anything the young woman was speaking again, firmly:

"I must inform you that the weapon shops take no action against individuals. We are not concerned with moral correction. That must come naturally from the individual, and from the people as a whole—and now if you will give me a brief account of your problem for the record and the court."

Sweating, Fara sank back into his seat; most desperately, he wanted more information about Cayle. He began: "But . . . but what . . . how—" He caught himself; and in a low voice described what had happened. When he finished, the girl said:

"You will procceed now to the Name Room; watch for your name, and when it appears go straight to Room 474. Remember, 474—and now, the line is waiting, if you please—"

She smiled politely, and Fara was moving off almost before he realized it. He half turned to ask another question, but an old man was sinking into his chair. Fara hurried on, along a great corridor, conscious of curious blasts of sound coming from ahead.

Eagerly, he opened the door; and the sound crashed at him with all the impact of a sledge-hammer blow. It was such a colossal, incredible sound that he stopped just inside the door, shrinking back. He stood then, trying to blink sense into a visual confusion that rivaled in magnitude the tornado of noise.

Men, men, men everywhere; men by the thousands in a long, broad auditorium, packed into rows of seats, pacing with an abandon of restlessness up and down the aisles, and all of them staring with frantic interest at a long board marked off into squares, each square lettered from the alphabet. The tremendous board with its lists of names ran the full length of the immense room. The Name Room, Fara thought shakily as he sank into a seat. And his name would come up in the C's.

It was like sitting in at a no-limit poker game, watching the jewel-precious cards turn up. It was like playing the exchange with all the world at stake during a stock crash. It was nerve-wracking, dazzling, exhausting, fascinating, terrible.

New names kept flashing on to the twenty-six squares; and men would shout like insane beings and some fainted, and the uproar was shattering; the pandemonium raged on, one continuous, unbelievable sound. And every few minutes a great sign would flash along the board, telling everyone:

"WATCH YOUR OWN INITIALS."

Fara watched. Each second it seemed to him that he couldn't stand it an instant longer. He wanted to scream at the roomful of men to be silent. He wanted to jump up to pace the floor, but others who did that were yelled at hysterically. Abruptly, the blind savagery of it scared Fara. He thought unsteadily: "I'm not going to make a fool of myself. I—"

"Clark, Fara—" winked the board. "Clark, Fara—"

With a shout, Fara leaped to his feet. "That's me!" he shrieked. "Me!"

No one turned. No one paid the slightest attention. Shamed, he slunk across the room where an endless line of men kept crowding into a corridor beyond. The silence in the long corridor was almost as shattering as the noise it replaced. It was hard to concentrate on the idea of a number, 474. It was completely impossible to imagine what could lie beyond—474.

The room was small. It was furnished with a small, business-type table and two chairs. On the table were seven neat piles of folders, each pile a different color. The piles were arranged in a row in front of a large, milky-white globe, that began to glow with a soft light. Out of its depths, a man's baritone voice said:

"Fara Clark?"

"Yes," said Fara.

"Before the verdict is rendered in your case," the voice went on quietly, "I want you to take a folder from the blue pile. The list will show the Fifth Interplanetary Bank in its proper relation to yourself and the world, and it will be explained to you in due course."

The list, Fara saw, was simply a list of the names of companies. The names ran from A to Z, and there were about five hundred of them. The folder carried no explanation; and Fara slipped it automatically into his side pocket, as the voice came again from the shining globe:

"It has been established," the words came precisely, "that the Fifth Interplanetary Bank perpetrated upon you a gross swindle, and that it is further guilty of practicing scavengery, deception, blackmail and was accessory in a criminal conspiracy. The bank made contact with your son, Cayle, through what is quite properly known as a scavenger, that is, an agent whose job it is to find young men and women who are in financial difficulties but who have parents with money. The scavenger obtains for this service a commission of eight percent, which is always paid by the borrower, in this case, your son. The bank practised deception in that its authorized agents deceived you by claiming that it had already paid out ten thousand credits to your son, whereas only one thousand credits was paid over and that not until your signature had been obtained. The blackmail guilt arises out of the threat to have your son arrested for falsely obtaining a loan, a threat made at a time when no money had exchanged hands. The conspiracy consists of the action whereby your note was promptly turned over to your competitor. The bank is accordingly triple-fined thirty-six thousand three hundred credits. It is not in our interest, Fara Clark, for you to know how this money is obtained. Suffice to know that the bank pays it, and that of the fine the weapon shops allocate to their own treasury a total of one half. The other half—"

There was a *plop*; a neatly packaged pile of bills fell onto the table. "For you," said the voice. Fara, with trembling fingers, slipped the package into his coat pocket. It required the purest mental and physical effort for him to concentrate on the next words that came.

"You must not assume that your troubles are over. The re-establishment of your motor repair shop in Glay will require force and courage. Be discreet, brave and determined, and you cannot fail. Do not hesitate to use the gun you have purchased in defense of your rights. The plan will be explained to you. And now, proceed through the door facing you."

Fara braced himself with an effort, opened the door and walked through. It was a dim, familiar room that he stepped into, and there was a silver-haired, fine-faced man who rose from a reading chair, and came forward in the dimness, smiling gravely.

The stupendous, fantastic, exhilarating adventure was over. He was back in the weapon shop of Glay.

CHAPTER NINETEEN

HE COULDN'T GET OVER the wonder of it. This great and fascinating organization established here in the very heart of a ruthless civilization, a civilizaton that had in a few brief weeks stripped him of everything he possessed. With a deliberate will, he stopped that glowing flow of thought. A frown wrinkled his solidly built face; he said:

"The . . . judge—" Fara hesitated over the name, frowned again in annoyance with himself, then went on: "The judge said that to re-establish myself I would have to—"

"Before we go into that," said the old man, "I want you to examine the blue folder you brought with you."

"Folder?" Fara echoed blankly. It took him a long moment to remember that he had picked up a folder from the table in Room 474.

He studied the list of company names with a gathering puzzlement, noting that the name Automatic Atomic Motor Repair Shops was well down among the A's, and the Fifth Interplanetary Bank only one of several great banks included. Fara looked up finally:

"I don't understand," he said. "Are these the companies you have had to act against?"

The silver-haired man smiled grimly, shook his head. "That is not what I mean. These firms constitute only a fraction of the eight million companies that are constantly in our books." He smiled again, humorlessly: "These companies all know that, because of us, their profits on paper bear no relation to their assets. What they don't know is what the difference really is, and, as we want a general improvement in business morals, not merely more skillful scheming to outwit us, we prefer them to remain in ignorance."

He paused, and this time he gave Fara a searching look, said at last: "The unique feature of the companies on this particular list is that they are every one wholly owned by Empress Isher." He finished swiftly: "In view of your past opinions on that subject, I do not expect you to believe me."

Fara stood quite still. He did believe it, with unquestioning conviction, completely, finally. The amazing, the unforgivable thing was that all his life he had watched the march of ruined men into the oblivion of poverty and disgrace—and blamed *them*.

Fara groaned. "I've been like a madman," he said. "Everything the Empress and her officials did was right. No friendship, no personal relationship could survive with me that did not include belief in things as they were. I suppose if I started to talk against the Empress I would receive equally short shrift."

"Under no circumstances," said the old man, "must you say anything against her majesty. The weapon shops will not countenance any such words, and will give no further aid to anyone who is so indiscreet. The Empress is personally not as responsible as might appear. Like you, she is, to some extent, adrift on the tide of our civilization. But I will not enlarge upon our policy. The worst period of our relations with the Imperial power was reached some forty years ago when every person who was discovered receiving aid from us was murdered in some fashion. You may be surprised to learn that your father-in-law was among those assassinated at that time."

"Creel's father!" gasped Fara. "But—" He stopped. There was such a rush of blood to his head that for a moment he could hardly see. "But," he managed at last, "it was reported that he ran away with another woman."

"They always spread a story of some kind," the old man said; and Fara was silent.

The other went on: "We finally put a stop to their murders by killing the three men from the top down, *excluding* the royal family, who gave the order for the particular execution involved. But we do not again want that kind of bloody murder. Nor are we interested in any criticism of our toleration of so much that is evil. It is important to understand that *we do not interfere in the main stream of human existence*. We right wrongs; we act as a barrier between the people and their more ruthless exploiters. Generally speaking, we help only honest men; that is not to say that we do not give assistance to the less scrupulous, but only to the extent of selling them guns—which is a very great aid indeed, and which is one of the reasons why the government is relying almost exclusively for its power on an economic chicanery.

"In the four thousand years since the brilliant genius, Walter S. de Lany invented the vibration process that made the weapon shops possible, and laid down the first principles of weapon shop political philosophy, we have watched the tide of government swing backward and forward between democracy under a limited monarchy to complete tyranny. And we have discovered one thing: *People always have the kind of government they want*. When they want change, they must change it. As always we shall remain an incorruptible core—and I mean that literally; we have a psychological machine that never lies about a man's character—I repeat, an incorruptible core of human idealism, devoted to relieving the ills that arise inevitably under any form of government.

"But now—your problem. It is very simple, really. You must fight, as all men have fought since the beginning of time for what they valued, for their just rights. As you know, the Automatic Atomic Repair people removed all your machinery and tools within an hour of foreclosing on your shop. This material was taken to Ferd, and then shipped to a great warehouse on the coast. We recovered it, and with our special means of transportation have now replaced the machines in your shop. You will accordingly go there and—"

Fara listened with a gathering grimness to the instructions, nodded finally, his jaw clamped tight.

"You can count on me," he said curtly. "I've been a stubborn man in my time; and though I've changed sides, I haven't changed that."

CHAPTER TWENTY

MOST OF THE HOUSES were known to the police. But there was an unwritten law in connection with them. When a raid was due to take place the owner was warned. But the names of the men who had been imprisoned on the premises *must* be discoverable in some easily accessible desk drawer. During the next few days a check-up would be made of passenger lists recording the names of indigents and criminals being sent to Mars, Venus, and the various moons. Government contractors were insatiably in need of men for work on other planets. And the houses, frequented as they were by wealthy women who could not afford scandals, supplied a constant trickle of labor with no questions asked.

In their dealings with the houses the police objected only to the idea that dead men tell no tales. Proprietors found themselves mercilessly hailed into court when they broke that one unalterable rule. After thousands of years, it had proved an effective method of keeping vice operating within the important limit, that the victim survived his grim experience.

Cayle stepped off the gangplank onto the soil of Mars. And stopped. It was an involuntary reaction. The ground was as hard as rock. The chill of it penetrated the soles of his shoes and somehow pierced the marrow of his being. With ice-cold eyes he surveyed the bleak town of Shardl. And this time a thought came, a hatred so violent that he shuddered. A determination so strong that he could feel the ice within him turning to steel.

"Get a move on you—" A stick prodded his shoulders. One of the soldiers directing the disembarkation of the long line of sullen men bawled the words, his voice sounding strangely hollow in that rarefied air.

Cayle did not even turn around. He moved—that was his reaction to the insult and indignity. He walked along, keeping his place in the line; and with every step he took the chill off the ground penetrated more deeply into his being. He could feel the coldness of the air now in his lungs. Ahead of him other men felt the constriction. They began to run. Still others broke past him, breathing hoarsely, the whites of their eyes showing, their bodies clumsily responding to the lesser gravity. The ground was rough and uneven and those who fell cried out as the jagged edges tore at them. Human blood stained the iron-hard soil of ever-frozen Mars.

Cayle walked on, unheeding, contemptuous of those who had lost their heads. They had been warned against the gravity. And the great enclosed plastic compound was only a quarter of a mile away, the intervening cold shocking but bearable. He reached the compound, his flesh tingling, his feet numbed. It was warm inside and he made his way slowly to the side of the building from which the main section of the town was visible.

Shardl was a mining town. It stood on a flat plain that was just beginning to blossom here and there with the green of warm atomic gardens. The shrubbery, spotty and incongruous, only emphasized the near desolation of every visible horizon.

He saw that men were studying bulletin boards over against one wall. He moved closer, and read what he could see of one sign. It read:

OPPORTUNITY

Cayle pressed up to it and read the rest of the words, then smiled and turned away. So they wanted people to sign up for Martian farms. Agree to remain fifteen years and "*Her Gracious Majesty, Innelda of Isher, will supply you with a completely equipped atomic-heated farm. No down payment, forty years to pay.*"

The offer concluded insinuatingly, "Go immediately to the Lands office, sign your application—and you will not have to do one minute's work in the mines."

Cayle was immune to the appeal. He had heard of this system of colonizing the cold planet of Mars and the hot planet of Venus. Eventually every acre of soil would be occupied, and the planet subjected to the beneficent influence of atomic power. And so, over the millennia, men would at last thaw all the icy habitable worlds of the Solar System and chill the burning deserts of Venus and Mercury. Men working out their lives on the drabber spawnings of their sun would create reasonable facsimiles of the far green Earth from which they had come.

That was the theory. In all those lazy days at public school, when he had read and listened to the accounts of colonization, he had not dreamed that he would one day be standing here, looking out at the half-light world of Mars, *standing here*, caught by a process too ruthless for any man, raised as he had been raised, to resist. He had no hatred now of his father. That was gone out of him into the hazy mists of the past, into that world of nothingness where his illusions had gone. The poor dumb fool—that was his thought now. Perhaps it was just as well some people never did comprehend the realities of life in the empire of Isher.

His own personal problem was solved in a simple, effective manner. He had been afraid. Now he wasn't. He had, astonishingly enough, been honest. Now, he wasn't. Well, in a way, he wasn't. It all depended on an individual's outlook on life as to how far he'd accept the theory that a human being must be strong enough to face the necessities of his era. Cayle Clark intended to face them all the way. Not for long would such a man as he had become remain on Mars. Meanwhile, he must sign nothing that would restrict his movements. He must be cautious, but seize opportunities instantly on an all-out basis.

Behind him a voice said slyly, "Am I addressing Cayle Clark, formerly of the village of Glay?"

Cayle turned slowly. He hadn't expected opportunity to come so quickly. The man who stood before him was small. He wore an overcoat of expensive material and he was very obviously not a person who had come on the boat, in spite of his shriveled and insignificant appearance. He spoke again.

"I am the local—uh—representative of the Fifth Bank. It may be that we can help you out of this unusual situation."

He looked like a toad, his gaunt face enframed in a high collar. His eyes, like black seeds, peered forth with a dull avaricious light.

Cayle shrank involuntarily, not from fear but from loathing. There had been a woman who came to the house, a woman bedecked with jewels and furs—with a face like that and eyes like that. And all the whips they had used on his bare back while she looked on with greedy eyes had not broken his will to have nothing to do with her. It cost Cayle an effort of mind to realize that he must not necessarily compare the two people or believe that they had anything in common.

"Interested?" asked the creature.

Cayle started to nod. And then a word that hadn't really penetrated before came through to his consciousness.

"What bank did you say?"

The human caricature smiled with the look of a man who realized he was bearing precious gifts. "The Fifth Bank," he said. "You made a deposit in our central at Imperial City about a month ago. In the course of a normal investigation of the background of any new depositor we discovered that you were on your way to Mars under unpleasant circumstances. We therefore wish to place our loan department at your service."

"I see," said Cayle carefully.

His eyes, sharp and alert, made another more detailed examination of this agent of the great bank. But there was nothing new, nothing to inspire confidence. And yet he did not think of ending the conversation. "Just what would the bank do for me?" he asked quietly.

The man cleared his throat. "You are the son of Fara and Creel Clark?" he asked pompously.

Cayle admitted the relationship after a moment's hesitation.

"You desire to return to Earth?"

There was no hesitation about his answer to that. "Yes," he said.

"The base fare," said the man, "is six hundred credits for the trip when the distance between Mars and Earth permits a twenty-four day journey. When the distance is greater the cost is ten credits a day extra. You probably knew that."

Cayle hadn't known. But he had guessed that the mine head wage of 25 credits a week would not provide a quick means of returning to Earth.

He felt tensed, conscious of how completely a man without resources could be confined to a planet. He had an idea of what was coming.

"The Fifth Bank," said the man in a grand tone, "will loan you the sum of one thousand credits if your father will guarantee the debt and if you will sign a note agreeing to pay back ten thousand credits."

Cayle sat down heavily. The end of hope had come more swiftly than he had expected. "My father," he said wearily, "would never guarantee a note for ten thousand credits."

"Your father," said the agent, "will be asked to guarantee only the one thousand. You will be expected to pay ten thousand out of your future earnings."

Cayle studied him with narrowed eyes. "By what method will this money be paid over to me?"

The gaunt face smiled. "You sign, then we give it to you. And just leave your father to us. The bank has a psychology department for handling co-signers and signers of notes. On some we use the dominating technique, on others—"

Cayle interrupted. "So far as I am concerned the money has to be paid over to me before I sign."

The other shrugged and laughed. "As you will. I see you are a sharp dealer. Come over to the mine manager's office."

He walked off, Cayle following thoughtfully. It was too easy and he didn't like it. Everything was happening too swiftly, as if—well, as if this were part of the routine of the end of a voyage. He slowed and looked around alertly. There was a long line of offices, he saw, where other men were being taken by well-dressed individuals.

It seemed to him that he could visualize the picture then. The first offer on the bulletin board. Volunteer to go on a farm. If they didn't get you that way, then along came a smooth tongued man to offer a loan on the basis of your family credit. The loan money would either not be advanced at all or it would be stolen from you almost immediately afterwards.

Thereupon, having exhausted all your available resources, present and future, you were on Mars to stay.

"There'll be a couple of witnesses," Clark thought. "Big fellows with guns on them to make sure that you don't get your money."

It was a good way to colonize an unfriendly planet, possibly the only way, considering that human beings were not too interested any more in pioneering.

He walked into the office. And there were the two men, well-dressed, smiling, friendly. They were introduced as, respectively, the mine manager and a clerk from the bank. Clark wondered cynically how many other persons, shanghaied as he had been, were being introduced at this moment to the "mine manager". It sounded very impressive and it must be thrilling to have a chance to talk in heart to heart fashion with so important a personage, to realize that he was human after all. Cayle shook hands with him and then turned to look the situation over. The important thing was to get the money legally. That meant actually signing the document and getting a copy.

Even that might not mean anything but, after all, there was a certain amount of law on the planets. The dangerous thing was to be without money and to arrive in court where other men could blandly deny one's story.

The room was not large but it was luxuriously furnished. It could have been a mine manager's office. There were two doors, the one through which he had come, and one directly opposite, where, presumably, the robbed individual made his exit without getting any chance to talk to people in the big room from which he had come. Clark walked over to the second door, opened it and saw that it led outside. There were scores of huts within sight and, standing in groups all around, were soldiers. The sight of them gave him pause, for obviously they would make it impossible for him to make a run for it if he succeeded in obtaining the money.

He used his body to block off the mob. With swift fingers he tested it to see if it were locked from the outside. It was. Quietly, he closed the door and, with a smile, turned back into the room. He shivered convincingly. "Sure chilly out there. I'll be glad to get back to Earth."

The three smiled sympathetically and the reptilian bank agent held out a document with ten one-hundred credit notes clipped to it. Clark counted the money and put it in his pocket. Then he read the contract. It was quite simple, apparently designed to ease the minds of people who were suspicious of involved forms. There were three copies, one to be sent to Earth, one for the Martian branch and one for him. They were properly signed and sealed and awaited only his signature. Clark tore off the bottom one and put it into his pocket. The others were inserted into the registered circuit. He signed the first one with a flourish—and then he stepped back and threw the pen, point first, into the face of the "manager".

The man screamed and put his hand up to his torn cheek.

That was all Clark saw. With a jump he reached the side of the toad-like man, grabbed at his neck just above the heavy coat collar and squeezed with all his strength. The creature yelped and struggled weakly.

For a moment then, Clark had the sharp fear that his plan of attack had been falsely based. He had assumed that the other had a gun also and would reach for it in panic. Long skinny fingers were clawing inside the voluminous coat. They came out clutching a little glittering blaster that Clark snatched, hand and all, and crushed into his own palm. Simultaneously, he squeezed the weapon away from the other's grasp.

He saw that the big "clerk" had his gun out, and was edging around, trying to get a chance to use it without harming the reptile. Clark took a snap shot at the man's foot. The radiant flame made a thin, bright beam. There was an odor of burning leather and a streamer of blue smoke. With a cry, the fellow dropped his weapon and sat down heavily on the floor. He writhed there, clutching at his foot. At Clark's urging, the "manager" held up his hands reluctantly. Swiftly, Clark relieved him of his blaster, picked up the one on the floor and backed toward the door.

He explained his plan briefly. The toad would accompany him as a hostage. They would go to the nearest airline base and fly to the city of Mare Cimmerium, at which point he would catch a regular liner for Earth. "And if anything should go wrong," Cayle Clark concluded, "at least one person will die before I do."

Nothing went wrong.

And that day was August 26th, 4784 Isher, two months and twenty-three days after Imperial Innelda launched her attack on the weapon makers.

CHAPTER TWENTY-ONE

CAYLE CLARK PLANNED AND SCHEMED. The days of the journey from Mars to Earth wound their clockwise course. The ship time switched gradually from Cimmerium Daylight Time to Imperial City Time. But the night outside, with its flashingly bright sun off to one side and everywhere else starry darkness, was an unchanging environment. Meals were eaten. Clark slept and dreamed and moved and had his being. His thoughts grew more direct, more determined. He had no doubts. A man who had put away fear of death could not fail.

The sun grew brighter. It splashed spiral-like across the darkness. Mars receded to a point of smallness, a reddish dot in a sea of night—hard to find among the starry brilliants of the jewel-case sky. Gradually Earth became a large, shining ball of light, then a monstrous, misty, unbelievable thing that filled half the sky. The continents showed through. And on Earth's nightside, partly visible as the ship swung past the moon, the cities shone with intermittent glitter that rivaled the heavens themselves.

Clark saw that vision of Earth in snatches only. Five days from destination he had discovered a stud poker game in one of the holds. From the beginning he lost. Not every game—an occasional win helped him recuperate a few credits. But by the third day of the endless game, the second last of the trip, the direction of his fortune was so marked that he took alarm and quit.

In his cabin he counted the money that remained to him—eighty-one credits. He had paid eight percent commission on the thousand credits to the representative of the bank. The rest had gone on fare, poker losses and one Imperial-style gun. "At least," Clark thought. "I'll soon be back in Imperial City. And with more money than when I arrived last time."

He lay back, amazingly at ease. The poker losses did not disturb him. He hadn't, when he came right down to it, planned to try gambling again. He had a different picture of his life. He would take risks, of course, but on a higher level. He had won five hundred thousand credits—at least—in the Penny Palace. It would be difficult to collect it but he would succeed. He felt himself patient and capable, ready for all eventualities.

As soon as he had the money he would secure a commission from Colonel Medlon. He might pay for it and he might not. It depended upon the moment. There was no vengefulness in his plan. He didn't care what happened to two venal creatures like Fatty and the colonel. They were stepping stones, it seemed to Clark, in the most ambitious scheme that had ever been planned in the Empire of Isher. A scheme rooted in a fact that seemed to have escaped all the creature-men who had risen to positions of rank in the Imperial Service.

Innelda of Isher meant well by the country. In his one contact with her he had sensed a personality frustrated by the corruption of others. In spite of the talk against her, the Empress was honest—on a machiavellian level, of course. Clark did not doubt that she could issue an order of execution. But that was part of her function as a ruler. Like himself, she must rise to the necessities of her situation.

The Empress was honest. She would welcome a man who would use her limitless authority to clean house for her. For two and a half months now he had been thinking over what she had said that day in Medlon's office and he had some pretty shrewd answers. There was her reference to officer-prospects staying away in droves because they had heard something was up. And her accusation of a pro-weapon shop conspiracy tied in with the in-explicable closing of the shops. Something *was* up and, for a man who had made a personal contact, it spelled massive opportunity.

To all his planned actions Clark made but one qualification. First, he must seek out Lucy Rall and ask her to marry him.

That hunger would not wait.

The ship came down into its cradle a few minutes before noon on a cloudless day. There were formalities and it was two o'clock before Clark's papers were stamped and he emerged into the open. A breeze touched his cheeks and, from the peak of metal that was the landing field, he could see the dazzling city to the west.

It was a view to make a man catch his breath, but Clark did not waste any time. From a 'stat booth, he called Lucy's number. A pause, then a young man's face came onto the screen. "I'm Lucy's husband," he said. "She went out for a minute, but you don't want to talk to her." Persuasively. "Take a good look at me and you'll agree."

Clark stared blankly. But the familiarity of the other's face would not penetrate through the shock of the words he had spoken.

"Look hard," the image in the 'stat urged.

Clark began, "I don't think that—"

And then he got it. He drew back like a man whose face has been slapped. He put out his hand as if he would defend his eyes from a vision that was too bright for them. He could feel the blood draining from his cheeks, and he swayed. The now familiar voice drew him back to normalcy.

"Pull yourself together!" it said. "And listen. I want you to meet me to-morrow night on the beach of the Haberdashery Paradise. Take one more look at me, convince yourself, and be there."

Clark didn't need the look but his eyes sought the image face. And there was no question. The face that was staring at him from the 'stat was his own.

Cayle Clark was looking at Cayle Clark—at 2:10 P.M., October 4, 4784 Isher.

CHAPTER TWENTY-TWO

OCTOBER 6TH—the empress stirred, and turned over in bed. She had a memory. The night before she had told herself that by morning her mind would be made up. As she came out of sleep she realized the uncertainty was still there. She opened her eyes, already embittered against the day.

She sat up, composing the tension in her face. And as she did so half a dozen maids, who had been hovering behind a sound-proofed screen, dashed forward. An energy drink was tendered. Sunlight adjustments were made, the great bedroom brightened for another morning. Massage, shower, facial, hair —and, again and again, as the routine proceeded, she thought, "I have got to get action or the attack will end in a personal humiliation. Surely, after four months, they cannot keep on delaying."

As soon as she had her dress on she began to receive palace officials. First, Gerritt, the chief of Palace Administration. He had a problem, many of them, and as usual, annoying ones. That was partially her own fault. Long ago she had insisted that all punishment of the palace staff be referred to her. Today the predominant motif was insolence. Servants defying their superiors and shirking their work. The offence was becoming common.

"For heaven's sake," Innelda said irritably, "if they don't like the limitations of their position, why don't they quit? Palace trained servants can always obtain positions, if only for what they are believed to know about my private life."

"Why doesn't your Majesty let me handle these personal matters?" said Gerritt. It was his stock remark, stolidly made. She knew that eventually he would wear her down but not to his own benefit. No stubborn old conservative was going to have full control of the huge staff of palace servitors. A heritage from the regency period, he and all his kind were going to be asked to vacate. She sighed, and dismissed him—and was back with her problem. What to do? Should she order attacks wherever possible? Or wait in the hope that new information would turn up? The trouble was that she had been waiting now for so many weeks.

General Doocar came in, a tall, thin man with slate gray eyes. He saluted with an angular motion and said, "Madam, the building reappeared for two hours and forty minutes last night, only one minute from the estimated time."

Innelda nodded. That was routine now. The pattern of reappearance had been established within a week of the first disappearance. She still insisted on being kept informed of the building's movements, just why, she couldn't decide.

"I'm like a child," she thought self-critically. "I can't let anything get out of my control." The analysis darkened her mood. She made a few sharp remarks about the efficiency of the military scientists under his command, then asked the question. The general shook his head.

"Madam," he said, "an attack is out of the question at the moment. We have a power machine dominating the weapon shops in every large city on this planet. But during the past two and a half months eleven thousand officers have deserted. The power machines are manned by guards who do not know how to operate them."

The woman flashed, "The hypnotic machine could teach them en masse in one hour."

"Yes." The hard voice did not change. The thin lips became a little thinner. That was all. "Your Majesty, if we are prepared to hand such information over to common soldiers, that is your privilege. You have but to command and I will obey."

Innelda bit her lip, vexed. This grim old man had her there. It was annoying to have come out at last with a thought that she had restrained so often in the past. She said defensively, "It seems that the so-called common soldiers are more loyal than my commissioned officers, and braver."

He shrugged. "You allow these tax creatures of yours the privilege of selling commissions," he said. "You do, generally, get educated people that way, but you surely don't expect a man who has paid ten thousand credits for a captaincy to take the chance of getting himself killed."

The argument began to weary her. She had heard it all before in different words. The same old meanings, reinforced by the same dramatizations, though it was some weeks now since the problem of commissions in the armed forces had been mentioned. The subject was not a pleasant one. It reminded her now of something she had almost forgotten. "The last time we talked of this," she said slowly, "I requested you to contact Colonel Medlon and ask him whatever became of that officer he was about to commission when I called him one day? It isn't often that I make personal contacts with lower ranks." Suddenly she became savage—"I'm hedged in here by a brigade of old men who don't know how to mobilize an army." She fought down her anger. "But never mind that. What about him?" General Doocar said stonily, "Colonel Medlon informs me that the young officer-prospect did not return at the appointed hour. The colonel assumes that he must have got wind of what was up and hastily changed his mind."

There was silence. She found herself thinking—that the explanation sounded wrong. He wasn't like that. And besides the Empress personally had talked to him.

She did not underestimate the power of such personal contact. People who met the Empress of Isher felt not only her personal charm but experienced the abnormal aura of her position. The combination was overpowering, not to be lightly dismissed on the word of a suspected "wino."

She spoke at last with a quiet determination. "General, inform the colonel *today* that he will either produce this young officer or face a Lambeth in the morning."

The gaunt man bowed but there was a cynical smile on his face. "Madam," he said, "if it gives you pleasure to destroy corruption, one individual at a time, you have a lifelong task ahead of you."

She didn't like that. There was a brutality in the remark that reached deep into her. She drew back. "I've got to start somewhere." She made a gesture, half threat, half frustration. She said querulously, "I don't understand you any more, General. When I was younger you used to agree that something ought to be done."

"Not by you." He shook his head. "The Imperial family must sanction, not personally direct, a moral house-cleaning." He shrugged. "As a matter of fact, I have more or less come around to the weapon shop idea that this is an age where people take to corruption whenever their adventurous instincts are denied normal expression."

The green, imperial eyes flashed. "I am not interested in weapon shop philosophy."

She was abruptly astounded that he should have mentioned the weapon shops in such a fashion. She flung the accusation at him. The grand old man was immune.

"Madam," he said, "when I stop examining the ideas and philosophies of a power that has now existed for three thousand seven hundred years you may have my resignation."

The woman rejected the argument. Everywhere she turned was this semiworship of the weapon shops. More, it was an acceptance of the shops as a legitimate facet of Isher civilization. "I must get rid of these old men," she thought, not for the first time. "They treat me as a child and will always treat me that way. Aloud she said icily, "General, I am not interested in hearing the moral teachings of an organization that at base is responsible for all the immorality in the Solar System. We live in an age where productive capacity is so great that no one need ever starve. Crime, because of economic need does not exist. The problem of psychiatric crime can be solved whenever we get hold of the afflicted person. But what is the situation?" She was hot now with remembered rage. "We discover that our psychopath has been sold a weapon shop gun. The owner of a house of illusion is similarly protected. True, in that case there is an understanding between the police and the houses whereby raids are allowed. But if any individual owner should decide to resist, we would have to bring a thirty-thousand-cycle cannon to defeat him." She paused to survey the job done by her hairdresser, felt satisfied, waved the woman away.

"Ridiculous and criminal!" she continued. "On every side, we are frustrated in our desire to end this eternal wickedness of millions of individuals, who sneer at the law because they have weapon shop guns. It would be different, if these—gun makers—would limit the sale of their products to respectable people. But when any sort of scoundrel can buy one—"

"A defensive gun!" interjected the general softly. "Defensive only."

"Exactly." said Innelda. "A man can commit any crime, then defend himself against justice. Oh—" furiously—"why do I even talk to you? General, I'm telling you. We have the weapon that can destroy these weapon shops once and for all. You don't have to kill the members, but get the army organized to destroy the shops. Get it organized, I say, for an attack within three days? A week?" She looked at him. "How long, General?"

He pleaded, "Give me until the new year, Madam. I swear that the confusion which was caused by the desertions has temporarily ruined us."

She had forgotten the deserters for the moment. "You have captured some of these officers?"

He hesitated. "Some, yes."

"I want one available for questioning this morning."

General Doocar bowed.

"As for the rest," said Innelda, "keep the military police after them. As soon as this mess is over, I'll set up special courts-martial and we'll teach these traitors the meaning of their oaths of allegiance."

"Suppose," said Doocar, and his voice was soft again, "they have weapon shop guns?"

Her reaction to that was so violent that she grew calm in her anger. "My friend," she said gravely, "when army discipline can be set at nought by an underground organization, then even the generals must realize it is time to destroy the subversion." She made a motion with her right arm. A gesture of decisiveness. "This afternoon, General, I shall visit the laboratories of Olympian Field. I want to see what progress has been made in finding out just what the weapon makers did to that building. Tomorrow morning, at least, Colonel Medlon must procure for me the young man he was supposed to have commissioned. If he cannot do it, one corrupt head will roll. You may think I'm being childish, concerning myself with one individual. But I must start somewhere. And that young man I know about. Him I can check on. But now," she said, "you weapon shop admirer, get out of here before I do something drastic."

"Madam," protested Doocar mildly. "I am loyal to the House of Isher."

"I am glad to hear it," said Innelda scathingly.

She brushed past him and went out into the hallway without looking back.

CHAPTER TWENTY-THREE

As SHE ENTERED THE SALON, she heard the faint sighing of relief of those already there. She smiled darkly. People who wanted to eat in the Imperial salon had to wait till she broke bread or sent word she wasn't coming. No compulsion existed for anyone to be present. But usually those who had access did not deny themselves the privilege. Innelda said, "Good morning!" Then sat down at the head of her table. She sipped a glass of water, which was the signal for the waiters to come in. After she had given her order, she looked around the room. Everywhere were graying heads; men and women over fifty; relics of the regency.

A half dozen young men and two of her younger secretaries sat at her own table. But they were a remnant; the residue of the emigration of young people that had followed the departure of Prince del Curtin.

"Did everybody have a nice sleep last night?" Innelda broke the silence sweetly. They hastened to assure her that they had. "How nice," she murmured—and settled into a moody silence. She wasn't sure just what she wanted of her companions. Lightness, perhaps. But how much? A year before, a newly introduced young man had asked her if she were still a virgin. And since she was, the incident still annoyed her.

Crudeness was definitely out of order. She had an instinctive feeling that immorality on her part would reflect on the reputation of the Isher family. But then what? She pecked at a piece of toast. What did she want? A positive approach—a belief in principles, with an ability to see the humorous side of life. Her own upbringing, severe and simple, had stressed the positive mind trainings. Very important, but seriousness could be overdone. She stiffened with an old determination. "I've got to get rid of these humorless, do-nothing, let's-be-careful-and-not-rock-the-boat, think-twice-and-stop—" She paused, self-pityingly, and prayed to her private gods, "Give me one good joke a day to make me laugh and one good man who can handle affairs of state and, in addition, know how to amuse me. If only Del were here."

She scowled in annoyance at the direction her thoughts were taking. Her cousin, Prince del Curtin, disapproved of the attack on the weapon shops. What a shock, when she had first discovered that. And what mortification when all the young men of his clique left the palace with him, refusing to participate in the adventure. Having killed Banton Vickers for threatening to inform the weapon shops of her plans, a treasonous utterance that would have destroyed her prestige if she had let it pass, she could not overlook the opposition. Tight-lipped, she recalled their final conversation, the prince cold and formal, marvellously goodlooking in his anger, herself uncertain but determined, as he said, "When you get over this madness, Innelda, you may call me back." He must have known that it was an opportunity for her to say, "That will be never." But she hadn't dared to say it. She had been like a wife, she thought bitterly. Wronged but unwilling to say too much, for fear that her husband might take her at her word. Not that she could ever marry the prince after such an action on his part. Still it would be nice to have him back—later—after the weapon shops were destroyed. She finished breakfast and glanced at her watch. Nine thirty. She cringed, involuntarily. The long day was barely begun.

At half past ten, free of urgent correspondence, she had the officer-deserter brought in. He was a man of thirty-three according to his file, country born and holding the rank of major. He came in; a faint cynical smile on his lips, but his eyes looked depressed. His name was Gile Sanders. Innelda studied him gloomily. According to his file he had three mistresses and had made a fortune out of a peculiar graft involving Army purchases. It was a fairly typical case history. And the part that was difficult to understand was why he, who had so much, had given it all up. She asked the question earnestly. "And please," she said, "do not insult me by suggesting that you were concerned with the moral issue of the war. Tell me simply and plainly why you gave up all your possessions for dishonor and disgrace. In one act you disinherited yourself. The very least that can happen to you is that you'll be sent to Mars or Venus permanently. Were you a fool or a coward or both?"

He shrugged. "I suppose I was a fool." His feet fumbled nervously over the floor. His eyes did not evade her direct stare, but his answer left her dissatisfied. After ten minutes she had got no real explanation out of him. It was possible that the profit and loss motivation had not influenced his decision. She tried a new approach. "According to your file," she said, "you were notified to report to building eight hundred A and, because of your rank, it was explained to you that at last a method had been found to destroy the weapon shops. An hour later, after having burned your private papers, you left your office and took up residence in a seaside cottage which you had purchased secretly—you thought—five years ago. A week later, when it was clear that you did not intend to do your duty, you were arrested. You have been in close confinement ever since. Is that picture fairly correct?"

The man nodded but said nothing. The Empress studied him, biting her lips. "My friend," she said softly at last, "I have it in my power to make your punishment anything I desire. Anything. Death, banishment, commutation—" she hesitated—"reinstatement."

Major Sanders sighed wearily. "I know," he said. "That was the picture I suddenly saw."

"I don't understand." She was puzzled. "If you realize the potentialities of your act, then you were very foolish."

"The picture," he said in a monotone, as if he had not heard her interruption, "of a time when someone, not necessarily yourself, would have that power without qualification, without there being anywhere to turn, without alleviation, without—hope."

She had her answer. "Well, of all the stupidity!" said Innelda explosively. She leaned back in her chair, momentarily overcome, drew a deep breath, then shook her head in irritation. "Major," she said gently, "I feel sorry for you. Surely your knowledge of the history of my family must have told you that the danger of misuse of power does not exist. The world is too big. As an individual I can interfere in the affairs of such a tiny proportion of the human race that it is ridiculous. Every decree that I issue vanishes into a positive blur of conflicting interpretations as it recedes from me. That decree could be ultimately mild—it would make no difference in the final administration of it. Anything, when applied to eleven billion people, takes on a meaningless quality that is impossible to imagine unless you have studied, as I have, actual results."

She saw with astonishment that her words had not touched him. She drew back, offended. It was all so crystal clear and here was one more obstinate fool. She restrained her anger with an effort. "Major," she said, "with the weapon shops out of the way we could introduce steadying laws that could not be flouted. There would be more uniform administration of justice because people would have to accept the judgement of the courts, their only recourse being appeals to the higher courts."

"Exactly," said Sanders. That was all. His tone rejected her logic. She studied him for a long moment, all the sympathy gone from her. Then she said bitterly, "If you're such a firm believer in the weapon shops, why didn't you protect yourself by going to them for a defensive gun?"

"I did."

She hesitated; then asked coldly, "What was the matter. Did your courage fail you when it came to the point of using it to defend yourself from arrest?"

Watching him; she knew she shouldn't have said that. It left her open to a retort which, she realized, might be devastating. Her fear was justified.

Sanders said, "No, Your Majesty. I did exactly what some of the other—uh—deserters did. I took off my uniform and went to a weapon shop, intending to buy a gun. But the door wouldn't open. It appears that I am one of the few officers who believe that the Isher family is the more important of the two facets of Isher civilization."

His eyes had been bright as he spoke. Now they grew depressed again. "I am," he said, "in exactly the position you want to put everybody into. I have no way to turn. I must accept your law; must accept secret declarations of war on an institution that is as much a part of Isher civilization as the House of Isher itself; must accept death if you decree it, without a chance to defend myself in open battle. Your Majesty," he finished quietly, "I respect and admire you. The officers who deserted are not scoundrels. They were merely confronted with a choice and they chose not to participate in an attack on things as they are. I doubt if I could put it more honestly than that."

She doubted it too. Here was a man who would never understand the realistic necessity of what she was doing.

After she dismissed him she noted his name in her check-file, commenting that she wanted to hear the verdict of his court-martial. The action of writing the words reminded her of her inability to remember the name of the man whom Colonel Medlon was to produce by morning. She leafed the pages, and found it immediately. "Cayle Clark," she said aloud. "That's he." She realized that it was now time to go to the Treasury Department and hear all the reasons why it was impossible to spend more money. With a tired smile, she went out of the study and took a private elevator up to the fiftieth floor.

CHAPTER TWENTY-FOUR

WE WERE MARRIED (said Lucy in her disjointed report to the coordination department of the weapon shops) shortly before noon, Friday, the day he landed from Mars. I do not know how to account for the fact that a later check-up revealed he had not landed until 2 o'clock, nor have I confronted him with this information. I will ask him about it only if I am specifically requested to do so. I do not desire to guess how he was able to marry me before the hour of the ship's arrival. There is no question in my mind, however. The man I married is Cayle Clark. It is impossible that I have been fooled by somebody representing himself to be Cayle. He has just made his daily 'stat call to me, but he doesn't know that I am making this report. I'm beginning to feel that it is wrong for me to make any reports whatever about him. However, the general circumstances being what they are, I am, as requested, trying to recall every detail of what happened. I will begin with the moment that I received a 'stat call from him on the morning of his arrival from Mars.

The time as I remember it was about half past ten. That conversation was extremely brief. We exchanged greetings, and then he asked me to marry him. My feelings about Cayle Clark are well known to the head of the co-ordination department. And I am sure Mr. Hedrock will not be surprised that I agreed instantly to the proposal, and that we signed our marriage declarations on the registered circuit a few minutes before noon the same morning. We then went to my apartment, where, with one interruption, we remained the rest of that day and that night. The interruption came at a quarter to two when he asked me if I would take a walk around the block while he used my 'stat for a call. He didn't say whether the call would be incoming or out-going but, on returning, I noticed on the 'stat meter that it had been an incoming call.

I do not apologize for leaving the apartment at his request. My acquiescence seems to me, normal. During the course of the day and evening, he made no further reference to the call but instead described to me everything that had happened to him since I last saw him in the house of illusion. I do confess that his account at times was not so clear as it might have been and he more than once gave me the impression that he was relating events which had happened to him a considerable time ago.

The morning after our marriage he was up early, and said that he had many things to do. Since I was anxious to call up Mr. Hedrock, I let him go without objection. The subsequent report of another weapon shop agent that a very expensive private carplane picked him up a block from the apartment and took off before the agent could summon transportation, puzzles me. Frankly, I cannot understand it.

Since then, Cayle has not been to the apartment but he has called me up every morning and told me that he cannot give me details as yet about what he is doing, but that he loves me as much as ever. I shall accept that until he himself tells me otherwise. I have no knowledge at all of the report that he has been for more than a month, a captain in Her Majesty's army. I do not know how he managed to obtain a commission, nor by what means he is pushing his interests. If it is true, as reported, that he has already been attached to the personal staff of the Empress, then I can only express amazement and speculate privately as to how he has managed it.

In conclusion, let me affirm my faith in Cayle. I cannot account for his actions, but I believe that the end-result will be honorable.

(Signed) *Lucy Rall Clark*
November 14, 4784 I

CHAPTER TWENTY-FIVE

THIS WAS IT. For a month Hedrock had delayed his reaction, waiting for new evidence. But now, reading Lucy's document, the conviction came. The unexpected turn of events that he had been waiting for was happening. What it was he had no idea. He felt a tensed alarm, the fear that he was missing vital clues. But doubt he had none—this was it.

Frowning, he reread the girl's statement. And it seemed to him then that Lucy was developing a negative attitude toward the weapon shops. It was not in what she had done but that she felt her actions might be misinterpreted. That was defensive, and therefore bad. The hold of the shops on its members was psychological. Usually, when anyone wanted to break away, he was divested of vital memories, given a bonus depending on length of service and shooed off with the blessings of the organization. But Lucy was a key contact during a great crisis. The conflict between her duty to the shops and her personal situation must not be allowed to become too disturbing.

Hedrock frowned over the problem, then dialed the 'stat. Lucy's face came onto the screen and Hedrock said earnestly, "I have just read your statement, Lucy, and I want to thank you for your cooperation. We appreciate your position thoroughly and I have been asked—" he worded it deliberately as if an executive group were behind what he was saying—"I have been asked to request that you hold yourself ready for a call from us night and day until the critical period is over. In return, the weapon shops will do everything in their power to protect your husband from any dangerous reactions that may result from what he is doing."

It was no light promise. He had already handed the assignment over to the protective branch. Insofar as it was possible to protect a man in the Imperial sphere the job was being done. He watched Lucy's face casually but intently. Intelligent though she was, she would never fully comprehend the weapon shop-Isher war. It didn't show. No guns were firing. Nobody was being killed. And even if the weapon shops were destroyed Lucy would not immediately notice the difference. Her life might never be affected and not even the immortal man could say what the pattern of existence would be when one of the two power facets of the culture was eliminated. He saw that Lucy was not satisfied with what he had said. He hesitated, then, "Mrs. Clark, on the day you were married you took your husband's callidity measurements and gave them to us. We have never told you the integrated result because we did not want to alarm you. I think, however, that you will be interested rather than anxious."

"They're special?" Lucy asked.

"*Special!*" Hedrock searched for adjectives. "Your husband's callidity at the time you measured him was the highest that has ever been recorded in the history of the Information Center. The index has nothing to do with gambling and we cannot guess what form it will take but that it will affect the whole world of Isher we have no doubt."

With troubled eyes he gazed at her. The devastating aspect of the affair was that Cayle Clark was not doing anything. There he was, attached to the personal staff of the Empress, his movements accounted for by a host of spies—well, almost all his movements. Several 'stat calls he had made from the palace had proved too private for interference. And twice he had slipped away from the palace, and eluded his shadows. Minor incidents—they could scarcely account for the fact that, according to his callidetic measurement, what was happening was happening *now*. The great event, whatever it was, was taking place. And not even the No-men of the shops were able to guess what it was.

Hedrock explained the situation, then, "Lucy," he said, "are you sure you have held nothing back? I swear to you it is a matter of life and death, particularly his life."

The girl shook her head. And though he watched closely her eyes did not change, showed not a trace of myopia. They widened, but that was another phenomenon. Her mouth remained firm, which was a good sign. It was impossible to tell definitely, of course, just by looking at her physical reactions—except that Lucy Rall was not known ever to have taken evasive training. Where Robert Hedrock could lie without giving one of the known lie-reactions, Lucy simply didn't have the experience or nerve-control training to stifle the unconscious signals of her muscles.

"Mr. Hedrock," she said, "you know that you can count on me to the limit."

That was a victory for his immediate purpose. But he broke the connection, dissatisfied, not with Lucy or with the other agents, but with himself. He was missing something. His mind was not seeing deep enough into reality. Just as the solution to the seesaw problem was eluding him, so now he was baffled by what must in reality be very apparent. Sitting here in his office, mulling over facts and figures, he was too far from the scene.

It was clearly time for an on-the-spot investigation by Robert Hedrock in person.

CHAPTER TWENTY-SIX

HEDROCK WALKED SLOWLY along the Avenue of Luck savoring the difference in its appearance. He couldn't recall just when he had last been on the street, but it seemed a long, long time ago. There were more establishments than he remembered, but not many changes otherwise. A hundred years did not affect the structural metals and material of a building made under the rigid Isher regulations. The general architectural designs remained the same. The decoration was different. New lighting façades, planned to attract the eye, confronted him in every direction. The science of refurbishing had not been neglected.

He entered the Penny Palace, undecided as to what level of action he should pursue. He favored the irresistible approach—he thought—better leave the decision about that for the moment. As he walked into the "treasure room" a ring on his little finger tingled. A transparency was probing him from his right. He walked on, then turned casually to examine the two men from whose direction the impulse had come. Were they employees or independents? Since he always carried about fifty thousand credits on him, independent sharpers would be a nuisance. He smiled gently as he came up to them.

"I'm afraid not," he said. "Forget any plans you had, eh?"

The heavier of the two men reached into a coat pocket, then shrugged. "You're not carrying a weapon shop gun," he said pointedly. "You're not armed at all."

Hedrock said, "Would you like to test that?" And looked straight at the man's eyes.

The gambler was the first to glance away. "C'mon, Jay," he said. "This job isn't the way I figured it."

Hedrock stopped him as he turned away. "Work here?"

The man shook his head. "Not," he said frankly, "if you're against it."

Hedrock laughed. "I want to see the boss."

"That's what I thought," the man said. "Well, it was a good job while it lasted."

This time Hedrock let them go. He felt no surprise at their reaction. The secret of human power was confidence. And the confidence they had seen in his eyes was rooted in certainties of which most men had never heard. In all the world there had never been a man armed as he was with mental, physical, emotional, neural and molecular defenses.

Lucy's description of Martin's office made it unnecessary for him to explore. He entered the corridor at the back of the gambling section. As he closed the door behind him, a net fell over him, neatly enveloping him. It drew instantly tight and pulled him several feet above the floor. Hedrock made no effort to free himself. There was enough light for him to see the floor five feet below, and the indignity of his position did not disturb him. He had time for several thoughts. So Harj Martin had become wary of uninvited visitors. It proved something; just what, he would leave to the moment of meeting.

He had not long to wait. Footsteps sounded. The door opened, and the fat man came in. He turned on a bright light and stood with a jolly look on his face, staring up at his prisoner. "Well," he said at last, "what have we got here?" He stopped. His eye had caught Hedrock's. Some of the jolliness faded from his expression. "Who are you?" he snapped.

Hedrock said, "On or about the night of October fifth, you were visited here by a young man named Cayle Clark. What happened?"

"I'll do the questioning," said Martin. Once again his eyes met Hedrock's. "Say," he said querulously, "who *are* you?"

Hedrock made a gesture. It was very carefully timed and estimated. One of the rings on his fingers dissolved the hard material of the net. It parted beneath him like a door opening. He landed on his feet. He said, "Start talking, my friend. I'm in a hurry."

Ignoring the gun that Martin snatched, he brushed past him into the large office. When he spoke again the confidence was in his voice. It required only a few moments after that for the resigned gambling palace operator to decide on cooperation. "If all you want is information, okay." He added. "Your date is right. It was October fifth about midnight when this guy Clark came in here. He had his twin brother with him."

Hedrock nodded, but said nothing. He was not here for discussion.

"Boy," said Martin, "they were about the most cold-blooded twins I ever saw and they worked together like a team. One of them must have had some Army experience because he stood—well, you know the hypnotic posture they get. He was the one who knew everything, and was he ever tough! I started to say something about not being a sucker and I got a blast across my legs. I made a bit too fast a move when I turned to pump the money out of the safe and another blast took off some of my hair."

He pointed at a bald spot on one side of his head. Hedrock examined it briefly. It had been close but obviously trained shooting. Weapon shop or Army. By elimination, Army.

"You're all right," he commented.

Martin shuddered. "That guy wasn't worrying whether I was all right or not." He finished, complainingly, "Life is getting too tough. I never knew the normal defense devices of Isher could be so easily nullified."

Outside Hedrock headed for a carplane stop in a meditative mood. The existence of the two Cayles was now established. And one of them had been in the Army long enough to receive more than the preliminary officer training. He had had that training on October fifth, a mere one day after Cayle Clark's arrival from Mars. By the morning of the sixth, the day Clark joined the Army, according to the record, he had had 500,000 credits.

It was a nice stake for a young man trying to get ahead. But it scarcely accounted for certain things that were happening. And, large though it was, it was a tiny sum when considered in its relations to Cayle Clark's callidetic index—if the callidity were due to follow a money pattern. His carplane arrived and the thought ended. He had one more call to make this morning—Colonel Medlon.

CHAPTER TWENTY-SEVEN

ROBERT HEDROCK RETURNED to his office in the Hotel Royal Ganeel shortly after midday. He examined the reports that had come in during his absence, then spent two hours on a private telestat with an economic expert at the weapon shop Information Center. Then he called the members of the weapon makers' council, and requested an immediate plenary session.

It required about ten minutes for the full Council to assemble in the council chamber of the hotel. Dresley opened the meeting. "Looks to me, gentlemen," he said, "as if our coordinator has struck a warm trail. Right, Mr. Hedrock?"

Hedrock came forward smiling. Last time, in speaking to a delegation of this council, he had had the pressure of the time map *and* the Empress on his spirit. The map was still in the building, its problem unsolved, becoming more urgent every hour. But now he had one solution. He began without preliminary. "Gentlemen, on the morning of November twenty-seventh, twelve days hence, we will send a message to the Isher Empress, and request her to end her war. We will accompany our request with facts and figures that will convince her she has no alternative."

He expected a sensation, and he got it. These men knew that, when it came to his job, he was not one to raise false hopes (they had yet to discover that his efficiency was equally great in other fields). Feet stirred, and there was excitement.

Peter Cadron said explosively, "*Man!* Don't keep us in suspense. What have you discovered?"

"Permit me," said Hedrock, "to recapitulate."

He went on. "As you are aware, on the morning of June third, four thousand seven hundred and eighty-four Isher, a man from the year nineteen hundred and fifty-one A.D. appeared in our Greenway weapon shop. The discovery was then made that the Empress was directing a new energy weapon against all Imperial City weapon shops. This energy was a form of atomic power, old in nature but new to science. Its discovery heralds another step forward in our understanding of the complex structure of the space-time tensions that make for the existence of Matter. The source of the energy in Imperial City was a building completed about a year ago and located on Capital Avenue. Its effect on the Greenway shop differed from its effect on shops further away. Theoretically, it should have destroyed any material structure instantly but, though the Isher rulers have never known it, weapon shops are not made of matter in the accepted sense. And so there was an intricate interplay of gigantic forces that took place predominantly in time itself. And so a man came seven thousand years out of the past."

He described briefly, using pure mathematical terms, the seesaw action of the man and the building, once they were launched into the abyss of time. He went on, "There are still people who cannot understand how there can be a time swing, when it is a macrocosmic fact that the sun and its planets move steadily through space-time at twelve-plus miles a second, in addition to which the planets follow an orbital course around the sun at varying speeds. By this logic it should follow that, if you go into the past or future, you will find yourself at some remote point in space, far from Earth. It is hard for people who think this to realize that space is a fiction, a by-product of the basic time-energy, and that a matter tension like a planet does not influence phenomena in the time stream, but is itself subject to the time energy laws.

"The reason for the balancing for two hours and forty minutes after every swing is obscure, but it has been suggested that nature unrelentingly seeks stability. The building, when it swings into the past, occupies the same 'space' as it did in normal time but there are no repercussions—for the reason that similarity is a function of time itself, not of its tension-product. McAllister started at seven thousand years, the building at two seconds. That is approximate.

"Today the man is several quadrillions of years away and the building swings at a distance of somewhat less than three months. The fulcrum, of course, moves forward in our time, so that we have the following situation— the building no longer swings back in time as far as June third, where the seesaw originally started. Please bear these facts in mind while I turn briefly to another division of this seemingly complicated but basically simple business."

Hedrock paused. There were quick minds in this room. It interested him to see that every face was still expectant. Now that he himself knew the truth it seemed queer that they had not yet grasped the reality. He continued: "Gentlemen, the Coordination Department discovered some months ago that there existed in the village of Glay a callidetic giant. With so much internal pressure pushing him we had no difficulty maneuvering him into coming to Imperial City. At first, our belief that he would influence events markedly was nullified by his ignorance of Isher realities. I won't go into the details but he was shipped to Mars as a common laborer. He was able to return almost immediately."

He went on to explain how Lucy Rall had been married to one Cayle Clark a few hours before the arrival of the ship that brought Cayle Clark back to Earth, how the two Clarks secured 500,000 credits, then visited Colonel Medlon, one of them disguised. The visit was a fortunate one for Medlon. He had just been asked by the Empress to produce Clark, or else. A captaincy was conferred on Clark, with the usual hypnotic machine training for officers. The following day he reported to the Empress.

"For a reason which she considers to have been impulse, but which is traceable to his callidity, she attached him to her personal staff and he is there now. Wherever his influence extends, he has followed a very interesting pattern of ruthlessly eliminating the more obvious corruption, and this has roused the interest of the ambitious Innelda. Even if nothing else worked in his favor, he would appear to be a young man destined to go far in the Imperial service."

Then Hedrock smiled. "Actually, the Cayle Clark to watch is not the one in the open but the one who remained elusively in the city. It is that Clark who has been making history since last August seventh. In the time since then he has achieved the following successes—and gentlemen, I warn you, you've never heard anything like this before."

In a few sentences, he described what had happened. When he had finished, the table buzzed with excited discussion. At last a man said, "But why marry Lucy Rall?"

"Partly love, partly—" Hedrock hesitated. He had asked Lucy a pointed question and her answer made his reply possible now. "I would say he grew immensely cautious, and began to think of the future. Basic urges came to the fore. Suppose something happened to a man who in a few weeks had accomplished the miracle that he had. Gentlemen, he wanted an heir and Lucy was the only honest girl he knew. It may be a permanent arrangement. I cannot say. Clark, in spite of his rebellion against his parents is essentially a well-brought-up young man. In any event, Lucy will not suffer. She will have the interesting experience of having a child. And, as a wife, she has community property rights."

Peter Cadron climbed to his feet. "Gentlemen," he said, "I move a vote of thanks to Robert Hedrock for the service he has rendered the weapon shops."

The applause was prolonged.

"I move further," said Peter Cadron, "that he be given the rank of unrestricted member."

Once more there were no dissenters. Hedrock bowed his appreciation. The reward was more than an honor. As an unrestricted member he would be subject only to the Pp machine examinations. His movements and actions would never be scrutinized and he could use every facility of the shops as if they were his own property. He had been doing that anyway but in future there would be no suspicion. It was a mighty gift.

"Thank you, gentlemen," he said, when the clapping ended.

"And now," said Peter Cadron, "I respectfully request Mr. Hedrock to leave the council room while we discuss our remaining problem, the seesaw."

Hedrock went out gloomily. He had momentarily forgotten that the greatest danger remained.

CHAPTER TWENTY-EIGHT

IT WAS NOVEMBER TWENTY-SIXTH, one day before the shops intended to inform the Empress that her war was lost. She had no premonition. She had come down to the building to see and, perhaps—perhaps to do as Captain Clark had suggested. She still felt repelled, though without fear. The feeling that she had was that the Empress of Isher must not involve her own person in hare-brained adventures. Yet the thought had grown, and here she was. At the very least she would watch and wait while Captain Clark and the scientists made the trip. She climbed briskly out of her carplane and looked around her.

In the near distance a concealing haze rose up lazily into the sky, an artificial fog that, for months now, had cut off this city district from the view of the curious. She walked slowly forward, her distinctive Isher face turning this way and that as she examined the scene. She beckoned Captain Clark. "When is the building due?"

The smiling young man saluted briskly. "In seven minutes, Your Majesty."

"Have you all the necessary equipment?"

She listened carefully to his recapitulation. Seven groups of scientists would enter the building, each with his own instrument. It was a pleasure to realize that Captain Clark had personally checked over the lists of machines in each group. "Captain," she glowed, "you're a treasure."

Cayle did not reply. Her praise meant nothing. This girl, who almost literally owned the world, surely did not expect intelligent people to be absolutely faithful to her in exchange for a few compliments and Army pay. He had no sense of anticipatory guilt and in fact did not regard what he intended to do as being in any way damaging to her. In Isher you did what was necessary and for him there was no turning back. The pattern of his action was already set.

The woman was looking over the scene again. The hole in the ground where the building had been was to her right. To her left was the Greenway weapon shop with its park. It was the first time she had seen one in which the glitter signs were not working. That made her feel better. The shop seemed strangely isolated there in the shadows of its trees. She clenched her hands and thought: "If all the weapon shops in the Solar System were suddenly eliminated the few thousand parklike lots where they had been could so easily be converted into almost anything that—in one generation, she told herself with a dark certainty—they'd be forgotten. The new children would grow up wondering what mythological nonsense their elders were talking.

"By all the gods of space," she said aloud, passionately, "it's going to happen."

Her words were like a cue. The air shimmered strangely. And where there had been an enormous symmetrical hole abruptly towered a building.

"Right on the minute," said Captain Cayle Clark beside, with satisfaction.

Innelda stared at the structure, chilled. She had watched this process once on a telestat screen. It was different, being on the scene. For one thing the size showed up better. For a quarter of a mile it reared up into the heavens, solid in its alloyed steel-and-plastic construction, as wide and long as it was high. It had to be large, of course. The engineers had stipulated oversized vacuums between the various energy rooms. The actual living space inside was tiny. It took about an hour to inspect all the levels.

"Well," said Innelda in a tone of relief, "the place doesn't seem to have been damaged in any way by its experiences. What about the rats?"

The rats had been placed in the building during an earlier appearance. So far, they had showed no sign of being affected. It was wise, though, to verify that they were still unharmed. She waited now in an upper room, glancing intermittently at her watch, as the minutes fled by.

It was annoying to realize that she was nervous. But, standing there in the virtual silence of an almost empty building she felt that she was being foolish in that she was even considering going along. She glanced at the men who had volunteered to accompany her if she went. Their silence was not normal and they did not look at her but stood moodily gazing through the transparent wall. There was a sound of footsteps. Captain Clark came striding into view. He was smiling and in his cupped hands he held a white rat. "Your Majesty," he said, "just look at him. Bright as a button."

He was so cheerful that when he held the little animal out to her she took it and stared down at it thoughtfully. On abrupt impulse, she drew it up and pressed its warm body against her cheek.

"What would we do," she murmured, "without lovely little rats like you?" She glanced at Captain Clark. "Well, sir," she said, "what is the scientific opinion?"

"Every rat," Clark said, "is organically, emotionally and psychologically sound. All the tests that show rats for what they are were favorable."

Innelda nodded. It fitted. At the beginning, on the day the first attack was launched, before the men inside the building knew what was happening, the structure had disappeared, causing an immense confusion inside, of which she had never received a coherent account. The moment, on that occasion, the building reappeared, all personnel was withdrawn and no one had been permitted to take the "trip" since then. But physical examinations of the men proved them unharmed.

Still Innelda hesitated. It would look bad now if she failed to go along, but there were so many factors to be considered. If anything happened to her the Isher government might fall. She had no direct heir. The succession would fall to Prince del Curtin, who was popular but known by many people to be out of her favor. The whole situation was ridiculous. She felt hedged in, but there was no use denying the reality.

"Captain," she said firmly, "you have volunteered to take this—journey— whether I go or not. I have definitely decided not to go. I wish you luck and wish, too, that I could go with you. But I'm afraid that I must not. As Empress I do not feel free for light-hearted adventures." She held out her hand. "Go with my blessing."

Less than hour later, she watched as the building flicked into nothingness. She waited. Food was brought. She ate it in her carplane, read several state papers she had brought along and then, as darkness fell over the capital city of her empire, saw by her watch that once more the building was due back.

It flashed into view and presently men began to troop out. One of the scientists came over. "Your Majesty," he said, "the journey was accomplished without incident except for one thing. Captain Clark, as you know, intended to leave the building for exploration purposes. He did leave it. We received one message from him, spoken into his wrist 'stat to the effect that the date was August seventh, four thousand and eighty-four Isher. That was the last we heard. Something must have happened to him. He failed to come back in time to make the return journey with us."

"But—" said Innelda. She stopped blankly. Then, "But that means, from August seventh to November twenty-sixth there were two Cayle Clarks in existence, the normal and the one who went back in time."

She paused, uncertain. "The old time paradox," she thought to herself. "Can man go back in time and shake hands with himself?" Aloud, she said wonderingly, "But whatever became of the second one?"

CHAPTER TWENTY-NINE

AUGUST 7—it was a bright day with a soft blue sky; and a faint breeze blew into Clark's face as he walked rapidly away from the building that had brought him to a period of his own past life. No one bothered him. He wore a captain's uniform with the special red insignia that indicated an imperial staff member. Sentries posted on streets adjoining the building snapped to attention as he walked by.

In five minutes he was in a public carplane heading purposefully into the heart of the city. He had more than two and a half months to pass before he would be back where he had started, but for what he had in mind the time would be short indeed.

It was late afternoon, but he was able to rent a four-room office before the close of business that day. An employment agency promised to have several stenographers and bookkeepers report by nine A.M. the following morning. And though the place was furnished as an office only, he was able to obtain a cot before dark from a twenty-four hour rental service. That night, he planned into the early morning hours, and then slept restlessly on the cot. He rose shortly after dawn and, carrying with him the sheet of paper on which he had his calculations, took an elevator down to the exchange room of one of the largest stockbrokerage firms in the city. In his pockets were some five hundred thousand credits which had been given to him by the "second" Cayle Clark. The money was mostly in bills of large denomination, and there were as many of them as one man could burden himself with, and still be able to move.

Before that day had run its course, he had made thirty-seven hundred thousand credits. And the bookkeepers upstairs were busy making records of his stock transactions; the stenographers were beginning to write letters; and a chartered accountant, hastily hired as office manager, hired more help and took on more office space on adjoining floors.

Tired but jubilant, Cayle spent the evening preparing for the next day. He had had one experience of what a man could do who had brought with him from the future complete stock market reports for a period of two and a half months. He slept that night with a sense of exhilaration. He could scarcely wait for the next day. And the next. And the next and the next.

During that month of August, he won ninety billion credits. In that series of deals, he took over one of the chain banks, four billion-credit industrial establishments and obtained partial control of thirty-four other companies.

During the month of September he made three hundred and thirty billion credits, and absorbed the colossal First Imperial Bank, three interplanetary mining corporations and part ownership of two hundred and ninety companies. By the end of September, he was established in a hundred-story skyscraper in the heart of the financial district, and he gave Employment Incorporated the job of setting him up as a big business. On September thirtieth, over seven thousand employees were working in the building.

In October he diverted his cash resources to investment in available hotel and residential properties, a total of three and one-eighth trillion credits' worth. In October also, he married Lucy Rall, answered the call from himself—just back from Mars—and made an appointment to meet the "other" Clark. The two young men, equally grim and determined, visited the Penny Palace, and secured from Harj Martin the money that had been stolen by the gambling house owner. Actually, the money mattered little at this stage, but there was an important principle involved. Cayle Clark was out to conquer the impersonal world of Isher. And no one who had ever put anything over on him was going to have that satisfaction for long. After Harj Martin, it was a natural step to seek out Colonel Medlon and so prepare the groundwork for the journey into the past.

Two Cayle Clarkes—really only one, but from different times—and that was the story that Robert Hedrock gave to the weapon shop council. That was the phenomenal incident that forced the Empress to end her war lest other officers or men wreck the financial stability of the Solar System by trying to repeat the success of Cayle Clark.

CHAPTER THIRTY

OUTSIDE, IT WAS NIGHT. Fara walked along the quiet streets of Glay, and for the first time it struck him that the weapon shop Information Center must be halfway around the world, for there it had been day.

The picture vanished as if it had never existed as he grew aware again of the village of Glay asleep all around him. Silent, peaceful—yet ugly, he thought, ugly with the ugliness of evil enthroned. He thought: The right to buy weapons—and his heart swelled into his throat; the tears came into his eyes. He wiped his vision clear with the back of his hand, thought of Creel's long dead father, and strode on, without shame. Tears were good for an angry man.

The hard, metal padlock yielded before the tiny, blazing power of the revolver. One flick of fire, the metal dissolved, and he was inside. It was dark, too dark to see, but Fara did not turn on the lights immediately. He fumbled across to the window control, turned the windows to darkness vibration, and then clicked on the lights. He gulped with awful relief as he saw that the machines, his precious tools that he had watched the bailiff carry away, were here again, ready for use.

Shaky from the pressure of his emotion, Fara called Creel on the telestat. It took a little while for her to appear; and she was in her dressing gown. When she saw who it was she turned very pale.

"Fara, oh, Fara, I thought—"

He cut her off grimly: "Creel, I've been to the weapon shop. I want you to do this: go straight to your mother. I'm here at my shop. I'm going to stay here day and night until it's settled that I *stay* . . . I shall go home later for some food and clothing, but I want you to be gone by then. Is that clear?"

Color was coming back into her lean, handsome face. She said: "Don't you bother coming home, Fara. I'll do everything necessary. I'll pack all that's needed into the carplane, including a folding bed. We'll sleep in the back room at the shop."

Morning came palely but it was ten o'clock before a shadow darkened the open door; and Constable Jor came in. He looked shamefaced.

"I've got an order here for your arrest," he said.

"Tell those who sent you," Fara replied deliberately, "that I resisted arrest—with a gun." The deed followed the words with such rapidity that Jor blinked. He stood like that for a moment, a big, sleepy-looking man, staring at that gleaming, magical revolver; then:

"I have a summons here ordering you to appear at the great court of Ferd this afternoon. Will you accept it?"

"Certainly."

"Then you will be there?"

"I'll send my lawyer," said Fara. "Just drop the summons on the floor there. Tell them I took it."

The weapon shop man had said: "Do not ridicule by word any legal measure of the Imperial authorities. Simply disobey them."

Jor went out, seemingly relieved. It took an hour before Mayor Mel Dale came pompously through the door. "See here, Fara Clark," he bellowed. "You can't get away with this. This is defiance of the law."

Fara was silent as his honor waddled farther into the building. It was puzzling, almost amazing that Mayor Dale would risk his plump, treasured body. Puzzlement ended as the mayor said in a low voice:

"Good work, Fara; I knew you had it in you. There's dozens of us in Glay behind you, so stick it out. I had to yell at you just now because there's a crowd outside. Yell back at me, will you? Let's have a real name calling. But first, a word of warning: the manager of the Automatic Repair shop is on his way here with his bodyguards, two of them."

Shakily, Fara watched the mayor go out. The crisis was at hand. He braced himself, thought: Let them come, let them—

It was easier than he had expected, for the men who entered the shop turned pale when they saw the holstered revolver. There was a violence of blustering nevertheless, that narrowed down finally to:

"Look here," the man said, "we've got your note for twelve thousand one hundred credits. You're not going to deny you owe that money."

"I'll buy it back," said Fara stonily, "for exactly one thousand credits, the amount actually paid to my son."

The strong-jawed young man looked at him for a long time. "We'll take it," he said finally, curtly.

Fara said: "I've got the agreement here."

His first customer was old man Miser Lan Harris. Fara stared at the long-faced oldster with a vast surmise, and his first, amazed comprehension came of how the weapon shop must have settled on Harris' lot by arrangement. It was an hour after Harris had gone that Creel's mother stamped into the shop. She closed the door.

"Well," she said. "You did it, eh? Good work. I'm sorry if I seemed rough with you when you came to my place, but we weapon-shop supporters can't afford to take risks for those who are not on our side."

"But never mind that. I've come to take Creel home. The important thing is to return everything to normal as quickly as possible."

It was over. Incredibly, it was over. Twice, as he walked home that night, Fara stopped in midstride, and wondered if it had not all been a dream. The air was like wine. The little world of Glay spread before him, green and gracious, a peaceful paradise where time had stood still.

CHAPTER THIRTY-ONE

THE EMPRESS SAID, "Mr. de Lany."

Hedrock bowed. He had disguised himself slightly, and taken one of his long discarded names so that she would not recognize him at some future date.

"You have sought an interview?" said the Empress of Isher.

"As you see."

She toyed with his card. She had on a snow-white gown that accentuated the tan of her face and neck. The room in which she received him had been made up to resemble a small south sea island. Palms and green growth surrounded them. And on every side was water, lapping on a beach as real as nature. A cool wind blew from that restless sea onto Hedrock's back and into her face. The woman gazed bitterly at Hedrock. She saw a man of earnest mien and commanding appearance. But it was his eyes that startled her. They were strong and kind and infinitely brave. She hadn't expected such special qualities. The visitor took on sudden importance. She looked down at the card again.

"Walter de Lany," she said thoughtfully. She seemed to listen to the name as she spoke it, as if she expected it to acquire meaning. Finally she shook her head, wonderingly. "How did you get in here? I found this appointment on my list and took it for granted that the chamberlain must have arranged it because it involved necessary business."

Hedrock said nothing. Like so many Imperials, the chamberlain lacked the defensive mind trainings. And, though the Empress herself had them, she did not know that the weapon shops had developed energy methods for forcing instantaneous favorable response from the unprotected. The woman spoke again.

"Very strange," she said.

Hedrock said, "Reassure yourself, Madam. I have come to solicit your mercy on behalf of an unfortunate, guiltless man."

That caught her. Once more her eyes met his, flinched from the strength that was there, then steadied.

Hedrock said quietly, "Your Majesty, you are in a position to do an act of unparalleled kindness to a man who is nearly five million million years from here, swinging from past to future as your building forces him ever further away."

The words had to be spoken. He expected her to realize instantly that only her intimates and her enemies would know certain details about the vanishing building. The way the color drained from her cheeks showed that she was realizing.

"You're a weapon shop man?" she whispered. She was on her feet. "Get out of here," she breathed. "Out!"

Hedrock stood up. "Your Majesty," he said, "control yourself. You are in no danger."

He intended his words to be like a dash of cold water. The suggestion that she was afraid brought splotches of color into her face. She stood like that for a moment and then, with a quick movement, reached into the bosom of her dress and drew out a gleaming white energy weapon. "If you do not leave instantly," she said, "I shall fire."

Hedrock held his arms away from his body like a man being searched. "An ordinary gun," he said in amazement, "against a man who carries a weapon shop defensive? Madam," he said, "if you will listen to me for a moment—"

"I do not," said the Empress, "deal with weapon shop people."

That was merely irritating. "Your Majesty," said Hedrock in a level voice, "I am surprised that you make such immature statements. You have not only been dealing with the shops the last few days, you have yielded to them. You have been compelled to end the war and to destroy your time-energy machines. You have agreed not to prosecute the officer-deserters but only to discharge them. And you have granted immunity to Cayle Clark."

He saw in her face that he had not touched her. She was staring at him, frowning. "There must be a reason," she said, "that you dare to talk to me like this."

Her own words seemed to galvanize her. She turned back to her chair and stood with finger poised over the ornamented arm. "If I should press this alarm," she said, "it would bring guards."

Hedrock sighed. He had hoped she would not force him to reveal his power. "Why not, then," he suggested, "press it?" It was time, he thought, that she found out her true situation.

The woman said, "You think I won't?" Firmly, her extended finger pressed downward.

There was silence except for the lapping of the waves and the soft sound of the lifelike breeze. After at least two minutes, Innelda, ignoring Hedrock as if he did not exist, walked twenty feet to a tree, and touched one of the branches. It must have been another alarm, because she waited—not so long this time—and then walked hurriedly over to the thick brush that concealed the elevator shaft. She activated its mechanism and, when there was no response, came slowly back to where Hedrock waited, and sat down in her chair. She was pale but composed. Her eyes did not look at him but her voice was calm and without fear. "Do you intend to murder me?"

Hedrock shook his head, but said nothing. More strongly now, he regretted that he had had to reveal to her how helpless she could be, particularly regretted it because she would undoubtedly start modernizing the defenses of the palace in the mistaken belief that she was protecting herself against superior weapon shop science. He had come here this afternoon prepared for any emergency, physical or mental. He could not force her to do what he wanted but his fingers blazed with offensive and defensive rings. He had on his "business" suit and even weapon shop scientists would have been amazed at the variety of his armor. In his vicinity no alarm energies would come to life and no guns would operate. It was the day of the greatest decision in the history of the Solar System, and he had come mightily girded.

The woman's eyes were staring at him with somber intensity. "What do you want?" she said. "What about this man you mentioned?"

Hedrock told her about McAllister.

"Are you mad?" she whispered when he had finished. "But why so far? The building is only—three months."

"The ruling factor seems to be mass."

"Oh!" Silence, then, "But what do you want me to do?"

Hedrock said, "Your Majesty, this man commands our pity and our mercy. He is floating in a void whose like no human eyes will ever see again. He has looked upon our Earth and our sun in their infancy and in their old, old age. Nothing can help him now. We must give him the surcease of death."

In her mind Innelda saw the night he pictured. But she was more intent now, seeing this event in its larger environment. "What," she said, "about this machine you have?"

"It is a duplicate of the map machine of the weapon shops." He didn't explain that he had built it in one of his secret laboratories. "It lacks only the map itself, which was too intricate to fashion swiftly."

"I see." Her words were automatic, not a real response. She studied his face. She said slowly, "Where do you fit into all this?"

It was a question that Hedrock was not prepared to answer. He had come to the Empress of Isher because she had suffered a defeat and, her position being what it was, it was important that she should not remain too resentful. An immortal man, who was once more interfering in the affairs of mortals, had to think of things like that. "Madam," he said, "there is no time to waste. The building is due here again in one hour."

The woman said, "But why cannot we leave this decision to the weapon shop council?"

"Because they might make the wrong decision."

"What," persisted Innelda, "is the right decision?"

Sitting there, Hedrock told her.

Cayle Clark set the controls so that the carplane would make a wide circle around the house.

"Oh, my goodness!" said Lucy Rall Clark. "Why it's one of these up-in-the-air places—"

She stopped and stared with wide, wondering eyes at the grounds below, at the hanging gardens, at the house floating in the air. "Oh, Cayle," she said, "are you sure we can afford it?"

Cayle Clark smiled. "Darling, I've explained to you a dozen times. I'm not going to do it again."

She protested, "That isn't what I mean. Are you sure the Empress will let you get away with it?"

Cayle Clark gazed at his wife with a faint, grim smile. "Mr. Hedrock," he said slowly, "gave me a weapon shop gun. And besides, I did a great deal for Her Majesty which—at least, so she told me on the telestat today—she appreciates. She doesn't dissemble very much, so I have agreed to continue to work for her in much the same way."

"Oh!" said Lucy.

"Now, don't get yourself upset," said Cayle. "Remember, you yourself told me that the weapon shops believed in one government. The more that government is purified the better off the world will be. And believe me—" his face hardened—"I've had just enough experience to make me want to purify it."

He landed the carplane on the roof of the five-story residence. He led Lucy into the interior, down into the world of bright, gracious rooms where she and he would live forever.

At least, at twenty-two or three, it seemed as it it would be forever.

EPILOGUE

MCALLISTER HAD FORGOTTEN about the personal decision he intended to make. It was so hard to think in this darkness. He opened his tired eyes, and saw that he was poised moveless in black space. There was no earth under him. He was in a time where the planets did not yet exist. The darkness seemed to be waiting for some colossal event.

Waiting for him.

He had a sudden flash of understanding of what was going to happen.

Wonder came then, and a realization of what his decision must be: resignation to death.

It was a strangely easy decision to make. He was so weary. Bitter-sweet remembrance came of the days in far-gone time and space, when he had lain half-dead on a battlefield of the middle twentieth century, resigned to personal oblivion. Then he had thought that he must die so that others might live. The feeling now was the same, but stronger and on a much higher level.

How it would be worked he had no idea. But the seesaw would end in the very remote past, with the release of the stupendous temporal energy he had been accumulating with each of those monstrous swings.

He would not witness but he would aid in the formation of the planets.